"I've never made out in the bed of a pickup truck." She'd blurted it out in the hopes that Beau would suggest—

"Maybe you should add it to your bucket list."

Was he simply making a suggestion? Was he flirting? Was *she* flirting? Where was the instruction manual? "I didn't bring the bucket list."

Dang it! Dumb thing to say dumb thing to say dumb thing to say…

"We could make out now and write it down later."

She swallowed loudly. There it was. He sounded so confident. Like he'd made out in the bed of a pickup truck a million times. Probably, because he had. He'd be a good teacher, right? And it wouldn't *mean* anything to him. This was Beau Montgomery. Kissing women was like breathing for him.

No big deal.

"Okay," she said softly. "Let's make out."

Praise for Carly Bloom's
Once Upon a Time in Texas series

"Spending any time in Big Verde is a delight, and Bloom has invented a place we want to hang up our hat and kick up our spurs any time she's got a story to tell."

> —*Entertainment Weekly*, on *Cowboy Come Home*

"Readers are sure to enjoy this sweet, gentle love story."

> —*Publishers Weekly*, on *Cowboy Come Home*

"Sexy, smart, sensational!"

> —Lori Wilde, *New York Times* bestselling
> author, on *Big Bad Cowboy*

"*Big Bad Cowboy* is sweet and sexy!"

> —Jennifer Ryan, *New York Times* bestselling
> author, on *Big Bad Cowboy*

"Heartwarming, hysterical and completely sexy and charming, *Big Bad Cowboy* was an outstanding start to the Once Upon a Time in Texas series...A series that I expect to be a huge hit with rom-com fans."

> —Harlequin Junkie, on *Big Bad Cowboy*

"Fans of Susan Elizabeth Phillips will delight in this funny, optimistic, quirky contemporary."

> —*Publishers Weekly* on *Big Bad Cowboy*
> (Starred Review)

Must Love
COWBOYS

CARLY
BLOOM

FOREVER

NEW YORK   BOSTON

Forever
Hachette Book Group
1290 Avenue of the Americas, New York, NY 10104
read-forever.com
twitter.com/readforeverpub

First Edition: April 2021

Forever is an imprint of Grand Central Publishing. The Forever name and logo are trademarks of Hachette Book Group, Inc.

The publisher is not responsible for websites (or their content) that are not owned by the publisher.

The Hachette Speakers Bureau provides a wide range of authors for speaking events. To find out more, go to www.hachettespeakersbureau.com or call (866) 376-6591.

ISBNs: 978-1-5387-6350-6 (mass market), 978-1-538-76348-3 (ebook)

Printed in the United States of America

OPM

10 9 8 7 6 5 4 3 2 1

To Ellie and Camille, the boldest, strongest, and smartest heroines I've ever created.

Must Love
COWBOYS

Chapter

One

❦

Alice Martin was wide awake, and the rest of the guests at the Village Chateau probably were, too. It was a fancy hotel—the nicest one in town—but it was also old, and the walls and ceilings were paper-thin.

Hopefully, the violently rocking ceiling fan was properly secured.

Oh GOD! Don't stop, baby…

Baby didn't stop.

Alice rolled over, put a pillow over her head, and tried to ignore the wedding hookup happening in the room above. She should have gone home after Casey and Jessica's reception instead of spending the night in Carmen's suite. But she'd had a bit of champagne, and besides, she liked hanging out with Carmen, despite them not knowing each other all that well.

On the surface, Alice and Carmen couldn't be more different. Carmen was a blue-haired, pierced, and tattooed celebrity chef with her own television show, *Funky Fusions*. And Alice was a brown-haired, single-pierced (each earlobe), and completely untattooed small-town librarian.

But in the town of Big Verde, neither of them quite fit in.

During a brief visit to Big Verde a couple of years ago, Carmen had bought the Village Chateau's struggling restaurant, renaming it Chateau Bleu. She lived in Houston and didn't come to town much—Jessica managed the restaurant—but she kept a suite at the hotel for when she did. The folks of Big Verde considered her a rare and exotic creature.

As for Alice, the folks of Big Verde seemed to find her rather odd, too. They were nice enough. Truly, they were. But Alice had never felt like she belonged. Maybe that's why she preferred to keep her nose stuck in a book.

Nevertheless, small-town etiquette dictated that nobody ever be left out, so Alice was invited to every graduation ceremony, birthday party, baby shower, and wedding. And because small-town etiquette also dictated that invitations be graciously accepted, Alice went to every graduation ceremony, birthday party, baby shower, and wedding.

She bit her lip and frowned. Brittany Fox's wedding was only six weeks away. And even though Alice usually flew solo at weddings (she was intentionally and deliberately single), she'd need a date for that one.

Brittany was the library's intern, and over the past two months she'd gone from a lovely ray of sunshine to the absolute worst bridezilla Big Verde had ever seen. And the "and Guest" she'd written on Alice's invitation—calligraphy with gold-infused ink—seemed to be more of a command than a polite suggestion.

Alice would typically ignore such a command. But Brittany was fueled by a combination of stubbornness and wedding-planning stress hormones. She cried easily, which made Alice uncomfortable, and she insisted that an odd number of guests made seating charts impossible. She'd made it her mission to find Alice a date, parading nearly every single man in the county through the library, which was awkward and disruptive.

Must Love Cowboys would be the motto of Big Verde's dating scene (if it *had* a dating scene), and although Alice had nothing against cowboys, she didn't have much in common with them. Nor did she have anything in common with Brittany's balding uncle, who, despite having recently found a cure for his hyperhidrosis—sweaty palms—was not anyone she wanted to spend time with. And he was who Brittany was currently threatening to fix her up with.

Alice needed a date for the wedding. But it would be a man of her *own* choosing. Preferably a non-sweaty one.

She groaned loudly into her pillow. All the men she knew were engaged or married. Such was life at thirty-two in a small town. Holy guacamole, who could she possibly take?

The lump of covers in bed next to her moved. "I can't tell if that noise was you or the woman upstairs," Carmen said. "If it was you, you're having more fun than I am."

"It was me. And I'm not having fun."

The ceiling fan was still rocking, so at least somebody was.

Scuffling sounds came from the nightstand as Carmen patted it down in search of the lamp switch. The unmistakable sound of a beverage falling over was followed by a whispered *dammit*.

The light came on, and Alice and Carmen squinted at each other. Then Carmen gasped and picked up a pair of Spanx off the floor to frantically slap at the bright red liquid edging toward their cell phones.

"I doubt that's very absorbent," Alice said, reaching over Carmen and snatching her phone out of the way.

Carmen, who had won a tequila shot contest with a young cowboy earlier in the evening, dropped the undergarment and flopped back onto the mattress. Her short hair stuck up in all directions, and she looked like a slightly deranged Cookie Monster. "Sorry. I opened that can and forgot about it. I heard energy drinks will prevent a hangover."

Alice climbed out of bed and hurried to the bathroom for a washcloth. Then she began wiping down the nightstand and floor. Her dress, draped over the back of a chair, was splattered with bright red spots. "Dang it. This is going to stain."

"Sorry. I'll have it cleaned," Carmen mumbled.

"You don't need to do that," Alice said. "It was an accident."

Carmen sat up to protest, but the woman upstairs started some interesting vocalizations. They stared at the ceiling.

"You don't think he's killing her, do you?" Alice asked.

"No. But I think she's died and gone to heaven at least three times already."

Oh my God, oh my God, oh my God …

"And she seems very religious," Alice said.

Carmen giggled. "It'll be over soon. He can't last much longer."

Alice held up a finger. "Actually, the average male lasts anywhere from four to six minutes during intercourse. But alcohol can reduce sensation, thereby making it more difficult to climax."

"Let's hope he's not drunk. Also, did you know you're like a walking, talking Wikipedia?"

It might have been mentioned once or twice, but Alice couldn't help it. Spouting facts had been her solution to shyness as a child, and it had become a habit. She was curious by nature, and as a librarian, she had ample access to all kinds of interesting and uninteresting facts about everything.

Facts were facts. Feelings were … messy. Why did people always want to talk about them?

Carmen checked her phone. "God. It's nearly two o'clock. And I've got a busy day tomorrow. Jessica will be off on her honeymoon, and half the restaurant staff is going to call in sick with wedding hangovers."

"Maybe you can call in sick with a wedding hangover, too?"

Carmen looked at the ceiling. "Nope. How long do you think someone can go with a numb penis?"

"Probably pretty long." Alice picked up her stained dress and slipped it over her camisole and undies. "I'm going up there."

Carmen got out of bed. "Up where?"

"We're in room 118. They must be in 218. I'm going to let them know they're keeping everyone awake."

The ceiling fan began rocking faster, and the woman upstairs moaned with more urgency. Carmen raised an eyebrow. "Hold on. Maybe they're about done."

Alice stared into Carmen's bloodshot eyes, and they both held their breath.

There was a long, piercing scream…

"Okay. Now he really has killed her," Carmen said. "Call nine-one-one."

Alice put a finger to her lips, and then…Silence. Beautiful, sweet silence.

Carmen started a slow clap. "Bravo!" she shouted at the ceiling.

Alice started to remove her dress. "Whew! I think he's finally spent."

Upstairs, a bed squeaked loudly. Voices murmured. And then…

The banging started.

"Oh my God," Carmen said. "I think they've just changed positions. Maybe they've gone doggie."

"It's unlikely she'll achieve another orgasm that way," Alice said. "Fewer than nine percent of women report being able to do so."

Carmen just stared at her. "I think I did once."

"You're drunk," Alice said. "Get back in bed."

"But—"

Alice opened the door. "I'll be back in a few minutes."

She climbed the stairs at the end of the hall and marched directly to room 218. Then she knocked and waited while tapping her bare foot, because dang it, she'd forgotten to put on shoes. Also, things were super quiet. Maybe they were done—

A bare chest suddenly opened the door. At least that's how it seemed. There were probably other body parts as well—a head and legs, for example. But she only noticed the chest, which was muscular, naked, and taking up the entire doorway. She and the chest were eyeball-to-nipple, which was awkward, yet somehow fascinating, and it took a bit of effort to drag her gaze higher, where it landed on a pair of bright blue eyes.

An irritating tingle sparked at the base of her spine and worked its way up to her mouth, where it came out as "Oh. It's you."

The source of the ruckus was Beau Montgomery. Not surprising.

Beau raised his eyebrows and ran a hand through his tousled sandy-blond hair. "Are you lost, Allie Cat?"

A lot of people couldn't tell Beau from his twin brother, Bryce. But Alice could. For one thing, nobody but Beau used that childish nickname for her. For another, Bryce wouldn't be inconsiderate enough to keep everyone awake with noisy, obnoxious sex. Also, Beau's face was thinner. And his chin cleft was just a tad deeper.

"Of course I'm not lost."

"Then might I ask why you're knocking on my door in the middle of the night?" His eyes drifted lazily up and down her red-stained dress. "And did you kill somebody?"

His gaze warmed her skin, made her head foggy, and . . . She'd come up here on a mission. "I was just about to ask you the same thing."

Beau raised an eyebrow. "Pardon?"

"Did you know there is a noise ordinance in Big Verde after ten o'clock?"

Beau rubbed his chin. "No, I don't think I was aware of that."

Alice rose on her toes and tried to peek over his shoulder. Unfortunately, he was too dang big, and she couldn't see who else was in the room. "You and your lady friend are keeping the entire hotel up," she whispered fiercely.

"Me and my—" Beau's eyebrows furrowed. Then they rose, touching a lock of hair on his forehead. Was it possible he was embarrassed? Or at least slightly chagrined? She took a step back as he moved into the hall, pulling the door shut behind him. He obviously didn't want her to know who was in there. And that was fine. Who cared? But Beau had a reputation for being a love 'em and leave 'em kind of guy, and she hoped that whoever was in his bed knew it.

Of course the woman knew it. That's how reputations worked.

Beau leaned against the doorframe with a grin. A myriad of laugh lines—another clue to distinguish him from his brother—appeared at the corners of his eyes. "Isn't there an ordinance against quoting ordinances after midnight?"

The answer to that was a solid *no*, but Beau was probably trying to be funny. Giving a response would be weird, so Alice swallowed down the explanation that you couldn't have an ordinance against quoting an ordinance because that would be an infringement of the First Amendment.

"You're being rude," she said. "You're keeping the entire hotel awake."

Beau produced a crooked little smirk that caused a dimple to appear in his right cheek. "Sorry, darlin'."

* * *

Beau wasn't sorry at all, and since the innocent aw-shucks routine had never worked on Alice, he figured she knew it.

He hooked a thumb in the waistband of his jeans, which he'd yanked on quickly to answer the door. He hadn't bothered with the button, and the jeans slid lower on his hips. He started to hike them up, but then he noticed Alice's gaze had dropped—so had her jaw—and the color in her cheeks had gone from rosy to fire-engine red.

This was interesting.

He let the full weight of his arm pull the waistband even lower—he hadn't bothered with underwear either—and flexed his abs.

Alice's chest rose and fell, and she brought a hand up to fan her face.

This was *very* interesting. Was it possible that Miss Martin was worked up? Turned on? *By him?*

"Cool your jets, Allie. The amorous activities are over."

He sure as hell hoped that was true. The noisy couple next door had quieted down about thirty seconds before Alice knocked on his door. But Alice didn't need to know that. Not while her cheeks were such a lovely shade of scarlet from irritation and...

Whatever it was that was making her pupils dilate.

"My jets don't need cooling, thank you very much."

"Well, you look pretty heated. Are you feeling okay?"

He loved ruffling her feathers. He'd been doing it since the age of nine, when his parents' list of babysitters for him and Bryce had dwindled down to one incredibly polite hard-ass thirteen-year-old named Alice Ann Martin.

"I feel fine except for being extremely tired and unable to sleep."

"Have you tried reading a book?" Beau asked. Because reading books was all Alice ever did.

Actually, that wasn't quite true. She also apparently stalked hotel hallways, hoping to make a citizen's arrest if folks were having too much fun.

Alice rolled her eyes. "Yes, and it was hard to concentrate because of all the moaning."

She turned her little nose up, as if she knew of a specific ordinance against orgasms.

Allie loved rules. And she'd had plenty for him and Bryce when she'd been their babysitter. Luckily, once he and Bryce finished eighth grade, their parents finally decided they could be left alone without burning the house down. It was right before Alice had gone away to college. Obviously, he and Bryce had changed a lot since then. Their cotton-top heads had turned sandy blond. They were tall—he had a good foot on Alice—and hard work kept them fit.

Hell, they were buff. And until now, he hadn't known Alice had noticed.

Her pulse pounded frantically at that sweet spot at the base of her neck.

She'd noticed, all right.

"Beau Montgomery, it's past midnight. You've been disrespectful to all the guests in the hotel. You'd better keep it down, or I'll—"

"Spank me?"

Alice pursed her lips and flared her cute little bunny nostrils. He hoped she'd go for the foot stomp. It was especially entertaining when she did that.

Her right foot—bare, with painted pink toenails—quivered. She was fighting the foot stomp. "I don't believe in corporal punishment."

"That's probably a shame," Beau said.

Alice rolled her eyes before spinning on her heel and heading for the stairs at the end of the hall. Was she really going to let him have the last word?

She stopped and turned around.

Nope.

"Beau Montgomery," she said. "Don't make me come back up here."

He laughed. He should probably 'fess up about Allie having the wrong room, but she was already halfway down the stairs. Which was fine, because Alice was going to think whatever she wanted to think, which was always the worst where he was concerned.

He went back into his room, shaking his head. He should have gone home after the reception, but Jessica and Casey had paid for rooms for everyone who'd helped out with the wedding. It was a nice room, and he'd anticipated having someone to share it with. Especially since his job had been to entertain all of Jessica's single out-of-town friends.

Just swing them around the dance floor and call them darlin'.
They're not used to real cowboys, and they'll be thrilled!

As one of the foremen of Rancho Cañada Verde—Bryce was
the other—Beau was definitely a "real" cowboy. And since he
loved to dance and charm the ladies, it had seemed like the perfect
assignment.

He stripped off his jeans and climbed back into bed, stretching
and yawning. The night had been a total bust. He'd danced with
every bridesmaid, cousin, and business associate of Jessica's. He'd
two-stepped, boot-scooted, and even whipped and nae-naed. He'd
fetched drinks and paid compliments. But after all that, here he
was, sprawled out in a double bed all by himself.

He'd thought things had started looking up when Jessica's
old college roommate began making some serious moves late in
the evening. To put it politely, she'd been an enthusiastic dance
partner. She'd probably be able to pick him out of a lineup if she
was allowed to do it with her pelvis. But while her body had been
all over him, her eyes kept landing on a sullen guy sitting all by
himself in the corner.

"Old boyfriend?" he'd asked.

The poor woman had wilted in embarrassment. Beau could have
been a dick about it, but it wasn't the first time he'd been used to
make someone jealous. He'd even helped her out by making sure
the guy had a clear line of sight while he pretended to whisper
sweet nothings in her ear. And judging by the sounds that had
come from next door, the couple was definitely back together.

Beau rolled onto his side and closed his eyes. He had to be up
early to take his grandmother to church in the morning. He'd been
sinning on Saturday and praying on Sunday ever since he was thirteen, which was when he'd sneaked his first cigarette, tossed back
his first shot of whiskey, and started having all kinds of conflicting
and inappropriate thoughts about the babysitter.

Chapter Two

❧

Sundays were busy at Chateau Bleu. Tourists visiting the Texas Hill Country's many wineries, shops, and swimming holes liked to drop in for brunch, and they were often joined by locals after the churches let out. Because of the wedding guests staying in the hotel, the restaurant was buzzing this morning. Luckily, Alice managed to snag a small table in the corner.

She tugged at the unfamiliar shirt riding up her midriff. When she'd woken up this morning, both her dress and Carmen were gone. A note explained that Carmen had taken the dress to have it cleaned. In its place were a pair of extremely short shorts and a pink cropped top with the image of a black cat. It said MEOW in glittery letters.

We're about the same size. Wear my kitty T!

A blue head caught Alice's attention. Carmen was darting in and out of all the tables, and when she spotted Alice, she headed right over.

She poured coffee in Alice's cup and plopped into the other chair. "Good morning, roomie. I fell asleep before you got back to the room, and you were in a coma when I woke up."

"Not quite a coma, but I did finally fall asleep. And, erm, thanks for the clothes?"

Carmen grinned. "You look cute."

That was doubtful. "Did the energy drink work?"

"Who knows? I spilled it all over your dress." She pointed at her head. "Raging headache."

Carmen looked great, as usual. Her hair was spiked up. She had on makeup, jewelry, and her signature classic white chef's jacket, monogrammed with a dark blue *B*, for *Bleu*, over ripped jeans with rhinestones on the back pockets. You'd never know she was hungover.

Alice had never been hungover. She had no desire to dehydrate her body, irritate her digestive tract, or cause her electrolytes to go out of whack, just to shed a few inhibitions. She was fond of many things, and her inhibitions ranked right up there with a good book and a snuggly cat.

"Well?" Carmen said. "How did the confrontation go?"

Alice poured some cream in her coffee. She doubted Beau Montgomery cared if anyone knew the noise had been coming from his room, but she wasn't one to participate in gossip. In fact, she hated it. And it was something small towns were particularly skilled at.

"Let's just say—"

"Dang it," Carmen said, standing up. "I'm being summoned by the hostess. You'll have to tell me later. Are you doing the buffet?"

"That's my plan."

Carmen gave her a thumbs-up. "There's good stuff on it this morning."

Alice didn't doubt it, and her mouth watered as she stood and headed for the spread, where she loaded her plate with a freshly baked croissant, a slice of German sausage quiche, and select pieces of cheese and fruit. When she looked up, Maggie Blake and Claire Kowalski were waving and pointing to an empty chair at their table. Their husbands, Travis and Ford, both smiled. Ford, who held baby Rosa, was the manager of Claire's family's ranch, Rancho Cañada Verde. Despite the bags beneath his eyes, parenthood looked good on him, and Alice smiled back and waved. Then she had the horrible thought that maybe they'd been waving at someone else. She briefly looked over her shoulder before sighing in relief.

Of course they were waving at her.

She collected her book, keys, and cup of coffee from her little table and then joined the group.

"Have a seat," Maggie said, pulling out a chair.

Maggie's short blond hair was a mess, her eyes were bloodshot, and she clutched a michelada in her small hand as if her life depended on it. A michelada was similar to a Bloody Mary, and paired with menudo, it was a popular hangover remedy in Big Verde.

"These are not as good as the ones you make," Maggie whispered. "They need more lime juice. Also, I'm digging your outfit."

Alice yanked on the shirt again. "I borrowed these clothes from Carmen."

"Well, you look cute! Great legs. Awesome butt. And you're pretty in pink."

That was the first time anyone had said she had an awesome butt. "Thanks. And don't let Carmen hear you criticize her micheladas."

Alice *did* make killer micheladas. They were popular at book club.

"What's wrong with my micheladas?" Carmen asked, swinging by their table with a coffeepot.

Maggie shrugged uncomfortably. "They need more lime juice. You should get Alice's recipe. Hers are the best."

Carmen put a hand on her hip. "Oh? How much lime juice per pitcher?"

"I'd say two limes, if they're juicy," Alice said. "Three if they're not."

"I'm still getting used to the ways of Big Verde," Carmen said. "None of my other restaurants offer hair of the dog selections on the menus."

Carmen's flagship restaurant was in Houston. The other was in Las Vegas. Both were named La Casa Bleu, and both were booked solid with reservations months in advance. And yet here Carmen was, holding a pot of coffee in Big Verde.

She looked at Maggie's husband, Travis. "How's the menudo?"

"Almost as good as Lupe's," Travis said.

Travis and Maggie owned Happy Trails Ranch, a small family ranch that sold directly to consumers. Lupe Garza handled shipping and booked their tours and field trips. From what Alice could tell, she was like a member of their family.

"*Almost* as good?" Carmen asked. "I think I need to get some hometown recipes. You locals have all the secrets."

Maggie eyed her bowl before pushing it away. "I know it's supposed to cure a hangover, but I've never been able to eat menudo. I shouldn't have ordered it."

Claire Kowalski held up a buttered croissant and said, "Menudo is just one of the many reasons I rarely eat meat."

Trista Larson showed up at the table, followed by her husband, Bubba. "I can't eat menudo. I've never cared much for tripe." She wrinkled her delicate freckled nose. "Texture issues."

Tripe was the stomach lining of a cow, and it was the main ingredient in menudo. Alice didn't much care for it, either.

Bubba held two plates, piled high with sausage links and bacon. "You have to have the stomach for stomach, which I do," he said. "Can I have a bowl, Carmen?"

"And do y'all have room for two more at this table?" Trista asked.

"You have the stomach for literally everything," Travis said. "Let's pull that table over," he added, pointing to a newly cleared table for two.

While Bubba and Trista got settled, Travis smacked his lips. "Time to doctor this bad boy up," he said, gazing at his bowl. He took a pinch of dried oregano from a nearby condiment bowl and followed it up with cilantro and a spoonful of raw onions and jalapeños.

Maggie made a face. "With all those onions, you can rest assured there will be absolutely no kissing—or anything else—for the rest of the day. And possibly tomorrow."

"Well, sweetheart, after what you put me through last night, I doubt I could muster the energy."

Maggie feigned embarrassment while everyone laughed.

"Was that you making all that racket last night?" Bubba asked.

"No," Maggie said. "I don't know who that was, but I'd like to meet whoever released the Kraken."

Alice knew, but she bit her tongue.

"I thought it would never end," Trista said. "And when it finally did, I turned to Bubba and said *I'll have what she's having*."

"You had it plenty," Bubba said.

Trista shook her head. "No. I don't think I did."

"Well, you had *something*," Bubba said. "And you weren't complaining about it."

"Hotel sex is the best," Maggie said. "There's just something special about a different bed and a do not disturb sign."

Claire sighed. "I can't wait until Rosa is old enough for sleepovers with my folks. She sleeps with us most nights, and we've had to get creative."

"Oh, please," Maggie said. "Like y'all ever had sex in an actual bed."

Alice sipped her coffee and listened to the easy banter. She had nothing to contribute to the conversation. Not even any facts or figures.

JD Mayes walked up, followed by his husband, Gabriel Castro. "Is there room for two more?"

"Absolutely," Bubba said, standing up and looking around for a couple of extra chairs. JD was Bubba's business partner, and they'd been friends since kindergarten.

Carmen came back with the coffeepot and gave JD and Gabriel each a kiss on the cheek. "You guys doing the buffet? Or are we talking hair of the dog?"

"Hair of the dog," JD said, running a hand over his handsome, but definitely haggard, face. "Thanks, Carmen."

Bubba dragged two extra chairs to the table as everyone shifted to make room. They ended up with four on one side and four on the other, with Alice relegated to the end.

Carmen brought two more micheladas to the table and set them in front of JD and Gabriel. "Menudo's coming out soon," she said, collapsing into the other empty chair on the end. "Whew! We're short on busboys, and as you all might have heard, my manager is on her honeymoon."

Bubba sat up straighter in his chair. "Do you need help?"

"Are you serious?"

"Sure I am. I used to bus tables at the Corner Café. My parents had all of us kids working there from the time we could walk."

"I doubt that's legal," Gabriel said. "But my menudo can wait. I'm happy to help, too."

"What do you need us to do?" Claire asked.

Carmen shook her head. "No, guys. You don't have to—"

Bubba had spotted a bus cart in the corner and was already headed that way.

Alice smiled at Carmen. "You indicated you needed help, and now you're going to get it."

"Y'all are so weird in this town," Carmen said, with a barely suppressed grin. "You help people and make direct eye contact, and I'll never get used to it."

"You're welcome," Maggie said.

Carmen laughed. "Seriously, I appreciate it. The church crowd is going to roll through that door any minute, and they're worse than my Houston A-list at nine o'clock on a Saturday night."

"People go to dinner at nine o'clock at night?" Travis asked.

Before Carmen could answer, the door opened and a mob of ladies waltzed in, tittering and chattering in their Sunday dresses.

Alice stood. Bubba was already clearing a table, and the one next to it could use clearing as well. She did a quick head count of the group at the door to see how many tables they'd need...*six, seven, eight*...

Ugh! Her skin prickled with irritation. Beau Montgomery was holding the door open, nodding and smiling at all the church ladies like he was a freaking choirboy.

"You okay, Alice?" Carmen asked.

Alice crossed her arms and narrowed her eyes as Carmen followed her gaze to where Beau stood, surrounded by his silver-haired harem of senior citizens.

"Aw," Carmen said. "Jessica says he comes here with his grandmother nearly every Sunday. Isn't that the sweetest thing ever?"

"Ha!" Alice said. "Beau Montgomery is no angel, believe me."

"I know," Carmen said, cheeks slightly flushed. "I hear he's a beast in bed, and that he never sleeps with the same woman twice."

"Everybody in the hotel knows he's a beast in bed," Alice said. "It's why we all have circles under our eyes this morning."

Carmen gasped. "That was Beau?"

Alice slapped a hand over her mouth. *Oops.*

* * *

Beau held his breath against the cloud of perfume fog and guided Nonnie to the hostess station, where Holly Vickers smiled brightly. "Hi, Mrs. Montgomery. That sure is some pretty turquoise you're wearing."

"Thank you, dear," Nonnie said, straightening the strand of blue beads. "It was a gift from Beau."

Holly raised an eyebrow at Beau. "Well, isn't he sweet?"

Beau returned the smile and removed his hat—white Stetson reserved for Sundays, weddings, and funerals—while watching Holly's cheeks turn as pink as a honey-baked ham on Easter. "Hi, Holly."

All he'd done was say hi, but Nonnie applied pressure to the sensitive flesh of his inner arm in a way that said, *Cut it out, Casanova.*

"Table for two?" Holly asked.

"Three," Beau said. "Bryce is joining us."

Holly looked into the dining room. "We're really packed this morning. And short-staffed. You might have to wait a few minutes while we clear a table."

"We can head on over to the Corner Café," Beau said to Nonnie. "I can text Bryce and let him know—"

Nonnie shook her head. "Don't be silly. We're already here."

"It looks like a table is being cleared right now," Holly said. "Just give us two minutes."

Beau followed Holly's gaze to a corner table, where a woman in extremely short shorts leaned over to grab some plates.

Damn. Very nice.

"Goodness!" Nonnie said. "Is that Alice Martin?"

Where?

Beau scanned all the nearby tables, but saw no sign of Judgy McJudgypants. But then a perky brown ponytail caught his eye, and it was attached to the woman he'd been eyeing in the super-short shorts.

"What is she doing clearing tables?" Nonnie asked.

Alice turned around. The pink T-shirt was too tight and stretched across her chest, glittering with the word *meow*.

Their eyes met, and Alice froze like a deer in the headlights. But after a few seconds, she seemed to decide to ignore him. She placed a tub of dishes on a cart and pushed it to the next dirty table without so much as a backward glance at him.

Those shorts, though.

Allie Cat had some nice, long legs.

Beau swallowed. Apparently, he was still having conflicting and inappropriate thoughts about the babysitter.

Chapter Three

🜂

Beau held a chair out for Nonnie and took the seat across from her. They had a nice table by a window, but he couldn't take advantage of the view. Not while there was a librarian loose in the restaurant.

"Help yourselves to whatever you want," Holly said, staring directly at Beau with a suggestive gaze that was probably not lost on his grandmother. "Hopefully, you'll see something you like."

"I'm sure we will," Nonnie said briskly. "There is plenty to choose from on the buffet."

Beau started to rise and head to the buffet bar, but his grandmother patted his hand. "We'll wait for Bryce."

Beau rolled his eyes but stayed put. He looked around and spotted Alice darting in and out of tables on the other side of the dining room. She glanced up, their eyes met again, and he couldn't help it. He smiled—nearly laughed out loud—remembering her shocked expression when he'd opened the door last night.

"What are you grinning about?" Nonnie asked.

"Nothing."

Nonnie gave him a look that said she didn't believe him but also that she didn't need to know everything. "I wonder why Alice Martin is clearing tables? She has a degree from a university and works at the library."

Actually, Alice had three degrees.

Undergrad from Rice, and two master's degrees from Texas Woman's University.

It had been hard to miss a big old photo of Alice Martin in the Big Verde News every time she'd hit a dean's list or earned another degree. Folks acted like she was the smartest person in town, which she probably was.

Carmen Foraccio, the blue-haired owner of the restaurant, stopped by their table. She said hello to Nonnie, and then she looked at Beau. "Well, well, well. Look what the cat dragged in."

She held a steaming coffeepot in her right hand, so Beau turned his cup over. "Good morning, Carmen. You're looking chipper."

Carmen raised a skeptical eyebrow and poured hot coffee into his cup. "You're either blind or being sarcastic, and I'm too hungover to care which."

Beau laughed. "I imagine you feel like you beat Worth Jarvis in a tequila shot contest last night."

Carmen's mouth dropped open. "Is that a thing I actually did?"

Beau nodded.

"Hopefully that explains the fifty-dollar bill I found in my bra this morning."

"You literally drank the poor kid under the table."

Carmen set a little pitcher of cream next to his cup. "Speaking of last night, if you need any help burying the body, just let me know."

Alice breezed by with an armful of plates and snorted.

Somebody had loose lips.

"What body?" Nonnie asked, eyes wide with alarm.

Carmen poured his grandmother a cup of coffee. "Everybody's fine, Mrs. Montgomery. I'm just messing with your grandson."

Beau narrowed his eyes, hoping the conversation would end right here. Luckily, his brother walked into the restaurant. "Look," he said. "There's Bryce."

Saved by the twin.

Nonnie accepted a kiss on the cheek from Bryce. "Carmen," she said. "Have you recently hired some new weekend staff?"

Carmen laughed. "I'm short on help today, so I've got some volunteers."

Ah. That explained it. Most of Chateau Bleu's staff had been at Jessica and Casey's wedding last night.

"You need help?" Bryce asked, just as Beau stood up to offer.

"No, no," Carmen said. "Thank you for offering—I should have seen that coming—but, it's totally under control. The group you came in with is the last wave. We're all good. Just relax and enjoy your meal like normal people."

Beau sat down. "If you say so."

"I do. Enjoy your brunch."

Bryce jerked his head toward the buffet bar, and Beau responded with a nod.

"I can see we've decided on the buffet," Nonnie said.

A few minutes later, Nonnie was daintily working her way through a pastry the size of her head while Beau and Bryce scraped their plates.

"Going back in for round three?" Bryce asked, patting his stomach.

Beau scooped up the last of his scrambled eggs. "I don't think I have room. And besides, we've got to ride later today."

"Gerome has you boys working on a Sunday?" Nonnie asked.

Beau shrugged. "Just a quick meeting."

"And then we're riding the fence lines," Bryce added.

They probably didn't need to ride the fence lines. There hadn't been any weak spots for months. But riding fence lines was enjoyable. Especially at sunset.

Alice walked by, and Beau tried hard not to look at her.

"Alice is not dressed very appropriately for working in a restaurant *or* a library," their grandmother said.

"Oh really?" Beau said. "I hadn't noticed."

Worn spot on the left back pocket of those shorts. Small stain on the T-shirt, right above the w.

Bryce cleared his throat, and Beau avoided eye contact. Bryce was the one person in Big Verde who knew about Beau's prepubescent crush on Alice. Which had lingered just a bit into post-pubescence.

What could he say? The teenage years were weird for everyone. Especially if you were fifteen years old with a raging boner for your nineteen-year-old former babysitter who was away at college, not thinking of you at all, because you were a baby, and a dumb baby, at that.

Why can't you pay attention like Bryce? and *You're not even trying!* were messages that had played on repeat. He'd heard it from his teachers and his mother. And he'd heard it from Alice whenever babysitting had included helping them with their homework.

By the time he was a senior, the crush had faded. Mostly. But then Alice, who'd already graduated from Rice—a year early and summa cum laude—had come home to Big Verde for the holidays. She was a grad student at TWU, and what the holy hell had made Beau think she'd want to dance with him on New Year's Eve at the VFW hall?

Jim Beam. He and the rest of his underage gang had been pouring it into their Cokes all night, and it had made him even cockier than usual.

At eighteen, he'd already had more than a little experience with girls. They liked him and he liked them. But by then, Alice was a grown woman.

It had taken courage (and cajoling from Bryce and their friends) to ask her if she wanted to dance. But he'd done it. He'd strutted over like a doofus, full of confidence he hadn't deserved, and asked her to dance in front of his friends.

She'd said no before reminding him of Big Verde's eleven o'clock curfew for unattended minors. He'd started to slink off, too embarrassed to correct her (he *hadn't* been a minor), when she'd grabbed his arm. For a brief moment, he'd thought she'd changed her mind. But no. She gave him a brief lecture on the dangers of underage drinking (he absolutely *had* been guilty of that) before offering to drive him home.

He'd jerked his arm away, and Bryce and their buddies had howled with laughter as he crawled back with his hat in his hands and his tail between his legs.

The server startled him out of his reverie by placing the check on the table, and in an effort to hide the blush spreading across his face, Beau grabbed it and stared at it.

Dammit. The words blurred and vibrated and generally refused to cooperate. He squinted and reminded himself that he *knew* what it said, so he didn't have to read it. They'd all had buffet plates and coffee.

He focused on the total.

Was that a nine or a six?

His skin prickled, sweat dripped down his back, and his pulse sped up. Bryce leaned over to take a look, but Beau shook his head.

Use logic. There are three people. The buffet is $21.95 per person. A nine doesn't make sense. It has to be a six.

He effortlessly calculated the tip for the bill, wrote it on the ticket, and handed a credit card to the server.

* * *

Beau had been side-eyeing her all morning. Why? He hadn't seemed upset over her knocking on his door. In fact, he'd seemed amused. Because of course he was. Everything was funny to Beau.

Yep. Everything was just a big old hilarious joke.

An old familiar hurt worked its way into her consciousness.

New Year's Eve.

She'd been home from school for the holidays, and there was a dance at the VFW hall. Claire had been home for the holidays, too, and she'd asked Alice if she wanted to go. She and Claire hadn't hung out in high school, but Alice had always liked her, so she'd nervously accepted.

She was in her first year of grad school, but as she'd walked into the hall, she'd felt sixteen again. And sixteen had not been a very good year. She'd been dorky. Nerdy. On the outside looking in. All the clichés had applied.

A band had played country music, and Claire was immediately whisked out onto the dance floor by someone they'd gone to school with. Alice had bought a beer—she'd needed something to hold—before assuming a position against the wall right between a fake tree and the American flag. A few folks smiled or said hello, but nobody stopped to talk.

She'd spotted two identical cowboy hats among the crowd, and realized in stunned amazement that they belonged to the Montgomery twins. And boy, had they grown up.

She'd spent five long years as the twins' babysitter. They'd been hellions, and she'd survived countless pranks (including one that turned her skin orange), put out literal fires, and confiscated cigarettes, alcohol, and a magazine called *Jugs*. Their parents couldn't leave them alone for more than ten minutes. No other babysitter ever came back a second time, but Alice survived out of sheer stubbornness and a consistent lack of anything else to do on a Saturday night. It hadn't hurt that Mr. and Mrs. Montgomery were desperate and therefore paid her like she was the last living babysitter in Verde County, which she basically was as far as their boys were concerned.

The twins had resented her, of course. So, she'd been pleasantly surprised when Bryce approached her at the VFW hall with a smile and an outheld hand. He'd inquired about school, and they'd made small talk for a few minutes before he wandered off, leaving her by the potted plant. Beau, on the other hand, had ignored her completely. He'd been surrounded by girls, and, like last night at Jessica and Casey's wedding, he'd danced with every single one.

By the end of the night, Alice had been more than ready to go home. And as the band announced the last song, the one that would usher in the New Year, Beau had sauntered over and asked her to dance. And behind him, his group of friends had been snickering and laughing.

That would have been bad enough, but then Alice had noticed the money. The boys had been holding dollar bills.

Beau had done it on a dare, making her the butt of his joke.

She might have gotten a little snarky—she didn't remember exactly what was said—and Beau had strutted off to howls of laughter.

He'd grown up since then. But he obviously still liked to taunt her. Isn't that what he'd been doing last night when he'd answered the door shirtless, with his jeans unbuttoned, smirking and oozing sex? He'd looked her up and down as if to say, *What's happening behind this door that's keeping the entire hotel up is something you'll never get.*

Which was fine.

Because she didn't want it.

Her phone rang, interrupting her thoughts. She reached around to the extremely tight back pocket of Carmen's cutoff shorts and yanked it out. It was her mother. Her parents were leaving for a month-long trip to Costa Rica today. It was the first vacation they'd taken in years, and they were probably just calling to say goodbye.

"Hi, Mom. Are you guys headed out?"

"Alice, we have a situation."

Scenarios began flashing through her mind. Had they been in a wreck? Were they at the emergency room? Maybe they'd just forgotten to unplug the coffeepot. She pulled her keys out of her pocket. "What's wrong?"

"We're already halfway to the airport, and—"

"Is it car trouble? Do you need me to come and get you?"

"No, honey. We're fine. But the doggie hotel called."

Oh great. The "doggie hotel" was where her parents usually boarded Gaston, their enormous Great Pyrenees. And he was a royal pain in the booty.

"What did he do?"

"Now, Alice. It isn't always Gaston's fault—"

"Yes, it is."

"He's being bullied."

"Bullied?"

"He had a run-in with another dog. Honestly, who could get along with a Labrador?"

"Pretty much anyone. Labradors are literally known for their cheerful dispositions."

"Can he stay with you? It's only for a few weeks."

Alice sighed and squeezed the bridge of her nose. Gaston was huge. Spoiled. And he was a walking blizzard of hair and dander. But she didn't want her parents' vacation ruined.

"Fine. But no matter how much he begs, he's not getting into my bed."

Someone bumped into her, and she turned to see Beau Montgomery—eyes twinkling—putting his hat on. He'd clearly overheard that last statement. And now he was going to say something stu—

"I'm sure there's an ordinance against that, Allie."

Chapter

Four

❦

Gerome Kowalski's study in the ranch house was the official business office of Rancho Cañada Verde, even though Gerome sat behind the desk less and less. He and Miss Lilly had stepped back from running the ranch, and now their daughter, Claire, and her husband, Ford, were the ones operating things.

Claire handled the marketing part of it, because Rancho Cañada Verde was more than just a ranch. It was also a brand, and its products were on shelves in grocery and department stores. They even had a ranch store in downtown Big Verde that sold everything from kitchenware to clothing and luggage.

Ford managed the ranch itself, with the help of Beau and Bryce. As foremen of Rancho Cañada Verde, they'd stepped into their father's boots. He'd been the foreman for twenty-seven years before retiring with their mom to a condo in Corpus Christi, where they spent their days fishing—bought a boat and everything—much like Gerome and Lilly spent theirs traveling around the country with a little travel trailer in tow.

People moved on, sought new experiences. But Beau and Bryce

weren't like that. They were happy to stay right here on the ranch where they'd grown up, living in the very cabin where they'd been raised.

Beau stared through the windshield at the Kowalskis' big wraparound porch. How many Popsicles had he licked on those steps while his daddy and Gerome had talked business inside? Hell, he'd tried to steal his very first kiss right there beneath the windchimes.

Claire had socked him good before acting like she was going to barf. He'd been fourteen and thought he was a full-grown man. Claire had been seventeen—much closer to being fully grown— and she'd had a good right hook. It had taught him a valuable lesson.

Real men don't steal anything, and that includes kisses.

Claire still occasionally stuck her finger down her throat and pretended to gag if he so much as looked at her wrong.

This ranch was his past, his present, and his future. If he had his way, he'd be buried beneath the ancient live oak up on Comanche Hill.

He climbed out of the truck just as Miss Lilly came out with a broom. "Good afternoon, boys. There's fresh coffee in the kitchen, and I think there might be some leftover cinnamon buns on the counter."

Beau flew up the steps, pausing briefly to give Miss Lilly a kiss on the cheek. "Your buns are absolutely delectable, Miss Lilly."

A broom connected solidly with *his* buns. "You'd better not let Gerome hear you talking like that, Beau Montgomery."

"You know darn well that Gerome would agree," he said. "And how do you know I'm not Bryce?"

That was a silly question. There were only five women alive who could instantly tell him and Bryce apart, and Lilly Kowalski was one of them. The others were their mom, Nonnie, Claire, and, for some godforsaken reason, Alice Martin.

"For one thing, Bryce has more sense."

True, but ouch.

"For another, you're a shameless flirt. Even old ladies like me aren't off limits, and that's a disgrace."

Beau winked at her, and then he nearly laughed as he watched her trying not to grin. Bryce walked up and gave her a chaste kiss on the cheek. "Is this person bothering you, Miss Lilly?"

"Never," she said. "Now get on inside, both of you. Gerome and Ford are waiting."

"Gerome?"

"Yes, he has something important to discuss with you boys."

Beau and Bryce glanced at each other. They loved Gerome like a father, and it would be good to see him. But what could the "something important" be? The warm scent of sugar and cinnamon greeted them as they walked through the door, and they followed their noses straight into the kitchen, where three cinnamon rolls sat on a plate.

Bryce grabbed two before Beau could stop him, cramming one into his mouth. Then he looked at his brother with satisfaction and bulging cheeks.

Beau grabbed the remaining roll. "Come on. Let's go upstairs."

By the time they got to the landing, the cinnamon rolls were history, and they were met by Gerome's booming voice—a welcome sound after the man's brush with throat cancer two years ago—and Ford's softer tone. The study door was open, so they walked on in.

Gerome stood and held out a hand. "Howdy, boys. I hope you don't mind me sitting in on your meeting with Ford."

Beau grinned and shook Gerome's big, warm hand. His grip was strong, and even though he was in his late seventies, he was an imposing figure. Nobody minded a bit that he was sitting in on a meeting about the ranch that had been in his family for multiple generations.

"I guess we'll tolerate it," Beau said with a wink.

Gerome chuckled. "Have a seat. We have some news."

We have some news could mean a lot of things. But judging from Gerome's relaxed demeanor, it wasn't anything too terrible.

They sat just as Claire waltzed in, baby Rosa in her arms. All four of them immediately jumped back up, seeing as how a woman had entered the room.

Claire rolled her eyes. "Good Lord. Would y'all please sit down?"

They did, and Claire deposited Rosa in Gerome's lap, where the baby immediately became enthralled with the snaps on her grandfather's starched white shirt. "I can tell by how calm they are that you haven't told them yet," Claire said, nodding her head in Beau and Bryce's direction.

Bryce looked at Beau, eyebrow cocked. *What could this be about?*

Beau shrugged. *No idea.*

Bryce snapped his fingers and narrowed his eyes. *You brought that bull to the pens like I told you to. Right?*

Beau rolled his eyes and shook his head. *Of course, I did... Asshole.*

"Are you two finished having your creepy telepathic conversation?" Claire asked.

Their mama always told them it made folks uncomfortable when they communicated with facial expressions.

Gerome cleared his throat. "Because of the drought, we need to thin out the herd."

Bryce stretched his legs and crossed them at the ankles. "Mother Nature's an indecisive bitch, isn't she?"

Big Verde had suffered a catastrophic flood a little over two years ago, and now they were in the middle of a drought.

"We've got some cows that haven't calved in a couple of seasons," Beau said. "And quite a few bulls to take to auction. How big of a cut are we talking?"

"We're not going to actually get rid of any cattle," Ford said. "We're just going to move them."

"Where? Are we leasing a place?"

Gerome grinned at Claire. "You tell 'em the plan. I don't have the balls."

Claire leaned against the desk and crossed her arms over her ample chest. She might be curvy and gorgeous and in possession of way more tiaras than the average person—rodeo queen, homecoming queen, prom queen, and Queen Crispin of the Big Verde Apple Festival—but she still typically had the biggest balls in the room.

"Have you heard of the Rockin' H Ranch?" she asked. "It's outside of Austin."

Bryce and Beau looked at each other and shrugged. "The only Rockin' H I know of is a dude ranch," Beau said. And then he laughed, because there was no way Gerome Kowalski was going to have any of his purebred, grass-fed, organic, free-range cattle lounging around a dude ranch while fake cowboys played guitars and sang songs around the campfire.

"That's the one," Ford said.

"What?" Bryce said. "You're kidding, right? We're moving our cattle to a—"

"Damn spa!" Beau said, interrupting. "I've seen their ads. They've got a swimming pool—"

Bryce cut in. "A restaurant—"

"Actually," Claire said. "The restaurant has closed."

Beau didn't really care about the restaurant. He just couldn't believe their cattle were headed to a resort. It didn't sit right. He prided himself on being a real cowboy. There weren't that many of them left. And on Rancho Cañada Verde, they did things the old-fashioned way. On horseback. No helicopters. No feedlot. They even still branded the old-fashioned way, with the same branding iron that Gerome's great-grandfather had used.

"And," Claire said, clapping her hands and bouncing on her heels. "There's more."

"Claire," Gerome said. "Don't go whistling before the water's boiled."

Claire actually did look like a teapot about to start whistling. She practically had steam coming out of her ears. "We're buying the whole place," she whispered.

Ford and Gerome sighed in unison.

"I'm hoping you two can keep a secret better than Claire," Ford said. "It's not a done deal. There's still financing and paperwork and whatnot."

"We're buying a resort?" Beau said. "Seriously?"

Gerome stood up and handed the baby back to Claire. Then he leaned over and got right in the little one's face. "Why don't you stick that chubby little fist in your mama's mouth instead of your own?"

Ford grinned. "What Princess Blabbermouth says is true. Initially, we were just looking to lease some land for grazing. But the Hills are itching to unload the place, and—"

"And it will be one more way that Rancho Cañada Verde can diversify," Claire said. "The property is a mess at the moment, but I feel confident that we can turn it around."

Gerome sat back down. "But for now, all we're doing is leasing a gorgeous one-thousand-acre paradise of irrigated pastureland."

That part of it sounded like a dream. Especially since most of Rancho Cañada Verde's twelve thousand acres were currently brown and crunchy.

Gerome smiled. "I'm looking for a cowboy who's willing to wrangle some cows on a dude ranch on the weekends, and if we do end up buying the place—"

"Which is likely," Claire said, eyes aglow.

Gerome shot her a side glance. "As I was saying, if everything goes through, I'll need someone to move there permanently. We'll know more in a few weeks."

Beau shook his head. Who the fuck would want to do that?

"I'll do it," Bryce said.

Beau gawked at his brother. What the hell had possessed the fool to say such a thing?

Gerome laughed. "I figured you would."

He did?

"If this goes through, you're both getting raises," Gerome said.

"Both of us?" Beau asked. "Why me?"

"You'll be the lone foreman on Rancho Cañada Verde," Gerome said. "You'll have more responsibilities and a bigger workload."

Beau clenched the arms of the chair as his world tilted. Other than the one semester that Bryce had spent at Texas A&M, they'd never really spent much time apart. And he fucking *needed* Bryce. How was he going to get through all the paperwork and correspondence by himself?

Ford slapped Beau on the back. "What do you say? Pretty exciting stuff, right?"

Bryce was now inspecting the hat in his lap with intense curiosity, as if he might pull a rabbit out of it.

Beau swallowed loudly. "Yeah. It's exciting."

That was a lie. Bryce was the only person in the world who knew that Beau still struggled with dyslexia. What was he going to do without his brother? And what kind of a grown man couldn't function without his twin?

*   *   *

Today had not gone according to plan. Alice snapped her gratitude journal shut as Gaston barked at Sultana. It was impossible to be grateful while a dog barked and a cat hissed. "Hush, Gaston! I've told you before, Sultana is just a kitty."

In Gaston's defense, Sultana didn't look like a typical cat. She had no hair, lots of wrinkles, and an impressive set of ears.

Gaston let out a high-pitched howl when Alice's front door suddenly opened and a blue head popped in. "Knock, knock."

Poor Carmen had probably been knocking for a while, but Alice hadn't heard her over the mayhem.

"Come on in!"

Carmen held Alice's dress in a clear plastic dry-cleaning bag. That sure was fast.

"Hold on," Alice said, grabbing Gaston by his collar. "Let me put this hellhound in the backyard."

By the time Alice returned, Carmen was sitting on the couch with Sultana curled up in her lap. "Where did you get this gorgeous creature?"

Finally, someone appreciated her cat. "From my neighbor, Dolly. Her little dachshund took one look at Sultana and had a stroke. The poor thing still walks with a limp."

"Is she a sphynx?"

"Yes. And with my allergies, she's the perfect pet for me."

"You just dragged a hairy dog out—"

Alice sneezed. "It's my mom's. I'm pet sitting."

She'd need to get to the pharmacy to pick up some more allergy meds tomorrow.

Carmen stroked Sultana and looked around. "Other than the dog and cat fight I walked in on, it's pretty Zen in here. I like it."

Alice was so pleased. She'd worked hard to make her little home comfortable. "My theme for this year is self-care."

"Your years have themes?"

"Yes. Last year was self-sufficiency. I learned to change my own oil and can pickles."

"Self-care sounds better," Carmen said. "Although it can be exhausting."

"So far, it's great. I've been trying to relax more with meditation, yoga, and journaling."

"See?" Carmen said. "Exhausting."

Alice *had* been rather tired lately. "Since I'm self-partnered—"

"Self-partnered?"

"I don't intend to ever get married."

Carmen raised a fist in solidarity. "Sing it, sister."

"I'm learning to be a devoted and caring partner to myself."

"Excellent idea! Does this self-care involve sex toys?"

Alice's cheeks warmed, which was stupid, because she was a grown woman in a relationship with herself, and sexual health was important. "Actually, yes."

"Awesome. We'll have to compare product notes. I just got a new vibrator."

Alice didn't quite know how to respond, so she simply said, "Orgasms improve the quality of your sleep."

Carmen nodded enthusiastically, rubbing Sultana between her Yoda-esque ears, making the cat wince. Or at least Alice thought she was wincing. She kind of always looked like that.

"I have an app for sleep stories on my phone," Carmen said. "My favorite one is read by Harry Styles."

"I've heard of that app. Does it help?"

"Not really. Instead of getting sleepy, I just get horny because it's Harry Styles. He's got that accent going on."

Alice laughed. "Maybe you should switch to a different narrator."

"Wouldn't be as fun," Carmen said. "I swear, you and I have so much in common! Who would have thought?"

There was a brief pause in the conversation, and Alice felt the usual urge to fill it. "You didn't need to rush having my dress cleaned. I don't intend to wear it again until the next wedding, which isn't for another six weeks."

"It was no problem. I sent it out with dirty linens, and it came back with a load of tablecloths and napkins. We were so busy today that I paid for same-day service. I think we ran out of just about everything."

Alice hung the dress, and then she filled the kettle to make tea.

When she came back into the living room, Carmen was looking at her goal journal, which was wide open on the coffee table.

Alice gasped, even though there was nothing in it to be ashamed of. She just wasn't… Well, shoot. It sounded childish, but she wasn't used to people looking at her stuff.

"Sorry. It was right in front of me."

"It's okay," Alice said. "I don't have many guests. And when I *do* have guests, like book club, for example, I tend to be prepared. No fighting animals, and no diaries left out in the open."

"Oh, shit," Carmen said. "Is this a diary? It looks more like a to-do list."

"It's a goal journal, which is kind of like a diary—"

"It's a to-do list. And it's a hefty one. I especially like how you've planned spontaneity." She pointed to a spot on the page. "*Be more spontaneous.* You wrote it right beneath zip-lining and…"

Carmen looked up, mouth open wide, eyebrows at the hairline. "You're going to bring a date to Brittany's wedding? It says *Find a plus-one for Brittany's wedding* right here in angry red ink."

Even Carmen, who didn't know Alice all that well, recognized that this was an unusual move on Alice's part. "Yes," Alice sighed. "I'm afraid I need a date."

"Who are you going to take?"

"No idea. Everyone is married or in a relationship."

Carmen wrinkled her brow. "Yep. All the good ones are taken."

"And a few of the bad ones," Alice added.

Carmen sat up straight. "Oh my God. I know who you can take."

"Who?"

"Beau Montgomery."

Alice gasped, and then she started laughing. Because Carmen was hilarious.

"I'm serious. He's the perfect choice!"

Alice couldn't think of a *less* perfect choice. "Beau and I have absolutely nothing in common—"

"You're self-partnered and not looking for a boyfriend. And Beau is definitely not boyfriend material. In fact, I hear he's a player. And that's what you want for a one-time date. Handsome guy. Loves a good time. No strings attached."

That might be true. But just thinking about being on an actual date with Beau Montgomery made Alice perspire. And her knees felt a little shaky. An uninvited image of Beau's bare chest popped into her head, and she sat down, fanning her face with her hands.

"Are you okay?" Carmen asked.

"Yes. It's a bit warm in here."

"I think it feels fine—"

"And anyway, there is absolutely no chance that Beau Montgomery would want to go on a date with me, even if I wanted to go on a date with him. Which I don't." Because, holy guacamole, she'd be a hot, sweaty mess the entire time. "What would we even talk about?"

"I don't know. But judging from the sounds his last date was making, I'd say that cowboy has a silver tongue."

Chapter
Five

❦

Beau leaned against a fence post and watched the sun come up. Yesterday, he and Bryce hadn't talked at all about the Rockin' H. After their meeting with Ford and Gerome, they'd ridden the fences as planned. But Worth Jarvis, Ford's brother and Rancho Cañada Verde's head herdsman, had ridden with them, making private conversation impossible. After that, they'd had dinner with the Kowalskis, a first-Sunday-of-the-month tradition. Ford, Gerome, and Bryce had talked nonstop about the dude ranch. Beau hadn't had much to say about it.

When they'd gotten back to the foreman's cabin, Bryce had gone straight to the shower and then to bed without so much as a word to Beau. The fucker never could handle confrontation.

This morning, Beau had gotten in the truck before Bryce was even awake. He'd driven to the northern cattle pens alone, because he could avoid confrontations, too, goddammit. And sometimes leaning against a fence post all by your lonesome and watching the sun come up was just what a man needed.

Tires crunched on the caliche gravel behind him. He didn't turn around to see if it was Bryce, because he knew it was. A truck door slammed. "Hey, why didn't you wait for me this morning? What's the point of bringing two trucks down here?"

"I woke up early and was eager to get to work."

"I don't see you doing any."

"I'm fixing to start. And anyway, we don't have to do everything together, right?" He shook his head. "A *dude* ranch, Bryce. Jesus Christ."

"A ranch is a ranch, and one of us was going to have to take it," Bryce said. "I knew you wouldn't want it. You're happy here on Rancho Cañada Verde."

"You're not?"

His brother sighed. "I'm just curious as to what it might be like to live somewhere else. To *do* something else. And this is the perfect opportunity. I'd still be working for Gerome, but I won't be stuck in the same spot where I was born for all of fucking eternity."

Even though it was warm and muggy, the words stung like freezing rain. Because being right here, where they'd been born, was exactly where Beau wanted to be. And he and Bryce had always wanted the same things. "When did you start feeling this way?"

"Since forever, I guess."

Forget the stinging rain. Now it was as if Beau had jumped into a pool of ice water. His body was frozen with shock. How had he not known this about Bryce? And why would his brother have kept such a secret—

Shit.

"Did you come home from A&M because of me?"

Unlike Beau, Bryce had been book smart. He'd been a good student, graduating from high school with honors. He'd received a scholarship to Texas A&M, and their parents had been so proud that they'd thrown a party, inviting the entire town. But Bryce had come home after a single semester, saying college wasn't for him.

But what if he'd only come home because he'd sensed how lost

Beau was without him? Because Beau *had* been lost. He'd felt left behind and abandoned. Hell, it had felt like somebody had fucking died, and he'd moped around for weeks, experiencing what their dad had jokingly referred to as "missing leg syndrome."

He'd done his best to mask his feelings during phone calls with Bryce. But apparently, he hadn't masked them enough.

Bryce stared at the dirt.

Great. He'd ruined his brother's life. "Well, did you?" Beau asked.

Bryce shrugged. "I came home because I was scared shitless up there. The classes were hard, I was used to being a big fish in a small pond, and I missed my brother. So, at least part of it was you. But our dependency on each other is a two-way street, Beau. Don't blame yourself for my mistakes."

Beau hoped that what Bryce said was true. Because he couldn't bear it if he was the reason his brother had given up on his dreams.

"We're grown men now," Bryce said. "We don't need four legs to stand on. Two is enough."

Beau frowned. Because Bryce had never really needed four legs. He'd always supported Beau. Now it was his turn to support his brother. "I hope things work out, and that you get to move to the Rockin' H permanently, if that's what you want. And I don't want you to worry about me. I'll be fine."

"It might not be permanent."

"Sounds like it will be."

Bryce sighed. "I know you're panicking."

Jesus. He wasn't *panicking*. But he was more than a little concerned about how he would handle the paperwork and correspondence aspect of being a foreman. Ford had recently implemented a new agricultural software program, and Bryce had been the one dealing with it. Now Beau would have to.

"There are apps and programs that will read out loud to you—"

"I'm not a child," Beau snapped.

"I know that," Bryce said. "You're a smart man. But you're one with an unaddressed learning disability."

Beau crossed his arms over his chest. "It's been addressed."

"That was with Mrs. Martinez in the third grade."

It wasn't just the third grade. It had also been fourth and fifth. And in junior high, their mom had started driving him to a special tutoring center in Austin. He hated going, because it meant missing Rodeo Club, which he and Bryce had been involved in since they were eight years old. He'd whined like any kid would, saying it wasn't fair that Bryce got to go to Rodeo Club while he went to tutoring.

But it was actually worse than that. *Nobody* was going to Rodeo Club. Not even Bryce. They simply couldn't afford it with the tutoring fees.

That's when he and Bryce had hatched their plan, and Bryce had started doing Beau's homework. Because his grades improved, it appeared that the tutoring was working. The next year, they were back in Rodeo Club.

They kept up the farce all through high school. Since Bryce was on the college track, they didn't have any classes together, so Bryce even slipped into Beau's seat in English when they had to do timed essays or tests.

Kids are pretty short-sighted, and they'd naively thought the battle was won.

"I'm sure they've made strides with treating dyslexia since we were in school," Bryce said.

"I manage well enough."

Silence. Because they both knew that he "managed" because of Bryce.

"I have to take some responsibility for this," Bryce said. "We shouldn't have hidden it. And we definitely shouldn't have let it go on this long."

Everyone believed that Beau had overcome his dyslexia. The thought of admitting that he still struggled with reading, as a full-grown man, was...

"There's nothing to be embarrassed about," Bryce said. "But you're going to need help, brother."

"I wouldn't even know where to start."

Bryce snapped his fingers. "What about Alice Martin? Doesn't she have some fancy degrees that have to do with reading?"

She had *two* fancy degrees that had to do with reading.

His chest tightened like it was in a vise. Alice was the last person on earth that he wanted to ask for help. But he'd already dragged his brother down once. He wouldn't do it again.

"We have to go into town for some errands later this morning. I'll swing by the library and talk to her then."

*　*　*

Most people hated Mondays, but Alice loved them. They were the beginning of the work week, which meant it was time to get busy. And getting busy was something Alice had always been good at.

Since this was the Year of Self-Care, she would start her day off properly, with a positive attitude and yoga. And then, according to her daily to-do list, it would be time to write in her gratitude journal. Then it would be time to go over her short-term and long-term goals—personal and career—followed by adding at least one thing to her bucket list.

Then she'd start marking things *off* her lists, because that was the very best part of keeping them.

1. Drink water!—Check!
2. Yoga!—Check!
3. Be happy!—Check!

Her jaw clenched over that one pesky to-do item.

Find a plus-one for Brittany's wedding!

Carmen had actually had the nerve to suggest Beau Montgomery. That was the craziest thing she'd ever heard. Beau Montgomery would never ever in a million years want to escort her to a wedding. And even if he did—which he didn't—she would never ever in a million years want him to.

Carmen had made some good points, but still... No way. Wasn't going to happen. Not in this lifetime.

Or the next.

She rolled out her yoga mat, popped her laptop open, and found *Sixty Days of Self-Affirming Yoga with Lauren* on YouTube (she was on day eight). Then she assumed the cross-legged Sukhasana pose and hit Play.

Lauren calmly instructed her to inhale deeply through her nose for five counts while clearing her mind.

Beau is an excellent dancer. Not that I've ever danced with him.

Out through the mouth.

He is the ultimate playboy, and wouldn't expect anything beyond one date.

In deeply through the nose.

He looks good in a suit.

Out through the mouth.

Brittany would lose her marbles if I showed up with Beau Montgomery.

In through the nose.

There is white dog hair on my black yoga pants.

Out through the mouth.

And all over the rug.

She shut her eyes—maybe a little too tightly—and brought her hands in a prayer position to her heart, which was beating more rapidly than usual.

She was failing to relax. And she didn't feel centered at all. Her cells vibrated with the intense desire to vacuum. She tried to think of something else, and Beau's gigantic bare-naked chest suddenly popped into her third eye. *No, no, no! Don't think about that!*

She thought about it. And it knocked all of her chakras out of alignment. In fact, she almost fell off her yoga mat.

The harder she tried to force Beau's bare chest out of her sacred mind's eye, the bigger it got.

She wasn't supposed to think of anything at all, much less bare chests. She scrunched her eyes shut, but the chest not only refused to leave, it inflated like one of those gigantic balloons in the Macy's Thanksgiving Day parade, bobbing happily right in front of her face.

Woof!

The chest popped at the sound of Gaston's barking. *Did he need out? Would he pee in the house?*

She opened her eyes. Oops! Lauren had moved into a mountain pose.

Alice jumped up and assumed the same position.

This is more like it! I'm not thinking about Beau now!

She leaned over into a flat back position and tried to force the muscles in her forehead to relax. They did not cooperate, and it made her frown. Also, her jaw was clenched. Jaws weren't supposed to do that during yoga.

She dropped to a plank just as Gaston barked again. Sultana, who'd been supervising Alice's yoga routine from her position at the foot of the mat, could tolerate one bark, but apparently not two, so she hissed. And even though Alice loved Sultana with all her heart, when the animal stood up and arched her back, it sent a shiver through Alice's spine, which made it hard to maintain a perfect plank.

"It's okay, Sully," she said, straining. "As soon as we're done saluting the sun with joy in our hearts, we'll put the beastie in the backyard."

She dropped to her least favorite pose of the sun salutation—knees, chest, and chin—just as Gaston began throwing himself against her bedroom door. Alice eyed it warily. It wasn't locked, and the latch was flimsy.

Just two more poses and then Alice would be done greeting the freaking day. She moved into upward-facing dog as Sultana began yowling, which was an ungodly sound.

Almost there…Don't quit…The cat won't explode…

Proud of herself for maintaining her focus, Alice pressed into downward dog, just in time for Gaston to burst into the room and leap onto Alice, flattening her into the mat.

She squealed and squirmed as a wet nose pressed against her ear. The dog had her pinned. And all she could do, as the first rays of the morning sun illuminated the cloud of dog hair suspended in the air, was greet the day with a middle finger.

It wasn't a typical gesture for Alice, but her finger was the only thing she could move.

Chapter

Six

❦

Alice had half an hour before the library opened. She'd done her guided meditation in her car, which was not how meditation was supposed to be done, but she could only squeeze in so much self-care before it was time to leave for work.

She checked it off her to-do list and leaned back in her chair, breathing in the scent of books. There was absolutely *nothing* that smelled better than books.

Her phone vibrated with a text from Carmen.

Would you like to meet for lunch?

She'd planned to pick up a sack lunch from the Corner Café and eat at the Rio Verde Park with a book as her companion. But meeting Carmen sounded better.

Don't you have to work?

Chateau Bleu wasn't open for lunch, but usually Carmen was busy all day getting ready for dinner.

The Bleu is closed on Mondays.

Alice hadn't known that. She hardly ever ate at Chateau Bleu, even though everyone raved about it. It was kind of a date place. Not really the type of restaurant you'd take a cozy mystery to.

I'll be free at 1:00.

It only took a second for Carmen to text back.

It's a date!

Her day might have gotten off to a rocky start, but things were looking up. At the top of her calendar, she'd written *Don't forget to schedule self-care! Be as kind to yourself as you are to others.*

Her self-care had nearly killed her this morning. She needed self-care to recover from her self-care. Lunch with Carmen would fit the bill.

The first thing on her morning schedule:

1. Grant applications

Like most libraries, they were perpetually underfunded. And since Alice wore all the hats, she was the official grant writer. She sighed. Grant applications were not fun, and this one required a bit of information she had yet to gather. She moved it to the afternoon.

2. Order books for the children's collection

Yay! She had a small budget to work with, but ordering new books was absolutely one of the greatest joys of her job.

3. Circulation desk

Yay again! She and Janie Ramos, the library assistant, worked the desk in shifts, and it was the most enjoyable part of the day. The people of Big Verde weren't at all shy when it came to telling her what they thought of a book. And when they loved a book that she'd recommended, it was the best feeling in the world.

Her afternoon schedule showed an appointment with a sales rep and a meeting with the city manager.

She had just enough time to check email, and ooh! There was one from someone with the Austin Public Library. Interesting.

A couple of years ago, the library had been destroyed in a flood, and there had been some doubt over whether it could be rebuilt. The building had been underinsured, and it hadn't had full flood coverage. Alice had preemptively applied for library positions in Austin, just in case the worst happened and she no longer had a library to call home.

Luckily, the community had come together to save the Big Verde Public Library, building a facility that was even better than the one before. But now, there was a job posting for a managing librarian of a lovely branch in Austin. It was much bigger than her library, and holy guacamole, it paid a *lot* more.

The person contacting her, Ms. Wilson, said they didn't normally keep an applicant pool, but that Alice had stood out because of the circumstances—Big Verde had been all over the news at the time. She wanted to know if Alice would like to update her résumé and apply for the job.

This was a lot to take in so early in the day.

The door opened, and at the familiar sound of Janie's bangle bracelets, Alice guiltily minimized her email. "Good morning, Janie," she called out.

Janie had been working at the library longer than Alice, and she was the only other full-time employee. The two of them were an excellent team. They had their routines down, and neither of them liked to vary from them much.

Brittany, on the other hand, who would unfortunately be skipping in around noon, was another story. She wanted to try a million different things at once. And the fact that she was an intern, and not a full-time employee, didn't slow her down at all. Luckily, wedding drama had saved them from redecorating the reading nook, rearranging the conference room, and researching mobile libraries, activities Brittany had been completely determined to supervise until her bridesmaids' dresses had arrived in yellow instead of peach.

There was a pretty big difference between yellow and peach, but Brittany had eventually adjusted, and now the decorative theme was sunflowers. She'd had a harder time adjusting to the reality of her venue—she'd wanted a destination wedding—which ended up being a somewhat rundown dude ranch outside of Austin instead of the Bahamas.

"Do you want me to open up?" Janie asked, stopping at Alice's door.

Alice rose from her chair. "I'll do it."

"Did you hear about Brittany?"

"What now?" Alice asked. Maybe the dude ranch had burned down. Or the cake-topper didn't look *exactly* like her and Zachary.

"She broke her foot. She's in a boot."

"Oh no! How?"

"I don't know. She said it was a stress fracture. Maybe from all the stress of the wedding," Janie said with a wink.

"How long does she have to wear the boot? Because if she has to wobble and limp down the aisle—"

"Her mom says it's been nonstop crying for the past forty-eight hours."

Alice grimaced. She didn't know if she felt worse for Brittany or her mom.

"Anyway, she's not coming in for the next few days. Have you thought more about who you're taking to her wedding?"

Alice headed for the door with the keys. An image of Beau's rock-hard chest and ripped abs rudely popped into her head. "Not really."

"You'd better get a move on," Janie said. "Otherwise it's going to be like a singles bar in here again. That girl is not going to give up."

Alice definitely didn't want the parade of single men to resume.

Before she turned the key to unlock the door, she stared through the glass at the town square, as if maybe a handsome bachelor she hadn't seen before would happen by.

But there were no surprises to be had in Big Verde. Alice knew every single person in town. And she knew their reading habits, as well. Across the street, Mr. Bowman chatted with Mr. Martinez in front of the Corner Café. Mr. Bowman was a World War I buff. He'd read every book the library had on the subject. And Mr. Martinez was a fan of Westerns. He'd read every Zane Grey in their collection at least twice.

George Streleki, the local real estate agent, paused to look in the window of the Dozen or So Bakery. Last Friday, he'd checked out books on beekeeping. His wife, Maryanne, had come in later, asking about books on menopause and depression.

Alice knew the folks of Big Verde as well as any therapist or priest. She knew who was concerned about symptoms of Alzheimer's, who was considering a second career, who was trying to get pregnant...

And their privacy was sacrosanct.

She touched the glass with her fingers. These were her people. And this was her town, where everything predictably happened the same as it had the day before. So why did she always feel as if she were on the other side of the glass?

Her muscles tensed as she thought about the job in Austin. Was she nervous? Or excited? Both, maybe.

"Who's volunteering today?" Janie asked.

Alice blinked and tried to think. "I'm not sure, actually," she said, unlocking the door.

A white Ford Escort pulled into the library's parking lot. A bumper sticker proclaimed YOU CAN FOLLOW THE CROWD. I'LL FOLLOW JESUS! "Never mind. It's Miss Mills. And she just arrived, so make sure your vices are all tucked in."

Janie laughed. "I no longer bother with tucking anything in."

Alice went to the desk, and Miss Mills entered a short time later. "Good morning, ladies. Did you hear about Brittany?"

"Sure did," Alice said. "Such a shame. I hope she's all healed up in time for the big day."

"If you ask me, this was the Lord's way of telling that girl to slow down."

Alice doubted that. "You can get started on the drop box books, Miss Mills. We had quite a few returns overnight."

Miss Mills fanned her face and sat down behind the circulation desk. "Maybe in a minute. Let me catch my breath first."

Miss Mills was a big fan of catching her breath. She reached into her enormous bag and pulled out a copy of *Breaking the Cowboy*. "I've got some catching up to do on my book."

"Ooh, that one looks steamy," Janie said. "Is it good?"

"It's not my cup of tea, but I'll read it—minus the racy parts—because it's the type of book Alice keeps choosing for book club."

Alice smirked. Miss Mills read every page, *especially* the racy parts. "Nobody came to book club regularly until we switched to romance."

"I did," Miss Mills said. "Religiously."

Alice had struggled for years to promote the book club. She'd tried choosing classics for back-to-school season. She'd tried horror at Halloween. Mysteries. Suspense. Nothing had built interest. But when she chose a romance novel— *Boom!* Six women showed up. And they'd been showing up ever since.

Romance was a huge genre with an inexhaustible number of themes and tropes to explore. There was literally something for everyone, and who didn't love a happy ending?

Their book club conversations might not be as sophisticated as the Self-Partnered Women meetings she attended in Austin, but they were always entertaining. More importantly, what was discussed in book club stayed in book club. And sometimes, they even talked about the book.

"Here comes our first patron of the day," Janie said. "A white Rancho Cañada Verde pickup just parked outside."

"It's Monday," Miss Mills said. "It must be one of the Montgomery boys coming to get their grandmother's books."

Alice nearly dropped the stack of books she'd just picked up. Hopefully, it was Bryce. Because she didn't really want to see Beau's chest saunter in. *Dang it!* She meant she didn't want to see Beau saunter in, with or without his chest. He was super annoying. He always loitered about, looking at books and mindlessly flirting with Janie and the volunteers. Heck, he would flirt with a tree stump if he happened to trip over it.

He did *not* flirt with Alice. And that was just fine. Why would she want him to? And what did flirting even mean? Besides, when you said it five times in a row, it started to sound weird. *Flirt, flirt, flirt, flirt, flirt.*

The door opened, and she was awash in irritation. Her Beau-dar had gone off, making her skin flush and her pulse pound.

"Alice, are you okay?" Miss Mills asked. "You're too young for a hot flash."

* * *

Asking Allie Cat Martin to tutor him in reading under the best of circumstances would be utterly humiliating. But doing it after she'd stood in his doorway lecturing him about noise ordinances while he was half naked was downright unbearable.

She'd probably say no, and then what was he going to do?

Deep down, Beau didn't really believe he could overcome dyslexia. He was an adult. Didn't that mean that his neural pathways were already set in stone? No matter. He had to try, because if he lost his job as foreman of Rancho Cañada Verde because he couldn't accurately use the new software program or analyze reports or correctly fill out forms . . . Well, he'd fucking die. The job and the ranch were his life.

He inhaled deeply while staring at the bulletin board by the door. It always smelled good in the library. Even though he didn't like to read them, he couldn't pretend he didn't like the smell of books. Also, he was procrastinating. Postponing the inevitable. And that wasn't going to get him anywhere. So, he squared his shoulders and cracked his neck. This was going to be awkward.

The first person to greet him was Miss Mills. "Good morning, Bryce. Are you out running errands for your grandmother?"

Alice snorted from behind the counter. Probably because she knew he wasn't Bryce.

"Yes, ma'am," he said, not bothering to correct Miss Mills. Between the two of them, he'd rather be Bryce anyway.

Alice came around the counter. "I haven't gathered her books yet."

She consulted a list as she went about collecting books from the stacks. "Her usual cozy mystery series," she said, snatching a book. "And she asked for something inspirational, so let's see . . ."

Alice put a finger to her lip, wrinkled her brow, and stared at a table of books marked *new*. She wasn't wearing cutoffs today, but she still looked pretty damn cute in a swirly kind of skirt with bright colors and a little white blouse. The skirt was knee-length, but thanks to the cutoffs, Beau knew exactly what her thighs looked like. Toned. Fit. Smooth. Longer than you'd expect.

Having apparently made a decision, Alice nodded her head once, bouncing her ponytail, and grabbed a hardcover off the table. "And she asked for a romance . . ."

There was always a romance novel in Nonnie's stack. Beau shook his head and grinned as Alice marched around behind the counter.

"This one will do," she said, picking up a book with a shirtless man on the cover. "We're reading it for book club."

"Not proud of it," Miss Mills said. "But I don't make the rules."

"Oh?" Beau said. "Who picks out the dirty books?"

He knew the answer, but he enjoyed the way Alice turned her little nose up and raised a single eyebrow before saying, "I object to the word *dirty* in regard to literature and sexuality. And I choose the books. Good ones."

Beau looked at the book. "That might be a matter of opinion."

He pretended to read the back of the book while watching Alice out of the corner of his eye. He'd love to rile her up to foot-stomping mode.

"Well, you're welcome to read it and form one. You can even join us at book club," Alice said.

"Goodness," Miss Mills said. "I'm not about to discuss a book where a man gets spanked like there's no tomorrow if Bryce Montgomery is in the room."

Holy shit.

"I thought you didn't read those parts," Alice said with a grin. "Also, that's Beau."

"Oh, sorry," Miss Mills said. "And if I don't at least skim those parts, how will I know to skip them?"

Typically, Beau would take that as a cue to try to get a rise out of Miss Mills, which wasn't hard, but he was here on a mission. And it was making him nervous.

Alice gave him a once-over that reminded him of the way she'd stared at his chest when he'd answered the door at the Village Chateau. Then she briskly began scanning Nonnie's books. "Hot outside? You're sweating."

He yanked on his shirt collar. "It's a bit warm."

How was he supposed to ask Alice for help right on the heels of a conversation involving Miss Mills and spanking? Especially when Miss Mills and Janie were both within earshot.

"I've been meaning to talk to you, Beau Montgomery," Alice said.

Why did his heart speed up like he was being called into the principal's office? "About what?"

"You're on the schedule for Cowboy Story Time next month."

"I am?"

She handed him Nonnie's bag of books, and then slid a piece of paper across the desk, tapping it with her finger. "Yep. It's your turn to read to the kiddos."

Beau looked at the Cowboy Story Time schedule. The library held the event once a month, and cowboys from local ranches showed up in full cowboy attire to read picture books to kids. Alice said it gave folks pride in their community.

"Okay, well, I'll be here then."

"No, you won't."

"Pardon?"

She leaned over the counter, giving him a quick peek at a lacy pink bra. He averted his eyes, because Allie Cat definitely wasn't flashing him on purpose.

"I know it's not you," she whispered.

"I have no idea what you're talking about, Allie," he said with all the innocence he could muster, even though he knew Alice could tell him and Bryce apart.

"It's Bryce," she said. "He's the one who comes in here and reads when it's supposed to be you."

Beau could read a picture book with no trouble at all…if he was by himself. Doing it in front of an audience, even if they were drooling and picking their noses, was another story entirely.

"Not that I'm admitting to anything, but why would it matter if Bryce took my turn? Maybe he enjoys it."

That might be a stretch.

"I guess it doesn't matter at all. I just wonder what it says about a man when he can't be bothered to read a book to children on a Saturday morning."

Well, it didn't say what she thought it said. That was for damn sure.

She thinks you're an asshole.

"Goodbye," she said, dismissing him. "I guess I'll see *you*"—
she made air quotes with her fingers—"at Cowboy Story Time."

He took the bag of books, the story time schedule, and once
again slunk away from Alice Martin with his tail between his legs.
Just like he had on New Year's Eve all those years ago.

Chapter Seven

The Corner Café was hopping. And it had been hopping steadily since early morning. However, things would wind down by midafternoon. It mostly drew a lunch crowd.

Sally Larson was behind the lunch counter, where she'd been since she and her husband bought the place thirty-nine years ago. "Hey there, Alice. Do you need a menu today? The specials are on the board."

Alice knew the weekly specials by heart. "No thanks, Sally."

There was a vacant booth in the back corner, and Alice headed for it, although she stopped constantly to acknowledge greetings and answer questions.

Did your folks get off okay?

I lost a library book. Can I just give you some cash?

Did you hear about Brittany?

By the time Alice plopped down in the bench seat, Carmen had walked through the door in electric blue pleather pants and a tight white T-shirt—sleeves rolled up to show off the ink. An excited murmur traveled through the café. Folks in Big Verde would never get used to being in the presence of a bona fide celebrity chef.

Carmen performed the part well with a red-carpet strut that was part runway model and part Captain Jack Sparrow. As soon as she sat down, Sally rushed over with a menu.

"I'll just have the special, Sally," Carmen said. "Whatever it is, I know it'll be good."

Carmen ate at the Corner Café every time she came to Big Verde, and Sally floated on air for an entire week after.

"Yes, ma'am," Sally replied formally. Because Carmen's celebrity status trumped the fact that Sally was her elder. "And would you care for iced sweet tea? It's freshly made."

"Sounds divine," Carmen said.

Sally smiled and hurried off as Carmen fixed her eyes on Alice. "Have you asked Beau out yet?"

Alice rolled her eyes. "We've been over this."

"Yep. And you couldn't give me one good reason why you shouldn't ask him."

"I gave you plenty. What I couldn't give you was one good reason why he'd say yes, even if I wanted to ask him. Which I don't."

Carmen held up a finger. "Reason number one is that you're super cute. Reason number two is that you're funny—"

"Ha! Since when?"

"It's not always intentional, but believe me, you're extremely entertaining. Reason number three—"

Sally set their tea on the table. "I'll be right back with your soup and sandwiches."

As soon as she walked off, Alice said, "No more reasons, please. I'm not going to ask Beau. It would be weird."

"Why?" Carmen asked, bringing the glass of tea to her lips.

"For one thing, I used to be his babysitter."

Carmen did a spit take, spraying tea across the table. "Oh my

God! How is it that you've withheld this juicy nugget from me? Like, are you fucking kidding me?"

Alice looked around. A few people were glancing their way, but most were trying very hard to act normal. "I'm only about four years older than him. It wouldn't be *that* scandalous. Not that I'm going to ask him."

"It's not the age difference. It's the circumstances. Totally adorable. Also hot and slightly porny."

Alice put a finger to her lips. "Shh, Carmen."

"How was he as a kid?"

"A hellion spawned from demon seed."

"And Bryce?"

"An angelic partner in crime."

"Now you *have* to ask Beau out. I mean, do it for me, would you?"

Sally set their lunch in front of them. And then she lingered, wringing her hands and nervously waiting for Carmen to try it.

Carmen inhaled the steamy aroma of the soup. "Split pea," she said with a dreamy smile. Because nothing made Carmen happier than food. "Do I smell tarragon?"

"Yes," Sally said, eyes glowing with excitement.

Carmen put her napkin in her lap and dipped her spoon into the soup. She took a sip and closed her eyes, swallowing slowly. "Oh, Sally. This is scrumptious."

Sally looked like she might collapse. "Do you really think so?"

"I do. Have you tried adding fennel? With the tarragon, it would be…" Carmen brought her fingers to her lips and performed a classic Italian chef's kiss.

"I'm not sure I can find fennel at the Tex Best Grocer."

"You could do bok choy instead."

Sally shook her head.

"Belgian endive?"

Sally's face went blank.

"Celery!" Carmen said, snapping her fingers. "That will do just fine."

"Celery!" Sally screeched. "Yes! I have that. I can do celery. Yes, yes, thank you, Carmen."

Sally backed up with what could only be described as a series of small bows, until she bumped into Bubba. "What the heck, Mom?"

"Sorry, honey."

Bubba waved at Alice and Carmen before giving his mom a kiss and following her to the register. He was probably picking up sack lunches for his construction crew. He did that most days.

Alice looked at Carmen, who had now moved on to chowing down on the chicken salad sandwich. "You are such a kind soul."

"Who, me?" Carmen said, wiping her mouth on her napkin. "Every word was sincere. I don't think Sally knows what a great cook she is. And anyway, the folks of Big Verde are the ones who are kind. They've been nothing but welcoming to me whenever I come to town. Even if they do stare at my blue hair."

"They secretly love your hair. Lisa's Locks now stocks a very similar shade."

Carmen beamed and looked around the café. "I can't even imagine what it must feel like to belong here," she said. "I was an army brat and never stayed in one place for too long."

Alice took a bite of her sandwich. It was the same thing she ate nearly every Monday, but Carmen was right. It was delicious. "That's kind of funny, because I've never really felt like I belong."

"Seriously? But you know everybody. And you do all the things with all the people. You go to the weddings. You go with Claire and Maggie to Tony's honky-tonk—"

"Actually, the honky-tonking is a pretty recent development. I'd never been until Claire invited me. It was on the day the library was demolished after the flood, and I'd desperately needed a pick-me-up."

The flooding of the town and rebuilding of the library had definitely brought her closer to folks.

"I love Tony's," Carmen said. "We should go while I'm in town."

"That sounds fun."

"So, you really don't feel like you belong here? How come?"

Alice toyed with a potato chip on her plate. "I moved away from Big Verde with my parents just before first grade, and I didn't come back until the middle of eighth."

"Why did you move?"

"My dad was accepted to medical school in Houston. It's where I went to school. My junior high was huge, with a debate team and a literary club—"

Carmen snorted. "How's the literary club in Big Verde?"

"Nonexistent. But I hear they have a debate team at the high school now. And of course, the library has its book club. Anyway, I didn't really spend my formative years here. I've always wondered if maybe that's why I don't fit in."

"My mind is blown," Carmen said. "I would have thought you were everybody's hometown girl."

Alice laughed. "That would be Claire. And she was my best friend in kindergarten. But by the time we moved back, everyone had changed. You know how it is at that age. Claire had emerged from her cocoon with big boobs and naturally wavy hair and clear skin, and I had emerged from mine with braces, glasses, acne, and a training bra bought just for the hell of it."

Carmen laughed. "See? You're funny."

Alice had never shared any of this with anyone, because she feared hurting their feelings. But she didn't have to worry about that with Carmen. "Everyone already had their friends. Their cliques. And even though I'm technically related to half the folks in town, I didn't really know them, and I kind of hovered on the perimeter. I finally stuck my head in a book and left it there until I graduated from high school."

"I was super popular in high school," Carmen said.

"Oh, that's nice—"

"I'm lying. Holy shit, Alice. Look at me."

Alice suddenly saw teenage Carmen. It didn't matter that grown-up Carmen had her own TV show where she traveled to exotic places eating delicacies most folks had never even heard of or that she had three successful restaurants. Everyone carried the wounds of their childhood.

"I am looking at you. And you're amazing and fantastic, and everyone in here is trying *not* to look at you, and it's impossible. Because you're magnetic."

Carmen's eyes actually teared up. She made a heart sign with her hands. "Back at you."

Alice practically blushed. If only Carmen were around more, maybe she wouldn't be so lonely.

"What did you do after high school? Where did you go to college?"

"I went to Rice for my undergrad studies—"

"Smarty-pants."

"And Texas Woman's University for grad school." She took a sip of tea. "I came back to Big Verde because they needed a librarian—Eunice Pickles was let go quite suddenly—and I figured it would be good to get my feet wet in a small library before venturing on to bigger jobs."

"And?"

"And then I just . . ." Goodness. It was like her lungs had suddenly run out of air. "Stayed."

"Maybe you're not really a small-town girl at heart. Like, maybe it's just not your natural habitat."

Alice bit her lip. "I've been invited to apply for a library management job in Austin," she said quietly.

"Oh my God, Alice. You should apply! Austin is great. It's amazing. Good music scene. Good food scene. And you'd still be in a library."

"I don't know…"

"What's holding you back? At least apply. You don't have to accept it if they offer it to you."

Carmen was right. What could it hurt? There was absolutely zero commitment involved in simply applying.

Carmen's eyes suddenly grew round and huge. "Oh my God."

"What?"

"That kid you used to babysit just walked into the café looking way tastier than the lunch special."

* * *

Beau wanted to turn right around and walk out. He should have known Alice would be here. He glanced at his brother, who suddenly didn't look so hot, either. Something weird had happened between him and Carmen, but Bryce had never talked about it.

Beau raised an eyebrow. *Want to head to the Dairy Dream instead?*

Bryce nodded once. *A burger sounds good.*

"Montgomery boys!" Carmen hollered. "Over here! Come sit with us."

"Oh God," Bryce said under his breath. Beau snorted, even though he was experiencing a similar reaction.

Carmen moved to the other bench, next to Alice, who looked about as happy to see him as he was her. This was going to be a fun lunch.

"Let's go," he said to his brother. "No way out now."

They nodded and said howdy to everyone as they made their way to the corner booth.

"I'll bring you boys some menus," Sally said.

"Don't bother, Sally," Beau said. "We know what we want." They always ate the chicken-fried steak for lunch. Cowboying was hard work, and they'd usually done a good bit of it before most folks had even arrived at the office. This morning they'd castrated bull calves and assisted with vaccinations before coming into town on some errands. The afternoon would be spent in the blazing sun moving herds and checking levels at the various watering holes.

Lunch didn't mean soups or salads for them.

"I'll bring one anyway," Sally said with a huge grin. "We have a new menu item."

Beau sat first and scooted over to make room for his brother. "Thanks for inviting us to sit with you."

"No problem," Carmen said.

Sally came to the table and set down two glasses of tea and a pitcher for refills. Then she placed a menu in front of Beau and Bryce. Bryce tried to hand it back to her. "We'll have the—"

"Chicken-fried steak. I know," Sally said. "But here, look at this."

She flipped the menu over to the breakfast side. "What do you think about that?" she asked, beaming. "Special number three."

Beau stared at the menu, and all the letters started dancing. Twerking. Blending together. He glanced at Bryce, saw his grin, and tried to emulate it. Then Bryce laughed out loud, so Beau did, too.

"The Montgomery Special," Bryce read. "Two identical pancakes, two identical eggs, two identical sausage links, and two identical buttermilk biscuits. If the Montgomery twins can gobble it up, you can, too!"

"Aw, that's cool, Sally," Beau said.

"It's what you boys have been ordering for breakfast since you were kids. Two of everything, and you always eat every bite!"

"That's pretty adorable," Alice said, looking at the menu.

"We're going to come up with some more items named after locals. Alice, how about Doc Martin's Heart-Healthy Breakfast?

I'm thinking a bowl of oatmeal, fruit, and those little chia seeds I keep special just for him."

"Oh, Dad would love it!" Alice said.

"Order up!" Rusty shouted from the kitchen. "Two chicken-fried steaks."

Rusty must have started it as soon as they walked through the door.

They all stared at each other while Sally got their plates and Alice chattered about chia seeds. Then they awkwardly ate, but not in silence, because Alice took that opportunity to fill them in on the origin of the chicken-fried steak, which it turned out was some guy in Lamesa, Texas. He'd misunderstood an order for fried chicken and a separate order for steak as "fried steak." And the chicken-fried steak was born.

It was kind of funny. And definitely more interesting than noise ordinances or chia seeds.

"Well," Alice said. "I'd better be getting back to the library."

Carmen's head snapped around, and she gave Alice some kind of look. Beau thought he detected activity beneath the table, too. As if maybe Carmen was kicking Alice. It was hard to tell, especially since Bryce was kicking *him.*

He narrowed his eyes at his brother. *Stop it, dumb shit.*

Bryce shrugged. *I will when you ask her.*

"I have some news," Bryce suddenly announced.

"What is it?" Carmen asked.

"I'm going to be managing a herd at the Rockin' H Ranch. And I might be moving there permanently."

"Wow!" Alice said. "That's close to Austin, isn't it? I think that's where Brittany is getting married."

"They have a restaurant," Carmen said. "I've eaten there."

"It's closed," Bryce said.

"Good. It was the worst barbecue I ever had."

"Are you going, too, Beau?" Alice asked.

"No. I'll be staying on as foreman of Rancho Cañada Verde."

"So..." Alice pointed at them. "Y'all will be, um, separated?"

She made it sound like something that required surgery.

Bryce laughed and stood. "Just by a few miles. Anyway, I need to be getting back to the ranch. It was nice having lunch with you ladies."

Beau knew he was supposed to stay behind and ask Alice for help. But he was mortified by the idea. He'd already tried once today. Shouldn't that be enough?

He raised an eyebrow. *Do I have to?*

Bryce gave a slight shrug. *Suck it up, brother.*

"I'll be going, too," Carmen said, standing up.

Alice began gathering her things...*Shit. Shit. Shit.* It was now or never. "Alice, do you have a few minutes?" he blurted.

Alice looked startled, and then she made a show of looking at her watch. "Just a few."

He waited until Bryce and Carmen had started walking for the door. "I need your help with something."

"I can't imagine what it might be."

"Do you have any experience with dyslexia? In adults?"

"Yes. I'm trained in two different programs that address adult illiteracy, which is often the result of dyslexia."

Beau winced at the word *illiteracy*.

"Two programs?"

"Often, it's a bit of trial and error to find what works. Everybody's different. Why?"

"Because, well..."

He could tell the moment she got it. First her eyebrows rose and her mouth opened in surprise. Then her face softened, and she folded her hands on the table. "Are you dealing with dyslexia?"

"I think *dealing with it* might be inaccurate. I've never really dealt with it."

"I see. And Bryce is leaving."

Okay. So, she *really* got it. "Yep. And I'm going to be the lone foreman. Ranching isn't what it used to be. We've got a new software program and I really need to be able to..."

"Read?"

"I can read. I'm just real slow. And sometimes I get the details wrong."

"We can definitely improve your fluency."

She said that as if she had zero doubts. Typical Alice. "So how does this work?"

"We just need to coordinate our schedules and figure out a time for you to come by the library."

"I'd rather not do this in the library, if you don't mind."

"Why on earth not?"

Beau shifted uncomfortably in his seat. Did Alice really not understand the crushing shame and embarrassment he felt over this?

"We'll be discreet," Alice said, finally catching on. "We can go into one of the private study rooms or even my office. We'll have complete privacy."

"Privacy? In Big Verde?"

Alice furrowed her brow. "You're right. You'll just have to come by my house, I guess."

"That will work. When can we start?"

"I think I have something scheduled nearly every night this week. How about Saturday?"

Beau sighed, because that seemed like a long way off. But Alice was always busy running here, there, and everywhere. He was lucky she was making time for him at all. "Sounds good. How much do you charge?"

Alice put a hand up. "No way. Community education and literacy is part of the library's mission."

"But we're not meeting at the library. We're doing it after hours. In your home. And I doubt you get paid overtime. So, consider it a tip, because I'm not letting you do this for free."

The last thing he needed was to owe Alice Martin anything.

Alice squirmed in her chair. She bit her lip. Picked at a cuticle. Examined an invisible spot on her blouse. Jesus, did his insistence on reimbursement make her *that* uncomfortable?

"I think we can barter," she finally said.

"Barter?"

Alice sighed. "I'm not happy about this, but I need a plus-one for Brittany Fox's wedding."

Was she asking him to be her *date*? And if so, how did he feel about it? On the one hand, she was totally obnoxious. On the other, she was offering to help him out. Also, he remembered how her legs looked in those cutoffs.

"She tried to fix me up with her uncle," she added.

"The one with the sweaty palms?"

"He's found special medication for it, but yes. That's the one."

Beau shivered a bit at the thought of Brittany's uncle putting his clammy paws on Alice. He leaned back in the booth and pretended to mull things over before reaching out a hand. "Deal."

Relief flooded Alice's face. She placed her hand in his. "Deal." And then she actually smiled. *At him.*

A weird, fluttery feeling expanded in his chest. It was probably just heartburn.

Chapter Eight

Beau got out of the shower and grabbed a towel off the rack. He ran it haphazardly across his body, wrapped it around his waist, and swiped at the fog on the mirror over the sink. He could probably use a shave, but why bother?

It was finally Saturday, and he was just going to Alice's for a little tutoring. What grown man shaved before tutoring? For that matter, what grown man went to tutoring?

He sighed. There was so much about this that he wasn't looking forward to. For one thing, whatever tricks Alice had up her sleeve probably weren't going to work. It was hard to be optimistic.

He stared at his face in the mirror. How could he look so different than he felt? He appeared to be a grown man, identical to his smart and capable brother. But his unaddressed dyslexia made him feel like a little kid. And he hated it.

He pulled out his electric razor. Maybe he'd shave after all.

A few minutes later, he stood buck naked in front of his closet. What should he wear to a tutoring session? There were starched and pressed dress shirts that he wore out to dance halls and whatnot.

And of course, there were a ton of work shirts. There weren't a lot of in-between clothes, because all he did was work and play.

He didn't want to wear a work shirt. Half of them were missing buttons or had stains or ripped pockets. That was the nature of ranch work. But he didn't want to look like he was going out on the town, either.

He abandoned the closet altogether and headed for his dresser, where he grabbed a clean pair of Wranglers from the bottom drawer and a plain blue T-shirt from the middle. Surely that wouldn't look like he was trying too hard.

Trying too hard to do what?

He stepped into a pair of black Ropers, brushed his teeth, and picked up a bottle of aftershave. Then he set it back down. Aw, hell. It wouldn't hurt to splash a little on his cheeks. Next, he turned around and examined his ass in the mirror, because women always talked about cowboy butts in Wranglers. It looked like any old ass to him.

His black hat would look good, but would it be too coordinated and planned? Probably. So, he grabbed the straw Stetson.

A snort came from the doorway, and he saw his brother's reflection in the mirror, smirking. "Somebody's hot for teacher."

"Shut up. I am not."

"You're primping and preening like a girl getting ready for the prom."

Beau breezed past his brother. "You're crazy."

"And you're wearing too much aftershave."

Dammit.

He should probably eat something before he left for Alice's. "Do we still have any of that brisket left in the fridge?"

"Not much. Maybe enough for a sandwich."

That sounded perfect, so Beau set about making one while Bryce leaned against the counter and watched. "Did Alice tell you to bring anything with you?"

Beau clenched his jaw and slathered mayonnaise on a slice of bread. "She didn't mention it."

"So, how much are you paying her?"

Beau finished off his sandwich with some spicy mustard and a slice of bread on top. "I'm not paying her."

"She's doing it for free? That's nice of her. Not surprising, though. She's always been a sweetheart. I feel bad for all the shit we pulled when we were kids. You should probably get her a gift or—"

"I should clarify that I'm not paying her in *money*, but believe me, she's being reimbursed."

Beau took a bite of his sandwich and thought about what it was going to be like to take Allie to a wedding. It probably wouldn't be too bad. He'd have to dance with her. Surely, she wouldn't turn him down if he was her date? He shook his head. With Allie, who really knew? She was definitely going to talk his ear off, all while bouncing that ponytail for emphasis.

"When you say reimbursed, you'd better not be talking about what I think you are. Because, brother," Bryce said with a sigh, "that is a horrible idea."

"What do you think I'm talking about?"

"Sex."

Beau nearly choked on his sandwich. His feelings were jumbled around like letters on a page, but one thing he knew for absolute certain was that he was *not* exchanging sex for tutoring with Allie Cat Martin. The suggestion made him want to laugh hysterically, even though he was currently clenching his jaw and trying to swallow a wad of sandwich down his suddenly tight throat.

He forced the chunk of sandwich down and wiped his mouth on a napkin while avoiding eye contact with his brother.

He couldn't have sex with Alice. For one thing, she wouldn't want to. And for another, well, she wouldn't want to. Even if he did make her blush now and then.

"I'm not having sex with Alice, Bryce. No need to concern yourself."

Bryce slumped in relief. "Good. But if you change your mind, don't do it before you've learned how to read. Because God knows you never hop in the same saddle twice."

"I know how to read," Beau said through clenched teeth.

"I know," Bryce said. "I was just kidding."

"And you're a real knucklehead if you think I would have sex with Alice."

"It was a logical assumption because you're..."

Beau raised an eyebrow. "I'm what?"

"You."

"It's not logical to assume I'm going to bang the babysitter."

Bryce laughed hysterically. "God. That sounds like a bad porno. And you have said absolutely nothing to dissuade my concerns, because you're clearly still carrying that junior high hard-on."

"I am not. And Alice wouldn't want to have sex with me anyway."

"You're probably right about that," Bryce said with a grin. "But if you're a good boy, maybe she'll let you stay up late to watch TV."

Beau crammed the last of his sandwich in his mouth. "Ha-ha," he said.

Bryce wiped his eyes. "So, what's your deal, then? What does Alice get out of this?"

"Believe it or not, she needs a plus-one for Brittany Fox's wedding. Otherwise Brittany is going to fix her up with her uncle."

"The one with the wet hands?"

"Yep. Anyway, it's just a wedding. One date."

"So, it's a date?"

"Well, not a *date* date."

"I know how dates end for you, Beau."

"Think of me as her escort."

Bryce cocked an eyebrow. "If you Google *escort service*, you'll see that you're not exactly digging yourself out of this hole."

"Remember when you and I escorted Nonnie to the church's Sweetheart Banquet for Valentine's Day? It's like that."

Bryce crossed his arms over his chest. "If you say so."

* * *

Alice frantically ran a lint roller over her royal blue chair and then ripped the little sticky sheet off in disgust. There was *still* a layer of hair on the chair, and she'd used at least six sheets already.

Woof!

"Hush," Alice said. "Or I'll make a rug out of you. Although maybe not, since you're apparently going bald."

As if she'd recognized the word *bald*, Sultana jumped up on the love seat, her eyes trained on Gaston's wagging tail like she was watching a tennis match.

"Oh my God! Sully, you're covered in dog hair, too."

Alice used three more sticky sheets on the chair before starting on the love seat. She sniffed the room and wrinkled her nose. Dang it. It was definitely eau de hound.

She lit a lavender-scented candle while giving stinky Gaston the side-eye. Then she went into the kitchen to set out some snacks. Beau wasn't *company*, but he was still a guest in her home. Chips, salsa, and a package of Oreos. They'd been Beau's favorite when he was a kid.

She only had a few minutes to get dressed, and Gaston followed her to the bedroom, where he immediately jumped onto her bed. There was no time to fight with him, so she ignored it and slipped into a pale pink sundress and white sandals. She redid her ponytail, applied a little lip gloss, and she was done.

By the time she got back in the kitchen, it was only five minutes until Beau was supposed to arrive. She snagged the bag of Oreos, ripped into it, and ate two before she'd even realized she'd done it. Then she put the rest on a plate.

Tonight, she'd try to discover what kind of a learner Beau was. They'd do a few sample tests that would give her a better idea of which program to start with.

Dyslexia didn't have a one-size-fits-all solution. But there was almost always a solution if you didn't give up. Her heart ached to think of how misunderstood Beau had probably been his entire life. Heck, *she'd* misunderstood him. Even though Mrs. Montgomery had told her that Beau had a hard time in school, Alice had been too young and inexperienced to connect the dots. She'd been impatient and frustrated, thinking Beau was just lazy. All the acting up he'd done was typical behavior for some kids with learning disabilities. They often misbehaved as a distraction from their challenges.

Having a twin had probably been both a curse and a blessing. She thought about Cowboy Story Time. Bryce was *still* covering for Beau.

Woof! Woof!

Gaston ran to the back door, and two seconds later, somebody tapped on it. She hadn't expected Beau to come through the kitchen.

She straightened her ponytail and opened the door.

Oh! It was just Dolly from next door. Ever since she'd given Alice the cat, Dolly had started doing pop-ins to check on Sultana. Alice didn't usually mind visiting with Dolly, but she preferred some advance warning.

"Hi, Dolly. Now is not really a good—"

Woof!

Gaston ran out of the kitchen and to the front window, where he nosed the curtains open.

Woof!

Dolly looked surprised, and possibly a little incensed that someone else had the nerve to visit Alice. "Who's here?"

"Nobody," Alice said. "I mean, obviously it's somebody. I'm expecting someone, actually. But it's just a person."

"Well, goodness," Dolly said, marching to the front door. "Let's let them in."

"Oh, wait. Let me get the dog—"

Too late. Dolly opened the door, and Gaston made a run for it. He didn't get far, though, because Beau grabbed him by the collar.

Alice ran over and wrenched Gaston's collar from Beau's hand. "Hi, Beau. Sorry about this. Come on in." She pulled Gaston inside and Beau followed, but the dog broke free just as Beau shut the door. He ran straight to Beau and sniffed hysterically, especially at the boots. And then he began to hump Beau's leg.

Alice had not anticipated the possibility of leg-humping. She'd never seen Gaston do such a thing, but then again, Gaston had never seen Beau, and on a certain level, Alice understood the reaction. "Oh God. Gaston! Stop it."

Beau shook Gaston off. Then he looked at Alice with a shell-shocked expression. "I didn't know you had a dog."

"It's not mine," Alice said, dragging Gaston through the kitchen to the back door as Beau and Dolly followed. "My parents are on vacation for a whole month, and I'm dog sitting."

She huffed and puffed and grunted, but Gaston had decided to sit, and it was like tugging on a boulder.

Beau opened the door and whistled. "Out, boy."

Gaston hopped right up and ran out the door. Beau shut it behind him with a grin. "You're not used to being around animals much, are you? You've got to be kind, but firm. Show them who's boss."

At that moment, Sultana sauntered in to gloat over Gaston's expulsion from the premises.

"Shit," Beau said, backing into the counter. "What the holy hell is that?"

Dolly walked through the doorway and picked up Sultana. "This is my cat."

"Actually," Alice said. "It's my ca—"

"I have seen cats before," Beau said. "That is not a cat. I don't know where you got it, but you should take it back. Before something bad happens."

Dolly waved him off. "She's a rare breed."

"Of what?" Beau asked.

Dolly narrowed her eyes. "Aren't you a Montgomery boy?"

Beau tilted his hat. "Yes ma'am. I'm Beau."

Dolly looked at the snacks on the table. Then she looked through the doorway into the living room where the candle was lit.

Uh-oh. Conclusions were being drawn. Incorrect conclusions.

"I guess three's a crowd, isn't it?" Dolly said with a huge smile, eyes darting back and forth between Alice and Beau. "I'll leave you two lovebirds alone."

Yep. Definitely the incorrect conclusion. "No, Dolly. Beau and I are just—"

Beau drew in a sudden breath, big blue eyes wide and frantic.

This was his deep, dark secret.

Alice desperately tried to come up with a reason Beau Montgomery would be at her house...*Think. Think. Think.*

Suddenly, she felt the weight of Beau's arm around her shoulder. He gave her a little squeeze, pulling her against him. And boy, oh boy. It sparked something weird. Something fizzy and electric and not entirely unpleasant that started at her toes and raced to her throat, where it tingled and prevented her from saying what she wanted to say, which was that Beau had come to work on the plumbing. Even though he wasn't a plumber and they all knew it.

Dolly put Sultana down and went to the back door. "You kids have fun," she said with a wink. "I've got to head to my Catholic Daughters meeting anyway."

Oh no. Not the Catholic Daughters. The only bigger gossip mill in town was the Lutheran Quilting Club.

Chapter

Nine

ॐ

This was awful! Dolly thought she and Beau were dating. In approximately ten minutes, the Catholic Daughters would think so, too. Alice would have to work overtime to prevent an engagement announcement from making its way to the front page of the *Big Verde News*.

She frowned and chewed on her lip. This was a complication she hadn't foreseen.

Beau looked at his right leg, which was covered in white dog hair. "At least *somebody* was happy to see me. I think your mom's dog found me quite charming."

Alice rolled her eyes. "Gaston was just trying to assert his dominance over you. Dogs do that."

Beau laughed. "Maybe he just found me attractive. Because I'm definitely not submissive." He leaned against the counter, crossing one boot over the other, tilting his chin, and hooking a thumb in his belt loop.

It was like watching a male peacock pop his tail feathers out at the sight of another male peacock. Alice didn't know how a male peacock would react to the show, but she was suddenly finding it difficult to breathe. "Can I take your hat?"

Beau removed his hat and ran his hand through his dark blond hair. He and Bryce had been nearly white-headed when they were little. Their mom had said the Texas sun kept their skin tanned and their heads bleached. "Do you have a hat rack?"

"No. I don't even have a hat. But you can put it on the table by the front door."

Beau went to the table and put his hat down, eyes sweeping the room. They paused on Alice's Buddha statue, yoga mat, and candles. He picked up a small bronze bowl.

Alice snatched it out of his hand. "That's a Tibetan singing bowl."

"It sings?"

"Yes."

"How?"

"You strike it with the mallet."

"Why?"

"It's relaxing."

"To you maybe. It doesn't sound so relaxing for the bowl. Maybe that's why it screams."

"It *sings*. And it is *very* relaxing."

"You don't look very relaxed, Allie Cat."

She didn't feel very relaxed. For one thing, Beau was standing so close she could smell his aftershave.

He'd worn aftershave.

"Maybe you should beat your bowl," Beau said with a smirk.

Alice set the bowl and its mallet down exactly where it belonged. Had Beau meant that to sound dirty? Because it had. She looked at him closely—she wasn't great at reading people.

He shrugged. "What?"

"Aren't you bothered that Dolly thinks we're dating?"

"Dating?"

"What else could she think?"

"Maybe she thinks we're just hooking up."

Alice gasped. And then she noticed that her fingers had somehow worked their way to her throat, where she would no doubt be clutching her pearls if she had any. She dropped her hands to her sides.

Beau laughed. "Relax, Allie Cat. Folks are going to think what they're going to think. There's not much we can do about it. And in a way, this will make it easier for the wedding, right? It won't come totally out of left field when we show up together."

Oh, dear God. She'd been so focused on avoiding Brittany's uncle—and on seeing Brittany's face when she showed up with Beau in tow—that she hadn't even considered what literally everyone else would think. She suddenly had a sinking feeling. "Are you friends with Brittany?"

"Not really," Beau said with his ridiculous blue eyes twinkling. "But I guess you could say we've met."

"Oh. My. God."

"What?"

"Have you gone out with Brittany? Because I swear to God, Beau. I am not showing up to the wedding on your arm if you've gone out with the bride."

"Settle down."

"Don't ever tell a woman to settle down."

Beau opened his mouth. Shut it. Opened it again. "Can I tell a woman to *calm* down?"

"That's even worse."

"But women are often prone to hy—"

"Don't say it."

"—steria"

Alice clenched her jaw. "Did you know that hysterectomies were the cure at one time for so-called hysteria? Women were punished for showing emotion by having their uteruses removed."

"We went to a dark place pretty quickly there, Allie Cat. I was just kidding."

"Did you date Brittany?"

"Nope. Just her cousin."

Alice sighed in relief.

"And her aunt. But not the aunt who is the mother of the cousin. That would be weird."

Oh God. Oh God. Oh God. What had she been thinking? She'd asked the town's biggest playboy cowboy, possibly a gigolo in chaps, to be her plus-one!

They should definitely hash out some details. The wedding was out of town. Surely, Beau wouldn't expect them to share a hotel room. But what, exactly, did he consider the obligations of a plus-one to entail?

"Before we get started," she said. "We need to establish some ground rules for our deal."

"Sounds good to me."

Alice went to her desk in the corner. "Let's type up a contract."

Beau laughed. "I don't think we need anything that formal. But listen, Allie. I'm just going to come out with it. This date for the wedding? That's all it is. I'm not looking for a girlfriend. I have no interest in relationships. You need an escort to an event. And I need some tutoring. That's all this is."

How dare he beat her to the *I don't do relationships* line?

"Everybody knows you don't do relationships. That's why I asked you. Because guess what? Neither do I. Believe it or not, I have no desire for a boyfriend. Not now, and not ever. I'm happily self-partnered."

Beau cocked an eyebrow. "Self-partnered?"

"Yep. Me and Emma Watson."

"You're dating someone named Emma? Why don't you just take her to the wedding?"

"You're exasperating."

"Not even trying."

"Emma Watson coined the term *self-partnered*. It means you're happy being single. That you're a whole and complete human without a partner. I'm even in a women's group. We meet in Austin, and we talk about how to be good partners to ourselves."

"My mom is in a women's group. They exchange recipes and knit slippers for the residents at the old folks' home. It's local, and I'm sure they'd be happy to have you. It would save you a drive."

Alice narrowed her eyes and glared at Beau, but then she saw it. The twinkle. Right there in the eyes. And the little dimple next to his mouth on the right side. "You're teasing me."

"You're too easy, Allie Cat."

"I've noticed, over the years, that I'm not exceptionally skilled at picking up on humor. I'm quite a literal person. So, I'd appreciate it if you didn't tease me."

Beau seemed surprised. After a few seconds of silence, which Alice desperately wanted to fill, he said, "Nonnie says teasing is my love language, but I'll try to rein it in."

"Thank you."

"And Allie, I'm sorry if I've made you uncomfortable. I didn't realize it was happening. So maybe I have a few blind spots, too."

As far as Alice could tell, he was being one hundred percent sincere. Or heck, maybe he was teasing. She couldn't tell. And that was the problem.

* * *

Beau couldn't believe they were actually typing up a contract.

"The wedding is on June twelfth, which is five weeks away," Alice said. "So, I think our contract should officially end at midnight the night of the wedding."

"What if we're still on the dance floor at one minute past midnight. Do we explode?"

Not teasing Alice was going to be harder than he'd thought.

"No. We turn into pumpkins," Alice said with a little smile. And then she added, "We're going to the wedding. We're going to make an appearance at the reception. And then we're going to get out of there."

"Can I at least eat first?"

"If you're quick about it."

The alien creature Alice pretended was a cat jumped in his lap. He choked down a scream and attempted to pet it. It felt like a plucked chicken, but it started purring loudly, as if it were, indeed, a cat.

"Aw, she likes you."

"It's a she? What's her name?"

"Sultana."

"It fits."

"Claire wanted me to call her Brazilian. But the breed originates from Canada."

Beau tried to hold in his laughter and failed.

"What?"

"I think Claire was making a joke."

"About what?"

Surely, Allie knew what a Brazilian wax was, but it was probably best to let it go. The hairless cat jumped off his lap. "Are you actually going to print up that contract? If so, we'd better go ahead and sign it."

Alice typed some more. "Hold on. I'm making it clear that my commitment to you ends when the contract expires. You should have all the tools you'll need for your reading toolbox by then. You might not be speed-reading Homer, but you'll have strategies in place. Our deal—all of it—ends at midnight."

Wow. Was that possible? If so, this was the first glimmer of hope he'd felt in a long time. He was scared to fan it into a flame, because he'd been disappointed before. All the tricks they'd tried in elementary school—red plastic films over pages that were supposed to make the letters stop moving around, sight-word flash cards, phonics games—had failed. And then there'd been the testing at the tutoring center in Austin, followed by more phonics and memorization.

He swallowed. He didn't want to stutter and stammer and struggle in front of anybody, and he especially didn't want to do it in front of Alice.

"And just so we're crystal clear," Alice continued. "No sex."

"Got it."

Alice read the contract to him—midnight blah blah no sex blah blah—and printed it up. Then they both signed it—as if it were something that needed signing—and went back into the kitchen.

"Would you like some tea? Or hold on…" She went to the refrigerator and grabbed a carton of milk. "How about milk? Are Oreos still your favorite?"

"Are you seriously offering me milk and cookies?"

"Yes."

He eyed the plate of Oreos. They were absolutely still his favorite. He grinned and reached for one.

"Still a dipper?" she asked.

Beau dunked his cookie in the milk. "Lickers are losers…" He looked up to see that Allie had twisted her cookie apart and was in the process of licking the filling. "Sorry."

Alice shrugged it off. "Before we get started on our lesson, it's very important that you understand something."

"I said I got it, Allie. Absolutely no sex."

"That's not what I was going to say. You need to understand that there is no correlation between dyslexia and intelligence. None whatsoever. Having dyslexia means you process information in a way that makes reading more difficult. That's it. That's the whole ball game. It doesn't affect your ability to predict outcomes or draw conclusions. And as far as creativity goes, which is its own

MUST LOVE COWBOYS 85

kind of intelligence, there is some evidence indicating that people with dyslexia are more creative and more likely to think outside the box. Dyslexia makes you a little bit different, but many consider it an advantage in problem solving."

Beau was speechless. He'd never in a million years consider dyslexia an advantage. But he'd also never heard it described in such terms. A small piece of shame seemed to melt away, and he felt lighter. He wished the folks he'd worked with as a youngster had described dyslexia in such a manner. Maybe it would have made a difference. "Do you work with kids?"

"When I'm asked to."

He swallowed a lump. "They're lucky to have you as their teacher."

Alice's cheeks turned pink and she smiled. The statement had really pleased her, and she was pretty when she was pleased. He wanted to please her some more.

Allie shuffled through papers to pull out one with the alphabet written on it. "Can you recite the alphabet?"

"Are you kidding?"

"Nope."

Beau sighed, crossed his arms, and effortlessly recited the alphabet like any five-year-old could.

"Good," Alice said. "Now can you write it?"

It took him a bit longer to do that, and by the time he handed the paper to Alice, his cheeks felt like they were on fire.

Alice looked over the paper. She put a few marks on it. Jesus. Had he made some mistakes?

When Alice looked up, her brown eyes were calm and friendly. There was no judgment. No disgust. No pity. "You're doing great."

His chest lightened a little. And that was all it took to get through the next half hour, during which Alice asked him to read a few words and try to figure out some sentences, even if he couldn't read them perfectly. A few times he had to guess, and Alice praised him. She said that using context clues was a coping strategy, and that he was very good at it.

"I have a better picture of your strengths now. And my plan is to use them to shore up the areas where you're weakest. In the meantime, what do you like to read?"

"Is this a trick question?"

"No. What's the last book you read?"

He started to say that the last book he'd read was in high school, but that wasn't even true. Bryce had been the one to read it, and he'd written the paper, too. "Wow. This is embarrassing, but—"

"Embarrassment is not a part of this process. Give me your phone."

"Why?" He pulled it out of his pocket, unlocked it, and handed it to Alice.

"I'm giving you some homework." She swiped a few times. "You've now got an app so you can listen to books." She put a finger to her lips. "Let's see…"

She stared at him intently, nodded her head once, and tapped the phone.

"This is the first book in a suspenseful, action-packed series. I loved it, and I think you will, too."

Beau took his phone and clicked on the new icon. A picture of a book popped up.

"All you have to do is listen to it. That's your homework," Alice said. "And I really hope you enjoy it."

Beau was skeptical. Books had never held his attention. And besides, he didn't want to overcome his dyslexia in order to sit around wasting time with books. He just wanted to be able to do his job.

Chapter

Ten

Alice rolled up her yoga mat and put it beneath her desk. Some people might enjoy doing yoga with animals—baby goats and puppies—but doing it with a full-grown Great Pyrenees was not in the same universe. So, she'd taken to doing yoga at the library.

She had a few minutes before Janie would arrive, so she opened the document she'd slaved over nearly all night.

Her résumé popped up. And it was pretty impressive for a small-town librarian.

When she'd come on board, the library had consisted of an old building filled with mostly donated books. She'd worked with the city to get real funding and a workable budget. She'd applied for grants and signed up for programs. She'd partnered with other libraries to offer interlibrary loans while building up the collection. She'd developed outreach programs—ESL, adult literacy, programming for children and teens—until the library was woven into the social fabric of Big Verde.

And when it had all been wiped out by the flood, she'd built it back up. Brick by brick, and book by book. But there really wasn't anywhere to go from here. There wasn't a higher position or promotion in her future. And her salary was a joke. What if Carmen was right, and she really wasn't a small-town girl?

She quickly changed out of her yoga pants and into a sweet little yellow A-line skirt she'd sewn herself. She was a beginning seamstress, but the skirt fit, and she was proud of it.

She spun in front of the door, watching the skirt twirl in the reflection of the glass. Then she jumped, hand to her throat, when she saw Claire on the other side.

Claire tapped on the glass. "Let me in!"

Alice went to the door. What had brought Claire to the library? She already had her copy of *Breaking the Cowboy*, the romance they were reading for book club. Whatever it was, it was urgent. Because Claire's eyes were wide, her cheeks were pink, and she was bouncing on her feet like she had fire ants in her shoes.

Alice opened the door. "Are you okay? You look like you might explode."

Claire blew a strand of hair out of her face and put her hands on her hips. "I think I'm in shock."

"What happened?"

Claire started tapping her toe. "That's what I'd like to know."

Alice flipped the sign on the library's door to OPEN. "Can you be more specific? Like are you asking me what happened on a specific day? In a specific year? Can we narrow it down a bit?"

Alice headed for the circulation desk with Claire hot on her heels. "I hear you have a *beau*," Claire said.

Alice nearly dropped the keys. She should have anticipated this. The rumor mill had been cranking for more than forty-eight hours. She went behind the desk and climbed on her stool. Claire leaned in, drumming her fingers on the counter. "Well? Are you seeing Beau?"

This wasn't going to be easy. Alice was good at a lot of things, but lying wasn't one of them. Although, technically, it wasn't a lie. She *was* seeing Beau. Twice a week. For reading lessons.

She could answer truthfully while withholding that last part, which was technically lying by omission, but she wasn't in the mood for technicalities.

"Yes, I'm seeing Beau."

Claire eyed her warily, and Alice blinked first. *Dang it!*

"How long has this been going on?" Claire asked.

Alice swallowed loudly and moved a small stack of books between her and Claire. It felt better to have a buffer. "Um, well, we just started on Saturday—"

"Well, what the heck happened last week then? Because I saw both of you at Jessica's wedding and there was nothing going on other than the usual drooling and whatnot."

Alice gasped. "The usual drooling and whatnot?"

Claire waved her hand dismissively. "Oh, please. You and Beau have always been gooey around each other."

"Gooey? What does that mean? It sounds gross."

"Y'all are weird around each other, that's all."

That wasn't very specific. Alice was kind of weird and awkward at times around everyone. And Beau just acted like he always had. There was no way he was attracted to her. He flirted with everyone *but* her.

What could she say? Beau's privacy—no matter how she felt about him—had to be protected.

The library door opened. *Janie! Yay!*

"Well, well, well. Look who took my advice and got busy."

That did not sound like Janie. It sounded like somebody with blue hair.

"Howdy, Carmen," Claire said. "What brings you to the library?"

Carmen leaned on the counter. "Gossip."

"Did you hear Beau and Alice are seeing each other?" Claire asked.

"Yes. And I take full responsibility."

The library door opened again, followed by a clunking sound. "Oh my God, Alice! I hear you have a date for my wedding!"

Everyone ran to assist Brittany, who was on crutches and wearing a boot bedazzled with rhinestones. As soon as she was settled, the door opened again. "Good morning," called Janie.

Janie wasn't a gossip. And she wasn't in a bunch of ladies' clubs. Maybe she hadn't heard anything. In fact, maybe not that many people were talking about Alice and Beau at all. Maybe it was literally just Claire and Carmen and Brittany.

"What's this I hear about you and Beau Montgomery?" Janie said.

Dang it. "Where did you hear about that?"

"At the Pump 'n' Go this morning."

"From who?"

"Anna Vasquez. She heard it from Trista Larson, who heard it from—"

"Sally Larson, who heard it from Dolly at the Catholic Daughters meeting," Alice said.

The library door opened again, and Miss Mills lumbered in. "Good morning," she said cheerfully.

"Miss Mills, you're not scheduled to volunteer today."

"The Good Lord whispered in my ear that the library might need my help, so here I am. Also, Alice, I hope what I heard at church isn't true."

Good grief. Alice was suspicious that the Good Lord didn't really think the library needed help today.

"I'm sure all you heard at church was how much Jesus loves you and how you shouldn't judge," Claire said. "Because good Christian women wouldn't have been gossiping about Beau and Alice hooking up."

Miss Mills dropped her keys in her purse and pulled out a book. "Someone's got some sass this morning," she said, tossing a glance at Claire. "And Alice, Beau Montgomery gets around. He goes from woman to woman like a bee in a flower garden, and honestly, I thought you had more sense."

"I'm responsible for the meet-cute," Carmen said. "I want full credit."

Brittany plunked her booted foot on the counter. "Oh? How?"

"Alice didn't want to go to the wedding with your uncle, so I told her to ask Beau. And apparently, she did. And then other things seemingly happened. Things about which I need to know every single detail."

What could Alice say? She glanced at Claire, who still had that eyebrow raised.

"What's wrong with my uncle?" Brittany asked.

"Not a thing," Alice said politely. "Beau and I enjoy each other's company. That's all there is to it." Surprisingly, that wasn't even a lie. She'd enjoyed their tutoring session.

"Since when?" Claire asked.

"Since recently."

"I just don't see how an *experienced* man like Beau would be able to control himself around a woman of virtue, such as yourself," Miss Mills said. "It's not a good match."

Claire snorted.

Alice opened the book on top of the stack in front of her. "Virtue has to do with adherence to moral standards, and I do not judge people's morality by how many adults they choose to have consensual sex with."

Claire snorted again, probably because she knew the effect these words would have on Miss Mills.

"Goodness!" Miss Mills said. "Alice, I would expect better moral standards from a librarian."

Carmen nodded her head vigorously, as if she agreed with Miss Mills. She then faked a pouty frown and brushed one index finger over the other, as if to say *Shame on you.*

"And Claire," Miss Mills continued. "You need to see a doctor. You sound like a pig clearing its sinuses."

Claire snorted loudly and then covered her mouth with her hand. "Sorry. That one just slipped out."

"Your generation doesn't understand the notion of behaving like ladies."

"There is no one way that ladies should behave," said Alice. "As for men being unable to control themselves around women of virtue, I say that's hooey."

"Miss Mills made Alice say *hooey*," Brittany said.

The library door opened again. Alice crossed her fingers and hoped for an emergency that only a librarian could handle...

But it was just Maggie, carrying two-year-old Maisy on her hip while pushing a gigantic empty stroller. "Hey, y'all! I hear Beau knocked up Alice!"

Miss Mills began frantically fanning herself with her daily devotional. "That didn't take long."

Claire dropped her head to her arms and started laughing in earnest.

"You did not hear that!" Alice said to Maggie. "Take it back."

"Oh, but I did hear it."

"Where?"

"At the drugstore. Carol Hawker was in there buying vaginal lubricant because she's going through menopause—"

Miss Mills dropped her ten-ton purse, making everyone jump. "That is not appropriate language for a library!"

"*Vaginal*? *Lubricant*? Or *menopause*?" Maggie asked.

"All three! And you'd better cover that child's ears, lest she turn out to have a potty mouth just like her mother and her friends."

"As soon as she says *menopause*, I'm going to wash her mouth out with soap for sure," Maggie said.

"That *is* a dirty word," Janie said. "Hot flashes kept me up all night."

"I had no trouble at all going through the change," Miss Mills said. "I prayed about it, and the good Lord answered."

"I'll try that next," Janie said. "Right after the CBD oil."

The library door opened again. Alice crossed her fingers, hoping to be saved by an elderly person needing help with the internet.

"Well, speak of the devil," Claire said.

Alice broke out in pins and needles. Her stomach dropped. Her heart pounded. She didn't even need to turn around to know who it was.

Her Beau-dar had gone off, and it felt different this time.

* * *

Oh, dammit. Beau had gotten here early, hoping Alice would be alone. Just how many people did it take to stick books on shelves? And what the holy hell was Claire doing here? And Maggie? And Carmen?

Janie smiled at him. "Good morning, Beau."

He removed his hat. Nodded his head. "Good morning, ladies."

Claire smirked at him. "Were your ears burning?"

"Pardon?"

One look at Allie's horrified face told him all he needed to know. She'd been right about Dolly starting up the gossip train. But Beau didn't care about all that. People in small towns gossiped. And people in small towns hooked up and then unhitched pretty regularly.

"Alice," Maggie said. "Do you and Beau need help planning your shotgun wedding? Claire and I would be more than happy to oblige."

Beau sighed. "Allie Cat, I need to talk to you."

"Aw," Claire said. "They have nicknames."

"In private," Beau said.

Miss Mills huffed and fanned as if they were going to do

something obscene. Which they weren't. It was specifically spelled out in the contract.

Alice came out from behind the counter, and he followed her to her office. She shut the door. "What on earth is wrong?"

"How do I get the second book?" he said.

"The second book to wha—" Alice's face erupted into a huge smile. "In the series? The one you're listening to?"

The first one had ended on a fucking cliffhanger. "Yes. I stayed up until nearly dawn listening, and now..." He fumbled around for words and finally decided on the truth. "I need the next book or I might die."

Alice squealed and clapped her hands. "I knew it! I knew you'd love it."

"Man, Allie, I just didn't know. I didn't know that listening to a book could be like watching a *Mission Impossible* movie—I love those, by the way—"

"I actually think reading a book is even better than watching a movie," Alice said.

Her big brown eyes shone, and her smile looked like it might outgrow her face. And Beau knew just what she meant. Watching a movie felt kind of passive. Even if it kept you on the edge of your seat, you knew you were in a seat. Listening to a book was like...*Like you were fucking there.* "This might be a stupid question—"

"There are no stupid questions."

"Does reading a book feel just as exciting as listening to one?"

Alice nodded her head. "Sometimes more so. Now give me your phone. I'll show you how to get the next one. And do you like scary movies? Stephen King type of stuff?"

"Of course."

Alice looked up slowly, grinning in a sly, almost evil way. "Wait until you read one of those. You won't be able to sleep without a light on for at least a week."

Beau watched as Allie found the next book. It looked easy.

"See? You can do it yourself. Also, the entire town is talking about us. They think we're dating. As in they think we're a couple."

"I figured as much when I saw the crowd out there."

"Doesn't it bother you?"

It should bother him at least a little. Because now he was definitely going to have to watch himself around women. No flirting. No other stuff. But instead of being irritated, he was just kind of excited to get together with Alice again. And it felt good to know that folks thought they were together. That someone like him could appeal to someone like Alice, who was literally the smartest person he knew. "It doesn't bother me."

Alice didn't say anything. It probably bothered her plenty.

"Don't forget that you get to break up with me in just a few weeks. And you can be as dramatic as you want."

"I'm actually not much for drama," Alice said.

"Maybe we'll just drift apart."

"It happens to the best of couples."

They grinned at each other, and then something caught Alice's attention behind him. He turned to see Carmen and Claire peeking through the doorway.

"Well, bye, darlin'. I'll see you tomorrow," he said with a wink. It would be their second tutoring session.

"Yes," Alice said. "See you then."

"It's a date," Beau said. "Oh, and you know what? Bryce will be out of town this weekend. Why don't you come by the cabin on Friday?"

"The cabin?" Alice asked, eyes big as saucers. "You want me to come to your place?"

"Sure." And since it seemed appropriate to the occasion, he leaned over and gave her a short and sweet peck on the cheek. And even though it was a humid day, there must have been some static electricity in the air. Because the contact made his skin sizzle.

Chapter

Eleven

❦

Beau sat in his saddle and looked at the sun, which was low in the sky. He should have been back at the cabin an hour ago, but when he'd come down to the river to bring the cattle up, he'd discovered a few of them missing.

The Rio Verde was so low in some places that a few trouble-makers had managed to pick their way across. Usually, the river was deep enough to serve as a natural barrier, but not during this drought.

The dang animals had ended up along the highway, and Deputy Bobby Flores had been forced to stop traffic—two pickups, a minivan, and a silver Lexus—until the cattle could be secured.

Two old farmers were in the pickups, and they'd happily gotten out and contributed to the confusion by chasing the cattle across the road and onto the wrong property. Bubba Larson had been driving the minivan, and he and his four kids had joined in the fray, chasing the animals even farther in the opposite direction. Anna Vasquez, Big Verde's one and only former debutante, put the cherry on top by laying angrily on her Lexus's horn.

Beau had finally managed to get the cattle back across the river, but he still had to run them up to the east pasture so he could close them in. They wouldn't be able to graze along the river anymore, where the grass was lush and green. He'd have to talk to Ford, because they needed access to every blade of grass they could get.

"Thank you, folks," he said to the so-called helpers. "Things would have been different if you fellas hadn't come along."

Faster. Easier.

The two old geezers tipped their hats, spit tobacco on the ground, and took their sweet-ass time heading back to their trucks. Anna honked again, which resulted in everything slowing down even more, because that's what honking always did. One of the farmers stopped walking to his truck to meander over to Anna to see what she wanted.

"Well," Bubba Larson said. "I guess me and the kids have done our good deed for the day."

Bubba's kids were splashing in the Rio Verde—fully clothed—and the racket was deterring one curious heifer who seemed to be considering making another run for the border. So maybe they'd helped a bit after all.

"Thanks, Bubba."

Bobby let out a quick blast of his siren, which caused the cows to start running back up the hill toward the pasture, including the renegade who'd been eyeing the river. All Beau would have to do was follow them through the gate. He waved at Bobby as he drove away, going around Anna, who was now trying to convince the farmer she was fine and just wanted him to move.

Beau looked at his watch. "Dammit." He was supposed to meet Alice in ten minutes. Since Bryce was at the Rockin' H for the weekend, he'd asked Allie if she wanted to come out to the ranch. He'd hoped to tidy up the cabin before she got there, but that wasn't going to happen. There was no way in hell that he was even going to get there before her.

"Got a hot date?" Bubba asked.

"No," Beau said. But then he remembered the local gossip. "I mean, yep."

As the day had worn on, he'd become less excited about seeing Alice tonight. And it had nothing to do with her—she was actually pretty cool—and everything to do with the hard work of trying to read. On Wednesday, they'd looked at the ranching software program, and he'd become frustrated.

Maybe tonight would go better.

"You don't look too excited, considering you and Alice just started dating."

"Where'd you hear about me and Alice?"

"Trista heard it from my mom," Bubba said. "And since the Corner Café is the official center of misinformation for Big Verde, I'd say at most, there's a fifty percent chance you're dating Alice, and a fifty percent chance you're not, and a fifty percent chance you are but it's not what it looks like."

"That's one hundred and fifty percent, Bubba," Beau said.

"I know that. I can add."

He studied Bubba's confused expression and decided it wasn't worth it. What mattered was that even Bubba was suspicious about his and Alice's "relationship." He knew with certainty that Claire was also suspicious, and probably Maggie, too. Carmen had seemed pretty gung-ho, though.

"Have you ever had an actual girlfriend before?" Bubba asked.

"I've dated lots of women."

"Uh huh. When's Alice's birthday?"

"February third." In seventh grade he'd sent her a birthday card. He'd remembered the date ever since.

"Huh," Bubba said. "That's mighty impressive."

"When is Trista's?"

"It's April twenty-second," he said. And then he scratched his head. "Or the twenty-third. Anyway, you know what I mean.

You've never really had a girlfriend. You've just had dates. There's a difference."

Beau was well aware of the difference. "Thanks for helping with the cattle. I've got to run now—"

"We're all fond of Alice," Bubba said. "Don't do her dirty, Beau."

Point taken.

"I'll do my best to be the man she deserves." Beau tipped his hat. "Thanks again."

He trotted off after the cows, leaving Bubba to gather his frolicking kids out of the Rio Verde. He'd never be the man Alice deserved. Someday, she'd end up with an educated man. Maybe a college professor or a lawyer.

Not a cowboy who could barely read.

He followed the cattle to the east pasture and closed the gate behind them. There wasn't much grass for them to chew on, but at least there was a well and a water trough. He'd have Worth set out some hay bales. The girls would make do.

With the river as low as it was, there were water restrictions in place. They couldn't irrigate using the Rio Verde, and that was why moving some of the herd to the Rockin' H was smart. He just wished it didn't mean losing his brother. He pulled out his phone to call Alice and tell her he was running late and she could go on in. They never locked the door.

He searched through his contacts—twice—and realized he didn't have her number.

With a sigh, he leaned forward in his saddle and galloped along the fence line of the east pasture. He slowed to a trot as they went over the low-water crossing, which was dry as a bone, at Wailing Woman Creek. He rode another mile until they came to a fork in the road. To the right sat the foreman's cabin. The gate was open, and there were fresh tire tracks.

He and Sofie, his favorite horse on the ranch, trotted down the lane. They went through a little clump of cedar trees and came out in the clearing where the cabin sat. Alice was on the front porch, and she stood and waved when she saw him. For some reason, Sofie started trotting a little faster.

"Sorry I'm late," he said when he got to the cabin. "We had cattle on the highway. I tried to call, but I don't have your number. Which is weird, considering we're a couple."

"We'll fix that. And you're not too terribly late. I was actually having a pleasant time on your front porch. It's peaceful here." She held up her phone, and he noticed she was wearing earbuds. "I did six minutes of guided meditation. And now I'm making a to-do list."

"Oh yeah? Do you ever just sit still and relax?"

"That's what guided meditation is."

"Nah. I mean, don't you ever just stare at the clouds? Or swing back and forth in a hammock?"

"Well, no—"

"That's what I thought."

There was a book on the porch railing, and it was the same one Nonnie was reading. The one with the shirtless cowboy on it.

"Whatever you're reading in that book is pure fiction. You're dating a real cowboy now, darlin'."

"Oh? And what's the difference between you and the cowboy on this cover?"

"For starters, I'm wearing a shirt."

Alice's eyes darted to his chest. She'd seen him shirtless at the Village Chateau. Was she blushing? Or were her cheeks pink from the heat?

He climbed down from his horse and stomped his boots to shake the dirt off his chaps.

Alice looked at Sofie. "I've never been on a horse. It's on my bucket list, though."

"Are you kidding me?"

"Nope."

"Well, let's cross it off."

Alice's eyes grew huge. "Right now?"

"Why not? Sofie is saddled and ready to go."

Alice bit her lip—fucking adorable—and furrowed her brow. "Is she a calm horse?"

"She's as gentle as a lamb. We'll just do a quick trip around the cabin. It'll be fun."

Alice stared warily at the horse. "It would be nice to cross something off my bucket list..."

One more jerk of the ponytail, and she was on her way down the porch steps.

* * *

She was going to ride a horse!

"Wait a minute," Beau said. "I didn't realize you were wearing a skirt."

Alice looked down at her bare legs. "Is that a problem?" That was a stupid question. Clearly, it was a problem.

Beau studied her skirt carefully, while rubbing his chin. "It's not a tight skirt. So, I guess it could work, but you'd have your bare..."

Alice frowned. "I'm wearing underwear."

Now it was Beau's turn to blush. "I figured you were. But, well, unless they're made out of denim or you happen to wear some pretty massive granny panties, you're basically going to be bare-assed on the saddle."

"I do *not* wear granny panties," Alice said. In fact, she was wearing some lacy, pale pink panties. But Beau was right. She would practically be skin-to-saddle, and that probably would not be comfortable.

Beau pulled the brim of his hat down low, shading his eyes. He rubbed his chin again, as if maybe he was imagining what her panties looked like. Maybe now would be a good time to forget about tutoring and horses and cowboys and just hightail it home.

Beau snapped his fingers. "Mom's gardening overalls. She always kept a small garden behind the house, and her overalls are still here. You can slip into those."

"Oh? Do you think she'd mind?"

"Not at all," Beau said, coming up the steps. "She's a bit bigger than you, but they're just overalls. It won't matter."

Alice followed him inside.

"Oh," she said, as soon as he shut the door and her eyes had adjusted to the dim lighting. "This is…"

Beau flipped on a lamp.

"Really nice," she said.

There was a dark leather couch and loveseat in the center of the room, and a rustic coffee table standing on a cowhide rug. Hanging over the rock fireplace was a painting of the Rio Verde, winding through limestone hills. The room was warm and cozy and masculine.

"Surprised?" Beau asked.

"A little."

"After living in the butt-ugly bunkhouse, it was nice to come back to the cabin where we were raised," Beau said.

"It looks like both of you."

Something flitted across Beau's face. An expression she couldn't quite identify. She'd just paid him a compliment, but Beau looked…

Oh. Of course. Bryce was leaving.

Alice had never had a sibling, much less a twin, but she could imagine what it must feel like to face separating from someone you were so close to. And Beau depended on Bryce for so many things.

Beau opened a closet door and took out a pair of overalls. "Just take off your skirt…"

The words seemed to echo in the room.

"There's a bathroom," he added quickly. "I'll wait outside. Just come out when you're ready."

Alice took the overalls and went into the small bathroom. She wasn't typically a nosy person, but she couldn't help but notice the items sitting next to the sink. Shaving cream. Two razors. Two different bottles of aftershave.

She picked one up, sniffed it, and set it back down. Then she picked up the other, sniffed it, and *oh my*. This one was Beau's. It was woodsy with just a bit of citrus. And it made her shiver.

She stepped out of her skirt and hung it on the rack next to the shower, where Beau took showers while completely naked like everyone else, and why was she thinking about that? It was weird and inappropriate.

Boom. Beau's bare chest popped up in her mind's eye. And it was even better than the one gracing the cover of her romance novel.

Holy guacamole, she needed to get the heck out of Beau's bathroom. It was hot in the small room, and it was making her have weird thoughts about Beau being naked or possibly naked except for a pair of chaps, which was nonsensical, because who would wear chaps in the shower?

She quickly stepped into Mrs. Montgomery's overalls. They were huge, but like Beau said, who cared? She leaned over and rolled the cuffs up before heading out to the porch.

Beau was standing with the horse—he'd called her Sofie—holding the reins. His face broke out in a huge smile at the sight of her.

"I know. I look silly."

"Not silly at all. You look…"

Alice waited for him to say something like *goofy* or *ridiculous*.

Beau shook his head and held out the reins. "Cute. Now come on over and climb up on Sofie."

Cute? She didn't know why that made her grin, but it did. She could feel it right there on her face. But it disappeared when she got next to Sofie. In fact, she broke out in a nervous sweat. She'd never been so close to such a large animal.

Beau took her hand and helped her rub the horse's nose and neck. "Sofie, this is Allie. Allie, this is Sofie."

"Hello," Alice said.

"You've got nothing to be afraid of," Beau said. "Sofie's a sweetie, and I'll be right here."

He guided her foot into the stirrup and, with a bit of help from his big, warm hands on her waist, she was up on the horse in a jiffy. *Way* up on the horse. It felt much higher than she'd imagined, and she got a bit dizzy. "Oh, dear. This is a little scarier than I'd thought it would be."

"You're doing great," Beau said. "Hold on to the saddle horn while I lead you around."

Beau made a little sound with his tongue, and then he gently pulled on the reins and started walking. Alice couldn't help it, she yelped—maybe it was a squeal—when Sofie started moving beneath her.

She felt clumsy and stiff, and she clenched the animal with her thighs while white-knuckling the saddle horn.

"Try to relax," Beau said. "Loosen up your hips. Just sit up straight and hold your shoulders square, but let yourself go a little Elvis from the waist down."

"Elvis?"

Beau stopped walking and Sofie came to a halt. "Like this," he said, swaying his hips this way and that, doing a little pelvic thrust and bump and grind, all while wearing a huge grin. "Loosen up, Allie Cat."

"I don't think I could do that without hurting myself."

"Oh, I bet it wouldn't hurt at all. In fact, I bet it would feel real good."

"That's enough out of you, Beau Montgomery."

With a laugh, Beau resumed leading Alice around. And she did somehow manage to relax a little and loosen up. By the time they'd circled the cabin three times, she was way less stiff. This was fun! Why hadn't she ever ridden a horse before?

"I hate to be a party pooper," Beau said when they came around to the porch. "But we've got some reading to do."

Alice sighed. She was having such a good time.

"You know what?" Beau said. "There's a real nice picnic area down by the dam. It's a pretty little ride, and I think you'd enjoy it. How about next week, we do our lesson outside?"

She would enjoy that. And she knew for sure that Beau would. He was probably happiest when he was outdoors. "That is a wonderful idea. I like it!"

"It's a date," Beau said. "I mean, tutoring session. It's not actually a date."

"Of course."

He came around and held out a hand. "Might I help you off your high horse, darlin'?"

Her heart was pounding. But was it because of the horse? Or because Beau had accidentally referred to their next tutoring session as a date while calling her *darlin'*?

Chapter Twelve

Beau had a crick in his neck from glancing back at Alice, but he was afraid of arriving at the dam—they'd stuck to their plan to have this week's tutoring session there—only to discover that she'd fallen off her horse at some point.

Although he wouldn't really need his eyes for that. Just his ears. Because Alice seemed to turn into quite the chatterbox when she was nervous, and being on a horse really opened the floodgates.

She'd talked to the horse.

She'd talked to the birds.

She'd talked to the sky.

And she'd talked to Beau.

He couldn't always make out what she was saying, but she didn't seem to need any response or prompting. All you had to do to set Allie on autopilot was say, *Hey, do you know what kind of tree that is?*

She'd go straight into a lecture about invasive species and whatnot, and then Beau was free to think about whatever he wanted, which was the quick glimpse of red panties he'd seen while helping her onto her horse. She'd worn jeans this time, but since they had to ride through some brush to get to the dam, he'd suggested she slip back into the overalls she'd worn last week. He hadn't peeked at her panties on purpose, but the overalls were huge and loose. He was quite a bit taller than she was, and when he'd looked down, well, there they were.

Lacy. Red. Tiny.

So tiny that they left quite a bit of curvy ass cheek exposed.

He'd looked away quickly, but the image was seared into his brain. And now he could pull it up whenever he wanted, like when Alice was blathering on about—he glanced over his shoulder and listened—deer ticks.

Lacy. Red. Tiny.

Did she always wear tiny little panties? Probably. Except for maybe when she wore none at all. Like maybe for dressy occasions when she didn't want those pesky visible lines some women were all concerned about. He remembered her at the Boots and Ball Gowns library gala a couple of years ago. That dress had been skin-tight.

Light peachy color. Lots of sparkly beads. Only covered one shoulder. And this was way more detail than a cowboy should be able to recall about a ball gown.

Beau shook his head, but his brain hopped right back on the track. Maybe she didn't wear panties when she slept. Or maybe she didn't wear anything at all while she slept.

"Beau! Did you hear me?"

She probably talked in her sleep. "Sorry. What did you say?"

"I asked if we're almost there. I think Sofie is tired."

Beau snickered. Sofie wasn't tired, but he bet Alice's butt and thighs were getting sore. Not to mention her mouth.

"Actually, we're here," Beau said, bringing his horse to a stop at the bluff overlooking the dam.

He climbed down and grabbed Alice's stuff, which he'd placed in the saddlebag. Then he helped Alice down, inadvertently catching another glimpse of her sweet little butt cheeks.

"Are your legs sore?" he asked.

"No. But I admit they're a bit shaky."

"Tomorrow, they'll be sore."

"You ride every day. Do yours get sore?"

"Nah. I'm used to it. My thigh and butt muscles get daily workouts." Riding a horse was better than a gym membership.

Alice's eyes flitted below his belt, as if checking out his thigh muscles, and he remembered how he'd gotten to her that night at the hotel. He'd been shirtless then, but it appeared she also enjoyed seeing him in chaps.

Most women did.

"How do we get to the river?"

Beau pointed at the bluff. "Down that trail. And you need to stick close. Maybe grab hold of me. Because those sandals weren't made for trails."

Alice looked at her feet with a frown. "Do you think they'll get ruined?"

"Just be careful. But next time, wear boots. You don't wear sandals to ride a horse."

Why was he thinking about a next time at the dam with Alice?

"I don't have boots."

"Then we'll have to get you some."

And now he was talking about boot shopping. With Alice.

He started down the steep trail with Alice on his heels. They hadn't gone very far when her sandal slid on some rocks, and she crashed right into his back with a dainty grunt. He was big and sure-footed, so he barely budged.

"Settle down back there, Allie Cat," he said. And then, because he felt like he had no option—Alice wore shitty shoes and was clumsy on top of it—he reached back for her hand. Without a word, she took it, and the two of them continued down the trail without further incident.

After they got to the riverbank, they picked their way over rocks and roots to get to the picnic table. He let go of her hand to set the bag on the bench, and for a moment they just stared at each other while his hand tingled.

The river flowed gently over the top of the dam, and the soothing sound calmed his nerves. It was so peaceful and quiet—

"Did you know that it's the limestone bottom that makes the water so clear? And there's a subterranean river here. We can't see it, but if it weren't for the dam, we'd probably be able to hear it if we got super quiet."

Beau snorted. "You'd have to stop talking for a minute, Allie Cat."

Alice crossed her arms. "What?"

Beau shrugged. "Nothing. You just talk a lot, is all."

Her foot started tapping, and Beau couldn't help but notice her little toes had gotten dusty on the trail. She opened her mouth as if she wanted to say something, but then she promptly shut it and stared at the ground.

Oh shit. He'd hurt her feelings. The silence was heavy. Oppressive. Guilt-inducing. And he swore he could hear that damn subterranean river, just like Alice said. It, along with the water trickling over the dam, was babbling away, saying, *Beau is an asshole Beau is an asshole Beau is an asshole.*

Beau cleared his throat. "I didn't mean that the way it sounded."

Alice leaned over and brushed the dust off her toes with her fingers. The pink toenails caught the sun and sparkled. Every second that she didn't speak was a second that made Beau feel worse.

Maybe he could get her chattering again. "The river is so low up by the highway that we've had cattle crossing it."

Alice straightened. Looked at him. Shrugged.

"And to think," Beau continued. "Just two years ago we had the biggest flood in our town's history."

Alice nodded. Silently.

"The weather is definitely becoming more extreme," Beau said. "There's a conference on how climate change is affecting ranching in Texas coming up next month."

Alice's eyebrows shot up. Her lips trembled. Her pink toes tapped. It was obvious she had climate change facts lined up, and they were banging their fists around in attempts to get Alice to open up her mouth.

"It sounds really interesting," Beau said.

Alice was now biting her lower lip. Clearly dying to say something. She probably had some pretty strong opinions about climate change.

"Of course, I don't know anything about it," he said. Because saying you didn't know something was like dangling a juicy peach in front of Alice.

Her eyes were big and round. She was probably holding her breath or biting her tongue.

Time to put her out of her misery. "Do you know anything about climate change and how it's affecting ranching?"

Alice let out a big breath, and Beau had to try very hard not to smile.

She searched his eyes, brows drawn together, as if trying to figure out if she was being played. Beau tried hard to appear earnest and sincere, because he was. Not only did he feel like shit about hurting Alice's feelings, he also actually wanted to hear what she had to say. And since she was the smartest person he'd ever known besides Gerome Kowalski, there was no doubt that she was a good source of information.

The little wrinkle in Allie's forehead disappeared and she took a deep breath.

Beau sat and leaned back against the picnic table, crossing his arms.

Alice started talking, and even though it was interesting… something about the difference between extreme drought and desertification…he couldn't stop noticing how pretty she was. The sweet spot at the base of her throat pulsed softly with excitement.

Damn. He'd drifted. He had no idea what this lecture was about anymore, but he was enthralled, nonetheless.

* * *

Alice was having a hard time staying on topic with Beau's long legs stretched out like that. For one thing, the chaps were distracting. So was the hat, which he'd pushed back on his head, presumably in order to see her better. His arms were crossed over his chest, an area she'd already spent way too much time ruminating about, and he had a silly little grin on his face that made her feel even more self-conscious.

She imagined the words pouring out of her mouth like soft-serve ice cream from the broken dispenser at the Chuckwagon Buffet— she had personal experience with that—and she wasn't even sure if she was spouting actual facts or total nonsense. Overgrazing, water tables, and changing climate zones. She was projectile vomiting all of it.

Occasionally, Beau's eyes drifted down to her neck and shoulders, where she was having a hard time keeping the straps of her overalls up. Oh God. Maybe his eyes weren't drifting. What if he was falling asleep? It wouldn't be the first time she'd caused someone to slip quietly into a coma. She paused, and Beau raised his hand.

"Um, Alice?"

"Yes?"

"This is all very interesting—"

"I'm sorry. I've probably bored you. As you said earlier, I talk too much."

"I never said you talk too much. I said you talk a lot, which you do. And that's fine. You have plenty to say. But I'm getting seriously heated."

Alice's pulse raced. Her skin prickled. She swallowed. "Heated?"

"It's hotter than Hades. Probably something to do with climate change. What do you say we move to the shade?"

He was hot. As in he had heatstroke. Also, he was hot as in *hubba-hubba*, but that was neither here nor there, because Alice didn't pay attention to such things. And somehow, she hadn't paid attention to the fact that her back was drenched in sweat. She fanned her face. "You're right. Can we drag this table underneath the oak tree?"

Beau stood up. "Sure."

He grabbed the edge of the table, and Alice ran around to the other side to push, but she ended up just kind of touching the table and following along. Because Beau was freaking strong. She'd always assumed horseback riding was a passive activity, but it wasn't. Her butt and thighs were definitely going to be sore tomorrow. No wonder Beau was in such good shape.

Understatement. Beau was a cowboy Adonis.

"I guess school is now in session," Beau said, once the table was settled on a level spot. "What books did you bring?"

Alice had a surprise for Beau. She dug in the bag and pulled out a paperback.

Beau's eyes widened, as if he were worried that he might be expected to pop it open and start reading.

"Just focus on the title," Alice said calmly.

A smile broke out on Beau's face. "*Jax Angle*. This is the book I listened to."

"Yep. Have you started the second one yet?"

"I'm on the third one. Listened to it all morning while I was doing some mindless ranch chores."

"Wow. Good! Anyway, I just wanted you to have the actual book. And you don't have to, but it might be good to listen to it again and see if you can follow along."

Beau took the book and opened it.

"It has a large font and more white space on the page. It's meant for people with poor vision, but it sometimes helps people with dyslexia, too."

"I see the word *Jax* all over the page," Beau said.

"Those are probably dialogue tags. They tell you who is speaking. And if you look carefully, you'll notice a visual pattern of quotation marks and dialogue tags. Searching for those patterns will help you distinguish dialogue from narration."

Beau flipped through a few more pages. "Here's the word *Foster*. He's the bad guy. And here's *Liv*. She's Jax's lady love."

"Don't get too attached to her," Alice said, and then she slapped her hand over her mouth. What had she just done?

"You mean she fucking dies?" Beau asked.

"No, I didn't mean anything by it. Let's put the book away now."

"She dies. Jesus. Which book? Does it happen in the third book?"

Alice just stared at him. She'd said enough.

Beau sighed. "Well, thanks anyway. When does this have to be back at the library?"

"Never. It's a gift."

Beau swallowed, loudly. "Thanks, Allie."

"You're very welcome. Now, let's get to work. We're going to start with sensory exercises. Lots of touching and rubbing and feeling."

Beau looked up slowly and grinned. He'd clearly misunderstood— or maybe she was teasing—because they were going to be using some tactile methods that had absolutely nothing to do with . . . Whatever it was he was thinking about.

Alice's tummy fluttered annoyingly in response to that grin. Maybe it was adrenaline and cortisol—fight-or-flight hormones— because Beau Montgomery looked like a saber-toothed tiger eyeing a tasty little bunny.

Chapter

Thirteen

It hadn't taken long for Beau's optimistic mood to take a dive.

He stared at the rock, leaf, and stick laid out on the table in front of him. He was trying not to be surly, but it was hard. Because this wasn't a reading lesson. This was utter nonsense, and he'd expected more from a woman with multiple degrees who considered herself a reading expert.

"You're not even trying, Beau."

Beau sighed. And then he touched each inanimate object. "Rock, leaf, stick."

Alice matched his sigh with one of her own. "No. Remember? These represent sounds. Touch each one again, and say the sound it makes. We're forming new pathways between objects and sounds, and then we'll turn those objects into written symbols."

"I'm too old to form new pathways."

"That's not true. It might take a bit more effort, but you're more mature than when you were a child. You have more patience."

He didn't feel like he had more patience. And he couldn't shake the notion that it was too late. That he'd never learn.

Alice pulled out a drawstring bag and opened it. Then she dumped a bunch of colored blocks out on the table. "Let's use these instead of the natural objects. They don't have a tactile element, but—"

"Those are toys." In bright primary colors. They looked like something you'd find in a kindergarten classroom. He yanked the brim of his hat down. "I'm not playing with children's toys, Allie. And I don't see how they'll ever get me to where I can read a book like *Jax Angle*, much less function as a literate foreman of a ranch."

"They're not toys. They're manipulatives."

"You can call them whatever you want, but they're blocks. For kids."

And I'm a fully grown man.

Just in case she hadn't noticed he was a fully grown man, he undid the top few buttons of his shirt. It was hot out, after all.

Alice bit her lip. Cleared her throat.

Got the message.

She put the blocks back in the bag and returned to the rock, leaf, and stick. Then she began digging in the dirt with her toe.

"What are you looking for?"

"Aha!" she said, leaning over and picking up an acorn. "We're going to try this again. Pretend these are sounds."

She spoke gently, but instead of calming him, her words made him feel jittery and strange. Damn, it was a good thing it was hot outside. Otherwise the heat in his cheeks might be visible. He might spend all of his time outdoors, and he might have a five o'clock shadow by noon, but he'd always been an outrageous blusher, and embarrassment was a trigger.

He yanked on his hat again. "I don't need to play pretend games. Just teach me the way you'd teach anybody. Let's do it the regular way."

"But Beau, the regular ways haven't worked for you. And this is a process that helps a lot of people. Every time you see the acorn, think of the soft *a* sound. And this"—she picked up the leaf—"is going to be a hard *c* sound."

This was beyond ridiculous. Where were the books? The letters? The tablets? Acorns and leaves didn't make sounds. Words weren't made out of acorns and leaves. Suddenly, he wasn't in the mood for this lesson.

He was hot.

Hot from the sun. Hot from the frustration. Hot from watching a small bead of sweat drip down Alice's chest and disappear between her breasts.

He looked at the Rio Verde. It would feel fantastic to dive into its refreshing depths and disappear with a little sizzle and a puff of steam.

He'd learned as a kid that when things got tough, it was time for a diversion. A distraction.

A bit of fun.

"Let's go swimming."

"What?" Alice stammered.

"Let's go swimming. We can cool off a bit, and then it will be easier for me to focus."

Alice glanced at the river. "I didn't bring a swimsuit, and I doubt you did, either."

"Who needs swimsuits?"

Alice raised her hand. "Me. I need one."

"Aw, come on. I think every kid in Big Verde had their first skinny-dipping experience right here at this dam."

Alice arranged the items. "This might look like a leaf, an acorn, and a twig. But together, they spell the word *can*."

It didn't look like *can* to Beau. It looked like a damn leaf, acorn, and twig. "How old were you the first time you went skinny-dipping?"

Alice moved the twig and replaced it with the rock. "Now it spells *cat*, and I've never been skinny-dipping."

Everybody had been skinny-dipping. She just didn't want to admit it. "You're fibbing."

Alice stared at the word she'd spelled. He glanced at it, too. She'd only changed out the last object—a twig for a rock—and that had changed the very last sound. Suddenly, he kind of had an inkling to see what would happen if he changed out the rock for something else.

Leaves and twigs didn't move around like letters.

"I've never even been to the dam before," Alice said softy. "Believe me, I was not at any of the parties held here, or anywhere, for that matter."

Beau thought back to when he was twelve and Alice was sixteen. He remembered that ponytail, and how it bounced around like it had a mind of its own. Alice swatted at a gnat, and he realized, with a grin, that her ponytail still seemed to have a mind of its own.

He remembered how she'd laughed at his and Bryce's jokes, and how it had made him want to do tricks and show off and be royally obnoxious, just to hear that sound. And he also remembered how much he'd wanted to impress her by being able to do his home-work quickly and correctly. By talking about books and whatnot, like Bryce did.

"Seriously, Allie? You've never been swimming here? Not even once? Not even on senior skip day?"

Alice had been pretty and smart, and his twelve-year-old mind had assumed she'd been popular. Was it possible he was wrong, and that maybe she'd sat at home while other kids were out having fun? It was hard for Beau to wrap his mind around. To him, Alice had been beautiful and sophisticated. Smart and talented. To him, she'd been . . .

Well, hell. She'd been everything.

* * *

Why did Beau have to look so surprised? Surely not *every* kid in Big Verde had skinny-dipped here. Alice swatted at a fly that was buzzing around. "Anyway, who cares about high school?"

She grabbed a notebook out of her bag and opened it. She tried to write the letters she planned to work with, but her arm was sweaty and it stuck to the paper, tearing it. "Dang it!"

"Come on, Allie. Let's cool off. Then we'll work."

How childish could Beau be? "That's not how it works. First you work, and *then* you play."

Beau raised an eyebrow.

Wait a minute. Had she just committed to playing? "Don't look at me like that. I have no intention—"

"I'll mess around with your rocks and acorns if you'll go skinny-dipping with me first."

"I'm not skinny-dipping with you, Beau. Get the idea out of your head right now."

"Okay, fine. You can keep your underwear on."

"I didn't come all the way down here to go swimming. I came down here to tutor you—"

"Bucket list."

"Pardon?"

"Write skinny-dipping on your bucket list, right below horse-back riding, and then let's cross it off."

She stared at him. He was speaking her love language, and he knew it.

"Let's cut a deal," he said. "Twenty minutes of swimming followed by twenty minutes of reading."

"I don't think—"

"You teach me how to spell with rocks, and I'll help you cross things off of your bucket list. And I bet I can even help you add some more stuff to it. Stuff that's not boring."

He winked.

"I don't have boring things on my bucket list."

Beau raised an eyebrow. "I bet you have a bunch of museums on it."

"They're mostly in Europe. And anyway, we've already cut a deal. I'm helping you with reading, and you're going to Brittany's wedding with me. That's our deal. We don't need to add silly things like—"

"Fun? And bucket lists? You might know a lot of things, Allie Cat. But I don't think you understand the concept of fun."

Ha! She had fun all the time.

"What's the last fun thing you did?"

Dang it. She tapped her toe and thought. Surely, there was something. Sweat dripped down the side of her neck. It *was* hot. And the Rio Verde looked crystal clear and cool.

"There are snakes in the river," she said. And snakes did not sound fun.

"Nobody has ever been bitten here. Stay away from the banks and the cypress roots, and you'll be fine."

"I have two words for you," Alice sputtered. "Amoebic meningoencephalitis."

Beau stood up. "That sounded like at least four words."

"It's a type of brain-eating bacteria that lives in warm water."

Beau unbuttoned his shirt. "Ah. Well, you only have to worry about that in non-flowing water. This section of the river is cool, spring-fed, and briskly flowing. It's perfectly safe."

"It's not *perfectly* safe. That would imply there is no risk at all, and statistically speaking—"

His shirt fell open, and it sucked up any and all words she'd been about to utter.

"If you're looking for a risk-free environment, Allie, you'd better go back to your little bubble of a library. Although it flooded a couple of years ago, so maybe it's not safe, either."

Alice crossed her arms and nervously tapped her foot. Because there was his chest. The same one he'd answered the hotel room

Carly Bloom

door with. Because of course it was the same chest. How could it be a different one?

"I'm going to get in the river to cool off so I can pay attention to you and your rocks and twigs and whatnot. You don't have to join me if you don't want to. But if you do want to, be sure to write it down on your bucket list first."

Alice stared in stunned silence as Beau removed his shirt and tossed it on the table. Next, he unbuckled his belt and yanked it through the belt loops so he could step out of his chaps. Finally, he removed his hat and handed it to Alice. "Watch and learn, Allie."

"Where are you going?"

"To the rope swing hanging off that old cypress tree."

She clutched Beau's hat. At least he hadn't taken his pants off.

"Beau!" she called. But he was already climbing up a series of boards nailed to the trunk of the tree. He quickly disappeared in the branches.

"Heads up!" he shouted as a boot landed with a thud next to her. Then another.

Zip.

A pair of Wranglers landed right on the table.

"Yee-haw!" Beau shouted as he swung out over the river. He let go of the rope, did a somersault, and splashed into the Rio Verde. Water droplets landed at Alice's feet.

She crossed her arms, expecting him to pop up like a cork.

Only he didn't pop up like a cork. Surely, he should have broken through the surface by now. He'd said the river was low. What if he'd hit his head on a rock?

She stood and walked a few feet down the bank. She'd known this was a bad idea! Why did Beau have to be so impulsive? She was in the middle of nowhere with only a horse for transportation and a man, who was twice her size, possibly in need of medical attention. And that was *if* she could even find him.

"Beau!" she shouted.

Nothing. Not a single ripple on the water.

Alice stomped her foot. "Dang it!"

With shaking hands, she bent over and unbuckled her sandals before kicking them to the side. Then she slid the straps of the overalls down both shoulders, because the last thing she needed was to be burdened by waterlogged denim while she was trying to drag a heavy man out of a river.

Just as the overalls slid down her hips, Beau broke the surface of the water.

Chapter
Fourteen

❧

Beau took in a huge gulp of air, filling his lungs to capacity. Then he let it all out with another "Yee-haw!"

He loved this river. And nothing felt better on a hot day. He kicked back, letting his feet float to the surface, and looked around for Alice. When he saw her—standing on the bank with her overalls down at her hips—he took in a mouthful of water. Then he sputtered and coughed. Alice was coming in!

Alice yanked the bib of her overalls up, flattening it against her chest. What was happening? Why was she getting dressed? "Aren't you coming in?"

Alice stared at him. "What took you so long to come to the surface?"

"I was just swimming around down there." He winked at her. "Big lungs."

Alice let out a huge sigh. "I thought you'd hit your head on something and were unconscious."

"Why would you think that?"

"Because you were under for so long!"

Her hands were shaking. Her sandals were off. Holy shit, had she been removing her clothes so she could come in and save him?

The ponytail bounced and swung as Alice fought with the buckles on the straps of her overalls. Her face was red and splotchy and shiny with sweat—probably not a look Alice wore very often—and a fly buzzed around her head. She swatted at it, and Beau thought he might have heard the word *dammit* seep through her lips, which was also probably a rare occurrence.

She'd been ripping off her sandals and clothes to jump in the river and save him.

He grinned at the thought, but then something warm and heavy slid past his heart and settled in his belly. The grin slipped away. *She'd been ready to save him.*

"Allie Cat, I'm sorry if I scared you."

She stopped fussing with her overalls. "It was very inconsiderate of you."

"You're right. I'm just not used to..." He paused and searched for the right words. "People being so easily alarmed."

"Any normal person would have been alarmed."

He wasn't sure that was true. "You look really heated. And you've already kicked off your shoes. Are you sure you don't want to get in for a few minutes and cool off? It'll clear your mind and put you in a better mood."

"There is absolutely nothing wrong with my mood." She swatted violently at another fly, nearly losing her balance in the process.

He shrugged. Then he put his hands behind his neck and floated on his back as if he hadn't a care in the world. "Man, this feels fantastic."

"You can't always put off the hard things, Beau."

A Mexican eagle soared against the backdrop of a few fluffy clouds floating lazily by. "And you can't always put off the fun ones. Or at least you shouldn't."

He squinted at a cloud. "Look. There's a hippopotamus."

"Where?" Alice said, looking over her shoulder.

Beau laughed, and Alice rolled her eyes in exasperation, or possibly it was embarrassment. She'd only gotten one strap buckled, and seeing her standing there on the riverbank, barefoot and sweaty and irritated, gave Beau all kinds of weird feelings. Soft ones.

Allie Cat Martin was out of her element… And it was cute. Sexy. Driving him nuts.

Alice looked at the clouds. "That's not a hippo. It's a duck."

"You're looking at it from the wrong angle."

Alice glanced at the river. Her bare toes were tapping, and it was obvious she wanted to get in the water.

He kicked his feet and just missed splashing her. "We both know you're hot." *So hot.* "And we both know you want to get in. So just do it."

Alice took a delicate step toward the river, looking intently at the rocks, before sticking her toe in the water.

"You can cross it off your list," Beau said in a taunting, singsongy voice.

"Fine. Turn around."

"Really?"

"Yes. But I'm keeping my underwear on. And you have to promise not to look."

Beau held up two fingers. "Scout's honor."

"You got kicked out of the Boy Scouts, if I remember correctly," Alice said.

"Yeah, but not for lying. Also, our troop leader had no sense of humor."

Beau turned around and stared at the limestone cliffs. He couldn't believe Alice was actually getting in. Damn, she was really going outside of her comfort zone to have a little fun.

Maybe he could do the same thing when it came to buckling down and tackling dyslexia. When they got out of the river, he was going to try really hard and do everything Alice told him to do.

*   *   *

Alice slipped the overalls down past her hips and stepped out of them. Next, with a quick glance at Beau's back, she slipped her shirt off. The sun warmed her skin, yet she still broke out in goose bumps. Why was she so stupidly nervous? She was a grown woman wearing modest-ish underwear. Her bra was padded, so it wouldn't be see-through when it got wet. It was full coverage and probably showed less cleavage than her swimsuit.

The red panties were another matter, but still. No smaller than the average bikini bottom. She crossed her arms to cover her breasts and carefully picked her way across the rocks. She eyed Beau. He had his back to her, but he'd come closer to the shore and was no longer treading water.

Her bare foot stepped on a sharp rock. "Ouch!"

Beau jerked and started to turn around. "I'm fine!" Alice said. "Stay where you are."

Beau froze, then returned to his previous position.

His blond hair was dark and wet, and his broad, tanned shoulders were dotted with droplets of water. The river came up just past his waist, and as she watched, he bent over and began wriggling around.

"What are you doing?" she asked, timidly taking another step. *You can do this, Martin. It's just a river. You're just getting in a river. In your underwear. With Beau Montgomery, who is also only wearing underwear.*

"Be careful on those rocks," Beau said over his shoulder. "They can be slippery. You should have swung in on the rope."

"It's safer to come in this way."

"Not true," Beau said, tossing something dark over his shoulder.

Alice ducked as it went past to land with a splat on the rocks behind her. "What was that?"

"I don't want to ride back in wet underwear. Those will be dry by the time we get out—"

"You're naked?"

"That's the local custom when it comes to skinny-dipping," Beau answered simply. "Are you in yet?"

"No! I'll tell you when."

She was having second thoughts. But dang it, she'd started this thing, and she was going to finish it. She took another step. Beau was right. The rocks were awful slippery. They were also covered in moss, which was squishy and unpleasant. A small fish darted out from beneath one and swam away. "You said snakes tend to hang out along the bank?"

"Don't worry. They're hiding in the cypress roots. You're fine where you are. Hurry up, I'm tired of standing here. I want to have some fun."

Fun? What kind of fun? Because if Beau thought she was climbing on his shoulders for a game of chicken, he could think again. She intended to tread water for about five minutes in order to cool off and then get out.

In her wet underwear.

She took two more steps and then stopped to consider where she should put her foot next. She was kind of getting used to the squishy feel, and the little fishies swimming around were cute. The water was nearly up to her thighs now, and maybe this wasn't such a bad idea.

She took a big step to make it to the next rock—a big, flat, and totally secure one—and missed. With an inhuman shriek, she hit the water.

Beau turned around just as she came sputtering up, gasping for air. "Are you okay, Allie Cat?"

He was grinning, and his blue eyes were absolutely ridiculous when surrounded by shimmering water.

"I'm fine. It's a bit chillier than I'd thought it would be."

"Come on," Beau said. "You'll warm up quickly. Let's head to the deeper water."

By the time they'd swum to the middle of the spring-fed swimming hole, she was smiling. This was exhilarating! And when Beau splashed her, she squealed and splashed him back. Before she knew it, she was laughing harder than she'd ever laughed in her life. It was the kind of laughing other people did while Alice stood awkwardly, watching the fun.

Holy guacamole, she didn't feel like herself at all. And it was fantastic.

Beau dove beneath the water, yanked on one of her toes, and then popped up behind her. Alice squealed, and their voices rang off the limestone cliffs, echoing up and down the canyon.

Things eventually quieted down, and they treaded water, side by side, admiring the beauty around them. "Look, Allie. Isn't that cool?" Beau gazed into the river. "You can see the bubbles from the spring."

A lone ray of sunlight poked through a cloud, slicing the water and illuminating the sandy bottom where the bubbles popped up from the spring. It was beautiful. Indescribable, really. And to think, this bit of paradise was readily available, practically in her backyard, and she'd never taken advantage of it.

"Aren't you glad you decided to strip down and, you know, fall in?" Beau asked. "I was going to say dive in, but that isn't really what happened."

Alice splashed him, laughing.

"I like the sound of your laugh," Beau said.

"Do you? Well, I guess there are worse laughs than mine."

"Yeah. Claire is a snorter."

He wasn't wrong, because Claire *was* a snorter. "I think I've laughed more today than I have in the past—"

"Week?"

"More like month."

"Damn, Allie. We need to work on that."

We?

His skin glowed. His eyelashes were all wet and stuck together. And his smile was so bright that Alice was afraid to look directly into his face. "Let's see who can touch the bottom first," he said.

"Wait—"

"One, two, three!"

Before Alice had a chance to take in a lungful of air, Beau had flipped over to dive. She caught a glimpse of fabulous butt cheeks and froze. But then her competitive drive kicked in. If Beau Montgomery could touch the bottom, so could she.

Alice took a deep breath and dove beneath the surface of the water. Everything became muffled and quiet, and she timidly opened her eyes, watching the bubbles from her mouth and nose float lazily up.

Then she looked down, kicking in earnest to catch up with Beau. But he was already at the bottom, grinning and holding both thumbs up.

And holy guacamole. Folks weren't kidding when they said the waters of the Rio Verde ran clear.

Chapter
Fifteen

❦

Beau swam behind Alice as they headed for the shore. He couldn't help but take in the view, which had nothing to do with the limestone cliffs, crystal clear water, and ancient cypress trees, and everything to do with Alice's shapely long legs kicking as she did the breaststroke.

And speaking of breasts…

Wait. Nobody was speaking of breasts.

But Alice's bra was waterlogged. It had slipped around quite a bit as she'd swam and splashed and generally had a good old time. Beau hadn't stared or anything even close to it. But he'd caught a glimpse or two of side boob. There had even been a possible nipple sighting, but he'd averted his eyes so quickly that he couldn't be certain.

Alice hit the incline of the riverbank first, and stopped swimming to stand. The water came up to her ribs, and she reached around and squeezed the water out of her ponytail. "How are we going to do this?" she asked.

"Do what?"

"Get out. How are we going to get out?"

Beau looked at the bank, where their clothes waited. "I figure we'll walk out since flying isn't an option."

Alice rolled her eyes. "I mean, which one of us is getting out first?"

He wasn't modest at all. In fact, he'd make a good nudist if cowboying accommodated such a thing. He liked nature. Loved being natural *in* nature. But he sure didn't want to make Allie uncomfortable.

"So?" Alice asked. "You? Or me?"

"I'll go first. That way I can help you out if you need it." He headed for the bank, and as he went to pass Allie, his inner fifteen-year-old came out, giving him the idea to play a tried-and-true Texas river prank. How could Alice have the full skinny-dipping-at-the-dam experience without it?

With a sideways glance at Allie, Beau faked being startled with a little jump. "What was that?" he asked.

Alice shrieked and scanned the water with eyes as big as saucers. Beau was just about to clue her in to the prank by humming the theme from *Jaws*—no need to drag it out too long—when, with no warning at all, Alice screamed, "Snake!" and headed straight for him.

He was pretty sure he was getting a dose of his own medicine, but water moccasins were both venomous and aggressive. "Where?"

The next thing he knew, Alice was climbing him like a tree.

"Alice—"

His face was suddenly pressed between her breasts, as she was doing her best to shimmy up to his shoulders. He somehow caught himself from tumbling over and grabbed Alice by the waist. "Whoa there, Nellie."

Alice glanced all around, and then after a moment, Beau felt her muscles relax. "Beau?"

"Yes, darlin'?"

"I think it might have been a stick."

Beau stifled a grin. "Confession time. I was just pulling your leg. Playing a little prank."

Allie slid down his body until they were face-to-face, and she wasn't smiling.

"Are you mad?" he asked.

He liked holding her this way. Especially the part where her legs were wrapped around his waist.

"No," she said. "I don't think I am anyway. I feel kind of—"

He lifted her a little higher, because he was in the danger zone of having his dick rub up against her ass. Her breasts were pressed against his chest, and her...Well, there wasn't an inch between them.

"Weird," she said, eyes dipping down to his lips. "I feel kind of weird."

The world tilted. He was naked and holding Alice in his arms. And she was staring at his lips. It was a teenage fantasy, only fantasies were blurry things with soft edges.

And this felt sharp and crystal clear.

* * *

Her legs were wrapped around a naked man. Holy guacamole, how many things could she check off her bucket list in one day? Not that she would have ever thought to add this to a bucket list. Like it wasn't even in Alice's bucket list universe.

But maybe it should be.

Her body tingled. In fact, it tingled so much that maybe she shouldn't even be in the water. What if she started to sizzle and spark and short out?

Very slowly, Beau let go of her, and as she drifted down, she bumped into something firm and *oh!* Beau's face turned scarlet. And the heat invading her cheeks indicated they were doing the same.

Right. He was naked.

Alice stepped back immediately, and then she covered her saggy, waterlogged bra with her arms. The water was just below Beau's hips, and his hands were cupped, hiding what she'd just felt bump against her inner thigh.

"Well, that was exciting," Beau said.

Alice tried to reply with a casual *yeah*, but only a squeaky croak came out. Beau had nothing to be embarrassed about. Men often got erections at surprisingly inconvenient times, and her legs suddenly wrapping around his naked body had probably been both surprising and inconvenient.

"I'm going to get out now," he said casually. "You might want to turn around. I'll give a holler when I've got some pants on."

Alice quickly turned.

There was splashing. There were a few muttered curses as Beau presumably stepped on sharp stones. There was rustling and then...a zipper.

"Okay, Allie Cat. It's safe to turn around."

Beau was shirtless and balancing on one leg while trying to get a wet foot into a sock. So, he was fairly occupied as Alice started for the bank, stepping gingerly on slippery rocks.

She didn't want to slide her T-shirt over a squishy bra, so she slipped the bra off and pulled the shirt over her damp skin. Next, she stepped into the overalls, only bothering with one strap, and slid into her sandals.

It was time to get down to business. They'd come here for a tutoring session.

Beau, still shirtless but now wearing his cowboy hat, stared at the rock, acorn, and twig. He picked up the twig and replaced it with a leaf. His lips formed the word *cat*.

"Hey," he said, looking up. "I think I get what you're trying to accomplish with this."

"Good! And I have a computer program I want you to work with that kind of does the same thing. We're going to slowly replace those objects with letters." She lowered her voice to a whisper. "Don't tell your brain, but we're going to trick it."

"That shouldn't be too hard," Beau muttered.

Alice watched as he fiddled with the acorn. During the times he wasn't laughing, grinning, pranking, or flexing a set of muscles, it was easier to get a glimpse of the real Beau. He was happy, but he wasn't necessarily carefree.

School had been so easy for Bryce. It had to have made Beau's struggle with dyslexia even harder.

His cowboy hat shaded his eyes, but they still peeked out, blue and brilliant and ringed with lashes. They traveled her body, probably taking in her clingy, damp T-shirt and the fact that she wasn't wearing a bra. She quickly buckled the other strap of her overalls.

"I think we need to add an amendment to our contract," Beau said.

"Oh?"

"Yep. Every time we have a reading lesson, we'll add something to your bucket list."

Today had been a blast. And she could probably count all of the blasts she'd ever had on both hands. "Okay. But I'm never going hang gliding."

Beau laughed. "Darlin', that makes you and me both. Open up your little book of lists, and we'll come up with something that requires less of a death wish."

Alice reached into her bag and took out her journal with the bucket list. She started to write *skinny-dipping*, but then stopped. She wrote *swimming without a swimsuit* instead. She hadn't technically skinny-dipped. She wanted to add *with handsome naked man*, but Beau was watching.

"Have you ever counted shooting stars?" Beau asked. "I imagine it's not as much of an adrenaline rush as hang gliding, but it's still a righteous bucket list item."

"I once toured the McDonald Observatory in the Davis Mountains during the Perseid meteor shower, which is—"

"I'm talking from the bed of a pickup truck. It'll be like our own private pasture party."

Pasture parties, like skinny-dipping at the dam, were another thing Alice had never done as a teen growing up in Big Verde. She'd heard about them on Monday mornings. This person had gotten drunk. This person had backed his truck into so-and-so's truck, and their dads were going to kill them. This person had kissed someone's boyfriend.

So much drama. Alice had not understood the appeal, and yet, if she were being honest, she'd always felt a bit left out.

"Okay," she said. "Let's do it."

She wrote down *Stargazing from the bed of a pickup truck* and *Pasture party* to her list.

"How about next weekend?" Beau asked.

"I've got a library board meeting on Friday. And Saturday is book club…"

"Don't you ever slow down? What time does your book club end?"

"Usually around five o'clock."

Beau's phone chimed with a text. He squinted at the screen.

"You can make that font bigger," she said.

"I don't need to," Beau said, still squinting. "It's from Ford, and I got the general idea. He just needs me to do some stuff while Bryce is at the dude ranch next week."

"Is he leaving already?"

"Not for good. We still don't know when or if that will happen." He said it casually, but she saw the tension around his eyes. Was she getting better at reading people?

"Anyway, how about you come over on Saturday after your book club ends? We can work for a couple of hours and then head out to stargaze."

"That sounds perfect," Alice said. "And Beau?"

"Yes, darlin'?"

Her tummy flopped. Why did it do that every time the man said *darlin'*? He called *everyone* darlin'. It didn't mean anything, and in fact, the women in her self-partnered group would probably object—

Oh no! She'd forgotten, but she already had plans for Saturday night after book club. The self-partnered group was meeting at a Chili's in San Marcos at seven.

"Something wrong?" Beau asked.

Alice looked into those blue eyes. Screw Chili's. It wasn't on her bucket list. "No," she said. "I was just wondering if maybe it would be helpful to let Ford, and probably Gerome, know about your dyslexia. That way, they could simply leave you a voice mail instead of a text message—"

His cheeks had turned pink again. "Maybe. But I think I've got a handle on it."

Alice just nodded. She hoped that was true.

Chapter
Sixteen

ॐ

The book club members would be here any minute. Alice straightened the stack of napkins next to the tray of cheese and crackers on the coffee table. The teakettle whistled, and she rushed into the kitchen to make iced tea. Maggie was bringing wine, but Miss Mills didn't drink alcohol.

She turned off the burner and poured the boiling water over the tea bags she'd dropped into her pewter pitcher. In another few minutes, she'd add sugar, ice, and cold water.

She walked back into the living room just in time to see Gaston finish off the cheese. "Gaston!"

The big doofus wagged his tail and barked.

Dang it. Luckily, the other women typically brought snacks. Nobody would starve. "You," she said to the guilty cheese thief. "To the guest room."

As soon as Gaston was settled in the guest room with his chew toy and a bowl of water, the doorbell rang. Alice peeked out the window to see Claire and Maggie. They were almost always the first ones to arrive.

She opened the door. Maggie held up a box of wine. "Let the festivities begin."

Claire held a plastic container with a blue lid. "Lemon bars. I know I said I'd bring something healthy, but…"

"They have vitamin C," Alice said with a grin. "Come on in."

Just as Claire and Maggie were about to step through the door, a minivan pulled into the driveway and parked. The door opened and two juice boxes and a sippy cup fell out, followed by Trista Larson. She tossed the trash and cup back in the van just as the sliding door opened.

"Goodness," Miss Mills said, holding the sippy cup. "Are you trying to kill me?"

"Sorry," Trista said. "I forgot you were back there. Why didn't you just sit in the front seat?"

"I don't trust the air bags in foreign-made vehicles," Miss Mills said, huffing to get a leg out of the van.

Just as she'd finally extricated herself from the van, a stack of papers fluttered out on the wind.

"Oh no!" Trista said. "Grab those, Miss Mills. They're Sammie's homework!"

"Dear Lord," Miss Mills said, grabbing for a sheet of paper and missing it.

Alice, Maggie, and Claire ran to help. Alice managed to step on a sheet of paper, while Maggie jumped after the airborne ones. Claire chased a page across the yard and then pounced, triumphantly impaling it with her stiletto heel.

"Woo-hoo! Teamwork!" Maggie said, carrying four sheets of paper to Trista.

Alice handed hers over, as did Claire. "Sorry about the hole."

Beep! Beep! A bright red Porsche pulled up.

"Yay! I didn't know Carmen was coming," Maggie said.

"She's in town for another couple of weeks," Alice said. "I thought it would be nice to include her."

Claire clapped her hands. "Great idea. She's so fun."

A silver Lexus pulled up and parked behind the Porsche. "And there's Anna," Alice said.

Nobody cheered, but Alice plastered on a smile. It was true that Anna was Big Verde's version of Nellie Oleson. She was snooty, entitled, and generally unpleasant to be around. But she'd chaired the successful Boots and Ball Gowns gala that had allowed the library to be rebuilt after the flood. Alice would be forever grateful.

Carmen, decked out in peacock harem pants and a silky turquoise tank, held up a platter. "Fried brie!"

Everyone cheered, because it wasn't every day that a celebrity chef brought her restaurant's signature appetizer to book club.

Anna cut in front of Carmen and held a plastic container over her head. "Cheese puffs. My grandmother's recipe."

The Lexus's passenger door opened, and a sparkly orthopedic boot popped out. "Oh, dear!" Alice said. "Anna, you left Brittany in the car!"

"I had my hands full. And anyway, she cried the whole way here. I needed a break."

Alice and Maggie rushed over to help Brittany. Her face was red and her eyes were swollen. "What on earth is wrong?" Maggie asked. "Other than your stress fracture right before your wedding, I mean."

"The caterer's food truck blew up," Brittany said. "My wedding is in two weeks, and I don't have a caterer."

"Oh, dear," Alice said, helping Brittany limp to the front door. "I'm sure you can find another one."

"No!" Brittany wailed. "Not at this late date!"

Everyone filed into the house, murmuring and fawning over Brittany.

"The wedding is in two weeks?" Carmen asked.

"Yes. Everything is ruined."

"I'll do it," Carmen said. "I'll cater the wedding."

"Really?" Brittany asked.

Carmen nodded, and Brittany took a flying leap at her, dropping her crutches with a loud clatter. "Thank you! You've saved my wedding."

Alice was confused. "I didn't know you'd still be here two weeks from now. Jessica and Casey will be back from their honeymoon. Won't you be heading out to film the next season of *Funky Fusions?*"

"I didn't want to say anything until I knew for sure," Carmen said, blowing a strand of Brittany's hair out of her face. "But the show has been canceled. And even though I know it's going to kill you guys, I really don't want to talk about it."

Everyone stood there, biting back overwhelming urges to comfort and spout useless platitudes.

"I'm sorry your show was canceled," Brittany said, taking a step back. "Can I still tell people that a celebrity chef is catering my wedding?"

"I've got another few weeks before I'm officially a has-been, so I vote yes," Carmen said.

"Are you going to be looking for a new venture?" Claire asked, eyes sparkling. "Maybe a shiny new project?"

"Absolutely," Carmen said.

Claire winked. "We'll talk later, then."

"I'm intrigued," Carmen said. "But I guess right now we talk about books? I've never been in a book club before, and I hope I don't get kicked out for not having read the book."

Everyone settled around Alice's living room with their snacks and beverages, and Maggie patted Carmen on the shoulder. "No worries. I didn't read it, either."

"I only read the dirty parts," Claire said.

Trista shrugged. "I read half of it."

Miss Mills pulled out her copy of *Breaking the Cowboy*. "I read the entire book, except for the racy parts."

"Seeing as how I only read the racy parts, together we have read the entire thing," Claire said.

Brittany looked at the cover of Miss Mills's book. "Wait a minute. That's not the book I read."

"It's *Breaking the Cowboy*," Miss Mills said. "Didn't you get your copy?"

"No. I read *The Bridal Wave*, which is the first book in the quintuplet wedding series."

"That's next month's book," Alice said.

Brittany sighed, leaned back, and plopped her booted foot up on Alice's coffee table with a loud clunk. She held a hand out to Anna. "Cheese puff me."

Claire also snagged a cheese puff. "My contribution to the discussion will be somewhat limited. But the sex scene with the ropes was super-hot. I might have read it out loud to Ford, and he might have liked it."

"Ooh," Maggie chimed in. "I got that far. And it was Travis's favorite scene, too."

"Goodness!" Miss Mills said. "You let your husbands read romance novels?"

"Travis loves them. They spice up our love life."

"I have never heard of such a thing," Miss Mills said, fanning herself with her daily devotional.

"I like this discussion," Alice said. "I don't think we've ever talked about how reading books together can bring couples closer. And I especially love that Travis and Ford don't care about gender stereotypes in regard to their reading choices. I personally feel that romance sometimes gets a bad rap simply because it's written primarily by and for women. And we're in a patriarchal cul—"

Woof!

"When did you get a dog?" Maggie asked.

Woof!

Alice sighed. "It's Gaston, my mom's dog."

"How does he get along with Sultana?" Maggie asked, as the cat glided exotically into the room.

Anna narrowed her eyes and made the sign of the cross.

"They've actually been getting along pretty well," Alice said. "I think they like each other. Anyway, as I was saying—"

Brittany raised her hand.

"Yes, Brittany?"

"Since I'll be on my honeymoon during the next book club meeting, can I share my thoughts on *Bridal Wave* if I don't give spoilers? And can I do it right now and then mentally check out?"

Alice sighed, because Brittany was definitely going to give spoilers. But she kept her expression pleasant. "Sure."

"First of all, it is a virgin trope."

"Oh, how nice!" Miss Mills said. "We don't read enough of those."

"Why is that nice?" Alice asked. "Honestly, I find the trope a bit problematic."

"Really?" Claire asked. "I think virgin stories are fun. Especially the historical ones."

"Well, they'd have to be historical, wouldn't they?" Anna asked. "Are there any modern-day virgins walking around?"

Maggie cleared her throat and dramatically nodded her head in Miss Mills's direction. "There might be a few—"

"I said there were no *modern-day* virgins walking around," Anna said, thereby indicating Miss Mills was historical.

Carmen looked at the back cover of Brittany's book. "This sounds really cute. I'm definitely going to read it."

Alice crossed her legs. "Again, I find the trope somewhat problematic."

"Why?" Anna asked.

"Because virginity is a social construct. It doesn't actually exist."

Maggie jerked her head in Miss Mills's direction again. "Oh, it exists all right."

Miss Mills, not noticing that she was the subject of interest, daintily bit into a lemon bar.

"I remember the night I lost mine," Trista said. "It was after graduation in the back of Bubba's pickup truck. We were all at the dam, remember?"

No, they hadn't *all* been at the dam. Alice hadn't been there.

"Oh my God," Claire said. "That's where it happened for me, too! Only it was after the homecoming dance with Bobby Flores. At least you technically made it out of high school still a virgin."

"Again," Alice said, "virginity is not a physical state. You don't *make it* out of high school with it intact or not intact."

Everyone looked at her like she was nuts. She clearly wasn't getting through to them.

"What about you, Anna? Who took your virginity?" Brittany asked.

Alice sighed. "Nobody *takes*—"

"My husband," Maggie said. "I'm pretty sure the first guy Anna banged was Travis."

"Goodness!" Miss Mills said.

Anna daintily crossed her legs and pretended to brush lint off her slacks while the room erupted in gasps.

"It was a *very* long time ago," Anna said. "In high school. And for Maggie's sake, I hope he's gotten better at it."

Everyone erupted in laughter, even though Alice didn't think there was anything humorous about it. "As I was saying, virginity is a social construct. It isn't something that can be given or taken, any more than you can give or take someone's experience of anything."

"You can give someone an experience," Maggie said.

Claire nodded. "Maggie gave me a gift certificate for a massage."

Frustration crept up Alice's spine. By the time it arrived at her throat, there was no holding back. "But the state of virginity isn't a thing. It's just someone walking around who hasn't had sexual intercourse. There are people who've never jumped out of an airplane. Is there a word for that?"

"Yes," Maggie said. "Smart."

Claire snorted. "I've jumped out of a plane."

"I know," Maggie said with a wink.

Alice squirmed on the couch. "I'm serious though. There are countless things any one of us or all of us have never done. We're not given freaking *titles* for it. If you have intercourse—"

"I really wish you'd stop being so profane," Miss Mills said.

"That's also a social construct," Alice said. "What's profane to one group is not necessarily profane to another. But as I was saying, you don't *lose* anything when you have intercourse for the first time—"

"Actually, I lost a bracelet the first time I did it," Anna said.

Everyone started laughing again, but Alice felt tears welling. It was so frustrating to know something was true and not be able to properly convince others. But she wasn't giving up. "We are not defined by our sexual experiences. After having intercourse for the first time, neither person *leaves* with anything—"

"Oh, I for sure did," Trista said. "And her name is Sammie."

Alice stood and stomped her foot. "There is no such thing as virginity! And furthermore, we don't need men in order to learn how to pleasure our own bodies. We're perfectly capable of pleasuring ourselves. Most women require clitoral stimulation—"

"*Goodness,*" Miss Mills said. "The only thing worse than pre-marital relations is a woman ringing the devil's doorbell."

At the mention of the devil's doorbell, the room dissolved into mayhem. Maggie laughed so hard that she slid off the couch, while Claire howled into a pillow. Anna giggled uncontrollably, and Trista and Brittany grabbed their phones, presumably to Google *devil's doorbell.*

Miss Mills just sat quietly, fanning herself frantically with a copy of *Ladies' Daily Devotions*.

Alice had lost control of herself *and* of the meeting.

"I just think this conversation is making people uncomfortable, is all," Alice said. "Particularly Miss Mills. How do you think she feels with all this talk of virginity? Miss Mills, I apologize if we've made you uncomfortable."

"No apology necessary. All is right with me and the Lord. He has forgiven me for my past transgressions, including the one in the church fellowship hall with the son of a Bible salesman in 1965."

Everyone gasped, and then Trista squealed as Alice covered her mouth with her hand.

"Miss Mills!" Trista said. "I just assumed—"

"The good Lord says that when you assume you make an *a-s-s* out of *u* and *me*," she said.

Alice didn't think that was anywhere in the Bible.

"And anyway," Miss Mills continued. "I was tricked by Satan. And I doubt very seriously, especially in this day and age, that there is a grown woman walking around who hasn't been. The devil is a rascal, and only the good Lord himself is perfect. The rest of us are sinners."

Everyone in the room had their mouths hanging open, and Alice was no exception. She snapped it shut.

Oh my God, was it possible that she was literally the only thirty-two-year-old virgin on the planet?

She squared her shoulders, crossed her arms, and harrumphed quietly to herself.

"I think it's time to change the subject," Alice said. "I have plans tonight, so we'd better discuss this book and be done with it."

Everyone went completely silent, as if what Alice had just said was even more shocking than Miss Mills's revelation.

Claire raised an eyebrow. "Are you okay, Alice?"

Alice was almost never rude. And by *almost*, she meant never.

Never ever. What had gotten into her? "I'm so sorry. Please excuse my manners. It's just that—"

Claire raised the other eyebrow.

"I'm seeing Beau later, and I'm looking forward to it," Alice finished.

Claire couldn't raise her eyebrows any farther without surgical assistance, so she switched course by narrowing her eyes. Everyone else nodded in understanding, as if it was perfectly reasonable for Alice to be so excited and anxious to see Beau that she'd let her manners slip.

But not Claire. She was still eyeing Alice suspiciously. Had she just figured out that Alice wasn't really dating Beau, and that on top of it, she was a virgin?

Not that virgins existed.

Chapter
Seventeen

❦

Beau sat on the porch with his feet propped up on the railing. He'd had to drive all the way to Fort Worth to pick up a new bull, a purebred Angus named Abiding Dude. Gerome said he didn't think anyone ever named a bull while sober.

In the nearly eight hours Beau had spent on the road, he'd finished listening to the third book. Now he was looking closely at the paperback Alice had given him. And he was doing more than simply picking out recognizable words on the pages. He was actually decoding the ones he didn't know, and it was getting easier and easier. Allie had told him that if he kept using the reading program, something would click. And it definitely had. You build words like you build anything. With parts. And the parts go in a certain order. And for some reason, they were now going in the same order every time.

Beau was feeling more and more confident by the day. Bryce had been at the Rockin' H nearly all week, and Beau had handled everything himself. By the time his contract with Alice was up, everything was going to be working out just fine.

His gut clenched. At exactly midnight on the night of the wedding, everything would go back to the way it was before where he and Alice were concerned. Which was to say, back to the occasional howdy in the library or the Corner Café. Unless maybe...

Nah. She wouldn't be interested in continuing their friendship. That's why she'd gone to the trouble of typing up a fucking contract. The woman wanted a definite end date for their arrangement. And why wouldn't she? They had absolutely nothing in common. She had her lady friends in Austin who were busy smashing the patriarchy and whatnot. Allie wasn't going to want to go fishing or skinny-dipping or stargazing with a cowboy.

He closed his book at the sound of tires crunching on the gravel road. Bryce was home—for now. He waved, and Beau headed down the steps to greet his brother. He was anxious to tell him how well everything had gone. "Howdy. It's good to have you ba—"

"I just drove through the pasture at Glen Oaks. We had some mighty thirsty cows penned up there. I let them out and they followed me over to Oak Springs. I've trapped them in there for now. But I thought we'd agreed to keep them out of that quadrant during the drought."

"We did. And I told Worth to keep them out—"

"How did you tell him?"

"What do you mean?"

"Were you talking? Or texting?"

"Ford sent me a text about moving that specific herd, and I told Worth—"

Bryce held out his hand. "Let me see."

"You don't need to look through my text messages. I'm telling you what happened, and—"

"And you have a problem with text messages. Give me your phone so I can see exactly what was said."

Fine. If Bryce wanted proof that Beau hadn't told Worth to pen the cattle up in a dry pasture during a drought, then he'd give him proof. He yanked out his phone, found the conversation thread, and slammed it into his brother's palm.

Bryce looked at it. "You told Worth to pen them up at Glen Oaks."

Beau yanked the phone back. "No way." His eyes went straight to Worth's message. Do we want that side herd over in Glen Oaks?

And then he saw his response. Yes.

"Dammit." He'd obviously mistaken Glen Oaks for Oak Springs. It seemed like the word *oak* was part of every damn name of every damn location on the ranch. He could read it clearly now, but earlier, he'd obviously been confused. He sighed and shook his head, feeling like shit. "I'm glad you caught it. Were they too terribly thirsty?"

"They seemed okay. And it was just a simple mistake, but Beau, you always need to seek clarification. Just call and ask—"

"I don't want to bother people with phone calls while they're busy."

"No. You just don't want anyone to know that you struggle with reading. And that fragile ego could have killed some heifers and calves. Get over yourself. Because I might not be here to save your ass the next time."

Beau hung his head, feeling stupid. As usual. And Bryce was right. He was absolutely embarrassed for anyone to know what his struggles were. But the necessity to hide it was so ingrained that he didn't know if he could shake it. How could he earn folks' respect if they thought he couldn't read? There was just so much fucking shame associated with the inability to perform that particular life skill.

At least he could own up to his mistakes. God knew he'd had plenty of practice at that. "As I said, I'm sorry."

"I don't want an apology," Bryce said. "We just need to keep it from happening again."

Beau held up the book Alice had given him. "I'm getting a handle on it."

"You're reading that book?"

"Yeah." Maybe he wasn't reading it very fast. And he was skipping a word here or there. But like Alice said, he was good at context clues.

"Well, that's awesome. I told you that Alice would be able to help you."

They walked up the steps and entered the cabin. Bryce inhaled deeply. "Do I smell Mom's special baked beans?" He sniffed. "And peach cobbler?"

"Yep."

Bryce looked around stupidly. "Is Mom here?"

Beau laughed. "No. I called her. She talked me through it. And I've got two steaks ready to hit the grill."

"I know you missed me, but you sure didn't need to go to all this trouble."

"Actually, Bryce, don't take your hat off. You're not staying. Alice is coming over for tutoring."

"It looks like a little more than tutoring. It looks like dinner. In fact, it might look like a date."

"I just wanted to show my appreciation."

"We've talked about this. Just don't appreciate Alice too hard, if you get my drift."

"Believe me, Alice is not at all interested in any tutoring appreciation activities."

Although, the memory of her warm, wet body pressed against his completely naked one popped up…The way she'd stared at his lips.

She'd seemed at least a little interested.

* * *

Alice helped Brittany into Anna's car and headed back inside. Trista and Miss Mills had left earlier, so it was down to Claire, Maggie, and Carmen. Hopefully they'd leave soon, too, because she needed a little quiet time to recover from her embarrassing outburst.

Nobody was gathering their belongings when she walked into the house. Instead, all three women sat on the couch, quiet and subdued with their hands folded in their laps. Hopes of alone time dissipated into thin air. She'd already briefly apologized for her behavior. Were they expecting her to do it again?

Claire spoke up first. "Alice, we're sorry."

"For what?" Maybe they'd accidentally broken something, although nothing appeared amiss.

"For making you uncomfortable," Maggie said.

"We just didn't know," Claire added.

"Know what?"

Carmen cleared her throat. "There is absolutely nothing wrong with being a virgin, Alice. Nothing at all. And if we said anything to make you feel self-conscious or embarrassed…"

Holy guacamole, this was not a conversation she wanted to have. "First of all, I'm *not* a virgin—"

"Whew!" Claire said. "We misunderstood."

"Right?" Maggie said with a nervous giggle. "We should have known, since she's dating Beau."

"Yeah," Carmen added. "And he's not exactly beginner material. I mean, size alone—"

What? Had Carmen slept with Beau?

Alice's head began to spin. Why hadn't Carmen told her? But then again, why *would* she? People didn't just go around reciting lists of who they'd slept with. And *of course* Carmen had slept with Beau. She was friendly and outgoing, and so was he. Also, he apparently slept with everybody. It actually *made sense* for them to have slept together. And that was fine, wasn't it? They were all adults here. Yay! Carmen had slept with Beau. Wasn't that awesome? She was so happy for Carmen!

"Why are you smiling like that?" Claire asked. "Are you okay?"

Alice's stomach churned as if she'd just eaten a bad burrito. And tears stung the backs of her eyelids.

"Oh God," Carmen said. "Alice, honey, sit down."

Alice's knees buckled and she collapsed inelegantly into the chair directly behind her. That was as close to sitting as she could come.

"I have never had sex with Beau," Carmen said. "It was Bryce."

Everyone gasped.

"Really?" Claire said. "Wow. Because, honestly, if we're still talking virgins, I'd have pegged him as a possibility."

"Believe me," Carmen said. "Bryce is no virgin. And since he and Beau are twins, I figure they have identical…"

Maggie grinned and raised her eyebrows. "Dongs?"

Claire snorted.

Penis size didn't interest Alice in the slightest. The way she'd nearly passed out thinking Carmen had slept with Beau, however, was something to ponder.

Maggie reached over and touched Alice's hand. "Now that we've cleared All The Things up…" She smiled. "We're sorry that while believing you weren't a virgin, we said some insensitive things regarding virgins, only to figure out you *were* a virgin and that we were assholes—"

Claire nodded enthusiastically. "Only to discover we were wrong again, and you *aren't* a virgin—"

"But just to be clear," Maggie interrupted. "We're still probably assholes."

Carmen laughed. "And then I had to top it all off by insinuating I'd seen your boyfriend's gigantic penis, when in fact, I have not."

"So, I guess this means you really are dating Beau?" Claire said. "Like, for real?"

It was nearly impossible for Alice to tell a lie of any kind, and all of her feelings over the past three weeks rose up her throat and sat on her tongue, waiting to come out.

She might not have gone skinny-dipping with these women in high school. She didn't get their inside jokes or understand what the heck they were laughing at half the time. But she *trusted* them.

Divulging Beau's secret wasn't a possibility, but she didn't have to carry on the charade of their "relationship" in front of Maggie, Claire, and Carmen. She sighed loudly as Sultana wove in and out of her ankles, purring. "Y'all were right the first time—no wait—the second time."

Claire stared at the ceiling while counting on her fingers. "So, you *are* a virgin?"

"No, because—"

"Virginity is a social construct," Carmen finished.

"Correct. But I have never had sexual intercourse with a man."

"Well, you're going to soon, right?" Maggie said. "Because you're dating Beau and he's…"

"Kind of a man-whore," Claire said.

The word *whore* was offensive, but Alice was too tired to say so. "Beau isn't my boyfriend. In fact, we're not even dating. He's simply agreed to accompany me to Brittany's wedding, and I'm helping him with something in return."

Claire opened her mouth, but Alice cut her off.

"And I'm not at liberty to say *what*, so please don't ask. We're just letting folks think what they want to think. And anyway, it'll all be over as soon as Brittany finally freaking gets married."

"Aw," Claire said with a pout. "Y'all are going to break up?"

"No, because we're not really dating." She thought for a moment, and then added, "But yes."

"Um, Alice," Carmen said. "Before you and Beau break up, you should definitely consider trying that sex with a human thing, at least once."

"Why? Sixty-five percent of women don't climax during intercourse. A vibrator provides a more satisfying experience."

"There are some things you can't get from a vibrator, though," Maggie said.

Claire nodded in agreement. "Like warm hands that aren't your own. The touch of another person is so…" Claire shivered instead of finishing her sentence.

"And then there's the emotional connection when it's someone you care about," Maggie said. "The first time Travis and I had sex, we were wearing Halloween costumes, and it was anonymous. And it was freaking *fantastic*. It was kinky and fun, and I was so turned on I actually had an orgasm. But the second time was even better. Because we knew each other then. And the connection we shared—the *love* we made—well, it was mind-blowing."

"With Ford," Claire said. "There's always been this sense of falling into him. I can't tell where I end and he begins. It's weird, and I'm not doing a very good job of expressing it. But it's practically spiritual."

"That was an excellent way of expressing it," Maggie said.

"The best sex I've ever had is with friends," Carmen said. "I don't really believe in romantic love—not for me anyway—but deep emotional friendship paired with physical attraction is my jam. There is nothing like it."

When Alice had been in Beau's arms, pressed up against his naked body, they'd been playing and laughing and enjoying each other's company—like friends—just moments before. But when she'd looked into his eyes, she'd had that brief sense of falling that Claire mentioned. And her skin had tingled and buzzed beneath his hands.

Sex would probably be pretty amazing.

The other women sat quietly, wearing little grins. They were all so different, yet deeply supportive of each other. Each one seemed lost in her own thoughts, yet the feeling of connection was almost palpable. Maggie smiled at her, and Alice realized they were sharing a moment of comfortable, companionable silence.

That was something friends did. And it was nice.

Chapter
Eighteen

❧

The crickets and tree frogs started up nature's sonata as Beau and Alice sat on the open tailgate, swinging their feet. He was doing his best to be jovial, but he couldn't shake the shame and guilt he felt over having told Worth to lock those cows in a dry pasture. God. He could have fucking killed them. What kind of a ranch foreman penned his cattle up in a dry pasture? He longed to unload his feelings, but he was too embarrassed.

Soon, everything would rest on his shoulders. He'd thought he was ready, but this had really shaken his confidence.

"It's so peaceful here," Alice said. "Do you come to this spot often?"

"Every chance I get."

A lot of the times when folks probably assumed that he was out chasing women, he was actually out here, lying in the bed of a pickup all by himself, staring up at the stars. There was nothing better than losing himself in the dark night sky.

"I bet you and Bryce played here a lot when you were kids."

"Not Bryce. Just me."

"By yourself?"

"Yeah. This is my special place." He winked at her. "Consider yourself special."

Alice looked down at her swinging boots—they'd gone boot shopping after tutoring on Wednesday—but Beau could see the little grin on her face.

"Anyway, I used to sneak off and spend hours out here, having adventures and whatnot. This was Beau Country, where it didn't matter if you struggled in school, or who was the smarter twin."

"Bryce is not the smarter twin. You're both smart."

"He's pretty dang smart, Allie. He got that scholarship to A&M. I never could have done that."

"There are plenty of students with dyslexia at A&M. They've just taken the necessary steps to mitigate it, and they take advantage of the tools and assistance available to them, which is something you seem a bit reluctant to do."

Beau rubbed his palms on his thighs and took a deep breath. "I messed up. I misread a text, and it could have killed some cattle." He stared straight ahead, too ashamed to look her in the eye.

The feel of Alice's soft fingers on his chin startled him. "Look at me," she said, turning his face to hers. "Everyone messes up. And I'm assuming the cattle are fine. But Beau, you probably shouldn't communicate via text if it's something important. And yes, that's going to mean telling people not to text you, and it's going to mean telling them why."

She hadn't removed her fingers, and her thumb lightly tracing the cleft in his chin made it hard to focus on words. But he still heard them, and Alice was right.

Her eyes dipped down to his lips, almost as if she wanted to—

"It sure is getting dark fast," she said, suddenly dropping her hand to her lap and staring up at the sky.

She'd chickened out, but Beau had no doubt that she'd wanted to kiss him. The idea of it had him tingling all over. "Good. It's kind of necessary if you want the stars at night to be big and bright…"

He waited for it, and after a few seconds, Alice grinned and performed the customary three claps, before singing the words, "Deep in the heart of Texas."

"Atta girl."

Alice giggled, and it was like windchimes, only windchimes didn't send a wave of butterflies through his belly. It was time for the first surprise of the evening.

"You know, if this were a traditional pasture party," he said, sliding the ice chest over, "you'd have your football player types over there on the left, and your rodeo types there on the right. And in the middle would be a keg of beer, brought by somebody who shouldn't still be hanging out with high school kids but can't get over his glory days."

Alice laughed. "And where are the cheerleaders?"

"All the girls are huddled along the back row of pickup trucks, needing to pee but not wanting to do it out here. And they're chugging cheap Strawberry Hill that somebody's older sister bought at the Pump 'n' Go."

"You're good with details."

"I attended many a pasture party." He opened the ice chest and pulled out a bottle of wine. "And since you and I can't handle an entire keg by ourselves, I purchased this."

Alice looked at the bottle. "I have never tried Strawberry Hill."

"Do you like a crisp, dry wine?"

"Yes, that's—"

"Not what this is," Beau said, unscrewing the lid. "You're going to hate it. And I didn't bring cups, so…"

Alice took the bottle. "Bottoms up."

Allie took a healthy, impressive sip with nary a wince. "Yikes," she said, passing the bottle. "That is toe-curling sweet."

"Hefty alcohol content. It'll get you in trouble pretty damn quick if you're not careful."

"I've never been drunk, and I have no intention of adding the experience to my bucket list."

"Smart woman," Beau said, taking a quick swig and handing the bottle back.

"I can't believe you fixed such a delicious dinner tonight. I'm not much of a cook, myself."

"My mom talked me through it, if it makes you feel better. And she told me I couldn't use paper plates, so you have her to thank for the nice dishes, too."

"Did she also tell you to pick the pretty flowers?"

"Nope. I did that all by myself." He hadn't had a vase, but a Mason jar had worked just fine. Next time he'd be prepared with candles. Allie would be pretty in candlelight.

"There's the Milky Way," he said, pointing at the sky. "Also, I brought a second surprise. Hold on."

He hopped off the tailgate and went around to retrieve the telescope from the back seat. He grabbed it before giving the door a shove with his hip. As he turned to walk back to the tailgate, he caught sight of Alice—feet swinging, staring at the stars, bottle of Strawberry Hill in her lap—and froze.

She looked as if she belonged here every bit as much as the giant oaks and the prickly pear cactus and sharp-scented juniper trees…It felt right. And that was weird. Because this is where Beau came to be *alone*. He shook his head and grinned. He could get used to this.

It was too bad he wouldn't get to.

"You okay back there?" Alice asked, looking over her shoulder.

"Yep. Have you ever peered through a telescope?"

Alice hopped off the tailgate. "You brought a telescope?" She clapped her hands and bounced on the balls of her feet.

Beau's heart seemed to expand inside his chest, making it hard to breathe. He was sharing his sky with Allie. And he'd never shared his sky with anyone.

* * *

Beau Montgomery was full of surprises. So many, in fact, that Alice was having a hard time keeping up. "This is a really good telescope."

"It's adequate," Beau said simply. "I bought my first one at fifteen, and I bought this one last year."

He quickly set it up, messed with some knobs, pointed it this way and that, and invited her to take a look.

"Wow," she said, staring through the eyepiece. And *wow* was a totally inadequate word, because the view was amazing! She wasn't even sure what she was looking at, but she didn't care. The view was dizzyingly beautiful, and for the next few minutes, Beau let her hog the telescope while he lectured on nebulas, galaxies, black holes, and probably some other things. It was hard to focus on the sky or his lecture when the only heavenly body she was interested in was right here on Earth. And standing so close.

He put his hands on her hips to gently nudge her aside so he could peek through the telescope himself. And when it was her turn again, he stood behind her, touching her in a myriad of what were probably mindless and unconscious ways.

A big warm hand on the small of her back.

Squeezing her shoulder.

A small oopsie when she stepped back and bumped into him.

It felt like one of those dumb movie moments where the hero assists a woman in improving her tennis game or golf swing. Or where he helped her shoot a gun or cast a fishing line or—

Beau's breath brushed the sensitive spot behind her ear. "Do you see it? Is it in focus for you?"

See what? How could she focus on *anything* with his hand

resting casually on her left hip? She wanted to step back and melt into him, to be completely enveloped in his arms...

"Shooting star," he said suddenly, pointing up.

Alice only caught the tail end of it, but she shivered from the thrill. She hadn't seen too many shooting stars in her lifetime. Probably because she was usually looking at a schedule or a calendar or a book.

"Are you cold?" Beau asked. "It can get chilly up here on the bluff, even this time of year."

She wasn't cold at all. Just excited. But Beau was already walking back to the truck.

"I have a sleeping bag," he said. "And since we just saw our first shooting star of the evening, it's time to crawl in the bed of the truck and do some proper sky-scouting."

Was he suggesting they lie down in the bed of his pickup? Next to each other?

Beau shook out the sleeping bag. Then he unzipped it and laid it out like a blanket, smoothing all the wrinkles. He held a hand out to Alice. "This time of year, we should see some more. Meteor showers abound."

Alice took his hand, hoping he couldn't feel how she trembled.

"Damn, woman. You don't have enough meat on your bones. You're shivering like a leaf."

He started to unbutton his shirt. That wasn't going to do anything to squelch the trembling, but she watched silently as he finished with the buttons. He wore a plain white T-shirt underneath, which was both a relief and a disappointment.

"Here, put this on," he said, wrapping it around her shoulders.

It was warm from his body, and it smelled like his aftershave.

Beau stretched out, flat on his back, placing one arm behind his head and extending the other out to his side. "I didn't bring any pillows, but you can rest your head on my arm, if you want."

She *did* want. Very badly. So, she tentatively leaned back, resting her head against his muscular arm, which was surprisingly comfortable. She looked up and...

"Oh," she said. "I feel so—"

"Small?"

"Yes." Beyond small. In fact, she felt lost. Unanchored. Like she might float away into the black abyss. But Beau was warm and solid. Maybe she wouldn't float away, after all.

"If you're this small, imagine how tiny your troubles are."

That was a delightful notion, and it made her smile. "Is this something that happened at pasture parties? Lying in the beds of pickups?"

"Yes, and no," Beau said.

"Oh?"

"Yes, people cuddled up in the beds of pickups, but no, they weren't typically looking at the stars while they did it."

"What were they doing?"

"Making out like fiends."

Oh.

"I've never made out in the bed of a pickup truck." She'd blurted it out in the hopes that Beau would suggest—

"Maybe you should add it to your bucket list."

Was he simply making a suggestion? Was he flirting? Was *she* flirting? Where was the instruction manual? "I didn't bring the bucket list."

Dang it! Dumb thing to say dumb thing to say dumb thing to say...

"We could make out now and write it down later."

She swallowed loudly. There it was. He sounded so confident. Like he'd made out in the bed of a pickup truck a million times. Probably because he had. He'd be a good teacher, right? And it wouldn't *mean* anything to him. This was Beau Montgomery. Kissing women was like breathing for him.

No big deal.

"Okay," she said softly. "Let's make out."

"For real?"

Holy guacamole, what if he didn't want to? His voice sounded weak and shaky. What if she'd made a rather large assumption? Beau was a playboy, but that didn't mean he played with just anybody. He'd never shown a lick of interest in her, and now she'd put him in this horrible position. "If you don't want to, that's fine—"

Beau rolled onto his side, leaning on his elbow and bringing his face mere inches from hers. "I want to."

"Okay, but we need some ground rules."

"Always," he said, grinning.

"Just kissing."

"Scout's honor that I will not try to sneak past first base."

"We've already established that you were kicked out of the Boy Scouts—"

Beau looked at her lips, and she lost her train of thought. He traced his thumb over her bottom lip, and holy guacamole, that felt nice. Even in places that were nowhere near her lips.

He cupped her chin and kissed her with lips that were soft, warm, and sweet, like Strawberry Hill, holding her mouth with a gentle suction that shot sparks up and down her spine. She was the one to intensify things with a timid flutter of her tongue, and Beau accepted the gesture, opening his mouth and deepening the kiss.

He pressed himself against her, and Alice's body became an entity completely separate from her brain. There were no thoughts or desires, just an aching, frantic need. Her skin wanted contact everywhere, all at once, so she pulled Beau even closer, loving the weight and feel of him. She explored the landscape of his back, and then ran her fingers up to his hair.

She wanted to touch every inch of him.

Beau groaned and thrust his tongue into her mouth, invading it completely, showing no mercy at all. True to his promise, he kept his hands to himself, and Alice began to regret the ground rules. Her body craved his touch so badly that it was almost unbearable, and she rubbed against him frantically, craving friction. Her hands went from his hair to his firm butt. She wanted him to *move* in a certain way...

She was out of control, and it was wonderful.

Beau broke the kiss and raised up. And then, while staring directly into her eyes, he began to move his hips with a fluid, gyrating motion. Alice gasped at the feel of his erection, and to keep herself from going mad and wrapping her legs around his waist, she reached up and pulled him back for more kissing.

She moaned and bit his lower lip. She was insatiable. Beau could kiss her from now until the end of time, and she would never get enough.

He stopped and looked at her, panting and gasping for air. Despite the chill, his cheeks were splotchy and red. "Damn, Allie Cat. For someone who's never made out in the bed of a pickup before, you're really good at it."

"Am I?" She sounded just as breathless as he did.

"Yes. You're driving me crazy."

He looked a little crazy. She'd thoroughly mussed up his hair, and his lips were swollen—as were other parts. She liked the feel of him, hard and thick. "Do we have to stop, Beau?"

"No, darlin'. I could kiss you forever."

Chapter

Nineteen

❦

Bryce parked the truck in front of the Kowalskis' ranch house. "Wake up, dumbass."

"I wasn't asleep."

Not technically anyway. But he was definitely lingering on the edge of dazed. Borderline comatose. Because after getting home at two in the morning and taking an extremely cold shower, he'd risen early to escort Nonnie to church, where he'd entertained deliciously dirty thoughts while Miss Mills played the organ and Nonnie sang off-key. That was followed by brunch at Chateau Bleu and Nonnie's endless inquiries about Alice.

When is her birthday?

Does she still play the piano?

Would she like to attend the Montgomery family reunion this fall?

He'd tried explaining that they weren't serious, but Nonnie wasn't having it.

Should we invite her parents to Thanksgiving?

Now he and Bryce had a quick meeting with Ford and Gerome.

"Jesus Christ," Bryce said, shaking his head.

"What?"

"Unless you've suffered an unfortunate incident with a vacuum hose, you've got a hickey on your neck."

"I do not."

Bryce jerked the rearview mirror around, indicating Beau should take a look. And there it was, right below the collar of his shirt. "Haven't had one of those since the eleventh grade."

"I thought we decided sex with Alice was a bad idea."

"It was just kissing." *And a little dry-humping.* "Adults should make out more. It's good times."

Making out with Alice had been more than a good time. With sex-as-a-destination off the table, the journey had been everything. Nothing was rushed; they'd stayed in the moment, which had stretched into hours. And as promised, he hadn't slid an inch past first base.

He grinned. Because Alice had made it halfway to second by grabbing the hell out of his ass, which he hadn't minded a bit. They might need to rethink some ground rules—

Bryce banged on the hood of the truck. When had he gotten out?

"Are you coming, Romeo? Ford's waiting on us."

Beau got out and followed Bryce up the steps. They knocked three times before pushing the door open, just like they'd been doing since they were old enough to know where Miss Lilly kept the cookies.

"Biscuits are on the counter," Miss Lilly said, without looking up from her knitting. "And Beau, you're welcome to bring Alice to first Sunday dinner. I'll make something special."

They each gave Miss Lilly a kiss on the cheek. "You don't need to go to the trouble," Beau said. "Allie and I just like hanging out."

"In other words, Miss Lilly," Bryce said. "I wouldn't go picking out a dress for the wedding."

Miss Lilly raised an eyebrow. "You never know. Beau and Alice are a perfect pair."

Guilt gnawed at Beau's belly. He hadn't believed folks would take their fake romance seriously. And now Nonnie was talking Thanksgiving and Miss Lilly had gone straight to the wedding. There were going to be a few broken hearts. And after last night, he feared his might be one of them.

Ford appeared at the top of the stairs with a baby strapped to his chest. "Are y'all coming up?"

They each grabbed a biscuit and climbed the stairs.

Beau nodded at the baby. "We didn't want to interrupt you, if you were, you know…"

"Breastfeeding," Bryce finished.

"Shut up, idiots. This is the only way she'll sleep."

Beau gave Rosa a gentle pat on the head. "We're just kidding. She looks good on you."

Gerome stood as they came in. "Howdy, boys. Thanks for coming in on a Sunday. We'll keep it short."

"No problem," Bryce said.

Gerome nodded and they all sat down. But as soon as Ford's ass hit the chair, Rosa began fussing. He hopped right up and started doing a ridiculous shuffle step, first with one boot, then the other.

"That's the Polish Granny Shuffle," Gerome said. "It puts babies to sleep like magic." He looked critically at Ford as Rosa squirmed in her little cocoon. "Put some more hip in it, son."

Ford glared at his father-in-law, but then he did seem to put some more hip in it, and the baby quieted right down.

"The cattle are sorted and ready to go," Beau said. "We've got our big trailer, and Mr. Kelsey is loaning us his."

"Good," Gerome said. "And how about you, Bryce? Are you ready to pack your bags?"

Bryce raised an eyebrow. "Like, now?"

"We bought the Rockin' H," Ford said.

Beau nearly choked. He looked quickly at his brother, whose eyes were big and round.

"For real?" Bryce asked.

"Yep. And you're going to run it like any old cattle ranch with a swimming pool, lodge, and guesthouse," Ford said, grinning and shuffling. "But don't worry. You'll mostly be in charge of the cattle. The existing staff is staying on board for now."

Gerome leaned forward in his chair. "But if you're not opposed, I'd like you to take a few online business classes specific to the hospitality industry."

Bryce removed his hat. "I'd love that, sir."

Beau felt nothing but happiness for his brother. And when he took a deep breath to say so, he realized his chest wasn't tight. For the first time in his life, he felt better prepared to stand on his own two feet. He wasn't an expert reader yet, but he was making real progress. In fact, he kind of loved reading. "This is exciting."

And just like that, the day he'd been dreading had turned into a day to celebrate.

"Can you be ready to go by next weekend?" Gerome asked Bryce. "You can live in one of the lodge's suites."

"I was ready yesterday," Bryce said. "Are we keeping the name? It's still the Rockin' H?"

"Hell, no," Gerome said. "It's the Rockin' Rio Verde now."

Ford danced over to the desk. "Gerome, can you grab those instructions and the solar panel diagram for Beau?"

Beau sat up straighter. He'd recently suggested buying some more solar panels and setting up a battery bank and a generator so the well's pump could keep going after dark. They needed all the water they could get in the troughs, especially now that the river was so low and the cattle couldn't graze along the banks.

Gerome dug around in a drawer and pulled out a pile of papers. "Beau, we took your advice to get us through this dry spell. The panels and battery bank came in, along with these instructions. Ford looked at them—at least some of it appears to be in English—and said you could probably handle hooking it all up. You've always been good at that sort of thing. But if you need help, let me know."

Beau took the stack of papers from Gerome. He was good at figuring out how to take things apart and put them back together again. Bryce leaned over his shoulder, looking at the instructions and diagram. The words were tiny, and there was hardly any white space on the page. It looked like gibberish, but Beau worked hard at keeping a neutral expression. "I can figure it out. No problem."

Bryce nodded at him. *You'll be fine, brother. I believe in you.*

* * *

Alice struck her Tibetan singing bowl with the little wooden mallet. Maybe it would center her. She hadn't slept a wink. It was as if she was inhabiting someone else's body. Because hers didn't normally feel this tingly and agitated. And it wasn't just her lips, which were overly sensitive from literally hours of kissing.

She'd been kissed before—twice in college and once since—but never like that. Nobody had ever kissed her so dang thoroughly. Or hungrily.

Or intimately.

And nothing in her previous experience had prepared her for the level of lust that had rolled through her like a tidal wave.

She broke the meditation position of her hands—the mudra—to fan her face.

His mouth had been warm and soft and freaking insistent. As if he couldn't get enough of her, either. Even though he could have any woman he wanted.

She'd bitten his lower lip. She'd never bitten anyone before. In fact, she'd never known she could even *want* to bite someone. Why had she wanted to bite him? And she'd licked his jawline, feeling the stubble beneath her tongue. That had led to his neck, which she'd literally feasted on.

She stood up. There would be no meditating today. She felt too big for the room. Too big for her house. Too big for her *skin*.

Maybe she'd go running. She'd never run before, but why not start? She'd take Gaston. Her folks were picking him up next weekend, and she was kind of going to miss the big furry monster.

She found a pair of sneakers. Then she grabbed Gaston's leash, hooked him up, and headed out.

Dolly was in her front yard watering her rosebushes. "Good morning, Alice!"

Gaston also wanted to water the rosebushes, so Alice was forced to stop. "Sorry," she said, yanking on the dog's leash.

"Going for a walk?"

"A run."

"You don't run."

"I do now. I've been trying lots of new things lately." Her lips tingled as if to remind her of those things.

"You should bring Beau to the fire department's Wild Game Dinner. Oh! And the Catholic Daughters are sponsoring a dance contest on Valentine's Day. Y'all should enter! Everybody knows Beau is a fine dancer."

The Wild Game Dinner? A dance contest on freaking Valentine's Day? February was *months* from now. She and Beau were going to be over in two weeks. And anyway, she'd planned to spend the evening at a Galentine's Day dinner with her self-partnered group.

"Valentine's Day has some rather dark origins, you know. And anyway, it's a long way off—"

"And you and Beau will still be together. I'm very good at predicting breakups, and I don't see one in your future."

Ha! How about midnight on the twelfth of June?

For just a moment, Alice imagined what it might be like to have a real boyfriend on Valentine's Day. The only heart-shaped box of chocolates she'd ever received had come from the library volunteers. And the only rose had been from a secret admirer her senior year of high school. She suspected the sender was her father, but she'd carefully dried it and saved it anyway. Just in case...

She sighed. "We're really just friends who enjoy each other's company."

"And that, my dear, is the secret to a long-lasting relationship," Dolly said. "Harold was my husband for thirty-nine years, but he was my best friend for forty-five."

Harold passed away a year ago, and Alice could see the loneliness in Dolly's eyes. What if all of the irritating little pop-ins weren't really to check on the cat? What if Dolly was really looking for *human* companionship?

Alice's phone chimed with an email notification. She glanced at it and *oh!* It was from the Austin Public Library. She opened it, right there in front of Dolly.

They wanted to set up an interview! For Friday afternoon!

Her mind raced. What did she have going on this Friday? It was rude to stare at her phone in front of Dolly, but she couldn't help it. Her calendar showed a meeting in the morning, but Janie could handle everything in the afternoon...

"Is everything okay?" Dolly asked.

Alice looked up. "Yes. Everything's fine. It's just an email." She couldn't tell Dolly about the interview. The rumor mill would be cranking before she was even done with her run. "It's work related." That was technically true.

"No wonder we have the best library in Texas. Our librarian never stops working."

Alice's phone, which she was still staring at, suddenly lit up with a call. It was Beau! She didn't want to answer it in front of Dolly.

"Well, I've got to run," she said as Gaston pulled on the leash. "Literally."

"Okay," Dolly said. "But I wanted to tell you that there's a hairless cat conference next month. I thought maybe we could go together. And also, I ordered a pirate ship for Sultana."

"A pirate ship?"

"It's cardboard. Four feet long! She'll love it."

"Where will I put a four-foot pirate ship? I might have to get rid of my couch."

"It comes with a little pirate hat."

The phone stopped ringing. Dang it.

Dolly clipped a pink rose and handed it to Alice. "Enjoy your run. We'll talk pirate ships when you get back."

Soon, Alice was at the end of the block, drenched in sweat with a cramp in her side, dying to see if Beau had left a voice mail. "Hold on," she said to Gaston, who'd apparently assumed they'd go farther than a block (he was wrong about that).

Yes! Beau had left a voice mail. She put the phone to her ear, and as soon as she heard his voice—*Hey, Allie Cat*—she broke out in goose bumps, despite the humid heat.

I'm going to be hauling cattle all week, so I can't get together for tutoring. But I promise to keep working on my own. And speaking of getting together...I had a great time last night. It was the best pasture party I've ever been to.

There was a bit of silence, and Alice thought maybe that was all he was going to say. But then:

I hope you had fun, too. So...

Another stretch of silence.

I guess I'll see you soon. And I, um...I have a few more ideas for the bucket list.

Alice's heart was pounding. Had she really made out with Beau Montgomery? Did she really have a job interview in Austin? And what the heck did Beau want to add to her bucket list? Holy guacamole, she might have to amend the contract.

Chapter

Twenty

❦

Alice had been super busy all week, but not nearly as busy as Beau, who'd been driving back and forth to the Rockin' H Ranch, which the Kowalskis had bought.

They hadn't seen each other in several days, but they'd texted. Which was absolutely wonderful because it was fun, but it also meant Beau was reading and writing. Their texts were silly stuff mostly; outrageous links and memes suggesting things to add to her bucket list.

Spend the night in an ice cave!

I hear roach milk is the new superfood!

Glamping in a yurt!

Nothing remotely sexy or flirtatious had been exchanged, and Alice was reminded that what they'd done in the bed of Beau's pickup was probably not all that out of the ordinary for Beau. Maybe when he'd suggested adding things to her bucket list, he really had been thinking of yurt glamping.

This morning, he'd texted to cancel their tutoring session tonight.

Bryce's last night in town. Going out with the boys.

She'd been disappointed, but she'd texted back that she understood, because she did. And then Beau had sent a picture captioned Blast from the Past!

It was a photo of her sitting on the Montgomerys' front porch. She looked about fourteen—braces, glasses, confused facial expression—holding a book. She vaguely remembered the boys pestering her with a camera that afternoon. Ugh. Why had Beau sent that? She'd responded, Yikes. How do you even have this?

Beau hadn't answered. In fact, he hadn't texted since. Which was fine, because she'd had her job interview today, and she was certain she'd blown it. She'd been anxious and awkward and weird—more so than usual. There was no way she'd get the position.

It sure was a gorgeous library, though. After the interview was over, the director had given her a tour and introduced her to a few people. There was someone to do every job that Alice typically did. They'd had a children's librarian, a resource librarian, a social media manager, and a program director, among others. It seemed like the only tasks left for her to do were the things she didn't enjoy all that much. Mountains of paperwork. Reports. Preparing for board meetings.

But still. If by some miracle they offered it to her, she'd be an idiot to turn it down, right?

She went into the kitchen with the intention of making tea and got down a wineglass instead. She had several of those tiny bottles of pinot grigio—single serving size—in the fridge. She grabbed one, unscrewed the lid, and poured it into the glass.

She kind of missed the Strawberry Hill.

And Beau's lips.

Sultana wove in and out of her ankles, purring. Gaston, who was finally being picked up tomorrow, was curled up in the corner. Everything was quiet and peaceful. Maybe what she needed was to cuddle on the couch with a good book.

Her phone chimed with a text from Carmen.

How did the interview go?

There was no way to adequately share how she felt about the interview in a text, so she said, Would you like to come over? Or go to Tony's?

Carmen responded with a thumbs-up, and Alice decided to invite Maggie and Claire, too.

This was the first time she'd ever invited anyone to go out for drinks. Not a big enough deal to go on her bucket list, but it was still a meaningful first.

By the time she'd showered and put on a pair of jeans, Carmen had arrived. "I'll drive," Carmen said. "Unless you want to?"

"I've never ridden in a Porsche before," Alice said. "So, I'd love for you to drive."

It only took ten super-fun minutes to get to Tony's in Carmen's red car, which they drove with the windows down and the music up. For a grown-up lady with a possible new job in a big library in Austin, Alice felt surprisingly young. And hip. And cool. And very much *not* the young girl in the picture Beau had texted earlier.

"There's Maggie and Claire," Carmen said, pointing to Maggie's yellow Jeep.

They had just parked, and when they spotted the Porsche, they waved and headed over.

Claire yanked Alice out of the car. "I'm on borrowed time. My boobs will explode in exactly two hours."

Music and laughter streamed out of Tony's as they filed inside. It took Alice's eyes a moment to adjust to the dim lighting as they walked past the small dance floor covered in sawdust to get to a table beneath a neon Dos Equis sign.

Carmen, always the hospitality person, automatically took their orders. "Is it beer for everyone? Whatever's on tap?"

"Soda for me," Claire said. "Because soon, I'll literally be what's on tap as far as Rosa is concerned."

"Beer," Maggie said, and Alice nodded her head.

For years, Tony's had been the place other people went when they had something to celebrate, or when they needed to blow off steam after a bad day, or when they wanted to catch a game with friends. It's where couples hooked up and broke up, and where dang near everyone—except Alice—bought their first legal drink. But tonight, Alice finally felt like it was her place as much as it was everyone else's.

"So, what's Travis up to tonight?" Claire asked Maggie.

"Dropping F-bombs all over Henry's third grade math homework," Maggie said. "And Maisy is potty training, so he's probably also begging and bribing and singing 'Itsy Bitsy Spider' while she sits on the potty playing him like a finely tuned fiddle."

Claire laughed. "I swear Rosa already has Ford wrapped around her little finger. And he loves it."

Carmen came back to the table, followed by Tony himself. "It's ladies' night, and Tony is treating us to fried mushrooms!"

Tony's was famous for its fried mushrooms.

"On the house," Tony said, setting the mushrooms and two beers on the table.

Carmen set the other two drinks down, gave Tony a high-five, and plopped into her chair. "I fucking love this town. Now, Alice, tell us how your interview went."

Maggie's eyebrows disappeared into her blond bangs. "Interview?"

Claire frowned. "For, like, a job?"

Alice cleared her throat. "Please don't tell anybody, but I interviewed for a library position in Austin."

Instead of squealing with excitement, Maggie and Claire just stared, mouths agape. "It's a much bigger library with a bigger staff, and"—she lowered her voice—"a bigger salary."

"But it's in Austin," Maggie said.

Claire nodded. "Have you asked for a raise here? In Big Verde? Maybe—"

"It's more than the money," Alice said. "I've done all I can do here. There's nothing else for me to achieve. There's no way for me to advance. If I stay in Big Verde, I'll be stuck doing the same thing forever."

"But we thought you liked doing what you're doing," Claire said.

"I do. But…" *But what?*

"She doesn't feel like she fits in here," Carmen said.

Claire gasped. "Of course you fit in."

Maggie, in her no-nonsense way, shrugged. "Maybe she doesn't. What's wrong with that? I certainly don't. Small towns aren't easy places for people who go against the grain. But when I decided to give folks a chance, they surprised me." She poked Claire in the arm. "I mean, look at me now, sitting here with the former Queen Crispin of the Big Verde Apple Festival."

"I'm not exactly known for blending in, myself," Carmen said.

A popular Tejano song came on, and a few people whistled as Gabriel Castro and JD Mayes took to the dance floor. Claire waved at them. "JD says the folks of Big Verde have surprised them, too."

Alice looked at their little table of misfits. "A beauty queen, a librarian, a celebrity chef, and a landscaper walk into a bar…"

They all laughed. "See?" Carmen said. "I told you you're funny."

Claire squeezed her hand. "If a job in Austin is what you want, then I hope you get it."

Alice swallowed. She wanted the job significantly less than she had an hour ago, and that was saying something. "Thanks," she said, fanning herself with a cocktail napkin. The air-conditioning in Tony's was crappy.

"So, what's Beau up to tonight?" Carmen asked brightly.

"He's out with the boys. I haven't seen him all week, actually. But last Saturday…"

Everyone leaned in.

"We made out."

Claire squealed and clapped her hands. "I knew it! Also, what do you mean by made out?"

"You know," Alice said. "Kissing and stuff."

Carmen dropped her head to the table in feigned frustration. "No pressure. But you've only got a week before this arrangement of yours comes to an end."

"I think you should just git 'er done," Maggie said. "I mean, why not? Beau's a nice guy, there are no strings attached, and I hear he knows what he's doing where sex is concerned."

Carmen looked over Alice's shoulder. "This might literally be your lucky night. Because guess who just walked in?"

Alice's Beau-dar went off. And for once, it was a rather pleasant sensation.

* * *

Like most of the cowboys in Verde County, Beau knew the layout of Tony's like the back of his hand. He didn't even need to let his eyes adjust to the dim lighting as he led the Rancho Cañada Verde ranch hands past the dance floor. It was Bryce's last night, and they were going to live it up.

Molly Newsom yanked on his sleeve. "Dance with me, Beau!"

"And I'm next!" Vanessa Ramirez said.

It was ladies' night. And normally, Beau would hit the dance floor the moment he walked through the door and stay there until it was time to go home—usually with a lady in tow. But as far as the town of Big Verde was concerned, he had a girlfriend. Also, he really didn't feel like dancing, and even though it was Bryce's last night in town, Beau would rather be with Alice.

He'd missed her.

"Sorry, ladies. I'm not hitting the dance floor tonight," he said.

"Oh my God," Vanessa said. "Is it true? You're dating the librarian?"

Bryce slapped him on the back and laughed. "It's true. He's out of commission."

Vanessa pouted, but then she smiled and grabbed Bryce's hand. "Come on. You'll do in a pinch."

"I'm always picking up your slack," Bryce said with a wink.

"It looks like quite a sacrifice."

"Get me a beer," Bryce hollered as he followed Vanessa onto the dance floor.

Two of the other guys also found dance partners, so Beau and Worth headed to the bar. "Let the single guys dance," Worth said. "You and I are going to warm some barstools while our women warm our beds. And honestly, if it weren't Bryce's last night in Big Verde, I'd be in mine right now, snuggled up with Caroline."

"I understand," Beau said, surprised that he really did. And then he stopped in his tracks. A familiar brown ponytail was swinging this way and that on the other side of the bar.

The toes of his boots automatically rotated in that direction, and he forgot all about beer and Bryce and what he was doing here.

Worth grinned, following Beau's gaze. "Oh. I see how it is." He slapped Beau on the back. "I guess I'm on my own tonight."

Alice looked up. And instead of wrinkling her brow, which is what she used to do whenever she saw him, her face broke out in a huge smile.

"Beau Montgomery," Carmen said when he arrived at the table. "What are you doing at Tony's on ladies' night?"

"The more important question is, what is my girlfriend doing here?" Beau said, sitting next to Alice and giving her a kiss on the cheek.

"Being a lady, of course," Maggie said with a mischievous grin.

Was it weird that none of this felt weird?

Carmen stood up. "Care for a beer?"

He'd forgotten he'd even wanted one. But before he could

answer, a beer bottle appeared out of nowhere. He looked up to see Worth. "Figured you'd want one."

The women immediately began fawning over Worth, calling him Baby, which was his rodeo name. He'd retired from bronc riding at the ripe old age of twenty-one in order to settle down and marry Caroline.

Alice, however, wasn't fawning over the young cowboy. She was staring directly at Beau, and it damn near stopped his heart. For a moment, he thought he might have to pound on his own chest.

She leaned in. "Where on earth did you find that awful picture?"

"What awful picture?"

"The one of me when I was fourteen."

"What was awful about it?"

Alice rolled her eyes, but what was so funny? He'd snapped that photo himself, at the ripe old age of ten, and then he'd stuck it in a birthday card that Alice had given him and Bryce for their tenth birthday. *Congrats on reaching double digits, boys!* It had been for them both, but Beau was the one who'd stuck it in a shoebox and kept it.

Even at ten years old, he'd known there was something special about Alice Ann Martin. She'd made him laugh. Sometimes she'd made him mad. But she'd always made his heart beat like a bass drum. Just like it was doing right now.

Even if the relationship was fake, his feelings were real. And this could become a problem.

"Are you okay?" Alice asked, eyebrows drawn into a frown. "You don't look so hot."

"I'm fine," he blurted, lifting his hat to wipe the sweat gathering on his forehead. "Would you like to dance?"

The last time he'd asked Allie to dance, she'd basically called him a child and sent him on his way. But he wasn't a child anymore. He was a man, and Alice was the woman who held his heart.

Heck, she was the woman who'd *always* held it.

Chapter
Twenty-One

❦

Oh God. Was he really asking her to dance? Right now? In front of everyone?

At least there were no snickering kids holding up dollar bills in the distance. Because Beau wasn't that cocky teenager anymore. And she wasn't the insecure girl in the photo. They were exactly what they'd been telling everyone they were: two people who enjoyed each other's company. Why shouldn't they share a dance?

"God, woman. You're killing me. I can practically hear the *Jeopardy!* music playing. Give me your answer."

"Are you wearing steel-toed boots?" She wasn't really joking. Because, while she could do an adequate two-step if she concentrated, she had a feeling it would be difficult to concentrate while dancing with Beau.

Beau grinned and held out his hand. "I'm not worried about you stepping on my toes. I'm a good enough dancer for both of us."

"And so modest," Alice said. "Just don't try to be fancy."

"I don't have to try. The fancy just leaks out naturally."

Uh-oh. She was in trouble.

They went onto the dance floor, and Beau took her in his arms. Crisp, starched shirt. The woodsy scent of his aftershave. He placed a big warm hand at the center of her back and started moving without any fanfare at all.

Alice frantically began her silent chant (short, short, long . . . short, short, long), but holy guacamole, she hardly had to concentrate. Dancing with Beau was like gliding on ice. Were his feet even on the floor?

"Relax, darlin'. You're awful tense."

"Am I?"

"Do you want to lead? I feel like you're trying to lead."

"No. I don't want to lead. Although, honestly, why do men always lead? Why can't women do it?" This was a bit of patriarchal nonsense that had totally escaped her until now.

"I imagine it's because women are typically shorter. It makes sense for the person moving forward to be the one who can see where he's going."

JD and Gabriel danced by, and JD, the taller of the two, was leading.

"Oh," she said. "That makes sense."

"But you can still be mad about it if you want."

Alice grinned and didn't feel mad at all.

"You ready to go for a ride?" Beau asked.

"What do you mean?"

"We're going to do some turns."

"Wait. I've never done turns before."

"Good. You can add it to your bucket list and cross it off."

"But I don't know how—"

Suddenly they were turning. One turn. Two turns. Three turns. Alice's tummy flopped. Then it flipped. She was a little dizzy, but there was a grin on her face—she could feel it—and before long, she was giggling uncontrollably. Actually, it was beyond giggling.

She was laughing. And she hadn't laughed like this since skinny-dipping in the Rio Verde.

Beau turned her into someone else. Someone fun and adventurous and—oh! He'd let go of her back and loosened his hold. "I'm going to spin you now."

Alice gasped. "No. I don't think—"

She was spinning! And then she was back in his arms as if nothing had happened.

"Again?" he asked. But before she could answer, she was spinning again. Spinning and giggling.

Then she was back in his arms. Closer than before. "You did that very well," he said.

"I'm pretty sure that was you," she said. "I have no idea what I'm doing."

"Must feel weird. You always seem to know what you're doing."

That wasn't true, and Alice started to say so, but the song was nearly over and Beau apparently wanted to finish big, because they were turning again. Faster and faster, and then everyone was applauding. Whistles rang out. Some folks hollered a few good-natured compliments and jabs. *Show her how it's done, Beau!* and *Boy, you still got them two left feet!*

The song ended, and Beau performed a polite bow before giving Alice one more twirl.

"That was beautiful, darlin'!" Bryce hollered, giving her a thumbs-up.

"Solid ten," Worth shouted, holding up all ten fingers.

Alice's heart was pounding. She was hot and sweaty. Who knew dancing could be such a workout? She didn't think she'd ever had so much fun in her life. And to think, it wasn't that long ago that she'd felt that she didn't belong in a place like Tony's. Not because she was too good for it, but because she just didn't, well, *belong*. Period.

The jukebox started up again, and the lights dimmed—they did that for the slow songs. Beau pulled her close. Real close. She turned her head so that her cheek rested against his chest as if it were the most natural thing in the world. All of the other couples on the dance floor seemed to melt into each other, and seamlessly, she and Beau did the same.

The beautiful melody of a steel guitar rang out, and Alice recognized the song immediately. It was George Strait, or King George, as JD called him, singing his beautiful old classic "The Chair."

Her breath hitched. This was the song that had been playing that night at the VFW hall. The night Beau had asked her to dance on a dare. She closed her eyes, but she could still see the boys laughing behind him, holding up dollar bills, watching to see if he'd go through with it.

Did he remember? She thought his body had tensed slightly at the first note, but maybe that was her imagination. The night had probably slipped from Beau's memory years ago.

It was ridiculous to hold on to the hurt for so long. Especially now that she'd gotten to know Beau better. He was kind and patient and sweet. A bit of a playboy, for sure. But none of the women he'd been with spoke ill of him. Not that she knew of, anyway.

She thought of the meditative exercises she did to let go of the things that caused pain. Generally, she wasn't especially good at it. But right now, in Beau's arms, she had no trouble letting it go. The pain from that night floated up and away...

Beau led her slowly to the center of the dance floor, and it was so smooth and effortless that she forgot to do her silent chant. He let go of her hand and wrapped his arms around her waist, and without even thinking, she wrapped hers around his neck. He was so solid. So strong. Like an anchor.

The people swaying around them were like small waves on an ocean. Next to them, Malcolm Ojeda's hand drifted down to Tina Wilson's butt, where it slipped inside the back pocket of her rhinestone-studded jeans.

Surely, Beau wouldn't try anything like—

His hand moved lower, and Alice's tummy fluttered as if an entire kaleidoscope of butterflies—that's what a group of butterflies was called—bounced around inside. She exhaled as his hand settled just above her back pocket. He didn't try to slip his hand in, but she wouldn't have stopped him if he had. She wanted his hands all over her. She was overcome with the same frantic need she'd felt when they'd made out in the back of his truck. Actually, *need* was an understatement.

She was starving. She wanted Beau to touch her in all the places she'd never been touched.

He tilted his head so that both their faces were shadowed by the brim of his Stetson, and as his warm breath brushed her cheek, he squeezed her even closer. What they were doing now could hardly be called dancing.

His belt buckle pressed against her—right where her belly button was—and so did something else ... *Oh!* Beau had an erection right out here in the middle of the dance floor. Should she put some distance between them? She didn't want him to feel embarrassed.

He pressed himself against her.

Not embarrassed.

Her heart pounded. When had her fingers started raking his hair? And why had her chin lifted as if she wanted to kiss him right here in a flagrant display of public affection? They'd stopped moving entirely now. No more shuffling. The world had shrunk to just the two of them. Alice was frozen except for the beating of her heart, which seemed to have slowed. In fact, everything seemed to have slowed.

Beau's lips parted, Alice rose on her toes, and then his mouth was on hers.

She was spinning again, even though they hadn't moved an inch.

* * *

Not only had Allie not pulled away at the feel of his embarrassing amateur-hour-on-the-dance-floor boner—hadn't had one of those since high school—she was kissing him. In front of people.

With tongue action.

This was the same song that the Baxter Brothers had so badly butchered on New Year's Eve. He remembered it well, because it had been such a humiliating evening. But right now, while kissing the hell out of Alice Martin, the hurt he'd been carrying since that night felt just plain silly. He'd been a teenager. Why would she have wanted to dance with him? What had he been hoping would happen?

This. He'd hoped this would happen. He'd fantasized about kissing her.

It seemed so ridiculous now. This never ever in a million years would have happened then. It was happening now though. And he never wanted it to stop.

Alice broke the kiss. "You asked me to dance to this song once." The words came out in a rush. "Do you remember?"

Jesus. She remembered the night, and she remembered the song. He hadn't been expecting this. He swallowed a lump in his throat. Maybe she was going to apologize. He hoped not, because she didn't need to. "How could I forget? I thought I was such a man that night." He laughed. "Until you turned me down."

He hoped she could see that he wasn't still sore about it.

"What do you mean? I figure you made at least ten dollars off of it."

This was confusing as hell. Ten dollars? For what? "Pardon?"

"I saw your friends holding up dollar bills. Did you do it on a dare? I mean, don't get me wrong. It was a long time ago, and I'm not upset. I'm just curious."

Good Lord. What was she talking about? He hadn't known anyone had held up dollar bills. If it had happened, Allie had misinterpreted it. "I wasn't a part of anything having to do with a bet or a dare. If anybody was placing bets, it was probably over whether you'd say yes. None of my pals expected a college girl like you to say yes to me. And I went straight home after you turned me down, to avoid all the ribbing. Hardly even glanced at those losers."

Allie looked as surprised as he'd ever seen anyone look.

"So... You really wanted to dance with me? You weren't making fun?"

"Allie, I would never make fun of you. *Ever.* My God, woman. I could never hurt you. And also, I don't think you see yourself the way everybody else sees you."

"No, I don't think *you* see me the way everybody else sees me."

He'd heard enough. He grabbed her and kissed her again. And she wrapped her arms around his neck and kissed him back. They didn't stop until someone tapped him on the shoulder.

Bryce wore a big old smile. "Dude, the song ended. And, any minute now, Tony is going to tell you two to get a room."

Alice's cheeks were bright pink.

Bryce laughed as they all walked off the dance floor together. "I can get another ride home if I need to."

Beau looked at his brother—kept his face straight, but Bryce got the message. *Yeah. You might want to do that.* Because he was definitely going to take Alice home. He needed her mouth on his in a bad way. This past week that they'd been separated had been torture.

"I'm heading out in the morning," Bryce said. "And then I need you to come to the Rockin' H and help me out on Wednesday. Ford said he could spare you for a couple of days."

Bryce was really leaving. Tomorrow.

But Beau would still rather hang out with Alice tonight. He could see his brother's ugly mug later. Heck, he saw it every time he looked in the mirror.

"I'll head up to the dude ranch on Wednesday. And I swear to

God, if you're singing trail riding songs while prancing about on a pony—"

"First of all, I don't prance. And also, it's worse than that," Bryce said. "I'm helping get the place ready for Brittany Fox's wedding."

Good Lord.

Also, *good Lord*—the wedding was next weekend. That meant his and Allie's contract would be ending soon. *Too soon.*

They went back to Alice's table, where JD and Gabriel had joined the group.

"It sure was fun to watch you two dancing," Claire said, pouting. "It's been forever since anyone has spun me around a dance floor like that."

"Let me finish my beer," JD said. "Then I'll take you for a spin."

"Thanks, JD," Claire said. "Who has little Brianna tonight?"

"My folks are visiting," Gabriel said. "They insisted JD and I get out and have some fun."

"And where's Ford?" Beau asked Claire. "Babysitting?"

"Not that I know of," Claire said. "He's supposed to be at home with Rosa."

"So...he's babysitting."

"No. Babysitting is something people do for other people's kids, and they get paid for it. Ford is at home being a parent."

Maggie nodded her head. "Dads don't babysit. They parent."

"And that's true if there's two dads, too," JD said.

"But speaking of babysitting," Claire said with a grin at Beau and Bryce. "Alice used to do quite a lot of it."

Oh damn. Leave it to Claire to go there.

"I heard you used to babysit for a pair of unruly twins," Carmen said. "Do you know whatever happened to them?"

Alice laughed. "I hear they've grown into nice, handsome young men."

"Best babysitter we ever had," Bryce said. "Cookies, milk, snuggles on the couch. Right, Beau?"

Beau's cheeks heated up.

"There were absolutely no snuggles," Alice said. "You two were too old, and anyway, you never sat still long enough."

Beau reached beneath the table to grab Alice's hand. He gave it a single squeeze, and without looking at him, she squeezed back.

There would definitely be some snuggles tonight.

Chapter
Twenty-Two

❦

Alice's mind raced along faster than Beau's truck. He'd asked if she needed a ride home, even though she clearly didn't since she'd arrived with Carmen and could presumably leave with her. So, his wanting to take her home had nothing to do with the logistics of transportation.

Was he expecting a tutoring session? Was he expecting to make out again? And why couldn't people just come out and say what they were thinking? She smiled to herself. He hadn't asked her to dance on New Year's Eve because of a dare. Was it possible he'd had a little crush? If so, it was quite a revelation.

He'd saved that silly picture all these years.

She glanced at him. He didn't look the slightest bit nervous. He probably took women home all the time. She, on the other hand, felt like she might spontaneously combust. How did she look to Beau? She knew her nervous tics—ponytail tossing, lip chewing—but maybe they weren't apparent to others. Maybe to Beau, she appeared calm, cool, and collected.

"Are you okay over there, Allie Cat? All that nervous energy is heating up the cab of my truck."

So much for being cool. She was apparently riding along in Beau's pickup with her hair on fire.

"I'm fine."

"Really? Because there's so much energy in here that my hair is standing up. You're like one of those static balls that shoots out electricity."

"That's a Tesla ball, and it's not actually—"

"You nervous about something? Because I can help you relax."

He probably wasn't talking Tibetan singing bowls or guided meditation. And he didn't seem interested in hearing about Nikola Tesla or the magnetohydrodynamic effect, on which she felt dangerously close to delivering a lecture.

A warm hand landed on the back of her neck and squeezed. "Yep. You're tense all right. Harder than marble. But luckily for you, I have magic fingers."

He rubbed her neck, and warmth spread from the base of her skull through her shoulders. She'd had a massage once, and she'd been fairly uncomfortable and tense throughout, but Beau's fingers had her muscles melting. Turning to liquid. And not just in her neck.

She heard a low humming sound and realized with a wave of embarrassment that it was coming from her. She'd literally moaned. "I think you do actually have magic fingers."

Beau laughed and pulled his hand away. It was all Alice could do not to place it right back on her neck, where it belonged.

"We're here," Beau said, parking behind her Prius in the driveway.

Alice's hands were sweaty. Her mouth was dry. Her heart beat so frantically that she feared Beau could hear it as he slowly turned to look at her.

She had one hand on the door handle and one hand clutching her purse.

"Allie, you look like you're about to march to the firing squad."

At the sound of his voice, her pulse slowed, and her heart settled back in her chest where it belonged. She let go of the door handle. "I'm fine."

"You keep saying that. But you look like you're in fight-or-flight mode, and you don't have to do either one."

"It's actually called the acute stress response, and it's a result of—"

"I was really hoping to kiss you some more. Would that be okay?"

"Right now? Here in the driveway?"

She wanted to jump him.

She looked up and down the street. It was dark. No neighbors were out. Who would even see them?

"Sure," Beau said. "Right here. In the driveway."

She dug around in the sludge of thoughts and emotions racing through her head and finally found the word she needed. And even though it was in enthusiastic all caps, she could barely breathe it out because her vocal cords were no longer connected to her brain. "Okay," she squeaked.

They simultaneously unbuckled their seat belts. And as waves of oxytocin surged through her body, Beau leaned over and kissed her. And just like the last time, it was shatteringly thorough. Hungry. There was nothing neat or tidy or quiet about it. And when Beau grabbed her ponytail and gave it a small tug, tilting her head so he could have even more access to her mouth—an alpha move—a wave of lust rolled through her.

Beau broke the kiss. His eyes seemed to have darkened a shade or two—which was not physiologically possible—as they stared deeply into hers. What did he see? He glanced at her lips, before pausing at her neck on his way to her breasts. Eyes couldn't radiate heat, so why could she literally feel his gaze warming her skin? Beau bit his bottom lip and stared at her like he was a starving man, and she was a cupcake sitting in a bakery window.

"Why are you looking at me like that?"

"Like what?"

"Like you want to—"

Beau raised an eyebrow. "Eat you?"

Alice blushed over the implication. Or at least over what she *suspected* he was implying.

"Because I do, you know," Beau said. "Want to eat you."

That did it. She was dead now. He'd killed her with sexy innuendo.

He placed his lips at her ear. "I bet you taste like honey."

He licked lightly along her jawline and then buried his face in her neck, where he kissed and sucked less gently, as if he really did want to devour her.

Alice leaned her head back and ran her fingers through his hair. He'd lost his hat. When had that happened? She opened one eye to see if it had fallen onto the seat, and noticed that Dolly's porch light had turned on.

"Oh no," she said. "Beau, stop. Porch light."

Beau's head snapped up.

"It's time for Dolly to walk her dog," Alice said.

Sure enough, Dolly came through her front door with Bidi-Bidi-Bom-Bom on a leash.

Beau sighed heavily, then he grinned and said, "I was going to try to slide into second base, but I didn't even come close. What do you say we take this ball game inside?"

"Junior high was a long time ago. Do you want to remind me what second base means?"

"Boobs," Beau said with a wink.

"Oh. We might need to amend our contract then."

"Can we, Allie?"

Alice swallowed loudly. "Can we what?"

"Can we amend the contract? Because I want to make love to you so badly that I can hardly stand it."

Holy guacamole. No more innuendo. He'd just come out with it. Which was great, because yay for communication, but nobody had ever told her that they wanted to make love to her before. She was both excited and outlandishly anxious.

She bit her lip. This was it. A new experience to cross off of her bucket list.

"Yes," she said.

"Oh, thank God," Beau said. "You had me worried for a minute there. It was like New Year's Eve all over again. I promise you won't regret this, Allie."

* * *

Beau followed Alice through the front door of her little house. He cleared his throat, squared his shoulders, and prepared to toss out a grin and wink if Alice turned back around. No need to scare Miss Happily Self-Partnered with a big set of puppy-love eyes.

"Would you like something to drink?"

He could see her pulse pounding at the base of her throat. Her pupils were dilated, and she was biting her lip. Damn, he loved the effect he had on her. Was it purely physical, though?

"No, thanks, I'm not thirsty." He gave her what he hoped was a sexy once-over with his eyes. "Just hungry."

Alice glanced at the kitchen as if she might offer to make him a sandwich. God, she was so literal. It was cute, but more importantly, it gave him license to spell it out. "Hungry for you," he clarified. "I've only had a tiny taste during that brief stop on first base."

Alice's cheeks turned bright pink, and she lowered her eyes with a bashful grin. "Oh, right. Well, I think we need to amend the contract first..."

He couldn't help it. He busted out laughing. "Allie, you do whatever you need to do."

He'd waited years for this moment, so what were a few more minutes?

"I guess we can just have a verbal agreement," Alice said. "For now."

"I verbally agree to have sex with you."

"And I agree to..." Alice swallowed. "Have sex with you."

They shook on it and he pulled her in for a kiss, but she put her hand on his chest. "Wait—"

Was she changing her mind? He readied himself for it.

"I just need to go freshen up. And change."

"You don't need to change."

"Aren't men visually stimulated? Because I have something to wear that might be more, you know, sexy."

Beau couldn't imagine Alice being sexier than she already was. He'd been drooling over those tight jeans all night. "You don't need to change on my account, Allie."

Not a single goddamn thing.

"Oh, okay. If you say so," Alice said with a pout.

All kinds of images began rolling through his horny brain. Lacy things. Sheer things. Well hell, if the woman wanted to put on something sexy, he was definitely not the man to stop her. "I'd probably enjoy it though," he said quickly. "If you have something you'd like to show off."

He doubted Alice had anything too kinky or sexy in mind. Cathy's Closet sold some lingerie. He'd seen it in the window. It was pretty tame, and Alice probably had something along those lines. And that was fine. If she wanted to slip into a flour sack, it would do it for him. The idea that she *wanted* to turn him on was what, well, turned him on.

Alice smiled shyly. "It was free. It came with something else I ordered."

Beau's head spun. What had Alice ordered that came with free lingerie? And how often did she order such things?

"And it's kind of practical," she added.

"Practical?" Maybe it was a flour sack after all.

"Yes. Earlier you referred to performing cunnilingus."

Alice had literally switched to Latin. And that really shouldn't surprise him. "Cun-a-what?"

Alice's cheeks, neck, and chest broke out in bright red splotches. "Cunnilingus means oral sex when performed on female genitalia. And if that's not what you meant when you said you wanted to eat me, then I'm seriously hoping to evaporate into thin air right now."

Beau cleared his throat and failed to produce words. Apparently, when all of your blood was currently holed up in your dick, your vocal cords didn't work.

Alice stared at her feet. "Dang it. I haven't evaporated, have I?"

She was embarrassed. And that wouldn't do. "That's exactly what I meant by *eating*," he said. "I mean, I was flirting and dirty-talking, but I meant every word. I'm just not used to Latin, that's all. And there's no need to evaporate. We're on the same page."

The corner of Alice's mouth curled up. "Good. Communication is important during sex."

We are going to have sex. And Alice is going to talk through all of it.

"The sooner you put on your sexy outfit, the sooner I can get you out of it."

"Aren't you skipping some bases?"

"Oh, darlin', don't you worry. I don't skip any bases. I take my time at each and every one."

Alice raised her eyebrows. "Oh really?"

"Yeah. Really."

"Well, just so you know," Alice said. "In regard to cunnilingus..."

He swallowed loudly. "Yes?"

"I fully intend to reciprocate. But I might need some instruction in how to perform pleasurable fellatio."

That word he knew. And it was a good thing the couch was behind him, because his poor knees finally gave out. They just flatly refused to continue supporting him, and he landed with a grunt on a couch cushion. "Okay," he said, after catching his breath. "I'll assist you in any way I can."

"Thank you," Alice said, nodding her head.

The sight of that bobbing ponytail damn near did him in.

"No problem," he wheezed through his constricted throat.

Alice marched off toward her bedroom. "Be back out in a bit," she said, glancing at him over her shoulder.

Beau shook his head and grinned. He had no idea what to expect from Allie, but that was one of the things he loved about her.

Chapter
Twenty-Three

☙

Alice stared at herself in the mirror. The sheer teddy looked cheap and flimsy, like a Halloween costume. She pulled at the droopy top, which she didn't quite fill out. The ribbons at the bottom tickled her thighs, and the stretchy, cheap elastic indicated this would be a one-time wear. She *had* gotten it for free for buying an expensive vibrator.

It even had crotchless panties, and they were... well, they were beyond ridiculous. They had a small slit in the crotch, but you couldn't really see it while standing. They just looked like regular panties if regular panties were made of itchy nylon netting with gaping leg holes.

She chewed her lip.

No man had ever seen her vulva. Beau would be the first. But it was no big deal. He'd probably seen plenty. And surely nothing about hers would stand out as memorable, right?

She was suddenly overcome by a wave of anxiety. What if she was unappealing? What if there was something wrong with her? What if Beau had a preference for one type of vulva over another?

Why hadn't she made an appointment for waxing? Did she have time to trim?

She stomped her foot. She wasn't about to start thinking like this. Her confidence in her own body shouldn't depend on anyone else's opinions about it. And besides, there was no such thing as normal when it came to people's genitals. She was perfectly fine.

She took down her ponytail and shook out her hair. Tonight, she was going to lose her—

There was no such thing as virginity.

She wasn't going to lose a dang thing. She was going to have an experience. And she was going to have it with Beau!

She fanned her face with her hands. She absolutely had to cool down, because this outfit was probably highly flammable. She'd hate to set herself on fire with sheer embarrassment.

There was no need to be modest. Modesty, like virginity, was a social construct.

She opened the door. Beau was sitting on the couch, hunched over a book and mindlessly rubbing Sultana. Alice smiled as he dragged his finger across the page, pleased by how quickly it moved. For a moment, she almost forgot that she was dressed like a blow-up sex doll.

"Look at you being a bookworm," she said, walking to the couch. "What are you reading?"

"I have no idea," Beau said, turning the page and continuing to read. "I opened it up to a random page and landed right in the middle of a sex scene."

It was next month's book club selection, the virgin trope. She cleared her throat. "Speaking of sex scenes…"

Beau quickly shut the book. "Shit. Sorry."

"It's okay—"

"Oh my God," he said, glancing up for the first time. "You look…"

"Silly?"

Beau's mouth had been hanging open, but he shut it and smiled. "That's not what I was going to say at all, Miss Martin."

Well, that was a relief.

Beau stood up, but his eyes didn't make their way to hers. They roamed her body, taking in every detail. His cheeks were a bit flushed, and there was a very small and nearly indiscernible twitch happening at the corner of his mouth.

Reading people was hard, and it was especially difficult while wearing crotchless panties. Was he turned on? Or was he about to laugh? "I can't tell what you're thinking. And it's making me really uncomfortable."

"I'm thinking a lot of things." He touched the hem of the teddy. "Like this must be itchy as hell."

"It is," Alice said, swatting at a ribbon. "And I'm sorry if it's not visually stimulating."

Beau let go of the teddy and took Alice's hands in his. "Oh, darlin'. I am highly stimulated. Would you like to feel how much?"

Alice glanced down to where his thumbs gently brushed across her knuckles. There was a definite bulge straining against the fly of his jeans, and yes, she wanted to touch it.

She pressed her hand against him. He was so hard. And thick. And even though she didn't entirely trust her ability to precisely assess measurement without a ruler (and was ashamed for even thinking about it), what was pressed into her palm was definitely longer than five point six inches, which was the average length of an erect penis.

"Can you feel what you do to me?" Beau whispered. "And it doesn't matter what you're wearing. God, Allie. Just being near you makes me dizzy."

That was so hard to believe, and yet, at this moment, she did. She believed him. She turned Beau on, and that made her feel sexy. *And powerful.*

She rubbed him, applying a little more pressure, and he groaned and dropped his head to her shoulder. He exhaled shakily right in her ear, and it made her warm and tingly.

"Should we head to the bedroom?" she asked.

Beau laughed softly, tickling her ear. "I'm not sure I can walk that far."

An erection shouldn't impede anyone's ability to walk, so Beau was probably teasing. But he didn't seem to be in any hurry to move. He kissed the side of her neck before pulling away to stare into her eyes. The usual glint of mischief and mirth was there, but so was lust and desire. His lids looked heavy and sexy and this must be what people meant by *bedroom eyes*.

"I can't decide if I want to walk to second base with my fingers," he said. "Or lips."

Why did he have to choose one or the other? Couldn't he do both? And could he hear her pulse pounding, or was it only in her head?

"Fingers first, I think," Beau said. "Then lips. Unless you have a preference? You're being uncharacteristically quiet."

That's because words were bouncing around in her head like bumper cars—*yes!* and *please!* and *both!*—and refusing to hook up and form sentences.

Beau raised an eyebrow. "No opinion?"

He trailed a calloused finger across her collarbone and slipped the strap of the teddy down her shoulder. Alice's instincts were to cover her breasts before they were completely exposed, but she kept her arms at her sides. She wanted to let Beau uncover her. And look at her...

The nylon lace of the teddy hung up on a very hard and perky nipple, and he seemed to like that. He let it rest there for a second before very slowly pulling it down, dragging the abrasive material over her sensitive skin.

Alice broke out in goose bumps. All over. There were apparently neural pathways from the nipples to *everywhere* in your body. Because she was lit up from head to toe.

Both nipples were exposed, and Beau was staring. "God. They're perfect," he whispered.

Breasts came in all shapes and sizes, and there was no standard of perfection. But Alice wasn't going to argue. Her perfectly average breasts were very much in need of Beau's attention. He trailed his fingers across them, up and down the sides. Across the tops and around the areolas. But he didn't touch her nipples, and she was dying for him to. They were sensitive, even to her own touch. What would if feel like when Beau—

He seemed to read her mind and rubbed his rough, calloused palms gently over her nipples, making her gasp and squeeze her thighs together. She lost all train of conscious thought as her body became a mass of nerve endings and pleasure receptors. "Oh, Beau," she whispered.

Beau dropped his head and kissed her neck. "You like that?"

She liked it so much, she couldn't formulate a response.

Beau kissed down to her collarbone and then lower. Alice rose on her toes, trying to get her breasts closer to his mouth, and then she felt it. A single lick.

Ecstasy. She'd tried to imagine what it would feel like so many times, and she had a pretty good imagination. But she'd missed the boat. This felt better than anything she'd ever imagined. She moaned in delight as Beau flicked her nipple gently before taking the entire thing in his mouth and sucking. Her vagina clenched in response. She hadn't known that could even happen without clitoral stimulation.

So far, sex with a partner was *definitely* better than solo good times.

Beau went to the other breast and gave it the same attention, and Alice couldn't stay still. In fact, her pelvis seemed to have a mind of its own and was seeking Beau's hard thigh. Or any part of him, really. It just needed some friction.

Beau appeared to sense her need, and while he gently sucked and flicked her nipple, his fingers trailed down her belly.

She shivered and trembled, enjoying the anticipation of what it was actually going to feel like when he touched her—

His fingers went between her legs, slipping through the opening in the crotchless panties, going right to her sensitive flesh that had never been touched by fingers other than her own. "Beau," she whispered. "Oh, Beau."

Beau jerked his head up and away from her breast as he removed his hand. "I'm so sorry, Allie. I didn't mean to touch you like that."

He didn't? Why not? God, had he felt something weird? Something unexpected? Was she literally deformed and hadn't known it? His touch had been so utterly thrilling and perfect that she hadn't wanted him to stop.

"I just meant to touch you through the fabric," Beau said. "I would never just, you know, barge in there like that."

He hadn't exactly barged in. "Oh, well—"

"And I think you have a hole in your underwear," he added.

"They're crotchless panties," she said.

Beau raised an eyebrow. Then he smiled. "Really?"

"Yes."

"Where on earth did you…" He shook his head. "Never mind. It doesn't matter. And you're sure you didn't mind that I touched you like that? Without asking?"

If she'd been turned on before, she was about to explode now. Beau Montgomery, a small-town, big-ranch cowboy who'd never been out of the state of Texas, fully grasped the concept of consent. And it was because he was *good*. Big-hearted, kind, and sensitive. That was Beau through and through.

There couldn't possibly be a better person to lose her—
To have this experience with.

"I want you to touch me everywhere," she whispered.

He placed his fingers back where they were. "How about here?" he asked, keeping his eyes on hers as his fingers brushed her panties, seeking the slit in the crotch. They both sighed when his fingers slipped in, parting her labia and caressing her sensitive flesh.

"Yes," she sighed.

"Is your clit sensitive?" he asked, rubbing his thumb over it gently and making Alice moan. "And yes, Miss Martin. I know where it is. Even with my eyes closed."

Oh, did he ever. Alice rotated her hips, first one way, and then the other, trying to get him to apply pressure in just the right spot.

Nearly half of all men couldn't properly identify the clitoris on a diagram. More than that couldn't find it on an actual woman, and most didn't know what to do with it if they did.

She sighed as her vagina clenched again.

Beau Montgomery was not most men.

Chapter
Twenty-Four

B eau willed himself to slow down. This was a moment that he'd dreamed of. Actually, it was more than a moment. It was an event. A dream come true. Only what he'd dreamed of had been a teenage fantasy. What was actually happening was so much better.

He brought his fingers to his mouth for a quick taste, and it made him weak at the knees. Because the smell and taste of an excited woman was the biggest turn-on in the world. And tasting Alice—*his Allie*—was more than a turn-on.

It was fucking nirvana.

He ran his palms gently over Alice's nipples, awed by the goose bumps breaking out all over her body. She was so sensitive. "I bet I could make you come just by playing with your breasts."

Alice sighed and shuddered. "I doubt—"

He pinched a nipple.

"Oh," Alice wheezed, squeezing her thighs together.

Beau covered the nipple with his mouth, and Alice made a low humming sound in her throat that set his senses on fire.

They probably should move things to the bedroom, but Beau

was literally too impatient, so he sat on the couch and pulled Alice on top of him. *Straddling him. In crotchless panties.*

She kissed him, and it wasn't a gentle librarian-style kiss. It was an impatient, hornier-than-hell kiss. She ran her hands through his hair while devouring his mouth, invading him with her tongue, as if she wanted to explore every nook and cranny.

Of course, she'd be thorough about it. And Beau didn't mind at all. He was one hundred percent on board for letting horny-on-fire Alice do whatever she wanted to him. He'd let her set the pace. No problem.

She rose up on her knees and guided his face to her breasts. Her devastatingly perfect breasts. He had what felt like a brief out-of-body experience while his brain tried to accept the fact that he was *finally* with Alice. Like, really with her.

Mind, body, and soul.

Alice's nipple brushed his cheek, and she moaned. Beau took her breast in his hand, kissed it, flicked the nipple with his tongue so Alice would make that sound again, and then he brushed it with his five o'clock shadow. Alice gasped, and he was worried he'd been too rough, but then she rubbed her nipple over his chin—where the whiskers were roughest—before teasing his lips.

He accepted the tantalizing nugget right into his mouth. Alice squirmed in response. Damn, she was cute when she was being driven crazy. And he was nowhere near done. He trailed his fingers up her inner thigh until Alice became very still. The only thing moving was her chest as she breathed, and Beau swore he could hear her heart pounding.

He brushed the edge of her panties. And then he touched right in the middle, where the slit in the crotchless panties was now spread wide open. His fingers met Alice's flesh and she moaned and squirmed and rubbed herself all over him.

His finger was right there at her entrance, and she pressed against it. "Please Beau," she whispered.

"Please what?"

"Can you…"

"You want me to finger you? Because that lands me squarely on third base, Miss Martin."

Her eyebrows went up at the sound of *finger you*. But who didn't like a bit of dirty talk? Also, if there was a technical term in Latin for the act, Alice would be sure to tell him.

She was practically sitting in his palm now, and she ground herself against him.

"Is that a yes?"

She nodded. "Yes."

She'd said it so quietly that he almost didn't hear her. He sensed an air of vulnerability, and it made him want to kiss her, to hold her, and to reassure her that he *wanted* her, and that he… Well, dammit. That he cared about her in a way he'd never cared about anybody.

He knew not to say it though. Instead, he slipped his tongue into her mouth, and she responded by deepening the kiss. And then very gently, he inserted his middle finger.

Alice stopped kissing him and froze. Then she dropped her head to his shoulder, breathing heavily against his neck. She made little sounds that began like kitten mews and evolved into soft moans when he crooked his finger and applied pressure right behind her pelvic bone, where women often liked it.

Alice's moans became lower. Deeper. And she moved her hips in a way that nearly drove him mad. In a way that suggested she knew just how to fuck a man.

But he wasn't interested in his own pleasure. He was only interested in hers.

"Is this okay?" he asked. "Does it feel good?"

"Yes," Alice gasped. "But…"

"But what? Tell me."

"I think I need more clitoral stimulation."

Yes! Man, it was so awesome to have a woman actually tell him what she wanted. He lifted Alice off his lap.

"What's happening?" Alice said.

Beau patted the cushion of the couch. "Lie down on your back."

Alice complied, resting her head on a pillow. Her knees were drawn up, and the toes of her pretty little feet dug into his thigh. He twisted to face her, kicking his boots off and bringing one leg and foot up onto the couch. "Open your knees, sweetheart. Let me see. You can show me what you like."

"Show you?"

"Yeah," Beau said. "Touch yourself. I'll watch."

He'd said that casually. As if he said it all the time. *Let me watch you get yourself off.*

But he didn't say that all the time. In fact, he'd never said it. Everyone thought he was so social and outgoing and had no filters, but in reality, he kept a lot to himself. Like most people with a secret, he was guarded, even if it didn't show. All the time. As if he had a million secrets that might come out if he didn't watch himself. But with Alice, it all fell away. And more and more, he found himself saying exactly what he thought when he was around her. If he didn't work on reinstalling some filters, he was going to blow it all by telling her how he really felt about her. By telling her that this was more than fun times for him. That it was way more than living out a fantasy.

That this was everything.

"I'm feeling a bit shy," Alice said.

This confession was so sweet that it made Beau's heart flutter around in his chest like a damn butterfly. He did a double take to make sure she wasn't joking, but of course she wasn't. When Alice joked, you knew it. Sometimes, she even pointed it out.

"You don't have to be shy," he said. "Not with me."

Alice bit her lip. "I know. And modesty is a social construct anyway."

"Every part of you is beautiful, Allie. Inside and out."

That was something people always said. But with Allie, it was true. Her outside checked all his boxes. From the big brown eyes to the full lips and curvy little figure...yep. Every box. But the other parts of her, the parts inside that made Alice *Alice*, that's where the indescribable beauty was. Her heart. Her soul. Her amazing mind and intellect. He couldn't see these things. But their beauty was real. Solid. Almost tangible.

"Beau?"

"What, darlin'?"

"I, erm...haven't really..."

"Haven't really what?"

Alice sighed. "I haven't really...Well, it's just that..."

Good Lord. He broke out in a light sweat. Alice wasn't a virgin, was she?

"I haven't really groomed to today's ridiculous societal standards," Alice said.

"Groomed?"

"My pubic area."

Whew! He'd misunderstood. Allie wasn't a virgin. "Darlin', women are beautiful. Specifically, *you* are beautiful. And I want to see every gorgeous natural inch of you."

He meant every word.

Alice smiled and seemed to relax. "In that case..."

She slowly opened her knees, and Beau found himself looking at a bit of heaven. And even though he wouldn't have thought it, the crotchless panties were a huge turn-on. "Those panties," he said. "They frame your pu—"

He caught himself. Alice probably preferred he use the proper verbiage.

"They frame your vagina"—the word caught in his throat a little, which was stupid—"very well."

"Vulva," Alice said.

It was hard, but Beau wrenched his eyes away from Alice's vagina so he could try to figure out what she'd just said. "Pardon?"

"Vulva," Alice said. "The vagina is the interior. It's inside. The vulva is the outside and it is comprised of the labia—"

"Which is where, Miss Martin?"

"You know where the labia are, Beau. Surely," Alice said.

The blush on her cheeks had spread to her chest. And Beau absolutely knew, but he wanted Alice to show him. He wanted to see her pretty fingers on her pretty pink pus—

Vulva.

"I'm afraid you need to show me."

Alice bit her lip and slowly ran a hand down between her legs to touch her labia. And it was such a fucking rush. It made Beau so hard he thought he might break his damn zipper.

"Oh, I see," he said, swallowing as Alice's fingers spread her labia apart.

"And here's the vaginal opening," she said, running a finger between her labia to the opening below.

Would she actually dip a finger in? Because he was going to lose it if she did.

"And even though you've already stated that you know where it is," Alice said, running her finger back up. "This is the clitoris."

Alice rubbed her finger in small circles right next to the little bull's-eye. Holy shit. This was probably the hottest thing he'd ever seen. And he'd seen some things.

"I usually need a vibrator to climax," Alice said softly. "Do you want me to get one?"

That was definitely going on *his* bucket list. But not tonight. He was going to show her that a vibrator wasn't necessary when he was around. "No, darlin'. I'm going to take care of you."

He didn't know how much longer he was going to be able to hold himself back. He needed to taste this woman. And he needed to do it now.

Alice moved her finger, spread her legs wider, and clasped the back of Beau's neck as he lowered his head. He kissed the inside of her thigh. And even though he was anxious to get to the pot of gold at the end of the rainbow, he took his time, enjoying the sensation of Alice's smooth skin on his lips and tongue.

Her breaths came quickly, like a panting puppy's, as he kissed his way up to the opening in the crotchless panties. He opened his eyes and saw that she was looking at him. No. Actually, she wasn't just looking. She was *watching*.

There was a difference.

He held her gaze as he dragged his tongue up her leg. When he got to the little slit in her panties—which was wide open—he heard her breath hitch. Her eyes widened, and her lips parted in anticipation.

He blew lightly on her skin, making her tremble. Good Lord, she was so responsive. So fucking sensitive. He wanted to strum her like a guitar.

Actually, he wasn't all that good on a guitar. He was way better at this.

He slowly extended his tongue and gave her clit the lightest, feathery lick.

* * *

Alice gasped when she finally felt Beau's tongue. And even though she wanted to keep watching, because *wow*, what a freaking turn-on it was to watch Beau, she couldn't keep her eyes open.

They were closing of their own free will, and her legs were spreading wider, and her back was arching, and her skin was tingly. In other words, she had literally zero self-control.

Beau was in control. And it was exhilarating. She hadn't realized how heavy self-restraint was. With it gone, she was lighter than air. Losing control was freeing, and she couldn't imagine feeling this way with anyone other than Beau. *She trusted him.*

His big, warm hands pressed against her inner thighs, opening her wider and getting her in the position that *he* wanted her in. And it was totally hot. She was at his mercy. This was *very* different than masturbating with a vibrator.

Alice could usually achieve orgasm with a vibrator within a matter of a few minutes, but Beau was going to get her there even quicker. She was already tingling and buzzing, and if he didn't alter what he was doing in some fashion...

She didn't care. This man could do whatever the heck he wanted to her. She was just going to lean back and enjoy the ride, which was a very un-Alice-like thing to do.

The tingling intensified. If the next touch of his tongue produced even a hint of a vaginal contraction, it was all over. She was going to explode.

She was gasping for breath, clawing at the cushions, and curling her toes. In other words, all of the stereotypical orgasm posturing was going on and then...

Beau stopped performing the soft fluttery licks.

Was he stopping? What was happening?

She grabbed him by the hair, slightly embarrassed by her desperation, but he was like a boulder. Immovable. He responded by calmly removing her fist from his hair and then effortlessly holding *both* of her wrists in his big hand.

"I'm in charge. And you're going to come when I decide it's time for you to come. Not a second sooner."

That was a line from the book! And it was a line that had irritated the hell out of Alice's feminist sensibilities. She'd found it to be completely ridiculous and annoying and downright offensive. Women were in charge of their own orgasms. She'd highlighted it so she could rant about it at book club.

Beau must have read it, because he winked at her. And it turned her into a mass of spineless, thoughtless, and inhibition-less jelly.

Beau delivered two soft licks, a kiss, and a short suckle before dragging his tongue lower. Alice tilted her pelvis to give him better access to...She didn't even know to *what*. But her body knew. It absolutely knew what it wanted.

And so did Beau. He entered her with his tongue. Repeatedly.

He was literally—she searched for words and the only one she came up with was one she never used—*fucking* her with his tongue. And he was moaning while doing it, as if he were enjoying it as much as she was.

She wanted to grab his head. To pull him even closer. Or maybe it was to push him away. She didn't really know. She just wanted to grab him. But she couldn't because he still held her wrists in his hand and holy guacamole, that was hot. She gave a little yank, just to see if he'd yield.

He squeezed tighter.

Something built deep inside. It swelled and vibrated and Alice had no idea where it was going to go. She literally wanted to explode. "Oh, Beau. I think I'm going to—"

He stopped thrusting and gave one final lick to her clit.

That did it. Her eyes literally rolled back in her head as she climbed higher and higher, reaching for an unattainable crest, before *boom!* She exploded in wave after wave of pure pleasure. Her vagina clenched and contracted over and over, more intensely than she'd ever imagined it could, until she had the overwhelming sensation that she needed to sob, or possibly belly-laugh, which was something she never did. Beau gently bit the inside of her thigh, and she opened her eyes to see him grinning and looking exceptionally proud of himself.

That was fine. He'd earned it.

She lazily floated down the crest, noticing that sounds and sensations seemed far away, as if after all that stimulation, her body had decided to go numb. And she didn't mind at all...

Beau abruptly lifted his head. "Did you hear that? It sounded like a car door."

No, she hadn't heard it. "Maybe it's Dolly going somewhere."

"It's eleven o'clock at night."

Woof! Gaston started going crazy in the guest room. His collar jingled and then he started to howl, something he only did around her mom, who encouraged it, calling it "singing."

Oh, no! She slammed her knees shut, smacking Beau's face in the process. "I think that might be my mom. She's not supposed to pick up Gaston until tomorrow."

There was a knock at the door, and since her mom tended to do the knock-and-enter, Alice hopped off the couch and grabbed Beau's hand. "Come on!" she said, rushing him into her bedroom and closing the door.

"Anybody home?" her mom called out. "We saw your lights on and thought we'd pick up Gaston."

We? It was both of them? "Hold on," Alice called, grabbing her jeans off the bed.

Gaston howled from the guest room. "Oh, poor boy!" her mom said. "Why did your sister lock you in the guest room?"

Beau raised an eyebrow at Alice. "Sister?"

Alice rolled her eyes and slipped a T-shirt over her head. What was Beau thinking? His eyes were twinkling, so something about the situation was clearly amusing to him. But his brow was also creased with concern. "You know, Allie. For a minute there, earlier, I thought you were going to tell me you were a virgin."

He had to bring this complicated subject up now? While her parents were standing in the living room? She wasn't opposed to telling Beau about her lack of sexual experience, but now wasn't the time.

"Are you? A virgin?"

She couldn't say yes. "No, virginity is a social construct—"

Someone tapped on the bedroom door. "Alice, whose truck is that out front? And whose boots are these?"

Alice put her hand on the doorknob. "Put your shirt on."

He shrugged with a grin. "I can't. It's in the living room, along with my boots and the sheer lacy thing you were wearing."

Oh God. She looked at the window.

"I'm a twenty-eight-year-old man, Allie. I am not climbing out your window." Beau stood behind her and gently squeezed her arm. "It's no big deal, darlin'," he said softly. "We're all adults."

He was absolutely correct, although she didn't feel very adult at the moment. She grabbed his hand, and with a deep breath, she opened the door. "Hi, Mom. Hi, Dad."

Her mom's mouth formed a perfect *o* and her cheeks turned pink as Beau leaned against the doorframe. "Howdy, folks. How was your trip?"

The reaction her mom was having to seeing Beau Montgomery, shirtless and taking up every inch of the doorway, was apparently hereditary. Because Alice knew just how she felt.

Chapter
Twenty-Five

ꕥ

Alice opened her eyes. And then she shut them, because it was super bright.

Why? Why was it so bright? She opened her eyes again and grabbed her phone off the nightstand. Ugh. It was nearly nine thirty! She must have forgotten to set an alarm.

Don't freak out—it's not your Saturday to work.

Sultana was curled up next to her, completely unconcerned.

Alice worked every other Saturday at the library. And today wasn't her day. Still, she never slept in. On her mornings off, she liked to do chores and laundry and shopping lists and journaling. And yoga and meditation and reading. Anything but sitting around listless.

She got out of bed, stretched, and wondered what Beau was doing. She smiled. After her parents had so rudely barged in on them, Beau had (finally!) put on a shirt, and then they'd all set about the ritual of awkward chitchat.

Goodness, Beau. You've grown up.

Alice, do you still meet with those women in Austin? The ones who hate men?

She actually giggled out loud sitting in her bed. Yes, Beau had grown up. And no, actually, she hadn't met with her group in a while. She'd been busy tutoring and all of the delightful things that apparently went with it.

At some point, the awkwardness had morphed into comfortable, casual conversation. They'd looked at her parents' photographs of Costa Rica and heard all about their many adventures. It had been...easy. Relaxing. Fun.

The yoga mat was rolled up neatly in the corner of the room. Alice eyed it, looked at Sultana, who was snoring softly, and decided yoga could wait. In fact, everything could freaking wait. The world wouldn't grind to a halt if she stayed in bed for a while, so she leaned back and lazily watched the pretty patterns the sun made as it shone through the lace curtains.

She heard a car pull up. It was probably Dolly. Or maybe it was Mr. Dean, the letter carrier. The rest of the world was busy as usual, but Alice felt as if her little corner had slowed down. And it was nice.

There was a knock on the door. Who the heck could that be? It figured that the one day she decided to sleep in was also the day someone stopped by unexpectedly to catch her at it. Whoever it was, they went from knocking to pressing the doorbell.

Holy guacamole. What was the emergency?

Alice scurried to the living room in her pajamas. She parted the curtains to see Claire standing on her front porch, baby Rosa on her hip. And behind her, a red Porsche pulled up. Carmen was here, too?

Alice opened the door and Claire rushed in. "Wait for me," Carmen shouted, slamming her car door and jogging up the walk.

"I don't have much time," Claire said. "Rosa and I are on our way to open the store."

"I'm actually not in a hurry," Carmen said. "Jessica is home from her honeymoon and back at work, so I'm not even going into

Chateau Bleu today. That means you don't have to leave out any juicy details."

"Details?"

"Oh, please," Carmen said, heading into Alice's kitchen. "Beau took you home last night. Also, why don't I smell coffee?"

"I just woke up," Alice said, following her friends into the kitchen.

Claire started opening the cabinet doors.

"The coffee is next to the fridge," Alice said, watching Carmen grab the carafe and fill it with water. "I'm going to go, you know, brush my teeth and use the restroom."

"Be quick about it," Claire said. "Chop, chop!"

By the time Alice came back in the room, Carmen was pouring coffee and Claire was scrounging around for spoons. "They're—"

"Found them!" Claire said, holding up a spoon.

Alice nearly tripped over the baby, who was sitting on the floor having a staring contest with Sultana.

Alice wasn't used to having people show up unexpectedly. And she definitely wasn't used to them opening drawers and cabinets and putting their babies on the floor like they owned the place. She sat down at the kitchen table as Carmen poured the coffee.

A huge smile took over her face. These two felt at home in her kitchen. And she loved it.

"First of all," Claire said, sitting next to Alice. "You don't have to tell us anything."

"I didn't agree to that rule," Carmen said, taking a seat. "I want to hear every little detail."

"Well, I don't think I'm going to give *every* little detail. It's personal, you know. Just between me and Beau."

"Oh my God," Claire said. "Look at that smile."

"That is not a virginal smile," Carmen said. "That is the smile of carnal knowledge."

Alice laughed. She wasn't even going to get into the virgin thing with them. There was no point, and besides, it absolutely didn't matter. "We did not have sexual intercourse."

The disappointment on the women's faces was enough to make her start laughing again.

"He did give me a spectacular orgasm though, which was something I didn't think could happen, because generally speaking, women are in charge of their own—"

"Was it oral?" Carmen asked.

Alice nodded her head shyly.

"You should definitely keep that cowboy," Claire said.

Alice sighed. "I'm not sure that keeping the cowboy is an option. Our contract expires after the wedding—"

"Wait. There's an actual contract?" Claire asked.

Carmen and Claire shook their heads as if trying to wrap their minds around it, and Alice had to admit that it sounded kind of silly.

"Listen," Claire said, reaching out and touching Alice's hand. "I know you can't tell us what your agreement with Beau is actually about."

"And we wouldn't want you to," Carmen assured her.

"But, honey," Claire said. "From where we're sitting, it doesn't look like Beau is your fake boyfriend."

Alice bit her lip. "What does it look like?"

"Like he's your real one," Carmen said.

"You don't dance the way y'all danced because of a contract," Claire said.

Carmen nodded in agreement. "And you don't look at someone the way you look at Beau—"

"Or the way he looks at you—" Claire said.

"Because of a contract," they said together.

Alice had only had one sip of coffee, but her pulse was racing. Her relationship with Beau certainly didn't feel fake. And neither did the friendship she had with these women. In fact, her life and relationships had never felt so real.

Rosa crawled over to Claire and started slobbering all over her slacks. Claire picked her up and wiped the drool and cracker crumbs off her chin. "I've got to run. We're late opening up the store. But Alice, I've known Beau my whole life. He and Bryce are the closest things I've ever had to brothers. If I were you, I'd rip that contract up. You will not find a kinder or sweeter man. Playboy antics aside—and at least some of that is overblown, by the way—Beau is what my mama would call a keeper."

"But he said he's not looking for a relationship—"

"And you've said the same thing ever since I've known you. But what do you want now?"

Beau. She wanted Beau.

Someone else knocked on the door. "Holy guacamole, it's like Grand Central Station this morning."

She answered the door and found Brittany, red-eyed and puffy-faced, sniffing on her doorstep.

"Oh no!" Alice said. "What's wrong?" She was proud of herself for not adding the word *now*.

"It would take less time to tell you what isn't wrong," Brittany said, limping her way into Alice's living room. "My cousin Margo has appendicitis."

"Oh dear," Alice said. "I'm sure she'll be fine. The mortality rate for appendicitis is extremely low."

Brittany looked at Alice like she was nuts. "My aunt says she can't be in the wedding now," she wailed.

"Oh."

Brittany threw her hands up. "So, I have an extra groomsman."

"How . . . tragic?" Claire said.

Brittany became very still, eyeing Alice carefully. "Aren't you about a size six?"

Dang it. She was a perfect size six.

* * *

Beau turned off the coffeepot and washed the plates in the sink. It was ten o'clock, and this morning he'd be following Bryce up to the Rockin' H to help him settle in. Then he'd be coming back here, to Rancho Cañada Verde, until Wednesday, when he'd head back to help Bryce get the place ready for Brittany's wedding.

The wedding. Just thinking about it set off a domino train of emotions. He'd get to be with Alice again, and barring uninvited parents, he was going to make love to her properly. And he was for damn sure looking forward to it. But it also meant the expiration of their contract. And he was not looking forward to that at all. He rubbed his temples. "Bryce! Better get a move on if you still want to hit the Rockin' H by noon."

He was trying to act as if everything was cool. Like today was like any other day instead of the day he was helping Bryce move out.

Memories played through his mind like a movie reel. Blanket forts and tree houses. Wrestling through the small living room and into the kitchen, their mama hot on their heels threatening to get after them with a flyswatter. The smell of fresh-baked cookies when they came home from school. A Christmas tree in the front window with two matching bikes beneath it. He had very few memories that didn't include his brother. Being half of a twin unit was a natural state for him. Unless he'd been at his special spot on the bluff—the only place he ever went alone—he'd always been half of a whole.

Bryce came in and smacked him on the shoulder. "I just packed the last box. Do you have room for it in your truck?"

"Yep. On the front seat."

Bryce pointed at the window over the sink. "Remember when you got stuck trying to sneak into the house while drunk on your ass? You finally managed to fall into the sink, breaking the faucet."

"I didn't have a choice. Mom locked the doors and all the other windows."

"Yeah. She really wanted you to work for it."

"And she was sitting in the dark, waiting for me, like some kind of freak in a horror film. Scared the shit out of me. And then she acted like it was my fault the faucet was broken."

"It was your fault. God, our poor parents. The emergency room visits alone should have sunk them."

No kidding. Their parents had earned their retirement on the Gulf Coast. "It's a good thing your new place is furnished. Otherwise we'd be fighting over the couch."

"We've already battled over the cookware and small appliances."

"I can't believe you're taking the spaghetti pot and the fucking blender."

"You don't use either one. And anyway, we might have to fight over the couch later. I'm thinking about getting an apartment in Austin," Bryce said. "And it won't be furnished."

Beau turned to face his brother. "Oh? Why would you do that? Gerome said you could live in one of the lodge's suites."

"I think it might be fun to live in the city," Bryce said. "It would only be about a twenty-minute drive out to the Rockin' H—"

"Ha. It'll take you twice that long just to get out of the city limits. Austin traffic sucks."

Bryce just shrugged as if city traffic didn't bother him in the least. "You ready to run this place all by yourself?"

"Yep. On Monday, I'm installing those new solar panels and getting the battery bank set up—"

"Were you able to read the instructions?"

"Good enough."

Bryce frowned, and it made Beau bristle. He was good at putting things together, and he had the diagrams.

"Do you want to fire up the new software program?" Bryce asked. "Take a look at it one last time? I'm still kind of figuring it out, myself…"

"Nope. Allie helped me with it last weekend. I know which tab takes me where and how to enter the correct information. I even emailed a report to Ford last week—no problem."

"That's great. I told you Alice would help you, and I was right. Looks like it's working out very well." He shook his head with a grin. "I'm surprised you came home last night."

"I wanted to be here with you this morning. Also, her parents barged in on us."

"No way! That sucks."

"It was fine. They're nice folks."

Bryce nodded. "So, from what I saw on the dance floor last night, you and Alice are really dating, right? Nothing about the way you two were clinging to each other looked like anyone was holding a gun to your heads."

Beau tried to hide a grin. Failed.

"That's what I thought," Bryce said.

"You think too much."

"Well, you've been pining for her ever since you sprouted your first ball hair, so—"

"I'm not sure the feelings are mutual."

"She's pretty straightforward. You should just ask her."

He was afraid of the answer. Because if he was nothing more to Allie than a buddy or maybe even an item on her bucket list, he really didn't want to know about it until the contract had expired. But what they'd done last night had felt different than the good times he'd enjoyed with other women. It had been so hot. And yet, strangely sweet and so...*Alice.*

She'd been sexy. Bossy. But he'd sensed moments of innocence and vulnerability, too.

Bryce crossed his arms over his chest and grunted softly.

"What?" Beau asked.

"I just find all of this interesting."

"Why?"

"Because it's you and Alice, dummy."

Beau grabbed the rinsed plates and put them in the drying rack. He and Alice *did* make an unusual couple, that was for sure. He shouldn't get his hopes up. "Bryce, do you know what a social construct is?"

Bryce rubbed his chin. "Hm...I suppose it's something that only exists because society says it does. Why?"

Beau frowned. "Oh, no reason. It's just a term I heard. Wasn't sure what it meant."

He still wasn't entirely sure, but it sounded like Alice's definitive statement that she wasn't a virgin might not mean what he'd thought it had. Not that it mattered, except that, well, it did.

He couldn't quite put words to the emotions swirling around his head as to *why* it mattered, but just thinking about being the first man to make love to Alice made him feel giddy.

He'd never been with a virgin before. It seemed like a huge responsibility. There were emotions involved. Expectations and whatnot. But hell, if Alice had held on to her virginity this long, didn't it mean it was special to her? And did that mean that *he* was special to her?

After all, she'd amended the contract.

Bryce poked him in the arm. "Keep your head on straight. I don't think Alice is the kind of woman who dates casually. And you're not usually the kind of guy who dates seriously."

"And you're typically not the kind of guy who dates much at all, so why would I take any relationship advice from you?"

"I'm your big brother."

Beau snorted, because it was by a whopping four minutes, but truth be told, he didn't mind the dynamic at all.

Bryce stood up straight. "Giving you advice is my job. Whether or not I know what I'm talking about is neither here nor there."

Beau laughed. "Grab that box, dumbass. I'm ready to have you out of here."

They went through the door, and Bryce didn't even linger on the porch steps. He was on his way to his new life.

Beau inhaled the crisp scent of juniper. Somehow, standing right here on the porch of the house where he'd grown up, he felt as if he was starting a new life, too.

Chapter
Twenty-Six

Beau took the toll road off of Interstate 35 so he wouldn't have to deal with Austin traffic—reading lots of signage while trying to remain focused on the road was hard—and the eighty-five-mile-per-hour speed limit made up for the extra miles.

All he could think about was Alice and when they could be together again. He hadn't seen her on Monday, because he'd worked so late on the dang solar panels. Yesterday, she'd had something to do in the evening. And today, he was heading back to the Rockin' H to help Bryce out. They had to sort the Hills' herd to get rid of some bulls, and of course there was a bit of work to do for Brittany's wedding.

But Alice was filling in as a bridesmaid for Brittany's cousin, which meant she'd be here a day early for the rehearsal. He smiled and shifted in his seat. He was looking forward to picking up where they'd left off the night her parents had shown up, but mostly he just wanted to *be* with her. He missed her. And he missed the way he felt around her. Capable. Smart. Confident.

He exited the toll to catch the farm-to-market road to the ranch. It was pretty country, although not in the same way that Big Verde was pretty country. There were no hills with twisting and turning roads. But there was plenty of bright green and heavily irrigated land for grazing, and that was a sight for a cowboy's sore eyes.

There was also urban sprawl leaking out of Austin. Interspersed between the pastures and farmland were brand new subdivisions and strip malls with their chain restaurants and shops. None of it appealed to him, but apparently, it did to Bryce.

He slowed his pickup to navigate a tight curve, and then followed the trail of YEE-HAW! signs with the Rockin' H brand (soon to be replaced) all the way to a super-fancy gate. He turned in and slowly drove up a curvy road bordered by lush green pastures and fat, sassy cows.

Up ahead he saw Bryce, sitting on a gate and waving his hat. Good Lord, but the fool looked ridiculous in his fringed chaps. And he was also wearing a vest like he was a fucking Walmart greeter. Beau stopped the truck and rolled down his window.

"Howdy, pardner," Bryce said in an exaggerated drawl.

"You look like an idiot," Beau said. "Get in the truck."

Bryce laughed, but didn't seem offended as he hopped off the gate. "Oh, brother, you don't know the half of it." He pointed at a little badge hanging on his vest. "I've got a name tag."

COWBOY BRYCE

Beau rolled his eyes.

"There's one for you back at the office," Bryce said. "Along with a vest and chaps."

Beau sighed and shook his head as Bryce climbed in the truck and slammed the door. "It's not so bad. In fact, it's kind of like being on vacation. You wouldn't be half bad at this gig. You're way more outgoing than I am."

That was true, but Beau had no interest in leaving Rancho

Cañada Verde. It was his home. And his work—as a *real* cowboy—was important to him. "I think I'll stay in Big Verde, where the cowboys cuss and spit and stink like proper ranch hands."

"Just pull up to the offices," Bryce said. "I've got to pick up the schedule for tomorrow."

"Schedule?"

"Yeah. It's a busy week. We've got a corporate group coming in, a family reunion, and of course, we're getting ready for Brittany's wedding."

"I didn't realize that you were going to have to deal with all of that when you took this job."

"Me either. It's kind of fun, though. And I can't very well chase cows through a wedding reception," Bryce said. "The herd has to share space with humans and their human-type shenanigans. The guests like to see us riding around and working. It's weird. But fun."

Beau pulled up to the building that housed the dude ranch's office. He waited while Bryce went inside to grab the schedule. A couple of guys wearing the same getup as Bryce walked by and waved, and then Beau saw a familiar blue head exit the restaurant connected to the lodge. What the heck was Carmen doing here?

Beau was just about to roll down his window and holler at her when Bryce came out and the two collided. He dropped the clipboard he was carrying, and Carmen dropped her keys. Then they both leaned over and bumped heads.

Even from this distance, Beau could see that Bryce was blushing. And that was strange, because Beau had always been the blusher. Probably because he usually had something to be embarrassed about.

Bryce handed Carmen her keys and watched her walk to her car. Like he *really* watched her walk to her car.

Good lord, his brother was barking up the wrong tree. Carmen would never fall for a cowboy. And even though she'd been hanging out in Big Verde while Jessica was on her honeymoon, Carmen would soon be off on some adventure doing God only knows what. That's just how she was.

Bryce fumbled his way back to the truck and climbed in.

"What's Carmen doing here?"

"She's catering Brittany's rehearsal dinner and wedding," he said, flipping through the pages on his clipboard. "She's using the old restaurant's kitchen."

"That's good."

"Can you keep a secret?"

"You know I can."

"She's going to buy it. Which would be fucking fantastic for the ranch. She says she's going to call it the Rockin' Bleu."

"You're right about that being great for the ranch. But is that the only reason you're excited?"

Bryce blushed again and pointed through the windshield. "Drive on over to the lodge. I'll show you where your room is, but first, let's head to mine so we can print up some paperwork to take to the cattle market on Friday."

Beau parked in front of the lodge, grabbed his shit, and followed Bryce inside. The suite looked a bit homier since the last time he was here, but it was still quite small. He could understand why Bryce might want an apartment in Austin.

Bryce dropped the clipboard on the bed, and Beau picked it up. He reached in his pocket and pulled out the little flexible ruler Alice had given him, placed it below the first line on the top page on the clipboard, and began reading. Initially, the words moved around a little, but the ones above the ruler mostly stayed put. Sight words stood out—no decoding necessary—and then, a few of the others were easily read. Soon, he was moving the ruler down the page at a pretty good pace.

"Are you really reading that quickly?" Bryce asked.

Beau smiled. "Yeah. Alice is a good teacher. She says dyslexia is just a different way of processing information, and that it can be common among creative people. Did you know that? Anyway, she believes in me."

"I believe in you, too, Beau. I always have."

"Thanks. I don't know what I would have done without you all these years."

"Well, we made some mistakes."

"Fixing them now, though."

"And don't worry. I'm going to keep you plenty busy for the next two days. School with Miss Martin will be back in session before you know it."

* * *

Alice stood in front of the full-length mirror and gasped in horror. Over her shoulder, Claire was likewise staring, clearly trying to suppress a giggle.

"Oh, Alice," Brittany said. "You look beautiful!"

Alice did *not* look beautiful in the hideous yellow dress. "You say your cousin is already up and walking around after her surgery? Are you sure you don't want her to be in the wedding?"

"God, no," Brittany said. "She looks awful. She's lost weight— we'd probably have to get this dress altered. And she has dreadful bags beneath her eyes. Can you imagine how that would look in the pictures? And she's whining and complaining constantly. Can't stand up straight. You'd think she fell off a twenty-story building."

"Well, she did have abdominal surgery," Alice said.

Brittany nodded. "Oh, I know. Bless her sweet little heart."

After the appropriate pause (typically about three seconds for a *bless her heart*), Brittany added, "I'm so glad you're a size six."

"Me too," Alice said, forcing a smile.

"Let me go grab the earrings," Brittany said. "I left them in the car."

"Are they yellow, too?" Alice asked.

"Yes," Brittany said with a bright smile, heading for the door. "Sunflowers! To match the theme. They'll look so great right up against your pretty face! Be back in a sec."

As soon as Brittany was out the door, Claire broke into hysterical laughter. "Oh my God," she said. "Right up against your face! Yellow is really your color, Alice. It brings out—"

"The sallowness of my skin?"

"I'm just kidding. You actually look lovely."

Alice flopped onto the bed. "How did I end up in this position?"

"By being too nice. Not knowing how to say no."

"Women, in general, are too nice," Alice said.

"We should rebel," Claire said. "We should just stop being nice. Kind of like when you broke the habit of mindlessly saying you're sorry—"

"Which is something *all* women do," Alice added.

Claire nodded her head. "Sorry. You're right."

Alice raised an eyebrow.

"Dang it! I said it, didn't I?"

"It's so hard to stop," Alice said. "But if I did it, anybody can."

Claire gave her a thumbs-up. "So, are you and Beau sharing a room?"

Holy guacamole. Alice hadn't thought about that. When they'd struck their bargain, she'd planned on doing a pop-in at the wedding reception and then driving back to Big Verde that night. But so much had changed. For one thing, she was a bridesmaid now and couldn't do a pop-in. And then there was the fact that her fake relationship didn't feel fake anymore. The prospect of sharing a room didn't freak her out at all. But she didn't want to make assumptions. Even if she and Beau had sex—and she was pretty sure they would—that didn't necessarily mean he'd want her in his bed all night. "Brittany says I can have her cousin's room."

Brittany limped back in. "Found the earrings!"

Oh dear. Big yellow sunflowers. Brittany handed them to Alice. "I think you have everything you need. Oh wait! Do you have a pair of cowboy boots? All the bridesmaids are wearing them."

"Yes," Alice said, faking cheerfulness. "A brand-new pair. Beau helped me pick them out."

Brittany sighed in relief. "Thanks, Alice. For everything. Also, your boyfriend is so cute! I always thought I'd end up with a cowboy. But here I am with a computer geek."

The glowing smile on Brittany's face indicated she didn't mind a bit.

"Thanks," Alice said, even though she wasn't sure if that was the appropriate response to someone complimenting your boyfriend.

"I've got to run and do like a million and one things," Brittany said. "Don't forget about the bachelorette party!"

"Bachelorette party?"

"You're invited since you're a bridesmaid. There are going to be strippers. Woot!"

Crap. Strippers always gravitated to Alice at these types of events. Claire said the mortified expression on her face was irresistible to them.

"Yay," Alice said, swallowing a lump of dread. "I'm looking forward to it."

"Okay," Brittany said, giving her a hug. "You're the best. Oh, and I already told the other bridesmaids that they can just call you Alice."

"What else would they call me?"

"Well, usually they refer to you as Miss Martin because you're so much older than us."

Claire made a noise that sounded like an old man choking on a chicken bone.

"Yes, I much prefer they just call me Alice. I'm not a card-carrying member of AARP yet."

"You're kind of a cougar, though," Brittany said. She formed her hands into claws and made a growling sound.

This was too much for Claire, who had moved past the chicken bone noise to general goose-honking.

"Well, I'm off," Brittany said. "I can see myself out."

As soon as Brittany had limped away, Alice turned her back to Claire. "Get me out of this thing."

"Okeydokey, Miss Martin. And then maybe you should take a little nap so you can keep up with that young whippersnapper you're dating."

Chapter
Twenty-Seven

❦

Beau put his bag in the corner of the room and hung his cowboy costume on the back of the closet door. Then he looked around.

The rooms at the Rockin' H were really nice, even if they were a little over the top with the cowhide theme. Normally he'd be in the employee quarters or the bunkhouse. But since he hoped to spend some private time with Alice—it might be their last weekend together—he'd gone ahead and booked the room.

He and Bryce had gone into town for supper. They'd waited for a table for forty-five minutes at a crowded steak place where the entire staff came out to sing "Happy Birthday" every three minutes. It was so noisy they could barely have a conversation, and the steaks were tough. But Bryce hadn't seemed to mind (well, he'd bitched about the steaks) and had even suggested taking in a movie before heading back to the ranch. But Beau had begged off. He had some work to do on his laptop, and also, he'd gotten the fourth Jax Angle book and was dying to get after it. He'd been following Alice's suggestion to alternate reading with listening, and damn if the reading wasn't actually getting a whole lot easier. He might try to forgo the listening altogether for the fifth book.

He stretched and cracked his neck as he opened up his laptop. The ranch program icon stared up at him, and he felt the familiar surge of agitation at the sight of it. But then he heard Alice's voice, calm and reassuring, in his head.

Just click on it—I promise it won't bite.

He clicked on it, and then he opened the folder he'd brought with him. It had all the tag numbers of the cattle they'd hauled in from Big Verde. He was surprised by how easily he was able to identify the spreadsheet for the Rockin' H. But there it was, and it was as clear as a bell.

Rancho Cañada Verde looked very different from *Rockin' H*, but he didn't even have to rely on the tricks he and Alice had devised. Because he was actually reading it. And he could hear the words in his head, which was something he'd never been able to do before.

It was kind of cool the way the program automatically removed the tag numbers from one database when he entered them into another. And tomorrow, when they hauled the Rockin' H bulls to auction, he'd be able to record that into the database, as well, along with how much they weighed, how much they brought in dollars, and who had bought them. And everyone—Gerome, Ford, and Bryce—could see it with a touch of a button or the swipe of a phone. Cool.

He leaned back in his chair, stretching his legs out in front of him. His belly was pleasantly full, and all he needed was a shower and then he was going to crawl in bed with Jax Angle.

That sounded wrong. He still couldn't wait, though.

He closed his laptop and peeled off his shirt. Tomorrow morning would come early. This might be a dude ranch, but it was still a ranch, and Bryce would no doubt have him up at the ass crack of dawn.

He went into the bathroom and turned on the shower, then came back out to grab a fresh pair of underwear while the water heated up. His phone battery was low, so he plugged it into the charger.

Five minutes later he was lathered up. The soap smelled nice. Kind of fancy for a cowboy, but whatever. He ran his head under the spray to rinse the shampoo out of his hair.

The heat eased his sore muscles, and he touched a cheek to each shoulder, loosening up some tightness there. He squeezed the taut ridge extending from his neck. Rubbing your own muscles never felt as good as when someone else did it, but he worked out some knots, anyway.

Alice had melted at his touch when he'd rubbed her neck in the truck. She'd actually moaned, and that's when he'd known how easy it would be to make her fall apart. And damn, had she fallen apart. He licked his lower lip as if maybe he could still actually taste her...

It made him hard.

He rolled his head and dropped his chin to his chest as trails of lather and foam cascaded down his belly and around his cock, which was now throbbing. That sucker was going to need some attention, or he'd never be able to concentrate on his book, much less get any sleep.

He closed his eyes, thinking about Allie walking out of her bedroom in that frilly, sheer get-up. She'd looked so fucking cute. And shy. And then she'd proceeded to spread her legs and brazenly give him an anatomy lesson.

Vulva

Labia

Clitoris

Latin was hot.

He stroked himself, long and slow, because he wanted to drag out the memory. The way she'd dipped her finger into her—

His phone rang from the other room.

He scrunched his eyes shut tighter, determined to ignore it. Whoever it was could leave a message. Unless it was Nonnie. He had assumed the responsibility of keeping an eye on her when his folks moved to the coast. And whenever she tried to leave him a voice mail, she talked before the beep and all he ever heard was *okay, bye now, see you then*, or, best of all, *but don't worry…*

Fuck. He turned the water off, and he and his raging boner hopped out of the shower and ran into the other room. He took a running leap for the phone; certain it was going to stop the minute he touched it.

Without really registering who was calling, he hit the slider on the screen.

Alice's face popped up.

He was on FaceTime.

* * *

Beau looked shocked to hear from her. Maybe she shouldn't have called. "Is this a bad time?"

Beau's mouth opened and closed. And his eyes were absolutely huge, as if she'd just jumped out from a closet and yelled *Boo!*

"Um…"

There were fumbling sounds, and she got a bit dizzy as Beau moved the phone around. There was a picture on the wall, a desk, the floor…

"Beau?"

His face came back into view. "Sorry. I didn't realize we were on FaceTime until I'd already answered."

He appeared somewhat calmer, but his eyes glanced around as if he were looking for something. He was shirtless. And wet.

"You caught me getting out of the shower," he said with a dimpled grin. "Let me grab a towel."

"I have the worst timing," she said. "I hope you didn't get out just for me."

A mirror came into sight, and for a brief second, Alice caught Beau's reflection in it. And he wasn't just shirtless. He was naked.

Her pulse started racing. Part of it was the surprise. But the other part was the sheer perfection of those muscular butt cheeks.

"You have perfect timing," Beau said, walking into the bedroom. "I'm glad you called."

Her eyes searched the tiny screen, just in case she'd get another mirror image of Beau's backside, but no such luck. Beau sat on the bed and smiled, and it set her heart to thumping even more than the sight of his butt cheeks had.

"I can call back if you want to get dressed," Alice said.

Beau leaned back against the headboard. "Nah. I'm good."

There was that twinkle. He was torturing her on purpose.

"I have a reason for FaceTiming," she said, as if he hadn't just leaned back naked on a bed right in front of her.

"Oh yeah?"

"I want you to see what I'm wearing." She'd put the yellow dress back on, just so he wouldn't be shocked by her outfit when it came time for their "date."

Beau's smile slipped away. "Is it crotchless?"

Alice rolled her eyes. "No. Hold on. I'll show you."

She reversed the image so Beau could see her in the full-length mirror in all her jaundiced, ruffled glory. "What do you think?" She flipped the image back so she could see his face. He was probably laughing—

Nope. Not laughing. "Oh my God, Allie. You look so beautiful."

Was he joking? Because she looked like a school bus.

"It reminds me of that princess dress you wore to Anna's Halloween party a few years ago."

Oh, dear God. She'd gone as Belle from *Beauty and the Beast*. And he was right. Did Brittany realize that her bridesmaids' dresses were Disney princess gowns? Also, Beau remembered what she wore to a Halloween party four years ago? They hadn't spoken. In fact, she hadn't even known he was there.

"You look pretty," Beau said. "You always look pretty. Even when you're wearing a bloodstained dress and yelling at me about noise ordinances."

"It wasn't blood. It was Carmen's energy drink. And you and your lady friend were being totally obnoxious."

Beau laughed. "Allie Cat, you had the wrong room. I was all by my lonesome that night. Nobody was with me."

"Why didn't you say so?"

"Because you'd have left. I'm sorry I've always annoyed you so, but it's the only way I can get your attention."

"You can have my attention any time you want. All you have to do is talk to me."

"About what? Cows?"

"Well, sure. Or any number of things. I like talking to you, Beau."

A slight blush crept across his cheeks. "I like talking to you, too, Allie."

"You don't have to go to any great lengths to get my attention," she said.

Beau grinned, and the devilish glint came back. "So, let's say, if a cowboy wanted to get your attention, he wouldn't have to do anything so extreme as this…"

Beau's face disappeared from the screen, and suddenly she was looking at his shoulders, dotted with water.

"What are you—"

And now it was his glistening chest. Had he lost control of his phone? Maybe he was resettling himself, or reaching for something, or…

The phone moved lower, to Beau's ripped abs. His hand made an appearance, lightly brushing over the delicious landscape, like a gameshow host showing off the big prize.

Silently, Alice urged Beau's phone to go lower, and it did. But the man was covered in a towel. What a tease!

Beau's face reappeared in the phone—lopsided grin—so apparently, the tour was over.

"Do I have your attention, Miss Martin?"

Alice nodded, because, boy, did he ever.

"You know," he said, with a bashful little gaze that was what Claire would call sin on a stick. "I was thinking about you in the shower."

"You were?"

"Yeah. I was thinking about you real hard."

Real hard. Maybe he meant it had taken a lot of concentration. Maybe *hard* didn't refer to an erection. Maybe she just had a dirty mind and...Dang it! She'd been trying really hard not to think of sex in those terms.

"And then I was um, interrupted by my phone. So, I didn't get to..." He raised his eyebrow. "Finish."

So, they *were* being dirty. And holy guacamole, dirty was fun. But was Beau admitting to masturbating in the shower? Not that there was anything wrong with masturbating *or* admitting to it. But he was clearly flirting. She should say something sexy back. "I hope you were able to rinse all the soap off."

She winced. What a stupid thing to say!

Awkward silence, followed by a sigh. "You're going to make me spell it out, aren't you?"

Actually, if Beau could spell *masturbation* that would be awesome.

"H-A-R-D..."

Oh. He wasn't going to spell *masturbation*.

"C-O-C-K."

Alice fanned her face. She was getting heated, no doubt the result of synthetic yellow fibers and the talk of a hard cock.

"That's what thinking about you does to me, Allie. Do you want to see it? I don't send unsolicited dick pics. So, you'll have to ask for it."

Things were crystal clear now. Which was actually how Alice preferred it. Still, she should probably try to be a little playful. "I've shown you mine, so yes, I think it's your turn to show me yours."

Beau raised an eyebrow. "You're going to have to do better than that. What, specifically, do you want me to show you?"

Alice bit her lip. Beau clearly wanted her to talk dirty (there was that word again), and she wasn't very good at it. "I want to see you," she said. "All of you."

"Like, my shins? My toes? My elbow? Can you be more specific?"

Beau was exasperating. "You know dang well what I'm talking about."

"I'm a little dense, darlin'."

"No, you're not, Beau Montgomery. And I would like you to show me your chest, followed by your abdomen, followed by your"—she lowered her voice to a whisper—"erect penis."

"That's assumptive."

"How?"

"We've been talking so long. How do you know it's still erect?" *Oh no!*

Beau laughed. "I'm just kidding, Allie. I'm as hard as a rock."

Whew. Good. "You can show me now. I'm ready."

Beau smiled. "Here we go. Feel free to take screenshots if you see anything you like."

She wasn't going to do that. At least she didn't think she was.

Beau's face left the screen, and it was quickly replaced by the sun-kissed skin of his muscular chest, and Alice licked her lips. Slowly, the camera went lower, down to his abdomen and its clearly defined six-pack.

Alice broke out in a light sweat. She liked to think she was attracted to men for their minds (and she was—Beau was super smart!), but she was only human. And humans were biologically and evolutionarily programmed to be attracted to strong physical specimens for the perpetuation of the species. Beau was a strong physical specimen. And even though she was not interested in ever having kids, her cells twerked and shouted, *This one looks good! Make babies with this one!*

She clenched her thighs. Science could be super irritating and uncomfortable. Especially when it made you want to lick someone's skin. Which is what she wanted to do right now, because Beau looked tasty.

White terrycloth came into view, along with Beau's fingers, which tauntingly toyed with the knot in the towel. And even though it wouldn't be the first time Alice had seen a penis—she could label a diagram—she'd never seen Beau's. Not clearly anyway (underwater at the river didn't count). And she'd certainly never seen one via FaceTime. It was playful. Sexy. Delicious.

He pushed the towel down to below his tan line, and Alice's mouth watered. But then he moved, and all she saw was his grinning face again. "You've got a bit of drool on your lower lip there, girl."

Alice rolled her eyes. Because she was absolutely not drooling. Much. And also, he'd called her *girl*.

Beau laughed. "So, do you want the towel to come off?"

Inside her head, Alice hysterically screamed *Yes!* But what came out of her mouth was: "If you're comfortable with it, then I'm comfortable with it."

"So you're saying…"

"Drop the towel, Beau."

Beau's smiled slipped away. "Yes ma'am," he said. And then he lowered his voice and added, "I like it when you tell me what to do."

Beau's chest and abdomen once again filled her screen, and then he opened the towel, revealing his very hard penis resting against his belly. It was slightly lighter in color than his tanned flesh, and maybe it was the screen's tiny size, but it looked...large.

The view tilted, and Beau's face came into focus in the distance. "Stunned speechless?"

"Yes, actually."

"Are you saying I've finally found something that will shut you up? And that it's been in my pants this entire time?"

Alice couldn't think of a single thing to say. So apparently, the answer to his question was yes. Her eyes were glued to her phone, and his penis came back into view, along with Beau's hand. He stroked himself. Just once.

"Is this okay with you?" he asked. "I mean, I don't know if you've ever messed around on the phone..."

"Does Candy Crush count?"

"Not even a little."

"Then no. I'll have to add it to my bucket list."

"Do you want to see me finish what I started in the shower? Because that's the kind of messing around I have in mind."

"Okay," she squeaked.

His hand continued stroking. And Alice watched closely, because she wanted to know just how it was done.

"You can talk to me if you want to," he said. "And I know you want to."

She did have a few questions. "Well, the glans is supposed to be the most sensitive part of the penis. So why aren't you touching it?"

Beau laughed. "So much for dirty talk. And I don't usually start out touching the head of my dick. Too sensitive in the beginning."

That made sense. Alice couldn't usually handle direct clitoral stimulation unless she was really aroused. "Some people are embarrassed over masturbation," she said. "But did you know it can decrease your risk of prostate cancer?"

Beau laughed again. "Oh, Allie, you really know how to turn a guy on."

"Sorry. I'll be quiet."

"No. Don't stop talking. I like the sound of your voice, no matter what you're saying."

She knew the kinds of things he wanted her to say, and she wanted to say them. But it was just so hard. She took a deep breath. "I'm really turned on right now."

"Oh yeah?"

"Yes. I like looking at your penis. It makes me..." She hesitated. She could feel the chastity belt tighten, and it seemed to have moved up to her throat. *Just say it!* "Wet. It makes me wet."

Beau groaned. "Fuck, Allie."

She felt a little naughty. And surprisingly, very in control. And being in control was her happy place. Maybe she'd say some more things.

"I want to taste it."

Beau breathed heavier. Louder. Faster. And speaking of faster, his hand was really moving now. Definitely no longer avoiding the glans. She'd turned him on. For real. With just a few words.

"And I want to feel it inside me," she said. The words had gushed out, as if the dam holding them in had finally broken.

Beau's hand was practically a blur now. Alice couldn't even see his penis. "Beau, I want to see your face."

His face came back into view. He opened his eyes briefly, startling her momentarily with their intensity. But then they rolled back and his eyelids fluttered shut. His lips parted. His breath came in quick gasps and pants, and his cheeks were flushed. *Very flushed.* Even for a blond.

"You're so beautiful," she said. "I'm never seen a more beautiful man."

Beau opened his eyes and smiled, although she could tell by his breathing and the shaking of the screen that he hadn't stopped stroking himself. "There's another guy who looks just like me so…"

"No. I see *you*, Beau. Just you. And you're beautiful to me."

The image stopped shaking and Beau stared right at her. *Right into her.* Then he let out a ragged breath and the activity started back up. "God, I want to come, Allie."

"Don't close your eyes," she said. "I want you to look at me when you do it."

Beau gasped and although he blinked a couple of times, he managed to keep staring into the camera.

"Oh, fuck, Allie," he groaned.

"Are you close?"

Beau's eyes rolled back, but he fluttered his eyelids, as if trying to force them to stay open. "Not until you tell me," he gasped.

She stared into Beau's eyes. He was a large, sexy hunk of a man— a sexually experienced one—and he was putting her in charge of his most intimate and personal act. He groaned, as if he couldn't hold out much longer, and his eyes pleaded for his release.

"Come for me, Beau."

She was surprised by the authoritative tone of her voice, but Beau didn't seem surprised at all. He was rolling with it. His lips parted. His cheeks flushed even brighter and his forehead shone with per-spiration as he panted and gasped, still somehow managing to hold on to his phone. "Oh God, Alice. Alice…Alice…Alice…"

He said her name as if it were a personal mantra, and then let out a long, shattering sigh. His eyes fluttered shut, and he just lay there, panting.

Alice was panting, too. The way he'd held her in his gaze while seeking his release was the most intimate moment she'd ever experienced. Even though he hadn't touched her. And oh, how she longed for his touch.

"Beau," she whispered.

He smiled, eyes still shut, and said, "Yes, darlin'?"

His speech sounded almost slurred, as if he was drunk on the pleasure hormones that were probably coursing through his body.

What had she wanted to say when she'd whispered his name? "I miss you," she finally said.

His smile grew even larger, but he still didn't open his eyes. "I miss you, too. Hurry up and get here."

Chapter
Twenty-Eight
❦

The young woman on the other side of the counter seemed to be using an unnecessary amount of pink tissue paper to wrap up such a small object, but maybe that's the way they did things in fancy lingerie stores.

"Are you sure we can't help you with anything else?" she asked, looking up at Beau through her fluttering false eyelashes. Her name tag identified her as Bekki.

Although he clearly hadn't purchased such an item for his mama, Bekki didn't seem to care. She had been on him like a fly on a horse since the moment he'd walked through the door, and it wasn't just for the sales commission.

"I think I'm good," he said, slipping his credit card back in his wallet. He was still reeling from the sticker shock. When he'd asked Carmen where a guy could buy some fancy underwear, she'd sent him to Uptown Boudoir. He'd known he was in trouble the minute he'd walked through the door.

Some places just smelled expensive, and Uptown Boudoir was one of them.

"This is a lovely gown," Bekki said. "Do you mind if I ask who it's for?"

"It's for—"

Shit. What could he say?

It's for my reading tutor.

It's for my former babysitter.

It's for my fake girlfriend.

"Never mind," she said. "We're trained in discretion. I shouldn't have asked."

Great. The woman thought he was cheating on someone. And if anyone was less trained in discretion than Bekki the underwear sales associate, he'd eat his hat. But he just smiled, took the fancy bag full of tissue paper, and exited the store to walk across the blistering pavement to where he'd parked his truck. Damn, it was always hotter in the city. Too much concrete reflecting the sun. He longed to get back to green pastures and Mother Nature.

He climbed in the truck and set the bag on the seat next to him. He wanted to pull the nightgown out and imagine it on Alice, but it was wrapped up tighter than Fort Knox. It would take twenty minutes just to locate it. He looked at his watch and quickly started the truck. He didn't have twenty minutes. He probably shouldn't have stopped to shop after dropping the bulls off at the market, but he'd wanted to get something nice for Alice.

His phone chimed with a text. He looked at it, and right away the words "bull" and "horny" and "fence" popped out.

He knew exactly what was going on without figuring out the rest. The bull had busted through that weak spot in the fence they'd been worried about. He'd gotten the gist of the message in like two seconds.

Now slow down and focus on context.

The rest of the message was easy to read.

Horny bull busted through the fence. Will ruin tonight's rehearsal dinner. Get your ass back here.

Beau responded with a thumbs-up emoji. Then he pulled out onto the highway, eager to get back and help. He absolutely didn't want Brittany's rehearsal dinner ruined.

He was going to have to round up a frisky bull and also repair the fence where the damn thing had busted through. It was hard to know how long it would take, but he was definitely going to be late for the rehearsal dinner. In fact, he and Bryce trying to round up a bull might end up being the entertainment.

And then after the dinner...

He shifted in his seat. He couldn't wait for tonight. He might be making love to Alice for the first time, and it might *actually* be her first time. It should be special. Hence the lingerie.

There was no hiding anything from Allie now. Last night, he'd fucking jerked off in front of her. Maybe it was just a fun and kinky thing for Alice to mark off her list—*FaceTime shenanigans—Check!*—but it hadn't been shenanigans for Beau. He might have blown more than just his load. He'd probably also blown his cover. Had she sensed how overcome with emotion he was? She claimed it was hard for her to read people, but he felt like an open book in front of her.

Christ. This was more than a crush. It seemed he was fucking in love with Alice Martin. And he didn't think there had been a single day, hour, or minute since he was twelve years old that he hadn't been.

* * *

Alice twirled in front of the mirror, admiring the way the navy skirt flared. She'd walked over to Carmen's suite after checking into her room. She wanted an opinion about the outfit she'd chosen. "What do you think? Should I add a string of pearls, or are they too blah for the cream blouse?"

"It's hard for me to say which is more blah, the blouse or the pearls," Carmen said.

"Really? The whole thing is blah?"

"Not for jury duty. But for a party? Yes. And you've got two to attend."

"Two?"

"Did you forget about the bachelorette party? It's right after the rehearsal dinner."

Alice groaned. She really wasn't looking forward to it. "I don't want to go to *either* party, honestly. And clearly, I have no idea what to wear—"

Carmen put a hand in front of Alice's face. "Shh. Let Auntie Carmen find you something appropriate."

Oh dear. The last time Carmen had given Alice something to wear, she'd ended up in cutoff shorts and a pink T-shirt that said MEOW.

"I think the dinner portion is kind of, you know, nice-ish," Alice said.

Carmen stopped digging in her suitcase long enough to give Alice a side-eye. "I'm literally catering the thing. And it's outside in the middle of a pasture. I don't think it's all *that* nice."

"Sorry," Alice said.

"I thought you'd stopped saying that."

"Dang it."

Carmen laughed and went back to scrounging in her bag. "Aha!" she said, holding up a pretty blue sundress with a small floral print. "This isn't quite my style, and I honestly don't know why I bought it. But I think it's going to look adorable on you."

Alice looked in the mirror. The dress was short, but not *too* short. And blue was her color. "Thanks, Carmen. It's really cute."

"You're very welcome. Now hurry up and put it on. I've got to head to the kitchen and check on things, so I might not see you until the bachelorette party."

"Are you catering that, too?"

"I'm showing up with a few trays of canapes and a margarita machine. But I'm staying for the strippers."

Alice groaned as Carmen headed for the door. "Loosen up, buttercup! I hear they're wearing chaps and not much else, so it's going to be a good time."

There was only one man that Alice wanted to see in chaps, and that was Beau.

She sighed. What did a person do when she'd developed very real feelings for her fake boyfriend? Every time her phone chimed, she hoped it was Beau. Every time she saw a cowboy hat, she hoped it was Beau. White ranch truck driving by? Maybe it was Beau.

When she was with him, she felt like herself, only *more*. She'd had a taste of Beau Montgomery, and now she wanted all of him.

Last night, Beau had shared his very essence in one of the most private and intimate human acts. And he hadn't just invited her to watch. He'd invited her *in*. He'd held her with his eyes, breathed her name with his release.

She shivered at the memory.

Tonight would be their night. They were going to make love. And Alice had no intention of marking it off her bucket list. Because it wasn't about that anymore. It was about being with Beau.

She stripped down to her undies, but before she slipped into the sundress, she removed her bra and covered a breast with her hand, letting the nipple peek out between her fingers. She snapped a pic, and then with a quick rush of adrenaline, she sent it to Beau.

She never thought she'd do something like that, but she never thought she'd fall in love—*was that what this was?*—with a cowboy, either.

With her heart still pounding, she got dressed. And Carmen knew what she was talking about, because the dress was absolutely darling. She took another picture and sent it to Beau, too. Then she brushed her hair. But instead of putting it up in her usual ponytail, she decided to leave it down. She felt different. So, why not look different?

Her phone chimed, sending a thrill coursing through her. What was Beau going to say about those pictures? Maybe he was sending one back—a quick peek at some delicious part of his body or just his gorgeous grin...

It wasn't Beau. It was an email from the Austin Public Library.

Subject line: Congratulations

Holy guacamole. She got the job! She plopped onto the bed, staring at her phone. Had she read it wrong? Nope.

She felt...proud. Pleased. Valued. Accomplished. And... somehow, not the least bit interested.

How was it that only a few short weeks had passed since she'd thought there was nothing keeping her in Big Verde? How had she been so blind? Her family was in Big Verde. Her friends— because yes, she had friends—were there, too. Not to mention her pride and joy, the Big Verde Public Library, which she'd basically built from scratch.

Why did she feel like such a different person?

Beau Montgomery.

It was true that she was a good partner to herself. And that she'd worked tirelessly on self-improvement. But it was being with Beau that had freed her. She'd finally emerged from her cocoon! It had taken seeing herself through Beau's eyes before she could fully appreciate her own uniqueness. She stood up and looked at herself in the mirror. She *was* pretty. And you know what? She had a sense of humor. And she freaking loved to have fun! All in all, she was kind of cool.

Someone knocked on the door. Maybe it was Beau! She opened it and...It was Claire and Maggie.

"Wow," Claire said. "I've never seen a more disappointed face."

"Sorry—"

"Stop saying you're sorry," Maggie said. "I'd be disappointed, too, if I were expecting a hunky cowboy and got me instead."

Alice laughed and stepped out of the doorway. "Well, I'm not disappointed. I'm delighted."

"And cute!" Claire said. "Where did you get that dress?"

"It's Carmen's. She found the skirt I brought to be a bit dour."

"Were we supposed to bring skirts or dresses for anything other than the wedding?" Maggie asked.

Although Claire wore one of those long maxi dresses, Maggie was distinctively more casual in a pair of shorts and a black T-shirt.

"Not unless you're going to the rehearsal and the dinner," Alice said.

"I'm invited to the dinner because I made all of the bridesmaids' bouquets," Claire said, sitting on the bed.

Maggie sat next to her. "We came a day early for a little getaway. Thank God I don't have to suffer through the rehearsal. Everybody acts as if the world will stop spinning if someone heads down the aisle one second too soon. That's why I didn't have a rehearsal for my wedding."

"Maybe if you had, you would have known not to walk down the aisle first," Claire said.

"I was the bride," Maggie said. "It made sense for me to go first. Also, Travis was standing at the end, and I was anxious to get the official part over with so I could rip his clothes off."

"Well, I was your maid of honor, and that's not how it was supposed to work," Claire said with a grin. "But Travis looked super hot that day. I don't really blame you."

Maggie sighed. "Bless his heart. He was so nervous." She seemed to lose herself for a moment, but then she snapped out of it. "What are they serving at the rehearsal dinner? Maybe I'll come."

"Brittany wanted a chuckwagon dinner," Alice said. "Carmen wasn't too thrilled about it at first, but once she started getting fancy with quail, venison, and baby back ribs—"

"I'm in," Maggie said.

Claire looked at her. "You weren't invited."

Maggie shrugged and popped her gum. "I'll pretend to pass out hors d'oeuvres or something."

"And then after the dinner, there's the bachelorette party to suffer through," Alice said.

"There's a bachelorette party?" Maggie asked, clapping her hands.

"How dare Brittany leave us off of that particular guest list," Claire said. "I mean, she's got strippers and everything."

Maggie jumped up off the bed. "Strippers?" She looked at Claire. "We're going, right?"

"Oh, absolutely," Claire said. "If nothing else, we'll pretend to serve as chaperones. All the bridesmaids are so young."

"Not all of them," Alice added dryly.

"Poor darlings," Claire said. "Personally, I am loving my thirties. And I think my forties will be even better."

"Same," said Maggie. "I feel like I've finally gotten my shit together."

"Speaking of getting one's shit together," Claire said. "Alice, have you heard from that library in Austin? Are you going to be moving on to bigger and better things?"

"As a matter of fact, I heard just a few minutes ago."

Both Claire and Maggie raised their eyebrows expectantly.

"I got it," Alice said.

Maggie pouted. "Oh. Well—"

Claire cleared her throat. "We're so happy for you! It sounds like a wonderful opportunity, doesn't it, Maggie?"

Maggie smiled, but her dark eyebrows were still drawn into a scowl. The result was somewhat hilarious, especially when Claire poked Maggie with an elbow, making her yelp. Alice's heart warmed. That was the only way to describe it. It was like having a chest full of honey. "Listen, you two—"

"Hold up," Claire said. "Before you say anything more, *we* have a few things to say."

"We really are excited for you," Maggie said, rubbing her arm where Claire had poked her. "And proud of you. And we'll help you in whatever way you need. Like, do you need to borrow a pickup truck? We'll help you move."

"No. I don't think—"

"What we're trying to say," Claire said, "is that we support you. But, Alice, I've thought back to our teenage years, and well, I'm sorry if you ever felt left out. And if you were ever hurt by anything I said or did—"

"Oh, never!" Alice said. "You were never anything but kind, Claire."

Maggie touched Alice's shoulder. "If you remember, I was a tomboy and mostly hung out with the FFA boys. The worst day of my life was the day Grandma Honey made me buy a bra. But if I ever did anything to hurt you—"

"Never," Alice said. "It was nothing anyone personally did. And thanks, guys, for your support and friendship. But I really should let you know—"

Someone pounded on the door, and Maggie rushed to open it. Bubba stood there, holding a beer. He poked his head around Maggie and looked at Alice. "Anna is barking orders at everyone, and she says you're two minutes late to the rehearsal."

Anna ran all the wedding rehearsals of Big Verdians. Nobody knew why. But she was good at it, and it gave her all sorts of opportunities to snap at folks, so she seemed to thoroughly enjoy it.

"Oh, yikes! What's gotten into me? I'm never late."

She grabbed her purse and headed for the door, thinking, *Happiness apparently equals tardiness.*

If this was going to become a habit, she'd need to set her watch ahead by two minutes.

Chapter
Twenty-Nine

❦

Claire caught Alice on her way out of the rehearsal, which had been long, hot, and boring. They'd practiced walking down the aisle over and over and over…

"This way to the hayride," Claire said, pointing to a large, noisy tractor pulling a flatbed trailer loaded with hay.

"Hayride?"

"How else would we get to the chuckwagon dinner?"

Alice immediately thought of multiple ways, but it didn't matter. She was already being herded onto the trailer, where she sat on a hay bale next to Claire. "Miss Martin, are y'all comfortable enough?" one of the bridesmaids asked.

"Yes, thank you," Alice said.

Claire leaned in and whispered, "You should have asked for a hemorrhoid pillow and a lap blanket. We're clearly the senior citizens on this hayride."

Alice snorted. "This is a little over the top, don't you think?"

"All weddings are over the top nowadays. I can't wait to turn this place into the Rockin' Rio Verde. We are going to throw the *best* events. And guess what?"

"What?"

"Carmen is buying the restaurant! She's going to call it the Rockin' Bleu. It'll be her first foray into fusing French and Western chuck and barbecue. Doesn't that sound fun?"

Alice nodded. It really did sound fun. And it also meant Carmen would be around more!

The trailer lurched forward. "Where's Maggie?" Alice asked.

"In the chuckwagon."

"What is she doing in the chuckwagon?"

"Trying to blend in, I imagine."

Alice raised an eyebrow. Maggie was good at a lot of things, but blending in with catering staff probably wasn't one of them. "Where's your hot date?"

"Out with another girl," Claire said. "The last time I saw Ford, he and Rosa were sleeping in a hammock next to the shuffleboard court."

"Aw, that's sweet—" Her phone chimed. It was a message from Beau!

How was rehearsal?

Just the sight of the simple question set her heart to hammering in her chest. Her cheeks warmed as she read it again, lingering over each and every word, simply because Beau had typed them. Goodness, she was an idiot. This was hardly a love note, so why did it feel like she had a giggle trapped in her throat?

Claire leaned over for a peek, and Alice jerked the phone away.

"Is it from Beau?"

"He's just asking about the rehearsal," she said. *And setting my heart on fire.*

She typed out her answer. It was okay. Are you going to make the dinner?

Three little dots appeared, and Alice bit her lip while waiting for his response.

Yes. Be there as soon as I can. Might be late.

Yes! She officially had a date for this shindig. And it wasn't just any date. It was Beau.

Her phone chimed again, and when she looked at it, she gasped. It was a picture of Beau's fly, and it was open. He had two fingers slipped inside, and there was a gigantic bulge in his jeans.

Thinking of you.

She quickly shielded her phone from Claire's prying eyes.

"What are you grinning about?" Claire asked.

"Nothing."

"Oh my God!" Claire shouted. "Did you just get a *dick pic*?"

Everyone on the hayride became deathly quiet. And they were all looking at Alice. She assumed a prim and proper pose, and then very quietly, she said, "Yes."

The hayride erupted in whistles and whoops of laughter.

* * *

Beau removed his work gloves and slapped them against a fence post to shake the dirt off. Then he crammed them in his back pocket. "Goddammit," he said. "By the time I get back to the room for a shower, I'll miss most of the rehearsal dinner."

Bryce slapped him on the back. "I'm sure Alice will understand. You had to work."

Beau sighed. His brother was right about both things. He absolutely did have to work, and Alice would totally understand. But he wanted to be there with her. He wanted to be there *for* her. As her date.

"I think you should hop on your horse and crash that dinner cowboy-style. Hell, I'll go with you. I wasn't invited, but Carmen will slip me a plate."

Beau looked down at his jeans and dirty boots. "We're dirty. We smell like cow shit."

"Speak for yourself. I smell like a spring bouquet."

Beau doubted that. "Well, let's at least ride by."

They mounted their horses and rode for about five minutes. When they came over the hill, the campfire area where they held the chuckwagon dinners was buzzing with activity. Beau's mouth watered when the scent of grilling meat hit his nostrils. Both he and Bryce picked up the pace, and soon they were galloping toward the party.

Folks saw them coming and started waving.

A blue head—Carmen—weaved in and out, and he looked for the familiar brown ponytail that got his blood boiling, but didn't see it.

They slowed to a trot, and then Bryce did a fancy dismount by swinging his leg over and riding sidesaddle before taking a leap. That particular trick had originally been devised to impress the ladies, but it seemed to be coming in handy on the dude ranch, because everyone cheered. And Beau had to admit that with the ridiculous fringe flying, it looked kind of cool.

He dismounted like a normal person and calmly tied his horse to the hitching post. While Bryce accepted applause and handshakes, Beau started looking for Alice.

He scanned the crowd. All he saw was blonde, blonde, redhead, blue head, bald head, wavy brown hair, black hair...Where the hell was Alice? His eyes flitted back to the wavy brown-haired woman, who stood alone, holding a drink, and his heart sputtered and knocked like an old Ford tractor.

Alice looked up, and their eyes met. Suddenly, the boisterous noise of the party dimmed, and Beau's vision narrowed until Alice was the only thing he could see. He quickly headed her way, single-mindedly ignoring the folks who tried to say howdy.

He removed his hat. "Sorry I'm late—"

Alice rose on her toes and kissed him. Her lips were warm and soft and tasted like wine. When she broke the kiss, he had to reach for her hand, because the sudden disconnect made the earth tilt.

Hold on to me…

"You look handsome," she said.

He grinned and shook his head as he replaced his hat. "I'm dirty and sweaty. I can go take a quick shower—"

She squeezed his hand. "Stay with me."

"Okay." He finally relaxed enough to get a look at her. And damn. Did she know how beautiful she was? He doubted it. "I like your hair that way."

"Thank you."

"I mean, I like it in a ponytail, too. Not that it matters. What I think. Because you don't make yourself pretty to please someone else—"

"I like pleasing you," she said. And then she bit her lip as a slight blush crept up her neck.

Beau bent his head to whisper in her ear. "You please me very much, darlin'."

Alice's breath hitched, and she put her hand on his chest. He thought for a moment that she might push him away, but then he felt her small hand grip his shirt, and she pulled him closer. "You please me, too."

God. It was such a simple sentence. Four little words. But they turned his insides to mush. He searched for something to say and came up empty.

They were yanked from the eye of the storm by a booming voice. "Y'all hungry?" The barbecue sauce on Bubba's shirt indicated he'd already eaten.

"Starving," Alice said. "Where's Trista?"

"Dropping the kids off in Round Rock with her sister. She'll be here tomorrow. And you should go get some food. Carmen said I can't have seconds until everybody's had firsts."

"I was just waiting for Beau."

"Well, he's here now," Bubba said, looking Beau up and down. "And wearing chaps."

"It's required," Beau said with a grin.

"Why don't y'all go grab yourselves some plates and come sit with us?"

Alice touched Beau's sleeve. "Go sit down. I'll bring you a plate."

Alice was offering to fix him a plate? No way. He was her date, and he was going to take care of her. "I don't mind fixing my own plate. In fact, why don't I get yours?"

Alice grinned. "If you insist."

"I do."

She did that thing again. The thing where she rose up on her toes and kissed him. Right in front of Bubba.

As Alice walked away, Beau was left grinning like an idiot. Bubba raised an eyebrow and tapped his beer bottle against Beau's. "Good save, bruh."

"Pardon?"

"If you let that girl fix you a plate, it's all over."

"I don't know what you're talking about."

JD walked up. "Are you tossing that plate theory around again, Bubba?"

"It's not a theory," Bubba said. "If a woman fixes you a plate at a social function, she plans to marry you."

"That's ridiculous," Beau said. "Alice doesn't ever want to get married to anybody."

Bubba shrugged. "I said what I said."

"What are you even doing here?" JD asked Bubba. "Which one are you related to?"

"The groom is the son of Trista's aunt's second cousin by marriage," Bubba said.

The ties that bound the folks of Big Verde to their ancestral trees were sometimes long and excessively thin, but they were strongly respected where weddings and funerals were concerned.

"Brittany is related to me somehow," JD said. "My mom started to explain it, but then she got confused and told me it was a *towels-only* relation."

Bubba nodded. "Yep. That's what Trista said."

"What the hell does that mean?" Beau asked.

"You buy them a couple of towels—"

"Or more if they're the small ones you just wipe your hands on," Bubba said.

"Yep," JD said. "There's a hierarchy. A full place setting of china is at the top—for like a first cousin if your mamas are on speaking terms."

"A can opener is for the marriages you think won't last or the ones you don't approve of, like when Misty Oliver married Sam Berhman after dating his brother for three years."

"Gabriel and I got a can opener from Miss Mills," JD said.

Gabriel, who was wearing little Brianna in a backpack, walked up and nodded in agreement.

Beau shook his head. Luckily, his mom didn't pay attention to all that uppity small-town social circle nonsense. She'd married a cowboy and stuck to her garden and horses. She always said she could tolerate horses a lot better than she could tolerate people.

Beau, JD, and Gabriel wandered over to the food line, where they found Carmen loading up a plate for Bryce. "Are you trying to work your way to my heart through my stomach?" Bryce asked.

"Nope," Carmen said. "Snatching your heart would only require undoing the top button of my blouse. I sure as hell wouldn't knock myself out with pheasant piccata."

Bryce laughed and took his plate. "Where are you sitting, little brother?"

"With the invited guests," Beau joked. "I think you might need to go sit behind the chuckwagon."

"Invitation or no," Carmen said. "Neither one of you should be anywhere near the white tablecloths."

"They're fine," JD said. "Bryce, there's plenty of room for you at our table."

"I tell you what," Carmen said. "I'll let you boys sit with the civilized folks if you do me a favor."

"What is it?" Bryce asked.

"I don't have time to explain right now."

"Well, I hate to agree to something without even knowing what it is."

Carmen crossed her arms over her chef's jacket, which was unbuttoned well past the mark that would win Bryce's heart, and raised a single eyebrow.

"Yes, ma'am," Bryce said.

Beau snorted. "I'm not agreeing to a damn thing."

"It's for Brittany," Carmen said.

Aw hell. Beau looked at the table where Brittany sat sniffling.

"Okay, fine," he said. "Can I have two plates? One is for Alice."

A few minutes later he was sitting at the table, barely tasting his food—which was no doubt delicious—while his knee bumped against Alice's, or her shoulder rubbed his, or she laughed at something somebody said, sending a waterfall of utter fucking delight washing over him.

She did not seem embarrassed at all by his dirty clothes or five o'clock shadow. In fact, at times, when she looked at him, he sensed something akin to…pride. Like she was both pleased and proud to be with him.

He wiped his mouth on a napkin and then brushed a strand of hair out of Alice's face. She'd been talking about genealogy—something about the origin of the pedigree chart—and stopped to smile at him.

That smile. It seeped into his pores and filled him with a skin-tingling warmth, like that first delicious moment of wrapping yourself in a towel fresh from the dryer. The grand clock of the universe slowed down, stretching the moment, as they linked hands beneath the table.

"Ahem," Carmen said.

When had she arrived? And why was everyone grinning at them?

"Beau Montgomery, did you hear a single word I just said?" Carmen asked.

"Nope. You must have been mumbling."

"She needs to speak with us," Bryce said.

"All the men at this table, please come with me," Carmen said.

Alice looked at Beau and shrugged. "No idea what's going on."

Beau and the rest of the guys followed Carmen back to the chuckwagon and gathered around.

"Listen," she said. "Nothing is going right for Brittany today."

They all nodded. That was pretty obvious.

"And her bachelorette party is tonight."

They all nodded again. Maybe Carmen was going to ask them to help set up tables or carry ice chests of beer.

"And her strippers canceled."

"Aw, hell no," Bryce said. "No way. Uh-uh."

JD's mouth opened as reality set in. "You've got to be kidding."

"Nope. Four of the Mount 'Em Cowboys ate some bad barbacoa last night. So Brittany's uncle Howard has offered to play the ukulele instead, and that is the saddest thing I've ever heard."

Bryce winced. "Well, we can't have that."

One of Brittany's bridesmaids came to the back door of the chuckwagon. "Do you have any more napkins? Brittany has saturated hers with tears."

"Jesus," Beau said, shaking his head.

Carmen handed the woman a roll of paper towels. "You tell Brittany to dry her eyes. She's going to have some cowboy strippers. Isn't she, boys?"

"I'll do it," Bubba said with a shrug. "No problem."

"Me too," Bryce said quickly. He rotated his pelvis with a wink, getting a blush and a grin out of Carmen.

"I'm in," JD said. "Why not? I've got the moves."

Carmen eyed him up and down. "Dad bods are in now, so thanks."

Gabriel busted out laughing, and JD raised the brim of his Stetson to look his husband in the eye. He was clearly trying to maintain a stern expression, but he couldn't swing it. He finally broke out in a grin and said, "Who's your daddy?" and everyone cracked up.

"I'm bowing out," Gabe said. "I've got to look after Brianna."

But then it got quiet. They were all looking at Beau.

"I've kind of got plans for this evening…"

"Alice is going to be at the bachelorette party," Carmen said. "Go take a shower. Wear your chaps—make sure these other guys get some—and meet us in the High Chaparral Party Room in an hour."

Chapter Thirty

🌹

Beau arranged the last two rose petals carefully on the bed and took a step back to admire the results of his labor.

A bottle of champagne chilled in the mini fridge. He'd snagged two crystal flutes from Carmen's stash of catering goods, and they sat on the small table, surrounded by more roses and a plate of chocolate-covered strawberries. Oh! One thing was missing.

He picked up the black bag with gold letters and waded through all the pink tissue paper to extract the negligee he'd bought at Uptown Boudoir. It was as light as air and as slick and smooth as the rose petals he'd just sprinkled on their pillows. It definitely wouldn't make Alice itch.

He draped it carefully across the end of the bed and set a single, long-stemmed rose on top of it.

If tonight was to be Alice's first time, he was determined to make it special for her. She deserved to be worshiped, and he was, well, he was going to church.

He jumped as someone knocked on the door. "Mount up, cowboy!"

It was Bryce. They'd come back to take quick showers and get ready for the bachelorette party.

"Just a minute," he hollered, grabbing his phone and wallet. He didn't want to let Bryce into the room, so he planned to quickly slip out.

Bryce tried to push his way in anyway. "I'm a little early," he said. "And Carmen said we shouldn't arrive too soon or we'll ruin the surprise."

Beau held his ground. "What do you say we head to JD and Gabe's room and pop open some beers?"

"Sure thing," Bryce said. "And damn, brother. Do I look as good as you do?"

Beau rolled his eyes. They both looked like idiots in chaps and hats with no shirts. "Nah. I look way better, as usual."

He started to pull the door closed behind him, but Bryce stuck his boot in it. "Hold up. I need to take a leak."

Before Beau could stop him, Bryce was in the room. "Don't get excited," he said. "None of this is for you."

"How about one of those strawberries?"

"Nope."

Bryce turned to face him. "You've gone to a lot of trouble here."

Beau just kind of shrugged.

"So, when you asked me about that social construct thing. What was that in regard to?"

Had he given it away with all the excess? It didn't matter, because he wasn't going to discuss it. "It's private."

Bryce sighed. "If this is about what I think it is, you should be careful. Make sure everybody is on the same page. You don't break hearts, remember? So, don't hurt Alice."

"Bryce, it's not Alice's heart you should be worried about. It's mine."

Bryce raised an eyebrow. "You've been crushing a long time.

But once you've scratched an itch, you don't tend to mess with it again, if you know what I mean."

"It's more than an itch. I think I'm in love."

"Oh. Wow. Well, how does Alice feel?"

"I know she likes me a lot. But beyond that... Do you think she could fall for a dumbass cowboy like me?"

"You're a damn good cowboy. And a fine man. Alice Martin would be lucky to have you. Now move out of my way, I drank a lot of iced tea with dinner."

By the time Bryce came out of the bathroom, someone else was pounding on the door. "That must be the rest of our dance team," Bryce said, rolling his eyes. "You ready?"

"As ready as I'll ever be."

Beau yanked the door open to a ridiculous sight. Bubba stood there wearing chaps, jeans, and a grin. Behind him were JD and Travis. And only two out of the three had the sense to look embarrassed.

"Pretty cool, huh?" Bubba said, flexing his biceps.

Beau and Bryce pulled the door—didn't want anybody peeking in the room—just as Carmen pulled up in her fancy car, tattooed arm hanging out of the window.

"Which one of you is willing to jump out of the huge cake I just rented?"

"A cake? Are you kidding me?" Travis asked.

"I'll do it," Bubba said. "Do I get the first piece?"

"It's not the kind of cake you eat, dummy," JD said. "And anyway, you won't fit in it."

"You don't know that for sure," Bubba said. "Carmen said it's huge."

"I'm sure there's a label on it that says if you've won the Apple Festival beer belly contest five years in a row, you shouldn't attempt to get in the damn cake," JD said.

"Hey, I was only runner-up last year—"

"Boys!" Carmen shouted. "The cake is gigantic. Probably big enough for Bubba. And let's be honest. Even though a couple of you look good enough to eat, everybody tells me Bubba is the best dancer in Big Verde."

Bubba crossed his arms over his chest and grinned.

All of this was going to make Alice extremely uncomfortable. She'd squirm and blush, possibly while quoting a study of some sort or another, and Beau was going to love every minute of it.

JD squinted across the parking lot. "Oh, hell no."

Gabriel and Ford were headed their way. And they weren't alone. Ford carried little Rosa, Gabriel had Brianna in the back-pack, and Henry pulled his sister Maisy in a wagon. "Hey!" Maisy called. "Where's your shirts?"

Maisy couldn't make the *r* sound very well, and it was fucking adorable.

"We lost them," Travis said, bending over to pick up his kid.

Brianna looked down at JD from the baby backpack. Then she grabbed one of Gabriel's ears and leaned around to shout in it. "Daddy lost his shirt, Papa."

"I know," Gabriel said, wincing. "Don't worry. We'll help him find it later."

"Why are y'all here?" Travis asked. "You're supposed to be babysitting the kids."

"You didn't think we were missing the show, did you?" Gabriel asked with a dimpled grin.

"This is entirely inappropriate," Carmen said. "But I guess you can't make anything worse than it already is. When I left the party, Brittany's uncle was tuning his ukulele, and I just bumped into Miss Mills, who's headed that way with her Bible. So, you might as well bring toddlers. But you'd better hurry, or you'll miss the whole dang thing. I can tell when a party's going to end early."

Ford shifted Rosa from one arm to the next, but she seemed particularly taken with Bubba. She reached for him, and Bubba took her from Ford without any hesitation. With four daughters, he was no stranger to girl babies.

"You'd better cover them titties," Ford said, nodding at Bubba's chest. "She's hungry."

* * *

Alice sipped her cocktail—it had an actual cock in it, hardy har-har—and waited for her team member to pass the cucumber. They were taking turns sculpting them with pumpkin-carving tools. They each had just a few seconds to whittle before passing the cucumber on to the next person. At the end of the game, they'd compare cucumbers to see which team's sculpture most resembled a penis. And at the end of it all, the prize would be...*a penis-shaped flashlight!*...to go along with the penis necklaces and the penis unicorn horn headbands.

"Alice," Claire said. "What's the plural form of penis? Is it peni?"

"No," Alice said. "It's penises."

"I figured it might be like octopi or hippopotami," Maggie said.

Claire gave Maggie a poke. "Stop talking and start carving." Then she leaned over and whispered, "This party blows."

"Oops!" Maggie said. "I just decapitated our penis."

The young women at the next table giggled and whispered as the timer buzzed, and Maggie passed the cucumber to Alice. "Here. Fix it."

"I heard them refer to our table as the senior citizen section," Claire said, nodding at their competition.

"I'm a proud senior citizen," Miss Mills said. "Alice, it looks like you're carving the Washington Monument. Have you never seen a penis?"

Nobody knew who had invited Miss Mills, but she'd dutifully shown up and insisted on leading an opening prayer before the penis unicorn horn headbands were passed out.

Alice felt badly for the pointy penis. Maybe she could save it, but it would be hard to carve a glans into it. Maybe she'd forgo the glans entirely and try to carve the dorsal vein.

Beau's rather large penis popped into her head—*Boing!*—and she momentarily forgot where she was or what she was doing. The result was another large chunk taken out of the cucumber.

"Oh my God," Maggie said.

Alice examined it. "It's not that bad. Maybe I can—"

"Henry is here."

"Hi, Mama!" Henry said, running up and giving Maggie a big hug. "What'cha doing?"

Maggie gasped and ripped the penis horn off of her head. "Nothing. What are you doing here?"

"I'm only nine. It's not like I can stay in the motel room by myself."

Someone at the next table stood up. "Um, Brittany? More elderlies have shown up, and they've brought kids."

Alice turned to see Ford and Gabriel standing at the door. Ford was carrying Rosa and pulling Maisy in a wagon, and Gabriel had Brianna in a backpack.

There was a flurry of activity as everyone began shoving penises into their purses and underneath tablecloths and, in some awkward cases, sitting on them.

Brittany looked like she might start crying again, so her uncle—the same one she'd been trying to fix Alice up with—started strumming his ukulele in an attempt to soothe her.

"We're just here for the show," Gabriel said. "You ladies can just carry on with whatever you were doing."

Ford swatted at the penis horn on Claire's head and said, "And what was it you were doing?"

Claire pulled the headband off. "What the heck, Ford? Y'all are a bunch of party crashers."

Ford shrugged and whispered, "It doesn't look like much of a party."

"There is no show," Brittany said. "The strippers aren't coming."

Alice had been the only person at the party who wasn't disappointed about it. She had a problem with the objectification of women *or* men. And also, with all the needless thrusting, she was afraid someone could get hurt.

Carmen walked onto the stage and cleared her throat. "May I have your attention? I know we're all bitterly disappointed that the Mount 'Em Cowboys had to cancel, but I'm excited to announce that we have a plan B. So, everyone, please raise your voices and lower your expectations for the Just Buckin' Around Boys!"

A few people clapped, but not enough to cover the sounds of Brittany crying.

Ford dragged a chair over, and he and Rosa sat next to Claire as Carmen wheeled a cake onto the stage. This generated some excitement, and when the music began and the top of the cake burst open, the women clapped and whistled with vigor.

After a small struggle, Bubba popped out, wearing a grin as big as his hat. Then, as the intro to "Save a Horse, Ride a Cowboy" rang out, Travis, JD, Beau, and Bryce strutted onto the stage.

Alice covered her mouth with her hand, and then she burst out laughing.

"They lost them's shirts," Maisy said with a tiny shrug. When she spotted Travis, she shouted, "Hi, Daddy! Daddy, over here!"

Travis smiled and made a heart sign with his hands, and the women went nuts.

"That was the sound of about twenty pairs of ovaries exploding," Claire said.

"Yeah," Maggie sighed. "I'm pretty sure Travis just made me pregnant again."

"I think he might have even made me pregnant," Miss Mills said. "And I no longer have a uterus."

Little Brianna bounced in her backpack. "Let me out, Papa!"

Gabriel turned so that Ford could extract Brianna. She ran straight to JD, who picked her up and put her on his shoulders.

By now, all of the men were line dancing, just like they did on Saturday nights at Tony's, only shirtless. And they were pretty dang good at it. Bubba served as their front man, wowing the crowd with his unexpectedly agile—and sexy—moves.

"Come on, Ford," Claire said, rising. "Let's go join them."

"Dammit," Ford said, following Claire with Rosa in his arms. "I thought I dodged the plan B bullet."

Maggie and Travis followed with Henry and Maisy, leaving Alice sitting at the table with Miss Mills. Someone tapped her on the shoulder and she looked up to see Beau. In all the commotion, she hadn't even noticed he'd left the stage. "Come on, darlin'. And you, too, Miss Mills."

"Beau, I don't know the steps. Believe it or not, I've never line danced."

Miss Mills stood up. "Oh, heavens. I'll teach you."

By the time they got to the stage, everyone in the room was dancing. And with the help of Beau and Miss Mills, Alice picked up the steps quickly. She laughed and turned, hands on her hips, and belted out the ridiculous lyrics with everyone else.

She was having the time of her life. In fact, she'd been having the time of her life for the past five weeks—ever since she'd signed the contract with Beau. What if it didn't have to end?

Chapter
Thirty-One

❦

Alice was a ball of nerves as Beau pushed the door to his room open.

"Allie, you should know that I kind of, erm…"

"What?"

"Decorated."

He flipped the light on and Alice gasped. Roses were everywhere. Along with candles, which Beau proceeded to light.

"I hope this is okay," he said.

Okay? He hoped it was okay? She'd never seen anything so romantic in her life. It was perfect.

"I hope you don't think I'm being too forward. If you're not into it, we can sweep all the rose petals off the bed, blow out the candles, and eat chocolate-covered strawberries while we watch TV."

She squinted at him. "Are you seriously worried about being too forward? You sent me a dick pic just a couple of hours ago."

"It was technically not a dick pic. I didn't actually let the horse out of the barn."

Alice laughed. "I think all of this is lovely. And we're on the same page. I want... Well, Beau, I want to make love."

Beau sighed. "Thank God. Oh, and I got you something. You don't have to wear it if you don't want to." He pointed at a gorgeous silk nightgown. "I saved the receipt. I can take it back. It's all good. Whatever you want. Like I didn't buy it for *me*..." He started laughing. "Sorry. Can you tell I'm nervous?"

Beau was nervous?

She picked up the nightgown. And wow. "Is this silk?"

"I think so," Beau said. "I thought it felt nice."

This had to be expensive. Surely, he didn't buy gifts like this for all of his lovers. None of this felt fake. Not Beau. Not the silk. And not their feelings. "It looks like a perfect fit. Thank you."

"You're welcome. Do you want to, you know, put it on?"

"Yes."

Beau sighed and took his hat off. *He'd been nervous!* God, it was charming and sweet. And also unbelievably sexy.

"What you guys did for Brittany tonight was pretty special."

Beau laughed. "Poor girl. She seemed to finally be having a good time though."

"It was way better than a typical stripper show. And at least Brittany didn't have to sit in the dreadful chair while some guy sweated all over her."

There was a light sheen of sweat still covering Beau's chest.

"So, ladies get lap dances, too? I didn't know that. I'm not a big lap dance guy myself. If a woman is going to rub herself all over me, I'd prefer she do it because she wants to."

"I bet plenty want to," Alice said.

Beau grinned and didn't deny it. "Want to sit in the chair?" He grabbed one from the little desk and set it in front of her.

"Like, for a—"

"Lap dance," Beau said with a wink.

"From you?"

"Who else?"

Holy guacamole. She suddenly couldn't remember a single thing she didn't like about lap dances, and she was trying really hard. Beau leaned over and kissed her on the nose. "Why don't you go put that fancy nightie on, darlin'? Me and this chair will be waiting for you."

Alice made a split-second decision. "Okay."

She went into the bathroom and slipped on the gown. Definitely silk. Definitely expensive. She turned this way and that, appreciating the way it felt on her skin, hugged her curves, and dipped low in the back. This was way better than the itchy little number with the crotchless panties.

She shook out her hair, squared her shoulders, and walked out of the bathroom.

Beau was leaning against the desk, his hand on the back of the chair. He'd put his hat back on. His thumb was hooked in the pocket of his jeans, one boot was kicked back, and boy, was he hot. He licked his bottom lip as his eyes traveled up and down her body.

"Damn, woman," he finally said. "You just knocked the air out of me. I can hardly breathe."

She was experiencing a similar reaction. And when Beau hit a button on his phone and Dierks Bentley's "Come a Little Closer" floated out, it was all she could do to continue standing.

"I believe this is your chair," Beau said. "So, have a seat. And hold on."

She sat down and took a deep breath as Beau began moving his hips to the music in a way that made his abdominal muscles do all kinds of wonderful things. He was a good gyrator.

She somehow managed to land her eyeballs on his face, and he was grinning from ear to ear. "You doing okay, darlin'? I'm not making you uncomfortable now, am I?" He tilted her head up with his hands. Ran a thumb across her lower lip.

She was dreadfully uncomfortable, but not in the way she'd

expected. Instead of being embarrassed and mortified, she was just...horny. Unbearably horny.

"I'm fine," she squeaked. "You're very good at this."

"Oh yeah? I've never done it before."

"I never would have guessed."

"You know," Beau said, reaching down for her hands. "Some places have a no-touching policy. But not this one. You can touch all you want."

He placed her hands on his warm, rock-hard belly, and wow. She'd known that each fingertip had more than three thousand nerve endings, but she hadn't known they were connected to her clitoris. She squirmed in her seat as Beau slid her hands up his sculpted abs to press one of her palms against his chest, just over his heart.

She'd been fantasizing about touching his chest in this way ever since the night he opened the door at the Village Chateau. And the reality was even better. She ran her hands over his pecs, feeling his nipples harden beneath her touch. Brazenly, she brushed them with her fingertips until Beau groaned.

He lowered himself until he was practically sitting on her lap, all the while continuing to move to the sensuous melody of "Come a Little Closer." Then he dipped his head until Alice's face was shadowed by the brim of his hat. He brushed his lips over her ear and whispered, "You make me crazy."

Alice shivered. She was the one going crazy.

Slowly, Beau stood up, dragging his chest and belly so close to Alice's lips that she could feel his heat. She wanted to taste him, so she brushed her lips against his skin. Beau shivered, and Alice kissed his flesh, sucking and licking as if he were a juicy peach.

She wanted to devour him.

Beau rose until she was staring at the fly of his jeans, which was perfectly framed by the chaps. He swiveled his hips, gyrating and yes...thrusting.

Every other guy she'd seen doing the thrusting pelvis move must have been doing it wrong. Because what Beau was doing was just plain right. In every way. In fact, it was utterly delightful, and when he slowed down, she dragged her hands down his thighs.

His hips stilled, and he tilted her chin up with a single finger. She looked up his long, lean, muscular torso to his mouth, which was set in a straight line. The upper half of his face was in the shadow of his hat.

He leaned down and brought his mouth to hers. He hesitated briefly, just touching her lips, and Alice nearly rose out of her seat. "Beau, I want you," she whispered.

He crushed his lips against hers, lightly grasping her neck with one hand while tangling the other in her hair.

She never wanted this to end. If Beau pulled away, she'd—

He pulled away. And she had not had nearly enough. She wanted more.

"God. Look at you," he said, his voice low and sultry.

Her lips felt swollen already, and her cheek was warm from his bristly stubble. Her hair must be a tangled mess. And Beau seemed to like it. A lot. His fingers trailed over the bulge in his jeans and then to the snap and zipper.

"What do you want, sweet thing?" he asked.

"You," she said simply, reaching for his fly.

Beau stood still as she slowly slid the zipper down. Her fingers trembled. What was she supposed to do next? Just reach in and grab it?

"Let me help," Beau said. He undid the button and pushed his underwear down. She could only see the back of his big hand as he lifted everything out, but then, when he took his hand away...There it was. Erect and pulsing slightly with the beat of his heart. Mesmerized, she slid her fingers along the shaft. The skin was so much softer and smoother than she'd imagined it would be. She longed to drag it across her cheek...across her lips. It was so very warm and she loved stroking it. But the best part about touching Beau's penis was what it did to Beau.

His head dropped back and he lost his hat. He flexed his stomach muscles and balled his hands into fists. His breathing was ragged and loud. When he looked back at her, his eyes were pleading.

He gently pressed her toward him. She stuck out her tongue and touched the very tip of his penis, making him moan. "Oh, Allie. Please. Take me in your mouth."

She did. He was warm and salty. All of her fears and insecurities about knowing what to do disappeared into thin air. She just did what she wanted... And she wanted to devour him. She licked. She sucked. She took as much of him in as she could manage. She was completely absorbed in the taste and feel of Beau Montgomery.

"Stop, Allie," he said. "I don't have the strength to pull away."

He pulled her to her feet and enveloped her in another crushing kiss. He moaned as if he liked the taste of himself on her lips, broke the kiss, and said, "Allie, darlin'. Come to bed."

Chapter

Thirty-Two

Alice lay on the bed surrounded by rose petals. The glow from the candlelight danced in her eyes. She looked like an angel, which made the fact that she'd just damn near tried to suck the life out of him all the hotter.

He kicked off his boots and dropped the vest. Then he unbuckled his chaps, causing them to fall in a heap at his feet. Last, but not least, he stepped out of his jeans and underwear. Alice kept her eyes glued to his cock the entire time, as if she couldn't wait to get her hands—and mouth—on it again.

He was every bit as hungry as she was. Possibly more. But he had to slow down. He lay next to her, on his side, and ran a finger down her chest, between her breasts. He heard her breath hitch, but he kept going, stopping just above her pelvic bone. "Allie, I need you to tell me something."

"Okay," she said, reaching for his throbbing cock.

He took her hand and brought it up to his mouth, kissing her wrist. They needed to talk, and if she started giving him a hand job, conversation would be difficult.

"What is it?" she asked.

"I have to ask you a question." He took a deep breath. "Are you a virgin?"

Alice sighed, as if that were a silly question. "I told you, virginity is a social construct."

"Have you had sex before?"

"No," she said quietly. "I've never done any of this before."

"*Any* of it?"

Alice was already a little flushed, but now she turned scarlet. He'd embarrassed her, and he hadn't meant to. But he was overwhelmed with emotion. Concern and empathy for Alice, but also a deep and gutting sense of responsibility. If he'd known she'd never touched a man's penis before...

Damn. He wouldn't have whipped it out and stuck it in her face while she sat in a chair getting a lap dance. He wished he could do that part over.

"Could you tell?" she asked quietly.

"Oh God, no, darlin'. I had no idea. It felt great. I didn't want you to stop."

She smiled. "Whew."

He kissed her forehead. "But I'm just wondering..."

"What?"

"Why? I mean, you're sexy and gorgeous and funny and smart and—"

"Whoa there, cowboy. You're trying too hard."

"I'm not trying at all."

"I think..."

"What?"

"You might be the only person who sees me that way, Beau."

How the fuck could she think that? Surely, she wasn't completely clueless as to how other people saw her. "That's not true—"

She brushed a strand of hair off his forehead with a casual sense of familiarity that rocked him to his core and made him forget the rest of the sentence.

"I think I'm smart. And sometimes I'm funny, but honestly, as Carmen pointed out once, I'm usually not trying to be—"

He laughed.

"Like that," she said. "It was clearly funny—you laughed—but I wasn't trying."

He kissed her nose, because she was precious. And then he rubbed his against hers, which was a silly little thing that Nonnie used to do with him when he was little, and it shouldn't feel appropriate at a time like this, but it did. And it made Alice giggle.

"Anyway," she said. "I don't think I'm unattractive, but sexy and gorgeous aren't attributes of mine. And I'm fine with that."

"Do you know what's sexiest about you?"

"What?"

"Your confidence."

Alice smiled. "I almost never feel confident."

"But you know so much. And you're never afraid to say what you think—"

"Here's a news flash, Beau. I memorize things and spout a lot of facts because I often don't know what else to do. I think most people find it awkward and weird."

"I find it attractive. Here's some hard evidence," he said, placing her hand on his cock.

Alice stroked him with a sly smile, and for someone who hadn't ever done it before, she did it very well. "So, you never answered my question," he said with effort. "About why you've never..."

He lost his train of thought.

"Been intimate with anyone?" she asked.

All he could do was grunt.

"I used to think it was just something I'd never gotten around to. Like I was busy with school and then with a job and then I woke up and bam! Thirty-two years old and a—"

Beau raised an eyebrow at her. She'd almost said *virgin*.

"Thirty-two years old and never been touched," she said.

Until him. He was the only one. He tried to sort out what he was feeling. Was it pride? That was stupid. Ownership? That was horrible, and if Alice caught a whiff of it, she'd be out the door before he could get his boots on. No, it was something else that he couldn't quite figure out.

He wouldn't adore Alice any less if she'd been with a thousand other men. He didn't have those kinds of hang-ups. He loved experienced women. Loved knowing them. Loved being with them. Loved their confidence. Loved their skills...

But being Alice's first made him want to bang on his chest and shout *Mine! Mine! Mine!*

It was a bunch of hairy macho bullshit, but there it was. Right in the center of his chest. And it didn't feel like a one-way street. Because, after all these years, she'd chosen *him*.

"I think I was just scared of intimacy."

Beau brushed a strand of hair off her forehead. "You want to hear something funny?"

"Sure."

"Being afraid of intimacy is why I've had so much sex. I never wanted to let anyone get too close, because if they did, they'd eventually find out how stupid I was."

Alice stopped stroking him. "You're not—"

"I know that now. I didn't understand dyslexia when I was a kid. And I took those feelings of stupidity and absorbed them right into the fabric of my being. Not being able to read very well is kind of a big deal in our society, Allie. Everybody I knew could do it. I just thought there was something bad wrong with me, and that nobody would want me if they knew."

"I want you," she whispered. "I want you so badly."

"I'm glad. And I'm happy to be your first, darlin'." *It means you'll never forget me.*

Alice started stroking him again. "I don't want you to feel any pressure."

"Pressure?"

"At least sixty-five percent of women can't achieve orgasm through intercourse—"

"Really?"

"Yes. And it's nobody's fault. Some of it is anatomical, of course. And some of it is psychological. But mostly—"

"Allie?"

"Yes, Beau?"

"Keep talking if you must, but I'm going to give you an orgasm now."

* * *

Alice was all in for orgasms. *Orgasms for everybody!* Especially if Beau was going to deliver it in the same manner that he did last time. Cunnilingus was probably the only way that she could actually reach an orgasm without some kind of mechanical stimulation from a vibrator.

But if she didn't have an orgasm, she wasn't going to let it stress her out. Because while she knew her own body well enough, Beau didn't. Not yet, anyway.

"I just want you to know I don't have ridiculous expectations, Beau. I'm going to enjoy the experience, wherever it leads."

Beau kissed her neck, just below her ear, and worked his way down to her collarbone, where he trailed his tongue, leaving behind a trail of goose bumps that quickly broke out over her entire body.

She was already tingling, and he hadn't even gotten to—

He brushed his fingers over her nipple, and then slipped the negligee down until her breast was exposed. "Why have you stopped talking, Allie?"

He really liked to toy with her. Instead of answering, she pushed his head down to her breast. She remembered what his mouth had felt like, and she wanted to feel it again.

"I'm sorry," Beau said. "But you're going to have to use your words. Communication during sex is important."

He wasn't going to make this easy on her.

"Is there something specific you want me to do with my mouth right now, Allie?"

"Breast," she said. "Mouth."

"I see we've regressed to caveman talk. You're lucky, because I'm fluent."

He was a smartass. A sweet, hot, delightful smartass. And when his mouth finally enveloped her nipple, Alice's language skills regressed even further, until all she could produce was a low moan.

Her clitoris tingled with every lick and suckle on her nipple. It was amazing how all those nerves were connected, and how touching your nipples yourself did not elicit the same response.

Sex was definitely better with another human. Especially when the human was Beau Montgomery, who was attentive and humorous and considerate and looked dang good in a pair of chaps and thought her confidence was sexy and—

Beau pulled the gown up to her waist, and then his big, warm hand trailed up her inner thigh. "Cat got your tongue, Allie? You're being awful quiet."

"I'm busy producing dopamine and noradrenaline."

"I don't think that's legal," Beau said, brushing his fingers over her skin.

She opened her legs to give him better access, and he dipped his fingers between her labia, stopping just outside the entrance to her vagina. He placed his lips at her ear and whispered, "I'm going to finger-fuck you now, and I'm going to watch your face while I do it."

She was starting to appreciate Beau's expertise at dirty talk.

He kissed her deeply, and when his tongue entered her mouth, his finger entered her vagina. She gasped as he moved it slowly in and out, pressing against the inside of her pelvic bone.

He broke the kiss and she opened her eyes to see his face, inches above hers. And while she could easily stare at that face all night long, her eyes drifted shut again when Beau moved his finger inside her, in a circular motion that she matched with her hips. She couldn't stay still. There was no way.

"Mm, Allie," Beau whispered. "You're so wet."

She wanted to say something about the importance of lubrication, but that would require stringing words together and there was no way that was happening right now.

"Can I add another finger?"

"Yes," she whispered.

He did, and then he crooked them, and began performing a deep vaginal massage that had Alice humming. The clitoris was actually a fairly sizable organ internally, and Beau was mapping uncharted territory with his fingers, stimulating pleasure receptors Alice didn't even know she had.

Sex toys didn't compare.

She drew her knees up and grasped Beau's arm. Her eyes briefly fluttered open, and there he was, watching her. He increased the rhythm, and the pressure, and suddenly her thighs were tingling along with her nipples. Hormones were definitely being dispersed. He was about to take her to a plateau higher than any she'd ever climbed with a vibrator.

She gasped and panted and reached for that plateau . . . Her body felt electric, like she might actually be glowing. And a pleasant ball of pressure expanded inside her, filling her with warm tingles. She wondered if she could hold it. Maybe she'd explode—

"Just stay right there," Beau whispered.

She did. In her mind's eye, she was right on the edge of a cliff.

But then, Beau removed his fingers.

Alice opened her eyes, "I wasn't ready for you to stop—"

"You're actually super ready," Beau said, reaching inside the nightstand drawer. He pulled out a condom packet and held it up.

"Oh," Alice said. Because this was it. They were going to have intercourse now, and she tried to tell herself it was no big deal, but it felt like a pretty big deal.

"Hey, Allie. Do you still want to do this? I mean, you're physically ready, but are you emotionally ready? Once you cross this line, there's no going back."

"It's an imaginary line, Beau."

"I guess that's true. My cousin Ida goes back and forth over it all the time. One week she's dating Jesus and she's a born-again virgin, and the next week she's dating a truck driver named Earl."

Alice snorted. "But she's the same person, no matter which side of the line she's on, and that's my point."

"Point taken. But you haven't answered my question. Do you still want to do this?"

"Oh yes," Alice said. "Yes, yes, yes. And hurry."

Beau laughed and slipped the condom on quickly. "Enthusiastic consent. That's what I like."

He kissed her deeply, and she felt his arousal as he pressed against her body. She also felt the smile on his lips, the general good humor that always seemed to surround him, and it made her heart flutter sporadically.

He broke the kiss and his smile disappeared. He moved so that he was on top of her, between her legs, and she felt his penis against her bare flesh. "I'll be as gentle as I can—"

Alice put a hand on his chest, pushing him away. "Wait, Beau. No."

Chapter
Thirty-Three

🖤

Oh God. She'd changed her mind.

Beau did his best to arrange his facial features as to not show his disappointment.

Alice laughed. "Don't look so sad. I just want to make a suggestion."

So much for controlling his facial features. And of course, Allie wanted to make a suggestion. "What is it darlin'?"

"I want to be on top."

Every time he thought Alice couldn't surprise him anymore, she...Actually, no. This wasn't surprising at all. This was pure Alice, and he loved it. "That's not exactly a beginner's move, but if it's what you want, I'm game."

He rolled over on his back, and Alice sat up. "It actually should be a beginner's move," she said. "I'll have more control, and research indicates I'm at least twenty percent more likely to achieve an orgasm in that position."

Beau was simultaneously turned on, amused, and educated. And when Alice leaned over and kissed his belly, he had a hard time forming a thought, much less a response. "Whatever you say, professor."

She slid her tongue up to his chest, where she paused to flick a nipple before adding, "And you don't need to worry about hurting me. It's not like I've never had anything in my vagina before."

"Like what?" he croaked. Because he could hardly talk. "What have you had in your vagina before?"

"You mean besides your fingers?" Alice asked.

He couldn't tell if she was asking a serious question or if she was trying to talk dirty, but either way, it had the same effect. He was so turned on he thought he might pop his cork if she so much as looked at him, which wouldn't help Alice's odds, no matter what position they were in.

"Yes, besides my fingers."

"Well," Alice said. "I have a hot-pink dildo I'm pretty fond of—"

"That's enough," Beau said. "Climb on. Before I embarrass myself. No more dirty talk."

"That wasn't dirty talk."

"Someday, I'd really like to hear your rendition of dirty talk. It's probably in Latin. But right now ..."

Alice peeled off the negligee and climbed on top of him, completely nude. Her breasts were beautiful. He reached out and cupped them in his hands, feeling the hard little nipples against his palms.

"But right now, what?" Alice asked, taking hold of his cock and rising on her knees.

Beau inhaled sharply, anticipating the ecstasy to come. His eyes met hers. "Fuck me."

There. That's how you dirty talk.

Alice raised both eyebrows. She didn't like being told what to do, and for a terrifying moment, Beau thought she might refuse, just on principle. But then she smiled and slowly lowered herself onto him.

Oh God. He closed his eyes and sighed as she slowly—very slowly—slid down his shaft.

"Oh," she said. "Oh, Beau."

The way she said his name, with such sweet surprise and rapture, made his heart thump and pound. Something was caught in his throat, and it terrified him, because it felt like a sob. And he was damn sure not going to start crying. There were some things a guy couldn't recover from, and crying during sex was one of them.

Alice slid down a little farther, and Beau watched her face break out in total bliss. It was like watching the sun come out.

But then she winced.

"Are you okay?" he asked quickly.

"Yes, but I think you might be a bit wider than my hot-pink friend."

She leaned forward and rested her hands on his chest and tentatively moved her hips. Beau groaned. He wanted to let Allie take her time and figure out what felt good and what didn't, and he absolutely didn't want her to experience any pain or discomfort. But good Lord, he was going to suffer.

She rose up and slowly slid back down. Then she did it again.

Yep. He was really going to suffer.

"You're also warmer than my dildo."

"That's because, even on my worst day, I'm not an inanimate object."

Alice moaned. "And you're harder."

Damn straight.

"And as smooth as satin," she whispered, eyelids fluttering. Her lips parted as she slid all the way down, taking every inch of him in. "Beau, I'm so…"

"What, baby?"

"I'm so full. You've filled me completely."

How stupid he'd been to worry about *taking* anything from this woman—not her virginity, not her spirit, not any living part of her.

As she moved on top of him, seeking her pleasure like a fucking goddess, all he wanted to do was *give*.

* * *

Alice moved her hips, searching for that sweet spot that Beau had managed to hit with his fingers. She rose and fell, and if she started to lose her rhythm, Beau grabbed her hips and helped her find it again.

She was in good hands. Good, strong, kind, and gentle hands.

"Is it okay, Allie?" His voice sounded strained, and his face was flushed.

Alice stilled. "Am I hurting you?"

He laughed. "No, darlin'. I've literally never felt better in my life. But are you having a good time?"

"Mm…yes," she said, rotating her hips. "A very good time."

"Do that again. With your hips."

"You like it?"

Beau moaned. "Damn, woman. You're driving me wild."

Driving Beau wild was an unexpected pleasure. It made her feel powerful and sexy. She loved watching the flush travel up his chest and neck—the way his cheeks turned splotchy and pink. She liked the sound of his breath hitching when she moved a certain way.

She rotated her hips. She moved back and forth, grinding herself against him and stimulating her clitoris. And then she rose up and came back down. Not quite *all* the way down. But pretty dang close. And yes, it hit the mass of nerve endings on the interior wall of her vagina, just where the elusive G-spot was supposed to be located.

She sat up straight—*ooh, yes, right there*—and took him all the way in.

Beau responded by bucking his hips. "Come on, Allie. Ride me."

She started moving again, up and down, and soon, she was desperate for release. She wanted it harder. And faster.

Beau, sensing her energy shift, lifted her up and brought her down like she didn't weigh a thing. And on every thrust—because he was thrusting now—she climbed higher and higher up the pleasure wave.

The headboard banged. Beau's pillow slid onto the nightstand and knocked the lamp over. Rose petals flew everywhere. And they didn't stop.

The room could catch fire, and they wouldn't stop.

Alice rode the wave higher and higher…She teetered at the edge of the abyss, where pleasure and pain blended together, frantic to get over the edge. Then Beau brushed her clitoris with his thumb.

She cried out…She was falling…

No, she was flying.

The moment stretched into an eternity as she contracted again and again. Beau cried out, too, and she collapsed on his chest as he bucked beneath her. Only the sound of Beau's frantically beating heart kept her from floating away.

He wrapped his arms around her, squeezing her tightly. "Oh, Allie," he sighed.

Oxytocin spread throughout her body—the love hormone—making her sleepy and content. Beau stroked her back, humming gently, and she felt almost high.

Words formed in her head and eventually worked their way to her tongue. "That was so much better than I ever dreamed it would be. Thank you, Beau."

He laughed softly. "Don't thank me, Allie. I just laid here. You did all the work, and man, you're a real hard little worker. I should have expected it."

She raised her head. "I'm serious. Everyone always talks about how disappointing, or even miserable, their first sexual experience is. And mine was, well, let's just say I have a super huge vocabulary, and I'm coming up short."

"It was good?"

"Yes," she said, smiling. "Let's go with that."

"It was good for me, too, Allie. I was nervous about being your first, but it was amazing."

"Why were you nervous?"

"Because I knew you'd always remember it. And I'd never want to be a bad memory for you."

She didn't want him to be a memory. "I think we might have broken the lamp," she said.

"And I imagine we pissed off the neighbors on the other side of this headboard," Beau added.

Alice sat up. "Oh no! Carmen is in that room. Do you really think she heard us?"

Beau laughed. "I think everyone on this ranch heard us."

"This is embarrassing."

"And possibly illegal. Do you know what the noise ordinances are in Travis County?"

Her embarrassment only increased. Beau was teasing, but now she realized how obnoxious she must have seemed, marching upstairs at the Village Chateau to tell two people who were lost in their own universe, making wild crazy love, to quiet down.

"I'm ashamed that I did that now," Alice said. "No wonder you've always found me obnoxious. I guess I kind of am."

Beau rose up to lean on an elbow. He touched her chin. "I've never found you obnoxious, Allie. A bit irritating now and again, maybe." He grinned and the dimples in both cheeks made an adorable appearance. "But that was only because I wanted to bang you so bad."

She slapped playfully at his arm, "I doubt that's true."

"Oh, it's true, all right. Also, that couple was seriously annoying. I'm suspicious she was faking it."

"I don't know, Beau. I just got pretty swept away. I mean, I broke a lamp. And I think I might have vocalized rather loudly."

"We both did. And Carmen is going to give us shit about it in the morning. Be prepared."

Beau removed the condom. His penis was no less beautiful resting lazily against his leg than when it was hard and pulsing. And she wanted to play with it.

"I see what you're eyeing, Allie. And it's going to take me an hour or so before I'll be ready for round two."

"Oh, that's not what I was thinking."

Beau raised a single eyebrow.

"Okay, so maybe I was," Alice said. "I'm going to go use the restroom, because some women get urinary tract infections after intercourse, and when I come back, we'll take a little nap."

"How about a medium-sized nap? I've rounded up cattle, loaded them onto a trailer, unloaded them at an auction, braved a strip mall, fixed a fence, danced at a bachelorette party, performed a private lap dance, and had sex with my ex-babysitter"—he looked at his watch—"all in the past eighteen hours."

Yikes! Sometimes she forgot just how hard Beau worked, and that what he did all day often involved physical labor.

She kissed him on the nose. "You can sleep as long as you want, Beau Montgomery. You've earned it."

He winked at her. "Give me two hours to rest my eyes, darlin'. And I want you in my arms while I'm doing it."

Chapter
Thirty-Four

A gap in the drapes allowed a sliver of light to enter the room, and in a flash, Beau threw off the covers. What time was it? If a cowboy opened his eyes to daylight, he was already late. He looked around for his boots, ready to jump into them like a firefighter rushing to a three-alarm fire.

But wait. He rubbed his eyes. This wasn't his room. Hell, this wasn't even Rancho Cañada Verde. He flopped back onto the mattress with a huge old grin as last night washed over him. He sighed contentedly. He had nothing to do today but help get the place ready for Brittany's wedding tonight.

The wedding. After last night, he was more confident than ever that what he and Alice had together was real. He was going to suggest ripping the contract to shreds.

Allie's side of the bed (if you could call it that—she'd pretty much slept on top of him) was empty. But there was a note on the pillow.

Beau squinted in the dim light. The first thing he saw was hearts. He grinned stupidly. Because she'd drawn hearts. Focusing more intently, he noted the first letter of each word as Allie had taught him. And then the rest settled into place. He heard her voice in his head as he read.

> *Bridesmaid breakfast. Busy all day. See you at the wedding!*
> *PS Thanks for the love lessons. You're a good teacher, Beau Montgomery.*

Love lessons. He wasn't exactly sure that he'd been the teacher.

He looked on the nightstand for his phone, and found it on the floor next to the broken lamp. Damn, it was a quarter after nine! He hadn't slept this late since... Well, he'd never slept this late. He grinned lazily. Allie Cat had worn him out.

Last night, she'd let him sleep for two hours before waking him up in a most enjoyable way, and then they'd gone at it again. You couldn't introduce Alice to a new subject and not expect her to do extensive research.

Beau, how long does it take for your penis to become flaccid after you ejaculate?

What happens if I keep touching it?

Why are you making that face? Is that a happy face or a pained face?

They'd tried every position he could think of, and a few he hadn't.

Beau, can we do it standing up?

The answer to that had been yes.

There were so many things left on Allie's bucket list. He wanted to be there for all of it, even the fancy European museums. He'd never been all that interested in traveling before, but doing it with Allie would be an adventure.

He stretched, and his heart filled up with hope just as surely as his lungs filled up with air. There was one thing he'd wanted for seemingly his entire life, and he'd just had her. Multiple times. Multiple ways. And goddammit. He planned to keep her.

Someone pounded on the door. It was probably Bryce, so he grabbed a pillow to cover himself, climbed out of bed, and answered it.

Bryce stood there with his left eyebrow raised. *Do you know what time it is?*

Beau stepped back and let him in.

"Jesus Christ. What happened in here?" Bryce asked, yanking the curtains open. The comforter was on the floor. The sheets were bunched up at the foot of the bed. Rose petals were strewn everywhere.

Beau winced as the light hit his eyes.

"Never mind. Don't answer that," Bryce said. "But you're going to pay for that lamp."

Beau picked the lamp up and set it on the nightstand. "I don't think it's badly broken."

It didn't matter if it was. He'd happily pay for it. Right now, he'd happily do just about anything.

"I'm going to meet up with Ford at the lodge and have a cup of coffee. Why don't you come join us? Then we'll get our day started."

"Sounds good," Beau said. Because everything sounded good right now. There was literally nothing on this earth that could bring him down.

"So, uh…" Bryce smiled. "I'd say things went pretty good between you and Alice last night."

Beau dropped the pillow. He was as naked a jaybird, but he had zero qualms. "Pretty good," he said with a wink.

Bryce shook his head. "I could have done without seeing the morning wood, brother."

Beau laughed. "You see it every day when you get out of bed. I'm hitting the shower, but I'll be quick. I'll meet you and Ford in a few minutes."

He stuck to his word, and it was only about fifteen minutes later that he walked into the grand lodge. Ford and Bryce sat by a huge fireplace—it would probably be really nice in winter—holding coffee cups and talking.

Beau helped himself to a muffin wrapped in cellophane and sat in a leather chair next to Bryce. "Good morning."

"Mornin'," Ford said.

There was tension across Bryce's brow. He looked at Beau. *Brace for it.*

Ford leaned back in his chair. "Worth called. The pump stopped working where you hooked up those new solar panels. He's called a technician and he moved the cattle down to the river."

Shit. Shit. Shit. "Who's watching the cattle? They can get across the Rio Verde right now."

"He's got a couple of guys on it."

Maybe Worth should be the fucking foreman. "So, the pump stopped working? Like, entirely? It was working when I left."

"Something must have happened. Don't fret over it. We should have paid someone to come out and hook it all up in the first place. I just wanted to keep you apprised because you're the foreman."

What kind of a foreman let his cows get thirsty during a drought? *Twice?* Fire-hot shame and embarrassment took over Beau's body, making him break out in a light sweat. "Yeah. Well, I'm real sorry about it."

Ford shrugged. "You tried to save us a buck or two. But next time, if you aren't sure what you're doing, just let me know. If Worth hadn't caught it—"

"The cattle could have died."

"This drought is a bitch for sure," Ford said. "Right now, everything is about the water. And that reminds me. Little Rosa and I are going to play in the pool while you two suckers work your asses off today. I'm on vacation."

"It hardly feels like working," Bryce said. "After years of wrangling cows, wrangling chairs and tables is easy."

"I suspect Anna will be a tough taskmaster," Ford said with a chuckle.

As if she'd heard her name, Anna walked in. She spotted them and came straight over. "I need you to haul a margarita machine to the bridesmaids' suite."

"Right now?" Bryce asked.

Anna shrugged. "It's five o'clock somewhere." Then she turned her attention to Ford. "Claire is looking for you. She wants you to take the baby so she can go to Austin."

"What is she going to Austin for?"

"Shoes."

Ford sighed. "I should have seen that coming. Tell her I'll be there as soon as I finish this cup of coffee."

Beau was hardly listening. He wanted to leave here and get back to Rancho Cañada Verde so he could check on things. Take a look at that solar panel hookup, make sure Worth wasn't going to let the cattle cross the Rio Verde...Dammit. Why hadn't he just admitted the instructions were over his head?

It hadn't felt like it, though. He'd understood the diagram.

Anna marched off and Ford stood up, downing the rest of his coffee in one gulp. "I'd better get going so Claire can buy all the shoes in Austin and be back in time for the wedding," he said. "And Beau, speaking of Austin, I heard Alice's good news. Claire probably wasn't supposed to tell me, but she did."

Alice's name got Beau's attention. "Pardon?"

"She told me Alice got that big, fancy library job in Austin," Ford said. "Claire's happy for her, but she can't believe Alice is leaving Big Verde."

Bryce looked at Beau. *What is Ford talking about?*

Beau had literally no idea. Ford leaned over and slapped him on the shoulder. "Long-distance relationships can be hard, but Austin isn't too far away. And when something's meant to be, it's meant to be, right?"

Alice had gotten a new job? In Austin? The ground seemed to tilt, and the sip of coffee he'd just swallowed rose into his throat, along with a healthy dose of bile. He worked hard to keep his face blank. He didn't want to look like he felt, which was sick. And stupid. Stupider, in fact, than he'd ever felt. And that was saying something.

How could Alice not have mentioned a new job in another town? Like, how could that have happened? Jesus. Their fake relationship really was fake. He'd fooled himself (easy to fool a fool). But he should have known better. What would a brilliant woman like Alice ever want from a guy like him?

The same thing every other woman wanted—a good time.

He was nothing more than an amendment to a contract. An item to be marked off of a bucket list.

How would he get through the rest of the day? He was gutted. Shattered. Nothing mattered anymore.

Everything he and Alice had shared together was fake.

Fake. Fake. Fake.

Fuck.

* * *

"Are you sure you wouldn't like a margarita, Miss Martin?" one of the bridesmaids asked. "We're going to be getting ready for a long time."

It's not even noon. "No, thanks."

They'd already had pedicures, which was silly, since they were wearing cowboy boots with their yellow dresses. Beau had taken her to the RCV Mercantile to help her pick out a nice, moderately priced pair. He'd said she could also wear them horseback riding and that they'd be good for walking on trails.

She smiled dreamily, thinking about sunset rides with Beau. Rides that ended on the bluff, where they'd wait for the stars to come out, big and bright—she quietly clapped to herself three times—deep in the heart of Texas.

Beau was deep in *her* heart. There was absolutely no way to deny it. And having him in her heart had changed everything, including her. She was a different person, more willing to take risks. And tonight, she was going to take the biggest one of all.

She was going to open her heart to Beau and tell him how she felt. She wanted to extend their contract. Indefinitely. Because nothing about their relationship felt fake, and although she wasn't all that great at reading people, she was almost certain that Beau felt the same way.

"Alice," Brittany said. "You're next to get your hair done."

"Oh, I was just going to pull it back—"

"No. You're getting an updo. Everybody is."

God. The dreaded Texas updo. Alice had lived thirty-two years without ever having to suffer the "do." Not for prom (she hadn't gone) or homecoming (she hadn't gone) or to serve in the Apple Festival court (she hadn't been asked).

Lisa from Lisa's Locks walked in the room and popped her gum. She wore what looked like a utility belt around her waist, and it was loaded with various bottles and spray cans and tools that looked like weapons. Her blond hair was curled and shellacked. She wore false eyelashes, dragon-length nails with rhinestones on them, and platform shoes that couldn't possibly be comfortable for someone who stood on her feet all day. "Whose do am I doing next?"

Brittany pointed at Alice. "Hers."

"My hair isn't very thick. Nor is it all that long. I don't think it's going to even go up in a do."

Lisa blew a bubble and popped it. "Honey, your hair will do just fine in a do. Hell, I got Misty Barnes's hair up in a do. That girl's got nothing but little baby hairs. Wispy like cotton candy. My mama says it's a vitamin deficiency. Anyway, did y'all see her prom pictures?"

All the bridesmaids nodded enthusiastically. "Magic!" one of them said. "Lisa is a magician."

Alice swallowed. There was no getting out of it. "Where do you want me?" she asked meekly.

"I've got my torture chamber set up in the adjoining room," Lisa said, gesturing at the door.

"Don't do just any do," Brittany said. "I want all the updos as big as you can get them."

Of course she did.

Alice followed Brittany into the other room, and suddenly, she didn't even care how awful her hair would look. Heck, she wanted the updo! She wanted the full Texas bridesmaid experience. The new Alice was in it for the fun of it. She wanted to live it up.

Beau's irresistibly fun nature had rubbed off on her. Actually, he'd more than rubbed off on her. He'd rubbed *all over* her. And in her. And—

"Goodness, Alice," Lisa said. "What on earth are you thinking about?"

Alice's cheeks became very warm. "Pardon?"

Lisa gave her a knowing smile. "Never mind. It's not a *what*. It's clearly a *who*. Now, let's get you all dolled up."

Chapter
Thirty-Five

❦

Beau slipped into the back row of chairs just as the music began. He'd had to squeeze past the bridesmaids on his way in—they were lined up and ready to go—and he'd somehow managed to smile at Alice as he passed.

He wanted to loosen his tie, because he was hot. And yes, he'd worn a suit and tie and a brand new dressy felt Stetson even though half the men in the room were in jeans. Because he'd wanted to look nice for Alice. He'd wanted her to feel proud when she was on his arm.

He swallowed. She'd kept her end of the bargain—it wasn't her fault he kept fucking up on the ranch—and he was going to keep his. He only had to make it to midnight without falling apart.

The first two bridesmaids walked down the aisle. Next came Alice, and the entire world stopped spinning as she passed, although nobody else seemed to notice. She gave him a sweet smile. And even though he was hurting, he returned it. Genuinely. The joy of seeing her, of having her smile at him, cut through the pain of knowing he was going to lose her.

He'd never really had her.

He watched silently as she floated down the aisle in the big, fluffy yellow dress. She was breathtaking, even though he knew she hated the gown. She probably also hated the way her hair was piled up in ringlets and curls, but she looked like a dream. And even though she didn't need to be dressed like a princess to render him utterly speechless, something about the way she looked right now appealed to the little boy inside him. The one who'd fallen for the babysitter.

Dammit. He had to get a grip. Otherwise, he was going to completely lose it right here in front of everyone.

It was time to let go of his childhood crush. He'd had a fantasy, and he'd been lucky enough to live it out for a few weeks. With time, he'd—

No. He wasn't a kid. He was a man who'd fallen in love with a woman. A real one. And he would never recover from it. Not in a million years.

He briefly closed his eyes. He had to grasp this moment and hold on tight. Instead of suffering, he'd will himself to enjoy every minute of it. He was going to shower Alice with attention. He'd hold her in his arms and spin her around the dance floor. He'd even kiss her if she'd allow it.

Because tonight was his last night as Alice Martin's fake boyfriend, and he'd be damned if he was going to miss any of it. He'd love her with every ounce of his being, right up to midnight.

And for every moment after.

The processional began, and everyone stood and turned to watch Brittany come down the aisle. Everyone except Beau.

He only had eyes for Alice.

* * *

Whew! The wedding had gone smoothly (except for the ringbearer refusing to walk and the unity candle refusing to light and Miss Mills refusing to hit the right notes on the organ), and this was absolutely the most fun Alice had ever had at a reception. She felt like the belle of the ball. But holy guacamole, she looked a mess!

She hardly recognized the woman staring back at her in the bathroom mirror. Smudged mascara, pink cheeks, and an updo that was slowly becoming a down-do.

She had no intention of fixing any of it, so she simply washed her hands.

The door opened, and Claire walked in with little Rosa. "Hey there, Alice. Are you having a good time?"

"I'm having a freaking blast. How about you?"

"I'm about to change a poopy diaper before calling it a night," she said, pulling down the wall-mounted changing table. "Does that sound like fun?"

Alice laughed. "Not really. But can I help you with anything?"

"You can reach into my bag and get out the wipes."

Alice dug around in the bag, which was filled with many things, most of them not wipes or diapers, until she finally found the little package. She handed it to Claire, who was holding down a fussy Rosa.

"Thanks," Claire said. "So, you haven't mentioned when you're starting your new job. Are you excited?"

Holy guacamole! Alice had practically forgotten all about it. "I'm not taking it."

Claire's head snapped up. "You're not? Oh, Alice. I'm so happy to hear that. Everyone would miss you so much."

"I think I was just excited over the prospect of doing something new. But I can do new things here. I *am* doing new things here."

Claire raised an eyebrow, and Alice's cheeks went warm.

"Anyway, I never really wanted it. I kind of enjoy wearing

all the hats at a small-town library. Probably because I'm such a small-town girl at heart."

"Of course you are," Claire said. "You always have been."

"And there are so many things keeping me in Big Verde."

Claire tossed the dirty diaper into the trash. "Three points, and the crowd goes wild." She handed Rosa to Alice and went to the sink to wash her hands. "Is one of the things keeping you in Big Verde named Beau?"

A little thrill traveled up and down Alice's spine, making her shiver. "He is definitely *one* of the things. And so are you."

"Aw, Alice," Claire said. "Come here."

Alice and Rosa were enveloped in a Claire hug, which was warm and soft and scented like milk and baby wipes and—

"I'm sorry it smells like baby shit while we're having a moment," Claire said.

Alice laughed again, because everything was perfect. It really was.

"You'd better get back to that man of yours," Claire said. "He hasn't taken his eyes off of you all night."

"I haven't been able to spend as much time as I'd like with him," Alice said. "The photographer constantly has us posing for pictures. And when we're not doing that, we're doing some kind of silly ritual."

"He's handsome tonight," Claire said.

Alice sighed dreamily. A lot of the men hadn't dressed up at all, which was typical of ranchers and farmers attending weddings. But Beau had gone all out with a suit, tie, dress boots, and a fancy black Stetson. There wasn't a single man who could hold a candle to Beau Montgomery, and that included his twin.

And even though Alice was constantly being yanked here or there for this or that, Beau was quietly waiting on her hand and foot. He'd fixed her a dinner plate so she wouldn't have to stand in the buffet line. He'd refilled her water glass and brought her champagne. And after Brittany and Zachary had cut the cake, he'd made sure she got a piece of both the bride's *and* groom's cakes.

They'd snuck off to make goofy faces in the photo booth, and he'd dragged her onto the dance floor for the chicken dance, which he'd managed to do while looking devilishly sexy.

Claire took Rosa back. "You'd better get going before you're missed."

Alice gave Claire another quick hug, and then she headed back to the party. Beau was waiting just outside the door. "How about another dance, darlin'? It's getting late."

Would she ever tire of hearing him call her darlin'?

No. Never.

She took Beau's hand and followed him onto the dance floor. A slow song had been playing, but it ended. A faster one started up, and everyone started grooving. Bubba moved to the center of the dance floor, and a small crowd gathered around to egg him on. Poor Trista knew to just get out of the way when that happened, because Bubba enjoyed putting on a show.

Hopefully, Beau would want to watch Bubba, too. Because the most Alice ever did during these types of songs was an awkward little step back and forth. Although maybe tonight would be the night she could finally shed the last of her inhibitions and get down.

Beau started moving, without taking his eyes off of her, and oh boy. He had moves galore. And rhythm. And timing. And a simmering sexy gaze.

She swallowed nervously, but then she started to dance. She closed her eyes and let the music enter her. The bass beat vibrated her bones. It was as if her heart started beating in time with the music, and soon, her hips were moving, her arms were in the air, and her head was thrown back.

She was dancing. Like *really* dancing. And she didn't care how she looked, or if she was doing it right. She just moved her body the way it was meant to move. The way it *wanted* to move. The crowd cheered—Bubba had probably dropped into the splits—and she opened her eyes.

Beau had stopped dancing and was just standing there, staring at her.

Oh God. Maybe she *had* looked stupid. So stupid that Beau had frozen in mortified embarrassment over being her dance partner.

He suddenly grabbed her, pulling her close. "Oh, Allie. You're so beautiful. I'll never forget tonight."

She wanted to say something back, but she couldn't find the words. She thought she might cry if she tried to speak. That's how freaking happy she was to be in this man's arms. And she never wanted to leave them.

Beau pulled her even closer, and she felt his desire. He moved his hips in time to the pulsing bass beat and forced a leg in between hers. She gasped. Could anyone see? Probably not—his leg disappeared into the yellow layers of the dress—and anyway, there were people doing worse things on the dance floor.

By the time the song ended, she was heated. Worked up. Super turned on and looking forward to all the things she and Beau were going to do when they got back to the room. Beau brought her wrist up to his lips and planted the sweetest kiss.

Bubba walked by, drenched in sweat, and smacked Beau on the back. "Decent moves," he said. "But I'm still the master."

Alice wasn't sure about that, but Bubba *was* a good dancer. Beau gave him a little nod and a hat tip.

The DJ's voice rang out. "All right, all right, all right! I need all the single ladies out on the dance floor."

Oh no. It was time for Brittany to toss the bouquet. This was usually Alice's cue to head to the ladies' room, but tonight she was a bridesmaid.

"Knock 'em dead, Alice," Bubba said.

"I'll be back," Alice said, rising on her toes and kissing Beau on the cheek. "I've got to go dodge a bouquet."

Only she didn't dodge it. She caught it. Or at least that's what people said when the dang thing smacked her in the face. She ran back to Beau, carrying the flowers. "Don't freak out," she said jokingly. "I didn't do it on purpose."

"I wouldn't think so. Listen, darlin', it's getting late—"

Someone tapped her on the shoulder. "We need a picture of you and Zachary's brother."

Zachary's brother had caught the garter.

"Oh, okay…" She looked at Beau.

"I'll be waiting," he said. "But it's almost midnight, Allie."

She started to laugh, but then something about the way Beau looked made her stop. What was it? She was so bad at reading people, maybe it was nothing. But Beau wasn't laughing. Nor was he even smiling. In fact, he looked almost sad.

The picture taking took way too long, and when she finally made her way back to Beau, he was standing at the back of the room, near the exit. Maybe he was ready to go. That was fine, because she was, too.

No matter how much fun she'd had at the wedding, she was looking forward to even more fun with Beau. "Ready to leave?"

"Yes, I think I am. It's a little past midnight now, and well, I should be getting back to Big Verde."

She started to laugh, because surely, this was a joke. But Beau wasn't laughing. There was no twinkle in his eyes. No dimple threatening to make an appearance in his left cheek.

"But I thought you and I were going to…"

She closed her mouth. Willed herself to shut up.

"The pump is broken at the ranch, and well, I've got to be up early to take Nonnie to church. Our deal ended at midnight, remember?"

Alice couldn't breathe. All the air in the room had been sucked out. Would she actually suffocate? She looked around frantically. How were other people breathing? And how could she have been so stupid?

Of course, Beau was going back to Big Verde. None of this had been real. She'd drawn up the contract herself. And, as Beau just so helpfully pointed out, it expired at midnight. Beau had turned back into a playboy who never slept with the same woman twice.

Her knees shook, and something that felt like a sob was working its way up her throat, threatening to come out of her mouth. She had to swallow it down. What good would it do to let him see her cry?

When she spoke, her voice sounded strangled and froggy. "I see. Well, thank you for being my plus-one."

"It was my pleasure," Beau said. "Thank you for all you've done for me, and Allie Cat, you can tell folks whatever you want. I'll go along with it."

And with that, Beau Montgomery tipped his hat and strolled out the door, as if shattering Alice's world was the easiest thing he'd ever done.

Maybe it was.

Chapter

Thirty-Six

❧

Beau walked up the steps to the Kowalski ranch house. It had been a week since the wedding, and he'd crawled through it like a zombie. This morning's herd report indicated they were missing two bulls, which wasn't the case. So, he'd entered the wrong number in the system after the auction. Or maybe he'd entered the right number but in the wrong place. Who knew? The bottom line was that he kept fucking up.

He was here to do the only thing that made sense. He was going to talk to Ford and suggest that Worth be promoted to foreman. Beau could be head herdsman. There was absolutely no paperwork involved with that. And honestly, none of it mattered. He'd be happy to just do the mind-numbing work of pounding in fence posts from sunup to sundown. He longed for that blissful state of exhaustion that made thinking or feeling impossible.

He was about to open the front door when it suddenly opened of its own accord. And there stood Claire, glaring at him as if he'd just kicked a puppy. What the fuck had he done now? Whatever it was, he wasn't in the mood for it. "Excuse me," he said, trying to get around her.

She didn't budge.

Her nostrils were flared. Her eyebrows were drawn into a menacing scowl. Hell, she practically had steam coming out of her ears. Claire wasn't just mad. She was what Gerome called *redhead mad*.

She poked him in the chest. "What the hell is wrong with you?"

"We don't have time to start that list. Now pardon me, I have a meeting with your husband and your father."

She poked him again. Harder.

"Ow. Jesus, Claire. Get out of my way."

"How dare you treat Alice like that?"

Oh. Allie must have concocted a story, and it sounded like it was a doozy. But he'd promised to go along with it. "I'm just a horrible guy, I guess. A real beast of a man. Now, if you'll excuse me—"

She shoved him. Like actually *shoved* him. And since he wasn't ready for it, he lost his balance and had to take a step back to catch himself. Unbelievably, Claire stayed on him, right in his face, pulling the door shut behind her.

Great. He'd lost his brother. He'd had his heart broken. He was about to give up his foreman position. And now Claire was literally trying to fight him on the front porch. "What the fuck, Claire? I don't know what you think happened between me and Allie, but believe it or not, it was all part of a plan."

"No doubt," Claire said, crossing her arms over her chest. "It's a tired plan, and you should retire it."

"I don't even know what that means—"

"You have more than enough willing victims for the one-shot game you play. Why did you have to prey on Alice?"

"*Prey on Alice?* I don't prey on anybody. And I don't play games. Every woman I see knows exactly what she's getting—which is a fucking good time, by the way—and Alice was no exception."

Claire gasped dramatically.

"In fact," he continued. "In Allie's case, there was an actual contract involved. Which she drew up. So, if you'll just get out of my way now, I have a meeting—"

"She gave you everything, Beau."

Beau's pulse pounded in his head. How dare Claire even engage him in this conversation? She had no idea what she was talking about. "She didn't give me a damn thing," he said. "She just took."

Took his heart and stomped on it.

"She. Was. A. Virgin."

"Virginity is a social construct."

He shouldn't have said that. Because he knew damn well that the first time was the first time, and that it meant something. It had just slipped out, much like a million other Allie-isms he often spouted.

"I'm so sorry you were her first."

Beau wasn't sorry. He would treasure that night for the rest of his life, and he hoped Allie would, too.

"You treated her like any old romp in the hay," Claire said. "I mean, Beau, this was Alice!"

Something snapped inside. He could hardly breathe or form a coherent thought, but it didn't matter. Feelings were rushing around inside of him, slamming into each other and exploding into a single, sloppy storm of grief and rage and disappointment, and it was all about to pour out of his mouth.

"I will never regret being Alice's first lover. *Ever.* I poured my whole heart and soul into making love to her, and you have no fucking right to stand here invading my privacy and forcing me to talk about something so personal and accusing me of…Of what, I don't even know. But I did not steal anything from Alice. I gave her everything. Her first time was with someone who cherished and loved her, and you will *not* talk shit about it to me or anyone else."

He yanked his Stetson down low, hoping the shadow would hide his face, because he'd already revealed more than he'd intended. "Now then, if you don't move your ass, I'm going to move it for you."

Claire didn't yield. "You're in love with Alice?"

There would be no getting past her. She was like a troll under a bridge, demanding a secret password, which seemed to be the baring of his soul. He lifted the brim of his hat, because fuck it. Let her go ahead and see the red-rimmed eyes and whatever other pathetic hints might be lurking in his expression. "Yes. I'm in love with Alice. I always have been, and I always will be. Are you happy now?"

Claire gave a shriek of joy and then launched herself at him. He was covered in redhead and totally confused. "Alice loves you, too, Beau. She's absolutely heartbroken. You need to go talk to her—"

Beau peeled Claire off of him. "No. You've got it wrong. Allie struck a deal with me, because..." Hell. Might as well let it all out. He had nothing to lose anymore. "I don't read very well, Claire. It's embarrassing, but it's the truth. Alice helped me with that. And in return, I took her to the wedding."

"First of all, that's nothing to be embarrassed about, and I'm glad Alice helped you. Secondly, you did a little more than take her to the wedding."

Beau shrugged. "I guess you could say that we amended the contract to include a few extracurricular activities. But believe me, Alice is not in love with me. Maybe, since I was her first, she's developed an understandable attachment. But she's moving to Austin to start a new job, and she didn't even bother to tell me about it. That's how important I am to her. The contract ended at midnight after the wedding. It's over."

"Who told you about the job?"

"Ford."

"Dang it." Claire chewed on her thumbnail. "That's what I was afraid of."

"It doesn't matter how I heard about it. What matters is how I *didn't* hear about it."

"She didn't take that job, Beau. I don't think she ever even seriously considered it, and that's probably why she didn't mention it."

"Why didn't she take it?"

Claire rolled her eyes. "You can be super dense sometimes."

Beau took his hat off so he could see Claire clearly. "Are you saying she turned the job down because of me?" If this was true, it melted his heart. But it also gave him pause, because he'd already held Bryce back. He didn't want anyone else giving up their dreams because of him.

Claire reached out and touched his cheek. "She thought your relationship was real. And she thought you felt the same way."

This information made his head spin. Like he literally reached back and grabbed hold of the porch railing to steady himself.

"Beau, why won't you let anybody love you?"

"What? You need to warn me when you're switching the topic."

"I think that's why you only land in a woman's bed once. You don't want anybody to get close enough to love you."

That wasn't true. He *wanted* to be loved. But letting someone get close meant letting someone know his secret, and that secret was shrouded in feelings of shame and worthlessness. But Allie knew his secret. And if what Claire was saying was true...

She loved him anyway.

But dammit. A job in Austin. With a big library. He couldn't be the reason someone didn't chase after their dreams.

Not again.

* * *

Alice marked off four more items on her to-do list.

Dust shelves—Check

Fluff beanbag chairs in children's nook—Check

Water plants—Check
Sharpen pencils—Check

The fact that she wasn't even scheduled to work today didn't stop her from performing mindless and mostly unnecessary tasks. She needed to keep moving. Because dang it, there were miniblinds to be cleaned. Also, if she slowed down for even a minute, she started to cry.

She grabbed the feather duster and headed for the blinds, but Brittany cut her off at the pass.

Brittany was home from her honeymoon but still riding the newlywed high. She was also out of her boot, which had her buzzing around like a bee on steroids. "Something came for you," she said, presenting a vase filled with red roses. "Maybe they're from Beau!"

For just a moment, Alice's heart fluttered. But there was no way the flowers were from Beau. She hadn't seen him since the wedding, and why would she? Their deal was up. The contract had expired.

She'd been such a fool to think their relationship was real or that it had a chance of continuing after the wedding. Beau had never hidden who he was. Everybody knew his reputation. *She* knew his reputation.

She'd written the contract herself. And signed it. There had been no reason to think their agreement had been anything other than what it was.

She took the roses. "These are probably from the library volunteers or something. Maybe it's a holiday." She didn't think it was, but she'd forgotten to eat for the past week, so who knew?

She went to go hide in her office, where she shut the door and held her breath while quietly pulling the tiny card out of its envelope.

From a Secret Admirer

She dropped into the chair behind her desk. She'd only received roses from a man twice, and it was her father both times. Who else would her secret admirer be?

Her dad knew she and Beau had "broken up." Heck, everyone in the entire town knew, because this was Big Verde, so of course they did. It was sweet of him to be concerned about her. But there was probably nothing sadder than a thirty-two-year-old woman receiving breakup roses from her dad disguised as a secret admirer.

Well, maybe there was something sadder. She opened her planner and wrote *Think of something sadder than Dad flowers*.

"Knock-knock!"

Ugh. That sounded like Claire. And Alice just wasn't in the mood to suffer through more attempts at cheering her up. "Come in."

Claire entered with Rosa on her hip and Maggie on her heels. Little Maisy was in a stroller being pushed by Henry. "We're here for Cowboy Story Time."

"That's today?"

"Yep," Maggie said, wearing a huge grin.

Alice pulled out the story time schedule and breathed a sigh of relief when she saw Worth's name. Not that Beau ever actually showed up for story time—

"Hello, Beau!" Brittany said. "Ready to read?"

Alice sank down in her chair, heart pounding. Dang it. She closed her eyes and repeated the plan she'd been practicing…

Polite smile

Cheerful countenance

No big deal

Although, maybe she should just shoo everyone out of her office, shut the door, and wait until Beau was gone.

Too late! He was in her doorway. Taking up every inch. And holy guacamole, he looked good. He'd worn the full cowboy getup—hat, chaps, boots, spurs, big belt buckle, rope at his side.

"You okay, Allie Cat? You look a bit heated."

And there it was. The playful twinkle in the eyes. The little dimple in the cheek. She was nothing special. Beau Montgomery would flirt with anyone.

"Hi," she croaked. Like an actual frog.

Folks began pouring in for story time. Bubba walked by with his two youngest. JD and Gabriel were right behind him with little Brianna. Miss Mills lumbered past for no discernable reason at all.

"Are you going to come listen to me read?" Beau asked.

Alice cleared her throat. "Sure." Reading story time was a big step for Beau, and broken heart aside, she wanted to support him. "The books are on the little table—"

"I brought my own," Beau said.

"Oh, that wasn't necessary—"

"It really was," Beau said.

He'd probably chosen a book he felt comfortable with.

She followed him to the children's nook, where everyone was busy finding their cozy spots on cushions and in beanbag chairs. And the entire time, her heart was flapping furiously around her rib cage, no doubt trying to get to Beau.

He doesn't want you, Alice. Get a grip.

"Would you like any water?" she asked.

"Nah, darlin', I'm good. Thank you, though."

Ha! She remembered when *darlin'*, which Beau used as often as other folks said please and thank you, made her knees go weak. Especially since it was just last week. And maybe right now.

She cleared her throat. "Thanks for coming to Cowboy Story Time, guys! Today we have Beau Montgomery. He's a real working cowboy from Rancho Cañada Verde. Let's give him a big cowboy welcome!"

All the kids cheered, and Beau's cheeks turned a bit pink. And even though she didn't want to be, she was nervous for him and wanted him to do well.

"Howdy," Beau said. "Before I get started, I have a secret. Do y'all want to hear it?"

The kids all screamed various versions of yes.

"My secret is that I don't read very well," Beau said.

Alice brought a hand to her heart. *Oh, Beau...*

Henry raised his hand. "But you're a grown-up."

"I know," Beau said. "But I struggle with something called dyslexia, which makes it hard for me to read. And for a long time, I didn't want anybody to know about it, because it's kind of embarrassing, you know?"

The kids all nodded.

"But if any of you ever have trouble reading, or maybe with math or other things, it doesn't mean you're not smart. People are smart in all sorts of ways. You just need to ask for help. And sometimes the first person you ask, or even the second or third, won't be able to help you. But you've got to keep asking until you get the right person. And do you want to know who my right person was?"

They all nodded their heads.

"Miss Alice," Beau said.

The kids craned their necks to look at Alice, so she smiled. "It's my job. I'll help any old person, really."

There was a snort, which probably came from Claire.

"Now then, who wants to hear the story of *Beauty and the Beast*?" Beau asked.

An unintelligible chorus rang out.

"I might need help as we go, so who wants to be my helper? I need a good reader at my side."

Literally every little girl and several of the moms raised their hands, ready to volunteer. But Beau pointed at little Dalton Reed, JD's young nephew, who'd really been blowing through books lately.

Dalton went to Beau's side, and they shared a high-five.

Before Beau opened the book, he looked at Alice. Reading aloud, in front of an audience, was one of his biggest fears.

You've got this, Beau.

"Before I begin, let me tell you what the story is about. You've got a beast—a big old ugly thing—who's under a spell. And there's only one thing that can break it—"

"True love!" a little girl shouted.

"That's right," Beau said. "But the Beast doesn't think he's lovable. And he especially doesn't think he can be loved by the smartest girl in the village, the one who reads books and likes going to museums and her special women's group in Austin and whatnot."

A women's group in Austin? Dear God. He was talking about her. About *them*. At story time. In front of everyone. She shifted uncomfortably as a few folks glanced her way with knowing smiles.

"But," Beau said. "The Beast loved the girl. He'd always loved her, and—"

"That's not how the story goes," a little girl said. "You're telling it wrong."

"Oh, am I?" Beau said. "I guess we'd better use the book then." He cleared his throat loudly and said, "Once upon a time…"

It was a really short version of the story, geared for little ones, and Beau got through it with no trouble at all. He consulted Dalton a couple of times anyway, seemingly for Dalton's sake, and the little boy beamed with pride.

When he closed the book and reached for another, Claire stood up. "I'll read the next one. You go grovel."

Alice was so confused. If Beau wanted to be with her, why had he left her all alone at midnight?

* * *

Beau looked around Alice's office, which was messier than usual. It seemed she'd started a million different projects, and hadn't finished any of them.

Alice Martin was not herself. And he understood, because he hadn't been himself for the past week, either. "I see you received the roses," he said.

"How did you know about those?"

"They're from me, Allie. Who did you think sent them?"

Alice stared at him, mouth agape, before finally answering. "I assumed they were from my father, because he sent me a rose in high school once, and he signed the card *from your Secret Admirer*—"

"No, darlin'," Beau said. "That was me."

Alice wrinkled her brow. "No, because you would have only been—"

"Thirteen," Beau said. "I was content to admire you from afar, because, well I was a kid. But then I grew into a man. And I was still your admirer, but I didn't think you could ever be interested in a simple, homespun, small-town cowboy like me. Not until we struck our deal, anyway."

"But you left me at the wedding…"

He took her hands. "I heard that you'd accepted a job offer in Austin and hadn't even told me."

"I didn't accept it. By the time they offered, I'd already made up my mind."

"I didn't know that. And I was hurt, Allie. I thought you didn't care about me at all, and that maybe *I* was the one who was bad at reading people. And that's why we need to talk it out. Right here. Right now."

"Okay—"

"Alice, I love you."

Alice stepped back, bumping into the desk and nearly knocking the roses over. Her pulse beat frantically at the base of her throat, and he could feel her fingers trembling. But she didn't say a word.

"I thought maybe I was just something to mark off your bucket list."

That did it. Her eyes filled with tears. "Oh, Beau..."

He took a risk and pulled her close. "It's just you, Allie. You're the only woman I want. And I am so sorry I hurt you. I didn't mean to. I didn't *want* to. And I swear to God, I will sign a contract right now stating that I will never do it again."

Allie lifted her head to look at him. Would she accept his pledge? Or had he hurt her too badly?

"I believe you, Beau. And I believe *in* you."

The relief damn near buckled his knees.

"And I'm not the only one who believes in you. You just need to believe in yourself."

This morning, when he'd gone in to quit his job as foreman, he'd ended up telling Gerome and Ford about his dyslexia instead. And they hadn't cared at all, other than being mad that he hadn't told them earlier. And it turned out that the broken pump had nothing to do with him—the dang thing had broken because it was old—and the inventory miscalculation had been Bryce's error.

Everyone made mistakes.

Alice brushed the hair out of his eyes, and the touch set him on fire. He wanted to kiss her, but did he dare? She still hadn't said—

"I love you," she whispered. "Just you. And nobody else."

She rose on her toes and kissed him.

They say that a man's life flashes before his eyes when he's about to die. But Beau's flashed before his at the touch of Alice's lips. He saw himself jumping into the clear waters of the Rio Verde. Riding his horse hard and fast. Chasing Bryce around the big oak tree. Trying his best to please the babysitter, who made him feel soft and squishy inside. All of this and more blew through his consciousness as he kissed Alice.

Dancing with Alice. Reading with Alice. Laughing and crying and making love with Alice. Growing old with Alice.

He broke the kiss, because he felt as if he might lose himself completely if he didn't. And anyway, he still had something else to say. "Listen, I think you should take that job in Austin. I don't want to hold you back. And I already talked to Gerome. He said I can move to the dude ranch. There are a few cowboy positions open and—"

"You'd do that for me?"

"I'll do anything for you."

"I don't want to go to Austin, Beau. I really don't. I love this library. I love this town. And I love my cowboy."

Oh, dear Lord. He nearly collapsed with relief. "I think we need to write up a new contract," he said, grinning.

Alice held up a finger. "With an evolving bucket list—"

"Beginning now."

Alice raised an eyebrow. "And ending..."

"Never, darlin'. Never ever."

The deal was sealed with another kiss.

And they lived happily ever after.

The End.

Epilogue

ॐ

Alice sat all alone at a corner table at Chateau Bleu, nervously twisting and untwisting the napkin in her lap. Something had probably come up at the ranch. Maybe a fence was down. Maybe there were cattle out. Maybe Beau was assisting the vet with a laboring heifer. These things happened, and as Beau often said, you just had to roll with it.

She was getting better at rolling, but Beau usually called to let her know when he was going to be late.

She checked her phone again. Still no message. No missed call.

A streak of blue caught her eye. Carmen had been dashing back and forth between the restaurant and the hotel all evening. Chateau Bleu provided room service for the hotel guests, but unless there was an event, there usually weren't that many guests. And Carmen wouldn't be the one delivering room service anyway. Carmen spotted her, smiled, and headed to her table.

"Is everything okay? Can I get you another glass of wine while you wait?"

"Everything is perfect," Alice said. "Beau is just running a little late."

Carmen sat and leaned forward. "I'll help you pass the time. How's your new job?"

Alice's nerves calmed ever so slightly with this welcome distraction. "Challenging, and I love it."

She'd recently been promoted to the previously nonexistent position of Verde County Library director. The Big Verde Public Library had joined with two other small rural libraries, and Alice oversaw all three.

"How about you? How are things at the Rockin' Bleu?"

"Great reviews from food critics. I've got a fantastic chef and a great manager, which is good, because my Vegas chef quit. I've been spending most of my time in Nevada."

"I've missed you," Alice said.

"I'm going to try to get home more."

"Did you just refer to Big Verde as your home?"

Carmen grinned. "I've got a suite here and one at the dude ranch. But I'm thinking of selling my house in Houston and making the Texas Hill Country my headquarters. It's centrally located, and the best part? I'll be closer to my bestie."

Nobody had ever called Alice their *bestie* before. It made her feel a bit gooey and soft inside. It also made her want to have a sleepover and do each other's nails.

Carmen's phone vibrated. After glancing at it, her eyes twinkled. "Your dinner is ready."

"My dinner? But I haven't even ordered it yet. And Beau's not here."

"Both are waiting in room 218."

Alice suppressed a squeal. She should have known Beau would do something special for the one-year anniversary of their contract.

"Don't forget this," Carmen said, snatching a red rose from a vase on the table. There was a little card attached: *From your Secret Admirer.*

Holy guacamole. She hadn't even noticed it! She took the rose, hugged Carmen, and rushed through the restaurant and hotel lobby to the stairs, which she took two at a time. Soon, she was standing in front of room 218, staring at the same door she'd knocked on a year ago.

She inhaled deeply and tapped softly. Would Beau answer in a sexy suit and tie? Her knees went weak just thinking about it.

A bare chest suddenly opened the door. At least that's how it seemed. There were probably other body parts as well—a head and legs, for example. But the chest, which was muscular and naked, was taking up the entire doorway. Her gaze drifted down to the unbuttoned jeans. It took some effort to drag it back up, where it landed on a pair of bright blue eyes.

A delightful tingle sparked at the base of her spine and worked its way to her mouth, which was turned up in a huge smile. "Oh, Beau," she sighed. "It's you."

I always want it to be you.

Beau winked. "Are you lost, Allie Cat?"

She threw her arms around his neck, giggling like crazy. "No. I'm right where I need to be."

Beau gave her a squeeze and picked her up like she was cotton candy. Then he carried her into the room, slamming the door with his foot.

There was a small table set with china, crystal, and candles, and the room smelled fantastic. "You didn't have to go to all this trouble, but it's lovely, and I'm glad you did."

Her stomach chose that moment to growl loudly, and Beau laughed.

"It sounds like we might have to eat before getting to the fun and games portion of the evening," he said.

Yes, but first, she had something to say. And she was going to go crazy if she didn't do it right now. "Can we sit for a moment? We need to talk."

"Sure, darlin'," Beau said, taking a seat on the bed. "What's on your mind?"

"I've been contemplating our current contract."

Beau shifted and pulled her onto his lap. "There's no expiration date, remember? You. Me. Together forever or until you get tired of me." His eyes widened. "Are you tired of me?"

"I'm never going to get tired of you, Beau," she said, running a finger along his cheek. "But I've been doing some research, and well…" She cleared her throat. "I think we might need a new contract. It seems there are many advantages to, you know, legally joining."

"Legally joining?"

She swallowed loudly, even though her throat was dry from nerves. "Like financial advantages. Some studies indicate there can even be long-term health benefits for married couples—"

Beau gasped. "Alice Ann Martin, are you proposing to me?"

"Marriage proposals are old-fashioned and archaic and often sexist. One person shouldn't ask the other for their hand in marriage. It should be a mutual decision, and I'm merely trying to open up some dialogue—"

"Yes."

"What?"

"Yes, Allie. I'll marry you."

Relief washed over her like a torrential downpour. She tried to inhale but discovered she couldn't. Had she forgotten how to breathe?

"Are you okay?" Beau asked.

"Yes. But are you sure? You don't want to talk about it some more?"

"We can talk about it for as long as you like, which is probably pretty long. I'm sure you came armed with facts and figures, but Allie, I want nothing more than to be your husband."

She absolutely *had* come armed with facts and figures. "Did you know that married people have better outcomes following major surgery and are more likely to—"

Beau leaned back against the pillow, pulling her with him, and she forgot all of her facts and figures.

"We need to add *Engagement celebration* to our bucket list," he said.

"How do you *propose* we celebrate?" She lifted her head to see if he got it. "I said *propose* as a joke."

Beau chuckled, and it vibrated her belly. "I have a few things in mind." He licked her bottom lip. "And I suggest we get started right away."

She liked the sound of that.

"And darlin', I did a little research of my own. The Village Chateau is point-four-six miles past the city limits."

"So?"

"So, noise ordinances do not apply."

Acknowledgments

What can I say? I wrote a book during a pandemic. And kudos to you, by the way, if you completed *anything* during the year of our Lord 2020. Seriously. Raise your glass if you made your bed or a sandwich, because you're a winner.

My biggest thank-you goes to my editor, Junessa Viloria, who managed to scoot me and this book across the finish line without ever uttering the word *deadline*. She's an author whisperer, and working with her is an utter delight.

Thank you to my copyeditor, Lori Paximadis, for getting down to the nitty-gritty with such aplomb (if I used that word incorrectly, she'll no doubt tell me), and to Bob Castillo for making sure that I'm happy with every single word. Extra-special thanks to Estelle Hallick for loving Big Verde and working so hard to promote my books. She's spectacularly creative and fun, and she's *still* my favorite Disney princess. Finally, thank you to my agent, Paige Wheeler, for always believing in me and my work.

Writing can be lonely for an extrovert (even when there's no pandemic), so I leaned heavily on a few folks to keep me energized and motivated. First, thank you to my family, who became my captive audience during quarantine. Their support never wavered, even when I had to break the news that they were my new social circle.

Thank you to Jessica Snyder, who literally babysat me every

morning while I drafted (via Zoom). If she didn't hear the keys clacking, she cracked the whip. She calls herself a writing coach, but she's more of a dominatrix.

Thank you to my community of writers, especially Amy Bearce, who was always available for a Zoom chat. As usual, she read every word of every version of this book, and she did it cheerfully. Thank you to Sam Tschida and the writers at Smut U, some of whom relentlessly wrote through wildfires in addition to a pandemic. I'm lucky to have them as cohorts. Thanks to Alison Bliss and Kamau Khary for their willingness to cyber-sprint with me when I didn't want to write alone, and to Erin Quinn, Sasha Summers, Jolene Navarro, Patricia Walters-Fischer, and Teri Wilson for their readiness to lend an ear.

Thank you to my assistant, Jenn Jaeger, and to my readers' group, Carly's Bloomers, for entertaining and encouraging me, particularly Gemma, Kristen, Anne, Brittni, and Addie. I love to write, but I especially enjoy doing it for them.

Last, but certainly not least, thank you to my readers. Big Verde is my escape and my refuge, and I love so very much that you join me there. Let's have lunch together soon at the Corner Café.

Turn the page to read a special bonus novel:

Big Bad Cowboy,
the first book in Carly Bloom's
Once Upon a Time in Texas series.

Who's afraid of the big bad cowboy?

After one too many heartbreaks, Travis Blake has hung up his cowboy hat and put Big Verde, Texas, behind him. But when he gets a call that his young nephew needs him, he knows he has to return home. His plan is to sell the family ranch and hightail it back to Austin, but there's a small problem: The one person who stands in his way is the one person he can't resist.

Maggie is pretty sure she hates Travis Blake. He's irritating, he's destroying her business, and...and he's just so frickin' *attractive*. But when they're forced to work together, Maggie discovers that the Most Annoying Man in the World is more than he seems. He's sweet with his nephew, he helps out in the community, and he makes her heart flutter. Maggie doesn't want to risk everything on a man who wants to leave, but what if she can convince this wayward cowboy to stay?

To Jeff, my real-life cowboy. You and your boots, cargo shorts, and Red Hot Chili Peppers T-shirt just plain do it for me.

Acknowledgments

It takes a village just to get me out of the house before noon. It took a global network of enablers to help me write *Big Bad Cowboy*.

Extra special thanks to my B Team—Amy Bearce, Alison Bliss, and Samantha Bohrman. You long-suffering ladies read every version of this manuscript with a bottle of wine and a stress ball. I see right through your empty threats of *Never Again!* and I know you'll be there for the next This Has to Be Fixed Right Now crisis. How awesome is that (for me)?

Thank you to Jessica Snyder for coming all the way to Texas for a taco-eating brainstorming session and for introducing me to the hilarious Pippa Grant! You make writing fun. And to Erin Quinn— I'd be a nobody without you! Thank you for "discovering" me.

Warm hugs and kisses to my reading group, Carly's Bloomers, and to my fellow SARA's in San Antonio Romance Authors. You inspire me every day.

Thank you to my wonderful agent, Paige Wheeler, for working so hard on my behalf. I still remember our first phone call, and how Freddy Mercury crowed his wicked heart out the moment I said *hello*. I might have been your first client to apologize for her rooster.

Thank you to Michele Bidelspach for letting me know that Travis's secret dream was to be a real cowboy. He'd have no hat without you!

And thank you to my editor, Madeleine Colavita, for pretending I don't have an italics problem. Your invaluable wisdom and guidance brought Maggie and Travis to life. Please don't ever stop dropping smiley-face bombs on my manuscripts. And to everyone else at Grand Central Publishing, especially Joan Mathews, huntress of dangling modifiers, thank you for knowing what you're doing!

Extra special thanks to my family. You are my world, and without your faith and support, I'd never reach *The End*.

Finally, thank you to my readers. You complete me.

Chapter

One

❦

White caliche dust clung to Travis Blake's boots as he slammed the squeaky door on the mailbox. Or tried to anyway. It was smashed nearly flat, because not much had changed in Big Verde, Texas, during the twelve years he'd been gone. There were still a few idiots who thought it was fun to hang out of truck windows while blasting down dirt roads taking out mailboxes with baseball bats.

Travis stuck the mail under his arm—he'd face whatever holy hell it contained when he got back to the house—and squinted up and down the dirt road. Whoever had destroyed his mailbox was long gone. He added *Replace mailbox* to his endless mental list of things to do and headed for his truck idling on the road.

He dumped the stack of mail on the center console and put the truck in Drive, just as a small voice piped up from the backseat.

"Uncle Travis, you're not s'posed to leave me in the truck while it's runnin'."

Travis jerked and looked over the seat, blinking slowly until reality clicked into place like a steel vault door. It had been eight weeks since he'd gotten out of the Army with meticulous plans for the rest of his life, and six weeks since those plans had been annihilated by a phone call from a social worker.

Six weeks since he'd met his nephew, Henry, for the first time.

"You were fine. You couldn't get out of that contraption you're buckled into to save your soul. And even if you did, why would you be stupid enough to try to drive the truck?"

"Because I'm a kid!"

Travis didn't have much experience with children, but Henry struck him as being smarter than the average five-year-old, which was probably the very worst kind of five-year-old.

Henry kicked the back of Travis's seat because he knew Travis hated it, and Travis clenched his jaw and ignored it because he knew Henry hated *that*. He slowly drove up to the big iron gate adorned by the ranch's brand, an H with a rising T in the shape of a horseshoe.

When Travis was thirteen, his father, Ben Blake, moved him and his brother from a trailer park on the outskirts of Houston to the two-hundred-acre Texas Hill Country ranch known as Happy Trails. Rags to riches. And often back again. That was high-stakes professional poker in a nutshell.

Being a naive kid, Travis had thought all three of them would immediately become real cowboys. His dad had even bought him a black gelding named Moonshine, who he'd promptly lost in a bet. The only thing the man had ever managed to hold on to was the ranch. Which was good, because Travis intended to sell it.

"Mrs. Garza says you don't know what you're doing," Henry said, seeking another button to push.

"Well, thank God for Mrs. Garza," Travis said. And he meant it, too. If it wasn't for Mrs. Garza taking care of Henry after school and on weekends while Travis did light landscaping work, he didn't know what he'd do. His final pay from the Army was being held up in a tangle of bureaucratic red tape, and he couldn't start his new job in Austin until he'd tied up the loose ends at Happy Trails. He glanced at Henry in the rearview mirror. The child was more of a thrashing, uncontrollable projectile than a dangling loose end. It was hard not to feel sorry for him, though. Henry's daddy was currently a guest at the Texas State Penitentiary in Huntsville. And his mama had just died of ovarian cancer.

The social worker seemed to think Travis was Henry's only living kin not serving time behind bars.

Yep. Definitely hard not to feel sorry for the kid.

Travis pushed the remote on the visor and waited for the gate to open.

And waited.

"Goddammit."

"That's a bad word," Henry spouted.

The remote for the gate didn't work. Travis got out—kept the fucking truck running so Henry wouldn't chide him about it—and trudged over to open the gate manually. A white piece of paper flapped in the breeze.

YOU ARE IN VIOLATION OF AGRICULTURAL CODE 246.4B AGAIN. IT IS NOT MY RESPONSIBILITY TO KEEP YOUR COWS OFF MY PROPERTY. IT IS YOURS. FIX YOUR DANG FENCES.

Travis yanked the note off the gate, crumpled it up, and dropped it.

"Litterbug!"

Henry was in prime form. He'd fallen asleep in the car seat, something he invariably did about three minutes before they got wherever it was they were going. Stopping the truck was like poking a nest of hornets, and that's why Travis had left it idling.

He leaned over and grabbed the wadded piece of paper, held it up for Henry to see, and then shoved it in his pocket. The gate groaned loudly as he pushed it to the post and hitched it on the wire. Then he got back in the truck, drove through the gate, stopped the truck, turned the goddam thing off while giving Henry the evil eye, and climbed out to close the gate behind him.

By the time he finally got back in, an audience had lined up on either side of the lane; young bulls on one side and heifers on the other. At least those fence lines were holding. The same couldn't be said for the one separating his east pasture from Honey Mackey's apple orchard. The crazy old lady kept leaving him threatening notes. He'd patched the fence multiple times, but it didn't hold. It needed to be completely replaced. The only things required were time and money, both of which were in short supply.

The herd followed them along as they drove up the lane, even though the bed of the truck was loaded with a lawn mower and a weed whacker—tools of his temporary trade—and not hay. Henry waved at the cows until the truck turned left at the split and continued up to the house.

The windmill rose above the trees as they hit the top of the hill, and Travis automatically depressed the accelerator at the tug of its familiar silhouette. His dad, always full of cowboy dictums, had said windmills made a horse's hooves trot a little faster and a man's heart long for hearth and home. The effect it had on Travis was surprising, since neither hearth nor home had ever quite risen to the occasion.

Unlike the windmill, the sight of the house stirred no warm, fuzzy feels. The attic windows stared angrily, like a glowering monster. A new coat of paint would probably do wonders. Make the place more _Southern Living_ and less _Amityville Horror_.

"Let me out!" Henry said. Then he convulsed and rocked in his seat until Travis reached back and sprung him.

"Stay out of the cookies. You've got to eat supper first."

Henry jumped down, leaving supper—a greasy paper bag from the drive-thru hamburger joint—on the seat next to his backpack. It was the best Travis could do after a long day at work, where he'd grubbed, dug, and planted at the Village Chateau, the fanciest hotel in Big Verde. And when he was done with all that, he'd helped get the place ready for Annabelle Vasquez's Halloween party. She'd kept a watchful eye on him as he'd installed a fake graveyard and set up a pumpkin patch. He'd politely turned down the invitation Anna had offered when he left. He didn't much care for parties, and this one seemed especially awful as it required a costume. He shivered at the thought as he followed Henry through the back door.

Anna had also invited him to bid on a landscaping project for her new house. He'd turned that down, too. For one thing, he didn't intend to remain in Big Verde long enough to complete a lavish Annabelle-style project that he was woefully unqualified to install. For another, it wasn't a good idea to work for someone you'd slept with.

*   *   *

Fishnet thigh-high stockings with silly bows on the back and a skirt so short it might be illegal—both in red. Maggie sighed. Why had she trusted Claire to rent a Halloween costume for her? She kicked off her sensible shoes and tossed her jacket on the bed while eyeing her best friend and co-worker, who had never owned a pair of sensible shoes in her life. With dark auburn hair and curves right out of a 1950s lingerie catalog, Claire was the opposite of Maggie, who looked more like your average little sister. Or—she ran her hands over the area where most women had hips—your average little brother.

"What do you think?" Claire asked. One corner of her mouth twitched. She knew exactly what Maggie thought and was clearly enjoying the hell out of it.

"Were they all out of stormtrooper costumes?"

Claire rolled her eyes and then held up a microscopic wisp of fabric with laces. "This is going to look fantastic on you. Way better than a stormtrooper costume."

"Is that a corset?"

Maggie had never seen a corset in real life, much less worn one. Maybe it would give her some curves if she yanked those laces real tight...

"Red will look great with your platinum blond hair."

"It's dirty blond, not platinum, and red washes me out. Also, stop trying so hard."

She took the corset from Claire and held it up against her yellow work polo with the green Petal Pushers logo. Pop, her blue-haired French bulldog, gave a bark of approval.

"I'm not trying. This *will* look great on you." Claire lifted a few strands of Maggie's hair out of her eyes. "And you call this pixie cut dirty blond?"

"Well, it's not platinum." Depending on how much Maggie was outdoors—which was a lot since she was a landscaper—her hair color ran the full gamut of sun-streaked caramel to light blond. People thought it was lighter than it was because of her ridiculously dark eyebrows and brown eyes. "And it's not a pixie cut," Maggie added, tossing her bangs out of her eyes. "A pixie cut is a hair-*do* and I don't *do* dos. Anyway, I can't wear this costume. It's demeaning."

"It's sexy. You can't clunk around a client's masked gala in a stormtrooper costume."

The client was Annabelle Vasquez, who was doing her best to spend a recent divorce settlement. "Would you stop referring to this silly Halloween party as a masked gala?"

"That's what the invitation said."

Annabelle was a pretentious snob. But Maggie really wanted to do the landscaping for the McMansion she'd plunked on top of the highest hill in Big Verde. It would be a challenge to make something out of that mound of limestone, but Maggie was looking forward to it. It wasn't often that she was able to work on a project in this small town that utilized her master of landscape architecture degree from Texas A&M.

"Travis Blake better not bid on that job," she said.

A couple of months ago it would have been a given for Petal Pushers, the garden center and landscape business Maggie owned, to win the contract. But now she had competition. *Travis Blake.* Just the thought of him made her shudder in revulsion.

"He's been aggressive about getting business since moving back to Big Verde," Claire said. "So, I'm actually not surprised."

"He's nothing but a glorified lawn boy," Maggie grumbled. "He's not remotely qualified, and besides, I bet his landscaping business isn't even a legit operation. You know he's an ex-con, right? He's probably a bookie, and the landscaping thing is just a front." She didn't know what a bookie did, but it was something shady and involved gambling, which was a known Blake family vice.

"I don't think it's a front," Claire said, picking up the micro-skirt Maggie was expected to squeeze into and holding it up to her own frame. "And besides, he's not an ex-con. You're thinking of his brother, Scott."

Nice boys, those Blake brothers. One of them—Maggie didn't even know which—had married Lisa Henley, knocked her up, and then, in the words of Maggie's dear dead grandmother, Honey Mackey, *That boy done run oft*.

Lisa had recently passed away, leaving behind a young child. Maybe that was why Travis was back. The kid must be his.

"Maybe you could take him a pie," Claire continued. "And sit down like neighbors to discuss his power grab."

Maggie laughed at the audacity of taking Travis Blake a pie. And only a girl like Claire, raised on a twelve-thousand-acre ranch, would consider Maggie and Travis neighbors. Maggie couldn't even see the Blake house from hers. And unbelievably, she hadn't seen Travis either. She wouldn't know him if he held a door for her while tipping his hat. Although she doubted he was that polite.

"You really shouldn't mess with him the way you do," Claire

said. "You know, just in case he is every bit as horrible as you like to imagine."

"I don't *mess* with him. I leave informative notes on his gate. He needs to keep his scraggly cows on his side of the fence." She smirked and added, "I quoted agricultural codes."

"You know agricultural codes?"

"No, but I'm betting he doesn't either."

Claire crossed her arms over her ample bosom. "You weren't terribly bothered by the cows getting into Honey's apple orchard before Travis got here. I think you're just itching for a fight with a Blake boy."

Grandma Honey had engaged in an epic battle of wills with Ben Blake over the damn cows getting in her apple orchard. But when he'd passed away four years ago, and Lisa and her baby had moved into the ranch house, Honey had merely chased the cows back in with a broom and a few choice words, because *That girl's got enough problems.*

Now that both Honey and Lisa were gone, and Travis Blake was back—stealing landscaping accounts instead of mending fences— Maggie had gleefully revived the battle in true Hatfield and McCoy style. "I won't have Blake cows destroying Honey's apple orchard," she said. "It's mine now, and I intend to defend it against all enemies."

Maggie walked to the window and squinted in the direction of the Happy Trails' ranch house. A patch of cedar trees blocked her view, which was just as well. Honey had said the place was pretty run down. It was more than Lisa had been able to keep up with on her own, even before she'd gotten sick.

"I hear he's really cute now," Claire said, joining Maggie at the window.

"I'd forgotten he even existed," Maggie said. He'd been a couple of grades ahead of her, and it wasn't as if she'd had a social life. Not unless you considered cow tipping with the Future Farmers of

America a social life. She'd been the only girl in Big Verde High's FFA program.

"Listen, there's something you should know," Claire said, chewing on her fingernail.

Nothing good ever followed *Listen, there's something you should know.* "Spit it out."

"Travis did the new landscaping at the Village Chateau."

The Village Chateau was the nicest hotel in town and the venue for the night's gala. More important, it was Maggie's landscaping account.

"Are you sure?"

Claire nodded while twisting an auburn strand of hair around her finger. "I'm sure. He started doing the upkeep a few weeks ago, and when they expanded the courtyard, they asked him—"

"But we have a maintenance contract with the Chateau. That's our job," Maggie insisted.

"We never had a contract."

They *should* have had the Chateau under contract. They'd been careless and overly confident.

"Why didn't you tell me earlier?"

"I wanted to! But I knew it would make you all splotchy…"

Maggie glanced in the mirror above the dresser. *Dammit.* "I can't attend a party at the Chateau—an account we just lost—dressed like a hooker."

Claire pulled a shiny red cape out of the Halloween store bag. "You're not a hooker. You're Little Red Riding Hood. And the fact that we just lost an account is the very reason you must go. We're going to make sure Petal Pushers wins Anna's project. Not Travis Blake."

Maggie crossed her arms over her chest and glared at the costume. She might as well be going as a sexy nurse or a French maid. "More like Little Red Riding Whore."

Claire snorted. "You're going to look sexy as hell while kicking ass. Maybe you'll even have fun. And JD will be there." She looked at Maggie as if she'd just said checkmate.

Maggie had chased after JD Mayes, with pigtails flying, since she was ten years old. Honey had always said, "You're like a dog chasing a pickup truck, Maggie. If you catch that boy, you won't have the slightest idea what to do with him."

At twenty-seven, Maggie knew exactly what to do with JD. *If* she ever caught him. Unfortunately, he was like all the other guys in Big Verde and saw her only as a friend. A good friend, which made it even worse. She held the corset up again, scrutinizing her image in the full-length mirror. She didn't look awful. Even with her grubby jeans on the bottom.

"You haven't seen the best part," Claire said.

What could possibly top the micro-miniskirt, corset, and snappy little cape and hood?

"Ta da!" Claire held up two shiny red boots. "You didn't think I was going to let you get by with garden clogs, did you?"

Well, no. But Maggie had thought maybe her red Converse high-tops would work in a sporty Red Riding Whore way. But these boots were better. "There's only one more fashion accessory I need," she declared.

"Earrings?"

"No." Maggie took the boots from Claire's hand. "A cowboy to wrap these around."

Chapter

Two

Travis put Henry's hamburger and fries on a plate and squirted ketchup onto a saucer, so it wouldn't touch the rest of his food. The kid was weird about that.

"Henry!" he shouted. "Come eat."

Henry was settled in front of the television, not budging, and prying him away from it would be a bigger battle than Travis had the energy for. He popped a TV tray up in front of Henry, set his food on it, and went back in the kitchen to get his own burger. Maybe he'd eat in front of the TV, too. He didn't even care what was on.

His phone rang as he grabbed a plate. It was the realtor, George Streleki. "Hey, George," Travis said. "What have you found out? When can we get this place on the market?"

"Well, that depends," Streleki stated simply.

"On what?"

"Your brother—"

"Scott and I inherited Happy Trails when our dad died. And we both want to sell." Was Scott's latest incarceration the problem? The idiot had been caught with drugs at the Mexican border.

"I believe you," George said. "But I've got to get something from your brother stating his intent to sell."

Travis should be able to get that. It would be unpleasant—every interaction with Scott was—but not difficult. "No problem."

"And did you know there's a lien against the property?"

This was news. "A lien? Why? How?" Shouldn't he have known about something this important?

Maybe if you'd ever bothered to check on your brother's wife and son, you'd know what the fuck was going on.

After their dad died, Travis had told Scott that he and Lisa could live on the ranch for as long as they wanted. What did Travis care? He didn't want it. All he asked was that they take care of the cattle to hold on to the agricultural tax exemption and...*pay the fucking property taxes.* He swallowed. Hard. Scott had been busted shortly after that conversation.

"You've got some back taxes built up," the realtor said. "You'll get a hell of a lot more money for the place if you can pay those off. Otherwise, folks will just be looking to take advantage of you."

The knot Travis had swallowed rose back up.

"Shit," Travis said. "I'll get back to you, George." He slammed down the phone.

"What's wrong?" Henry asked. He was covered in ketchup.

"Nothing." *Everything.*

He was going to need real money to pay off the taxes. There was no point in hitting Scott up for it. And the change he was bringing in mowing lawns was putting food on the table, but that was about it.

He chewed his lip. Where the hell could he come up with a big chunk of money? The check he was expecting from the Army most likely wouldn't cover it. He stared at the invitation to Anna's costume party resting on top of the mail, the one she'd handed him as he left the Village Chateau. The *Dia de los Muertos* skeletons and their taunting, garish grins stared back.

"Henry, I've got to go out tonight. Will you be okay if Mrs. Garza comes over?"

Henry's eyes lit up. He'd seen the party invitation in the truck. "You're going to the costume party? Can I go?"

"Believe it or not, it's just for grown-ups."

Henry shot past him and ran up the stairs. "I've got a mask for you!"

Travis wasn't going to wear a mask. He dumped his hamburger in the trash and went upstairs to the bathroom. He needed a shower if he was going to the party. He sniffed a pit. And even if he wasn't.

While Henry scrounged around for a mask Travis had no intention of wearing, Travis stripped and stepped into the shower. He turned the water on full throttle, nice and hot, so it could pummel his sore shoulders and back.

God, he dreaded this party. He'd intentionally kept to himself since moving back to Big Verde. He hadn't exactly made a ton of friends here as a kid. And of all people, it sucked that it was Anna holding this power over him. But there was a chance her landscaping project would pay enough to take care of the back taxes.

He snorted, remembering himself at seventeen. He'd been a clueless, puny bookworm, and Annabelle Vasquez had never paid him any mind until he started mowing her family's lawn. He could still see her standing at her bedroom window, curling a strand of shiny black hair around a finger and licking her lips while she watched him work.

She'd been his first crush, and it had been a thrill. But after doing an awful lot of Anna's homework assignments, he'd realized he was being used. He'd tried to end things as politely as possible, but it was Anna's first taste of rejection, and she hadn't much cared for it. She accused him of stealing a bracelet out of her car. Her father had even filed a police report. Nothing had come of it.

There had been no witnesses, and of course, Travis hadn't stolen the damn thing. But he was embarrassed by it.

He'd worked so hard to be the *Good Blake Boy*. But he and his family were outsiders in Big Verde. Folks had believed Anna, their hometown girl, and everyone suddenly claimed to have seen it coming:

Apple doesn't fall far from the tree. Poor kid didn't have a chance. How else was he going to turn out?

He groaned as the shower head did what it was supposed to, and his muscles melted beneath the pounding stream. He'd work up a bid for Annabelle as soon as he got out of the shower. How hard could it be? It wasn't as if you needed a damn degree in landscaping to move dirt or plant shrubs. Although *some* people seemed to think so.

Mary Margaret Mackey had gone to A&M and earned a degree in landscape architecture. Travis knew this because he'd stalked her LinkedIn profile after damn near every business in town had told him Petal Pushers did their landscaping: a college degree, an internship at a big company in Fort Worth, followed by a questionable move back to Big Verde, where she obviously hoped to impress everyone with her vast knowledge of potted plants. *Petal Pushers*—what the hell kind of name was that? Did she flounce around in a pink sundress and fancy hat?

He turned off the shower and shook his head like a dog as Henry pounded on the door. "Uncle Travis!"

Travis ran a towel over his body and wrapped it around his waist. He didn't trust the old lock and didn't need another bathroom invasion resulting in an awkward conversation about the size of his penis.

"What is it, Henry?" It could be something as simple as wanting a cookie. But it could also be the beginning of a fit. Travis hadn't spent any time around Henry before Lisa died. He didn't know if the fits were typical shenanigans for a five-year-old kid, or if they were the result of loss. Either way, he dealt with them. He seriously doubted his idiot brother could do half as well. He'd had little more to do with Henry than Travis had.

"I found the mask!"

"That's awesome, buddy," Travis called back. "But I'm not gonna wear a costume."

Holding the towel in place, Travis opened the door. A disappointed face met him on the other side, but it didn't appear Henry was about to go ballistic.

"I've decided to go to the party as a ruggedly handsome man, so I don't need a mask." He gave Henry his best cheesy smile and puffed out his chest.

Henry didn't laugh. "I don't think people will know you're dressed up in a costume. You'll just look like yourself, and you're butt ugly."

Travis laughed and mussed Henry's hair, and Henry threw his skinny little arms around Travis's waist. Travis took a step back at the sudden display of affection, dragging Henry with him. Then he patted Henry's back, feeling the tiny shoulder blades poking against his Spider-Man T-shirt. The contact was getting a little less awkward each day.

"You always tell it like it is, Henry."

"That's because you're not supposed to lie."

Travis peeled Henry off and squatted so he was eye level. "You going to be okay with Mrs. Garza tonight? I might be late."

"Yes," Henry said, lowering his voice to a whisper. "But you have to tell her about my bedtime problem."

"You mean how you're a very sound sleeper and sometimes don't wake up to go to the bathroom?" Changing sheets and pajamas in the middle of the night was a pain in the ass, but Travis refused to shame Henry about wetting the bed. His own dad had been an asshole about that sort of thing, and Travis wasn't going to follow suit.

Henry nodded.

"I'll tell her. But go to the bathroom before she puts you to bed, okay?"

"It don't help," Henry said.

"It doesn't help," Travis corrected.

"That's what I said."

Travis sighed. "I wish I didn't have to go to this stupid party."

"*Stupid* is a bad word."

"Did your mom tell you that?"

A watery expression floated across Henry's face. Travis hated bringing Lisa up, but the lady at school who provided Henry with grief counseling told him he shouldn't avoid it.

"Mom didn't like the word *stupid*."

"I'll try not to say it so much then."

Henry's little eyebrows turned down for a frown. "I wonder when my dad's gonna come get me."

Henry couldn't have many memories of Scott. He'd seen him only a handful of times, and Henry had been awfully young. "Remember what we talked about? Your dad can't come to Big Verde right now."

Henry's lower lip began to tremble. "He don't want me."

"He *doesn't* want—" Travis shut his mouth. "You know what, big guy? I think you're right. I need a costume. Let's see that mask."

Just like that, Henry snapped out of it. "I've got three little piggies and *this*."

Two yellow eyes and a pair of wicked fangs.

Who's afraid of the Big Bad Wolf?

Chapter Three

❧

Maggie watched through the windshield as Claire picked her way across the Village Chateau's parking lot on stiletto heels. The full October moon lit up the witchy silhouette, complete with broom and pointy hat.

Maggie flashed the Jeep's lights to get Claire's attention, and then got out and leaned against the door. She ran her hands over the corset, barely recognizing her own shape. It was as snug as she and Claire could get it, and came just below her breasts, which were probably supposed to be pushed up and out, but Maggie owned no contraption capable of achieving such a feat. Instead, she wore a stretchy bandeau bra beneath the white off-the-shoulder blouse because it was the only strapless bra she owned. The boots were above the knee, and the red fishnet thigh-high stockings stopped about four inches from the bottom of her skirt.

She felt both sexy and silly.

A truck pulled into the parking lot, shining its headlights in Maggie's face. She squinted as it swung around before backing into the space in front of her. She rolled her eyes at the bright blue "bull balls" hanging from its hitch, swinging obscenely to the bass beat of a Rascal Flatts song. Why did guys hang scrotum sacks on their trucks?

The music stopped abruptly as Bubba Larson opened his truck door and climbed out. "Howdy, Mighty Mack."

When would guys stop referring to her as Mighty Mack? It had been cute in high school, when she'd earned the nickname by being the only kid in FFA who could get Mini-Might, a two-thousand-pound Brahman bull, into the chute. But now it was just childish and unwomanly and didn't go with her new corset.

The lighting was too dim for details, but it seemed Bubba had poured his portly self into something tight. In fact, it looked like he might be *wearing* tights.

A light breeze blew Maggie's cape open.

"Goddamn, girl," Bubba said. "I'm Superman, but what are you supposed to be?"

"She's Little Red Riding Hood," Claire said, arriving just in time to give Maggie backup. "Isn't she cute?"

Bubba raised his eyebrows. "I don't know that *cute* is the word I'd use."

Humiliation crept in, and warmth spread across Maggie's cheeks. They were probably the same color as her cape, which she quickly yanked closed. Why had she let Claire talk her into wearing this outfit? She felt like a little girl who'd been caught in her mother's lingerie. She must look laughable! Since feeling humiliated was not something she enjoyed, she became pissed off instead. "Listen here, Bubba. You're one to talk. I mean, if anybody looks more ridiculous than me—"

"Who said you look ridiculous?" Bubba asked. "You look smokin' hot, Mighty Mack." He nodded at Claire and added, "You, too."

Claire curtsied with her broom, but Maggie shifted nervously from foot to foot. Bubba looked as serious as a large man with a muffin top over his tights could look, so she let go of the cape.

"Come on," Bubba said, offering an arm to each of them. "Let's light this place up."

"Isn't Trista coming?" Claire asked.

"She's already here," Bubba said. "Came early to help out."

"Is she a superhero, too?" Maggie asked, taking Bubba's arm.

"Nah. She's dressed as a nun."

Claire laughed. "She must be at least eight months along by now."

"Seven," Bubba said. "Baby is due around Christmas. She just looks like she's about to pop. Don't tell her I said that."

"Do you know whether it's a boy or girl?" Maggie asked.

"We'll find out when it gets here. I figure it's another girl."

Bubba and Trista had three daughters. As Bubba liked to say, his swimmers wore skirts. He worshipped those baby girls, though. He and Trista had been together since high school.

Maggie's heel hit a pebble and she wobbled. "Don't let go of me." She might look smokin' hot leaning against her Jeep, but walking turned her into a spindly-legged newborn calf.

"You'll get the hang of it," Claire said. "Just try to walk normally."

"Which one of you is going to cut a rug with me?" Bubba asked. "Trista can't do it. Not unless we want this party to get a lot more exciting than it should."

Maggie loved to dance. But she'd break her neck doing it in these boots. "I'm just learning to walk in these," she said. "No way I could keep up with you on the dance floor."

Bubba was a lumbering alligator on dry land, but set him on some sawdust and he turned into a sleek and nimble creature. He could drop into the splits and pop right back up. A crowd always gathered once he got going, and Maggie didn't need an audience watching as she stumbled around in her red porn star boots.

"You've got to dance tonight," Claire said. "Those boots were made for it."

Short of snowshoes, Maggie couldn't think of anything made *less* for it.

They passed the final row of parked cars. "There's the white horse," Claire said, pointing to a gigantic white King Ranch Special Edition Ford F350 pickup. "JD is here."

Maggie tripped, almost impaling herself on the iron railing of the Gothic fence surrounding the Chateau. Her heart hammered in her chest. "I wonder who he's with."

"It doesn't matter. You're dressed better. If JD keeps you in the friend zone after seeing you like this, then he just doesn't like girls."

Bubba snorted, and so did Maggie. JD liked girls all right. And they liked him. He'd probably dated every single woman in Big Verde, *with one obvious exception.*

* * *

The lobby of the hotel was covered in cobwebs, flickering lights, and ghoulish displays. Maggie had to give Annabelle credit for throwing a different kind of Halloween party. Instead of renting the VFW Hall, she had transformed the Village Chateau into a proper haunted castle for a party nobody would soon forget.

Maggie rolled her shoulders. Time to focus. She was here for one reason and one reason only. Well, two, really. But the first order of business was to show off her cinched-in waist and nice round ass (optical illusion) to JD Mayes. "You go kiss up to Anna," she said to Claire. "I'm going to find a certain cowboy."

"Both of us need a drink before our missions," Claire said. "Let's get some witch's brew."

A waiter whisked past with a tray of smoking goblets, and they each snatched one. Witch's brew was basically trashcan punch, and it went down easy. Maggie wiped her mouth on the hem of her cape. Then she looked around for JD.

Something shiny caught her eye, and since every cell in her body gravitated toward it, she knew it was JD. His boisterous laugh rose above the din, and Maggie's feet automatically headed toward the source. The crowd parted, and there he stood, dressed as a knight in shining armor.

"Go get him," Claire said. "I'll go compliment Anna on the party, and her hair, and her costume…"

Maggie kept her eyes on the prize—gosh, he was cute—but her mind went to business. "Remind Anna that I'm the only landscape architect within a hundred miles and that Travis Blake is a guy with a lawn mower."

Claire sauntered off and Maggie inhaled deeply, squared her shoulders, and strutted toward JD like America's Next Top Model if America's Next Top Model were wearing heels for the first time and was slightly buzzed on trashcan punch. JD stood with Alice, the town's librarian, who wore the familiar yellow ball gown from *Beauty and the Beast*.

"Hi, Alice."

"Oh my!" Alice squealed. "Look at you." She turned to JD and poked him in the ribs with her finger. "JD, look at Maggie."

JD took a long, hard look that turned Maggie's legs to jelly. Then he flashed his two-million-dollar smile. "I don't know who you're supposed to be," he said, "but red agrees with you."

"I'm Little Red Riding Hood."

JD wore a breastplate over his starched white shirt, and metal plates were strapped over his Wranglers to his thighs and shins. There was even a gilded faceplate attached to the brim of his white Stetson. He gave a deep, squeaky bow. "M'lady."

"Isn't he just precious?" Alice asked. She winked at Maggie from behind an open book.

"Oh yeah. He's just precious." Alice had pulled off coquettish, but Maggie sounded like she was having an asthma attack.

JD pulled a fake sword out of a scabbard hanging from his belt. "Check this out."

Why wasn't he drooling over her newly corseted curves? Maybe some pleasant conversation about his outfit would lead to some more comments about hers. She nodded at his boots. "You're wearing the white tops."

JD could afford hand-tooled Tony Lamas, but he always wore Justin Boots because that's what George Strait wore. *What's good enough for King George is good enough for me.*

"Of course," he said with a wink. "The prettiest girl in Big Verde helped me pick them out."

She grinned and fluttered her eyelashes. "Maybe we can do that again sometime. I love hanging out with you, you know." They'd gone to San Antonio to shop for boots, eaten dinner downtown, and then watched the Spurs game at a sports bar. Unfortunately, the evening had ended with a friendly pat on the back.

JD shrugged. "I don't really need any boots right now."

Alice patted Maggie's arm sympathetically. "Is Claire here?" she asked. "I need to see if she's coming to book club this month."

Maybe the conversation could move beyond swords and boots if it was just the two of them. "She was headed to the ballroom."

Alice nodded and swooshed off, popping open a book and nearly taking out a waiter. Dimples appeared in JD's cheeks, and Maggie made sure her cape was open and pushed her chest out. *Look! Boobs!*

"You want to hit the bar for a drink?" JD asked, taking her empty goblet and ignoring her boobs entirely.

"Um, sure." Feeling deflated, she renewed her effort at puffing out her chest and damn near threw her back out.

"You okay?" JD asked.

"Yeah, just stretching."

JD cocked a brow and shook his head. "There's a portable bar set up in the corner. We don't have to go into the ballroom yet if you don't want to." He knew Maggie always needed a few moments to warm up before jumping into the fray. He was thoughtful and observant like that.

"Do you want another one of those misty things? Or your usual Dos Equis?"

A nice Mexican beer sounded delicious, but she didn't want to be predictable tonight. "Another misty thing, please."

While they waited for their drinks, JD folded his arms across his breastplate and gave her another good once-over. "So," he said. "What happened to the stormtrooper costume?"

"Claire picked this out for me instead. Do you like it?" Her heart pounded while she tried not to blurt out that she'd worn it just for him.

"Like I said before, red looks good on you. You should wear it more often."

The bartender set her drink down and JD doled out some money before picking up his beer. Was that all he was going to say? That she looked good in red?

"Bottoms up, Mighty Mack."

She grabbed her trashcan punch and guzzled it down. Maybe JD was just dense. Maybe he was so used to the two of them being buddies that he couldn't see what was right in front of him. A warm, tingly sensation spread throughout her body. *Time to show him.*

A graveyard had been set up in the courtyard. She'd seen it when they'd parked. "Let's get some air."

They started for the courtyard with JD squeaking at every step and Maggie hobbling along beside him. "You'd better pace yourself with the drinking or you're going to regret it in the morning."

He offered his arm, but on a whim, Maggie grabbed his hand instead. He hesitated a moment, but then resumed his squeaky gait. Was he surprised? Maggie stared straight ahead, not daring to glance at his face. He didn't let go and scream *girl cooties*, but he didn't give it a sexy little squeeze either.

The courtyard was unreal. Tombstones leaned this way and that, casting long, sideways shadows across the ground. Every now and then a dismembered hand clawed its way out of the dirt.

"Hey, look," JD said, pointing at a tombstone. "They have names of people we know on them." He let go of her hand and started wandering around. "Listen to this one. 'Here lies Dr. Martin—finally got something in the hole.'"

"I sincerely hope that's referring to his horrible golf game and not his dating life," Maggie said.

JD laughed. "Knowing him, it could go either way."

There were more amusing tombstones, but Maggie wasn't interested. "Isn't that the most gorgeous harvest moon you've ever seen?" she asked, sliding next to JD and slipping her arm through his. "It's very romantic."

JD looked at her. At least she thought he did. It was hard to tell because his Stetson cast the upper part of his face in shadow. But she could see the lower half, and his mouth was set in a stern, straight line. Either he was about to grab her and take her right here on the fake tombstones, romance novel–style, or he was not in the mood at all—*at least where she was concerned.*

She decided to press the issue by mashing her breast into his arm. Actually, it was probably the trashcan punch making that decision, but whatever. It seemed like a good one. JD's biceps flexed against her breast, and then she felt it—a small shiver. It passed through JD's body and into hers. *She was getting to him.*

"It's a little chilly out here, isn't it?" she asked, giving him an opportunity to deny it was the cool night air giving him the shivers.

JD cleared his throat and stared at his boots. Then he slowly lifted his gaze to hers. Maybe it was just the neon glow from the Pump 'n' Go sign across the street, but his hazel eyes gleamed like they'd been struck by moonbeams. Maggie held her breath. This was it. She reached up and softly traced the outline of his jaw with her finger. And he . . . *flinched.*

It was just a flash of a flinch. If she hadn't known him so well, she might have missed it or been able to talk herself out of having seen it. But there was no doubt in her mind about what had just happened. JD Mayes had flinched at her touch.

It felt like a slap piercing the alcohol buzz as easily as a cartoon cannon ball shot through a cloud. Her mouth dried up. Her skin broke out in a light sweat followed by a chill. She wrapped herself in her cape.

"Maggie—"

"No." She held her hand in front of JD's face like a shield. She needed to block the words before they ripped her apart like bullets from a machine gun.

I don't like you in that way.

Let's just be friends.

You're not my type.

She'd known it. So why had she made such a fool of herself?

It was the stupid corset, the ridiculous boots, and Claire's infuriating optimism. Claire had never known rejection. She hadn't been stood up by Scott Flores for the eighth grade Sadie Hawkins dance, nor had she sat home the night of the senior prom, pretending she hadn't wanted to go anyway. Women like Claire were never tucked away into friend zones, forced to watch the objects of their affection cry into their beers over other women. They never stood in front of JD Mayes while dressed like the world's least shapely porn star, watching him flinch and shiver at their touch.

JD moved her hand away from his face. The contact was electric. Not the sexy shock of fireworks, more like sticking your wet finger into an electrical outlet.

"I need to tell you something, Maggie."

Her eyes stung. She hadn't cried since Honey died. She couldn't blink. If she did, a tear might escape. *Hold it in, Mackey.*

"No. You really don't need to say anything," she said.

Blink.

Dammit. A tear slipped out. JD wiped it away with his finger. How dare he touch her tenderly on the face?

"You need to know—"

"I got the message, okay? Loud and clear."

JD dropped his hand to his side. "Let me talk, Maggie. You're my best friend—"

"Not anymore," she said. "It's too cruel."

She couldn't look at JD's face for one second longer. She turned and walked steadily—how, she didn't know—in the direction of the bar. She needed to find Claire and tell her she was leaving. Corsets, red porn star boots, and smoky eyes weren't meant for women like her. She could only imagine what people were thinking.

Look at little Mighty Mack trying to be sexy.

"Maggie, wait!"

She walked faster. A blur of unrecognizable faces rushed past as she stormed into the hotel, pushing her way through throngs of people, ignoring the few who called out greetings. She held the cape tightly closed.

Through her watery eyes she saw the tip of a pointy hat. *Claire!* She sped up, zigzagging through people toward the circular bar. But just as she got there, the hat disappeared. She headed for the one empty seat at the bar. She'd sit there and wait for Claire. Just like always.

She started to hoist herself onto the stool—they were tricky things for short people in tight miniskirts—and her heel missed the rung. She lurched forward and landed in a pair of strong arms.

"Are you okay?"

The voice was deep and held a hint of humor. She looked up to see vicious fangs, a tapered snout, and pointed ears. She gasped, even though it was a mask.

"I'm fine," she finally said. "But my, what big teeth you have."

Chapter

Four

❦

The entire night had been so surreal that Travis didn't know why he was surprised when a pretty woman in red—almost elfin with large eyes set in a small heart-shaped face—fell into his arms with a sarcastic comment about the size of his teeth. He couldn't help it; he ran his tongue over them. They felt perfectly normal.

"Thanks a lot," he mumbled, helping to get the little blonde upright again.

He assisted her onto the barstool, getting a good look at the red boots she wore. They were probably the reason she'd flopped into his arms, but damn, they looked good on her legs.

Her eyes crinkled in amusement. "Your mask," she said. "It has fangs. I wasn't referring to your actual teeth."

He smiled with a dumb sense of relief. The child's mask only covered the upper part of his fully adult-sized face, and his mouth was framed by long, sharp, and appropriately named plastic canine teeth. "I'm not used to having fangs."

"Admit it. You thought I had a tooth fetish."

Travis leaned over and whispered, "Do you?"

She grinned, but her eyes were shiny, as if maybe she'd been crying or trying not to cry. And her makeup was smudged. "Wouldn't you like to know? Maybe I have a mask fetish. I think that's an actual thing."

Her voice was smoky and sultry, like a jazz singer's, and surprisingly low for such a small woman. And yes, he would definitely like to know if she had a fetish of any kind whatsoever. "Wolf masks, in particular, seem to turn women on," he offered.

He wasn't even kidding. He'd initially left the mask in the truck, but even though he did his best to avoid socializing, he'd been forced into a couple of awkward conversations with people he didn't know but who seemed to know him. He'd retrieved the mask and quickly found Anna to give her the bid. She'd seemed pleased and insisted he stay long enough for one drink. Since then he'd been growled at, petted, and a woman who might have been his freshman English teacher had called him a good puppy.

His new blond friend seemed fascinated by the dance floor, staring at it intently. "My, what big eyes you have," he said.

He cringed as the eyes in question turned their gaze back to him. He couldn't seem to stop the stupid from pouring out of his mouth.

"That's my line," she replied.

He swallowed. Her voice was such a turn-on. She practically channeled Kathleen Turner with a little Emma Stone around the edges. It made it hard to follow a conversation. "Pardon?"

"You said, *My, what big eyes you have.* I'm Little Red Riding Hood. That's my line."

She didn't look anything like the Little Red Riding Hood in Henry's bedtime storybook. "I'm the—"

"Big Bad Wolf. Yeah, I get it," she said, waving a hand dismissively. "Fancy meeting you here."

She called the bartender over with just a nod of her head. "Dos Equis," she said. "With lime."

Travis pulled out his wallet. "Let me get that for you."

"No, thanks. I've got it."

Was that a rejection? And if so, a rejection of what? He wasn't exactly looking for a romantic relationship, and even a hookup seemed complicated now that he had a kid at home. It wasn't like he could stay out all night, or even real late, for that matter. And he certainly couldn't show up at the ranch with Little Red Riding Hood in tow. What would Mrs. Garza think?

Little Red Riding Hood dug around in her purse while the bartender looked on. In only a few seconds there was an impressive pile of crap on the counter, but she hadn't scrounged up any money. She sighed in resignation. "Just water, I guess."

"I've already opened the bottle," the bartender said.

She turned her big brown eyes on Travis. "Do you mind?"

Heck, no, he didn't mind. It was why he'd offered. He handed some cash to the bartender as the blonde took a big swig of beer. And then another.

"Argument with a boyfriend?" he asked.

Her big eyes grew even larger. He probably shouldn't have said anything. "You just look a bit . . . out of sorts."

"Great. I look out of sorts."

He couldn't say the right thing to save his soul. "I didn't mean anything by it. Just wondering why your makeup is smudged."

"My makeup is smudged?" She dug through the pile of crap still on the counter and pulled out a small mirror.

"You look fine."

"Fine? Aren't you a sweet talker. And oh wow"—she stared in the mirror—"in what universe do I look fine?" She licked her finger and rubbed it beneath her eye. "And there is no boyfriend," she added. "Zero, zilch, nada."

A flicker of hope popped up and settled inconveniently in Travis's crotch. He had no intention of fanning it into a flame, so he took a sip of beer and tried to ignore it.

"I guess I do technically have a boyfriend."

Good. The flicker of hope fizzled out.

Little Red Riding Hood rubbed a cocktail napkin across the condensation on her beer bottle and smeared it under her eyes in earnest. "Lots of them, actually. That's the problem."

She was a player. The flicker flared back up. "Oh, I see."

"Oh, stop. You don't see a thing. I mean there are lots of men and they're all friends. Friends, friends, friends..." She wadded up the napkin and took another sip of beer.

Her makeup was more smeared than ever, and it was kind of sexy, just like the rest of her. "Would you like to dance?" he blurted. His hands immediately became damp with perspiration. Why had he done that? He hated to dance. It must be the mask. He felt like a different man with it on. He hoped the motherfucking wolf knew how to dance.

Little Red Riding Hood stared at him as if he'd just told her where he'd last seen Elvis.

"You want to dance with *me?*"

Had he been too pushy? "Only if you feel like it." He tried to make it sound like he didn't care one way or another.

Little Red Riding Hood's adorable mouth curved up into a slight smile, and she fluffed her hair. She wasn't pissed. She was pleased. And the little flicker of a flame that had started in his crotch moved higher, warming his insides and making him grin like a jack-o'-lantern.

Something squeaked behind them, and Little Red Riding Hood stopped fluffing and frowned. Travis turned to see JD Mayes dressed like the Tin Man. JD had been one of the few people who'd been friendly to him in school, and they'd had a few pleasant run-ins since he'd moved back to Big Verde. But JD didn't look friendly now. His lips were drawn in a tight line, his fists were clenched, and his hat was pulled down low, hiding his eyes. What had JD's blood boiling?

"What do you think you're doing, Maggie?" he asked.

So, her name was Maggie. Travis hadn't even thought to ask.

"I'm about to dance with the Big Bad Wolf, not that it's any of your business."

He should probably lift his mask, so JD could see who he was and stop glowering. He reached for it, but then something rubbed against the inside of his calf. He looked down to see a red boot delicately working its way up and down his leg.

Tonight, with this pixie in her sexy boots and little red cape, he didn't want to be Travis Blake and all it entailed. He wanted to be the Big Bad Wolf.

Little Red Riding Hood had said there was no boyfriend in the picture. But with JD flaring his nostrils in and out like a bull ready to charge, it seemed a good idea to keep the mask on. The last thing Travis needed was to get on the bad side of the town's golden boy.

* * *

Maggie had half expected JD to follow them onto the dance floor. Not because of jealousy. They were good and clear on that. The idiot was protective, which was offensive, because she didn't need protecting. She wasn't his sister. Heck, she wasn't even his buddy anymore.

The wolf was huge. And he smelled good, like woods and sunshine. His hand spanned her back from below her bandeau bra to her waist. She shivered all over, and it was becoming increasingly difficult to continue simmering over JD.

Friends and acquaintances blew past them, a blur of mind-dizzying motion, two-stepping across the dance floor with hardly a glance. But the wolf steered her through the melee until they stood in the center of the dance floor, arms around each other, settling into stationary swaying and rocking. They danced in the eye of the storm. She reveled in the sexiness of the slow, warm pace, and her body melted into his as the long, hard feel of him swiftly led to the blissful Zen of *JD Who?*

The song ended, but the wolf pulled her closer, as if he didn't want to let go. She tightened her grip around his neck...*yes, let's dance some more*. She nestled in just below his chin as the next song began. It was a slow dance, and this was typically when her partner thanked her kindly and escorted her off the floor. She was good for a fun spin through the sawdust, but her usual buddies looked around for women like Claire when it came time to get their slow groove on.

For the first time, Maggie wondered just who the hell the Big Bad Wolf was. He couldn't be local, or he'd have gotten the memo that she was basically a guy. It felt wonderful to be perfectly anonymous. She was just a woman in a corset, stockings, and sexy boots dancing with a mysterious stranger.

The song ended, and the driving beat of electronic dance music started up. The wolf let go and stood there, stiff as a board, and gave a little shrug. "Not much of a dancer," he said.

"I beg to differ." He'd been doing just fine a minute ago. The man had rhythm in his hips. She grabbed his hands and started to move, hoping he'd become inspired. But dancing in red porn star boots was about a thousand times more difficult than swaying in them, and she felt like she'd just put on her first pair of roller skates. And from the grin on the wolf's face, she looked like it, too. "Fine. Let's head back to the bar."

The wolf practically wagged his tail in relief, and he grabbed her hand and steered her through all the sweaty, bobbing bodies, including Bubba and the crowd that had already formed around him. Their drinks still sat on the bar, but hers had gotten warm, so she pushed it aside. She didn't need any more alcohol anyway. The trashcan punch buzz had worn off as she'd danced, and that was a good thing.

"What are you thinking about?" the wolf asked. He held his

head slightly tilted. He looked every bit the part of a curious puppy, and Maggie wanted to offer him a belly rub. She knew from slow dancing that the belly in question was lean and hard. She fanned her face with a napkin.

"I'm thinking that you are a very good distraction from my troubles," she said. Not to mention an excellent and timely ego boost.

"Troubles," he said. "We've all got 'em." He took a swig of his beer, no easy task since he had a snout.

She scanned the rest of him. Nice suit, excellent fit. Maybe he was a businessman. He clearly didn't know who she was, so he wasn't from around here. "Are you a friend of Anna's?" she asked.

"Not exactly."

It must be a business relationship then. Except Anna was engaged in no business to speak of…Oh! Maybe he was a divorce lawyer. She waited, but he didn't offer anything further. Maybe he enjoyed the feeling of being anonymous as much as she did.

Her gaze journeyed to his feet. Square-toe boots—dressy, but very worn—provided no clue. Almost every man in Big Verde wore boots, no matter their occupation.

The wolf set his beer down, and the corner of his mouth turned up in response to her scrutiny. "They're comfortable."

"I love a man in boots," she quickly assured him.

He gazed pointedly at her legs. "And I love a woman in boots."

Her cheeks grew warm at the compliment. Was it possible that this was leading to a *hookup?* She'd never had a one-night stand. She'd had a couple of boyfriends in college, and she enjoyed the occasional romp with a seed salesman who called on Petal Pushers. But she'd never hooked up with a stranger. The idea was exciting, and considering her extremely recent rejection, it was also one humdinger of a rebound. *Swoosh! Nothing but net.*

The Big Bad Wolf jerked as if poked by a cattle prod, and then began digging in his pockets. "Sorry," he said. "Got a text."

He'd better not claim that his poor, sick mother had suddenly taken a turn for the worse. Maggie watched the wolf fumble with his phone before breathing a visible sigh of relief. "Everything's fine," he said.

Maybe he'd just gotten the results of a biopsy or been approved for a loan. Whatever it was, she wasn't about to ask. She was determined to keep the Big Bad Wolf as her mysterious, sexy stranger.

Clearing her throat, she turned on her stool and brought her legs out from under the bar. The wolf picked up on the motion. Very slowly, Maggie uncrossed her legs, and then crossed them again. This was one of Claire's signature sexy moves. Maggie's skirt climbed up from the activity, and the wolf noticed. He set his phone on the bar. "Where were we?"

"Here," Maggie said, running her leg up his calf. Her skirt slid even higher, and she was rewarded by a very wolfish smile. This man oozed sex, and he was directing it all at her.

"I knew it!"

They both swiveled on their barstools to see Claire, standing with her hip thrust out, a broom in one hand and a drink in the other, pointed hat set properly askew. Speaking of oozing sex...

"Knew what?" Maggie asked. She hoped the Big Bad Wolf wasn't about to trade her in for a witchier model. But his warm knee pressing against the outside of her thigh indicated he liked his women in little red hoods.

"Y'all are the perfect pair. As soon as I saw this guy"—Claire poked at the wolf with her broom—"I knew you would end up together."

They hadn't *ended up together*. Not yet.

Claire stuck her broom beneath her arm and thrust out a hand. "I'm Claire Kowalski."

Oh no! Claire was going to blow their covers. If the wolf introduced himself, she'd be forced to introduce herself, and once she said the words *Maggie Mackey*, the magic would disappear.

"I'm..."

The wolf seemed to have forgotten his own name.

"I'm the Big Bad Wolf."

Whew! He was just as determined to remain undercover as she was. He pointed to an empty seat next to him. "Want to join us?"

"Absolutely," Claire said. Without falling, tripping, or otherwise planting herself onto the wolf's lap, she sat on the barstool. As if she'd blown an invisible dog whistle, the bartender trotted over, ignoring the throng of other guests holding out money and trying to get his attention.

Claire leaned over the bar, gave the guy an eyeful of cleavage, and ordered a whiskey sour. The wolf winked at Maggie. His eyes hadn't strayed. *Good boy.*

"Listen here," Claire said to him. "This is my best friend. No leg humping on the dance floor."

Awesome. Claire was talking about leg humping.

The wolf grinned. "I admit to being a leg man, but I'm not much of a humper. You're thinking of Labrador retrievers. Wolves have more self-control."

"Really?" Claire said. "I thought wolves were wild, untamed animals."

"Wild, yes. Drooling, excitable idiots, no."

The wolf clearly had experience with Labrador retrievers.

"I think we're done dancing anyway," Maggie said. The dance floor was not the wolf's natural habitat. Although she would love some more body-to-body contact.

"You are not," Claire said with a mischievous grin.

The DJ's voice came over the sound system. "I've had a request," he announced. "Better get your howl on, folks, it's 'Li'l Red Riding Hood,' by Sam the Sham and the Pharaohs."

Claire started laughing and scooted a mortified Big Bad Wolf off his stool. Maggie began to apologize—give him an out—but then the familiar opening howl of the song rang out. The Big Bad Wolf grinned and extended his hand. "They're playing our song."

Chapter

Five

❦

Travis was unbelievably turned on. It took everything he had to avoid the dreaded leg humping that Claire Kowalski had brought up.

He'd almost choked when Claire had introduced herself. Her father, Gerome Kowalski, owned the famous Rancho Cañada Verde, which bordered Happy Trails. Although they'd been neighbors of sorts, he and Claire hadn't hung out in high school. She'd probably never given him a second thought, but he'd coveted everything she had: beautiful ranch, good family name, a dad whom everybody looked up to.

It was doubtful that Claire would be trying to hook him up with her friend if she knew who he was. And for that matter, what about Little Red Riding Hood? Travis had probably gone to school with her, too. But for the life of him, he couldn't place her.

He couldn't take the mask off. Not that she'd recognize him if he did. He was hardly the scrawny, thick-lensed-glasses-wearing runt he'd been at Big Verde High. But if his name came up, it might ring a bell, and then Little Red Riding Hood would politely excuse herself from the dance floor. Luckily, she hadn't shown any interest in exchanging information. Maybe she wanted to remain anonymous, too.

Maggie. JD had called her Maggie. It sounded vaguely familiar, but that was it. Unless they belonged to former tormenters or super popular kids—often one and the same—the names of his past were mostly forgotten. He let go of Little Red Riding Hood briefly to make sure his mask was secure, and then pulled her close again.

They were attracting a bit of attention, which he hated. They'd even garnered a few comments made in jest.

Make him keep his paws to himself, girl!

Watch out for that full moon!

He didn't feel comfortable dancing as intimately as they'd done earlier. People might not know who he was, but they sure as hell knew Little Red Riding Hood, and he didn't want to embarrass her.

Little Red Riding Hood didn't seem nearly as concerned about what people thought. She pushed her pert breasts into his chest, and his mind went blank as all the blood drained out of his head. He tried to put a couple of inches of space between them, but she was having none of it. She rubbed against him in a way that surely allowed her to feel every inch of his—more painful by the minute—*interest*.

The music wasn't helping. How could a song be so dirty without actually being dirty?

It's your mind that's dirty, bonehead.

It had been a while. There wasn't much room in his life for anything other than Henry. There was certainly no room for a relationship. But a little fun? Maybe. Especially if it was anonymous.

A soft hand ran up his back, briefly squeezed his neck, and then ran through his short hair.

"Are you staying at the Chateau?" she asked.

She must assume he was from out of town. Would it be intentionally misleading to let her think so?

"No."

There. That was the truth. And any lingering misgivings about honesty were promptly extinguished when he realized why she'd asked. She wanted to hook up just as much as he did, and was thinking about a place to do it.

Where could they go? Not to Little Red Riding Hood's house. That was too personal. She'd expect him to remove his mask.

There was an equipment shed on the grounds. It was on the other side of a patch of cedar trees, at the very edge of the property that backed up against a utility easement. It wasn't exactly a first-class solution, or even a second-class solution, but if the way Little Red Riding Hood was currently grinding on his thigh was any indication, he just needed a quick solution.

"There's a place we can go if you want to be alone," he whispered.

"Does it entail me following you through the woods?"

"Yes, actually. It does."

Little Red Riding Hood raised her eyebrows. For about five horrible seconds he thought she might say no thanks. But then she smiled and grabbed his hand.

"Into the woods."

* * *

Maggie followed the stranger—*stranger!*—through the trees and away from the party. He yanked on her hand, and it was all she could do to keep up.

She would never forget the look on JD's face as she walked out of the ballroom with the wolf. *Ha! Take that, JD. This could have been all yours—* She almost toppled to the ground as one of her heels snagged on a root. The wolf caught her, helped get her steady, and then gave a tug to get her going again.

"Hey, hold up," she said. "Where's the fire?"

The wolf stopped, and she bumped into him. After the giggling was over, he grabbed her by the waist and pulled her close. She rose up on her toes and wrapped her arms around his neck. It was hard to tell who kissed who first; their lips practically melted together. Maggie parted hers at the urging of his tongue, and he explored her mouth hungrily...impatiently...*deliciously*. Her head spun. She had never been so thoroughly kissed in all her life.

He straightened up to his full height and her feet left the ground. Pressed up against him as she was, she felt where the fire was. *In his pants.*

"You're so small," he whispered.

Like it was a good thing.

His mask was adorably crooked from the kissing. She straightened his snout.

"Have you caught your breath?" he asked.

Not even a little. But she nodded anyway.

The wolf set her down, and for the first time since she'd taken his hand and followed him into the woods—a generally bad idea for Little Red Riding Hood or anyone else—she wondered where they were going.

"The shed is just behind that clump of trees."

"The shed?"

"We're not headed to Grandma's house."

A shiver went up Maggie's spine. "We're going to do it in a shed?"

The wolf cocked his head. "God, I hope so. And it's actually a pretty nice shed."

"That's probably the worst pickup line ever."

The wolf laughed. Then he leaned over and planted a whisper-soft kiss along the side of her neck, setting off a domino effect of goose bumps up and down her arms. He followed it up with a little lick. "Mmm..." he said. "Tastes like chicken."

"What?"

"Chicken. Big time."

He flapped his elbows and made squawking sounds. Maggie laughed, and the wolf made one final cluck before holding out his hand with a grin. Maggie took it without hesitation.

The shed was clearly visible in the light of the full moon. It was an old stone structure with a tin roof—kind of romantic. The wolf pushed the door open with a loud creak.

This was it. She could turn back if she wanted. She knew this man wouldn't stop her. But she didn't want to. She wanted to be ravished by a tall, sexy man in a mask. And it wasn't entirely to make up for the fact that she'd been rejected by a tall, sexy man in a cowboy hat. She really liked this guy. She liked his looks—what she could see of them. She liked that he was an awful dancer. She liked his laughter and his chicken imitation. She officially liked him enough to justify jilted sex.

She stepped inside and shivered as the wolf shut the door.

"There's no lock on the inside," he said. "But I don't think anyone will walk in on us."

Moonlight streamed through the dirty window, casting shadows. Frogs and crickets performed a raucous symphony that competed with the music floating through the woods from the reception. But it all paled in comparison to the sound of her pounding heart.

The wolf's chest rose with each breath, but other than that, he didn't move. His mask was still on. Menacing sharp fangs, frightening eyes... Maggie backed up slowly until she bumped into an old weathered worktable.

"Are you still down with this?" the wolf asked.

So, so down with it.

"I'm not afraid of the Big Bad Wolf," she whispered.

He closed the distance between them with one step. Her breath caught as he tilted her chin up with his fingers. Then that bit of gentleness disappeared, and he pulled her to him by grasping the back of her head. His fingers tangled in her hair as his mouth covered hers. She felt the mask slip up as his tongue slipped in. She opened her eyes, but all she could see were shadows playing off the angles of his face and the waves of his dark hair.

Her eyes drifted shut again as his hand moved to her neck and trailed down to her collarbone. Breaking the kiss, he followed his fingers with his lips. The mask slipped up on his forehead even higher as he cupped her breast.

She couldn't see his face, but that was okay. He was her Big Bad Wolf. She gave in and let herself be swept away by the fantasy. She'd never role-played before. Was this what they were doing? If so, it was fun, thrilling, and turning her knees into jelly.

With one move, the wolf had the laces of her cheap costume corset free and her blouse lifted. She wanted to cross her arms over her unsubstantial bra, but she resisted. The wolf pulled it up with a single finger, exposing both breasts to the kiss of the cool night air. Her nipples hardened in response.

"My breasts are small," she said, hating herself as soon as the words spilled out.

The Big Bad Wolf's mask had slipped back down. All she could see was the lower half of his face. He smiled wolfishly and licked his lips. "They're perfect. They match the rest of you."

He brushed both nipples with the tips of his fingers, and Maggie squeezed her thighs together. Her nipples were a Candy Land shortcut to other areas.

"And besides," the wolf added, "it's responsiveness that turns me on."

Her nipples were almost painfully hard. Definitely responsive. The wolf ran his tongue along the side of her neck. He palmed her breasts and squeezed. Not too hard, but hard enough to get her attention, and she inhaled sharply.

"Do you like that?" he whispered.

Yes. She wasn't sure if she said it out loud or merely thought it. Forming words wasn't a priority.

"I'm a hungry wolf," he said with a raspy voice. "These look good."

He covered a nipple with his hot mouth. The rest of her breast, exposed to the night air, had gooseflesh. But her nipple was on fire. The wolf sucked and tugged, moaning in the back of his throat like Maggie was the best thing he'd ever tasted. When he'd had enough of one, he went to the other.

The wolf was a wonderful mixture of rough and gentle. He gripped her breast firmly—almost painfully—and stopped sucking to brush her nipple with his tongue like a whisper. Fingers trailed up the inside of her thigh, past the top of her stocking, leaving a path of molten heat. When he bit a nipple, her knees buckled.

Her knees had never buckled before.

The wolf clasped her firmly around the waist with his other arm, steadying her.

"Can I see what Little Red Riding Hood has in her basket?" he asked, skimming the edge of her panties with his fingers.

"Yes," she whispered.

He pulled her panties aside, but he didn't touch her. He kissed her mouth softly and lifted her skirt, exposing her fully to the autumn air's sensual caress.

But he didn't look. And he still hadn't touched. She was desperate for it.

He leaned over and kissed her again, this time parting her lips with his tongue while he teased the sensitive skin of her inner thighs with his warm hand. Then he gently inserted a single finger.

She moaned, barely recognizing the sound of her own voice.

"Is that good?" he asked.

"Yes," she hissed. "So good."

He moved his finger slowly in and out, and she rocked against his hand. He picked up on her neediness, and his finger moved faster, with less gentleness.

And she loved it.

She moved against him, wanting his finger deeper. He obliged, and added a second.

He stopped kissing her. His face was inches away, mask intact, as he watched her intently, soaking up her reactions.

"I want to make you come," he whispered. "Just like this."

Orgasms were elusive things and usually required a vibrator. But Maggie didn't want to burst the wolf's bubble. And besides, something was building from a place deep inside that had never been touched like this. Not with this force, this rhythm...she moved against his hand and wasn't even embarrassed. Her need was too great. She wanted to explore this new sensation, this deeper, rougher arousal she'd never experienced before. "Harder," she whispered.

She braced herself on the table and let her head fall back. The table creaked from the force of his thrusting fingers. Her entire body shook. She tingled. She buzzed. And still, it wasn't enough. It left her starving and desperate and wanting more.

"Come on, baby," the wolf growled.

Pressure built. Instead of stilling and pulling her energy in, Maggie pushed, and her orgasm exploded in deep, rhythmic contractions that radiated from her very core. *This* was a different kind of orgasm. It rocked her entire body until she melted into the wolf, collapsing against his chest. She couldn't even open her eyes. Her lids were too heavy.

"You've ruined me," she mumbled.

The wolf jerked. "Did I hurt you?"

Maggie snorted into his chest. "No, you didn't break me with your big, strong man hands. But you just raised the orgasm bar to a ridiculous level. All the orgasms I have from here on out will be disappointments."

"Oh," the wolf said. He stroked her hair, and she sensed a smile in his voice as he said, "I think we can raise it higher if you're not too…"

"Too what?"

"You talked in tongues near the end. Are you coherent enough to move on to the next part of the story?"

"What part is that?"

The wolf put his lips to her ear and whispered, "The part where the Big Bad Wolf eats Little Red Riding Hood."

Everything below Maggie's waist woke back up. She wasn't about to ruin the moment by informing him that the Big Bad Wolf actually eats Little Red Riding Hood's grandmother. No need to be a buzzkill.

Chapter

Six

❦

Was it the fucking mask? Travis didn't know and didn't care. He'd driven a woman wild with just his fingers. He'd never done that before. Maybe Little Red Riding Hood was especially orgasmic, or maybe he was just a badass.

He wanted to do it again, but without fingers. He pushed her back against the worktable and adjusted his mask to make sure it was still firmly in place. She leaned back on her elbows, smiling contentedly. She might have had her fill, but he sure hadn't. Her shirt was still pushed up and her perfect breasts were on display. They were an offering he couldn't refuse. He leaned over and kissed each nipple, which made her gasp. Then he pinched them, which made her gasp harder. The sound set him on fire.

Little Red Riding Hood spread her legs. *Nice.*

He still held her nipples, pinching them both a little harder. She closed her eyes and dropped her head back in response. *She liked it.*

He tugged gently, pulling her away from the table by her nipples, which was a huge fucking turn-on, and even though she winced,

Little Red Riding Hood raised her head and her glassy gaze told him she was totally on board.

"Turn around," he ordered.

It was very unlike him to order a woman to do anything, and he almost followed it up with a *please*. But they were role-playing. That much was clear. And he was the Big Bad Fucking Wolf, and the wolf didn't say please.

Little Red Riding Hood turned around.

"Bend over the table."

"I should have known this would be your position of choice."

Damn, she was cute. And incredibly sexy as she complied with his request, sticking her perfect little ass out in the process. She grinned at him over her shoulder as he flipped her skirt up. He wanted to give each exposed cheek a hard slap and see what replaced that grin. *Where had that come from? He'd never felt compelled to spank anyone before. Wolf was a dirty dog.*

He didn't dare spank her. He caressed each cheek instead, then squeezed. It opened her up and she gasped. Her panties were still pulled over to the side, and with a single finger he pulled them over farther. He wanted to see. "Spread your legs."

He'd lost some of his commanding tone. In fact, he could now barely find his voice at all. But she'd heard him and did as she was told. He dropped to his knees and gazed. Her stockings rose to mid-thigh and had sexy red bows on the backs. Might as well start there.

He licked from a bow to a sweet ass cheek. Damn, he wanted to *bite* her. He could just imagine her warm skin between his teeth. He couldn't do such a thing, though. It might hurt her or frighten her. Hell, it kind of frightened *him*. Little Red Riding Hood arched her back and spread her legs wider.

"Good girl," he said. He had never said *good girl* to a woman before.

He threw off the stupid mask because wet-nosing a woman

wasn't sexy. He squeezed her ass again, still wanting to smack those perfect round cheeks. She moaned with that sexy voice of hers. He wished they were in an actual bed with an actual locked door. He'd make her moan all fucking night.

The sight before him made him weak. He gave her a long, slow lick. Her thighs quivered, and he did it again. And again. Then he sought out the hard little nub with his tongue to give it the special attention it deserved. She responded by pressing against his face, forcing him to behave like a hungry wolf.

When he couldn't take it anymore, and he sensed she couldn't either, he gave her one last lick and stood up.

She reached for him. He placed a hand firmly on her back and she stilled.

"Patience," he said, although he had none at the moment himself. He unbuckled his belt and pulled his zipper down.

"Condom?" she asked.

He knew he had a condom in his wallet. It taunted him every time he pulled out money to buy more shit for Henry.

"I've got it covered," he said.

His voice sounded solid, but he was a mess, fumbling with the condom wrapper as his pants fell and pooled around his ankles.

His rested his penis on her lower back, noting the contrast in size between what he had and where he wanted to put it. He was by no means a freak of nature, but larger than average would be an apt description. And Little Red Riding Hood was so tiny. But man, she seemed ready as hell. He had to step out of his pants to reposition his stance and get low enough to reach her.

Little Red Riding Hood squirmed with impatience. "Please," she said.

He edged in slowly with a groan. She opened up like a flower and pressed against him. Everything fit just fine. "I want to hear you," he said. "Make some noise for me."

She breathed raggedly, but that was all.

He increased the intensity with a forceful thrust, eliciting a gasp. It still wasn't the reaction he wanted, so he pulled almost all the way out and slammed it home. She cried out and it fed a fire inside him. "Do you want me to do it again?" he asked.

"Yes," she gasped.

"Tell me how you want me to do it, baby." Holy shit—who the actual fuck was he? He didn't recognize himself at all.

Little Red Riding Hood wiggled her ass, but she didn't say a word. It was very naughty to disobey him. "How do you want it?" he asked again.

Another silent wiggle.

Somebody needed to be taught a lesson. He pulled all the way out. "I asked you a question."

"Hard," she whispered. "I want it hard."

He obliged, and she responded with the most delightful moans he'd ever heard. Her voice alone could make him come, and he was close. Too damn close.

He wanted this to last forever. Right now, the back taxes and a million other worrisome details could go fuck themselves. He didn't have a care in the world. There was just the rhythm of their bodies, the sound of the workbench banging against the wall, and their ragged breathing.

She stilled, and then he felt her contracting around him, squeezing the last bit of his willpower. He let everything go. The emotional relief that poured through him was as intense as the sexual one. For about ten blinding seconds, he just *was*.

His normal senses returned slowly. He was bent over Little Red Riding Hood, panting, skin damp, pulse pounding. The music from the party floated in and out of his consciousness.

The woman beneath him was warm, still, and silent. She'd had an intense orgasm; he'd felt it. Maybe she was as wrung out as he was. "You okay?" he asked.

"Mm-hmmm," she mumbled.

He stood, peeling his shirt off her damp body. He'd never un-buttoned it, hadn't even taken his jacket off. He quickly discarded the condom in the trash and pulled up his pants. Little Red Riding Hood flipped her skirt down and started to straighten up.

"Wait," he said. He grabbed his mask and slipped it on silently. "Okay."

She turned and pulled her shirt down. He almost groaned at the loss. He could stare at her breasts forever. He tucked his shirt in while she went about putting herself back together. He watched, mesmerized by every move. Her short hair was mussed, her makeup was still smeared, and she looked like a woman who'd been thoroughly fucked and had enjoyed the hell out of it.

"That was…" Every word he came up with—*hot*, *good*, *amazing*—seemed woefully inadequate.

"Soul shattering?"

That was it. He nodded.

They stared at each other. Now what? Little Red Riding Hood seemed almost too good to be true. She was sexy. That much had been established. The little conversation they'd shared had shown her quick wit. She was flirtatious but completely unaware of the effect it had, which charmed the pants off him. *Literally.*

Maybe they should exchange names and numbers like normal people. Maybe after what they'd just done, she wouldn't care that he was a Blake.

What the fuck. He'd go for it. The worst thing that could happen was she'd say she didn't date Blake trash. He felt for his phone, quickly patting down all his pockets, including the ones in his jacket.

"Lose something?"

"Yeah. Have you seen my phone?"

"You had it at the bar. Did you leave it there?"

Shit. Had she had him in such a state that he'd left his phone on the bar? "What time is it?"

Little Red pulled her phone out of her purse. "It's about eleven."

"Crap." He'd promised Henry a bedtime phone call over an hour ago. "I need to get my phone."

He held the shed door open for Little Red Riding Hood. Cool air rushed in—they'd really made some heat in the small shed. A light fog had settled along the slope of the riverbank, and the full moon created a phosphorescent dreamscape. Travis reached for Maggie's hand, so she wouldn't lose her footing in the ridiculous boots. He would have enjoyed the romance of the moment if he weren't panicked about his phone.

The music got louder as they approached the party, which was still in full swing.

"Don't worry," Little Red Riding Hood said. "I'm sure Zeke picked it up."

"Who's Zeke?"

Maggie laughed. "You'd know Zeke if you were from around here. He's the bartender."

Travis swallowed the unease of his deception. But the farther away from the shed they got, the less certain he became about everything.

Maggie stopped in her tracks when they came to the parking lot. "You know what? I'm just going to cut out here. It's getting late."

She was right. It was getting late, and he needed to get home. But was it rude to end the night so abruptly? "Are you sure?"

Maggie glanced in the direction of the courtyard that led to the ballroom. Maybe she was worried their reentrance would come off as a walk of shame. "Yeah, I'm sure."

They stood awkwardly in the grass. This was the time to ask for her number. To tell her who he was.

She suddenly stuck out her hand. "Safe travels."

Stupidly, he accepted, and they shook. Before he could find the words to steer events away from the awful direction they were headed, Little Red Riding Hood spun on her heels, nearly fell, and then took off at a rapid pace for the parking lot.

Fuck it. This was for the best anyway. He'd had some fun, so had she, and now everybody needed to resume their usual personas. Little Red Riding Hood glanced over her shoulder at him but didn't stop walking. He gave a feeble wave, before heading for the bar.

Zeke held up his phone as soon as he saw him. "Claire handed it in," he said.

Relief washed over him at the familiar weight of his phone in his hand. But it was short-lived. He had six text messages, all from Mrs. Garza. They started with Henry woke up with a stomach ache and ended with On our way to urgent care clinic.

Chapter

Seven

❦

Henry was nestled in the crook of Travis's arm, breathing deeply and radiating heat. He didn't have a fever. He was just a little furnace while he slept. Travis had been the same way as a kid.

The room didn't look much different than when Travis had slept in it. It still had a stain on the ceiling that looked like a vagina if you squinted. Travis hadn't been much older than Henry when Scott had decided to dispense a bit of brotherly wisdom and point it out. "That looks like a pussy," he'd said.

No matter how hard Travis had tried, he'd been unable to convince himself that the stain resembled a cat. He'd said as much, and Scott had laughed at him. Then he'd pulled a ratty magazine from beneath the mattress and showed Travis a series of pictures that had further complicated matters.

Staring at the stain made him think of Little Red Riding Hood. Not a cool association, but he couldn't help himself. An image of that part of the female anatomy, even if you had to squint to see it, was just too tempting an invitation to begin ruminating on last night's activities. That soft skin, those perky breasts with their perfect pink nipples…

Henry shifted, flooding Travis with guilt and embarrassment. He placed his hand on Henry's chest to settle him back down—he could use a few more minutes of peace before the little scoundrel woke up—and wondered if he'd ever been that innocent. If he'd even had a chance to be. His mom had run off when he was little. And his dad, instead of shielding his sons from things most people would consider solidly within the *adults only* realm, had practically reveled in exposing them to his vices. Travis had little to no doubt that Scott, if he was man enough to raise his own kid, would do the same to Henry.

He pulled Henry in a little closer, swallowing the unease that plagued him almost constantly now. *What was he going to do about Henry?*

Scott was not father material. But neither was Travis. Henry deserved better than either of them. And didn't Travis deserve better, too? He hadn't asked for this. Was it his fault his brother was a loser and the kid's mom had died? He was fresh out of the Army with his whole life ahead of him. His buddy had a pipe outfitting business and was holding a job for him in Austin. It wasn't as glamorous as being a rancher, but it was a hell of a lot more realistic. He was stuck in limbo until he could sell the ranch and get Henry settled.

He needed to call the social worker again. Surely there was a long-lost aunt or cousin somewhere who would be a good fit for Henry. Foster care had been mentioned, but Travis hoped it wouldn't come to that. Scott would get out of prison eventually and then… Well, hell. Travis didn't exactly want it coming to that either.

Henry stirred and opened his eyes.

"How are you feeling?" Travis asked. "Still up for our trip?"

Travis had chiseled out a chunk of time he didn't have to

take the kid camping. Henry had never been, and that was a fucking sin.

Henry's foggy, sleep-encrusted eyes turned bright and clear. "That's today?"

"If you feel good enough."

Henry tossed off the sheet and launched himself like a rocket, jumping on the small bed and narrowly missing Travis's crotch. It was hard to believe he'd been in an urgent care clinic just a few hours ago. Who knew severe constipation could mimic appendicitis? And who knew little kids got constipated?

The doctors at the clinic had been all over him. *When's the last time he had a bowel movement?* Travis had no idea. *How much fiber does he get per day?* Again, no idea as to how much fiber the kid even needed per day, much less how much he got from a cherry Pop-Tart. *How much water does he usually drink?* Does juice count? Or milk?

Henry needed more fruits and vegetables. Less junk food.

Henry stopped bouncing as Travis stood up. "I want some Cocoa Balls with chocolate milk."

Travis had already thrown the box in the trash. "How about oatmeal? I'll put some raisins in it."

Henry looked at him as if he'd just suggested tarantulas with piss sauce.

"All the bad food I've been feeding you is what made your tummy ache. We've got to eat better."

Henry scrunched up his face, and then opened his mouth to protest.

"The longer you whine, the longer it'll take us to hit the road."

Henry switched gears. "Will we see bears?"

"Nah," he said. "The only bear you're going to see is me after a week of not shaving." By most men's standards, Travis's five o'clock shadow was more of a starter beard. A week would leave him pretty wooly.

"You won't turn into a bear, Uncle Travis. That's just silly."

Travis winked at Henry. "You're right," he said. "I'm more of a wolf."

* * *

Maggie pulled into the parking lot of Petal Pushers. It had been hard getting out of bed this morning. She stretched, noting the familiar soreness in her shoulders. It came with the business. She'd had trouble getting the weed whacker started at the courthouse and had dang near put her shoulder out.

She opened the door of her Jeep and leaned back in her seat expectantly. Pop flew over her lap and onto the asphalt like he'd been ejected from a cockpit. Then he ran straight for the fence that enclosed the outdoor garden area, barking and shaking his stub of a tail. He looked over his shoulder at Maggie, snorting impatience through his little smashed-in bulldog nose.

"I know you've got trees to water. Settle down."

Stepping down from the Jeep brought a second ache into focus, somewhat unfamiliar but not at all unpleasant. And it wasn't located anywhere near her shoulders. She slammed the door, catching a glimpse of her face in the side mirror. There was that stupid grin again. She'd been walking around like a brainless idiot all morning.

"Snap out of it, Mackey," she said aloud.

But no matter how hard she tried to tone it down, she was bouncing around like one of those people with a spring in their step. Surely it would wear off by the end of the day. It wasn't like she had a freaking boyfriend. She'd had sex with a stranger. And they had made no plans for future interludes. But he'd found her sexy. And irresistible. And it was just so dang utterly delightful that now she was stuck with this irritating bounce when she walked.

"Snap out of it, Mackey," she said again. Because she didn't need any man to boost her step *or* her ego.

He couldn't keep his hands off me.

She resigned herself to the bounce. But she was limiting it to twenty-four hours.

She unlocked the gate and Pop shot through to begin his daily watering. He would only squirt a little on the first two or three trees. After that he'd shoot blanks until he exhausted himself.

She followed him in, scanning the rows of plants and shrubs, breathing in their magic elixir. She tiptoed among the balled and burlapped trees heeled-in at the back of the nursery, as if not to wake them, and stepped gingerly over the trickle irrigation lines, working her way to the small building that used to be a farm implement business owned by her grandfather. Upon his death, Honey had made it a nursery. Maggie had moved home to be a partner, and Petal Pushers had flourished under the management of the grandmother-granddaughter duo. Honey had kept up her end, which included floral arrangements for all the funerals and weddings in Big Verde, while Maggie developed a successful landscaping venture.

Claire had recently stepped into Honey's shoes as florist, and they seemed to fit pretty well. But nobody would ever fill the hole Honey had left in Maggie's heart. Or her life.

She strolled among the blooming plants, removing a leaf here and there, deciding what needed to be moved into the direct sunlight of the nursery's entrance and what needed to be loaded onto the truck for the River Mill subdivision.

The Texas Hill Country was a beautiful region, and although Big Verde might not attract a lot of industry, it did attract tourists and wealthy folks looking for pretty country homes. River Mill was a great addition to her portfolio, and she was ninety-nine percent certain she'd be adding Anna's project, as well. There was no way Anna would hire Travis Blake for something that important.

He was a nobody.

She let herself in through the nursery's back door and started flipping on lights. She checked on the shelves of gardening tools, gloves, and bulbs, noting which ones looked bare and needed restocking. She turned on the ceiling fans to make the wind chimes jingle pleasantly, and then went to the counter to boot up the cash register—a fancy new one she barely knew how to operate. Honey's gloves and shears sat by the business cards like a memorial.

While the cash register came online, Maggie pulled out her phone to check e-mail.

She had a text. According to the time stamp, it had been sent last night from an unknown number.

Who's afraid of the Big Bad Wolf?

Her heart leapt straight to her throat. The wolf had texted! But then a sense of unease crept in. She scowled. How did the wolf get her number? Did he *know* her? If so, why hadn't he said anything?

Her stomach lurched. She'd assumed he was a stranger. What if she'd been wrong?

The best night of her life had suddenly turned creepy.

Someone tapped at the front door and Maggie jumped. She had the jitters. With her heart pounding, she slowly approached the glass door while hugging the fertilizer aisle so whoever it was wouldn't see her. She sighed in relief. It was just Norbert. He was here to start loading the trailer for River Mill.

Maggie unlocked the door with trembling fingers.

"Sorry," Norbert said, breezing in. "Forgot my key to the back."

"No problem." She hoped she didn't look as freaked out as she felt. "I haven't made coffee yet."

Norbert hung up his cowboy hat and put on his Petal Pushers cap. He looked at Maggie with a glint in his eye. "I would have thought coffee would be your top priority this morning."

The blood in Maggie's veins turned to ice. She hadn't seen

Norbert at the party last night, but maybe that's because he'd been *wearing a freaking wolf mask!* Even though her veins were now officially frozen, her face was on fire.

Surely, she hadn't banged Norbert in a shed.

Norbert whistled and headed for the coffeepot in the break room. Maggie followed, watching him as he rinsed out the carafe and dumped yesterday's grounds. She had to remind herself to breathe as she sized him up to be about the same height as the wolf.

"I'm going to add an extra scoop," he said. "That was some gala last night, wasn't it?"

He'd been there. Maggie swallowed and clenched her hands into fists.

Norbert turned around. "Maggie? Are you okay?"

She took in his build. He was fit, but stockier than the wolf. And his hair was darker and longer. His hands...definitely not the wolf's. She closed her eyes and imagined the wolf's hands. *The things they'd done to her...*

"Whoa," Norbert said, putting down the coffee scoop and heading her way. "I think you need to sit down."

"No, I'm fine." She waved him off. Norbert's text wouldn't have shown up as an unidentified number. She was being freakishly paranoid. "You're right. I probably had a little too much to drink last night."

Norbert looked doubtful, but he turned back around and flipped the switch on the coffeepot. It sparked and sizzled. Norbert said something in Spanish and jumped away from the counter. The smell of ozone filled the small room.

"No coffee this morning," Norbert said, unplugging the coffeemaker.

Maggie didn't care about coffee this morning, which was saying a lot, and her mind went straight back to wondering who the Big Bad Wolf was. She turned and felt paper stuck to the bottom of her boot. Something yellow poked out—a sticky note. She peeled it off, noting Claire's handwriting. COFFEEPOT IS TOAST. LET'S GET A KEURIG!

She crumpled the note and tossed it in the trash. She'd only recently convinced Claire to start washing and reusing a real mug, and now she wanted to blow through plastic K-Cups.

Whatever. Back to the endless loop of anxiety and panic.

"Who was that wolf you were dancing with?" Norbert asked, like a mind reader.

"Um, just a guy," she said. "He was from out of town."

Unless he was the mailman. Or the guy who kept the books for Petal Pushers. Or the man who drove the UPS truck... She felt faint again.

Once Norbert was adequately occupied and Maggie's heart rate had dropped back into the normal zone, she went into the small office and closed the door. She stared at the message again.

Who's afraid of the Big Bad Wolf?

Her thumb hovered over her phone. Maybe she should just ask the idiot who he was. Then again, maybe she didn't want to know.

After twenty minutes of fretting, she decided to ignore it for now. And by ignore it, she meant think about it constantly while pretending not to.

She still hadn't checked her e-mail. Maybe that would provide a decent distraction. She opened her in-box. First up was a Groupon for a spelunking tour. In an earnest effort to continue ignoring the text from the Big Bad Wolf, she bought two. Next were erectile dysfunction drugs from Canada, political appeals, and an Indonesian prince who wanted to give her lots of money. *Delete. Delete. Delete.* But then she hit pay dirt. An e-mail from Annabelle!

Dear Maggie and Travis,

Wait...what? Why was Travis Blake included in the greeting? Why were their names side by side? Why were they being addressed as a single entity?

I am happy to award the landscaping and architecture bid to Maggie (gorgeous design). The labor bid is going to Travis (great price). I'm sure the two of you will work well together.

Congratulations!

Annabelle Vasquez

Maggie set her phone on the desk like it was radioactive. That dirty rotten scoundrel had weaseled his way in on her job! Maybe if she'd spent less time banging the wolf and more time talking to Anna at the party, this wouldn't have happened.

Whatever Travis Blake's price was, she'd go lower. She supplied her own labor: herself and a small crew. She was not going to share this job.

This had turned into a shitty day. In less than an hour, her mysterious sexy stranger had turned into a stalker, and her unqualified competitor had become her brand-new work buddy.

She might not be able to do anything about Travis at the moment, but she could confront the Big Bad Wolf. Was he trying to scare her? Well, it wasn't working. Much.

She pulled out her phone.

Who's afraid of the Big Bad Wolf?

Ha. Screw him.

Not me.

She sent it and strummed her fingers on the desk. Would he answer?

Five minutes went by with no response while she cleaned out her in-box. She picked up her phone.

And if you text me again I'm calling the cops.

There. That would put an end to it.

Pop started whining at her feet. She mindlessly leaned over and rubbed him between the ears while contemplating all the ways she could make Travis Blake miserable enough to walk off the job and go back to doing lawns with his little push mower.

Pop barked as someone began pounding on the front door.

Maggie stormed out of the office. What type of gardening emergency couldn't wait fifteen minutes for the store to open? She was full of bluster and ready to shout, "We're closed!" But then she remembered she had a stalker.

Pop had beaten her to the door, and she listened for his ominous, protective growl. Instead, she heard his whiny *rub my tummy* growl. And from the frantic toenail ticking, she deduced he was doing his happy feet circle dance, too. Just when she'd thought the day couldn't possibly get any worse, she rounded the fertilizer aisle and saw the white Stetson.

She crossed her arms over her chest. JD had stopped pounding and now tapped politely on the glass.

"We're closed!"

Pop wasn't buying it. He kept whining. JD kept tapping.

"Fine," Maggie muttered, unlocking the door and yanking it open. JD walked in quietly. His hat sat firmly above his ears. He adjusted it once, twice, and then once more.

Oh, for heaven's sake. JD didn't realize it, but that stupid hat was an interpretive device. JD having a good day meant it was high on his forehead. JD having a bad day meant it rode low. JD hiding from everyone because of some shit he'd pulled meant it was yanked *way* down low, and JD setting the damn thing squarely on the ears meant he was shooting for a confidence he didn't deserve.

Maggie wasn't going to make it easy on him, so she said nothing. They didn't have a thing in the world to talk about. Pop clearly hadn't gotten the memo and ran figure eights between JD's ankles, yapping to be picked up.

JD removed his hat. *Dear God, he was going to do the Grand Gesture.*

"Maggie—"

"Save it, JD."

"Too soon?"

"Massive understatement. I'll reevaluate when Hell freezes over."

"I think it's best to do it now."

"I'd prefer to let it fester. And believe it or not, I have bigger things—"

"We need to talk about your feelings for me," he said, taking a step toward her.

"How about we talk about your feelings for *me?* Shorter conversation."

JD cleared his throat. "Maggie, you mean the world to me, and there's something I need to tell you."

He'd practiced! She could hear it in his voice. He had a speech ready. Well, she wasn't going to let him deliver it. "I was drunk. That's pretty much it." She put her hand on his chest and tried backing him to the door. "Bye now."

"I've seen you drunk. You were maybe a little buzzed."

"Okay, fine. I was on my period."

"I've seen that, too. You weren't telling me to fuck off—"

"Fuck off."

"And your skin is perfectly clear. You don't have those puffy things you get beneath your eyes from fluid retention."

She got puffy things beneath her eyes from fluid retention? "File it under temporary insanity. I've been under a lot of stress lately. Or"—she snapped her fingers—"I was horny. How about that? Even girls like me get horny."

"Girls like you... What does that mean?"

"You know what it means."

"No, I don't."

Maggie turned and started for the counter. "Do, too," she said over her shoulder. It was habit to argue childishly with JD. They'd been doing it for fifteen years.

"Do not," said JD. "So do you want to go to Tony's tonight and catch a game?"

Maggie stopped in her tracks, overwhelmed by the repetitious, deadening familiarity of it all. She didn't want to fall back into the same old rut of being one of the guys. And she didn't appreciate her feelings being swept under the rug by JD, even if she had refused to talk about them.

She turned. "I need some space. I don't think we should hang out anymore."

JD's jaw dropped. Hurt shone in his hazel eyes—genuine hurt. But Maggie couldn't handle going back to the way things were. Not yet anyway.

"Fine. If you don't want to be friends anymore, then we just won't be friends." JD resettled his hat, giving it an extra yank. "It was going to happen anyway."

What was that supposed to mean? Before she could ask, JD yanked the door open, violently jingling the little bell on top. He looked over his shoulder. "Stay away from that goddamn wolf."

Chapter Eight

Claire breezed in with a cardboard tray of steaming coffee cups. "JD just blew past me in the parking lot. What was that about?"

"Nothing," Maggie said.

Claire walked to the counter, her heels tapping out a Morse code of sexiness across the concrete floor. She perched on her usual stool and set the coffee on the counter.

"Is he jealous of you and the wolf?"

"Hardly."

"Are we in a one-word-only mood today?" Claire asked. "Because I need more from you. Like who is he? How was it? Are you seeing him again?"

"Dunno. Great. No." *At least she hoped she wouldn't.*

Maggie just couldn't believe the wolf was someone she knew. Nor could she believe the way he'd made her feel. Even as she sat there in her Red Wing work boots and grubby clothes, the thought of his touch weakened her knees. She'd been so feminine and sexy in his hands. He'd teased out a side of her she hadn't even known existed.

"Why don't you want to see him again?"

She wanted to tell Claire about the text, but she was afraid Claire would immediately begin accosting every man in Big Verde. *Did you bang Maggie in a shed?*

"I told you not to wear those high heels to work." The only time Claire wasn't wearing heels was when she was rock climbing. Although now that Maggie thought about it... "Hey, you don't wear those when you climb rocks, do you?"

"Oh my God. Are you seriously not going to give me details? And of course I don't wear them when I climb. I wear them to work because they're the only shoes that keep my leather pants from dragging in the muck."

"I told you not to wear those either."

"Stop telling me what to do, or I'll take back your skinny pumpkin spice latte with an extra dash of cinnamon and no whip."

Maggie picked up the cup and looked at it. "Is that really what's in here?"

Claire laughed. "Of course not. Where would I get something like that in Big Verde? It's a bitter cup of black goo from the Pump 'n' Go."

Maggie took a sip and grimaced. "It's dangerous to walk around here in those heels."

"I promise not to sue you if I fall. Now start squawking."

What could she say? She'd never had sex like that before. And it wasn't just that she'd never had sex with a masked man while bent over a workbench in a toolshed. It was that she'd never done *anything* remotely kinky before. The Big Bad Wolf had seemed to know every secret desire she'd ever had and just how to meet it. She'd been putty in his hands. A pliable, quivering mess of need that only he could fulfill.

She shivered at the memory of the low rumble of his voice when he'd said, "Good girl." She'd have done almost anything at that moment to please him. She'd trusted him completely. And look where it had gotten her. The freedom of letting go might have been exhilarating, but it had also been stupid. Her stomach churned as she considered the consequences. What if he tried to blackmail her or something equally sinister?

Maggie pushed her coffee away and then quickly hid her hand beneath the counter, so Claire wouldn't see it shaking.

But Claire had seen it. "Oh, honey, what's wrong?" The concern in her eyes was intense. In fact, Claire appeared almost panicked. "Did he hurt you?"

Maggie twisted her hands. "I'm just a little shaken up. I'll give you the details, but you have to promise not to tell anyone until I decide what to do."

Claire set her cup down. "What do you mean, until you decide what to do?" She grabbed Maggie by the shoulders and shook her. "What happened?"

"I was stupid. That's what happened."

Claire pulled Maggie in for a bone-crushing hug. "It wasn't your fault. Whatever happened; it wasn't your fault. Shit, Maggie what have I done?"

What had *she* done? Maggie pushed Claire off because she really wasn't much of a hugger, and because she suspected Claire was off her rocker. "You didn't do anything but request a song for us to dance to, and we'd already danced anyway. None of this is your fault. It was my decision to follow him to the shed—"

"That dirty bastard assaulted you in a shed?"

Before she could answer, Maggie was again enveloped in an awkward and brutal hug.

"He didn't—"

"And I've given him your number," Claire whimpered. "Now he's going to stalk you."

"You *what?*"

Claire released her. "Don't be mad. It's just that I could tell things hadn't gone well with JD—I'd seen him sulking—and when I saw the wolf, I just thought maybe he could make you feel better…"

Boy, had he ever.

"And so, you gave him my number?" What a relief! The wolf wasn't a creepy stalker out to blackmail her. Claire had given him her number. And he'd texted her!

"Not exactly," Claire said. "He left his phone on the bar while y'all danced, which is careless if you ask me, and—"

Everything clicked into place. "You sent the text."

"Yes. In case you were too shy or too stupid to exchange numbers, you know?"

Maggie's mind raced to keep up. She pulled up the text to confirm. Who's afraid of the Big Bad Wolf? She pushed the phone toward Claire. "This was you?"

"Yes." Claire had the good sense to avoid eye contact.

What a freaking roller coaster. First, Maggie had thought she'd accidentally banged Norbert in the shed. Or possibly the UPS guy. And that he might be planning to blackmail her. Then she'd learned it hadn't been Norbert or the UPS guy, just her glorious and mysterious Big Bad Wolf, and that he'd texted her, probably because he wanted to see her again. *Elation!* But then it turned out to just be Claire. *Disappointment.*

"Oh, well," she mumbled. "At least we had one great night."

"You had a great night? You mean he didn't, you know…"

"Goodness, no! He didn't do anything I didn't want him to do." Her face felt like it was on fire and she lowered her eyes. She'd wanted him to do all kinds of things. "We had sex."

"In a shed? Are you kidding me?" Claire bounced on her seat and clapped her hands. "That sounds incredibly kinky and possibly uncomfortable. Tell me everything."

"I just did."

"I doubt that. Are you going to text him back? He might not even know he's texted you since he didn't really."

"I already did."

Claire clapped her hands. "What did you say?"

"I threatened him with calling the cops." She took a sip of her coffee before adding, "And that would be your fault, not mine."

"Apologize. And then send something clever or witty."

All Maggie could drum up in her head was white noise. "I got nothin'."

"Sext him," Claire said, eyes shining with mischief.

"I couldn't!" Maggie said. "And besides, I'm not so sure about this. We know absolutely nothing about this guy. What if he's married?"

"He's not," Claire said.

"How do you know?"

Claire took a gulp of coffee, hiding behind the cup.

"You looked through his text messages, didn't you?" Maggie asked.

"I have morals, Maggie."

Maggie mentally counted to five before Claire coughed it up.

"He was texting with the babysitter."

Maggie swallowed loudly. "He has a kid? How do you know he doesn't also have a wife?"

"Because *he* was the one texting the babysitter. And there was no wife at the gala. The situation just doesn't have a married vibe."

He *had* been at the party by himself. Dressed in a costume. It certainly didn't sound like he was married. But who was he? And should she try and see him again? She shivered as the memory of his hands on her bottom rudely crashed into her thoughts.

She took out her phone and started texting.

Chapter
Nine

❦

Travis stared at his phone while he pumped gas. He hadn't had any service in the state park, so he'd expected his phone to go berserk as soon as they got through the winding hills surrounding Big Verde. But he hadn't expected a series of nonsensical and mysterious texts from a person he assumed to be Little Red Riding Hood to come pinging in just as he pulled into the Pump 'n' Go.

It was odd because he'd never given the woman his phone number, and what was even more puzzling was that he'd supposedly texted her first.

Who's afraid of the Big Bad Wolf?

He had not sent that text. Something was fishy. And Little Red Riding Hood had responded.

Not me.

Followed by a threat.

And if you text me again I'm calling the cops.

Followed by several humdingers that made absolutely zero sense.

Never mind. I'm not calling the cops LOL.

Why would I do that?

Claire sent the first text and I didn't know it.

What did that even mean? How had Claire sent the first text?

Are you mad?

Do you want me to stop texting?

Those had all been sent within five minutes. Then there was a three-day pause, which he hated, because that meant she'd thought he was ignoring her.

Hey, it's me, Little Red Riding Hood. I understand if you don't want to text.

She'd waited almost fifteen minutes before sending the next set.

But if you want to text I'm fine with it.

Unless you're married. I don't want you texting me if you're married.

Not that you are.

Texting me.

Or married.

His pulse sped up. He'd like to see her again. She hadn't been far from his mind during the entire camping trip. Heck, he hadn't been able to be fully present with Henry, although God knows he'd tried. He'd been haunted by Maggie. More like obsessed. Unable to keep the hooded pixie out of his head for more than five minutes at a time. But he hadn't known how to get in touch with her, and now that he did, he wasn't sure he wanted to.

First off, she seemed a tad anxious. Second, she thought he was a mysterious stranger in a nice suit from out of town. The reality of who he was couldn't be further from the truth.

But all he had to do was close his eyes and he could see her. Feel her. Taste her. *Oh shit. Don't go there again.*

He went there.

As the display on the pump continued its upward climb to twenty gallons, his mind replayed the well-worn reel of their night in the shed. The softness of her hips, the sound of their skin slapping together. He could practically hear her moaning and begging—he'd made her beg—as he'd fucked her senseless.

"Uncle Travis?"

He landed back on Earth with a deadening thud. The pump had stopped. The guy in line behind him scowled, waiting for him to finish up.

Travis hastily put his phone in his pocket, removed the gas nozzle, and closed the cap on his tank.

"Why were you standing there with your mouth hanging open?" Henry asked. "Were you daydreamin' or something?"

Travis climbed in the truck. "Or something. Put your seat belt back on."

Henry had learned how to unbuckle the harness on his car seat, a development that was making Travis's life a living hell. Travis thought the five-point contraption was overkill for a five-year-old and didn't blame Henry for not wanting to ride in the damn thing, but Lisa had left very specific orders. Henry was to ride in the car seat until he achieved the recommended weight and height for getting out of it.

"It's for babies!"

In retrospect, a week in the wilderness had probably been about four days too long. Henry was worn out and melting down.

Travis started the truck and slowly pulled away from the pump even though Henry wasn't buckled in yet. The little guy was just getting wound up—Travis could hear it in his voice—so it was best to find a safe spot to park and ride it out.

He pulled into a space in front of the store just as Henry delivered a punch to his kidneys through the seat.

Travis swallowed the urge to yell as he turned the engine off. "Stop it, Henry," he said, knowing it wasn't going to stop.

Henry screamed like a banshee and gave Travis's left kidney another good kick. Then he flung himself to the floor and curled up into a ball. This was extremely bad timing. Little Red Riding Hood hadn't been the only female frantically texting him while they'd been camping. Annabelle had also repeatedly texted, asking if he'd received her e-mail about the bid—he hadn't—and letting him know about a meeting at her new house thirty goddamn minutes from now.

Travis reached back and tapped Henry on the shoulder, which caused him to explode in a mass of arms, legs, and shrieks. It would be impossible to get the stinker back into his seat like this. It would be easier to get an octopus into a straitjacket, so Travis turned back around and pulled his cap down to wait it out.

Kick.

Henry had climbed back in his seat to kick the shit out of him again.

Kick.

It was bad timing because Henry wasn't the only one who was cranky and worn out.

Kick.

"Henry, stop it right now, or I'll never take you camping again. In fact, I'll never take you anywhere again. Got it?"

Kick.

It was hard to tell over all the sniffling and muttering, but he could swear Henry had just called him a rat bastard.

Travis rolled out of the truck with a grimace and limped to Henry's door. He yanked it open just as a small foot shot out, pegging him in the nuts. Blinding white pain bent Travis over for about twenty seconds. On the twenty-first second, he grabbed Henry by one ankle and pulled him out of the truck. He quickly took hold of the other ankle, and before Henry knew what had him, he was dangling upside down.

"Now listen," Travis wheezed. "You don't have a choice about whether to ride in your car seat. No choice."

"I hate you!"

"I'm not real fond of you right now either. And you're going to hang here until you're calm enough to get back in the truck and act like a human."

Henry made a vicious grab at Travis's leg, but Travis dodged him. "You missed me," he chided, feeling about the same age as Henry.

"Butthead!" Henry shouted.

Travis swung wide so that Henry went back and forth like a pendulum. "Yeah? Well, you're a wiener head."

They'd long passed the point where one of them needed to be an adult, and besides, sometimes the word *wiener* made Henry laugh. But not today.

Henry spit at him and wiggled like an earthworm. Travis tightened his grip, so he wouldn't drop Henry on his head. Just when he thought he might have to sit on the kid to get him buckled in, Henry wound down and quit wiggling. Which was good, because a car had pulled up next to them—an older couple in a big silver Cadillac. The woman in the passenger seat, no more than three feet away, gawked openly. Travis smiled all friendly-like, hoping that would be the end of it.

"Help! Help!" Henry shouted.

Great. The passenger window of the Cadillac rolled slowly down.

"Can we be of any assistance?" the lady asked.

"No thank you, ma'am," Travis said. "We're just having a seat belt debate."

"Are you his father?"

"Stranger danger!" shouted Henry.

Travis pulled Henry up even higher, so he could see his beet red face. "Are you nuts?" He hoisted the kid to his shoulder to get him right side up again, and Henry proceeded to pout like a pro, but that was it. Maybe the battle was over. "I'm not his father. I'm his uncle," Travis said to the woman. He held out a hand and introduced himself. "Travis Blake."

"My dad is in prison," Henry added helpfully. Travis's face heated up with embarrassment, just as it had been doing his entire life.

The woman looked at his hand like it was a rattlesnake, but her husband reached across and shook it. "I'm Judge Samuel Monroe, retired. I knew your brother."

"No doubt," Travis said.

"And your daddy," he added, just in case Travis needed to be reminded of all the times he'd driven the truck—with no license— to haul his dad out of the drunk tank. After he died, they'd retired his barstool at Tony's with a brass nameplate.

The good judge's wife recoiled in her seat. Travis couldn't blame her. After a week in the wilderness with no shower and no shave, he probably looked like an escaped convict. He was on his way to being Grizzly Adams, or worse, a hipster from Austin. He couldn't wait for a shave and a haircut.

"Henry is just about to get in his car seat, aren't you, Henry?"

Henry was redder than boiled beets, a combination of rage and all the blood rushing to his head while he'd hung upside down. He stuck his tongue out at Travis.

"Y'all have a good afternoon," Travis said. He plunked Henry into the seat, buckled him in, and started the truck. With a final wave at the busybodies, he backed up. Henry's red, tear-streaked face was visible in the rearview mirror.

"Listen, Henry, I'm real sorry about the way I handled that."

"That man was a judge. Is he gonna take me away from you?"

Where had that come from? "Of course not. Why?"

"Before she went to heaven, Mom told me I'd better be good for you or a judge might put me in frosted care."

"You mean foster care?"

Henry sniffled. "That's what I said."

Something had changed on the camping trip. Keeping Henry alive had been exhausting, and Travis had started to worry a bit about letting just anyone do it. But that wasn't what had caused the shift. It was the other stuff. The storytelling. The endless question-answering. The warm sleeping bag hugs that kept away the things that went bump in the night. But mostly, it had been the moment he'd reentered the tent after a middle-of-the-night whiz to find Henry sitting up, eyes wide and lips trembling. He'd said, "I missed you, Uncle Travis."

But what he'd meant was, *I thought you'd left me.*

"Over my dead body," Travis said. "You're not going to foster care."

But where would he go? It wasn't like Henry could stay with *him*. Hopefully the social worker would turn up someone soon. Or maybe Scott would get out of prison, straighten out his life, and take being a dad seriously.

And maybe pigs would fly.

* * *

Maggie sat in her Jeep seething with rage. She'd just witnessed some jerk holding a poor child upside down at the Pump 'n' Go. She'd been about ready to jump out and do something when an older couple had pulled up and handled it.

She should have been more proactive—maybe gotten his license plate number—but she'd been struck dumb by the ridiculous scene. If she ever ran into that idiot, she'd give him a piece of her mind. But she hadn't recognized him, which meant he was probably just passing through Big Verde.

Still shaking, she pulled out of the Pump 'n' Go and headed north on Main Street. It was Friday, so every storefront bore bright green messages in shoe polish cheering on the Big Verde Giants in tonight's game against the Sweet Home Beavers.

FEE FI FO FUM!

KEEP THOSE BEAVERS ON THE RUN!

There were other cheers about the Sweet Home Beavers— it was just too easy—but most weren't appropriate for storefront windows. The Big Verde pep squad usually managed to sneak in an oldie but goodie, though, and she smiled to see Mr. Chavez seated in front of a checkerboard in the Rite Aid drugstore window with

LICK THE BEAVERS! scrawled above his head. Every single person in Big Verde got the reference, but since they'd all been feigning innocence since their own pep rally days, nobody could admit it.

As Maggie passed her alma mater, Big Verde High, the Jeep vibrated with the powerful cadence of the school fight song. The pep rally was in full swing. When the song ended, the entire stadium would yell *Ho ho ho, Big Verde!* It was a take on the Jolly Green Giant jingle and was totally lost on the current generation, but they used it anyway because tradition was important.

Maggie drove on by. It wasn't that she minded reliving what were certainly not her glory days; she just had a meeting at Annabelle's. And she was determined to talk Anna out of splitting the contract between Petal Pushers and Travis Blake.

Her phone buzzed on the seat next to her. She was the only car on Main Street, so she risked a glance with her heart in her throat and her spine on fire, because the wolf hadn't texted back yet, and it had been a full week.

Ugh. It was her mother. And it was long. She'd read it later.

She imagined the wolf receiving her texts. He hadn't seemed like a jerk, so why hadn't he at least responded with a No, thank you? How could he just leave her hanging like this?

Maybe he'd figured out who she was. He wasn't from Big Verde, but he knew Annabelle, didn't he? What if Annabelle had teased him about dancing with her? She could just hear it…*Saw you dancing with poor little Maggie Mackey. Bless her heart, Big Verde High didn't know whether to name her FFA Queen or FFA King. So sweet of you to give her some attention.*

The road turned curvy as soon as she passed the Big Verde city limit, and her cares automatically lightened. Nature did that for her. It was one of the reasons she spent so much time working outdoors even though she had a landscape architect degree and could basically have a desk job.

She rolled her window down. Perfect autumn day for the Hill

Country. Clear blue skies and eighty-five degrees for a high. Her ears popped as she gained a little altitude, and the landscape changed slowly from scrub brush and cactus to juniper and cedar. The highest hill was her destination, and she could see the road switchbacking up its side in the distance.

When she drove over the cattle guard, a cloud of dust met her, stirred up by the truck ahead. It went left at the fork, and so did she, continuing to eat its dust all the way up to the top of the hill, where the house was still under construction.

Three trucks were already parked beneath a giant live oak, and the one she'd been following pulled up under a big cottonwood, leaving absolutely no space for her in the shade. Leave it to a bunch of men to try and squeeze her out. She parked next to a pile of gorgeous white rock she assumed would go on the outside of the house and jumped down from the Jeep with Pop on her heels.

Two of the trucks bore L&M Construction emblems. One belonged to JD, the other to Bubba. They were partners. She spotted JD's white Stetson right away.

With her plans in hand, she strode with confidence toward the group of men. JD wore a starched white shirt and a pair of Wranglers with perfect creases pressed into each long leg—his Sunday attire. Trying to impress Annabelle? It seemed to be working. Anna had plastered herself to his arm.

Bubba smiled and waved. "Hey there, Mighty Mack."

JD tilted his hat and nodded, then pulled it all the way down to "hiding" mode. Annabelle projected her usual beauty queen smile, looking at Maggie as if she were a stray puppy she'd love to take in if only it didn't have fleas. Her right boob was displaced by JD's biceps, rising out of the hot pink scoop neck sweater. Not fair. Anna had enough cleavage without the help of JD's biceps.

Because he was a good doggie, Pop jumped up on Annabelle's legs. She squealed and gave a delicate kick that Pop artfully dodged. "Do you have to take that dreadful little dog with you everywhere?"

Maggie wanted to offer Pop a high-five, which was one of his very best tricks. "Sorry." She pointed at Anna. "Pop, show some love!"

That was another one of Pop's tricks. *Show some love* meant *lick person on face* and Pop happily obliged, jumping up to give Anna some tongue when she bent over to brush the dirt off her jeans.

"Oh!" Annabelle said, scrunching up her face. "Get away from me!" She stood and delivered a sizzling glare to Maggie. *I'll get you and your little dog, too.*

Bubba scooped Pop up into a football hold while JD walked over to Maggie. "She's your client," he said in her ear.

He was right. Being in Annabelle's presence turned Maggie into a thirteen-year-old. "I'll have those jeans cleaned for you."

"Don't bother," Anna said. She'd already lost interest and was headed toward the dark truck Maggie had followed to the house. Its driver had finally gotten out, and Maggie gasped when he turned around. It was the jerk from the Pump 'n' Go! And even though she didn't think he'd seen her, his stunned, slack-jawed expression suggested he recognized her, too.

Chapter

Ten

❧

Travis couldn't believe it. The mask had not done as good a job of concealing his identity as he'd thought. Little Red Riding Hood had shown up at his job site—*why?*—and recognized him immediately. He'd been thinking of ways to respond to her texts the entire ride here, and now she was right in front of him, looking seriously pissed off.

He stood like a deer in the headlights, glued to the spot as Maggie stomped her way toward him with those adorable eyebrows drawn into a menacing scowl. She pushed the sleeves of her sweatshirt up like she was heading for the center of the ring, and his heart nearly burst through his chest. Not only was it responding to what it perceived as a pint-sized, but potent, threat, but something stupid located in the part of the brain housing primal instincts screamed, *That's my girl.*

"I recognize you," she said, stating the obvious.

That voice. He wanted to pick her up and spin her around, maybe push her up against the side of his truck and kiss her senseless, but he remained where he was, entirely paralyzed, while Ms. Hood went around him to peer into his truck. He couldn't help but notice her perky breasts responding to the enthusiastic stomping. And he wasn't entirely paralyzed. One part of him had definitely moved.

"It's good to see you again," he said as she breezed by. Little Red Riding Hood had practically mowed down Annabelle on her way to his truck, but now Anna was also standing there staring at the two of them and looking every bit as confused as he felt.

Little Red Riding Hood seemed interested in Henry, and damn near poked her head through the window of his truck. Luckily, Henry was sound asleep. "Listen," Travis tried again. "I've been out of town. I was going to answer—"

"Is this child okay?"

"What?" He looked at Anna, but she just gestured with her finger near her ear in a circular motion while mouthing *loco*.

"Is he *okay?*" Maggie repeated, very slowly, as if Travis had a comprehension problem.

"Of course he's okay. He's sleeping. The window's rolled down. What's your problem?"

His exhilaration over seeing her had journeyed from excitement to confusion and had settled at irritation. Maybe Anna was right. It figured that his one and only hookup in months had been with a crazy person.

"Are you sure?" She opened the door.

"Please don't wake him. You have no idea what you're doing."

He'd kept his voice nice and calm, as if he were talking to someone on a ledge. He didn't want to make any sudden moves that might cause her to screech or anything else that might rouse Henry. Travis felt bad enough about bringing a child to the meeting—it wasn't professional—and the last thing he needed was a huge fit that would make Anna reconsider her decision.

"Well, a few minutes ago he was hanging upside down over the asphalt."

She'd seen him at the Pump 'n' Go? Did she know he was the wolf?

"I hope he hasn't had a seizure or something," she added.

She said that last part without much conviction, as by now JD and Bubba were also standing around—with dumbass grins—and she seemed to notice she was the only one freaking out.

"He wouldn't get in his car seat," Travis said, even though it was none of anybody's business. "I had to calm him—"

"That is not how you calm a child down."

She had no idea who he was. She just thought he was some sort of—

"People who abuse children might think it's calming," she continued. "But nobody else does."

Child abuser. Great. Not a good time to suggest a date, then. Plus, he was kind of getting pissed at Ms. Hood.

"I'm sure Travis isn't a child abuser," JD said.

"Thanks, JD."

Maggie's mouth dropped open like she had a steel ball attached to her chin. "Travis?" she sputtered. "Travis Blake?"

Travis stuck his hand out, but he couldn't muster a pleasant expression. "Did you follow me from the Pump 'n' Go all the way out here just to harass me?"

Maggie jutted out her chin, frowned, and grabbed his hand with surprising force. "I'm Maggie," she said, giving his hand one vicious pump.

"Don't hurt yourself," he said.

She yanked her hand back and glowered at him. "I did not follow you. I'm here on business."

"I explained it in my e-mail," Annabelle said. "Petal Pushers is doing the design, you're just doing the labor."

"But Petal Pushers is Mary Margaret Mackey's business," Travis said. Alarms went off in his head. He gulped and looked at Little Red Riding Hood. "I take it you're Mary Margaret?"

She stared angrily with her arms crossed, tapping a toe in disgust. "Only if you're my mother."

Travis's head spun. This couldn't get any worse. Mary Margaret Mackey thought he was a child abuser and had no idea he was the Big Bad Wolf she'd recently had very filthy and satisfying sex with in a shed.

Beneath Maggie's heated and somewhat quizzical gaze, he muttered, "I guess we'll be working together."

She stared at him even harder. Holy shit, did she recognize him as the wolf? This probably wouldn't be a good time for that to happen. She was glaring at him intently. Putting two and two together? He'd been clean shaven the night of the gala. Now he was scruffy with a starter beard, and she'd never seen the upper half of his face. She averted her eyes.

Henry chose that moment to wake up and contribute to the conversation. He muttered a few unintelligible words before his dull eyes settled on Travis. "I just peed my pants."

He hadn't even been home to change clothes before being thrust into a meeting over a bid award he didn't fully understand, only to be accused of child abuse, and now he had a kid with wet pants. He opened the truck door. A dark stain was spreading across Henry's lap, probably soaking the car seat.

Henry was already unbuckling the harness. Travis lifted him out, holding him at arm's length.

"I imagine that seat liner comes out," Maggie said, looking at the car seat, which was soaked. "Just throw it in the washing machine. Do you have a towel for when it's time to buckle him back in?"

"I'm not getting back in that car seat," Henry said, crossing his arms. "You can't make me."

Maggie raised her eyebrows, then glanced at Travis and those big brown eyes—like mood rings—clearly said, *Okay, I get it.* She smiled and shrugged.

Henry moved on to the next item on his agenda. "I'm hungry."

Travis set him down.

"Goodness, you're dirty, too," Maggie said, taking in Henry's appearance.

"We've been camping for a week," Travis said.

"That must be why you smell like a campfire."

"I'm always dirty," Henry said. "And I'm always hungry."

Travis glared at Henry. He was laying it on pretty thick—probably hoping Maggie had a candy bar.

"You can have a banana," Travis said.

"I don't want a banana."

Of course he didn't. "Granola bar?"

"Nope."

Maggie reached into the bag hanging off her shoulder. "I have a bag of chips—"

"Thank you," Travis said. "But we're trying to eat better, right, Henry?"

"I want what she has."

So did Travis, but it was doubtful they were thinking about the same thing. Maggie waited, arm in the bag, for him to give her permission to hand over the chips. He nodded. "Fine," he said. "Thanks."

"You've got a naked kid," JD said.

"What?"

Henry had stripped to his underwear in record time. "I'm all wet."

"Wait a minute there, Henry—"

"Anyone have an extra shirt?" Maggie asked, just as the undies hit the ankles.

Nobody did.

Travis had a bag of camping clothes, but unfortunately it had rained last night. Everything in their tent had gotten wet.

Henry kicked the underwear off and stood there, butt naked. "I'm cold."

"Aw, hell." Self-consciously, Travis pulled his T-shirt over his head, eliciting a whistle from Bubba.

Travis ignored Bubba and slipped the shirt on Henry's skinny little frame. It dragged the ground, but it would keep Henry from getting chilled and cover his willy. This scene couldn't get any weirder. He was at a business meeting and both he and Henry were partially naked. Bubba and JD looked entirely too amused.

"Ooh, nice ink," Annabelle said. Her eyes took their time tracing the dragon tattoo that went from his shoulder to his biceps. His face heated up as she gazed at the falcon spanning the width of his chest, and he really became uncomfortable when she dropped her eyes to the rattlesnake coiled on his lower abdomen. He turned slightly, feeling stupidly modest.

Maggie tilted her head as if watching Henry inhale chips, but she was doing an obvious bit of peripheral peeking. He was damn glad he'd kept his shirt on in the shed.

"I have a tattoo," Bubba said.

"That hula girl quit dancing a long time ago," JD said. "Keep your shirt on."

Bubba faked a sad frown. "She's still got some sway, bruh."

"That's just jiggle," JD replied.

Anna had finished her site survey of Travis's body. "I'm done with Tweedledee and Tweedledum here," she said, waving a hand at JD and Bubba. "Now it's time to talk landscaping."

* * *

This was insane. Maggie had come ready to protect her turf with actual facts and figures—she absolutely *could* match Travis Blake's bid on the labor and do a better job with more equipment and a crew—but it was all she could do to yank single-syllable words out of the vocabulary soup threatening to explode through her ears.

Him bad. Me good.

"Do you think you can work that little bit out between the two of you?" Anna asked.

Little bit of what? What had Anna been saying? While Maggie

had been trying to form a sentence in the presence of a half-naked male centerfold covered in tattoos that dipped down into his low-riding jeans, Anna had been blathering on about something involving her and the said half-naked male centerfold.

She remembered Claire's description of Travis Blake in high school and thought, *Quiet skinny bookworm in glasses, my ass.*

"We can work it out," Travis said. "No problem."

Work what out? Also, he looked like he worked out plenty.

She leaned on the newly installed granite bar and pretended to know what they were talking about. "Sure. No problem." *Maybe we can work it out naked.*

What was she doing? Ever since her night with the wolf, she'd been—for lack of a better word—horny. She shook her head and focused on why she was here. "Anna, I'd like to discuss the contract in private if you don't mind."

"We don't need to discuss anything in private. You two are a team. You *do* know how to collaborate, don't you?"

"Yes, of course. And I'm pleased you like my plans. But splitting the contract seems unnecessary. I can match Mr. Blake's—"

"Call me Travis."

She risked a glance at the gigantic lumberjack sucking up all the air in the room with his chiseled pecs. Big mistake. "Okay—Travis. Whatever. Anyway . . ." What had she been saying?

"It's too late," Anna said. "It's been decided. You're going to work on this project together, and if one of you refuses, you'll be replaced."

Replaced? Oh, hell no. Good sense finally overcame the pheromones leaking out of the gigolo lawn boy. "There's one—*one*—landscape architect in town. And it's me."

"There's plenty in Austin," Anna said.

"They're more expensive, though."

Anna shrugged her shoulders and grabbed Travis's arm, leaning in and displacing her boob again. Someone should shield poor little Henry's eyes—she glanced around—wherever he was.

"He's not going anywhere," Anna said.

Travis was Annabelle's man candy. To his credit, he appeared somewhat mortified. What little skin she could see through his beard was flaming red, and his delicious full lips—*stop it, Mackey!*—were not smiling.

He pulled away from Anna and folded his arms across his bare chest. "I better go find Henry," he said.

Annabelle smiled at him sweetly. "Run along then."

Travis hesitated, as if he had something to say. But he apparently thought better of it. He nodded at Maggie before heading out in search of Henry.

"Oh, don't look at me like that," Annabelle said.

Maggie tried to adjust her snarl into a more pleasant expression. "Like what?"

"It's not what you're thinking," Anna continued. "I'm just trying to help him out. I mean, good Lord, he's a pathetic case. No education, living in that trashy house at Happy Trails, and now he's inherited a kid that belongs to his prison inmate brother."

Wow. When she put it that way...

She looked through the French doors to where Travis squatted next to Henry, who was poking at an ant mound with a stick. Henry squealed, dropped the stick, and slapped at his hand. Travis brought the little fingers to his bearded face and delivered a quick kiss to make it better.

More than just man candy, then.

* * *

Henry had just learned his lesson about poking at a fire ant mound. Travis had already kissed his knuckles—Henry had taught him all about magic kisses—and swatted another twenty or so ants off his little legs before the fuckers had a chance to bite again. Henry's eyes were brimming, but he wasn't wailing. Yet.

"Suck it up," Travis said. Then he winced. That's what his dad used to say to him. "Sorry," he muttered. "You can cry if you want to."

Henry sniffled but kept a lid on the waterworks.

Travis looked toward the house, where Anna stared at him through the window just like old times. It was clear that she'd awarded him the bid to relive her lawn boy fantasy from high school. That hadn't ended well. Maybe he didn't need this job that bad.

Except that he did need it that bad.

He swallowed his pride—it got stuck about halfway down but he powered through—and waved at Anna. She wanted a lawn boy? She had a lawn boy. He didn't have to be happy about it, though.

He stood, brushed off his pants, and picked Henry up. "You ready to go home?"

Henry yawned in response.

Maggie came out. "Did you get attacked by some fire ants?" she asked Henry.

Henry nodded.

"Hurts like the dickens, doesn't it?"

Maggie mussed Henry's hair but didn't look Travis in the eye. "Can you be here at nine on Monday? We'll start clearing out the rocks behind the patio."

"Make it seven," he said. His voice was brusque. "An earlier start is better for me."

So much for being the Big Bad Wolf. He was Anna's goddamn lawn boy.

He loaded Henry into the car seat and climbed behind the wheel, yanking his phone out of his back pocket. Little Red Riding Hood's texts stared up at him. A sly grin crept across his face. Maybe he couldn't get the upper hand with Maggie Mackey, but he knew who could.

Her last text had asked him if he was married. He'd start there.

Not married. I'm a Lone Wolf. Sure you're not afraid?

Chapter

Eleven

❧

Maggie jerked awake and slammed her hand on Darth Vader's head to silence the "Imperial March" alarm. She'd bought herself ten more minutes. Pop recognized the beginning of the snooze loop and settled in at her hip with a satisfied grunt.

Maggie sank back into the blissful abyss. She'd been dreaming about a snake.

A snake tattoo! Today was her first day on the job with Travis Blake. Forget the snooze. She threw the covers off. Pop cocked an ear, looking offended.

"We've got to get up. That jerk insisted on seven o'clock and I'll be damned if he's going to get there first." She swung her legs over the side of the bed. The floor was cold, and she headed for her robe and slippers. No point in cranking up the ancient gas wall heater she always half expected to explode. It was supposed to hit the upper eighties by early afternoon. Such was life in central Texas.

She shuffled into the kitchen and unlocked Pop's doggie door. You couldn't live in the country and leave a doggie door unlocked at night. Not unless you wanted a skunk in your house. Pop shot through and disappeared into the early morning fog.

She rinsed out the stovetop percolator and filled it with coffee. She should probably buy a coffeepot like a normal person, but the percolator had belonged to Honey. She hadn't done much to the cottage since Honey died, and she had a half-baked idea to turn it into a vacation rental. It was originally built in 1901 by German settlers, and Maggie had been approached by several people wanting to buy it. Since she wanted to keep the cottage in the family but didn't necessarily want to continue living in it herself, turning it into a weekend rental was the perfect solution.

She turned on the gas burner. The wolf had responded to her texts on Friday—finally! And it had been a fun exchange. She didn't know what she'd expected, maybe a little innocent back and forth, but they were dirty texting. She couldn't wait to tell Claire.

She looked at the texts again.

Not married. I'm a Lone Wolf. Sure you're not afraid?

I've already followed you through the woods. Seen you at your wildest.

What makes you think that was my wildest? Wear sexy panties to work tomorrow.

The wolf wanted to play games. Maggie wasn't sure she'd be very good at it, but last night she'd set out a pair of red lacy panties.

Pop bolted back through the doggie door and skidded to a stop in front of his empty bowl. Maggie dumped a little kibble in it.

She wasn't looking forward to working with Travis Blake. He wasn't qualified. He didn't deserve his half of the contract. He was getting by on his looks, while Maggie had to work hard to get what she wanted. Her entire life had been a struggle to prove she was tough enough, big enough, and smart enough to compete with the boys.

She headed to the bathroom to get dressed. The red lacy panties were on top of her work clothes. The Big Bad Wolf probably thought she wore sexy lingerie all the time. As far as he knew, she worked in an office. She tried to imagine herself in a pencil skirt and heels and couldn't. But thanks to a gag gift she'd taken home from Lou Stewart's bachelor party (because of course she'd been invited to a bachelor party) she did have those panties.

She picked them up, biting her lip. She'd never worn them. Not exactly her style. But she yanked the tag off and slipped them on, feeling a bit like Little Red Riding Hood. She grabbed a stretchy sports bra, but it ruined the mood. As did the white utilitarian one from Walmart.

Forget it. She didn't need a bra.

Instead of her work clothes, she grabbed a cinnamon-colored long-sleeved T-shirt with a scoop neck and a black sweater. Black jeans and boots completed the ensemble, and three minutes later a toothbrush and toothpaste had completed her morning beauty routine. She ran her fingers through her short hair and was done.

The coffee was finally ready. She poured it into her PETAL PUSHERS—WE'RE DIGGIN' IT travel mug, grabbed her bag, and followed Pop to the Jeep. It was forty minutes after six when they headed down the bumpy dirt lane that led to Peacock Road.

Dang it. The cows were in her apple orchard. She slammed on the brakes and honked the horn. Two of the cows looked up, apples in their dumb mouths. Maggie rolled down the window. "Shoo! Go home! Get back on your stupid happy trail to Blake land!"

Pop, excited by the shouting, flung himself out the window. Before Maggie could get the door open, he was running circles around the cows, nipping at their hooves.

"Stop it, Pop!" The cows were getting jittery, and Pop was going to get kicked or stepped on.

Pop did not stop. Focused on the biggest cow, he darted in and out of her hooves, growling and yapping, until he managed to sink his sharp little teeth into a leg.

The cow did not appreciate it. She dropped the apple and ran.

The rest followed suit, and Maggie jumped back in the Jeep to avoid being crushed in a stampede, which would be a stupid way to die. And the worst part was, the damn things were running in the wrong direction.

* * *

Travis pulled up to the construction site, noting the absence of a certain yellow Jeep with extreme satisfaction. He'd figured Miss Mary Margaret for an early bird. Maybe he'd been wrong.

He wondered if she knew her grandmother regularly left threatening notes on his gate. Yesterday's had been, YOU KNOW WHAT WOULD LOOK GOOD IN MY LIVING ROOM? TEN COWHIDE RUGS.

JD's truck was here. He'd been one of the few kids to be kind to Travis when he'd been an outsider in a town where most other kids absolutely knew they belonged. Their families' names were plastered all over the town. KOWALSKI FEED AND SEED, MACKEY DRUGS, MAYES CARPENTRY AND CONSTRUCTION. The same names over and over, linking aunts, uncles, grandparents, and cousins. There was only one Blake family, and they were known for gambling debts, theft, and, thanks to Scott, drug smuggling.

And not paying property taxes. Couldn't forget that one.

Travis hadn't known how to find his place in the community, and his family's antics hadn't helped. He'd been a loner by necessity.

But the Mayes family had been kind. JD's dad had never failed to shake Travis's hand and ask him how he was doing when most adults acted like he was invisible or eyed him warily. And his mom had been nice, too.

Travis opened the console in his truck and dug through yesterday's mail and Henry's stash of snacks to find his work gloves. *Yesterday's mail...* He pulled out two envelopes. One was alarming—unopened letter from the tax office—and the other was depressing—his bank statement. He sighed heavily and crammed them both back into the console. Then he climbed out of his truck, stuffed his gloves into his back pocket, and gathered the tools he'd need: wheel barrel, pickax, shovel, and hoe. There was nothing glamorous about digging up rocks.

He wheeled the tools around to the back of the house. Little Red Riding Hood hadn't marked anything off yet, so he wasn't sure where he should start. He looked through the French doors and saw JD on a ladder, hammering away on some molding.

He went inside. "You're here awful early."

JD missed a nail. "Dammit," he muttered.

"Sorry."

"No problem. And Annabelle wants to move in like yesterday, so I'm not early enough."

Travis nodded. "Nice house."

"Divorce settlement. You remember Jim Henderson? His dad had the Chevy dealership on the highway."

"Obnoxious kid who wrecked a Corvette on his sixteenth birthday?"

"That's the one. Three years ago, he wrecked his life by marrying Anna. I kind of thought they were perfect for each other."

Anna was on the rebound. Great.

JD went back to hammering. "What'd you do after high school?" he asked.

"Oilfields, mostly. Then the Army."

JD stopped hammering. "Were you deployed?"

"Afghanistan."

JD set the hammer down on the top of the ladder, and then made a motion to tip his hat, realizing too late that it wasn't on his head. He grinned in embarrassment—being without his Stetson probably felt like being completely naked—and said, "Thank you for your service, Travis. You should have had a hero's homecoming here in Big Verde."

Travis didn't know what to say. He was no hero. He'd met some real heroes, and he didn't like being elevated to a pedestal that he didn't deserve to approach, much less stand on. "I didn't see combat."

"Doesn't matter. You signed up. You went. Most people don't."

Travis waved him off and pretended to admire the molding.

"When did you get out?" JD asked, picking up the hammer and sticking a couple of nails in his mouth.

"Just before coming to Big Verde."

JD lined his hammer up with a small nail. "Well, welcome home," he mumbled, careful not to spit nails. "Glad you're back."

Travis swallowed. Welcome *home*. Big Verde had never felt like home. It had felt more like an unkept promise.

"It's so sad about Lisa," JD said. "Mrs. Garza says you're really good with Henry."

And there it was. That uncomfortable feeling when you realized everyone in town had been talking about you. Another aspect of small-town life he could never get used to. And he didn't think he was all that good with Henry. But he was better than Scott would be, and he was starting to get a little worried about it. He shrugged his shoulders—a gesture JD probably mistook for modesty.

"I hear the ranch is looking good," JD said.

Was JD out of his mind? "Where'd you hear that?"

"Gerome Kowalski says you've got the herd separated, fixed some fences…"

Gerome Kowalski had been talking about Happy Trails? More gossip. Travis felt sick at his stomach. The enormous Rancho Cañada Verde bordered Happy Trails on its western fence line, and with its pristine, perfectly maintained fences, manicured pastures, and award-winning Black Angus herd, it was the gem of the Texas Hill Country, and it made Happy Trails seem all the more pathetic.

"I've patched the fences in several places, but they need replacing. And I've managed to get the heifers and young bulls separated, but that's about it. The herd needs to be thinned out."

"Nothing that can't be done with a little help," JD said.

"I just need to get it in good enough shape to sell. I've got a job waiting for me in Austin."

JD's mouth hung open and three nails slipped out, bouncing off his boots. "You're selling Happy Trails? What about Henry?"

"I'm not real sure. There's a social worker looking into the possibility of other relatives and whatnot," Travis said, stuttering just a bit.

JD furrowed his brow. Reached for his nonexistent hat. And then he changed the subject, for which Travis was grateful. "I'm going to Tony's with Bubba and a few of the guys to watch the first Spurs game of the season tonight. You want to come?"

"Sorry, but I've already got some plans."

JD looked down at him like he didn't believe him. "Maggie will probably be there."

Travis's head snapped up in a completely involuntary gesture. He tried to cover it up by swatting an imaginary gnat. "So?"

"I realize she can be intimidating."

Intimidating? That tiny little thing? "I don't find her intimidating at all."

And I know just how to make her behave herself.

"You're a rare man then," JD said with a grin. "Anyway, I saw the way you were looking at her."

"What way was that?"

"Like she was a piece of cake and you hadn't eaten in three years."

"I think you're mistaken."

"And she was looking at you the same way."

"I *know* you're mistaken."

Whatever it was that was going on between Little Red Riding Hood and JD, it wasn't of a romantic nature. Because it sure as hell felt like JD was trying to fix him up.

JD set his hammer down and picked up a thermos. "If your plans change, you know where to find us. We'll keep a stool warm for you."

Although Travis appreciated the invitation, Tony's was one place he hoped to avoid. His dad had spent too much time there. Besides, he really did have plans. "I promised Alice I'd build a gazebo in the children's reading garden. Alice is the librarian," he added. "She reads to Henry at story time every week, and I couldn't turn her down."

"I've known Alice all my life."

Of course JD knew Alice. Everyone knew everyone in Big Verde. He wouldn't be surprised if Alice was JD's cousin or if maybe her granddaddy had married JD's great-aunt on his mother's father's side. That's how all the introductions went in Big Verde. *You know Sally...she married that nephew of Bob's down at Bippo's Shop...his mama was a Polinski*...and so on, and so on.

"Alice's uncle married my Aunt Fran," JD started. Then he grinned and reached for his missing Stetson again, cheeks turning pink as he realized the pattern he'd fallen into. "Sorry. You don't need to know all that. Anyway, I wasn't aware Alice needed help at the library. Maybe Bubba and I will sacrifice our barstools tonight and come by to help out."

This was another small-town phenomenon. Folks dropping everything to help out.

"Really?" Travis asked. Alice had already recruited some local teens for the project, but it sure would go a shit-ton faster with JD and Bubba on-site.

"Sure," JD said. "It'll be fun. And maybe we'll get done in time to catch the second half of the game."

A car door slammed. It was followed by the excited yaps of a little dog.

"Look," JD said, pointing out the window. "There's that woman who doesn't intimidate you."

Travis looked, but as he watched Maggie head his way, no amount of bracing could prepare him for what his heart did next, which was damn near grind to a stop.

Chapter Twelve

⸙

Twenty minutes late! All because she'd had to chase a bunch of cows off her property. She marched across the area where the back-yard was going in and blew through Anna's French doors to find JD and Travis shooting the shit like they had nothing better to do.

She was going to light into Travis about his fences. Set his ass on fire. Toss him into a volcano of burning lava—

He smiled. Blue eyes. White teeth. A dimple she hadn't noticed before, just above the beard, only on the left side. Her heart flopped over like a fainting pygmy goat on a YouTube video. Maybe it wasn't professional to chew him out in front of JD.

"Good morning," he said.

His voice was low and echoed in the big room—the *great room*, as Anna insisted on calling it—vibrating its way through her bones, snaking its way up and down her spine, and generally making her feel warm and tingly all over. Which was mighty inconvenient and vaguely familiar. Every time the man spoke, she had an uneasy sense of déjà vu. Her head spun for a moment.

"Sorry. I'm late because I was...I was—"

"Trying to decide what to wear?" JD was grinning like an idiot. "Because you sure look nice today."

She glared at him. "I was reevaluating my initial plan to install agarita bushes. Thinking about going with Anocacho orchids instead. It'll do better here, and it won't attract as many deer as the agarita." This was technically true. She had recently made this decision.

"Why don't you want to attract deer?" JD asked.

"Probably because they'll destroy the landscaping," Travis suggested.

"That's partially it," Maggie said. "It's also because I suspect Anna hates anything furry and cute with doe-eyes. She wouldn't think twice about eating Bambi."

JD laughed. "I would only eat Bambi if the Martinez Meat Market turned him into sausage first."

"Chicken-fried venison steak is the best way to eat Bambi," Travis added, rubbing his extremely flat and presumably hard stomach.

"Mm," JD agreed. "Or Polish kielbasa." He took to rubbing his own *Mr. October* abs with delight.

Maggie fanned herself with her landscaping plans. It was getting very warm in this room.

"Sausage talk getting to you?" Travis asked.

JD laughed. "It's getting to me."

Maggie raised her eyebrows slightly. "Oh, really?"

JD stopped laughing, and then blushed furiously.

Maggie snorted. "Keep going. You're doing so well."

"Nothing like a good, thick ring of sausage," Travis said with a wink.

"Y'all are awful." Maggie refused to blush. She literally willed the rising red tide creeping up her chest to stop at her neck. "And I'm not the slightest bit embarrassed by this banter, so you can stop trying."

"I don't know what you think we're talking about, Maggie," Travis said with a grin that indicated the opposite. "We're merely discussing the merits of venison in its many delightful forms."

Maggie grabbed his sleeve. "JD is already being a bad influence on you. Let's get to work."

The cool autumn air felt good on Maggie's flushed skin. She closed her eyes, stretched, and inhaled the scent of cedar and sage. When she opened her eyes, Travis was standing there with his mouth hanging open. Did the man not know how to dig up rocks? "Just start at the house and work your way out."

Travis blinked, and seemingly snapped out of whatever trance he'd been in. Who knew what ridiculous nonsense was going through his mind? Probably chicken-fried venison.

"Sure. I'll do that." He gave her a sharp salute, and then yanked up a pickax.

Maggie got right to work marking off plots. Within a couple of minutes, they were comfortably laboring side by side. Maggie measured, hammered in stakes, and strung lines while Travis dug up rocks, loaded them into his wheelbarrow, and piled them up at the edge of the site.

"I'm going to use some of them for terracing," she called to Travis. "So separate the good ones."

"That'll look real nice," Travis said. "And it'll be a good way to deal with the steep slope."

Yep. That's why she'd planned terracing. She didn't need him mansplaining her own business to her. She started to say as much but managed to bite her tongue. If they were going to survive the duration of this project, she'd have to keep a lid on the snark; the gate notes were bad enough.

By eleven o'clock the cool autumn air was long gone, and it had taken Maggie's sunny disposition with it. Sweaty and uncomfortable in her dumb clothes, she was seriously regretting her life choices. She ditched the black sweater and rolled up the long sleeves of her T-shirt. She'd ditch the boots, too, if she could. Both of her sweaty feet had blisters. The damn things were made for two-stepping, not for squatting and measuring gradations. They also weren't very flexible, and when she swatted at a gnat, she lost her balance and ended up on her bottom with a grunt.

Travis looked up. Because if you're going to squat, swat, and fall, you should do it when a handsome man is around to see it.

"You okay?" he asked.

"Yes," she said. She gave him her best *why do you ask* look. "Taking a little break." *Right here. In the middle of this pile of dirt.*

"Do you need to sit in the shade for a few? It's getting warm, and it's humid as all get-out." To demonstrate his discomfort, Travis dropped his hoe and grabbed the hem of his shirt.

He was going to take it off.

With the leisurely air of a stripper—not that Maggie had ever seen one outside of the movies—he slowly pulled the DON'T MESS WITH TEXAS shirt over his head. *Oh, hello, snake, falcon, dragon...*

"What did you say?" she mumbled. Or maybe she thought it. It was hard to know, because her mouth no longer seemed to be connected to her brain, which was probably a good thing.

"I said it's getting hot, and you've been working hard. Do you want to take a seat in the shade for a minute?"

Maggie managed to work her eyes up to his. They were so incredibly blue against the Texas sky. Maybe she did need to sit in the shade for a bit. "Shade sounds good."

Also, your eyelashes are unreasonable.

"I've got some tea in a cooler."

Cooling down sounded good, too. "You're going to get sunburned without a shirt."

Travis looked down at his lean, tanned torso. "Nah. I work outside like this all the time. You, on the other hand, could use some sunscreen on that pink nose."

Maggie started to get up, but the damn inflexible boots threw her off and she sank back into the dirt. Travis plucked her up like a dandelion, and she suddenly found herself smashed against his bare chest, eye to eye with the falcon.

"Oops!" Her fingers involuntarily grazed his abs on their way to his chest, which she only touched in order to push her face away from his warm, salty skin. It was a hard, unyielding chest. Pretty decent, as far as chests went. Her fingers might have lingered a moment. She might have pretended she needed the contact to steady herself as her head spun.

"Sorry," Travis said, lowering his eyes to where her fingers still rested.

The sight of a blushing lumberjack did nothing to help matters. She removed her fingers without looking to see if they were on fire, and then followed Travis to where his cooler rested beneath an ancient live oak. He opened the lid and grabbed a thermos. Then he snapped the cooler shut, brushed it off even though it was spotless, and invited her to sit on it as he lowered himself to the ground with a groan. Gosh, why did he have to be so—

"Sweet?" he asked.

"Pardon?"

"I hope you like it sweet." He held the thermos up. "Sweet tea. It's all I brought."

"That's fine," she said, hoping her ears didn't appear as bright red as they felt.

"Your ears are getting pink, too," Travis said.

Dammit. She was an ear-blusher. An ear-blusher with super short hair so everyone who witnessed her falling on her ass and then damn near kissing a bare chest could also witness the after-effects on her ears.

"You should probably put some sunscreen on them. And that cute, upturned nose."

Did he just call her nose cute?

The ears. They were literally on fire now. She was like the "extra" version of Rudolph.

Travis poured tea into the thermos lid and handed it to her. "Bottoms up," he said with a wink.

Why didn't her voice work? Not even a squeak. She tapped her cup to his thermos and took a sip. It was good. She hadn't realized how thirsty she'd been. Travis must have been thirsty, too, because he tilted his head back and greedily drained the entire thermos.

"Hits the spot, doesn't it?" he said, wiping his bearded chin on the back of his hand.

There was definitely a spot she'd like him to hit.

Silence. *Talk, Mackey! How hard can it be?*

"There's supposed to be another cold front blowing in tonight," Travis said. "We might even get a frost."

Maggie nodded, the sound of her silence screaming in her head. This was so weird. Maybe all the blood rushing to her ears had left her vocal cords paralyzed. The same way erections caused stupidity in males. *Erections. Why was she thinking about erections?* She forced herself to grunt, "Uh-huh." Which was way better than *Me horny*, the phrase playing on repeat in her head.

"It's still mighty hot in the sun, though," Travis continued.

"Uh-huh."

"Not so bad in the shade."

Holy cow. He was a weather rambler. A hot, topless weather rambler.

"In the shade it's downright nippy."

Then why did he wipe a bead of sweat from his temple?

* * *

It was all over. He'd spent the last three hours trying not to notice Maggie's breasts, and in an attempt at conversation, he'd chosen a tried-and-true category—*I'll take weather for four hundred, Alex*—and said *nippy.*

But damn, she wasn't wearing a bra. His mouth watered. He knew what those delicious buds tasted like. Could she see it on his face? What if she was putting two and two together and figuring out he was the Big Bad Wolf? He yanked his cap out of his back pocket and put it on, pulling it down low. Combined with the itchy beard he longed to be rid of, it might be a passable disguise.

Or he could just tell her that he was the man she'd had sex with in the shed. *Hey, want to hear something funny?*

Only she was kind of being nice to him at the moment. Why fuck it up? He slipped his shirt back on, so she wouldn't see the goose bumps she was giving him.

"When will you be finished with the rocks?" Maggie asked.

She sounded a bit breathless and shaky. The woman really couldn't take the heat, and it wasn't even summer. "Another day or two will do it."

"Do you think you might need some help?"

"No. I got this." Tomorrow would be a bitch, though. His back was already killing him, but he couldn't afford any help. He'd bid on the project, and now he had to deliver.

"On Wednesday we can start filling in with soil. I'll see about having it delivered that morning. Can you have a front-end loader here?"

"I'm just going to shovel it in by hand."

"You can rent one," she said.

"Nah." It cost too much. He couldn't swing it.

Maggie unrolled several sheets of plans on top of the cooler. "If you're thinking about doing it manually, you'd better have some help," she said, tapping the paper. "Big job."

For the millionth time, doubt crept in. What had made him think he could go from mowing lawns and planting shrubs to doing a large residential installation with no equipment and no crew? Why had he bid on this job? *Because you need the money, you idiot.* And why had Anna hired him? *To toy with you, you idiot.*

"I can provide a crew," Maggie said.

She might be cute, and he might know what her inner thighs tasted like—and want to taste them again—but the woman wanted him off the job. She'd been clear about that, and here he was sharing his tea and worrying about her sunburned ears. Time to toughen up. "You're just in charge of the design," he said. "I'm the crew. How I get shit done is up to me, and I'm going to get it done with my bare hands."

The dark eyebrows disappeared into her blond bangs, and she crossed her arms over her still-very-nippy chest. "But you're not a crew. You're one man. I honestly don't know what Anna was thinking when she split this contract."

Okay. Now his blood was starting to boil. She wasn't the boss of him, and she wasn't going to steal his half of the project.

"If you want to split the labor," Little Miss Hood continued, "I'm sure we can talk some sense into Anna." She looked him up and down. As if the idea of him tackling this project was the most nonsensical thing she'd ever heard. Which it probably was.

Travis clenched his jaw. It was easier to ignore her hard little nipples poking through her shirt now that she was pissing him off. "You stick to your part of the bid, and I'll stick to mine."

Maggie stood and re-crossed her arms below her breasts, stretching the T-shirt even tighter.

Not so easy to ignore, after all.

"Just consider it. You might be in over your head here."

Why didn't she just cut off his balls and hand them to him on a platter? He snatched her plans, rolled them up, and handed them to her. Then he picked up the cooler. "Break's over," he said, heading for his truck to put the cooler away.

"Just think about it," Maggie called after him.

He could feel her eyes boring into his back. Why was he so

fucking embarrassed? He'd known he was in over his head with this project. But he needed the money and was going to make the best of it. What he *didn't* need was to care what Maggie Mackey thought of him.

He did, though.

He remembered the way she'd melted at the Big Bad Wolf's touch. The way she'd acquiesced at the sound of his voice. The way those big brown eyes had looked at him as if he were the most important man on Earth. He climbed in his truck and pulled out his phone. He had a sudden desire to send a text.

*   *   *

Maggie stared at Travis sitting in his truck. She'd upset him. But dang it, he was going to slow down the entire project. He was behaving like a man-baby, and she had zero tolerance for man-babies. His feelings weren't her problem. Getting this project completed was.

Ping!

It was her phone.

How is your day going, LRRH?

She stifled a squeal and hurried to her Jeep for some texting privacy. It would just look like she was checking e-mail. Pop hopped onto the seat, put his little paws on the window, and started panting. "Chill out. We're not going anywhere."

Maggie tried to adopt an air of professionalism as she composed her text—in case anyone was watching—but she probably looked just like Pop, all slobbery and impatient.

How to answer the question? She tried to come up with something cute or sexy, but she wasn't good at cute or sexy, and decided to go with honesty instead.

Meh. At work.

You don't like work?

He didn't ask what she did. That was good. Let him think she had a fancy job somewhere sitting behind a desk in heels while everyone fell all over themselves doing her bidding.

I do. But I have a difficult co-worker to deal with.

Oh really?

Yeah. Thinks he knows everything.

Maybe he's all bark and no bite.

How about you? Are you all bark and no bite?

You know very well that I bite.

He'd never actually bitten her. But the thought of her skin between his teeth while he held her down and forcefully—holy cow, where did these thoughts come from? The wolf had a strange effect on her. And it was not one that would make anyone's mama proud.

You might need obedience training.

You just gave me some ideas. Are you wearing sexy underwear like a good girl?

She was curious. Where did the wolf work? She remembered the look of his suit. The feel of his closely shaven skin, short-cropped hair. The square-toe boots—dark slate, not the usual black. He probably worked in a high-rise somewhere. But he'd just posed the question she'd been waiting for.

Red lacy panties.

She glanced around. Travis was messing with something in his truck, JD had left, and Anna still hadn't shown up. Nobody was paying any attention to her.

Little Red Panties for Little Red Riding Hood?

So very little.

Is there a Little Red Bra to go with them?

Not wearing one.

That was the truth.

Are your nipples hard?

Her face exploded in crimson.

Yes.

She couldn't believe she was having this conversation. In her Jeep. At work. With some businessman dressed in a suit with his secretary out front. Or maybe a client in front of him.

Pinch them.

She gasped. No way! She bit her lip, trying to think of a single reason to comply with the wolf's request. She came up with two: it was delightfully dirty, and it gave her a thrill.

Pop had caught on to the fact that he wasn't going anywhere and started whining. Maggie opened the door and let him out. No need to expose him to the depths of depravity to which she was about to sink. And then, after another quick glance to make sure Travis wasn't looking, she slipped her hands inside her T-shirt and did as she'd been told. The thrill was more psychological than physical, but it was intense. She fumbled for her phone.

I did it.

I knew you would. Enjoy the rest of your day.

A door slammed. Travis stood next to his truck, stretching. He glanced in her direction, smiled, and peeled off his T-shirt again.

It was going to be a long afternoon.

Chapter

Thirteen

❦

Travis had barely had time for a shower, much less dinner. Luckily, Mrs. Garza had seen fit to provide tamales. And not just enough for him and Henry. She'd made enough for everyone who was going to help with the library.

"Mrs. Garza, you didn't have to do that." He sure was glad she had, though.

Mrs. Garza, wearing jeans with rhinestones on the back pockets and a shiny purple blouse, continued packing foil-wrapped packages of tamales into an old, beat-up ice chest. "It was no trouble. And Henry helped."

Travis was certain it had been a lot of trouble. And he also knew that Henry's help generally amounted to the job taking twice as long as it should. But looking at Henry's face, beaming with pride, Travis realized he needed to let the kid help with ranch chores more often. Even though it was a pain in the ass.

"I didn't even know I liked tamales!" Henry said. "But the ones I made are real good."

"You have the magic touch, *mijo*," Mrs. Garza said.

"I do?"

Mrs. Garza stopped what she was doing and put her hands on her hips. "I said so, didn't I?"

Henry had something that looked suspiciously like chocolate on his chin. Travis grabbed a paper towel and wiped it off.

"We made cupcakes, too."

"I see that."

"I gots the magic touch for all kinds of cookin'."

"You *have* the magic touch."

"That's what I said," Henry replied, with no attempt at hiding his irritation. "And it's a good thing, too, because you can't cook."

Travis couldn't argue with that. Mrs. Garza had no doubt noticed all the frozen food in the freezer and the fast-food bags in the garbage. When she babysat for Henry, she almost always made dinner.

Beneath the aromas of cumin, garlic, and chocolate was the faint lemon scent of furniture polish. Looking around the house, it was clear that the one with the magic touch was Mrs. Garza.

"I don't expect you to cook and clean while you're here taking care of Henry." He didn't pay her near enough for that. He didn't really pay her near enough for anything.

"Well, the child has to eat," Mrs. Garza said. "And he needs a clean, safe place to play."

Mrs. Garza had zero filters and spoke her mind. She and Henry were alike in that way. You were getting the truth whether you liked it or not.

He picked up the mail from the counter. The notice from the tax collector's office glared up at him. He should open it. Face the music. See exactly how much he owed. He took a deep breath and...set it back on the counter. Covered it with a flyer from the local tractor dealership. Front-end loaders were on sale.

"I talked to my cousin about painting this place," Mrs. Garza said, closing the lid on the ice chest. "He says he can do it."

Travis gulped. He hadn't asked her to do that. The house needed painting, but he couldn't afford it. "I'm sure he'd offer me a good deal, but—"

"He wants a quarter."

Travis couldn't have heard that right. "A quarter?"

"That's for the interior. If you want him to do the outside, too, then he's asking for a half. He'll tell you how he wants it."

"How he wants it?"

"Is there an echo in here?" Mrs. Garza asked. She shook her head. "Anyway, I told him to stick with skirt steak for *fajitas*, some ribs, and to get the rest ground."

Beef! The man wanted beef. Travis might not have time or money, but he had sixty-two head of cattle, which was too much for the property in its current state. He'd forgotten how folks in Big Verde purchased large amounts of beef directly from the rancher. Almost everybody had a chest freezer on the porch for that specific purpose. Families went in together to buy a quarter, half, or even whole cows. Why hadn't he considered using beef to barter?

"Martinez Meat Market will process it," Mrs. Garza said.

Travis's bump of optimism took a dive. He didn't even have the cash to pay for processing. His concern must have shown on his face, because Mrs. Garza patted his arm. "Beto Martinez is my brother. He'll work something out."

Mrs. Garza was related to at least half the people in Big Verde. "You don't happen to have a cousin or a brother down at the tax office, do you?"

"Sorry, but no." She smiled and continued patting his arm. "Everything will be fine. You just keep doing what you're doing."

Ignoring things. Putting off unpleasant tasks. Sure, he'd just keep doing what he was doing.

A few minutes later, loaded with tamales, cupcakes, and an ornery five-year-old kicking the back of his seat, Travis headed down the lane. Movement caught his eye in the east pasture. About twelve cows—he'd nicknamed them the Dirty Dozen—were walking in single-file, toe to tail. And they were headed straight for the weakest spot in the fence and Honey Mackey's motherfucking apples. He'd already come home to one note with a thinly veiled threat of poison. No doubt there would be another one tonight.

* * *

Maggie pulled to a stop in the back lot of Petal Pushers. She was pooped from her day at Anna's, having sweated her ass off in her stupid clothes while Travis paraded around half naked. Between his hot, gleaming torso and the wolf's dirty texts, she could use a cold shower. Too bad she didn't have time for one. The first frost of the season was on its way, and she had a ton of plants to move.

She got out of her Jeep. Norbert and Claire were already loading up carts.

"Can you believe this weather?" Norbert asked. "Hot as hell all day and dipping into the freezing zone tonight."

"That's Texas for you," Claire said.

Maggie picked up the handle on a cart loaded down with pallets of perennials and gave it a yank. What they couldn't haul inside would have to be covered with tarps.

As tired as she was, Travis had to be way worse. He'd chipped away at the limestone forest all afternoon, one rock at a time. He'd made a decent amount of progress, but there was still so much more to do. Stubborn man.

Maggie dragged the cart backward, being careful not to trip on any hoses.

"Let me help you with that," Norbert said.

"I've got it. You just make sure all the faucets are dripping." She could damn well drag a heavy cart as well as any man, and the last thing she needed was frozen pipes.

She gave a huge tug on the handle, lost traction in the mud, and fell flat on her ass, which was apparently today's theme.

Claire covered her mouth with her hands, eyes wide, and nostrils quivering as she tried not to laugh.

"Not funny," Maggie said.

Claire held out a hand. "A little funny. And if you were wearing heels, this wouldn't have happened. Mine are dug in like anchors." To demonstrate, she lifted a foot. Clumps of dirt and roots hung from the narrow heels of what were ruined and probably very expensive shoes.

"Those are more like tent stakes," Norbert said.

Claire yanked Maggie up. "Either way, I'm not going down."

Maggie wiped herself off, picked up the cart handle, and went right back to grunting.

"Why do you have to do the heaviest and hardest job when you're the tiniest person here?" Norbert asked.

"Because she's trying to prove she can do everything Travis Blake can do," Claire said.

"He's the one who thinks he can do everything himself," Maggie said, noting with satisfaction that once she got the wheels out of the ruts, she could drag the damn cart quite well, thank you very much. "There's just no reason for it," she said, wiping her brow and leaving a smear of mud on her face. "We have a crew. We have equipment. He just has himself. Anna just wants him around because he looks good." *Boy, does he.*

Claire had finished covering the citrus trees and picked up a handle on a cart of succulents. "He is easy on the eyes."

"But he's not qualified. You can't hire someone just because he's hot."

"Men do it all the time. They have their secretaries and assistants in their short skirts running around. Why can't women have a little fun, too?"

"Because it's wrong," Maggie said. "No matter who does it."

She deserved the contract. The *full* contract. This project was right up her alley, and she didn't appreciate having to share just so Anna could have a boy toy. Although he did work ridiculously hard. She'd give him that.

"Anna and Travis have a bit of history, you know," Claire said.

"Really? What kind?"

"The high school kind."

How could Anna and Travis have high school history when Maggie didn't even remember Travis from high school?

"They dated?"

"I don't think you could call it dating. But he used to mow her family's lawn after school. I heard they messed around."

"He was literally Anna's lawn boy? And now he is again?"

"You could say that. And supposedly Travis stole jewelry from her. God, Maggie, did you ever lift your head out of the dirt and look around when we were in school?"

She'd noticed lots of things in school—like JD, for instance. But oddly, she hadn't noticed Travis. "There's no way he stole anything. He's not that kind of man."

"Know him well, do you?"

"Are you absolutely sure he went to school with us?"

Claire laughed. "He's a pretty amazing case of metamorphosis. He's a hunky butterfly." She parked her cart next to Maggie's. "I think that's it. We've got all our babies inside."

"Yuck," Maggie said, lifting a boot. "Look at our feet."

"At least it's just mud," Claire said, taking the rag offered by Norbert and wiping off her heels. "We've stepped in worse. And that reminds me, you did have a run-in with Travis in high school."

"I did?"

"Remember when Danny Moreno put cow patties in your locker and they fell out when you opened the door?"

Yes, she remembered. It had gone splat onto her shoes, then she'd screamed and dropped her books in it, and then the vice-principal had walked by and told her to clean it all up. Danny was a pharmacist now, but Maggie still didn't trust him.

"The kid who helped you clean up the mess was Travis."

Maggie dropped the cart handle. "Get out," she said. "That was *not* Travis. It was some new kid."

"Why do you think that?"

"Because I'd never noticed him before." Or after, for that matter. Had she even said thank you? She tried to remember the boy who'd stopped to help her. He'd been small. His backpack was bigger than he was. He'd had brown hair and wore glasses—she'd been startled by his magnified blue eyes and *oh my God it was Travis.*

"Bingo," Claire said. "I can see from your dumb expression that you remember."

"This does not compute."

"It computes all right. He had a growth spurt. Lost the glasses. Hubba hubba."

"Wow. I mean, *wow.*"

"I know."

Norbert pulled the outside gates shut and locked them. "We knocked it out with just the three of us."

"Is there a big party or something going on tonight?" Maggie asked. "I texted Derek and Frank to see if they could help, but they were both busy."

Derek and Frank were high school seniors who sometimes helped out at Petal Pushers.

Norbert's naturally dark complexion darkened some more. "Yeah, there's a . . . thing," he mumbled.

"What?" Maggie said.

"They're working at the library," Claire said quietly.

Maggie snorted. Derek and Frank didn't strike her as being big readers. Stoners? Yes. Readers? No. "Good one. What's really going on?"

"No, really. The library is redoing the children's reading garden and—"

"Redoing it how?" The library was city property, and Petal Pushers had the contract for landscaping.

"A gazebo is going in. And some new play equipment."

"Oh. That sounds nice. I should swing by and have a look. I bet we can propose some new landscaping to make it even nicer."

"Yep," Claire said, and then mumbled something over her shoulder as she headed for the garden center doors.

"What did you say?"

"She said Travis Blake is in charge of the project," Norbert said.

Maggie was speechless for almost two seconds, which felt like an extremely long period of time. Travis was going to ruin her. "You're kidding me, right?"

Norbert shook his head.

"How did he land that? Is every single person in this town so easily swayed by a bare chest?"

Norbert furrowed his brow. "What are you talking about?"

Maggie didn't have time to explain her theory about the gigolo lawn boy. Instead she held her fist in the air and proclaimed, "I'll go to City Hall! I'll stage a protest—"

"Hold on there, Norma Rae," Claire said. "I don't think we've lost a contract just because Travis is building a gazebo and installing playground equipment. Neither of those things are services we provide."

"He'll weasel his way into that contract. He'll be very polite about it. He might blush stupidly and say *aw shucks* and then, he'll take off his shirt!"

"Okaay..." Norbert said.

"And when he does that," Maggie continued, "nobody can think straight and there goes our contract."

She stomped over to the utility sink to wash the mud off her hands. He had weaseled into her business. He couldn't keep his cows on his side of the goddamn fence. "Enough is enough," she spat.

"Are you about to make a big scene at the library?" Claire asked.

"Don't try to stop me."

"I wouldn't dream of it. Hold up while I put on some lipstick."

Chapter

Fourteen

Maggie pulled into the library at the same time as Claire. She wasn't quite ready to go in like the Terminator, so she waved Claire over. They needed to strategize.

It was after hours, but the small lot was filled with cars and bikes. Mark Polinsky's monster truck had its tailgate down, and two girls sat on it, legs swinging. An ice chest with its lid propped open was behind them in the truck's bed.

"It looks like a tailgate party," Maggie said as Claire climbed out and closed the door. "Travis has no idea how to direct a crew of young people. He thinks he can just turn on some loud music and set them loose."

They weren't exactly running around loose. Several were unloading bags of concrete while another group stacked lumber. Travis came around the corner. He wore a black T-shirt. Its hem rose when he hoisted a bag of concrete onto his shoulder, exposing nice ripped abs. Claire made a barely muffled sound of approval in her throat.

Something settled in Maggie's belly. It quivered and shook and sat at attention. Apparently, irritation and annoyance had slinked off like a twitchy-tailed cat, and dumb, dark desire had bounded in like a dog in heat.

"It looks like he's doing pretty well to me," Claire said. "Very well, in fact." She raised an eyebrow in a manner that suggested she was thinking of all kinds of non-concrete-related things.

Travis dropped the bag next to a wheelbarrow. He had to be dying after all he'd already done today. Yet here he was. Her eyes narrowed.

They must be paying him big bucks.

Alice came out of the library with a bag of books. Her face lit up when she saw Maggie and Claire.

"Oh no, she's going to ask me about book club again," Claire said. "Just tell her no. Do you even read?"

"You know how hard it is for me to say no."

Maggie was so upset about Travis and his business-stealing bullshit that she let that little gem slide.

"Would you come to book club with me? You can read the book and tell me about it like you did for Honors English."

Maggie sighed. It wasn't that she didn't like to read. But she didn't relish the idea of talking about a book with a bunch of women who, like Claire, probably hadn't even bothered to read it and were just there for the wine.

Alice tapped on the window. Maggie rolled it down. "Hello, Alice. Heading home, are you?"

"Goodness, no. Not with this party getting started. Are you here to help us get the gazebo put together before the front blows in? We're expecting some freezing rain and whatnot—Travis doesn't want the lumber getting warped."

Maggie crossed her arms over her chest. "Oh, he wants everybody to help, does he?"

Alice shifted her bag to her other shoulder. "Of course! And everybody seems happy to do it. Travis even brought tamales."

Travis, Travis, Travis.

"That sounds nice," Maggie said through gritted teeth. "Claire and I were just going to check out a book, and I see we're too late so—"

The Jeep shook as Claire's door slammed.

"Where are you going?"

Claire shrugged. "Travis brought tamales."

"What book did you need?" Alice asked, opening Maggie's door.

Maggie's mind drew a blank. "What are you reading for book club?"

Alice bounced on the balls of her feet. "Are you coming to book club? We're reading *Bound and Determined*, Reyn Taylor's latest. It's just delightful—"

"Isn't she a romance author?" Maggie asked. She didn't think she'd ever read a romance novel.

"Yes, she is." Alice glanced around to see if anyone was listening and then whispered, "A dirty one. The genre is erotica."

"Sign us up!" Claire said.

"Wait—no—"

"We have one left and I'll put it on hold," Alice said. "Can you two share?"

"That won't be necessary—"

"You bet we can," Claire said with a wink at Maggie. Then she whispered, "I'm just going to read the dirty parts."

"Oh, goodie," Alice squealed, clapping her hands. "We could use some fresh blood. Between you and me, Miss Mills isn't going to last much longer. Of course, we've been saying that for twenty years."

"Miss Mills is reading erotica?"

"Yes. When she's not teaching Sunday school at First Baptist."

Maggie snorted.

"This evening she's helping Travis by handing him nails—and no doubt a bit of heavenly advice—while he hammers on the gazebo."

The waver in Alice's voice and the red splotches creeping up her neck said she very much approved of Travis Blake's hammering skills.

The three of them walked up the sidewalk to the reading garden behind the library. Sure enough, Miss Mills sat as stiff as a board in a folding chair next to the gazebo, holding a nail up to Travis.

Maggie cleared her throat. It was time to broach the subject of the visit. "Alice, I'm a little surprised that Travis is here. Petal Pushers has a landscaping contract with the city—"

Alice smiled and patted Maggie's arm. "And they still do. Travis offered to build the gazebo and install the play equipment for free."

Cue gag reflex.

"I got some teenagers to help him because he was planning to do it all himself. Can you believe that?"

That aggravating, bull-headed man.

"He has touched up the landscaping a bit, though. You know, just in the places where it needed it," Alice added.

Maggie bit her tongue. The landscaping did *not* need any touching up. She went by regularly. And as for the Saint Travis act—ha! He was trying to worm his way into getting the city's contract for the following year. Which would include the parks, the courthouse lawn, city hall, the public pool...

"Well, we'd love to help," Maggie said with a forced smile. Because she could work for free, too, damn it.

"We would?" Claire asked.

"Absolutely. I just need to find a hammer."

"You're not going to kill him, are you?"

"I'm not planning on it. Accidents do happen, though."

"Oh, look! Bubba and JD are here, too."

"Goodie," Maggie said.

Ping.

A text! Claire raised an eyebrow. "Is it him?"

"I don't know." Maggie clawed her way to her back pocket, spinning around like a dog chasing its tail.

"Who?" Alice asked.

"A guy Maggie is sexting."

Alice stopped in her tracks. "That kind of thing goes on in Big Verde?"

"It goes on everywhere," Maggie said. "But we're not sexting. That's ridiculous." She looked at her phone and almost dropped it.

You've been wearing those panties long enough. Take them off.

"Well?" Claire asked.

"We're sexting."

Alice tried to sneak a peek at the phone.

"Alice, can I get in the library for a minute? I need to use the restroom."

Because good girls removed their panties when the Big Bad Wolf told them to.

* * *

Ping.

Travis grinned. That was fast. "Hold on a minute," he said to Miss Mills, who held up a nail.

He'd told Little Red Riding Hood to take off her panties. The red ones she'd supposedly worn to the job site this morning. The ones he'd been thinking about all day.

He looked at his phone under Miss Mills's watchful gaze.

They're off.

He laughed. Who knew if she'd really done it? She might not even own a pair of red panties. For all he knew, Maggie had worn boxer shorts under her jeans at work today. No matter. He didn't care what kind of underwear she wore. It was what was in them that turned him on.

Henry yanked on his shirt. "Guess who's here, Uncle Travis."

"Just a minute." He needed a few seconds to think of a response.

"You young people and your phones," Miss Mills said.

"Uncle Travis—"

"Hush, Henry."

"Is it a woman texting you, Travis?" Miss Mills asked. "I swear you're blushing beneath that beard."

Could a guy not sext without commentary from an old spinster lady and a five-year-old?

"If it's a woman, she's a hussy. Young ladies shouldn't make overtures."

"Don't be jealous, Miss Mills."

Miss Mills huffed and fanned her face with a copy of *Ladies' Daily Devotions*. Travis grinned and added, "You can't keep me all to yourself."

Miss Mills stopped fanning momentarily. "Why, I *never*—"

"Maybe you should."

"Travis Blake! You should be ashamed of yourself for talking to a Christian woman this way."

"It makes your day," Travis said. "Now if you'll just give me a moment to respond to this hussy, I'll get back to hammering your nails in a jiffy."

Miss Mills fluttered her *Ladies' Daily Devotions*, but her cheeks were pink, and one corner of her mouth curled up. She daintily poked a hairpin back in her bun while looking at Travis over her horn-rimmed glasses.

"Uncle Travis—"

"One sec, Henry."

The thought of Maggie without her panties, eagerly awaiting instructions, made it hard to think. But he needed to type something.

"Hi, Maggie," Henry shouted.

Travis nearly dropped his phone. There stood Maggie and Claire, chatting with Bubba and JD. He quickly stuffed his phone back in his pocket and took a nail from Miss Mills to look busy. He poised the hammer and pretended not to see Maggie approaching in his peripheral vision.

"Hi, Henry. Are you working hard?"

That voice. *Goddamn, it was sexy.*

"Yes, very," Henry said, even though he was stuffing a cupcake in his face.

"And what about Uncle Travis? Is he working hard?"

"Nah, he's just hammering."

"It looks hard from where I'm standing," Maggie said.

Travis missed the nail and smashed his thumb. "Jesus Christ," he said, sticking it in his mouth.

"Don't take the Lord's name in vain, Travis," Miss Mills said. "And pay attention to what you're doing."

Travis glanced at Maggie, who was grinning from ear to ear. He took in the rest of her appearance—tousled blond hair, big brown eyes—and his heart seized. Why did she have such an effect on him?

Because she's Little Red Riding Hood and you know the kind of effect you have on her.

Inexplicably, Henry threw his arms around Maggie's knees and hugged her.

"Let go, Henry," Travis said. "You're going to make Maggie fall."

Henry didn't let go. If anything, he hugged Maggie tighter.

"You're going to get chocolate on Maggie's pants."

"Oh, it's okay. These pants are already ruined," Maggie said.

She turned around, taking Henry with her, and gave Travis a truly spectacular view of her ass. It was covered in mud.

"Have you been rolling around in a pigpen, Miss Mackey?"

"Practically," she said. "Not that it's any of your business."

And that's when he saw it. A small triangle of red lacy fabric poking out of her pocket.

She'd taken her panties off. Her tiny red panties. The ones she'd worn just for him.

She saw him looking, and her face lit up like a fuse. She quickly poked the bit of fabric back in her pocket. "Allergies are awful this time of year. I carry a hankie."

If there was a person less likely to carry a red lacy hankie than Maggie Mackey, Travis couldn't think of one. Of course, he also wouldn't have bet on red lacy panties. He cleared his throat and tried to act clueless.

"Anyway," Maggie said. "I just came down here to—"

"Rip me a new one?"

Maggie's eyes grew round as she feigned innocence. "To help with the gazebo, of course. Do you have an extra hammer?"

Those big brown eyes lined with thick, long lashes looked straight at him. His stomach did something—it felt like a flip but maybe it was a flop—as she crossed her arms and stuck out her hip.

"You're a good girl, Maggie Mackey."

The last time he'd said that, she'd been bent over a table.

"Petal Pushers takes care of the library, you know," Maggie said. "It's our account."

Ah. That's why she was here.

"Good for you."

"Not interested in sharing it."

"Not asking you to."

She sure was cute when she was defensive, territorial, and pissed as hell.

"Come on, Uncle Travis. What do you want to nail next?"

Travis grinned. He knew *exactly* what he wanted to nail next. And it must have shown on his face because Maggie's eyes widened, and her cheeks turned pink. She fluttered her eyelashes like a prissy pants. "Well, I never—"

"That makes you and Miss Mills," Travis said with a grin.

And yes, you have.

Chapter

Fifteen

☙

It had gotten dark over an hour ago. Maggie stretched, feeling every vertebra in her back pop, and watched Travis load his tools into his truck. "Need help with anything?"

"Nope. I got this."

I got this. If Travis had a motto, that would be it. And as much as Maggie wanted to believe he'd taken on the gazebo to steal her business, it just didn't feel that way. Travis might be a Blake, but in his case, the apple had fallen from the tree and rolled far, far away.

"I'm waiting on Claire anyway. Have you seen her?"

Travis scooped Henry up and put him on his shoulders. "I wouldn't wait around if I were you." He nodded to the parking lot between the library and the Green Giant Burger Spot, where a pickup and horse trailer was parked.

It was right beneath a streetlight, and Maggie could clearly see the silhouette of a man leaning against the trailer with one foot kicked back on a tire and one arm wrapped securely around Claire's waist.

"Who's that?" Travis asked.

"If I'm not mistaken, that's Ford Jarvis," Maggie said in amazement. Why hadn't Claire told her she was hanging out with Ford? "He's a bit of a legend around here. Reclusive cowboy born in the wrong era. He's a throwback to the days of trail rides and chuckwagons."

Hardly Claire's type.

"Did he go to school with us?" Travis asked.

This was the first time Travis had acknowledged they'd gone to school together. Did he remember her? She swallowed the lump of disappointment. She kind of liked the idea of him not remembering her as Mighty Mack from high school. If she was honest with herself, that was a big part of her attraction for the Big Bad Wolf. Well, that and a few other things...

"No. He's from..." Maggie thought for a while. She had no idea where Ford was from. "He just showed up. Ranchers hire him when they need work that can only be done on horseback."

Travis perked up. "He's one of the Rancho Cañada Verde cowboys?"

The cowboys who worked for Gerome Kowalski, Claire's daddy, worked cattle on horseback, not with ATVs or helicopters like other big ranches.

"I don't think he's a full-time employee. Claire says he comes in to help with roundups, but he travels all over Texas doing contract cowboying."

"Wow," Travis said, wide-eyed like a little boy. Maggie couldn't help but grin when he added, "Cool."

"Have you ever been on a horse, Travis?"

Travis frowned. "Just because I wasn't born in Big Verde doesn't mean I've never been on a horse."

"Just so you know, I was born and raised here, and I've never been on a horse," she said. "I didn't mean anything by it. How many horses do you have?"

"We don't got no horses," Henry said.

"We don't have any horses," Travis corrected.

Henry, still perched on Travis's shoulders, yanked on one of his ears. "That's what I said."

Travis winced, but didn't do what Maggie would have done, which was put the little toot down.

"I had a horse as a kid," Travis said. His eyes turned wistful. "For one glorious summer."

"What happened to him?"

"My dad lost him in a bet," Travis said with a shrug.

"Oh, Travis. I'm so sorry..."

He smiled. "It's okay. It was a long time ago. And thanks for your help tonight. I guess Henry and I need to get going."

He hoisted Henry off his shoulders and plopped him into his car seat. Henry started to struggle and whine immediately. "I don't want to be buckled in! It huuuurts. I can't breathe! I can't move!"

Travis grunted and struggled to keep Henry in the car seat. "You're moving just fine. Settle down."

"No!" Henry yelled. Then he kicked the headrest of the seat in front of him.

Travis let go and rubbed his temples while Henry appeared to melt and slide halfway out of the seat. "I'm all out of tricks, kid. With Maggie standing right here, it's not like I can hold you upside down by your ankles."

Henry responded by jerking his body into a rigid imitation of one of the two-by-fours in the bed of Travis's truck. From jelly to rigor mortis in under two seconds. It would be hard to get him strapped in like that, and Maggie was beginning to see the logic in hanging him upside down.

"I want to ride up front like a big boy."

"You can't," Travis snapped.

Maggie had an idea. "Henry, do you like basketball?" He was wearing a San Antonio Spurs jersey, so it was a pretty safe bet.

"Yeah. Do you?"

"Of course! And the Spurs are playing tonight. First game of the season. It's on television. I bet you can still catch it if you hurry and get in your car seat."

"That's right," Travis said, giving her a look of utter gratitude as Henry resumed a normal posture and allowed himself to be buckled in.

"Can we watch it with Maggie?"

Whoa. She hadn't seen that coming. Surely Travis wouldn't want to.

"It's fine with me," Travis said.

Maggie's stomach began fluttering. It was annoying.

"I'm sorry," Travis said. "Awkward."

"No! It's fine. Really." Was it? Her hands were sweaty.

"Okay. I'll bring the leftover tamales to snack on. What's your address?"

They were meeting at *her place?* And why did he need her address when they were neighbors? Who did he think had been leaving him the slightly salty notes on his gate—the ones she may, or may not, possibly be regretting right about now?

"Are you sure it's okay?" Travis asked, probably sensing her hesitation because she was doing some serious hesitating. "JD said something about meeting you and Bubba at Tony's. I don't want to keep you from that."

She tried to organize her facial features into some semblance of normal as she pondered possible strategies. *Yes, I already had plans. Sorry. Bye. Ignore the note on the gate where I threatened to summon the Chupavaca to drain your cattle of blood.*

"We kind of invited ourselves over," Travis continued. "We'll understand."

Maggie looked at Henry. If you had to stick a label on him, it would say, PERSON LEAST LIKELY TO UNDERSTAND. How could she rescind an invitation to a five-year-old? "I'd love to have you both. I live at Honey's place. On Peacock Road."

Oh Lord. Watching it dawn on Travis's face—*you're the crazy lady who's been threatening me*—was both painful and hilarious. Maggie didn't know whether to laugh or cry. She fluttered her eyelashes and waved her fingers. "Howdy, neighbor."

Travis looked at her like she'd just smashed an ax through a door and said, *Here's Johnny!*

He was about to back out. Maybe he'd fake a sudden onset of stomach cramps. That's what she would do.

"Let's go!" Henry said. He'd clearly run out of patience. "Let's go to Maggie's *now*."

Travis rubbed his beard as if trying to decide which one of them was scarier: her or Henry. "You sure you want us to come over?"

"Yes. Don't make me beg. It's weird."

Travis raised a single eyebrow in a way that made her tummy flutter again. Like maybe he'd like to make her beg. She pretended to be interested in her feet, so he wouldn't see the blush creeping up her cheeks.

"I'm going to stop at my house and put Henry in his pajamas first," he said. "Then we'll be right over."

Nothing like mentioning a five-year-old in his pajamas to vanquish the sexual tension. If there had even been any.

"I'm not tired! And I'm not wearing pajamas."

"Really?" Maggie asked. "I'm going to wear mine."

Travis raised the other eyebrow, and Maggie's cheeks heated up again.

"They're Spurs pajamas," she said. Just in case he was imagining something else. Something sheer. Or lacy. Or...*He wasn't thinking that, Mackey. Stop it.*

Travis grinned. Dammit. That dimple on the left side just plain did it for her.

"I have Spurs pajamas, too!" Henry shouted. Like it was literally his job to keep her from having inappropriate thoughts.

"Good. You wear yours and I'll wear mine."

Henry clapped his hands.

"If you're not wearing Spurs pajamas when we get there, Henry is going to have a royal fit. And I'll be a bit disappointed myself."

"I'm a woman of my word," Maggie said, watching Travis climb behind the wheel of his truck.

"I don't doubt it," Travis said. Then he rolled down his window and stuck a GO SPURS GO flag on top of his truck.

Well, hell. She was in trouble.

* * *

The headlights illuminated the Happy Trails' gate and the note flapping in the breeze.

I live at Honey's place, she'd said. She had to know about the notes. There was no way Maggie's crazy grandmother was keeping all the cow rage to herself. Maybe Maggie thought it was funny. Travis felt like an idiot.

He got out of the truck and yanked the note off the gate.

FIX YOUR FENCE OR I'LL SUMMON THE CHUPAVACA.

He tried not to smile, which should have been easy, considering how he felt. But he had to give the old lady her due—this was funny. According to Mexican folklore, the Chupacabra was a mythical creature who sucked the blood out of *cabras*, or goats. Travis had never heard of such a thing until he'd moved to Big Verde, where at least once a year, the local newspaper featured stories about Chupacabra sightings, usually next to pictures of dead goats who'd most likely fallen victim to mountain lions. It caused a lot of chatter at the Corner Café, where farmers and ranchers laughed it off before going home and making sure their shotguns were loaded.

Honey had replaced *cabra* with *vaca*, the Spanish word for *cow*. Probably thought she was clever.

Having to face Honey Mackey on her own turf with her feisty

granddaughter as backup on the very night she'd literally threatened to drain his cattle of blood didn't sound like fun. What if
tonight wasn't about basketball, but an ambush?

"Are we at Maggie's?" Henry asked.

Travis sighed. "Not yet. We're home. Let's get you in your PJ's."

Maggie wouldn't ambush a five-year-old. He was being paranoid.
The thought of her in San Antonio Spurs basketball PJ's—
possibly plotting an ambush—made him grin, though. It also gave
him an idea, and before he knew it, he was sending a text.

* * *

The wind kicked up, stirring Maggie's wind chimes into hysteria.
She pulled her shoes off on the back porch just as the screen door
slammed with a wham. She banged them together, shaking off the
dried mud, and hightailed it inside to get the wood-burning stove
going. The house was still warm, but it would be chilly within
the hour.

A smile tugged at her lips as she lit the kindling. She was
glad she'd helped with the gazebo. It felt good, and she'd enjoyed
working with Travis.

She added some logs and sat cross-legged on the floor, watching them catch flame. No matter how handsome Travis was, or
how noble or perfect or adorable, she couldn't be sucked in. It
would cloud her judgment, and she needed to protect her business.
Despite what her mother might think about her decision to move
back to Big Verde—*you'll waste away at Honey's flower shop until
you marry some small-town man with a small-town mind and start
having his small-town babies*—Maggie was on the road to success.
She'd used her degree to turn Honey's beloved flower shop into a
real business. She was building an impressive portfolio. One of her
projects had even been featured in *Better Homes and Gardens*. By
Big Verde's standards, she was a freaking rock star and had thus

far not been approached by a single small-town man about making babies. *So there.*

And that was fine with her. Mostly. Maybe she was just one of those women who only needed fulfilling work, good friends, and a sexting relationship with a guy in a wolf mask. There were probably lots of women like that, right?

The fire popped, bringing her back to the issue at hand, which was getting ready for company. What did "in a little while" mean? She was filthy and needed a shower. She stood up with a groan and headed for the bathroom, just as her phone pinged.

Wear sexy lingerie tonight. I'll be thinking of you.

She didn't own any sexy lingerie, but even if she did, she could hardly wear it tonight with company coming. And anyway, she'd promised Henry she'd wear her Spurs PJ's.

She decided to respond honestly.

No can do. Having company.

Are you seeing another wolf?

Ha! Hardly.

Believe it or not, it's a man who's trying to ruin my business.

She waited a few minutes, but the wolf didn't text back, so she hopped in the shower. What had she expected? That her anonymous sexting buddy would want to have a deep and meaningful conversation about her job insecurity? He didn't know she worked in a male-dominated industry. He could never understand the scrutiny she underwent every single time she bid on a large job, just because she was a woman. She could handle the ribbing and jabbing and jokes at her expense. It was the lack of confidence that men—and women!—expressed in her ability to do the job because of her gender that really got her hackles up. She had to work twice as hard, and often for less money, to prove herself.

It wasn't Travis's fault that Anna had hired him to do a job he wasn't qualified for. But he should have turned it down. Or at least accepted some help.

After a super quick rinse off, she felt blindly around for her towel, shivering the entire time. It took only about twelve seconds before she was zipped up into her warm San Antonio Spurs footsie pajamas. Then she swiped at the foggy mirror with her hand and towel-dried her hair.

Ready for company.

She checked her phone to see if the wolf had texted back— he hadn't—and padded down the chilly hallway to check on the wood-burning stove. It was going gangbusters.

Note to self: Wolf just wants to talk dirty. No more personal revelations.

Travis was bringing tamales; but shouldn't she at least offer some chips and dip or something? She opened the refrigerator and stared for the obligatory five seconds before moving on to the pantry. It was a bust. All she had to offer were stale crackers and an expired carton of yogurt. She was a horrible hostess.

Pop started yapping. Maggie peeked out the window above the sink to see headlights coming up the lane.

"Settle down, Pop. It's just company."

Other than Claire or JD, Pop wasn't much used to company. He tilted his head as if considering what she'd said. Then he began yapping and growling again. He really got going when the headlights hit the house.

"Hush up, Pop. Do I look scared? It's not a serial killer. It's just Travis Blake."

Yap!

"Coming to our house."

Yap!

"Because that's not weird at all."

Yap!

She stepped onto the screened-in porch with Pop running circles at her feet as the truck pulled to a stop. It took a few minutes for Travis to extricate Henry from his car seat, but then she was covered in five-year-old.

"Hi, Maggie!"

Pop stopped barking to actively sniff the hell out of Henry. That turned to enthusiastic licking, which broke Henry out in a rash of giggles.

"Look, Uncle Travis. She still gots her dog!"

"She still *has* her dog."

"I know. That's what I said."

Travis sighed and smiled at Maggie. He wore a big wooly green sweater. *And glasses.* She hadn't expected those. Combined with his longish black hair and scruffy dark beard, it made him look like Rustic Outdoorsy Guy Who Likes to Read. She approved.

"You look nice in glasses."

Travis paused at the compliment, and then smiled. "My contacts were bothering me." He lifted his glasses and rubbed his eyes. "Cold fronts get me every time."

"Does your dog have a name?" Henry asked.

"It's Pop."

Travis eyed her Spurs basketball pajamas, took a closer look at Pop, and proclaimed, "I see the resemblance."

"Did you just insinuate that I look like my dog?"

"No. I insinuated your dog looks like Greg Popovich."

Greg Popovich was the head coach of the Spurs. And Travis had successfully noted the resemblance between him and the little blue-haired bulldog. "Impressive," Maggie said.

"It's the stubby silver hair and the, no offense, face only a mother could love."

Maggie laughed and picked Pop up, petting him between the ears. "Don't call my dog ugly."

"So, are you a real fan or just one of those girls who wears NBA lingerie and names her dog after Greg Popovich to attract guys?"

"Aw...you nailed it. I'm just trying to attract guys. I know nothing about sportsball."

"I bet you know more about it than I do."

Henry looked nosily through the open door to where Maggie's television glowed. "Let's go inside. I want to watch the game."

Travis came up the steps and reached over her head to hold the door open. He smelled good, like woods and sunshine.

How had this even happened? She took the bag of tamales from him and went into the house, where Henry was already rolling around the floor with Pop. Their relationship status had gone from Mortal Enemies to Comfy Pajamas Complicated in one afternoon.

Chapter
Sixteen

❦

Travis looked around the old farmhouse. Although he didn't see Honey Mackey—hopefully she was infirm and bedridden—evidence of her was everywhere. Gingham curtains, those ugly lace things that went beneath lamps, and about a zillion salt and pepper shakers shaped like roosters.

Maggie caught him. "It's my grandmother's house."

"Oh, I know. I just didn't realize you lived here, too."

Maggie looked at him quizzically. "I live here alone. I moved in after Honey passed away."

He was confused. And then it dawned on him. Miss Mary Margaret aka Little Red Riding Hood aka the Chupavaca Summoner had been leaving him the nasty notes.

She looked up at him with an angelic smile.

He folded his arms. "Sorry to hear about Honey."

"I'm surprised you didn't know, small towns being what they are."

"I haven't been back very long. And everybody still refers to this property as Honey Mackey's place."

Maggie nodded. "And they will still be referring to it as Honey Mackey's place a hundred years from now. Just like that drugstore on the corner is still called Harmon's, even though the Harmon's sign is long gone, and it's owned by a chain. You could say we're a little resistant to change."

"No kidding." Travis bet Honey's underwear was still in a drawer somewhere in the house. A mug on the counter said WORLD'S GREATEST GRANDMA. Travis picked it up. It had about an inch of cold, stale coffee in it. "Unless Honey died last week, I'd say you're resistant to change."

Maggie stared down at her hands quietly.

Dammit! He was no good at making jokes. Especially ones about somebody's *dead* grandmother.

Maggie sniffled. "Actually..."

Oh, no. No, no, no, no. Her grandmother had *not* died a week ago.

Maggie sniffed again.

Jesus Christ. Maybe she had.

Maggie's pink cheeks slowly deepened to scarlet red. Her lips trembled, her eyes brimmed with tears, and it took everything Travis had not to turn around and fling himself out the window. This was worse than when he'd asked a nonpregnant lady when her baby was due. When would he learn to engage his brain before his mouth? No wonder Maggie had been so ornery. She was grieving a fresh loss.

"I'm so sorry. I didn't know."

Maybe Henry would barf now—he sometimes did that for no reason whatsoever—and they could make a hasty retreat.

Maggie covered her face with her hands. Her shoulders began to shake.

Instead of fleeing, Travis gathered her in his arms. And even though everything about the scenario was mortifying, a party had started in his pants. He kept the necessary three inches between it and Maggie, so she wouldn't get the invitation. "There,

there," he said stiffly. "It'll be okay. I have a horrible sense of humor."

For some reason, the sound of his voice seemed to unleash the beast. Maggie's shoulders shook so hard she rocked them both. He held on tightly as the first sob came. It cut through his bones and went straight into his heart. "Shhh..."

"Why are you lovin' on Maggie?" Henry asked.

When had Henry come into the kitchen? "Her grannie just died, Henry."

"Then why is she laughing?"

"She's not laughing—"

Travis loosened his hold as Maggie's sobs turned into howls. Travis held her at arm's length and stared into her face, which was distorted from *laughing*. Tears streamed down her cheeks.

Henry started to laugh, too, even though he had no idea what was going on. Laughter was contagious. In fact, Travis felt a little something stirring up, but he did his best to squash it.

"What's so funny?" Henry asked between giggles.

"Your uncle," Maggie wheezed to Henry. "God. He's gullible."

"Okay, so I fell for it," Travis said. "Big deal."

"Uncle Travis, do you have your feelings hurt?"

Now he felt even sillier. "Nah, it was a good joke." He'd love to make a joke about how the Big Bad Wolf was currently in Little Red Riding Hood's grandmother's house. What would Maggie's reaction be? He tried to imagine it. She'd be shocked. Embarrassed. Mortified, most likely. And he'd have to explain why he hadn't said anything sooner. It was just one more thing he'd put off, and now it seemed too late. It was like when someone called you by the wrong name and you didn't correct them, and before you knew it, it was past the point of awkward, so you just pretended to have a new name.

It would be fine. Once the ranch sold and Henry was settled, he and Big Verde—and Maggie—would part ways. In the meantime, he should probably stop sexting her.

"Good," Henry said decidedly. Then he looked at Maggie. "Because it's not nice to hurt people's feelings."

Maggie rolled her eyes. "His feelings aren't hurt. Want some hot cocoa, pookie?"

"Yes, ma'am!" Henry said.

"I was talking to Uncle Pookie, but you can have some, too."

Maggie kicked a small stool over to the kitchen counter, while Travis glanced awkwardly around. Was Honey Mackey really deceased? Maggie had said she was, but she'd also indicated the woman was freshly in her grave, which obviously wasn't the case. Was the joke that Honey hadn't died recently? Or that she hadn't died at all? And who joked about dead grannies? Travis cleared his throat. "We're not disturbing your grandmother, are we?"

"God, I hope not," Maggie said. "She's been dead for nearly a year."

Okay. So that answered his question. Maggie Mackey joked about dead grannies. While wearing Spurs pajamas in a house full of rooster knickknacks. A grin took over Travis's face, and he realized he kind of liked twisted girls. Or at least he liked this one.

Maggie winked, but pain creased her forehead and her smile trembled. Honey Mackey was definitely dead, and her granddaughter, whacked sense of humor notwithstanding, was heartbroken.

"Were you close?"

"She was my best friend."

"That's pretty close," Travis said. "I'm sorry you've lost her."

"Thanks." Maggie looked down at her hands, took a breath as if she had something else to say. "She was the only person who truly believed in me."

Who wouldn't believe in this sexy dynamo of a woman? While Travis searched for something to say, Maggie turned away and opened the cabinet above her head. "Honey would have loved the little joke I just pulled on you." She stood on her tiptoes and still couldn't quite reach whatever it was she was looking for. "We had identical senses of humor."

"That's horrifying," Travis said. He walked up behind Maggie. "What are you looking for? I can get it."

Maggie came down to her heels just as he reached over, gently bumping into her. He backed up quickly, but the response of his dick had been swift. He now stood behind a grown woman in footsie pajamas in a dead lady's kitchen—with a raging hard-on.

"Oops," Maggie said. "Watch what you do with that thing."

"Excuse me?"

"You're gripping a cast iron skillet. I'm pretty sure my grand-mother used it to kill my grandfather."

"Really?" Henry asked.

"No," Maggie said. "Another joke." She looked at Travis and whispered, "Somebody's as gullible as his uncle."

Travis let go of the skillet. He hadn't even known he'd grabbed the damn thing.

"The saucepan behind it," Maggie said. "That's what I need to heat the milk in."

"Got it." He handed Maggie the pan.

"Do you have whipped cream that squirts out of a can?" Henry asked.

Maggie set the pan on the stove and went to the refrigerator. "I might. Let's see."

Travis let out a low whistle at the sight of two bottles of beer, some ketchup, and a half gallon of milk. "That's some stock you've got there. Sure you're not a guy?"

Maggie frowned. Had he said something wrong? *Again?*

"Not a guy," she said with a sigh. "But thanks for asking."

He kept his mouth shut for fear of what might fly out next, and because the sight of her bending over looking in the fridge stunned him speechless. His penis kept hopping to attention like Maggie was a five-star general. He knew what they'd done together…

And she didn't.

"Ah ha! Look what I found, boys." She held up a white can with a spout in triumph. "Whipped cream."

Travis tried—and failed—not to think about all the places he'd like to put that whipped cream.

Maggie slammed the door shut with her hip, squinting at the can. "And it only expired two months ago. This is practically straight from the cow."

"I don't think that's ever seen a cow," Travis said.

Henry licked his lips. "Squirt some in my mouth, Maggie!"

"No, Henry. That's not a good—"

"Party pooper," Maggie said, breezing past him with the nozzle aimed at Henry's mouth. The unmistakable sound of the depressed tip of a whipped cream can came next, followed by hysterical giggles. Travis tried not to grin. Somebody had to be the grown-up.

"Go see what the score is, Henry," Maggie said, nodding at the television. "I'll bring the plates in."

"We can eat on the couch?"

"Where else would we eat on game night? Travis, grab those TV trays, would you?"

TV trays. The woman ate on TV trays while watching basketball and doing weird shit with whipped cream. She was a dream come true.

* * *

Maggie couldn't believe that she was sitting on the sofa sipping hot cocoa with Travis while the Spurs creamed the Mavericks. Henry sat between them, his little head already nodding. She pulled him in for a snuggle, and he curled right up.

A commercial came on. "I think Henry's asleep," she said, muting the television.

It was already the fourth quarter. The game would be over

in a few minutes. Travis probably wanted to get home and put Henry to bed.

"Did Honey raise you?"

"Not initially. But when I started high school, my mom took off for Los Angeles. She's an artist, or at least that's how she sees herself. Big Verde stifled her creativity. She wanted me to come along, but even at fourteen I knew I didn't want that life. I'm a small-town girl at heart, which my mother finds terribly disappointing. Small towns, small minds, she used to say."

"You went off to A&M, didn't you?"

She raised an eyebrow.

"LinkedIn," he said. "Every time I tried to solicit business in town, I was told Petal Pushers had the account. I got curious. Had to scope out my competition."

"Stalker. And yeah, I did an internship at a landscape architect firm after graduation—"

"Vector."

She paused. "Seriously. You're a stalker. Anyway, it was a lot of sitting around behind a desk. I hated it. I decided to make a go of it here. I prefer sunshine to desks."

"Sunshine looks good on you."

She wasn't super adept at picking up social signals, but was that a flirtatious statement? It sounded like it. But what if she was wrong, and her ears were glowing for no reason at all? Travis was unbelievably hot, and surely, he knew that. What would he be flirting with her for? It hadn't been half an hour since he said, *Sure you're not a guy?*

Lord knew Travis wasn't the kid he'd been in high school— that skinny, short boy who'd helped her clean up the cow patty mess...Although when she looked in those blue eyes behind the lenses of his glasses, it was obvious at least part of him was still that sweet boy.

"I recognized you as soon as I saw you tonight," she blurted.

Travis sat up and inhaled sharply, as if bracing himself for an onslaught of high school memories. "I was going to tell you," he stuttered. "I wasn't sure you'd recognized me with the beard, and I thought maybe it was best to just not say anything. It's kind of embarrassing, isn't it?"

"High school is *supposed* to be embarrassing," she said. "It was the glasses that gave you away."

"High school?"

"Ho Ho Ho Green Giants!" She winced. That had come out of nowhere with comedic timing.

Travis stared at her as if she were performance art. Maybe she was. "Do you recognize me?" she asked.

He frowned at her. "Is this a trick question?"

"Aw, you don't, do you? Does a cow patty cleanup outside a locker ring a bell?"

Travis looked beyond confused. His blue eyes searched hers, and she did her best to look like fourteen-year-old Maggie, which wasn't nearly as difficult as it should have been. Then his eyes widened, and a huge grin broke out on his face. "I do remember you! I knew we'd gone to school together, but you were a couple of years behind me. And I really didn't have any friends…"

He blushed, and it broke her heart.

"Anyway, you were the Future Farmers of America girl that hung out with all the redneck boys."

"I think that's what it says beneath my unfortunate yearbook photo."

"You had a nickname. What was it?" He rubbed his beard.

"Mighty Mack," she said. "And I'm trying really hard to out-grow it."

His eyes left hers and traveled down her face to the rest of her, and even though she was wearing what amounted to a blanket with a zipper, his voice deepened, and he said, "Oh, I'd say you've outgrown it. There is nothing remotely childish about you, Maggie Mackey."

Maggie could swear her ears were bathing the room in a rosy glow.

Travis's eyes worked their way back up to her lips, where they settled, making Maggie's heart pound in her chest. "I recognize you," he whispered.

All he'd said was that he recognized her. But it felt as if he'd said, *You're mine.*

Maggie cleared her throat. "I never said thank you for helping me that day."

Travis moved closer. They were practically nose to nose. His lips smelled like cocoa. They'd probably taste like it, too, but Maggie didn't have the guts. Instead, she kissed him sweetly on the cheek. "Thank you."

"You're welcome," he whispered. Then he gave her a feathery soft kiss on the lips.

He did taste like cocoa. Maggie didn't want him to pull away, so she parted her lips in invitation, and Travis accepted. With a quiet groan that nearly caused Maggie to come undone, Travis slipped his tongue between her lips. There was nothing feathery soft about the kiss now. His hand came up her back and settled at the base of her skull. She hadn't been kissed this way since her night with the wolf, and it awakened every cell in her body. This man who'd taunted her with his tattooed chest, his dimpled grin, and his end- less blue eyes was now kissing her as if she were the best-tasting thing since chocolate ice cream. As if he wanted to devour her— *just like the wolf had.* She'd give anything to feel Travis's lips on her neck, trailing down to her breasts and maybe even lower. The only thing between her and Nirvana was the zipper on her PJ's.

Travis's beard was rough and soft all at the same time. It scratched and tickled—a delightfully wicked combination. She'd never kissed a man with a beard before. It was foreign and exciting, but somehow comforting, too. She brushed the side of his face with her fingers before tangling them in his wavy hair. With her other hand she toyed with the tag of the zipper at her neck. Should she do it?

A sensation of warmth spread across her upper thigh and soaked the leg of her pajamas.

She broke the kiss instantly, gasping in horror. They'd forgotten all about poor little Henry!

"What's wrong?" Travis asked.

"I think Henry wet himself."

Travis looked like he might say, "Henry who?" but then his eyes widened. "Holy shit."

Henry yawned and stretched. "Did the Spurs win?"

Maggie had no idea who had won the game, and from the dazed look on Travis's face, neither did he.

Chapter
Seventeen

❦

Travis collapsed on the couch and looked around in defeat. The place was hardly a model home under the best of circumstances, but after a bout of Hurricane Henry, it was a disaster. Spilled cereal under the table. An upturned laundry basket of clothes. All the couch cushions, save the one Travis was sitting on, dumped on the floor.

And it was only eight o'clock in the morning.

When he'd finally dragged Henry to the breakfast table, he'd discovered they were out of the little tyrant's favorite cereal. The socks Henry liked were dirty. The toothpaste wasn't the right flavor. By the time Travis had shoved Henry onto the bus, he felt like he'd been through the wringer.

Ping!

He looked at his phone and grinned. Hey wolfie. Cat got your tongue?

Close call last night. He thought for sure she'd recognized him as the wolf. It was an odd moment. Part of him had been relieved. He was ready for the deception to end, for Maggie to know the truth, and *choose him anyway*. He should ignore the text. Why make it worse? Maybe because making things worse was his specialty...

Just can't stop thinking about my tongue, can you?

He didn't like being deceptive. But Jesus, she thought he was trying to ruin her business. Other than Anna splitting her project between the two of them, what business had he officially stolen? He just had a few piddly-assed small businesses as clients. Although come to think of it, piddly-assed small businesses made up the overwhelming majority of Big Verde's business community. Had he inadvertently stolen clients from Maggie?

He'd stolen clients from Maggie.

Shit. He hadn't meant to fuck with her life. He'd finally met someone he really liked, and she thought he was out to ruin her. He doubted she'd take kindly to him being a lying dog—literally—on top of it.

He'd kissed her.

Thinking about it gave him a rush. If it hadn't been for Henry, they might have made out like teenagers for hours. Maybe they'd have done more than make out. He knew what was hidden inside that shapeless mass of fuzzy fabric Maggie had worn, and he'd wanted nothing more than to pull down its zipper and run his hands all over her smooth, warm skin.

You've got a pretty nice tongue.

A dumb smile took over his entire face. What did Miss Mary Margaret think about last night? Maybe he could get her to fess up.

How was your evening? You entertained the enemy. Refused to wear sexy lingerie.

What would she say? That she'd made out like a fiend with the guy she thought was ruining her business?

It was okay. He's a nice guy.

A nice guy? There were probably worse things than being a

nice guy. Like being a lying bastard business-stealer who'd had sex with an unsuspecting business-maiden in a garden shed.

Should I be jealous?

He wanted her to say yes, that she was completely hot for the guy she was with last night.

He's no alpha dog.

Travis laughed, even though it was a slap in the face. How could he be jealous of the wolf when he *was* the wolf? Being both the alpha dog who made Maggie do dirty things and the nice guy who brought his nephew over for hot cocoa was emotionally confusing, to say the least.

But nice guy or not—I need to shut him down.

Travis raised an eyebrow. She wanted to shut him down? Irritation crept up his spine, along with a healthy dose of respect.

The back door slammed. Mrs. Garza wasn't supposed to come today, but Travis's nose picked up garlic, onions, and cumin. Not only had Mrs. Garza come on a day she wasn't expected, she'd brought food. His stomach growled as he went into the kitchen.

He smiled. Even with her jet-black hair teased high on her head, Mrs. Garza couldn't be much more than five feet tall. Today's outfit was a zebra-striped pantsuit, complete with a rhinestone-encrusted cane hooked casually over one arm.

"I brought you *carne guisada* and homemade tortillas. And I brought in the mail. It looks like nobody's done that for a few days. The box was overflowing."

"Thank you. The food smells delicious. I didn't realize you were coming today." He glanced at the huge stack of mail on the counter with dread, and then sighed and started thumbing through it. Magazines and other things addressed to Lisa, flyers...nothing from the Army. And finally, on the very bottom, a pink envelope from the tax office. He'd open it later when he had some privacy.

"I need to clean up a bit before Albert gets here."

Travis scratched his head. "Albert?"

"My cousin." She opened the foil-wrapped tortillas and a cloud of steam escaped. "He was supposed to paint the Janskys' house today, but they're not quite ready for him. He's going to work here instead."

"Today?" Panic. The place was trashed. "He's going to paint the interior today?"

"He'll at least get started on it. And my brother, Beto, is happy to process the beef if he can keep half of the cow. Plus the head, of course."

"The head?"

"*Barbacoa.* His is the best."

"He can have whatever he wants."

Mrs. Garza pushed him aside with her cane as she reached for a plate. "You'll eat some of this now, *sí?* I can hear your stomach grumbling. But save some for tonight. Henry will need dinner."

"Yes, ma'am."

She walked into the living room. "What happened in here?"

"Henry didn't want to go to school today."

"I'll clean up this mess. You make your taco."

She bent over to pick up a couch cushion from the floor. Travis rushed to snatch it up, fearing she'd topple on top of it. He set the couch cushion in place and gestured for Mrs. Garza to have a seat, but she spotted the cereal under the coffee table and headed for the broom in the corner.

"No, ma'am," Travis said. "You have a seat and I'll take care of that."

Mrs. Garza stopped and raised one of her eyebrows, which was quite a feat since it was painted on and already arched just below her hairline. "Did you say no to me?"

Travis swallowed. "Sorry, ma'am." He got her the broom and she briskly swept the tiny pieces of cereal into a pile.

"Go eat," Mrs. Garza said, shuffling to the trashcan to empty the dustpan.

"Maybe after I'm showered. I'm running late for work."

"Go on, then," Mrs. Garza said. "You get in the shower and I'll fix your tacos and warm up a plate."

"Oh, no, really. You don't have to—"

"Are you saying no to me again?"

Travis knew when he'd been beat. He went upstairs to the bathroom, took off his clothes, and got in the shower. Turned out it was the right thing to do. The stress of the morning dissipated under the rhythmic pounding of the showerhead.

He needed to tell Maggie he wasn't planning to remain in Big Verde. She'd probably be relieved to know he had no plans to take over her evil landscaping empire.

He shouldn't keep texting her. But it was fun. And so damn hot. Even as his mind pondered the depressing reality of his current predicament, his hand wandered down to the pressing, aching need that had risen in response. He closed his eyes and teased up an image of Maggie's sweet ass bent over the workbench in the shed. The bows on the backs of her red stockings had driven him wild. He gripped his cock, thinking about what she'd tasted like when he'd licked the bare skin of her thighs all the way up to her hot little—

The bathroom door opened. *Dammit, Henry.*

But Henry was at school. Travis frantically poked his head out of the shower curtain. "Mrs. Garza? What the—"

"Don't mind me, *mijo*," she said, standing in the steam like a zebra-striped apparition. "I'm collecting dirty towels, so I can start a load of laundry."

He was naked. Mrs. Garza was two feet away from him. And he still had his dick in his hand. Flustered, he let go and made sure the shower curtain wasn't gaping. "You don't need to do that," he said. "I can get to it later."

Mrs. Garza opened the laundry hamper and bent over, a vision that chased away any lingering fantasies involving Little Red

Riding Hood. "It looks like later never comes around here. I'm happy to help."

Mrs. Garza grunted as she stood up, arms overflowing with towels, socks, and underwear.

"Thank you," he said with a feeble smile, hoping she'd quickly be on her way.

"Don't worry about getting this load in the dryer," she said, turning toward the door. "I'll do it while you're gone."

Ten minutes later, Travis blew through the back door, but then immediately screeched his heels to a halt at the sight and sounds of three men hammering and sawing right behind his house.

"Mrs. Garza!" he hollered, continuing to watch as the men climbed in and out of the mass of wood and metal that made up the long-useless cattle pens.

Mrs. Garza opened the door and poked her head out. "What is it, *mijo?*"

"Who are those men, and what are they doing?"

"Those are my cousin's sons. They're fixing up your cattle pens."

"Why?"

"Because he wants his *fajitas*," Mrs. Garza said. "That means getting a cow to the processor. Which means getting one into a trailer. And first you've got to get it into a pen."

Travis hadn't given that a bit of thought. More evidence that he had no business being a rancher. *Wait, when had he thought about being a rancher?*

He walked over and watched the men work for a few minutes. They asked him some questions, he thought about the answers, and by the time he got in his truck, he had a good idea of how to get cows into the chute and trailer, and some plans for improving the design.

* * *

Travis pulled up to Anna's to see an entire herd of pickups parked beneath the trees. He found a spot and got out, gathering his tools from the bed of his truck.

JD stood with a group of men next to a pile of rocks. He waved his hat, inviting Travis over.

"Here's the brawn," JD said. "Where's the beauty?"

"I imagine she'll be here any minute." Travis nodded at the other men, most of whom looked vaguely familiar. That was the recurring theme since coming home to Big Verde—vaguely familiar.

"Beauty?" one of the other guys said with a smirk. "I thought you were going to say brains."

"Maggie's got both," JD said.

"I agree. She's a beauty with brains," Travis added, with a nod to JD.

"I don't think either one of you should get your hopes up," one of the guys said.

"Travis, do you remember Bill?" JD asked. "He was probably a year behind you in school. He's doing the masonry on the house."

Travis didn't remember him, but he nodded as if he did, and Bill did the same.

"I heard Maggie's a lesbian," Bill said.

"She is not," Travis and JD said together. Then they awkwardly eyed each other until Bill piped up again.

"I bet she's a virgin then."

"Definitely not," Travis and JD chorused. Then they stared each other down with what were no doubt identical expressions of surprise before Travis looked away first.

JD finally cleared his throat. "Bill, not every woman who turns your ugly ass down is a lesbian or a nun."

Mark Langley, who Travis remembered because his dad had been the high school principal, laughed heartily. "That's true," he agreed. "Unless ninety percent of the women in Big Verde are lesbians or nuns."

"Aw, fuck off," Bill said. "And I've never even hit on Maggie. I just have a very sensitive gay-dar. I mean, have you seen the way she dresses? Lesbian all the way."

"She dresses like a landscaper," JD said. "Stop stereotyping."

"Well, I've never seen her with a man," Bill said, crossing his arms as if that decided it.

JD yanked the brim of his hat down. "You obviously weren't at Anna's gala."

Mark Langley glanced around and lowered his voice. "I was there. She sure wasn't dressed like a landscaper that night."

Travis didn't like this one bit. The whole scene put a bad taste in his mouth. And as for how Maggie dressed, these were the kind of guys who catcalled. How was she supposed to dress? Who could blame her for wanting to be taken seriously?

JD stirred, and his fists were clenched. "She was Little Red Riding Hood at the gala. And I'd better not ever run into that wolf."

Travis broke out in a light sweat and pretended to squish a bug with the toe of his boot, keeping his face lowered because he figured it was fucking on fire.

"Who was that guy?" Mark asked.

"I have no idea," JD said. "I asked around, but nobody knew."

"You got a thing for Maggie?" Mark asked JD. "You guys more than friends?"

Bill, who Travis liked less and less by the second, broke out in hysterical laughter. "Are you kidding? JD here could have any woman he wants. Why would he be with Maggie?"

"Don't make me punch you in the face, Bill," JD said through clenched teeth.

If JD didn't do it, Travis might.

"Don't lose your shit. I'm just kidding."

It was doubtful that JD, in his pressed blue jeans and starched white shirt, ever *lost his shit*. But he could probably pack a powerful punch. The air was heavy with tension as all the men stood around worried that a fight might break out—and kind of hoping it would. But the sound of tires crunching on gravel drew their attention elsewhere.

"Speak of the devil," JD said.

The men scattered, getting busy at whatever tasks they had to do, but Travis stayed put, watching as Maggie parked. Pop sprang out the door, peed on all four tires, and then sniffed the air like he could smell the previous conversation. And it stank.

Maggie slammed the door. Then she looked up and smiled.

It was a big, genuine, beautiful smile. Her cheeks were already pink from the brisk autumn air, her light blond hair whipped around her face, and Travis nearly melted into his steel-toed boots.

Would it be weird to give her a hug? Because he wanted her body pressed against his in a bad way. Pop ran up, wagging his stubby tail, so Travis bent over and gave him a good rub.

"Did you have a hard time getting Henry up this morning?"

"It was awful. You're too much of a party animal for us."

"Just wait until the play-offs start. Then we're really going to party."

"Maybe I'll enlist the help of Mrs. Garza on school nights," Travis said. "That way we can watch without Henry."

Maggie raised an eyebrow. Travis grinned, put his head down, and headed for the patio. He'd just leave that there and see what Maggie did with it.

Pop barked as another car pulled up. Travis looked over his shoulder. Two young men got out of a beat-up blue pickup. He recognized one of them from last night—his name was Norbert—and waved.

"Hey, Maggie," Norbert called. "Where do you need us to start with the rocks?"

Travis stopped in his tracks. "What are they here for?"

What was it Maggie had texted? *I need to shut him down.*

"I thought you could use some help. These guys weren't doing anything today so—"

"I told you I didn't need any help."

"I know, but you really *do* need the help. You've got to be so tired, and it's no big deal to just let these guys join in. Y'all can be done by this afternoon."

Only it was a big deal. He couldn't spare any money to pay them. And he couldn't afford to get kicked off this job if Anna thought Maggie was having to help him.

He looked at the two men, who stared back in confusion. It wasn't their fault. He started for the rock mine. "Come on."

His pulse pounded in his head.

Maggie scurried along behind him, her feet scattering gravel, her breath coming in short pants. He had at least a foot on her in height, and she was no match for his long legs, so he increased his stride.

"Travis, are you mad?"

"Nope."

"Wait up. I was just trying to help."

He doubted that. She was competitive. And she'd been pouty about sharing this job from the beginning. If he didn't do something to put a stop to this, she'd have a full crew out here by next week, and he'd be out of a job.

He'd chat Anna up today. Make sure she remembered why she hired him.

Chapter

Eighteen

❦

Stop the truck!" Henry hollered as soon as Travis pulled onto Pea-cock Road. They were almost home, but Travis hit the brakes.

"Why?" There was nothing blocking the road. What in the world was he yelling about?

"Horse! Horse! Look, a horse!"

For a kid raised on a ranch, Henry sure had a strange reaction to seeing livestock.

Gerome Kowalski rode his chestnut mare down Peacock Road like it was the most natural thing in the world. Travis slowed down so as not to spook the animal, and Gerome waved and stopped. Travis rolled down his window.

"Howdy," Gerome said with a tilt of his straw Stetson.

"Out for a ride? It's a gorgeous day for it."

"That it is."

Gerome was an imposing figure, eyes shaded by the brim of his hat. Henry, for once, was quiet in the backseat.

Should Travis introduce himself? Surely, Gerome didn't re-member—

"I haven't seen you since your daddy's funeral," Gerome said. "Have I changed as much as you have?"

"Not a bit," Travis said, flattered to be recognized. And Gerome hadn't changed much at all. Maybe a little grayer at the temples, but that was about it.

"My condolences about your sister-in-law. She was a good neighbor," Gerome said, not missing a beat. "Lilly thought highly of her, and of course, she's fond of that little man in the backseat."

"Hi, Mr. K!" Henry called out.

"Howdy, Henry. Your cows are looking good today."

"Yours, too," Henry said nonchalantly. Like it was normal for a five-year-old to discuss cattle with the owner of Rancho Cañada Verde.

Gerome gazed at the front pasture of Happy Trails, and Travis wilted beneath the scrutiny. "You need to make some hay, or the cattle won't survive the winter. Manual Lopez will cut and bale it if you go in halves with him. He used to do it for Lisa."

Jesus. As big of a pain as Happy Trails was, Lisa used to manage it all herself. And here he was, not having given a single thought to what the herd would do for food for the winter. He hadn't planned to be around that long. "I'll give him a call this evening."

"And you need to thin out this herd. Sell some yearlings if you're not going to turn them into steers."

This was humiliating. Travis wanted to mumble, *Yes sir, thank you sir*, but he manned up enough to say, "Thank you for the advice."

"It'll help with your cash flow if you can sell a few."

Just when Travis thought it couldn't get any worse, Gerome had brought up his cash flow. "How much is beef bringing right now?"

Gerome scratched his chin. "At market, I'd say these yearlings would get about a dollar a pound on the hoof."

Travis wasn't entirely sure what that meant, and it must have shown on his face, because with a barely perceptible grin, Gerome added, "They look to weigh about five to six hundred pounds each."

That was easy math. And a lot of fucking money.

"But they'll bring quite a bit more at the Texas Farmer's Market in Austin."

"Really?"

"And it's a better way to sell beef. Meeting with folks who want to know where their food comes from, selling them a healthy product you've raised while being a good steward of the earth... Well, it just feels right."

Travis's mind whirred with possibilities. It was surprising that he could make more money selling beef that way, but he trusted Gerome to know what he was talking about. "I never even considered that. And I agree, it sounds like a better way to sell beef."

"I'm going to miss it. But Cañada Verde can't keep up with demand now that our focus is retail and we're the sole supplier to three big grocery chains."

Gerome wasn't bragging. Just stating facts. He stopped staring at the pasture and looked down at Travis. "Would you like our stall at the Texas Farmer's Market? You grow good grass and good cattle. Hell, thanks to your wandering bull and piss-poor fences, they're the same bloodline as my own. I'd be happy to endorse you."

Travis couldn't believe his ears. This would be a way to earn some quick cash, and well, it sounded like fun. "Mr. Kowalski, I would love nothing more than to take over your stall. Let's shake on it."

"Done," Gerome said, grasping Travis's hand in a firm shake. "You'll need a permit, but that's easy. And I'll send Claire with you to help out and show you the ropes. She loves working the market."

Henry started kicking the back of Travis's seat.

"Somebody's getting restless," Gerome said. "I'll let you two get back to your business, and I'll finish my ride."

Travis watched Gerome through his rearview mirror, literally riding off into the motherfucking sunset like a god.

Was it possible to make enough money to pay off the taxes with a stand at the farmer's market? He drove through the gate and past the cedar patch, whistling the whole way.

"Hey! Our house is clean!" Henry said as they rounded the bend.

It was only white primer, but by God, the house was painted. And yes, it did make it look cleaner. The place looked downright respectable. "It's just the primer," Travis said. "The real coat of paint hasn't even been applied yet."

"It sure looks real to me."

"Let's go see what the inside looks like." Travis didn't know which one of them was more excited, and they burst through the back door together.

"What's that smell?" Henry asked.

"Paint."

"Where's all my stuff?"

"Beneath those drop cloths." Albert had covered everything up.

Henry walked right up to a wall and put his hand on it. "Don't touch!" Travis shouted.

Henry snatched his hand back and stared at his white palm. Then he touched the wall again.

"Goddammit, Henry." Travis grabbed his tiny wrist. "I said don't touch. What the hell is the matter with you?"

Henry's bottom lip jutted out and his eyes started filling up with tears.

Here it comes.

Travis's entire body vibrated with frustration. He bit his tongue to keep from saying hurtful words. But man, they would feel glorious spilling out of his mouth. He could almost taste them.

"I don't want the house painted," Henry said. "I want everything just like it was!"

Travis started to count to ten. It was supposed to be a good idea, but for the life of him, he didn't know why. It only postponed the inevitable. "Get in the tub," he said through gritted teeth. "I'll have your supper ready when you get out."

Mrs. Garza had left tacos in the refrigerator. At least he wouldn't have to cook or feel like shit for going through a drive-thru.

"No! I don't want a bath."

Travis glared at Henry. *One, two, three...*

"You can't make me."

A dull ache began to throb behind Travis's eyes, and he brought his fingers to his temples. He was so fucking tired he could hardly move. And now he had a house full of wet paint and a five-year-old hellbent on touching every surface. And he still had forms to fill out for Henry's school and sandwiches to make for tomorrow's lunchbox. And there was the social worker to touch base with and the letters from the tax office to open—but he didn't plan on doing that without a beer.

Four, five, six...

"I want a cookie," Henry said quietly.

That was it. He'd only made it to six. "Do you know what I want, Henry?" The first words slipped out, and there was no going back. "I want to come home from work and not have to deal with a difficult little shit who isn't even mine."

Henry took a step back, as if Travis had slapped him. A wave of remorse and disgust rose immediately like bile. He'd just glimpsed the depth of his dark side, and it was fucking fathoms deep. If only he could take back those words.

Travis reached for Henry—his heart sinking—but it was too late. Henry turned away. What if he'd done irreparable damage?

"I just want things the way they were," Henry repeated with a sniffle.

Jesus. The poor kid wasn't talking about the paint. He wanted his mom, not an uncle he hardly knew who yelled and called him names. Some days were so trying that Travis had a hard time remembering how much Henry's world had been turned upside down. Travis squatted so he could look Henry in the eye. The one thing he'd longed for when his dad got drunk and said mean things was an apology. He'd never gotten one. But he could damn well give one. "I know you wish things were the way they used to be. You miss your mom, and I don't blame you. I'm sorry you're stuck with me instead. And I didn't mean what I just said. You are not a little shit. I'm tired and cranky is all. But that's no excuse for talking ugly to you, and I am deeply sorry. Can you forgive me?"

"Yes," Henry said, and his ready forgiveness somehow made Travis feel worse. "But you meant the other part."

"What part?"

"I'm not yours. That's why you don't love me."

Now it was Travis's turn to be stunned. Slapped by words. "You *are* mine. We're family, remember? Same blood running through our veins. And of course I..." It wasn't easy. He wasn't raised hearing or saying those words.

He took Henry by the shoulders. "Look at me."

Henry looked up, and it damn near broke Travis's heart. The pain in those little eyes was almost too much.

"I love you, Henry. I know you can't see it right now, especially when I'm like this, but everything I'm doing is for you. Do you understand? When we sell this place, you'll be set—"

"What does that mean?" Henry asked.

Not a good time to answer that question. "Just that we have better times ahead of us. I'm trying to do that for us, okay?"

Henry shrugged. He didn't understand. How could he?

"You say lots of bad words," Henry said.

"Sorry. I'll work on that."

"Can I say one?"

Travis couldn't squat any longer. He sat on the floor, popping his back and pulling Henry onto his lap.

"Just one. Make it good."

Henry put a finger to his chin, leaving a spot of paint, and considered which filthy word to utter. Travis felt bad that he had so many to choose from.

Henry straightened up—he'd made his decision. "I love you, too, Uncle Travis."

That wasn't what Travis had expected. "I'm happy you said that instead of a bad—"

"But sometimes you're a shit."

Travis bit the inside of his cheek to keep from laughing. When he had it under control, he solemnly said, "Thank you, Henry. I'll try harder."

"Can I have a cookie now?"

The kid knew when to strike a deal. "I'll split one with you. Then a bath."

Henry struggled out of Travis's grasp and grinned. "You need a bath, too. You stink."

Ten minutes later Travis finally popped open a beer and filled out Henry's field trip permission form. Then he wrote an e-mail to the social worker, asking if she'd had any luck locating extended family for Henry. His fingers froze when he tried to hit Send.

He'd leave it as a draft. Maybe he'd send it tomorrow.

He took a sip of beer and fingered the envelope from the tax office. Why was he so fucking afraid to open it?

Because he was an avoider and a runner, plain and simple. When things got bad, he took off. When Anna had done her stupid teenage drama bit with the stolen bracelet, he'd left Big Verde rather than stay and defend himself. When his dad got sick, he joined the Army. What if the amount owed in taxes was too much to fathom? Just the thought of it made him want to pack his bags.

Henry squealed and splashed in the tub.

He couldn't run this time. Not until he'd taken care of business.

He tore at the corner of the envelope just as his phone buzzed.

Fuck. Collect call from a third-party provider. It was Scott. Prison calls usually meant money for cigarettes or some stupid shit like that, and Travis often ignored them. But he needed to make sure Scott had signed the paperwork about selling Happy Trails. He downed his beer before answering.

"Collect call from a resident at the Texas State Penitentiary at Huntsville. Will you accept the charges?"

As usual, Travis hesitated for about seven seconds before replying that he would. The hesitation was real, he dreaded talking to Scott, and it had the bonus of making Scott nervous.

"Took you long enough," Scott said.

"Did you sign the papers about selling the ranch?"

"Whoa. No small talk? Can't I just call to talk to my little brother?"

"Not on my dime."

Henry screeched and laughed in the tub, and something tightened around Travis's heart like a noose. Would this dumb shit even ask about his kid?

"I haven't seen the papers yet. It's not like I have a butler skipping in with my mail and slippers every evening."

"Did you know we owe back taxes on this place? You said you and Lisa would take care of property taxes in exchange for living on the ranch."

"I didn't really get to live on it all that long, now did I?"

"That's your own fault. Your wife and son lived on it and somebody should have paid the taxes."

Henry and Lisa had probably never been more than a blip on the radar of Scott's self-centered universe, so Travis wasn't surprised by Scott's dismissal. "I figured Lisa would do it."

"Well, she didn't."

"Just pay it. Didn't the Army give you some money?"

"I haven't gotten my final check yet. And it probably won't be enough."

"*Probably* won't be enough? How much do we owe? Do you even know?"

Travis put his phone on speaker mode and set it down. He peeled back the corner of the envelope while sweat prickled the back of his neck. Slowly, he grasped the pink paper. He only had to pull it out about an inch before the number came into view.

"Jesus Christ. It's thirty-six thousand dollars."

"What?" Scott yelled, his voice ringing like tin through the phone's speaker.

This was more than three or four years' worth of back taxes. Their dad hadn't paid up during the final years of his life. Why hadn't Travis known anything about this?

Because you ran, dumbass. And never looked back.

"Brother, you better get your money from the Army and pay—"

"It won't be enough," Travis hissed. "How much do you think an enlisted man makes?"

"Don't you have a job waiting in Austin? Call that buddy of yours and ask for an advance."

"An advance of more than an entire year's pay? Are you kidding me?"

"Well, you'd better do something. Otherwise we'll lose the whole place. You realize that, right? But we'll both be rich if you can sell Happy Trails. Make sure it happens."

"You're going to set aside a chunk for Henry, right? This could take care of college for sure, and probably set him up pretty well with some proper investing."

There was a long pause.

"Did that social worker lady ever find a family for him?"

"You and I are his family." Poor kid.

"I'm not really daddy material—"

"No shit."

"It might be better for Henry if I just terminate my rights."

Travis let that sink in for a moment. The bastard didn't want to share his piece of the pie with his own kid. That's all it amounted to. Without another word, Travis softly touched his phone and hung up.

Chapter

Nineteen

❦

Maggie lay in her darkened room, propped up on one elbow, replaying the day in her head. It was like a stupid broken record.

She couldn't shake the look on Travis's face when he realized she'd brought Norbert and Alex to help. She should have known he'd bristle. He was stubborn and hellbent on doing everything himself.

He'd practically ignored her for the rest of the day.

He hadn't ignored Anna, though. Maggie had felt small and invisible, the total opposite from last night when the world had shrunk to just her and Travis. When she'd looked into his eyes, and it hadn't felt like remembering someone from her past. It had felt like looking into a future she hadn't seen coming but had always known existed. Those blue eyes behind the lenses of his glasses...they'd felt like *home.*

And they'd avoided looking at her all day.

But that kiss, though. It had been so hot. So sweet. And it had sent familiar shockwaves coursing through her body, which had initially cried, *Wolf!* But she hadn't needed a sexy costume to get a rise out of Travis. Unlike the wolf, who wanted a fantasy in fishnets, Travis had desired *her*.

Until today.

She rolled over, getting twisted up in her nightie, before flopping onto her back, lifting her ass, and dragging the hem back down where it belonged. She'd bought the stupid thing—black and lacy—at Cathy's Closet in town. Cathy had been curious, and Maggie had told her it was a gift for a shower. She'd been too embarrassed to admit it was for herself. That she'd bought it because the Big Bad Wolf had asked her to wear sexy lingerie last night, and the truth was, she hadn't had any.

Now it was serving as a torture device. She'd never get to sleep tonight, not with her nightgown trying to kill her.

She eyed the nightstand drawer. Five minutes with her silver bullet vibe—endearingly nicknamed Mr. Tatum—would take care of at least some of her restlessness. She slid open the drawer and dug around. Aha! He was hiding beneath *Bound and Determined*, the paperback she'd checked out for book club. She'd barely started the silly thing, and book club was next week. She squinted at the cover—a woman's near-naked ass and bound wrists. She might as well read it since she would soon be forced into idle chitchat about it. Maybe it would take her mind off things.

Leaving Mr. Tatum behind for Plan B, she pulled out the book, leaned back, and opened it to page twenty-seven, which she'd dog-eared. There were probably library rules against dog-earing pages, so she tried to un-dog-ear it by bending the corner back the other way. This made the whole situation worse, possibly permanent, and she'd just flunked book club with what the other readers would consider a crime against humanity.

With one more fluff of the pillow, she began to read:

Celeste didn't have time to ponder her predicament or how she'd managed to land herself in Ethan's bedroom. She

needed to talk her way out of this, and she needed to do it
quickly. She wasn't some drunken sorority girl who couldn't
look out for herself. She was Celeste Harrington, CEO of
Harrington Inc.

"Ethan, I demand you take these handcuffs off this very
minute."

"Or what?" Ethan said, easy smile on his lips, as if he didn't
have a care in the world. As if he didn't have to return to
work the next morning, hoping he still had a job as Celeste's
assistant. "Are you going to fire me?"

"I'd love nothing more than to fire your ass," she spat.

Ethan moved closer, but Celeste didn't flinch. "And I'd
love to set fire to yours—with this paddle."

"You are so out of a job."

"Time to show you who's boss, Ms. Harrington."

Why were her panties so wet?

Surprisingly, Maggie related to that question. The book was effec-
tive. Unless, of course, you were trying to go to sleep. She could
turn to Mr. Tatum. But he wasn't much of a talker. And right now,
she wanted somebody to talk to her the way Ethan talked to Celeste
Harrington.

Forget Mr. Tatum. She pulled out her phone.

Full moon tonight, Wolfie. Are you in control of yourself?

She counted the seconds. When she got to ten, she picked up
her book.

Ping!

She dropped the book like she'd been caught with porn. Because
she basically had.

Total control. As usual.

A chill went down her spine. When it hit the end of the
road, it raced back up as a thrill. She should respond with something awesome. She waited for a brilliant bit of witty banter to

materialize out of thin air. It didn't, so she typed out a very clever Ha.

Her wolf responded immediately.

I'm sure you're texting me in the middle of the night because you want to discuss lunar cycles. Not because you're horny.

Her thumbs hovered, hesitating. But then she went for it.

Up late reading erotica.

The phone was silent. She'd stunned it. Shocked it. It was probably dead. Then finally, Is it a fairy tale? I like those.

A fairy tale would be convenient. But alas, Maggie was reading plain old smut.

BDSM tale.

Seconds ticked by before the wolf finally spoke up.

???

Could it be he didn't know what BDSM was? Come to think of it, Maggie didn't even know what all the letters stood for. And it wasn't as if most guys had read *Fifty Shades* or the latest issue of *Cosmopolitan*. Not that she had, either, but didn't everyone know about this currently popular kink? Time to school the wolf.

The heroine has been a very bad girl. She's bending over for a spanking.

There. That should do it. She'd spelled it out for him.

Children's book?

Or not. How was she supposed to sext with the wolf if he thought she was reading *Anne of Green Gables*?

No!

The wolf responded with a devil emoji. He'd been messing with her. Wolves do not sleep in clothes. How about LLRH?

Oh! She wouldn't even have to lie.

Black lace nightie. Very short. Very sheer.

She rubbed her legs together and waited.

I want to do some very big bad wolfish things to you.

Now they were getting somewhere.

Like what?

Discipline first. You're wearing a naughty nightie.

The wolf wasn't as naive as he'd seemed.

It is so naughty. You can see everything.

Was she really doing this?

Like your hard nipples?

Maggie shivered. Her nipples were rock hard and rubbing against the lace.

Yes.

Bad girl. Are you wet too?

Maggie gasped. She should have seen that one coming.

Maybe.

She couldn't bring herself to tell him the truth, which was yes, of course she was. The tiny strip of satin that barely covered her bits felt cool and damp against her skin.

Take off your panties.

She could keep them on and say she'd taken them off. The wolf would never know.

NOW.

Maggie jumped at the sight of the all caps. The wolf using all caps was hot. Quickly, she slipped her panties down her thighs, past her knees and ankles, and then kicked them to the floor.

Okay! I did.

She couldn't believe she'd done it. She should feel incredibly silly, but she didn't. She was a bit embarrassed, though. But she could always fake it. She could pretend to do what he asked. He wouldn't know.

Don't even think about faking.

Geez! He was good. She sent an awkward "thumbs up" and waited. He didn't respond. The thumb probably killed his boner. If he'd even had one. What if *he* was the one faking? What if he was sitting on the couch in a pair of dirty sweats watching television and drinking a beer and pretending to sext?

Spread your legs. Nice and slow.

Okay. He was good at pretending. She obeyed. And it felt so very dirty.

Wider. Pull your knees up.

It felt like the wolf was watching her. Heat spread across her cheeks as she pulled her knees up and did as ordered. Then she picked up her phone.

Somebody's an impatient puppy.

But you're the one in obedience training. Pull up your gown and expose your breasts.

The room was chilly, but Maggie was on fire. She slowly pulled the lace up her body, shivering as it brushed her nipples. The light sheen of perspiration on her chest turned into gooseflesh when the cool air kissed her skin. Her nipples puckered as if touched by the wolf's breath.

Lick your finger and brush it over your nipples.

Oh God. They couldn't possibly get any harder, but she did as he said. She was completely under his control now. The day spent ordering people around and making decisions melted into a hazy bliss as she became the wolf's pliable puppet to do with as he pleased. Her muscles relaxed beneath the surrender, yet at the same time every nerve in her body was hypersensitive. Her blood warmed the surface of her skin and flooded to parts that swelled with need. She felt like a flower that had just opened under the sun. Without waiting for the wolf's orders, she arched her back and pulled her knees up higher.

Ping!

It took all her concentration to see what he'd ordered her to do now.

If I were there I'd check to see how wet you are. Since I'm not you have to do it yourself.

She didn't need to check. But she knew what he wanted her to do, and she did it. As soon as she touched herself, she dang near had an orgasm.

Don't you dare come.

The man was psychic.

I'm very wet.

Hard nipples. Dripping wet. You need a spanking.

Just like Celeste Harrington!

Yes. I'm a bad girl.

As soon as she sent the message, she realized the silliness of it. The difference between her situation and Celeste's was that there was nobody in Maggie's bedroom to administer punishment.

Three slaps LRRH. I'm going easy on you.

She couldn't very well spank herself, now could she? Were they going to pretend?

Did you do it?

Do what? Maybe he really did expect her to do it herself.

I'm not in the right position. Also, you're killing the mood with junior high ass slapping dance moves.

Who said anything about your ass? And you're in the perfect position.

The perfect position...What? He wanted her to spank herself *there?* Even poor Celeste hadn't been asked to do that.

Maybe this was the place where she'd lie—Sure, I did that. It was great. Bye now!

Ping!

Maggie jumped and shamefacedly looked at her phone.

A picture popped up. Lower abdomen with a thumb hooked inside the waistband of a pair of black Hanes briefs, pulled down low enough to show off one side of his "V" and a nice leftward leaning bulge. She was weak with need and impatient for that waistband to dip lower.

Need some encouragement? I go lower after you've done it.

It was all so very encouraging! Maybe she would consider it—*Ping!*

NOW. Three slaps because you're a bad girl.

She closed her eyes. Could she do this? More important, *why* would she do this? Because she was a bad girl, that's why. And because the wolf had told her to. She braced herself for the possible sting and definite embarrassment and then: *Slap! Slap! Slap!*

Okay, so it wasn't very hard. But it still stung. Maggie let out the breath she'd been holding just as the sting was replaced by tingling warmth. *Ooh.* She didn't want to wait for further instructions. She *couldn't* wait for further instructions. Her fingers brushed the spot where her nerves were lit up, where she was swollen with the need for release. Without the wolf's permission, she reached lower, rocking her hips. Her own breath filled her ears as she sought the perfect balance of touch and imagination— and oh, how her imagination went into overdrive. *Those abs. That bulge.*

It didn't take long. Mr. Tatum had just been put to shame.

Ping!

WHAT DID YOU JUST DO?

How did he know? Still panting and engulfed in flames, she fumbled with her phone.

I only did what you asked.

Plus a bit more.

I think you did too much.

No! He couldn't possibly know.

Her pulse had just begun to slow down but now it raced back up. Did she accidentally have FaceTime on? Had he been watching? Listening? She frantically checked. Nope. The wolf was just guessing.

Took way too long Little Red Riding Hood.

I'm a slow spanker. Do I still get another pic?

What you get is another punishment.

Ooh! That sounded like a decent idea.

Give me a minute to recover from this one.

A minute was probably all it would take.

Not tonight LRRH. This was fun but I've had a bad day. Should probably call it a night.

This was jarring. She'd nearly forgotten the wolf was a real person. A man she'd teased with, danced with, *had actual sex with*...and he'd had a bad day.

Want to talk about it?

Maggie stared at the phone for nearly five minutes before the wolf texted back.

No. And you already made it better. Get some sleep LRRH.

Her phone stayed quiet, and Maggie turned off the light. The wolf had had a bad day. He hadn't told her about it, per se. But he'd shared something personal. A weird thing was cropping up between them. It felt like trust.

Maggie rolled over and snuggled into her pillow. She was fully sated and pleasantly sleepy. But then her eyes popped open.

How could she trust a man in a mask who hadn't even told her his name?

Chapter Twenty

❧

Travis sat bleary-eyed at his kitchen table. He'd just returned from driving Henry down the lane to catch the bus. He had about ten minutes to chug down some coffee and scarf a Pop-Tart. His eyes darted to the clock on the wall. *Make that five minutes.*

He'd snagged only a couple of hours of sleep last night, thanks to Little Red Riding Hood. He felt as if he'd been smacked by a train and then run over by a semi. Come to think of it, that's what he felt like most of the time lately—a wreck. But this morning's exhaustion didn't carry the usual tension associated with the single working parent gig. His muscles felt like putty and he almost had a buzz going on. He had that wrecked, exhausted, loopy feeling that followed a good massage. Or a night of amazing sex.

It hadn't been *real* sex. But close enough. Without it, he'd have been up all night clenching his jaw with worry over the back taxes. He appreciated the distraction.

He took a gulp of coffee and leaned back in his chair, grinning. Maggie had absolutely zero self-control. He was glad he hadn't sent the second promised photo. It required some artful maneuvering to keep his tattoo out of the frame, and dick pics were generally a bad idea anyway. Last night he'd been like a drunken teenager, thinking everything sounded like a good idea, including using his only phone to carry on an incognito sexting conversation with the woman who was basically his boss.

He hadn't expected things to go so far. A couple of jokes or a few sexy comments were all he had in mind. But Miss Mary Margaret had surprised him. Who would have guessed she was into erotica? More specifically, who knew she was into *BDSM* erotica? And since he'd still been a little heated over her bringing her own guys in to finish the rocks, the Big Bad Wolf had doled out some punishment. *And she'd liked it.*

He laughed, thinking about her sleepwear. Black lacy nightie, his ass. She'd probably been wearing her basketball pajamas. Although, on second thought, she was honest to a fault. He swallowed. *Damn. She'd been wearing sexy lingerie.*

There were so many sides to Maggie, and he wanted to get to know them all. His Pop-Tart popped up. He grabbed it and licked some cherry goo off his fingers, thinking about how Maggie's fingers had surely dipped between her legs. Had she really done everything he'd asked? Had she really spanked herself in that way?

Yep. She had.

It was as if they'd been physically together in the room. The energy connecting them had been tangible. *Real.* All his problems had disappeared, and he'd been right there with Maggie. Watching her. Touching her. *Wanting her.*

He crammed half the Pop-Tart into his mouth and shifted in his seat. There was absolutely no way for a decent outcome. He could never fess up about being the Big Bad Wolf now. Not after what he'd made her do. How could he look her in the eyes?

There would be no next time. He meant it. If nothing else, he was going to fuck up and call her Maggie instead of Little Red

Riding Hood. And there was the phone situation. It was sheer luck that they hadn't already exchanged numbers.

He mentally made a note to get a new phone—like *today*—then crammed the last bit of Pop-Tart into his mouth before standing up and grabbing his sack lunch off the counter. There was absolutely no part of his day he was looking forward to...except for one.

Maggie.

Ping!

Dropping his lunch back on the counter, he frantically dug his phone out of his pocket. Was Little Red Riding Hood ready for some early morning shenanigans?

Hey Big Guy. Hope you got some sleep last night.

Yep. The intelligent decision to never, ever sext Maggie again went straight out the window.

You know exactly how much sleep I got last night. I hope you learned your lesson.

He waited for her to text back, like a puppy panting for a treat.

My lesson about what?

She wanted to play dumb. Where was she right now? Sitting in her Jeep at the work site? Maybe she was in her office at Petal Pushers, with the door locked, the shades pulled, and a dirty little grin on her face as she egged him on.

Do you need another spanking? Who cared if he was late for work? Maggie was being a bad girl.

Who do you think you're talking to?

He knew exactly who he was talking to. A very bad girl who needs another spanking. This time on her bare ass.

His mind hummed as he considered his options. Maybe he'd make her remove her panties and go commando. Nah. They'd already done that. Maybe he'd make her masturbate at work. He started to text, but she beat him to it.

I am a bad girl. It's been a long time. I'm glad you remember.

His brow furrowed, and a sense of unease crawled up his spine. That didn't make much sense. He squinted at the screen.

Holy shit. He was sexting Annabelle! He damn near dropped the phone. He had to think. The truth seemed to be the only option. I am so sorry. I thought you were somebody else.

He broke out in a delayed sweat as a wave of nausea washed over him. This was no game. What was he doing?

Too bad. If you ever need another ass to spank—or need a spanking yourself—you obviously have my number.

What should he say? *No thanks. I'm full up on asses to spank.* Seconds ticked by before he finally tucked the phone back into his pocket. Best to pretend it never happened. Maybe Annabelle would do the same.

* * *

Maggie poured coffee into her travel mug and grabbed her bag. She was late again! But the Big Bad Wolf hadn't let her get any sleep.

She blasted through the door with Pop in pursuit. She needed to beat the dump truck. Otherwise, the driver would automatically dump the topsoil in the place farthest away from where it needed to go. Murphy's Law ruled construction sites with an iron fist.

She'd call Travis. He was probably already there, and he could make sure the dirt was dumped in a convenient spot. She started the Jeep and her phone synced up with a pleasant chime. Time to give a shout out to her drunk girlfriend, Siri.

"Siri, please phone Travis."

"Okay," Siri said.

Maggie breathed a sigh of relief. Siri was being uncharacteristically cooperative.

"Calling Mavis now."

Maggie slapped the steering wheel in frustration. "No. Not Mavis. *Travis.*" Mavis was her hairdresser. The last thing Maggie needed was a thirty-minute conversation during a fifteen-minute ride about why she wasn't married.

"Who would you like me to call?"

"Siri, call Travis."

"I am sorry. There is no one in your contacts by that name."

Maggie frowned. Surely, she'd called Travis before, although now that she thought about it, she couldn't remember ever having done so. "Are you sure?"

"I am one hundred percent certain there is no one by that name in your contacts."

Well then, she'd call JD. He was usually on site early. "Siri, please call JD."

"Jay-Z is an American rapper and music producer, and he is also not among your contacts."

"Jesus Christ," she murmured.

"Jesus Christ is not among your contacts either."

"Siri, let's start over. Please call JD Mayes."

"Calling Jazzy Maids now."

When Maggie finally pulled under the big oak tree and parked next to JD's truck, her nerves were rattled, she was covered in dog hair, and someone was coming by to clean her house at three. She looked around for Travis's truck and didn't see it.

"Well, that figures," she said to Pop. "Hard to find good help."

She reached for the handle, but the door opened of its own accord.

JD Mayes, always the gentleman, stood in a golden ray of sunshine. "Good morning, pretty girl," he said with a wink.

"Why do you do that?"

"Open the door for a lady? It's how I was raised."

"No. I mean the flirting."

"I don't flirt. I give genuine compliments."

"Whatever."

Pop flew over Maggie's shoulder in a cloud of hair and landed in JD's arms.

"There's my pooch," JD crooned.

"Oh, brother." Maggie sighed, hopping out of the Jeep. JD even flirted with dogs. That should tell her something.

"How long are you going to be mad at me?"

JD stood there, earnestly staring at her, while giving Pop a groan-and-drool-inducing ear massage. Both looked totally clueless.

"Now's not the time to get into it."

JD shrugged his shoulders. "Well, I've got a few phone calls to make. I'm going to go sit in my truck for a while."

"You do that."

JD turned and headed toward his truck, pulling his phone out of the back pocket of his Wranglers.

Maybe it *was* time to get into it. "JD, wait."

He stopped in his tracks and turned, removing his hat as if somebody had died, which Maggie knew was merely his *I'm just a little boy—please don't hurt me* gig. He gazed at her through his lashes, and there it was. The glint. The hint of a grin.

"Stop flirting with me."

The hint of a grin turned into a full smile. "Aw, Maggie—"

"No. I'm serious."

The flirty pretense slipped as JD held his hands out. "Why are you acting so weird? And why don't we ever hang out anymore?"

"Because you're not interested in me, and yet you flirt with me constantly. It's rude, JD. And quite frankly, it's mean."

JD's mouth hung open as if she'd smacked him over the head with the plans she held in her hand. After a few seconds he replaced his hat, his signal that things were getting serious. "I'm sorry if you've misinterpreted my friendliness for flirting."

"I haven't. You're a flirt. Everyone says so. You just flirted with Pop for crying out loud. And I don't know why I didn't see it all these years. I don't know why I didn't get it, that your flirtation with me was no more significant than your flirtation with Pop."

"You know I care about you."

"Do you want to make out? Or maybe even have sex? Because that's what flirting insinuates."

JD tilted the brim of his hat down—nervous gesture that had the added benefit of shielding his eyes. But it didn't hide his cheeks, and they were flaming red. "I'm sorry. It's a habit. I've been doing it my whole life." He pulled the brim of his hat even lower and stared at the ground.

Maggie didn't care if she was making JD uncomfortable. He'd done it to her for years. "Well, stop it."

JD removed his hat again and held it in front of his belt buckle with both hands. He didn't look up, though. She rolled her eyes. He was doing the *Let us pray.*

"Yes, ma'am," he said with the earnestness of a Boy Scout. "But Travis flirts with you, too." His earnestness was replaced by a playful grin. "I bet he wants to make out with you."

"He wouldn't even look at me yesterday. Spent his time chatting with Anna."

"You shouldn't have hired labor. That's his part of the job."

"I was trying to help."

"It wasn't your place. It was unprofessional."

That stung. "I won't do it again."

"Good. Because he needs this job. Maybe that's why he gave Anna a bit of attention. Had you thought about that?"

No. She hadn't. Time to turn the topic back to JD. "His flirting doesn't hold a candle to yours. And you should be ashamed. There are rumors going around about you."

JD looked up sharply. "Rumors?"

"Bubba says you're going to Austin an awful lot. You're seeing someone, right?"

JD's mouth opened and shut again, as if he were going to deny it but had then thought better of it. She'd struck a nerve.

"You should know you can't keep secrets in Big Verde," Maggie chided.

His pink cheeks faded, and he turned a little pale.

"That's what I thought. Whoever she is, I doubt she'd appreciate all the flirting you do. So, knock it off."

JD pulled his hat down as low as it would go. "Maggie, I need to tell you—"

Beep! Beep! Beep!

The topsoil was here, and sure enough, the truck was backing up to dump it in the worst possible spot. Maggie didn't have any more time for JD. "If you've got something to tell me, you can do it tomorrow. Claire's coming over for the game."

"I'm invited? Does this mean we're hanging out again?"

She acted like she didn't hear him and ran off to catch a dump truck.

Chapter
Twenty-One

❦

Travis pulled up to the job site just in time to see Maggie and Pop attacking a dump truck. Or at least that's what it looked like.

He grabbed a shovel out of the back of his truck. Today was going to be spent spreading dirt the old-fashioned way: with his two hands.

His nose picked up on something floral and spicy.

"Hey there, Big Bad *Dom*."

His heart seized over the words *big* and *bad* as he turned to face Anna. *Calm down. She doesn't know.* He'd talked to her at the gala, so she'd seen him in the dumb mask. That's probably all she was referring to. She didn't know he was sexting with Maggie.

"Uh, yeah, about that spanking thing," he sputtered. "I was just messing around. Texting a friend. I'd prefer we not talk about it."

Anna licked her lips. "I didn't figure you for a spanker," she said, boldly ignoring him. "Who's the lucky bad girl? Anyone I know?"

Yaps cut through the air, coming closer and closer. Pop was heading their way, and his bad girl owner was right behind him. "Look who decided to show up," Maggie said.

She was out of breath from chasing the dump truck, and it made her voice even sexier than usual. He didn't have time to think about her sexy voice, though. Not with warning bells going off in his head—along with red alerts and whatever that sound is that submarines make right before they dive. He needed to get rid of Anna before she continued blabbing about spankings in front of Maggie.

He downed the rest of his coffee and held out his mug to Anna. "I sure could use another cup." Anna took the bait immediately.

"I have a fresh pot in the house."

"Great," he said. But instead of taking his mug, Anna took his arm.

"Why don't you come inside with me? You can fix your coffee however you like—"

"I just take it black," he said, digging in his heels. "Thanks."

Anna gave his arm a jerk. "Come on, silly. You haven't even seen the new crown molding yet."

And he didn't want to. But Anna was about to rip his arm off. He'd follow her inside, get his coffee, and come back out. Hopefully without Anna. "Okay. Sure."

Maggie narrowed her eyes at him. "Don't stare at molding for too long. You've got a crap-ton of dirt to spread."

"Maggie sure is cracking the whip," Anna said, pulling him to the house. Then she let go of his arm and slapped his ass. *Hard.*

"Jesus, Anna. Stop it."

She laughed. "I don't like being left out of the fun."

The urge to turn around and see if Maggie was gawking—he could feel her eyes on his back—was overwhelming. But he kept walking to the patio and opened the French doors for Anna to pass through like a queen.

The great room smelled of sawdust and fresh paint. Their feet echoed across the tile as Anna led the way to the coffeepot, which was about the only thing on the pristine black counters. "Place looks great," he said.

"Do you think so? I don't like the countertops. I'm not sure this is the color I chose, and I've changed my mind about the texture on the walls. I already told JD about it."

She must be driving Bubba and JD fucking crazy. He held out his mug as she filled it, standing way closer than she needed to. He took a small step back and brought his mug to his mouth.

"It's going to be a warm day today," she said.

Weather. Safe subject. "Yep. Another front's coming in, though. Not as big as the last one, but they're back to back—"

"Umm," Anna said, licking her lips. "I like front to front better." She closed the space between them and took his mug away, setting it on the counter.

"Wait a minute. I'm not done with—"

"Oh, you're done."

Her breasts pressed against his chest. She could probably feel his heart rattling his rib cage. He felt seventeen again as his body battled his brain. *This* is what it had been like all those years ago. Anna's relentless pursuit. His resulting awkwardness. And to think women experienced this shit all the time—some on a daily basis. How did they stand it? He took another step backward. "Anna, I've got a lot of work to do—"

"Who's your bad girl, Travis? I'm dying to know."

"I told you. I was just messing around with a friend."

Anna took another step, and Travis backed up against the counter. She had him cornered. "We're friends, aren't we?"

Travis swallowed loudly. "Um—"

The door swung open, and Bubba strolled in. He looked around the room, took in the two of them, and kept a poker face.

"What do you want?" Anna asked.

"I heard rumors about you not liking the countertops," Bubba said. "They're what you ordered." He pulled a wrinkled piece of paper out of his back pocket. "Got the order right here, with your signature. And the receipt."

"Do we have to talk about that right now?" Anna asked, as if she didn't really care about the countertops at all. "Travis and I are having a private conversation."

This was his out. "I'd better start shoveling," he said, scooting around Anna. Bubba gave a subtle wink as Travis passed, so subtle that Travis nearly missed it. As soon as he got outside, he inhaled deeply to clear his mind. He felt almost like he needed a shower and he hadn't even started working yet.

He pulled his cap down and grabbed the shovel just as JD rounded the corner of the house. "I have some good news for you, partner."

"I could use some. Shoot."

"The truck that was coming out here to haul off my front-end loader can't make it until Tuesday. Maggie says you might need it—"

"Maggie needs to mind her own business."

JD laughed. "That might be true, but it's not going to happen. Trust me. I know. But Maggie or no Maggie, the front-end loader is just going to be sitting here, taunting you while you shovel, unless you swallow your pride and use it."

The shovel handle was already burning against the blisters the pickax and wheelbarrow had given him yesterday. It sure would be easier with a front-end loader. And faster—which was even more important.

"Okay. Thanks," he said. "I appreciate it."

Maggie was watching them, and JD gave her a nod. She headed their way, and Travis grinned. Goddammit, he couldn't help it. The wind blew the hair out of her face, showing off the dark eyebrows that didn't quite go with her light blond hair but nevertheless looked perfect on her face.

"You got plans tomorrow?" JD asked. "Claire and I are watching the game at Maggie's. I'm sure she wouldn't mind if you joined us."

Travis stuffed his hands in his work gloves. "Your matchmaker is showing, JD. It's weird. Put it away."

* * *

Travis and JD had been talking about her. That could mean any number of things, but hopefully it meant Travis was going to use JD's front-end loader and get the dirt spread today.

"Do you mind if Travis comes over to watch the game tomorrow?" JD asked.

Instead of rolling out a welcome mat, she rolled her eyes. "Why, JD? Do you need a buffer?"

"No. Well, maybe. But I thought Travis and Henry might enjoy hanging out with us. It's the weekend, you know. People do that on the weekends."

Oh, sure. Drag poor little Henry into this. She looked at Travis, who stood there like a kid waiting to be picked for the softball team. Although maybe he'd rather spend the evening with Anna.

"You're welcome to bring Henry," she said. "I'll need someone intelligent to talk to."

"You might be all talked out by tomorrow evening," JD said. "What's that book you're discussing at book club again? *Down and Dirty*?" He looked at Travis and stage-whispered, "They're reading porn."

She wanted to slap that silly expression right off JD's face. "It's called *Bound and Determined* and it's not porn. It's erotica."

She gave JD a look that would thaw an iceberg.

"I'm not sure Henry and I will make it for the post-erotica book club festivities," Travis said. "But we'll try. It'll depend on when I get back from Austin. I'm going to the farmer's market. We'll be selling Happy Trails beef at the Rancho Cañada Verde stand."

"Oh?" Maggie said. "That sounds awesome."

"Claire is coming to help. Do you want to come along?"

A slight flutter started in her tummy. Butterflies! Maybe they were over the rock thing. "That sounds like fun. But I've got book club in the afternoon."

"You could just come for the morning."

"Y'all are cute. You know that?" JD said.

"Go away, JD. I came *this close* to not even inviting you over for the game. Maybe I'll un-invite you."

JD and Travis looked at each other and shrugged, and then JD adjusted his hat and shook his head with a smirk. "You do what you've got to do, Mighty Mack. And I was just leaving for another site anyway."

Bubba stepped out. "What's up? Are we meeting at Maggie's for the game tomorrow?"

"Shush, Bubba," Maggie said as he closed the door behind him. "I don't want Anna to hear." The absolute *last* thing she wanted was Anna rubbing all over Travis on her own damn couch.

"She went upstairs to her bedroom to pout about something," Bubba said. "I'll bring some wings and beer tomorrow. Trista is going to her sister's place in Round Rock. That means I'll be both hot *and* single. Tell all your friends."

Travis shuffled from one foot to the other. "So, about Austin…"

"I promised I'd take brownies to book club. I'll definitely need to leave early, but it sounds like fun! I'll go."

"Fantastic," Travis said.

Maggie started to turn, but then remembered about the phone number. "I didn't realize it until this morning, but I don't have your phone number."

"I have it," Bubba said, pulling out his phone.

"No, wait!" Travis said. "New number. I got it this morning. I need to give it to everybody."

After they'd exchanged contact info, Bubba took off, leaving them alone.

"Will you be wearing lingerie tomorrow night?" he asked.

Her face erupted into flames. How did he know she'd bought new lingerie? "Pardon?"

"Spurs PJ's. Henry will want to know."

God. She felt stupid. "Sure. We'll make it another pajama party."

Travis did that magic trick—the one where a dimple appeared out of nowhere in his left cheek, nearly obscured by his beard. Then he took off his flannel shirt and tied it around his waist. "Maybe I'll wear some, too," he said casually. "Although I don't usually sleep in any."

And with that, the jerk sauntered off with a shovel perched over his shoulder. He looked back to see if she was watching, and dang it, she was.

Chapter
Twenty-Two
❦

The Texas Farmer's Market was a madhouse of activity. Travis didn't know what he'd expected—booths of zucchini and onions maybe. But it was so much more than that. In addition to every fruit and vegetable in season, there were eggs, meats of every variety, honey, cheeses, herbs, and even growler stations from local breweries.

Taking over the Rancho Cañada Verde stand was easy. Martinez Meat Market had processed several cows, keeping a percentage for themselves. Everything had been packaged, labeled, and frozen solid before being loaded into coolers. Claire had even made a banner with the Happy Trails' brand as a logo.

It looked official.

Luckily, Claire worked the counter, interacting with customers who wanted to know why the sign said HAPPY TRAILS instead of RANCHO CAÑADA VERDE.

"That's right," Claire said to a customer. "Same Black Angus beef. Raised on a small farm right next to Rancho Cañada Verde.

All natural and grass fed. Rancho Cañada Verde is thrilled to endorse Happy Trails beef products."

"Travis, we need a chuck roast," Maggie said. Her eyes twinkled. "This is fun, right? Maybe I could sell some of Honey's apples here, you know, if my neighbor ever gets his cows under control."

Travis ignored the side-eye she gave him, weighed the roast, marked it, and handed it directly to the customer, a young woman in tie-dye. "Enjoy," he said. "It's grass and apple fed. You won't find that just anywhere."

"Cool."

Maggie snorted and poked Travis in the ribs. "Watch it. This is Austin. Apple-fed beef will become a trend."

"Beef bones," Claire said. "And move it. We've got a line."

Travis reached in and grabbed a package. The beef bones were a surprising hit. Maggie said folks made broth out of them, that it was good for fortifying the immune system and aided healing. He might give it a try. It seemed like Henry had the sniffles every other week.

"Here's a bag!" Henry shouted.

It was his job to bag the merchandise, or at least hold the bag open for Claire. And he was obviously having the time of his life.

"You planning on growing into that hat?" Maggie asked him.

Gerome had given Henry a gigantic cowboy hat. "I think I already did," he said, wiggling the hat down over his ears. "See?"

Maggie laughed, then her eyes landed on Travis. "And what about you, cowboy? It looks like you've grown into yours."

Gerome had told him he couldn't sell Black Angus beef while wearing a knit cap like a hippie. And then he'd pulled out a very nice straw Stetson. He'd dropped it on the ground and stepped on the brim before handing it over...*so it doesn't look like you just bought it at a department store.*

As if reading his mind, Maggie reached up and gave his beard a slight tug, which sent a tingle up and down his spine. "I like it," she whispered. "I like it a lot."

Her brown eyes darkened, and the tips of her ears turned pink.

Okay. The woman liked a man in a cowboy hat. Good to know.

"Excuse me," a man asked. "Do you raise turkeys at Happy Trails?"

"Turkeys? Um, no. Sorry," Travis said.

"That's too bad. We used to get our Thanksgiving bird from a small farmer near Moulton. We're looking for someplace closer."

"I'm pretty sure you can get one at your local grocery store," Travis said.

The man raised his eyebrows. "Do you know the conditions those turkeys are raised in? We don't eat meat that's been tortured. We're looking for naturally fed, free-range turkeys. Pigs and chickens, too."

Claire cut in. "And you can be sure that Happy Trails cattle are completely grass fed on one hundred and fifty acres of beautiful Texas Hill Country property. They drink the sweet, crystal-clear water of the Pedernales River, and are not treated with hormones or antibiotics, nor are they finished on corn in feed lots."

Damn. The woman knew her spiel. And it was obvious she felt strongly about it. Just like her daddy.

"Humane husbandry? Like Rancho Cañada Verde?" the man asked.

Travis could answer this one. The cattle had gotten used to eating hay in the pens in preparation for the roundup. All they had to do was close the gate behind them, and then Gerome had shown him how to single out the ones they wanted in the chute. "They're rounded up calmly," he said. "No prods. No loud noises. Heck, we don't even make eye contact—"

"Completely humane," Claire finished. She gave him a look that said, *Don't bore them with the details—these people do not realize the animals get slaughtered before they eat them.*

He shut his mouth. She was probably right. People didn't want to know the truth about where their meat came from. But most folks ate meat, and there were lots of ways to raise it. Most of those ways were downright awful, and Gerome Kowalski had opened Travis's eyes. It was fascinating to learn about the humane husbandry Rancho Cañada Verde was known for. Roundups could be extremely stressful for animals unless done a certain way. Gerome had taught him how to stand quietly where you *didn't* want the cow to go. You didn't look at it directly—just watched with your peripheral vision. No sudden moves while you slowly shuffled forward, while your buddies did the same, until the animal had no place left to go but the chute. Then you closed the traps behind it, one by one, until it walked on into the trailer, happily chewing hay the whole time.

Gerome had told Travis he had a knack for it.

"And do you help?" the man's wife asked Henry.

"Yes ma'am," Henry said. His hat wobbled as he vigorously nodded his head. He hooked his thumbs in his belt and puffed out his little chest. "Happy Trails is my ranch."

* * *

This morning the social worker had called: "Henry has no family other than you and his biological father." Travis had felt like collapsing beneath the weight of those words, and it wasn't until he exhaled that he realized it was from relief. There was no way he would have sent Henry off to live with strangers. His heart had already decided that.

Being all Henry had in the world might be terrifying, but they were family, and one way or another, they'd make it work.

But where would they make it work?

Travis climbed in his truck as a guy on a bike rode past in lime green skinny jeans and an ugly argyle sweater. "Thanks for the beef, man!"

Travis waved. The dude's man-bun was coming loose, but he was doing his best to keep Austin weird. Before Travis knew it, he'd shouted, "See you next month!"

Next month. He wanted to come back next month.

What was it Henry had said earlier? *Happy Trails is my ranch.* What right did Travis have to take him away from it?

None. He had no right to take Henry away from the ranch. And he realized he didn't want to. Henry had been so cute peddling beef. In fact, Travis wasn't sure who'd drawn more customers: Claire in her tight rhinestone-studded jeans, or Henry in his ten-gallon hat.

The farmer's market had given Travis all sorts of crazy ideas about raising free-range turkeys and chickens, goats, bees...maybe even planting a lavender patch. A lady had asked him about school field trips and eco-tourism. His mind was humming with fantastical notions. He couldn't wait to talk to Maggie about it. She'd left early and taken Henry with her. She should have dropped him off with Mrs. Garza by now.

He and Maggie had made such a good team today. Heck, they made a pretty good team as landscapers, too, even though Maggie was a micromanager to the nth degree and couldn't keep her nose out of his business. He liked her nose. And the thought of her being Suzy Homemaker and baking brownies for book club put a grin on his face.

It also gave him an idea. He pulled out his old phone; the one he'd stashed in his glove compartment, so it wouldn't tempt him. *The wolf's phone.*

Just one last time...

What are you doing today? Being a good girl?

He started the truck.

Ping!

That was fast.

A very good girl. I'm about to bake brownies.

He couldn't answer her right away. She needed to wait for it, worrying that bottom lip of hers while wondering what he'd make her do. And what would he make her do? A sly grin spread slowly across his face.

Do you cook often?

The response was immediate. HA HA HA HA HA. (That means nope.)

Do you have an apron?

Since she still probably had Honey's dentures in a jar somewhere—he shuddered a little—she probably also had an apron. Although like Honey's dentures, she'd probably never worn it.

Yes.

Bingo.

Good. Wear it. And nothing else.

He was very pleased with himself.

Nothing?

Nothing.

He was grinning from ear to ear when he decided to use the wolf's phone for good, instead of evil, and search for a nearby place to eat. Since this was Austin, he started to narrow the search by specifying *non-vegan*. But then he stopped. After all he'd learned about raising beef, did he really want to eat meat if he didn't know where it came from? He tailored the search by adding the words *local*, *organic*, and *beef*.

Hot damn. A grass-fed burger joint was ten minutes away. He headed for South Lamar Street, satisfied that he was about to enjoy a good meal while Little Red Riding Hood baked brownies in her birthday suit. A stream of X-rated images flowed through his mind. He particularly liked the one where Maggie was bent over, retrieving brownies from the oven. He was able to entertain himself with that all the way to the restaurant.

The parking lot was packed. A big white pickup caught his eye. White pickups weren't a rarity, but this one had the L&M

Construction logo on its door. What was JD doing in Austin? Travis headed inside, happy he wouldn't have to eat alone.

There were three or four folks in line in front of him, so he looked around. All the indoor tables were full and there was no sign of JD. He must be sitting outside. Travis went back to examining the menu, which had his mouth watering with its pictures of thick, juicy burgers.

It was almost his turn to order when his phone rang. It was Mrs. Garza. "Everything going okay?" Travis asked.

He expected her to give him a blow-by-blow of what Henry was doing because that's what she usually did. But all she said was, "We're fine, Mr. Blake. But when are you coming home?"

She'd never called him Mr. Blake before. And her voice was filled with tension.

"I'm grabbing a bite to eat, then I'll be on my way. You sure everything's okay? I can skip lunch and come straight home."

Travis had a bad feeling. Maybe Henry was sick.

"Everything is fine now, but earlier—"

"What happened earlier?" Had there been a fire? Had Henry choked on a pretzel? Did he have a rock up his nose? The list of alarming things that had possibly gone wrong was endless.

"It's just that we had a visitor."

Who would be stopping by to visit?

"Your brother, Scott," Mrs. Garza continued. "I didn't know what to do. I told him he'd have to come back later. Was that okay?"

There it was. The clenching of dread in his belly, the tightening of the noose around his neck. Scott must have gotten out early.

"Did he see Henry?"

"No. He was upstairs, and I didn't invite your brother in."

"You did the right thing, Mrs. Garza."

"Should I let you know if he comes back?"

"Yes, ma'am. Please do. I'll be home as soon as I can."

Travis wasn't hungry anymore, but it was his turn at the counter, so he mechanically ordered. Then he took his number and wandered out to the patio. He felt so numb he could hardly tell which way his feet carried him. There was no way he could let Scott take Henry. But did he have any right to stop him?

A white Stetson stood out among the crowd, and the sight of it calmed his raw, nervous energy. He was in bad need of a friend. Travis waved, but JD didn't see him. He didn't want to shout across the restaurant, so he quietly wove in and out of the tables, carrying his number and making his way toward JD, who was nursing an ice-cold beer. There was a second bottle on the table, so maybe JD wasn't alone. Didn't Maggie say he was seeing a lady in Austin? Travis hesitated. He didn't want to bust up a lunch date.

While he stood indecisive, a man in a gray suit entered the patio from the parking lot. JD looked up and smiled at the guy, who had a sharp haircut to match his suit.

Not the type of guy JD usually hung out with. Maybe this was a business lunch.

He expected JD to push his chair back, remove his hat, and rise for a handshake like the gentleman cowboy he was. But JD remained in his seat, smiling, as the newcomer walked over. He removed the cap from the second bottle of beer and pushed it toward the man just as he leaned over and gave JD a kiss. *On the lips.*

Travis's mind clicked along, gears grinding, and arrived at the only logical conclusion. JD was obviously not *out*. At least not to folks in Big Verde. He wouldn't appreciate being spotted by Travis. Maybe there was a free table inside now. Or fuck it, maybe he should just cancel his order and leave.

JD looked up just as Travis was about to turn. Their eyes locked.

Nothing to do now but smile and act normal. He waved and walked to their table.

The other man looked to see who JD was gawking at.

"Hi, JD," Travis said as normally as he could muster. "What are you doing in Austin today?" He sure hoped his outside didn't match his inside. And that his voice only sounded unusually high in his own ears.

JD stood. Travis expected him to pull the brim of his hat down, but he didn't. Good for him. The other man stood, too, and held out his hand. "Hi, I'm Gabriel Castro."

Travis shook Gabriel's hand and waited for JD to finally find his voice.

"Gabriel, this is Travis Blake. He's from Big Verde."

A huge smile appeared on Gabriel's face. "Nice to meet you."

Awkwardness descended in the form of silence. Travis wished there was a way to act as if a big secret hadn't just been unwittingly revealed, but saying, *How 'bout them Spurs?* seemed like a bad idea. In fact, he should probably find another table.

"Well, it was nice to meet you, Gabriel. I'll see you later, JD."

JD still didn't have a speck of color in his face. Even his lips were white. Did he think Travis was going to run back to Big Verde and blab?

"I haven't met many of JD's friends," Gabriel said. "Why don't you join us?"

JD's mouth tightened into a straight line.

"I don't know…"

A man arrived with a tray holding a gigantic double hamburger and a side of onion rings. "Number eighty-nine?"

"That's me," Travis replied.

"Sit with us," Gabriel said. "There's plenty of room. No need to take up another table."

The server set his food down and hurried off. It would be more awkward to leave than to just graciously accept Gabriel's offer.

"Thanks," he said, taking a seat. JD and Gabriel followed his lead and sat down, as well. "I wasn't looking forward to eating by myself. I saw JD's truck in the parking lot and came in here looking for him. I've been at the farmer's market."

Gabriel began snatching fries out of JD's basket. "No problem." Then he elbowed JD. "Thanks for waiting, cowboy. Did you even order me a burger?"

"You can have mine. I'm not hungry anymore." Only the lower half of JD's face was visible. But he looked pissed.

"Aw, come on," Gabriel said with twinkling eyes and a smile that lit up the room. "Eat up, man. It's your coming-out party."

Travis somehow managed to hold back a grin.

JD lifted the brim of his hat and narrowed his eyes at Gabriel. "This isn't anything to joke about."

Gabriel sighed. "I know, cowboy. But aren't you at least a little relieved?"

"No," JD said, adjusting his hat on his head. *Once, twice, three times.* He jerked his chin at Travis. "I guess you're pretty surprised."

Travis wiped his greasy chin and fingers on a napkin— motherfucking excellent onion rings—and took a sip of iced tea because he hadn't had the foresight to order a beer. "Not really."

JD's mouth fell open and he raised the rim of his Stetson. His eyebrows rose in incredulity. "You aren't?"

"Nah. You can't keep a secret in Big V."

"It's the pressed Wranglers, right?" Gabriel said with a grin. "With the seam down the front?"

"There've been a few rumors going around," Travis said.

JD looked downright incensed. "About me?"

"Who else? People have been saying you're seeing someone in Austin. We just didn't know who."

JD grunted. "Well, just wait until they find out."

"I'm not going to tell them," Travis said. And he meant it. He wasn't even going to tell Maggie, although he sure wished JD would.

"Have you two known each other a long time?" Gabriel asked.

"I went to school with him and his brother, Scott."

"Is Scott still in Big Verde, too?"

"Scott's in prison," JD said.

It irked Travis just a little that JD blurted that out. But maybe he wanted to share somebody's secret, too.

"Oh, wow," Gabriel said. "That's rough."

"Actually, he's out," Travis said. "Mrs. Garza just called and said he came by the ranch."

JD leaned forward in his seat. All his embarrassment and misery seemed to fade away as he said, "Did he see Henry?"

JD cared about Henry. Shit, it seemed the whole motherfucking town cared about Henry. It was his home. Maybe the crazy ideas creeping into Travis's head about turning Happy Trails into a real ranch—one that earned money—weren't so crazy. Something inside him shifted. It didn't quite settle yet, but it had definitely shifted.

"Travis, did you hear me?" JD asked. "Did he see Henry?"

"No. But he'll be back. Jesus, I hope he doesn't want to stay at the house."

"Who's Henry?" Gabriel asked.

"My five-year-old nephew."

"Your brother is the boy's father?" Gabriel asked.

Travis nodded.

"And where's the mom? Out of the picture?"

"You could say that," Travis said. "She died earlier this year. Cancer."

"That's too bad," Gabriel said. "My condolences."

"Anyway, I'm Henry's only family, other than Scott. And I think I'd like to…" He swallowed, knowing the words he wanted to say but fearing the reality of giving them form. He cleared his throat. "I'd like to adopt Henry. That is, if Scott goes through with giving up his parental rights."

There. He'd said it. And the noose that had been tightening around his neck for the past few weeks was finally loosened.

"That's great news!" JD said. "Really great news, Travis. You and I both know Scott has no business—"

"Are you sure your brother will relinquish his rights?" Gabriel asked.

"Scott doesn't want Henry," JD said. "He's a selfish bastard. Everybody in Big Verde knows that."

Travis agreed. "And even if he didn't want to give Henry up, wouldn't the courts see that I'm the better choice?"

"That would depend on a lot of things. But the state of Texas generally tries to reunite families. Scott is the biological father, so as long as he makes a good faith effort to turn himself around and live by the rules—"

Travis snorted. "He can't."

"Still. If he wants his son, it won't be an easy termination," Gabriel said.

A throbbing pain began building behind Travis's eyeballs. He didn't like the thought of Henry caught up in anything messy. "I think I might need a lawyer."

"Well, today's your lucky day," Gabriel replied. He pulled out a card and set it on the table next to a ketchup-smeared napkin. "I practice family law."

Travis took the card with gratitude. "Thanks, man. I might take you up on it. I don't have a lot of money right now—"

"Let's not talk about that. You're a friend of JD's. I'll do whatever I can to help you and Henry."

Relief washed over him. A month ago, it had been him and Henry against the world. Now he had friends and people who felt like family.

Chapter
Twenty-Three

༄

Maggie sat awkwardly on Alice's sofa, watching as everyone took dainty bites out of the brownies. Something was wrong. You shouldn't look like you had a cockroach in your mouth when eating a brownie.

"Mm," said Alice. "Yummy."

If it was so yummy, why did Alice look like she was suffering from a leg cramp?

"I'll just save the rest for later," she said, setting her plate on the coffee table.

Claire raised her eyebrows at Maggie. *What the heck did you do to the brownies?*

Maggie shrugged. She'd followed the recipe. Maybe she'd been a bit distracted because she'd been wearing an old frilly apron of Honey's and nothing else.

She picked up a brownie. It looked perfectly fine. She sniffed it. It smelled fine, too. She took a small bite, and her taste buds seized. Her salivary glands gushed in an attempt to wash out the offending foreign object. Maggie shuddered, looking for a place to spit.

"Here," Claire said, holding out a napkin just as a string of chocolate drool escaped Maggie's mouth in a slow descent toward Alice's carpet. Maggie took the napkin and spit the brownie into it.

"Well, now I'm intrigued," Claire said. "And clearly a glutton for punishment." She picked up a brownie and took a tiny bite. She managed to keep it in her mouth, but her scrunched-up face said she definitely detected what was wrong.

"God, Maggie. How much salt did you put in these?"

"I think just a spoonful."

"What kind of a spoon?"

"I don't know. Just a spoon."

"A big spoon? Or a teaspoon?"

How was she supposed to know? There were soup spoons, serving spoons, dessert spoons, and teaspoons. Who could keep them all straight? "It was one of the medium-sized spoons, I think."

"Do you even own measuring spoons? Next time you can bring the wine."

Maggie was more of a beer girl. And she wasn't too sure about a next time. So far, book club was like pretzel sticks—salty with very little substance.

Alice brought out glasses of water for everyone, and they guzzled them down like parched shipwreck victims on a desert island.

"Maggie, we're just so glad you're here," Alice said. "All you ever need to worry about bringing is yourself. But if you want to practice your cooking or baking skills, the Big Verde Book Club is happy to be your guinea pigs."

"Hear, hear," Claire said, raising her empty water glass.

Maggie laughed. There was nothing but kindness in the smiles of everyone in the room, except for maybe Anna, but kindness wasn't her strong suit, and she was at least looking pleasant. There were worse ways to spend an afternoon.

"You know, I once used baking soda when it called for baking powder," Alice said, blushing. "I took the cookies to the library's Christmas party and they tasted like copper. At the end of the evening, paper plates were scattered about, and the only thing on any of them were my cookies, each with a single bite taken."

"I put chili powder instead of cinnamon on the toast at Sammie's tea party," Trista said, rubbing her pregnant belly and bouncing a toddler on her hip. "Bubba ate it, of course. But the little girls, not so much."

"Oh, goodness," Miss Mills said, fanning herself with her daily devotional. "I still remember the first time I baked a buttermilk pie. The custard didn't set, and when I cut into it at the church potluck, it was a runny mess. I managed to sneak it into the trash when nobody was looking."

"You make delicious pies now," Alice said.

"Practice makes perfect. I had a particular young man in mind when I baked that buttermilk pie."

Maggie wondered if she'd baked it while wearing only an apron and thinking about being pushed up against the counter and ravished by a man in a wolf mask.

Miss Mills let out a long, ragged sigh. "It broke my heart that he didn't eat my pie that night."

"Yeah, I bet," said Maggie, avoiding eye contact with Claire, because that would be disastrous.

"That's what bakeries are for," Anna quipped. "I've never baked a pie in my life. But I set the kitchen on fire once when I tried to fry an egg."

Soon all the women were telling stories about their culinary catastrophes. It escalated into a weird competition between Alice's burned lemon bars, Claire's twenty-five-pound frozen turkey, Miss Mills's cornbread full of weevils, and Trista's chicken and dumplings dripping from the ceiling.

Alice finally stood and spoke above the din, "Would everyone like to begin a discussion of the book now?"

One by one the ladies regained their senses, took their seats, and picked up their copies of the latest in literary porn. Claire leaned over to Miss Mills. "If you sat this one out, everyone would understand."

Miss Mills set her devotional down on the coffee table and dug in her bag. "Goodness, no. I never fail to complete a reading assignment." She pulled out a ragged and well-read copy of *Bound and Determined*. Post-it flags popped out from between every other page.

Somebody had done some deep, reflective studying.

"I really found myself identifying with the heroine," she said. "Sometimes you just want to let everything go—all of the trials of life and infinite worry with decisions."

You could have heard a pin drop. Alice recovered her voice first. "I guess it's a *let go and let God* type of thing, isn't it?"

Well, hell. It was going to be extremely disappointing if this discussion strayed from smut to Bible study.

Miss Mills looked at Alice as if she'd grown a second head. "Oh, goodness, no! Let's not bring the dear sweet Lord into this. And I don't approve of the premarital sex in this book. Not at all. And there was just so much of it. Nine sex scenes total, eleven if you count oral only."

There was a pause while everyone let that sink in. Then Trista said, "But who's counting?"

A few giggles here and there turned into howling laughter pretty quickly, and Alice had to fight to regain control. "I think Miss Mills is probably referring to letting the story's hero, Ethan Manning, take control with that paddle he loves so much."

Miss Mills picked her devotional back up and commenced fanning. "Ethan reminds me of Mr. Barret Hymes. Do you girls remember him? He taught sixth grade when I worked as a secretary at the school."

A general murmur went through the group. Who could forget

Mr. Hymes? He was the meanest teacher Big Verde Middle School had ever seen or would likely ever see again. And he'd dressed like an undertaker.

Anna shuddered. "I was terrified of him in school. What in the world could he possibly have in common with our hot, sexy Ethan?"

"He had that paddle hanging by the door, didn't he?" Miss Mills asked. "I used to think about it sometimes."

It took another few seconds for Alice to get everyone settled down. She was like a referee. "Miss Mills, you never cease to surprise us."

"Don't think I've joined the ranks of those for whom fornication is the sin of choice. And I didn't choose this book, remember?"

"I'm sure Jesus understands," Alice said.

"I admit to enjoying the occasional spanking," Trista said out of the blue. "Once the kids are in bed, of course."

"Really?" Alice asked, eyes round. "I think I might have a problem with it in real life. And I hate to see women submit to men."

"Who said I was the one getting the spanking?"

"Bubba lets you spank him?" Claire squealed. "You realize we're all imagining it now. And that we can't unsee it?"

"Sometimes he's a bad boy," Trista said with a shrug and a wink.

"Goodness," Alice said. "I just didn't know that sort of thing went on here in Big Verde. Spanking, sexting—"

Anna perked up. "Sexting? Who's sexting?"

What the actual heck? Was Alice about to spill the beans?

"Yes," Alice said with a grin. "You might want to ask Maggie about it."

Shock must have shown on Maggie's face, because Alice immediately began apologizing.

"Oops. I'm sorry. I got carried away with the conversation and wasn't think—"

"Who on earth are you sexting?" Trista asked. She was clearly surprised that *anybody* would be sexting Maggie. "I mean, it's a man, right?"

"Not everyone with short hair is a lesbian," Maggie said. "And no, Trista. It's a cat. I'm sexting a cat."

"I'm not sure that's legal," Miss Mills said.

Anna had a fork of pea salad halfway to her mouth, but she set it back down on her plate. "I'm sure Maggie is sexting with a big, handsome hunk of a man. Am I right, Maggie?" Anna wore a sly grin that made Maggie distinctly uncomfortable. But that was the only kind of grin Anna ever wore.

"If you all must know, yes."

"Oh! Maggie has a suitor," Miss Mills happily exclaimed.

"And it's not a cat," Claire added helpfully. "He's distinctly more canine."

Anna's eyes narrowed as if she were connecting dots. The chance that Anna knew the wolf—he'd been at her party—both excited and terrified Maggie. Sometimes she forgot to think of him as a real person. Like, the Big Bad Wolf had a name. And a car or truck. Friends. And Anna might know all those things about him. It felt weird.

"It's just a guy and I don't want to talk about it."

"What's his name?" Trista asked.

"She doesn't know," Claire said.

Maggie shot Claire the evil eye and then risked a nervous glance at Anna, who'd set her plate on the coffee table and was dabbing her mouth with a napkin. She was grinning like a Cheshire cat.

"You don't know his name? What if he's a serial killer?" Miss Mills asked.

"He's not a serial killer. But he wishes to remain anonymous. And so do I for that matter." Another glance at Anna.

Anna cleared her throat. "I recently received a very dirty text," she said.

"From who?" Claire asked.

"It was a wrong number," Anna said.

"How odd," Alice replied.

"It was hot, though. He sounded like a Big Bad..."

Maggie's breath caught in her throat.

"*Dom*," Anna finished. "A big, bad dom. Which reminds me, let's get back to this book."

Maggie pulled her library copy of *Bound and Determined* out of her bag. A vague hint of unease hovered about, but she swatted it away by taking two big gulps of sweet wine fresh from a box. She wiped her mouth on the back of her hand as Alice asked the group if they could all relate to the heroine's desire to relinquish control.

Maybe she just had something in her eye, but Maggie could swear Anna winked at her.

Chapter
Twenty-Four

☙

Travis slammed the truck door and stared at the windows of Maggie's little house. They glowed with a warm yellow hue. Pop blazed through his doggy door, yapping hysterically. But he stopped and wagged his stub tail when he saw Travis, who leaned over and patted the French bulldog. "Nobody's sneaking up on Miss Mary Margaret while you're on the job, huh, fella?"

Travis straightened, looked around, and realized his truck was the only vehicle here except for Maggie's Jeep. Where was everybody else? He wasn't especially early. Maybe they were just running late.

"Let me out," Henry whined.

Travis reached in and unbuckled him, and Henry hopped down and began rolling around in the grass with Pop. "Don't get dirty," Travis said absentmindedly. "You're already in your pajamas." So was he. He'd stopped by Walmart and picked up a pair of Spurs pajama bottoms, which he'd paired with a black T-shirt. Henry was over the moon about the pajama party scenario.

He grabbed the bag of organic chicken nuggets he'd picked up at the burger joint and started for the porch. Henry wouldn't eat wings, but he'd do nuggets.

"Can I give a nugget to Pop?" Henry asked.

"You'll have to ask Maggie. He's her mutt."

"Kind of like Maggie asks you before she'll give me anything sweet," Henry said.

"Yeah. Because you're my mutt."

Henry laughed and dropped to all fours, yapping like a puppy.

"Get up. You're getting dirty."

"I don't care." Henry began digging a hole with his hands, tossing the dirt between his legs.

Travis bent over and scooped him up, then carried him to Maggie's screened-in back porch. Maggie opened the door and Pop jumped up and licked Henry on the nose. Henry dissolved into a fit of laughter. Travis set him down and held out the paper bag. "I brought some chicken nuggets to go along with Bubba's wings."

She stood back and held the door open. "Bubba's not coming. Neither is Claire or JD."

"Why not?"

"Let's see. JD says he has a headache. Claire is washing her hair. And Bubba says he has to watch some paint dry."

"Oh."

"Yeah. *Oh.* I suspect they're at Tony's gossiping about us."

Henry began running around on all fours, yapping and growling. The kid really knew how to make an awkward situation even worse.

"We can leave," Travis said.

"Why would you do that? You've already missed the first quarter. Come on in."

Henry upped the yapping to full-blown barking.

"Sorry, Henry. I don't have room for another dog in this house, so you'd better turn back into a boy."

"I don't know how. I'm a dog forever now." To prove it, he

started to howl. Pop tilted his head to the side as if witnessing a freak show.

"Cut it out. And wipe your boots off."

"I don't understand people talk," Henry said.

"What was that, Pop?" Maggie said.

"Pop didn't say anything," Henry said.

"Oh, yes he did. He said that if you spin around two times and then touch your nose, you can turn back into a boy."

"How does he know that? Did he used to be a boy?"

"I don't really know. But I guess if he ever was a boy, and he wanted to turn back into one, he could."

"I want to stay a dog, too," Henry said.

"That's too bad," Maggie said. "Did you know dogs can't have chocolate?"

"They can't?"

"Nope. It makes them very sick."

Henry seemed to think about that for a while. Then he turned around two times and touched his nose. "Do you have any chocolate, Maggie?"

"I have a bag of miniature candy bars I've been hoarding since Halloween."

Henry scrambled into the house while telling Pop he was dumb for staying a dog.

"Thank you," Travis said.

"For what?"

"You just turned Henry back into a boy."

Maggie walked past him, and he caught a whiff of something very un-Maggie-like. Something fruity or floral.

"If you hadn't stepped in with your dog magic," he continued, "I was going to listen to Henry bark for at least three more days."

Maggie dismissed it with a wave of her hand. It hadn't even taken any thought. She just knew what to do around kids, and he never did.

"Are you wearing perfume?"

She avoided his eyes and fidgeted with the hem of her shirt as he pushed the back door open. "It's just some lotion for my hands. I went shopping with Claire, and now I smell like a girl."

"You look like a girl, too."

Maggie blushed all the way to the tips of her ears. She was dressed appropriately for their pajama party, but not in the footsie pajamas she'd worn last time. What she wore *this* time left less to the imagination—tight black leggings that went mid-calf and a little white NBA T-shirt. No bra.

She walked over to the refrigerator and grabbed a beer, stuck it in a koozie, and handed it to him. "You're not mad at me anymore?"

He pushed his glasses up on his nose. The combination of the season's cool dry air and dusty landscaping work was making it hard to wear contacts. "About what?"

"The guys I hired to help you. JD's front-end loader. We didn't have time to talk about it at the farmer's market today."

"I was never mad at you."

Maggie crossed her arms. "You sure acted like it."

"I acted like a pouty baby who had his ego poked. Not the same thing." He stared deeply into her chocolate drop eyes, hoping she could see what he felt. *I could never be mad at you, Maggie.*

"It wasn't my place. I'm sorry I hired help without talking to you about it. And I'm sorry you paid them—I'd intended to do that."

"Water under the bridge. And thank you for wanting to help. I don't know that my back could have held out for two more days. And you should know that I'm not out to ruin Petal Pushers. I don't intend to—"

"I know."

"You do? Because just recently you threatened to shut me down to save your business."

Maggie's eyes grew huge and round. Travis's heart nearly

stopped. That was information Little Red Riding Hood had shared with the Big Bad Wolf.

"My, my," she muttered. "This is a bit embarrassing."

No shit. Travis took a sip of beer and wiped his brow.

"JD Mayes needs to learn to keep his mouth shut," Maggie added.

Whew! Travis took another sip—more like a gulp—and willed himself to relax between near-misses. "Anyway," he said, "I'm not sticking with landscaping. The farmer's market today gave me some—"

"JD told me. You've got a job waiting in Austin." Maggie looked in the direction of the living room, where Henry played with Pop. "You're not planning to stay in Big Verde."

"You're right. JD needs to learn to keep his mouth shut. And anyway, I'm kind of recon—"

"It would have been nice to hear it from you," Maggie said. "Because I kind of thought we were getting to be friends."

She came closer, the top of her blond head not quite reaching his shoulder, and looked up with her big, brown eyes. Travis lost his train of thought. "We were," Travis said. "We *are* . . . I hope."

Her eyes tugged at his like a magnet, and he lowered his head as she rose on her toes. "Austin's not that far away," Maggie said.

"You're wrong," he whispered, softly brushing Maggie's bangs off her forehead so he could fall deeper into her dark brown eyes. "It's too far away." Right now, anything farther away from him than Maggie was at this very instant was *too far*.

He set his beer down on the counter and cupped Maggie's face in his hands. She seemed so small and delicate, yet she was tough as nails, and he loved it. She pinched his bearded chin and gave it a small tug until their lips met.

Travis had kissed his share of women, but nothing compared to the way his mouth was a perfect fit for Maggie's. He'd heard the *two become one* line before. It was sappy and sentimental and exactly what happened when his lips touched hers.

His decision was made at the sound of her soft sigh. He was staying in Big Verde. Staying at Happy Trails. Staying with Maggie.

He wrapped his arms around her, lifting her up effortlessly. He deepened the kiss as Maggie's breasts pressed against his chest. He could turn and perch her on the counter—

Pop barked, and it was immediately followed by the unmistakable sound of someone gagging.

Travis nearly dropped Maggie. Jesus, what kind of a...*parent? uncle?*...was he? He looked at the doorway, expecting to see Henry barfing over his and Maggie's inappropriate display of affection. But it was empty.

Maggie quickly disentangled herself from him, straightened her shirt, and then shouted, "What happened?" as she hurried into the living room.

Travis stayed behind in the kitchen. He needed a minute for a certain part of his anatomy to return to the state it had arrived in.

Maggie was back in under a minute. "It's okay," she told him. "Henry threw up a little. It's an old pillow and I'll just toss it."

Great. So much for a fun evening. "Is he sick?"

Maggie went to the sink and washed her hands. "No. Just a gag reflex."

"Shit. The sight of us kissing literally made him vomit?"

Maggie shut the water off and briskly dried her hands. "No. It wasn't that."

"Then what was it?"

Maggie tossed the towel on the counter and turned to face him, hands on hips. Her cheeks and ears were pink, but he doubted it was from the steamy kiss they'd just shared. What the fuck was she so heated about?

"He ate one of my brownies, okay?"

One of her brownies. The ones she'd baked while wearing

nothing but an apron. Travis tried to reel in the smile taking over his face. "Jesus, Maggie. Are they that bad?"

A grin tugged at Maggie's lips. "Want to judge for yourself? There's about a thousand or so left."

Travis grabbed her hand and gave a light yank, pulling her close. "You should steer clear of the kitchen and stick to things you're good at."

"Like digging in the dirt?" Maggie asked.

"No," Travis said, putting a finger beneath her chin and tilting her face up. "Like kissing."

Chapter
Twenty-Five

The game was over. Travis had talked about Happy Trails through most of it. It was weird how excited he was about the place, considering he was going to sell it. It figured. She'd had two men notice she was a woman. One hid behind a wolf mask and the other was moving to Austin. And both seemed perfectly happy to carry on with her—one via sexting and the other through hot, steamy *yet completely temporary* kisses. Maggie had hinted that Austin wasn't that far away—JD was in a relationship with a woman in Austin— and Travis had responded that it was too far!

Message received.

She'd kissed him anyway. It was just a kiss, so what did it matter? If he wanted to smooch and rub his rock-hard body against hers while he was still here in Big Verde, who was she to protest?

Then again, maybe she should. Maybe she should end it right now. Kick him out. Say, *Adios, muchacho, it's been super fun swapping spit now buh-bye*. Of course, that meant saying good-bye to Henry, too. And she and Pop weren't ready for that.

She glanced at him, all stretched out with his long legs in front of him and his hands resting behind his head like he hadn't a care in the world.

It was ten thirty. He'd probably want to grab Henry from where he was passed out in the guest room and head home.

Only he wasn't moving.

Maggie's pulse sped up, which was stupid. Just because a tired man with a full belly wasn't jumping right up off the couch to sprint out the door didn't mean he wanted to make out.

Which was *fine*. Really. She'd only recently decided she could even tolerate Travis. She should ask him to leave right now, this minute, so she could begin the process of not kissing him ever again.

She cleared her throat to tell him it was time to pack up his hot self and his adorable nephew and get the heck out of Dodge. But what came out was, "Would you like another beer? Tomorrow's Sunday, and I don't have to get up early."

A small grin caused that dimple to pop out. "Nah. It'd probably put me to sleep." He closed his eyes.

Maggie let her eyes wander. Maybe it was because she'd baked brownies while almost completely naked. Maybe it was because of the book club discussion of *Bound and Determined*. Most likely it was because of their earlier Last Kiss Ever. Whatever it was, she really wanted to jump Travis.

The black T-shirt stretched across his chest and firm stomach, riding up just a bit. She'd love to slide it up and get another look at his tattoos. The waistband of his underwear peeked out of the top of his PJ's, and she tried—really, she did—not to look at the bulge.

Failure. She'd love to climb on top and rub herself all over him.

"How was book club?"

He was gazing right at her. Had seen where she was looking.

Her ears burned. "You're asking me about book club? When we could be talking about the flagrant foul that happened under that blind ref's nose?"

"Yeah, you went, right? Took the poison brownies? Tell me about it."

He just wanted to hear about her day? That was . . . *nice*. It was also a bit disappointing, considering there were other, more interesting, activities floating around in her head. "It was at Alice's house, and I kind of had fun. I think I might go back next month."

"That's good. I'm glad you enjoyed it. Alice seems nice."

"She is. She's a blabbermouth, though." *Could have done without her telling everyone I'm sexting the wolf.*

"What was the name of the book again?"

"*Bound and Determined.*"

"Is it the one on top of the microwave? The one with the bare-naked ass on it?"

She'd left that out? She turned to look at the microwave. At least it was too high for Henry to have seen it. "That's the one. I should put it away."

Travis stood up with a groan, stretched, and then lazily strolled toward the microwave. "Don't put it away. I might want to read it."

"You definitely do not want to read it."

"You're right," he said, picking up the book and looking at the cover. He glanced up at her with a very judgmental expression. "I'm not going to read it. You're going to read it to me."

"You've got to be kidding."

Travis brought the book to the couch, where he adjusted his glasses and read the back cover. He somehow managed to keep a straight face while Maggie sat quietly, engulfed in flames and wanting to disappear.

When he was done, he said, "Okay. This seems like a fine piece of literature. Let's take a peek."

The book automatically fell open to the nastiest scene. She should really stop dog-earing pages.

Travis scanned the page, a smirk forming at the corner of his mouth. He looked at Maggie with a raised eyebrow. "Seems like a good place to start."

He tossed the book at her and it landed in her lap.

"I have no intention of reading any of this out loud. You can forget it."

She held her hands up in the air as if she were under arrest, making no move to touch the book. Travis sighed and shook his head.

"Do I have to do everything myself?"

He reached for the book, but Maggie grabbed it first. "You're not reading any of this out loud either."

Travis took hold of the book with a big hand and tugged. "Yes, I am."

Maggie held on tightly. "No, you're not."

"Let go," Travis said.

"No."

"I can easily wrench this out of your scrawny little hands, but I'd prefer you graciously let go so I don't have to."

Maggie snorted. "Like that's gonna happen."

One yank, and it happened. She hadn't even felt it leave her fingers. "I'm not going to listen to you read that out loud."

Travis nodded to let her know he'd heard and registered her comment before opening the book. Then he dramatically cleared his throat.

Maggie crossed her arms over her chest and concentrated on actively not listening.

"Ethan firmly pressed Celeste against the bed."

It wasn't working. She'd had zero success in tuning that line out. So, she put her fingers in her ears and began humming because *Hey, we're all adults here.*

But she could still hear the low rumble of his big deep man voice as he read. He didn't even glance at her, just pretended she didn't have her fingers in her ears.

"Now that her wrists were bound to her ankles—"

He stopped reading.

He was probably shocked that Maggie and the other book club ladies had read such smut. He furrowed his brow and then said, "I'm not sure how that works."

"How what works? What do you mean?"

"How are her wrists bound to her ankles?"

"With those leather wrist cuff things."

He grinned and raised an eyebrow. "Leather wrist cuff things? Some girl really knows her bondage gear lingo."

Okay, she was sitting with Travis Blake in her very own house on her very own sofa and he had just said *bondage gear*.

Travis looked at the book again, as if he were studying a math problem in a textbook. "So, she's lying down, but where are her ankles? Does she have her legs lifted up?"

"Oh my God," Maggie said in exasperation. "Can you really not visualize this?"

"I guess I'm a little slow about these things. You might have to explain it to me. You seem to be the expert here—tossing out technical terms like *leather wrist cuff things*."

"I'm not explaining anything to you."

"Ah. You don't get it either. That's what I thought."

She did, too, get it. It wasn't rocket science. She got onto the floor—knowing full well she was playing into his hands—and lay down. She slid her feet up toward her bottom, but kept them on the floor because she was sure as holy hell not raising them into the air.

Travis got off the couch and kneeled next to her. He radiated heat. Maybe she should turn the ceiling fan on. Was it hot in here? She felt a bit warm.

"Okay, now see if you can reach your ankles with your hands."

Her neck was getting splotchy. She could feel it. Because nothing said *aren't I sexy* like a splotchy neck. Her arms were at her sides and she straightened out her fingers to clasp her ankles. Only she couldn't do it. She'd pulled her feet up so far that they practically touched her ass, but—

"You're shy a few inches," Travis said.

Why didn't her wrists meet her ankles? Were her arms too short? How had she lived all these years not knowing how disproportionate her arms were to the rest of her?

"It's like I'm a T-rex," she said.

Travis laughed. "I've heard there's an erotica market for that, too."

"And you would know this *how?*"

"Made the mistake of asking a lady in the doctor's office what she was reading. And anyway, your arms are fine. I don't think you can visualize this either."

"Okay, well, this doesn't work but I'm done. Who cares anyway? It's just a book."

"Now wait a minute," Travis said. "Don't be so hasty. This woman took the time to write a book. The least we can do is figure out what the hell she's saying."

He put the book down and touched a finger to his bearded chin. "Hmm," he pondered. "How about this?"

He moved so that he knelt at her feet. He took an ankle in each hand and said, "May I?"

Of course not!

"Sure," Maggie said.

Travis pulled one foot, and then the other, out to the side of her hips. It was hard for a girl to keep her knees together like a lady when a man was yanking her feet apart. But she tried, achieving a knock-kneed spread that was probably a negative three on the sexy scale.

"See?" Travis said. "This would work." He grunted as he gave her feet an extra shove. "Relax a little."

With his left hand, he managed to ensnare her ankle and wrist. "There we go," he said, seemingly very pleased with his accomplishment. He looked at Maggie as if she were a Rubik's Cube he'd just solved. He quickly snagged the other ankle and wrist with his right hand, and Maggie was rendered completely helpless.

There was a brief surge of panic, but then something inside her stilled. Travis was smiling like a goof, but she trusted him completely. All the tension seeped out of her body and dissipated like mist. It felt almost like being with the Big Bad Wolf, which was stupid because Travis was not the Big Bad Wolf and they were *not* going to have sex.

He smiled with a mischievous glint in his eye. "So, this works."

She couldn't speak.

"The question is, works for what?" he said.

He let go, and she crumbled inside. Her wrists and ankles had been so secure in his grip, and now she felt unanchored.

"Let's keep reading," Travis said, snatching the book up.

Maggie hesitated to move. Should she hold her position? No, now that he'd let go, that would look stupid. She stretched out her legs and clasped her hands over her stomach, feigning relaxation. Like she was just chillin'. While Travis read erotica out loud.

Travis cleared his throat again. *"He pushed her knees open, displaying her for his pleasure, and she shivered in excitement."*

Travis's voice had become distinctly lower. Raspier. She glanced at his cheeks—what she could see above his beard—and they were pink. Bright pink. She crossed her ankles and tried to look casual. She remembered this scene. Next Ethan would—

"He firmly grabbed the spreader bar—"

Travis lowered the book, and Maggie quickly averted her eyes to examine the ceiling in great detail. "Oh, look," she said. "There are cobwebs up there."

"Maggie, what's a spreader bar?"

She really didn't want to admit to knowing what a spreader bar was. "How would I know?"

"Haven't you read the book?"

"What? Oh, well yes, obviously. But I don't remember every single detail and I don't remember a mention of spreader bars."

Except that she totally did. She'd broken out in a light sweat, even though it was cool inside. And she could hear her pulse in her head. "There's a moth hanging up there," she said, pointing at the ceiling.

Travis looked up. "I don't see anything."

Oh. It seemed her dilated pupils improved her vision. She now had special horny powers.

Travis looked down at the book again.

"He firmly grabbed the spreader bar and pulled her wrists and ankles up. Celeste was startled by this move. Slowly, Ethan pressed the bar over her head, lifting her ass up with his other hand, until the toes of her feet came to rest just above her head."

He set the book down and squinted at Maggie in concentration. "I think I know what a spreader bar is now. But this seems like an advanced move. Not real sure I have a firm grasp of how she's positioned."

Maggie knew but she wasn't saying.

"I guess we'll keep reading." Travis turned the page.

He was really playing this up. It was adorable, sexy, and infuriating.

"Ethan held the bar close to the ground—no chance for Celeste to break free. She was exposed, open, and Ethan's face was so close to her—"

Maggie faked a sneeze.

"Gesundheit."

"I think I'm catching a cold. You should go now so I can get some rest."

"We can't stop here, and you know it. Also, that was the worst fake sneeze I've ever heard."

"It was the best I could do on short notice."

Travis shook his head and looked back at the book but then stopped and chuckled. "Jesus Christ, Maggie. Y'all read this with Miss Mills?" He was grinning from ear to ear.

"She loved it. Said it made her think of Mr. Hymes. Remember him?"

Travis's mouth dropped open. "That teacher who looked like a mortician—the guy with the paddle?"

"That's the one."

Travis closed his eyes. "Oh God," he said. "It's in my head. It's seared into my brain and I'll never ever get it out."

"Just imagine Miss Mills bent over Mr. Hymes's lap—"

Travis moved his hands to cover his ears. "I'm warning you, Maggie. Stop it or I'll—"

"You'll what?" She lightly shoved his knee with her foot. "What are you going to do, tough guy? Give me a spanking?"

She regretted it as soon as she said it.

Travis dropped his hands from his ears, having obviously heard every syllable she'd just uttered. He gave her a crooked grin. "You sure as shit deserve one."

"Me?" she asked innocently. "I deserve no such thing."

Travis narrowed his eyes. "I don't know about that," he said, rubbing the palms of his hands together as if gleefully contemplating the sound they would make on her bare ass. Her heart sped up at the thought of it. So, she quit thinking about it.

Travis picked the book up again. "Where was I? Oh yeah. He has her in a complicated martial arts situation. I'm not sure I understand the scene at all. I mean, where the hell are her feet?"

"What's wrong with you? Do you have to have every little thing you read explained?"

"It's just that—unlike some people—I'm completely innocent when it comes to this stuff. How long is a spreader bar?"

"No idea," Maggie said. "A foot maybe?"

Travis pulled out his phone.

"You're Googling it?"

"Yes." A few seconds later he looked up. "There's a lot of stuff on here."

"I bet. How long is the spreader bar?"

"This one is twenty-five inches. And forty-nine dollars."

He did a couple of finger swipes on the phone and then put it down. "It was Prime."

"You did *not* just buy a spreader bar."

Travis waggled his eyebrows before picking the book back up. "Okay, so we've got her ankles by her ears and her ass in the air. Sounds like yoga."

Maggie laughed. "X-rated yoga, for sure."

"I bet you can't even do it," Travis said.

Was he serious? She could do it. She wasn't going to, though. She had nothing to prove to Travis Blake.

"You'd have to be pretty fit and flexible to do this pose."

Maggie sat up. "I'm fit and flexible. And when I lived in Fort Worth, I even took a yoga class. I was so flexible I had to quit because I made everyone else feel inferior and it messed up their zen."

"I don't believe you."

"You are not tricking me into putting my feet by my ears."

"Okay."

"Seriously. I'm not doing it. I *could*, though. And that's what matters."

"Whatever you say."

"You don't believe me?"

Travis didn't answer. Just gazed at her calmly.

"Fine," Maggie huffed. "Watch this."

She sat up, curved her spine, and then shoved off to give herself some momentum. Up and over she went—easy peasy. But she couldn't stay that way without supporting her lower back with her hands.

"Ha! I told you." She held her position like a pro.

"Not really," Travis said. "You're supposed to have your wrists connected to your ankles, remember? You're holding your butt up with your hands like that lady on the senior fitness channel."

"That's just to get me started," she said. "Hold on. I got this."

She tried four or five times to remove her hands and to place them up by her ankles, but her rear end started to come down each time, pulling her legs and feet with it.

"Here, let me help," Travis said.

Before Maggie could stop him, he'd shoved his knees into her lower back and grabbed her wrists. He pulled them over her head, bringing them to rest beside her foot on either side of her head. He leaned over to do so, up between her legs, pressing his weight against her.

She was trapped beneath him. In a very naughty position that was obviously meant for a very specific activity. They were nose to nose and other parts to other parts, and his pajamas had developed a distinct tent.

"Breathe, Maggie."

She'd been holding her breath. She let it out.

"I can see where the spreader bar would come in handy right now," he said. His blue eyes were so intense. They looked like they'd darkened at least two shades. "I could hold it with just one hand, which would free up the other one for...other things."

Maggie lost all muscle control. She went limp.

She'd surrendered.

"Uncle Travis?"

"Shit," Travis said, letting go of Maggie and sitting up in the frantic and time-honored *I wasn't doing anything* tradition.

"What are you doing?"

Henry's hair was tousled, his eyes were puffy, and the likeliest reason for his wakefulness was spread across the front of his pajamas in a dark stain.

"Aw, man, Henry. Did you wet the bed?"

Obviously, he had, and there was no reason to fuss at him about it. Maggie stood up. "Let's get you out of these wet PJ's. Did you bring any extras with you?"

"Nah. But what were you and Uncle Travis doing?"

"We were reading a book."

"It didn't look like you were reading a book. It looked like you were wrestling."

"It was a book about wrestling," Travis said, standing. "Maggie, can we borrow a T-shirt or something?"

"I'm not wearing a girl's shirt," Henry said.

"You have to wear something, and your pants are wet."

"I'm not wearing a girl's shirt," Henry repeated.

With a sigh of resignation, Travis did a glorious thing. He pulled his shirt over his head. And there it was. The tattooed chest and ripped abs. To think it had all been on top of her just moments before.

"Excuse me," Travis said, yanking her out of her daze. "I don't mean to interrupt whatever it was you were just thinking about, but do you have a plastic bag for Henry's wet clothes?"

"You didn't interrupt a darn thing," she said, reaching under the counter for a grocery bag.

"Uncle Travis, when we get home, I want you to read me that wrestling book."

"That ain't gonna happen."

Travis slipped his shirt over Henry's head. Then he scooped him up. "Maggie, this has been a very entertaining evening, and I'm sorry it had to end." He glared a little at Henry, who seemed oblivious.

"I guess I'll see you tomorrow?"

"I look forward to it," Travis said with a wink. "I'll, uh…let you know when that bar comes in."

The more she blushed, the bigger he grinned. He pushed his glasses up on his nose and carried Henry to the truck.

She watched as they drove away, then she went inside and stripped the bed in the guest room. Before she even made it to the washing machine, she'd sent a text. Because a woman had needs, dang it.

Hey, wolfie. Want to play?

Chapter
Twenty-Six
☙

Travis rushed into his bedroom, quietly closing the door behind him. Henry was sound asleep, hadn't woken up even with the jostling of being removed from the car seat. He'd gone smoothly into bed without a problem, which was a relief, because Little Red Riding Hood had texted.

He'd sworn not to play the Big Bad Wolf role again. But after reading that book and doing those things with Maggie, he was just so fucking lit up. And Maggie was, too.

He'd looked straight into her eyes as she'd lain beneath him at his mercy—*she'd wanted it. So bad.*

The wolf was going to give it to her.

He'd pulled to the side of Peacock Road just long enough to text Get naked. Now he was finally in his bedroom. Did you do it?

Yes. And freezing. You sure took your sweet time.

Because he'd had to drive home from her house first.

You better not have taken matters into your own hands.

Although the idea of that excited him.

It's just me and Mr. Tatum.

Who the hell was Mr. Tatum?

??

My vibrator has a last name and it's T-A-T-U-M.

She named her vibrator.

Whatever you say.

First name is Channing.

That sounded familiar. He Googled Channing Tatum. What he found brought up all his old insecurities. This is what turned her on? For a moment he felt like his old long-limbed, skinny, stuttering self. But then he remembered he wasn't that kid anymore. He stood and looked at himself in the mirror. He was still shirtless. And he could give Channing Tatum a run for his money.

He picked up his phone. She should put that damn vibrator away. Mr. Big Bad Wolf was on the scene now. On second thought...

Just what are you doing with Mr. Tatum?

Getting warmed up for my wolf.

She'd called him her wolf. He wanted to be hers. And for her to be his.

I thought you were cold.

Not all of me. One part of me is very warm. And inviting.

He swallowed. He knew damn well just how warm and inviting that particular part of Maggie was. *Maggie.* He couldn't think of her as Little Red Riding Hood anymore.

He'd give anything if he could have her right here in this room. But since he couldn't, he'd have to let Mr. Tatum do the work for him.

Set the timer on your phone for 30 seconds.

Why?

Because I said so.

He knew she'd do it.

Done.

Now let Mr. Tatum tickle your right nipple until the timer goes off.

From what he knew of her nipples and their sensitivity, thirty seconds was going to be a long time. He grinned. He was a very bad wolf.

He busied himself with extremely filthy thoughts for the next thirty seconds. Then his phone finally pinged.

You're a horrible wolf. Don't make me do that again.

Now the left one. Thirty seconds.

NO.

Make that thirty-five seconds.

Silence. It was going to be about thirty-five seconds before he heard from poor Little Red Riding Hood again. He stared at the ceiling, thinking about her rock-hard little nubs and how he could outmaneuver Mr. Tatum with his tongue if only he could get to them. He pulled the waistband of his pajamas down to let his aching hard-on get some air. He took it in hand and stroked firmly. He could taste Little Red Riding Hood—no, *Maggie*. Maggie with her legs spread wide and his tongue buried deep inside her wet—

Ping!

Breathing heavily, he let go of his cock and fumbled for the phone. There wasn't just one text. There were three. How had he not heard them?

Done.

Hey, I said I'm done.

WHAT ARE YOU DOING?

Shit. He'd been caught.

I was in the bathroom

That's not sexy, wolfie.

No kidding.

I was slappin the salami.

LOLOLOLOL

Beating the bologna

Stop

Buffin the banana

I'm dying

Choking the chicken

I get it! I get it! Did you choke the life out of it? Are we done?

Nowhere near done. But you're talking disrespectfully to your master and his choking chicken. Go get an ice cube.

M'kay.

She sure fell in line quickly. Good girl. He imagined her running naked through her cold house and struggling to get an ice cube out of the tray while Pop looked on quizzically. He laughed out loud.

Got it.

Now what did he want her to do with it? His face burned. He knew exactly what he wanted her to do with it.

Put it in your mouth until I tell you to stop.

A second or two passed.

OK. I'm sucking furiously because I want this thing as small as possible before you make me put it somewhere else.

He swallowed at the words sucking furiously and then grinned over her realizing exactly what was going to come next.

Right nipple. 5 seconds.

You're mean!

10 seconds.

He counted to ten.

Left one.

I have a completely numb nipple. Is that what you were going for?

No, that was not really what he'd been going for. God, he'd love to warm it up with his mouth.

OK 5 seconds on the left one.

He counted to five.

Still have ice left?

Yes. Where is it going next?

You know where to put it next.

For how long?

Until it's gone. And put Mr. Tatum to work too.

How long would it take? What if she got frostbite? Nah. It would melt quickly inside her hot—

He couldn't stand it. His hand went back to work. He groaned as the images took over. It wasn't his own hand sliding over his painfully hard cock. It was Maggie's hand. Maggie's mouth. Maggie's hot sweet—

In his mind, she was on top of him, riding him hard. Then that vision morphed into her beneath him, legs wrapped around his waist, hands clawing at his back. Now he was behind her pounding it home and...*Shit*. His strangled groan of release was enough to wake the neighborhood. He lay there panting and listening— all was quiet. No rustling sounds of Henry rousing. All the stress seeped out of his body and he waited for relaxation to take over and turn his muscles into putty. But it didn't. He was in *anguish*. He needed Maggie. Not this pretend relationship.

Maggie. He'd forgotten about Maggie.

Maggie? You still there?

His mind snapped to attention before he hit Send. That was close. He deleted her name. You still there?

Kind of. Partially. Sorry but I couldn't wait. It was so cold and Mr. Tatum was so warm and everything was all melty and oh my god that was good.

He wished they could melt into the warm afterglow together. He'd love nothing more than to hold her all night long, only to wake up in the morning and treat her like a queen. He'd bring her coffee and breakfast in bed, and then Henry would come in for some morning cuddles.

Jesus. He was thinking in terms that could only be described as family. His pulse pounded. It should be coming down now, right? Not increasing?

His phone pinged.

Where are you wolfie? Not finished yet? Because I know what you're doing you dirty dog.

He laughed.

I'm here. You drove me wild though. I'm crazy for you.

He stared at the phone, waiting for a response. None came, so he added, You're my moon. That was romantic, right? Poetic? Also, it was true.

He got up and put on fresh boxers and a T-shirt. Then he peeked at Henry—sound asleep—and brushed his teeth. He checked his phone again before getting in bed. Maggie hadn't texted back. And even though he was dead dog tired, he had a very hard time going to sleep.

Chapter
Twenty-Seven

☙

Maggie yawned and put the windshield wipers on to get rid of the mist droplets coating her Jeep. Thanks to Travis's X-rated story time, she hadn't gotten a bit of sleep last night. Playing with the wolf had only served to make her more restless. And even worse, she felt kind of *ick* about it.

Travis had made it clear that they weren't in a relationship of any kind, so why did she feel like she'd cheated on him with the Big Bad Wolf? And for that matter, why did she feel like she was leading the wolf on, seeing as how he'd shown no interest in ever actually seeing her again, much less, removing his mask? *Because he'd gone all sweet on her last night, that's why.*

He'd called her his moon. She sighed dreamily, and then jumped when Pop barked. They'd just come around the curve and the apple orchard was filled with mother-luvin' cows!

She slammed on the brakes and honked the horn. As usual, the cows looked up briefly, then went back to what they were doing, which was destroying the orchard. It was a good thing her window was up, and Pop couldn't get out to start a stampede.

She texted Claire. Going to be late. Cows in the orchard. AGAIN.
As soon as she set the phone on the seat, it rang. It was Claire.

"Why don't you call your cowboy and have him fix his fence?"

"Ha! Who says he's my cowboy?"

"JD. And everyone else."

"Who is everyone else?"

"Me. Anyway, I'm going to call my dad. His boys can have that entire fence line replaced in a few hours."

"Travis won't allow it."

"Just quote another agricultural penal code, summon the Chupavaca, whatever you have to do. Tell Travis he has no choice."

It was tempting. Maggie was tired of dealing with his cows. "Okay. Call your dad."

* * *

Travis's belly was nicely stuffed with *huevos rancheros*, and he had a sack lunch in his hand, filled with homemade pimento cheese sandwiches, pickles, chips, and cookies. Mrs. Garza patted his cheek. It felt good to be mothered.

Happy Trails was a hub of activity this morning. Men climbed up and down the scaffolding, putting the final coat of paint on the outside of the house. The inside was finished, and Mrs. Garza was busy hanging pictures like she owned the place.

Henry swung in the big tire that hung from the giant live oak out back, content for the moment. It was a crying shame Travis had to go work at Anna's. It was a good day to get some stuff done at the ranch. All the activity around him made him want to join in.

"How do you like the white?" Mrs. Garza asked, looking out the front porch window. "My cousin thought the personality of the house called for classic white."

Travis agreed. "I like it."

"He's getting a bid for central air conditioning," Mrs. Garza continued. "He thinks you might be able to work something out with the Jenkins brothers. They help out with St. Anthony's church picnic every year, and they'll need meat for the BBQ plates."

Travis hoped he didn't run out of cows. "We might have to hold off on that for a while." He grabbed his keys and headed for the door. "Listen, we'll talk about this later. I've got some work to do at Anna's. If my brother comes by, don't let him in. Okay?"

"Okay. Will you see Maggie today?"

"Yes. Why?"

"You should invite her to Thanksgiving." Mrs. Garza stared silently at him for a few seconds before adding, "Henry says she's your girlfriend."

"That little turd…"

"Well, I sure don't believe she's your wrestling partner."

Travis tried not to grin. This had escalated quickly. His heart started a weird rhythm—a fucking flutter—at the idea of Maggie here, in his house.

"I'm baking a turkey," Mrs. Garza continued. "And all the sides. You just need to get Maggie here with an appetite."

Mrs. Garza was having Thanksgiving at Happy Trails? "Don't you have plans with your own family?"

"My sister's daughter had a baby. First grandchild for her. The whole gang is going to East Texas, but my hip aches. I don't want to ride in the car that long. We'll just have Thanksgiving here. You, Henry, me, and Maggie. Smaller than I'm used to, but we'll have fun. You just wait and see."

Before he could say anything else, the old lady shooed him out of his own house. His head was still spinning as he stood on the back porch. *Thanksgiving.* He didn't usually celebrate, but he should probably do something now that he had Henry.

Lost in thought, he climbed in the truck, headed down the lane, and almost didn't notice the activity at the east fence.

"Whoa," he said out loud. To his fucking truck. As if he were thirteen years old again, dreaming of being in the saddle. Which he wasn't.

There were half a dozen guys working on the fence. Cedar posts were piled up on a flatbed trailer, and a tractor with an automated post hole digger was going gangbusters. Shit, it looked like half the fence was done. *Who the hell…*

And there she was. One hand on her hip and the other waving around in the air as she flapped her gums at Gerome Kowalski, who was leaning against a fence post, staring at the ground, and nodding silently, as cowboys were prone to do when women talked.

Travis stopped the truck and got out. He took a deep breath and starting walking.

"Oh, hi, Travis," Maggie said as he approached. She had a smile plastered on her face, but insecurity clenched her brow and shone in her eyes.

"I hope you don't mind me replacing this fence," Gerome said. "I understand you've got your hands full."

Maggie had complained about his cows to Gerome? "Not at all," he lied, wondering how he was going to pay for this. His current bartering tool of beef didn't make much sense. "I feel bad about putting you out this way, though."

"It's nothing. We'll be done in no time, and then you won't have to suffer any more of Maggie's rage." With a wink at Maggie, he added, "And won't that be a relief."

Travis attempted a smile.

Silence settled in, except for the hum of the post hole digger and the clanking of hammers nailing wire to the fence posts.

"I'm not real sure when I can pay you for this fence," Travis finally blurted.

"See that bull out there?" Gerome pointed to a huge Black Angus in the pasture, swishing his tail at flies. Travis didn't know much about bulls, but he admired the straight back, large neck, and powerful shank of the animal.

"You need to trade him out. It's a shame, though; he's a producer. I should know. He used to be a real pain in my ass, visiting my herd regularly. I figure I owe you for all the calves he's sired. So, don't worry yourself over this fence."

"Are you sure?"

"If I said it, I'm certain of it."

Travis was overwhelmed. And grateful. Because it really would be a fucking relief not to have his cows traipsing into Honey's apple orchard. He looked at Maggie, who was gnawing her lower lip and twisting her hands.

"Does this mean the threats will stop?" He tried to stare sternly at her, because watching her simmer tickled the hell out of him. Possibly turned him on a little, too.

"I don't have the slightest idea what you're talking about," she said.

Gerome looked at Maggie, glanced at Travis, and went back to contemplating the Black Angus. "Your daddy sure had an eye for bulls. I loved to watch him at the cattle auctions. He was rarely buying, but he'd advise anyone and everyone about which bulls to bid on, and they almost always took his advice."

"Are you shitting me? Dad didn't know a damn thing about cattle."

"I beg to differ. He had good instincts."

"I didn't know that."

"I figured you didn't."

Travis swallowed a knot in his throat. Learning something new about his dad, seeing him through the eyes of someone else, caused a small chunk of resentment to thaw and break away.

"In my experience, it runs in families," Gerome added.

And if Gerome said it, he was certain of it.

Chapter

Twenty-Eight

❦

Maggie unlocked the front door of Petal Pushers, and Pop sprinted in. It was eleven thirty, so she had about half an hour before customers began showing up. People liked to do Sunday projects, and fall was a good time to plant shrubs and perennials. She wished she could get out to Anna's today. All the dirt had been spread, and it was time for the shrubs and trees to go in. Norbert had delivered them yesterday.

She walked through the garden center to the counter, where she booted up the computer. Then she went into the back to retrieve some more wind chimes to display by the cash register.

As she pulled a fourth box out to add to the stack, the bell on the door jingled and Pop went off like a car alarm. Claire was supposed to have the day off, but Maggie smelled Chanel. She came out of the stock room, carrying boxes, just as Claire slipped behind the counter.

"What are you doing here? I thought you were rock climbing today."

"Canceled," Claire said. "Everybody but me had other plans. I figured if I came in and worked in the shop, you could get back out to Anna's and hurry that project along."

"Sure you don't mind?"

"Not at all. And I've been meaning to talk Thanksgiving with you."

"No worries. I'll bring a vegetable tray again." She'd spent last Thanksgiving with Claire. And she assumed she'd spend this one the same way.

"I'm going to Abilene with Ford for Thanksgiving. But my folks say you're still welcome—"

"Did you just say you're going to Abilene with Ford for Thanksgiving?"

"Yes."

"Ford Jarvis the Cowboy? That Ford?"

"Good Lord, Maggie. Unless you know some other guy named Ford who happens to be a working cowboy, yes, *that* Ford."

"Does your daddy know?"

Mr. Kowalski's parenting advice to every new mother in Big Verde was basically *Mamas, don't let your babies grow up to date cowboys.*

Claire drew her mouth into a thin line. Finally, she sighed. "Nope. Grown woman. Going anyway."

"Good for you! Also, I knew it! I knew you had more than just the hots for him."

"Who says I have more than just the hots?"

"Thanksgiving, that's who. You don't do Thanksgiving with someone unless it's serious, Claire. And don't worry about me. I'll go to JD's. Or maybe Bubba and Trista's."

"Speaking of cowboys, I hear yours is getting a fantastic new fence."

"Once again, he's not my cowboy. He's not anyone's cowboy. He's selling the ranch and moving to Austin."

Claire laughed.

"What's so funny?"

"My dad says Travis is a cowboy. And you know he doesn't say that lightly. Travis isn't going anywhere."

Maggie was filled with hope. Gerome Kowalski was never wrong.

* * *

Travis stood and wiped his hands on a rag as the rumble of tires on the gravel road made its way in from the distance. He'd finished early at Anna's and decided to paint the Happy Trails gate. It seemed a shame, with the house painted and the new straight fence lines in, to have a rusty gate at the entrance.

He took a big swig of water and wiped his sweaty face on the sleeve of his shirt.

The tire noise grew louder. Maybe it was Maggie coming down Peacock Road to get to her place. The cloud of dust made it difficult to make out the vehicle, but he was disappointed to see it wasn't a yellow Jeep.

It was a blue pickup. And it was slowing down.

With dread, Travis watched it turn in. All the painters had left, and nobody was coming back until tomorrow. The setting sun reflected off the windshield, concealing the driver's identity. But it had to be Scott.

The door opened, and a pair of grubby boots hit the dust. Travis inhaled and steeled himself for a confrontation, but the man who emerged was not his brother. "Hey there, runt, remember me?"

Runt. That brought back memories. Travis hadn't seen lowlife John Sills since he was seventeen. Because he didn't know what else to do, he offered a hand. "Hi there, John. What are you doing out here?"

"Shit. Look at you. I heard you got big, but *damn*, boy, I don't think I'd pick a fight with you now."

Walking up to someone who wouldn't fight back, smacking

them in the face, and breaking their glasses was not a fight. And those were the kind of fights John picked. "I wouldn't if I were you," Travis said. "I hit back now."

John laughed and pulled his hand away. He hollered over at the truck. "You were right! He's a badass."

An arm dangled out of the passenger-side window, flicking ashes off a cigarette. Travis recognized the tattoos. "Are you going to get out of the truck, Scott?"

The cigarette was flicked to the ground. "Howdy, little bro." Unlike John, his brother was not grubby or disheveled. Menacing— yes. Messy—no. He could emerge from the flames of wreckage with his shirt pressed and hair combed. Today was no exception. He opened the door of John's decrepit truck with the cracked windshield and busted-out headlight as if he were climbing out of a Mercedes-Benz.

Scott walked over and thumped Travis on the back. "I feel like we're drifting apart. You never call or come by anymore. And when I stopped by yesterday, your *sancha* wouldn't let me in the house. She's a little old for you, by the way."

John laughed again. Travis just stared Scott down. "What do you want?"

"Maybe I just want to see my kid."

Travis worked at keeping his face blank. "Do you really think that's a good idea?"

"I need a phone. Then maybe money for a place to crash, unless you want me at Shitty Trails."

Travis broke out in a sweat. In addition to paying the back taxes, he'd have to buy out Scott's half of the ranch if he ever wanted to be rid of him.

"My wallet's in my truck. I'll give you some cash for a prepaid phone and a motel room. But then you're on your own."

Travis walked to his truck to get some money.

"Somebody's coming," John said.

Indeed, there was another dust trail headed their way, and a yellow Jeep was the cause.

"Who's that?" Scott asked.

"The woman who lives down the road," Travis said, pressing a wad of cash into Scott's hand. "This should take care of things. I have to get back to work." *Just leave.*

"That crazy old lady who fought with Dad all the time? What was her name...Sweetie? Darlin'? It was something stupid."

"Honey," Travis said through clenched teeth. "She died. Somebody else lives there now. You should get going."

Travis nearly groaned as the yellow Jeep slowed down. Maggie stuck her arm out and waved. Then she turned in.

"Is that the little somebody?" Scott asked as Maggie pulled up behind John's truck. "She's cute."

Pop shot out the window. He pissed on all four of John's tires before trotting over.

"There's a good dog," Travis said. Scott bent over to pet him, but Pop responded with a low growl.

"Pop, stop that," Maggie said.

She wore her usual work jeans and long-sleeve polo with a flannel over it. But the flannel was open, exposing a pair of perky breasts. No bra. Travis glanced at Scott. He'd noticed, too, but wasn't openly staring. John, however, was not as suave as Scott. He leered, and Travis's pulse pounded like a jackhammer in his head.

"Are you going to introduce us to your friend?" Scott asked pleasantly.

Maggie smiled at him. She had no clue who she was dealing with. Scott was good looking, smart, and practiced at playing a nice guy, but Maggie's brows furrowed. She was wary.

"This is Maggie Mackey. She's a landscape architect."

Scott raised his eyebrows. "Holy shit. Mighty Mack grew up."

Maggie frowned. "Scott?"

"He's just leaving," Travis said.

Scott shook his head and laughed. "Received loud and clear, bro. Let me know when you get this place sold. I'm assuming you came up with a plan to pay the back taxes?"

Travis hadn't really wanted to do this in front of Maggie, but he was planning on telling her everything anyway. "I'm working on the back taxes," he said. "But I've decided not to sell Happy Trails. I'm staying on the ranch."

There was a deep intake of breath, and Travis looked to see Maggie with her hand over her mouth, eyes wide in surprise. Then those same eyes crinkled a bit as a smile crept out from behind her fingers. That was the reaction he'd hoped for. He winked at her.

Scott's face was a mirror opposite. Lips drawn. Nostrils flared. Vein pulsing next to his right eye. Travis dared a glance at his brother's fists. Both were clinched, and Travis took a step back. He wouldn't be surprised if Scott threw a punch, so he stuck his chest out and clenched his own fists, ready for it.

Scott raised an eyebrow.

That's right, motherfucker. I can take you now.

Relaxing his demeanor and adopting an easy smile that would have been pleasant on anyone else, Scott reached out and squeezed Travis's shoulder. Still wearing the smile, he said, "Sell the ranch, or you'll regret it."

Travis snorted. "Is that a threat?"

Scott stopped smiling. "Tell my son that his daddy will be back to see him real soon. It's time he and I got to know each other."

Travis tried to remain passive. Blank. Stoic. But the confirmation of his failure was reflected in his brother's satisfied gaze.

He'd just given away his weak spot.

*   *   *

The sun was setting in a brilliant Texas Hill Country display of orange, pink, and blue. Travis had pulled Maggie into his truck to talk, and it could have been the moment he'd been waiting for—the one where he confessed his feelings and his secret—but he was too frantic.

"He doesn't want Henry," he spat. "And he couldn't possibly take care of him."

"Exactly. So you have nothing to worry about," Maggie said.

"You don't know Scott. He's going to try and force me to sell the ranch. He obviously needs the money for something. Who knows what's hanging over his head? Scott's dangerous when he's desperate."

"Do you think he'll try to take Henry? Like blackmail? Sell the ranch, or else?"

That took the wind out of his sails. That's exactly what he thought Scott would do, but he didn't like hearing somebody say it out loud.

"What kind of custody do you have?" Maggie asked.

"I have temporary custody. That's all."

"Well, what do we do?"

She'd used the word *we*. God, he could kiss her. He could kiss her because she clearly didn't want him to think he was in this fight alone, and because she loved Henry. She really did. It was right there in those big brown eyes.

"I've got a lawyer," he said.

Her eyes melted with relief. "Good. Where did you find him?"

"He's a friend of JD's."

"JD is friends with a lawyer?"

Travis tried to keep his eyes on hers, but he couldn't. He was a horrible liar. He performed all the telltale *liar liar pants on fire* signs when he did it. Like avoiding eye contact. "Yeah. Just a guy he knows in Austin."

He glanced back at Maggie. She scowled in thought, trying to figure out who JD knew that she didn't. "You want *just a guy* to be your lawyer?"

"JD knows him well," he said, watching a moth flutter around the cab of the truck. "I trust him." He ran his hands through his hair. "Man, I really thought I had more time to get all this settled. Scott got out early. Gabriel thinks—"

"Who's Gabriel?"

"JD's lawyer friend." Back to the moth tracking. "He says the courts try really hard to keep kids with their biological parents. And even though Scott's been in prison, if he can pull off looking like he's making a good faith attempt at turning his life around…"

"I just saw him. He's not pulling anything off."

"I know. But he's a goddamn sociopath. He can be charming when he wants."

"Really? I think you're the charming brother."

Maggie looked at him almost shyly, and his heart thumped away like a tail on a dog that had been praised by its master. He was a roller coaster of emotions. "I should have jumped on this sooner. But I was reeling from my new responsibilities." He looked her straight in the eye. "Maggie, I didn't want to be all Henry had in the world. I held off because I secretly hoped something else would work out." His voice hushed to a whisper. "I didn't want him."

"But you do now, and that's all that matters," Maggie said, touching his hand. "It'll be fine. We'll make sure of it."

There was that *we* again, settling over him like a comforting blanket. He brushed her bangs out of her eyes, and then he just fucking went for it. Leaned over and kissed her softly on the lips. Her fingers floated up to caress his cheek, then entangled in his hair. She parted her lips and moaned softly as he deepened the kiss.

Travis's heart thudded, threatening to burst out of his rib cage. When Maggie's tongue brushed up against his, all of his worries disappeared into thin air. *Well, maybe they didn't disappear. But they retreated to a respectable distance.*

There was only room for one concern, and that was to kiss the hell out of Maggie Mackey.

Chapter
Twenty-Nine
꧁

Maggie sat in the break room at Petal Pushers, staring at her phone. She and Travis had gone at it like teenagers in his pickup truck yesterday. And Travis wasn't selling Happy Trails! Even better, he'd told her she was one of the reasons. Henry was the other one, so she was in good company.

She needed to do something about the wolf, though. His last text stared up at her. You're my moon.

It was the most romantic and sweetest thing a man had ever said to her. Especially since the man was a wolf. But she had to let him go. Travis was real. The wolf was not. The choice was easy.

Hey, wolfie. You there?

The response was immediate.

Right here, Red.

Best to just come out with it.

I can't play with you anymore. There's someone else.

She stared at her phone and counted...one, two, three...She'd never broken up with anybody before.

Is it serious?

I'd really like it to be.

Four, five, six...

Here's to your happily ever after.

Relief washed over her. Also, a bit of sadness. She'd miss her wild wolf, no doubt about it. But mostly, she was looking forward to kissing Travis again. Which would hopefully be sooner rather than later, since he would be dropping Henry off any minute.

Claire breezed in, carrying a tray of paints and paintbrushes for the craft class she was leading this morning. "Did you do it?"

Maggie nodded. "Yep."

"Good. Because you can't be two-timing on your cowboy when he just pulled into the parking lot."

Maggie's pulse picked up. "He's here to drop Henry off."

"He's leaving a five-year-old in our store?"

"Just for a few hours. It'll be fine."

The bell on the door jingled and Pop bounded out of the break room. Soon he came trotting back with Henry in tow. "Hi, Maggie!" Henry said, climbing onto a stool.

"Hi yourself. Where's your uncle?"

"He's in the truck lookin' at himself in the mirror. I got tired of waiting on him."

Claire laughed. "Aw, Maggie. He wants to be pretty for you."

"Boys aren't pretty," Henry said.

Travis walked into the room, proving Henry wrong. His shirt was pressed and tucked into his Wranglers, and his smile lit up the room. Honey would have referred to him as a *long, tall drink of water*.

"Thanks for watching him while I go to Austin," Travis said. "I wasn't prepared for a teacher workday, and Mrs. Garza has plans until three."

"No problem. I'm happy to have him hang out at Petal Pushers." Maggie went to the mini-fridge and grabbed a carton of milk. "Want a cookie, Henry?"

"Did you make them?"

"No."

"Then yes."

Travis poked Henry. "Manners."

"Yes, *ma'am*."

Maggie laughed and set a store-bought bag of cookies on the counter. Henry was a truth-o-meter. He didn't get all the subtleties involved in sparing someone's feelings. Not that her feelings were hurt. Baking was clearly not her strong suit. Now if someone were to criticize her landscaping, that would be another story.

"We're going to have fun today, Henry. It's time to decorate for Christmas."

"It is?"

"Not really," Maggie said. "But in the retail world we don't let that stop us."

Henry stuffed a cookie in his mouth and nodded as if he understood.

"The trees were unloaded early this morning. And we have all the Christmas goodies to set out. I'm talking snowmen, reindeer, You Know Who with the sleigh—"

"Santa!"

It wasn't usually this easy to make someone happy. It felt good.

"When are we getting a tree, Uncle Travis?"

Travis frowned. "Trees are a fire hazard and they make an awful mess."

"You're not serious," Maggie said.

"We never had one for those very reasons."

"You probably never had a lot of things. That doesn't mean Henry doesn't deserve them."

Travis rolled his eyes. "It's all a bunch of clutter, if you ask me."

Maggie wasn't exactly a glitter cannon of Christmas herself. In fact, she found a lot of it nauseating. But she was not going to let Travis Blake deny this kid a tree just because he'd never had

one and apparently harbored an inner five-year-old who thought he
didn't deserve one.

"We have ormy-ments at the house. And lights, too." Henry
toyed with a second cookie but didn't eat it. "From before," he
added quietly.

Maggie pulled gently on Travis's beard, so he'd look at her.
"This is Henry's first Christmas with you." She gave him her very
best *no way in hell you're denying this kid a Christmas tree after
his goddamn mother died* glare. "He needs a tree."

"Fine. A small one."

Maggie gave a little yank on the beard. Travis winced. "Or a
medium-sized one."

"Yay!" Henry took an enormous bite out of the cookie and
began humming "Jingle Bells."

Maggie rose up on her toes and planted a kiss on Travis's cheek.
"Thank you."

"What about you?" Travis asked.

"What about me what?"

Travis lowered his voice. "When are you trimming your tree?"

That sounded filthy, and Maggie's ears lit up like she wanted to
pull Travis's sleigh tonight. "They're fire hazards and they make
a mess."

"Are you kidding me?"

She wasn't, and she grinned to let him know it. "No tree for me.
I'm hardly ever home, and anyway, I'm surrounded by them here."

"Maggie can come to Happy Trails and trim our tree," Henry
announced.

Travis raised an eyebrow at Maggie. "How about it?"

"Sounds like fun," she said, heart fluttering. She'd never been
inside Travis's house.

"I get to put the star on top. Uncle Travis will have to hold me
on his shoulders like in the movies."

Something about the expression on Travis's face told Maggie that

Henry wasn't the only little boy who'd imagined having a made-for-TV Christmas. This year they were both going to get one.

"I'd better get out of here. Are you going to be okay with Henry?"

"Of course. And he even gets to do a craft class with Claire. Right, Claire?"

"You bet," Claire said. "He'll like that."

"I'm not painting pots with a bunch of old ladies," Henry said. "That's what Uncle Travis says Claire does in her classes."

"Uncle Travis spouts off a lot, doesn't he?" Claire said.

"It's part of my charm," Travis said with a wink.

"They're making ornaments today. I think Claire should at least wait until after Thanksgiving, but some folks just can't help themselves." Maggie gave Claire the side-eye.

"If I ran the world, it would be Christmas all year long. Maggie's a Scrooge." Claire held out a hand to Henry. "Come on, let's go set up."

"Okay," Henry said, grabbing two more cookies before hopping off his stool. "What's a Scrooge?"

The tapping of Claire's heels and Henry's questions receded as Travis cleared his throat. They were alone. And Travis looked like he had something on his mind. If it was the same thing she had on hers, they might need to lock the door.

"Do you have plans for Thanksgiving?"

This was unexpected. And somewhat delightful. "Are you inviting me?"

"Yes."

What was it she'd said to Claire? *You don't do Thanksgiving with someone unless it's serious.* She swallowed. "I'd love to come."

"Good," Travis said. His voice was tinged with relief. It was so sweet! "I should be back by suppertime. You behave yourself now."

Maggie looked around the room. "Are you talking to me?"

"Is that the best De Niro you got?"

"It's the only De Niro I got, and I always behave myself."

"I doubt that, Miss Mackey." He kissed her on the nose. "I'll see you later."

He headed for the door and then stopped. "I've been meaning to tell you that package came in."

"What package?"

Travis waggled his eyebrows. "The long, skinny one. I think we determined it's about twenty-five inches."

Maggie's ears lit up like beacons. "You did not really order that."

Travis picked up a wooden ruler—MEASURE UP WITH PETAL PUSHERS!—and smacked it against his hand. Maggie jumped and squealed.

"Scare you? Guilty conscience got you thinking about a spanking?"

This was getting more and more Big Bad Wolfish by the minute. Was there an animal lurking behind Travis's twinkling blue eyes? As she watched, they darkened a shade or two.

"Don't you need to be somewhere?" she asked.

Travis blinked like someone had just turned on the lights. "Yeah. Wow. I'd better get out of here. Don't forget about Thursday."

Like she could forget about Thanksgiving. "Wait! What should I—"

"Anything but brownies," he called over his shoulder.

* * *

Travis hoped his jeans were clean. And his shoes. And his hands. He'd never been inside a room that was so *white*. White rug. White furniture. White walls.

Gabriel Castro did not have kids.

Gabriel came back into the room with two cups of coffee. "It's black. Do you need cream or sugar?"

Travis took one of the mugs with extreme care. If Henry were here, he'd choose now to jump on his back. "Black is fine. Thank you for meeting with me."

Gabriel sat down and set his mug on the coffee table. "I'm happy to help. Any friend of JD's is a friend of mine."

Time to get some unpleasantness out of the way. "Listen, before we start, I need to know how much this will cost."

"I told you not to worry about that."

"I have to worry about it."

"It's pro bono, brother."

"You don't need to—"

"Yes, he does."

JD strutted out of the bedroom. Shirtless and damp from a shower, he wore nothing but athletic shorts.

"Jesus Christ, JD. I've never seen your legs before. Where are a pair of sunglasses when you need them?"

Gabriel grinned. "When I decided to go for a white boy, I went for a *white boy*. Check out that sexy farmer tan on his arms."

"I'd have worn a shirt, but I didn't know you were coming." JD glared at Gabriel.

"I forgot to mention it."

JD disappeared—probably to grab a shirt—and Gabriel popped open his laptop. "Has Scott ever paid child support?"

"Are you kidding?"

Gabriel wasn't smiling.

"No child support. Ever."

"So, you support the child?"

The child had a fucking name. "His mom used to support Henry. Now I do. Lisa had some life insurance—not much—but it's in trust. Henry gets it when he's eighteen. And there's some social security."

"Scott has been incarcerated multiple times, correct?"

"Yes." This was sounding better and better. What judge in his right mind would grant custody to Scott?

"Has he been involved with Henry at all?"

"Not enough to be noteworthy."

"It's all noteworthy. And I've talked to his parole officer. Scott took a parenting class in prison, and as of this morning, he's signed up for a series of parenting workshops that start next month."

"Shit. That was fast."

"He's looking for work. Doing all the right things."

What had seemed black and white was now murky as fuck.

JD came back into the room wearing jeans, a T-shirt, and a red face. He glanced at where his hat hung.

"Not in the house, cowboy," Gabriel said, and JD sat down and crossed his arms, staring straight ahead. Hatless.

Gabriel typed on his laptop, JD scowled, and Travis became more nervous by the minute.

"Scott reports that he's attempted to see Henry twice since his release. The first time was the day he got out—it was supposedly the first thing he did. And then he tried again yesterday."

"He did not try—"

"Says he did."

"I have custody. I don't have to let anybody see Henry if I don't want them to." He was getting pissed.

"Actually, you have temporary guardianship. You do not have custody."

Travis tried to quell the rising panic. "Are you sure?"

"Yes. Guardianship was granted due to parental incarceration. And that has ended."

"Early," Travis said. "It ended early. And he said he wanted to relinquish his rights."

"Verbally?"

"Yeah. I bet that doesn't mean shit, does it?"

"That's right. Verbal doesn't mean shit."

Travis rubbed the bridge of his nose. "I should have jumped on it when I had the chance."

"His crimes were not violent," Gabriel continued.

"Oh, he's plenty violent."

"I can only go by his convictions. And according to those, he's not violent, and none of his crimes are against children."

Gabriel typed for a few minutes while Travis and JD fidgeted. Finally, he looked up. "I don't want to give you a false sense of hope. But my gut says Scott doesn't want Henry, especially if he verbally agreed to relinquish his rights. He's fucking with you. I'm going to petition for nonparental custody. That's our first step. And since he's looking for a job, I'll also begin the paperwork to garnish future wages for child support. He'll hate that."

"What if it doesn't work? What if he still goes after Henry to try and force me to sell the ranch?"

Gabriel raised an eyebrow. "He'll have to prove to a judge that he can care for Henry better than you can. But we'll cross that bridge when, and if, we come to it. If you think there's a chance Scott isn't going to relinquish his parental rights voluntarily, then we need to go on the offensive and file."

After a few minutes of idle chatter to wind things down, Travis asked about Thanksgiving plans. "Having Thanksgiving with your folks, JD?"

"No. Not this year."

Gabriel sighed. "I hate being the reason you're not with your family."

"I'd rather be with you." JD grabbed Gabriel's hand.

"What about you, Travis?" Gabriel asked. "You got big holiday plans?"

"Believe it or not, I'm having Thanksgiving at Happy Trails. Mrs. Garza and Maggie are coming over."

"Maggie?"

"Yeah," Travis answered. "We're kind of dating, I think." Although he hadn't taken her anywhere. He should probably do that.

The corner of JD's mouth curled up; the little smirk that drove women—and at least one man—wild. "You think?"

Travis didn't want to talk about Maggie. He wanted to talk *to* her. Badly. Time to head back. "I can't thank you enough, Gabriel," he said, standing. "I feel better knowing you're on my side."

"We both are," JD said.

Gabriel stood. "We'll walk you out. I need to get the mail."

When they got to the door, Travis had a thought. "Would you guys like to come for Thanksgiving?"

JD looked at Gabriel, whose eyes were hopeful.

"Mrs. Garza is cooking, if that's any incentive."

JD put an arm around Gabriel's shoulders. "As long as it's not Maggie."

Travis laughed, but then he turned serious. "Don't worry. It'll all be fine."

Chapter Thirty

The house was warm from the oven and the wood-burning stove, and the best part was it smelled like apple pie. Satisfied and basically pleased as punch, Maggie removed her apron. She was fully clothed—no naked baking this morning.

She hoped two pies would be enough. Travis had said JD was coming with a date. It seemed everyone was getting serious with somebody.

A few minutes later she pulled through the freshly painted Happy Trails gate. Travis had done some gorgeous landscaping with cactus and sage. The fences, she noticed with satisfaction, were straight and strong. Round hay bales sat majestically in the west pasture, surrounded by apple-deprived cows.

When the house appeared, she literally gasped. She didn't know what she'd expected, but it wasn't a gleaming white two-story with a wraparound porch and hanging baskets of blooming Christmas cactus. It looked like a home. A real one.

Travis was really staying.

She grabbed the pies and climbed out of the Jeep, just as

Travis opened the front door. He wore a black long-sleeved Henley and jeans. He'd tamed his wavy hair and trimmed his beard, and his blue eyes twinkled as he said proudly, "Welcome to Happy Trails."

Maggie stepped onto the porch and handed him the pies. They were still warm. "You baked these?"

"Yes. Technically, I baked the shit out of them."

"Technically?"

"I put them in the oven raw and took them out done."

"And before that, did you take them out of a box and let them thaw?"

"Look at you knowing where your food comes from."

The door opened and Mrs. Garza, decked out in a gold lamé dress covered by a well-worn apron that had never seen a store-bought *anything*, waved them inside. "Come in, come in. Henry's been waiting for you, Maggie."

"Maggie! Come watch the parade with me." Henry wrapped himself around her knees.

"Let me see if I can help Mrs. Garza first, okay?" She looked around. "Travis, I'm... Well, heck. I guess I'm speechless." The living room was warm and inviting. Picture windows, high-beamed ceilings, a view of the valley called Cañada Verde. "No wonder you've decided to stay here."

Travis took her hand and grinned. "The reason I'm staying here has pink ears."

"SpongeBob!" Henry shouted. "Look, Maggie!"

Henry was mesmerized by a gigantic yellow balloon being led down a street lined with freezing New Yorkers. He let go of Maggie's legs and plopped himself back in front of the parade.

"Travis, I need you to get down the turkey platter," Mrs. Garza said. "Maggie, you can set the table."

"It's such a relief to have someone in charge," Maggie whispered to Travis.

"Don't cross her," Travis whispered back as they followed Mrs. Garza into the kitchen.

"Wow. This kitchen is bigger than my living room."

It was nothing fancy. Some might even say it was strictly utilitarian, since it was clearly built for making big meals for hungry cowboys. But it was charming. It had tons of cabinets, endless countertops, and a walk-in pantry. Maggie wasn't the type of woman who typically got excited over such things, but she was still pretty dang impressed. And was it weird to imagine her landscape plans all rolled out under the bright and cheerful lighting?

"The plates are up there," Mrs. Garza said, pointing at the cabinet to the left of the stove. "I put the silverware on the table already."

The cabinet doors were glass, which Maggie knew was kind of "in" since Anna had chosen them for her new house. A stack of mismatched plates nearly hid the pretty white ones in the back. Maggie pulled them down. Adorned with a cheerful bluebonnet pattern, they were absolutely perfect. Had they been Lisa's Sunday dishes? Would she be pleased about their use today? Maggie tenderly carried them to the table, which was a long, rustic polished pine beauty.

"Where did you get this table?"

Travis handed Mrs. Garza the turkey platter he'd retrieved from the top shelf. "My dad made it for my mother. It went with us everywhere we lived. Sometimes it literally took up half the house—or trailer. We never ate on it, though."

"Goodness, why not?"

"I don't know. My mom left when I was little. My dad kind of lived in suspended animation after that. I think he was waiting for her to come home so we could be a family again. Until then, it was TV trays and frozen dinners."

Maggie had never asked Travis about his mom. She'd assumed the woman was dead since he and Scott were raised by their dad. "Do you know where she is?"

"The last I heard, she was a showgirl in Vegas." Travis smiled sadly. "But I doubt that's where I'd find her now."

Maggie couldn't imagine a woman abandoning her children. Sure, her mom had taken off, too. But Maggie had been a teenager, and her mom had begged her to come along. They still talked as often as Maggie could tolerate, which was about once a month.

"I'm glad we're going to be sitting at this table today," Travis said, snatching Henry's backpack off the back of a chair. "Oh, and I'd better put this out of the way, too," he added with a grin, holding up a skinny box.

Maggie nearly dropped the plates.

"I'm going to run upstairs and put it in the bedroom. Care to join me?"

"Travis, stop it," Maggie whispered. "It's Thanksgiving."

"I know. I need to talk to you for a minute." He grabbed her hand and pulled her to the stairs. She followed him up, and he opened a door and shoved her through. A king-size bed took up almost the entire room.

"We need to talk about JD," Travis said.

So much for being thrown on the bed and ravished. "What about him?"

"He's bringing someone."

He'd already told her that. She took a moment to compose her facial features into *Great!* before saying, "It's weird that he's bringing her here. Why isn't he doing Thanksgiving with his family?"

Travis shook his head slightly. "Listen, JD's a little nervous. Just be a good friend."

It finally dawned on her what this was about. "Oh my God. What else would I be? Does he think I'm going to launch into a jealous rage? What an ego!"

"It's not that."

Ha! The hell it wasn't. This was infuriating. Embarrassing.

Humiliating. "Wow. I just went through the seven stages of grief in, like, three seconds flat. Easy peasy. I'm at acceptance."

"That's where you need to be," Travis said, rubbing his bearded chin.

"Travis, come here." She grabbed a few whiskers. "I don't have the hots for JD."

"Prove it."

She was happy to. His mouth was so soft. She felt his hand at the nape of her neck and things became unmistakably less gentle. Her heart pounded when he ran his fingers through her hair, pulling it a little and tilting her head back. It gave him better access, and she nearly collapsed when he parted her lips with his tongue.

The man meant business.

Maggie wanted to climb him like a tree and shout *Timber!* before pushing him onto the bed.

Travis closed his hand into a fist, pulling her hair a little harder and tilting her head back even more. Her pulse raced like someone had waved a flag and said *Go!* Thrills and chills ran up and down her spine at this unexpected show of... whatever the heck it was. She hesitated to think *dominance*. This wasn't *Bound and Determined*, and Travis wasn't the hero of an erotic novel. Nor was he the Big Bad Wolf.

Which made the whole thing way hotter.

Travis's lips left her mouth and worked down her jaw to her neck. She went limp as a noodle. At the same time, she felt like she might possibly be on fire. Every bit of skin his lips touched was set aflame.

"Oh, Travis," she whispered.

He responded with a groan. This was going someplace good!

Although now the groan sounded a little high-pitched and whiny—

"Gross, Uncle Travis."

Travis and Maggie let go with a start. "Jesus, Henry," Travis said, running his fingers over his mouth. His face looked like it might explode. "Can't you knock?"

"Why would I?"

Travis's hair was a mess. Maggie imagined hers was just as bad. She was still out of breath, her knees were knocking, and she wanted to send Henry packing. But instead, she said, "So you don't require therapy later."

Henry backed out of the room and shut the door. Then he banged on it.

"Come in," Travis said.

Henry opened the door. "JD is here in a fancy car."

"We'll be right there. Now close the door."

Henry slammed the door. "I'm gonna tell Mrs. Garza that y'all were wrestling again!" he shouted.

"Do you think we've traumatized him?" Maggie asked.

"Nah. We were just kissing. He's seen worse on television."

If that was *just kissing*, Maggie was the Queen of England. "You should probably do a better job of monitoring what he watches on TV."

"Probably. Brace yourself," Travis said, opening the door. "Be nice to JD."

When they got downstairs, Mrs. Garza was staring out the kitchen window. "Who is that handsome man?"

Maggie walked up and peeked over the older woman's shoulder. No white pickup. A sleek, black Audi coupe had parked next to her Jeep. She didn't recognize the car or the dark-haired man standing next to it, but she sure recognized the white hat that got out next. It was pulled down very low, shading the upper part of JD's face. *Hiding.*

Mrs. Garza fanned herself with her hand. "That's some Latino sexiness out there." She fluffed her hair as she ran to the door.

The guy with JD was handsome all right. And dressed up in a nice shirt and tie. He carried a platter of pastries, and JD held some flowers, although they hung limply at his side as if he'd forgotten about them. The two of them stood together, looking at the house but not moving.

Mrs. Garza opened the door. "Welcome! Come inside!"

They came up the steps, the stranger with a smile and JD with a frown. Was this guy holding JD hostage? Maggie didn't see a gun to his head, but that was the vibe.

Travis shook hands with both men, did some back-pounding and other ritualistic whatnot, and then everyone stood around awkwardly because men were absolutely horrible at introductions.

"Who's your friend, JD?" Maggie asked. Otherwise they'd never know.

JD cleared his throat and pulled his hat down even lower, if that were possible, as if he were trying to drag it down over his entire body.

"No hat in the house, cowboy," the other man said.

Holy cow! They were going to begin Thanksgiving with a fistfight. Nobody told JD Mayes to remove his hat. JD could wear his hat in a church if he wanted to, and nobody would dare say a thing about it.

JD removed his hat.

"This is Gabriel Castro."

His lawyer friend—the one Travis had gone to see. The one Travis had been reluctant to share details about. The one who'd just called JD "cowboy" and ordered him to remove his hat in the house.

Not just friends then.

Numbness spread throughout Maggie's body. This is what JD had been trying to tell her! She'd been so focused on her own feelings that she'd been an awful friend. JD's hands were trembling, so she took one and squeezed it.

She glanced at the others. Mrs. Garza smiled reassuringly. Travis looked normal. And Gabriel grinned brilliantly—gosh, he really was handsome—while JD looked like he might drop dead on the spot.

Travis smacked Gabriel on the back. "I'm glad y'all could make it. Gabriel, this is Mrs. Garza. She's responsible for all the delicious smells coming from the kitchen."

Mrs. Garza blushed as Gabriel took her hand and gave it a soft kiss. "The way to my heart is through my stomach," he said. Then he looked at Maggie. "And I've heard all about the infamous Maggie Mackey."

"You have?"

"You've been partners in crime with JD since you were little kids, correct?"

She nodded.

"And that's Henry," Travis said, pointing to where Henry sat in front of the television.

Henry looked up. "That's who I am all right. And I can't hear the TV with y'all standing in here talkin'."

"Henry," Travis said in his warning voice. "Manners."

"I can't hear the TV with y'all standing in here talkin', *please, thank you, sir, and ma'am.*"

Everyone laughed, and Henry rolled his eyes in annoyance.

Mrs. Garza took the platter from Gabriel. "Pumpkin empanadas!"

"I made them myself."

Mrs. Garza stroked his cheek as if he were the baby Jesus.

"I baked an apple pie," Maggie said. "Two of them, in fact."

Travis rubbed her back. "Yes, you did, sweetheart. You and Mrs. Smith."

Maggie smacked his arm. "And what's your contribution to the feast?"

"I'm offering up the elegant digs. *Mi casa es su casa.*" He opened his arms in a wide, welcoming gesture.

"*Gracias, hermano,*" Gabriel said.

While Gabriel was being talkative and outgoing, JD was being uncharacteristically quiet. He'd wandered over to stare at the television with Henry.

"Is he okay?" Maggie asked Gabriel.

"He will be."

"Television off," Mrs. Garza demanded. "It's time to eat."

Henry began whining, but when he saw all the food on the counters, bar, and table, he stopped. "Come on, JD. We gots to eat."

"We *have* to eat," JD said.

"That's what I said."

Gabriel grabbed JD's hand as they entered the dining room, but JD wrenched it away. Then Gabriel touched the small of his back, and JD stilled. Mrs. Garza's eyes flitted to where Gabriel's hand rested.

"You two sit here," she said, pulling out chairs. Then she nodded to Maggie and Travis to take their seats, as well.

"Where do I sit?" Henry asked.

Mrs. Garza pulled out a chair. "Next to me, *mijo*."

"Can I sit on the big books?"

"You've grown a bit," Mrs. Garza said with a critical eye. "I'd say A through E ought to do it."

"He refuses a booster seat," Travis said in answer to their quizzical expressions. "It gives us something to do with the outdated encyclopedias."

After Henry had scaled a sixth of the alphabet, the rest of them took their seats. Henry immediately reached for the turkey. "Hey, slow down," Travis said. "I drove all the way to Moulton to get that bird."

"Why would you do that?" Gabriel asked.

"I wanted to try a fresh, free-range turkey. Thinking of maybe raising some."

"Nobody's touching it until we say grace," Mrs. Garza said. "Travis, would you do the honor?"

Travis was quiet for a moment. "Why don't we all say something we're thankful for?"

That was an excellent idea to Maggie.

"I'm thankful for unexpected blessings," Travis said. "The past few months have brought one surprise after another. I fought against every single one. And I'm glad I lost."

Maggie squeezed his hand. It was quiet for a moment, as nobody seemed to want to go next.

Mrs. Garza spoke up. "I'm thankful that we can choose to make our own families."

"I thought you had to be related to be family," Henry said.

"Not always, little one. I think of you as my grandson, did you know that?"

"You do? Can I call you grandma?"

"Of course. Or you can call me *abuela*. That's 'grandma' in Spanish. And Travis, I'm tired of you calling me Mrs. Garza. Lupe is fine. We're family."

Travis reached over and squeezed Lupe's hand. "I couldn't have made it without you."

"It's my turn," Henry said in his bossy tone. "I'm thankful for *abuelas*. I never thought I'd have one!"

Maggie glanced at Travis. This had turned into a Hallmark movie. The kind that usually made her want to stick a finger down her throat. But now she had something in her eye. Lots of somethings. She dabbed them with a napkin.

Gabriel shifted in his seat and reached for JD's hand. JD stiffened but didn't pull away. "I'm thankful for love," Gabriel said. "And for finding it where you least expect it."

Everyone looked at JD. Would he take a turn? He sat silently for a moment, but then in a blur of motion, he pushed his chair back and stood.

"I'm just not ready for this." He looked at everyone sitting around the table, then shook his head and headed for the door. "I need some air."

"Are you in love like Maggie and Uncle Travis?" Henry asked as he passed. "You and Gabriel?"

JD stopped cold. Maggie's heart stopped cold, too, because Henry had just suggested she and Travis might be *in love*. She kept her eyes on JD, trying to be a good friend for once and focus on someone other than herself. JD grabbed his hat off the hook by the door, crammed it on his head, and walked out.

"I'm sorry," Travis said to Gabriel.

"No, I'm the one who's sorry. I forced this on him. He talks about Big Verde and all of you so much, and I'm just ready to be a part of his life—his *real* life. I'm tired of being his dirty secret." He put his napkin on the table and started to rise.

"Sit," Maggie said. "You don't deserve to be anyone's dirty secret. JD is being a gigantic dick."

Henry laughed. "Maggie said *dick*."

Maggie stood. "Sometimes it's called for."

Without another word she stormed out the door, where she found JD standing on the porch.

"What the hell is the matter with you?"

"I'm gay. That's what."

Maggie made an X with her arms and imitated a loud buzzer sound. "Wrong. Try again."

"What do you want me to say?"

"I have never seen this side of you, JD Mayes, and I don't like it. I don't like it one bit. You are being an awful guest and a worse host to poor Gabriel."

JD turned, his mouth agape. "You're upset about my *manners?*"

"That, and the fact that you didn't trust me. That you hid something from me—something this *big*, for crying out loud. And I'm also regretful of the opportunity you just passed up with Henry."

JD shoved the brim of his hat up. "What opportunity with Henry?"

"Henry just asked you point blank, with all the innocence and honesty of a five-year-old, if you and Gabriel are in love. And you could have said yes. You could have shown him that love doesn't always look the same for everybody, but it's still love. You could have shown him that it's *normal*, JD. But instead, you chose to be a shamefaced weasel. And that will be what he remembers about this, probably for the rest of his life. You'd better hope that kid's not gay."

The red tint that had stubbornly stuck to JD's face throughout her entire tirade drained away, leaving him pale. "It's just that I—"

"Come inside, JD."

Maggie offered her hand. JD grabbed it and pulled her close. "I do love you, you know."

When they came back into the dining room, Henry was attempting to cram an entire roll into his mouth. JD sat next to him, picked up his fork like nothing had happened, and said, "Yes, Henry. Gabriel and I are in love."

It took Henry about ten seconds to finish swallowing, but then he said, "I didn't know I could have an *abuela*, and I didn't know boys could love boys."

"Well, now you do," Mrs. Garza said. "It's a good day for learning."

"I don't want to see any kissing, though," Henry said. "I've seen enough of that today already."

Chapter
Thirty-One

❦

Travis brought Maggie a glass of wine. She leaned against his shoulder with a soft sigh, and he put his arm around her. The house was quiet, as Mrs. Garza had taken Henry to the bingo hall, a weird Big Verde Thanksgiving tradition for a certain older crowd.

Maggie pulled her knees up and settled into him. "You smell good," she said.

He'd put on cologne today. It wasn't something he did very often. Just for special occasions.

"It's familiar," she said, leaning in to sniff in earnest.

Travis's pulse sped up. He didn't know if it was because of her warm breath on his neck—which felt nice—or if it was because he'd worn cologne on the night of Anna's Halloween party.

"It's just the cheap stuff most guys wear." That wasn't entirely true. It was a department store sample.

"Well, I like it," Maggie said, nestling her head beneath his chin. "And Thanksgiving was wonderful. I'm glad you invited me."

Travis sighed with relief. "I half expected Scott to show up. Made it hard to relax."

"He doesn't seem the type to drop in for family holiday celebrations. What are you going to do about him and Happy Trails?"

"Buy him out someday. Until then, I'm not selling, and there's not a damn thing he can do about it. My dad set it up so that both of us had to agree in order to sell. He knew what he was doing, since Scott and I have never agreed on anything."

"Can't Scott just insist on splitting it in half? You each get a hundred acres?"

"Dad thought of that, too. Property can't be split. It can be sold as two hundred acres, or not at all."

"Scott mentioned back taxes. Have you paid that yet?"

Travis winced. "I don't have all of it. As soon as Anna pays me the rest of my fee, I'll have about a third of what we owe. I'll have to see if the tax office will accept that for now."

Maggie brushed the hair out of his eyes. It really was getting too long. He wanted to cut it and shave off the beard. Would she recognize him if he did? Now that she'd broken things off with the wolf, it wasn't like he *had* to tell her about his hidden identity. Maybe he'd just keep the mop of hair and itchy beard forever...

No. Their relationship couldn't be built on deception.

"I can't believe JD didn't tell me he was gay."

"He was scared." Travis could fully relate to being afraid of sharing a secret with Maggie. "It's always a risk to let someone know who you really are. Most of us hide behind masks."

"But what was he afraid of?"

"Losing you," Travis whispered. He closed his eyes. He wasn't talking about JD any longer. "He was afraid of losing you if you knew."

"That's ridiculous. I would never abandon a friendship, and certainly not over something like a person's sexual orientation. What do I care? But the lying... I just feel kind of played, you know? He lied to me about who he is."

The words Travis wanted to say—*I'm the Big Bad Wolf*—were swallowed up by the room. He could practically see them escaping through the ceiling. What would Maggie do if she found out he'd been harboring his own secret? That he'd also lied about *who he is* . . . She thought JD had played her? Holy shit. She'd go through the roof over what the Big Bad Wolf had done.

He decided to change the subject. "So how about you come over this weekend and we'll trim the tree with Henry?"

"Are you nuts? Tomorrow is Black Friday. This weekend will be insane at Petal Pushers."

Travis snorted. "I can't quite picture a horde of frothing-at-the-mouth shoppers taking over Big Verde's thriving business district. I mean, we're talking the oil change place, Pump 'n' Go, and Petal Pushers."

"Make fun all you want," Maggie said. "You haven't seen Miss Mills when she's got her eye on the last inflatable baby Jesus. Can we tree trim on Monday?"

"You've got an inflatable Jesus?"

"And three wise men."

Travis shook his head in amazement and tried not to think about Miss Mills blowing into spouts to fully inflate three wise men. "I'm hauling some calves to market on Monday. Does Tuesday work?"

"Tuesday evening. Tell Henry we've got a date. And speaking of Henry, I wonder how late he and Mrs. Garza will be out? How late do bingo halls stay open? I mean, I wonder if they'll be gone long enough for us to—"

"For us to what?" Damn, she was cute. She was panting like a puppy. "Play a game of Scrabble?"

"I'm not much for board games."

"Well, it so happens that Henry is going home with his *abuela* after bingo. We've got the whole night. What do you want to do to pass the time? Maybe read a book?" He grinned at her. "We never finished the last one. I recall that when we left off, our heroine was in the very indelicate position of having her legs up over her head, separated by a twenty-five-inch spreader bar."

"You must have thought a lot about it to remember it in such detail."

"Well, you did that nifty demonstration. It left an impression."

Maggie laughed. "I bet."

"It probably left one on Henry's mind, too."

"Oh God," Maggie said. "I don't think he knew what we were doing."

Travis scooted closer and raised an eyebrow. "What were we doing, Maggie?"

She started to speak, but nothing came out. He should give her mouth something to do.

He kissed her gently at first, but urgency soon took over. He wanted her on her back, legs in the air, inviting him to do whatever the fuck he wanted.

Go away, wolf.

Maggie broke the kiss first, but only to say, "This is so much better than Scrabble."

Travis agreed. "Let's go upstairs."

By the time they got to the bedroom, he was ready to give orders. *Take off your clothes. Lie down. Spread your legs.* But he didn't. That was the Big Bad Wolf's way. Not his.

He pulled Maggie's sweater over her head and dropped it to the floor. She stood in front of him in a red lacy bra. Again, orders bubbled up out of nowhere—*Take off your bra. Push your breasts out. Twist your nipples*—but he kept them to himself.

"I want to see you," Maggie said.

"I'm right here, darlin'."

She rolled her eyes. "Travis, take off your clothes."

"You want me naked?"

"Yes. I want you naked. Now."

"You're a bossy little thing."

If she wanted him to take off his clothes, he'd take off his clothes. But he was going to do it nice and slow. Make her suffer a little. "Okay. Sit on the bed."

Maggie sat, and he slowly lifted his shirt, flexing to define his abs. He might have lost a little ground since settling down with Henry, but he was still in good shape—better than most men—and he knew it. Maggie stared intently at his exposed skin. Not that he let her see very much. Yet.

His jeans rode low, and he hooked a thumb in his waistband, pulling it down a little as Maggie licked her lips. Turning her on was turning him on.

He was no dancer, but he knew how to move his hips, and so he did...a little. He flexed his muscles the entire time, keeping a close watch on Maggie's face, because if she started to laugh, it was game over.

She was not laughing.

He raised the hem of his shirt to reveal the three rows of muscles making up his six-pack. Maggie's eyes followed the shirt's path, leaving a heated trail on his skin. He ran his hand over the snake tattoo that coiled across his lower abdomen, and then raised the shirt higher. He stepped closer to Maggie. So close that her breath grazed his flesh. She kissed his belly, and he clenched his fists and fought for self-control.

Her fingers traced the fly of his jeans, and he backed away.

Too soon, princess.

He turned around to show off his back. Maggie exhaled a long, shuddering breath. He pulled his shirt off and dropped it to the floor. The belt came next, and he yanked it through the loops in one swift move.

"Gosh, Magic Mike much?"

Maybe he'd been a little too dramatic. He looked over his shoulder to see her grinning, but she wasn't making fun of him.

She seemed to be enjoying the hell out of herself. He unzipped his fly and lowered his jeans to mid-thigh. With his feet hip-distance apart, he pulled his underwear down and flexed his glutes, one at a time. Maggie squealed, so he did it again.

He had a dumb smile on his face now. Maybe he had a little Magic Mike in him after all.

He pulled his pants up, which made Maggie boo and hiss, and then spun around. He ran a hand over his abs and up his chest, flexing his pecs as he walked toward her. Maggie covered her face with her hands, but she peeked between her fingers.

"Travis, you're prettier than me. There is no way I'm taking my clothes off now."

When he was mere inches from her face, he pulled her fingers away. "Oh, yes you will."

Maggie's eyes went to his fly. He hooked his thumbs in the waistband of his briefs and slowly dragged them over the head of his penis. Maggie licked her lips. Then she licked him.

He groaned and pulled his briefs the rest of the way down, letting his cock free. Maggie took it in her warm hands, and he watched as she slid them up and down his shaft.

"This is pretty impressive," she said.

He just smiled and tried not to come all over her. She took him in her mouth and he had to try even harder. His eyes met hers—big and round above her sweet mouth so full—and that damn near did it. He pulled back.

"Your turn. Lose the bra."

Maggie bit her lip and furrowed her brow. He was surprised by her shyness, until he remembered that, to Maggie, this was their first time. An uncomfortable wave of guilt crept up, threatening to ruin the mood.

* * *

Maggie couldn't believe the gorgeous man in front of her. He was like one of those guys on a calendar—all he needed was a firefighter hat and a cute puppy. What on earth was he doing here with her? And how the hell was she supposed to get up the nerve to take off her bra? It was possible Travis's pecs were bigger than her breasts. "I'm not much in the cup size department."

Travis knelt before her. "You're the perfect size. The perfect shape."

"Do you have your contacts in?"

Travis laughed. "I see just fine, sweetheart."

"It's really bright in here. Maybe we can turn off the overhead light and put a lamp on. Do you have a scarf to drape over it and set the mood?"

"I'm all out of scarves."

"Oh. Well, maybe we could—"

"You're killing me here. How about I count to three? On three, you lose the bra."

That might work. Maggie scrunched her eyes shut. "Okay. Count."

"You look like you're about to rip off a bandage."

That was kind of like what it felt like. "No. I'm fine. Start counting."

"One...two...three!"

Maggie tried. She really did. But nothing happened. Her fingers were frozen. What she needed was her red cape and porn star boots. Little Red Riding Hood would have no trouble losing the bra. If only she could feel that free and sexy again. But Travis was very unlikely to growl—or bark—orders at her. He was too polite. Too sweet. And she should be totally turned on by that, especially given the adorable striptease he'd performed.

"Try again," she said.

Travis sighed. "One...two...you're not going to do it."

"Sorry! It's just that you're all—you know—Channing Tatum-ish and whatnot. And I'm—"

"Sexy. Gorgeous. Making me so hard I could die."

"Really? Even in bright lighting?"

"Especially in bright lighting." He traced a finger along her collarbone, leaving a trail of gooseflesh, and dragged it around the curve of her breast. "Perfection," he whispered.

Maggie wanted to believe him. She saw his pulse pounding in his neck, watched as he licked his lips.

Slowly, she unclasped her bra and let it slide down her arms. She tried not to melt as she closed her eyes and let him look.

Warm breath brushed her skin. She shivered as his mouth covered her nipple. She was on fire. Places Travis wasn't even touching were lit up in anticipation, and Maggie arched her back when fingertips brushed her other nipple.

She didn't care about the bright lighting anymore.

Travis tugged at the button on the waistband of her jeans. "Let's lose these."

"You first."

Without an ounce of hesitation, Travis stood. And before Maggie could snap her fingers, he was butt naked, except for his socks. And he was clearly anxious to get on with things.

"Come on. Your turn." He pulled her off the bed with a glint in his eye. "Do I have to count to three?"

"Probably. But let me get my boots off first."

She yanked them off. Then she looked at Travis and waited.

"One."

She unbuttoned.

"Two."

She unzipped.

"Three."

Maggie pulled her jeans down, stepped out of them, and did a little dance in her red lacy panties. "Whoo-hoo! I did it!"

Travis offered her a quick high-five, then pulled her close as they collapsed onto the bed. Oh, but it felt good to have his naked body pressed against hers. She pushed on the top of his head, encouraging him to give attention to her breasts again. He seemed more than happy to oblige, and soon Maggie was floating on air, tingling with euphoria.

Travis kissed, sucked, flicked, and grazed. Maggie writhed beneath him, willing him to go lower down her body, but not wanting him to abandon any part of her. He moved against her, warm and hard, kissing down her abdomen, paying homage to her rib cage and belly button, making her giggle with his beard. "Sorry, I'm ticklish."

"I'm filing that info away for later," Travis said, blue eyes sparkling. "Now, let's see what else you've got for me to play with."

Maggie couldn't help it. Her eyes immediately darted to the long, skinny box on the nightstand.

"What are you looking at?"

Ugh! He'd caught her. And he was enjoying it.

"Nothing."

"Are you sure? Because it appears you're interested in that box over there."

Play dumb, Maggie. "What box?"

Travis dragged his finger lightly down her tummy, leaving a trail of goose bumps. He followed it with his lips, and even though his beard tickled, Maggie wasn't laughing. "You want to know what's in that box, baby?"

His voice had gone distinctly lower, gruffer, and there was something about the way he said *baby* that caused her to tremble. "Yes," she whispered.

Travis licked her just above the waistband of her panties, and Maggie could barely catch her breath.

"It's a—"

He licked her lightly again.

"Fully retractable—"

He kissed her through her panties.

"Self-assembly—"

He licked a little lower.

"Cardboard telescope for Henry."

What? Maggie smacked Travis lightly on the top of his head. "You big tease!"

"What did you think it was?"

"You know what I thought it was, and you're infuriating."

Travis pulled at the waistband of her panties. "I bet you won't stay mad long."

Holy cow. That beard. Those lips. *That tongue.* He was right. Irritation no longer registered on her radar. She just wanted him to keep doing what he was doing, only lower.

As if he needed any more tricks, Travis proved to be a mind reader and hooked his thumbs in her panties, yanking them down in one swift move before tossing them over his shoulder. "Open your legs."

Ooh…there was that voice again. Low. Commanding. A hint of a growl. But it couldn't stamp out the stupid sense of modesty currently keeping her knees glued together. "It's really bright in here."

"I'm not turning off the light. We just got to the best part."

Maggie chewed on her lip and pulled her knees up.

"One," Travis said.

The menacing undertone nearly did it for her.

"Two."

She could do it.

"Three."

Nothing.

Travis put his hands on her knees. "Give me permission. It'll be over before you know it."

Maybe… "Okay—"

Bam. He slammed her knees open before she could add, *I guess.*

Travis held her knees firmly in place. She was trapped. At his mercy. *Displayed.*

"You're so beautiful," he whispered. "I have to taste you."

This is the part where the Big Bad Wolf eats Little Red Riding Hood.

Maggie stilled. Why had the wolf's voice butted in? There was no room for him in here. Was her mind playing tricks on her?

Travis's warm mouth erased that thought, and any that tried to form after it. *Rough beard. Soft tongue. The sensation of being devoured.* A low primal moan that she vaguely recognized as her own voice resonated in her head.

Her skin tingled. Her bones hummed. And when Travis's fingers traveled up her rib cage to pinch her nipples, she completely fell apart, trembling beneath waves of pleasure. And then she was floating…until Travis wrenched her knees apart with a gasp.

She'd been squeezing his head between her thighs.

"Sorry," she wheezed, still trying to catch her breath.

Travis grinned goofily. "It would have been a good way to die."

Slowly, he crawled up her body until they were nose to nose. She lost herself in his blue eyes, and even though she was thoroughly wrecked, she was madly looking forward to what came next.

"This has to be a dream. Pinch me."

Travis's eyes became a shade or two darker. "I just did. And you tried to strangle me with your thighs."

The flush crawled up Maggie's chest, spread to her cheeks, and lit up her ears. He'd noticed what had pushed her over the edge.

"If this is a dream," Travis continued, "I hope we never wake up."

She pulled his face back to hers, wanting his lips, wanting the full weight of him crushing her and holding her down. The bed shook as Travis fumbled around in the nightstand drawer without breaking the kiss. He was getting a condom. At least one of them still had the mental faculties to be responsible.

After he'd slipped it on, he kissed her sweetly and then gently— *oh so gently*—eased himself inside her. She wrapped her legs around him as he moved slowly and rhythmically. The man knew what he was doing. This was a delicious prelude, but Maggie longed for the pace to quicken, the intensity to deepen—

Travis moaned and bit his bottom lip as if trying to control himself. He was holding back, and she didn't want him to. She wanted him to give her everything, but how could she ask for what she needed? She dug her heels into his very fine butt cheeks and pulled on his shoulders.

"You okay?" he asked.

"Yes, I just want…" She couldn't finish.

"What do you want, baby?"

There it was again. The way he said *baby*. The sound of it made her tremble to her core.

"Maybe faster. Try it faster. Or harder. Or…something." She squeezed her eyes shut in embarrassment. "I think I like it hard."

Travis quit moving. He was frozen above her, inside her. She opened one eye for a quick peek at his face. Had she stunned him into silence?

Those eyes. Heavy lidded yet so intense she could feel their gaze. His mouth was drawn in a tight, straight line. Nostrils were flared. A tiny vein pulsed on his forehead.

Maggie dug her fingernails into his shoulders. He winced, and after a sudden, gasping breath, he grabbed both of her wrists easily with one hand. Before she could even squeak, he pinned them above her head.

Oh, yes. This was it. This was what she wanted. "Travis—"

His breath teased her ear, setting her on fire. "Open your legs and take this cock."

Her breath caught. She was so turned on she couldn't move.

"Now," he growled.

Her legs responded like good little soldiers, unwrapping themselves from his back and falling open, knees raised. "Take me."

Luckily, he didn't need to be told twice.

* * *

Maggie lay next to Travis, listening to his soft snores compete with the ticking of the clock in the hall. While he'd done the man-thing and immediately fallen unconscious, she was wide awake. Her mind hummed along like a hamster on speed.

Best. Sex. Of. Her. Life. Not only was it steamy and, well, just the way she apparently liked it, it was sweet and funny. That striptease! Those ridiculous countdowns to get her clothes off! Followed by heat. So much heat. How had she gotten this lucky? Travis was literally everything she'd ever wanted.

So why was she unsettled? She felt as if she'd missed a doctor's appointment or failed to pick up the one thing she'd gone to the store for. Maybe it had something to do with work. It would come back to her if she could just freaking relax.

Travis had left the nightstand drawer open after rummaging for a condom. She'd somehow ended up on that side of the bed, and the open drawer stared up at her. She wasn't much of a snooper, but as she went to close it, the light from the hallway made it easy to spot condoms, sore muscle cream, and a book—*Bound and Determined*! How adorable and hilarious. She covered her mouth to keep from laughing.

She was about to close the drawer when a phone caught her eye. It wasn't the one Travis regularly used, but it was the same model. Why would he have a second phone in his drawer? She frowned. This shouldn't give her pause. She probably had four or five old phones tucked away in various places.

Her hamster mind spoke up. *Phones are used for texting. By wolves.*

Maggie sat up, pulling the sheet against her. This meant nothing. Absolutely nothing. And why was she thinking about the wolf anyway? She was just doing that worrying thing she sometimes did in the middle of the night.

She looked down. One of Travis's boots poked out from beneath the bed. A square toe. *Dressy, but very worn.* Just like the wolf's.

She sniffed the sheet. At one point tonight, Travis's cologne had sparked a flashback to the night in the shed. She'd brushed it off, feeling guilty for fantasizing about the wolf while she was with Travis.

Open your legs and take this cock.

Maggie gasped. She dropped the sheet and stood up, naked and shivering. She looked at Travis, sleeping peacefully. What was his jawline like beneath the beard? Her eyes darted around the room and spotted her jeans on the floor. She grabbed them and slipped them on, because she suddenly couldn't stand being naked. Too vulnerable. Her red sweater was also on the floor. Where her bra? No matter. She pulled the sweater over her head. Stepped into one of her boots while looking around for the other one.

"Maggie, is everything okay?"

That voice!

A lamp flicked on, and she winced in its harsh light. Travis sat up sleepily, rubbing his eyes.

His eyes. She'd believed their familiarity was because of high school. But it was more than that. Way more than that.

She limped to the side of the bed, wearing only one boot. Maybe its partner had been kicked underneath when she'd tossed it off with wild abandon. This was all she needed to focus on... *getting dressed*. Nothing else. Not the way Travis's body had felt like the wolf's. Not the way his forceful thrusts and animalistic groans had driven her insane, or the way she'd gleefully submitted, feeling safe and secure—what a joke—and *just like Little Red Riding Hood.*

She looked under the bed.

"I figured you'd stay the night," Travis said.

Maggie had to stop searching for her boot to find her voice. "Henry will be home in the morning. It would confuse him."

"I don't think he'd be confused. He knows we're wrestling partners."

Don't be cute and funny right now. "Tomorrow's Black Friday, remember? I've got to work."

"Just get up early—"

"No, I've got stuff to take care of at home."

"Like what?"

"Pop needs to go out."

"Go get him. He can stay over, too."

He wasn't going to give up. "What part of *no* do you not understand?"

She'd snapped at him. His blue eyes widened in response. His mouth opened as if to speak, but then he faltered. *That's right, buddy. I've got your number. Or the wolf's number. Somebody's number.*

Travis got out of bed and slipped on his jeans.

"What are you doing?"

"Getting dressed. I'm not going to walk you out naked."

"Why would you need to walk me out? I'm perfectly capable of finding my Jeep."

"I don't know. Maybe because we just had soul-shattering sex?" He stuck his foot in a boot, not realizing he'd also just stuck it in his mouth.

Soul-shattering sex. That was how she'd described their night in the shed.

The two of them stood eyeing each other suspiciously, each wearing a single boot.

Maggie looked away first and picked up the bedspread they'd knocked to the floor. Where was her godforsaken boot? Maybe she'd kicked it through the open closet door.

"Listen, Maggie. We need to talk."

Maggie walked to the closet. There was a very nice suit hanging up. Same color as the wolf's. She touched the jacket sleeve. Same fabric. The feel of it against her finger triggered memories in high definition. She shivered, then she turned to look at Travis. "I think it might be a little late for that."

Travis paled. "I can explain."

She didn't want to hear it. *Couldn't* hear it. "What a fun little game you've been playing."

"It wasn't a game. I just didn't—"

"Is the mask in here, too? Do you keep them together?" She dug through the closet. Flannel shirts, T-shirts, jeans...no wolf mask. But it didn't change anything. She was certain. Everything clicked into place. She'd recognized his very first kiss, hadn't she? And tonight, she'd known who he was with every pant, groan, and forceful thrust. *Her wolf.*

And then there'd been Anna. Holy cow, just how many hints had she dropped? *Of course* she would know Travis had come to the gala as the Big Bad Wolf. And Maggie had been providing her with entertainment ever since.

What an idiot she was.

"I was going to tell you—"

She stomped her booted foot. "But you didn't! All this time, and you didn't say a word. Did you think it was funny?"

She didn't stick around to hear his answer *or* to find her stupid boot. She grabbed her bag—it was right next to Henry's telescope and wasn't *that* another hilarious piece of the humiliation puzzle— and limped out the door.

Chapter
Thirty-Two

❦

Black Friday. In more ways than one.

Petal Pushers would rake in more money today than it had in the previous two months, and normally this obscene amount of consumerism filled Maggie's heart with cheer. But today, instead of doing the happy dance of a retail mogul smothered in jingle bells, she sat at the cash register with her head in her hands, mindlessly rubbing Pop's tummy with her foot.

She was ignoring Travis's texts. She should probably block him. And the stupid wolf, too. Although he hadn't texted since she'd broken up with him. Ugh! She had to stop thinking of Travis and the wolf as two different people.

They were one and the same.

All those texts. She'd sat in her Jeep taking orders from the wolf while Travis sat in his truck! She'd removed her panties at the library while Travis hammered nails in the gazebo! And she'd even talked to the wolf *about* Travis. And he'd never said a word. She'd been so thoroughly played.

She groaned and raised her head. Petal Pushers looked like

Christmas had vomited all over it. Every surface was covered by wreaths, trees, bows, and ornaments. It had been cheerful earlier, but now it was disgusting. And if she heard Wham! sing "Last Christmas" one more time, she was going to explode in bloody chunks of green and red.

See? She could be festive.

Where was Claire when she needed her? Well, she knew where she was—somewhere between here and Abilene—but that wasn't the point. Maggie pulled out her phone to send another emergency text.

Claire, where are you???????

Claire.

Claire.

Claire.

Claire.

The door jingled, followed by the tapping of Claire's heels. It was music to Maggie's ears, and she jumped off her stool.

"What is wrong with you?" Claire asked. "My phone thinks it hit the jackpot."

"Travis is the Big Bad Wolf." There. She'd spilled the beans. Said it out loud for the very first time. Right in front of Ford Jarvis. "Hi, Ford."

She'd never heard Ford's voice; not that she could remember anyway. And today was no exception. He nodded and smiled.

"Ford, why don't you head out? I'll see you later," Claire said. Her voice sounded normal—even and tempered. But her eyes were huge and clearly said, *My friend has lost her mind.*

Ford seemed anxious to comply and, with a final nod at Maggie, quickly vacated the premises.

"Oh my God," Claire said. "Have you been eating chalk?"

"What?"

"Sometimes when people have nervous breakdowns, they eat chalk."

"Get some coffee and sit down. I've got a story to tell, and it begins with *Once upon a time there was a Big Bad Wolf.*"

Ten minutes later, Maggie's voice was hoarse, Claire's coffee was untouched, and George Michael was at it again, singing about how someone had thrown his heart away. "And I thought I loved him. The end," Maggie said.

"Okay. I admit this sounds incriminating. It really does. So, let's assume you're right."

"He lied to me!" Maggie wailed. "Like over and over again."

"Well, I imagine it got kind of awkward, you know?"

"I had no idea who he was, Claire. And he knew who I was. He had all the power—"

"Why do you think he knew who you were? Initially, I mean…"

Maggie thought back to the gala. She *had* intentionally avoided introducing herself to him. She'd assumed he was a stranger from out of town. Maybe he'd had similar misunderstandings about her.

"But as soon as he saw me at Anna's—that first day we worked together—he recognized me. He should have come clean."

Claire took a sip of her cold coffee and made a face. "True. Although he was probably pretty dang shocked. And there were other people around, right? What was he supposed to say? That y'all had already met via a shed bang?"

"He could have at least said that we'd met before. And then later, when we were alone, he could have told me—"

"You accused him of child abuse at that meeting, right? Maybe he wasn't anxious to add insult to injury."

The boiling rage in the pit of Maggie's stomach settled down to a simmer. Claire sounded reasonable. "It's just that he dragged it out for so long."

"It doesn't mean his feelings for you aren't real."

"How could they be real? How could *anything* he said or did be real?"

"Are your feelings for him real?"

"He lied to me," she said stubbornly.

Claire leaned closer to Maggie. "You were excited by it. So was he. This isn't necessarily a bad thing. You know what would wrap this up nicely?"

"What?"

"You, agreeing to be pre-surgery Meg Ryan in *You've Got Mail*. You meet Travis at the park. He's wearing a wolf mask. And you say, *I wanted it to be you so badly*. Then you kiss. And we all go, *Yay! And they lived happily ever after!*"

"Real life isn't a fairy tale, Claire."

"I was shooting for a romantic comedy."

The bell jingled on the door, and a blast of cold air hit Maggie in the face. She sighed. "We'll finish this conversation later." She turned to face the next round of customers.

It was JD. And Gabriel was with him. "Mighty Mack, we need a Christmas tree. What have you got?"

JD and Gabriel were buying a tree. Together. In Big Verde.

"I've got an eight-foot noble fir. That's what you usually get, right?" JD had a gorgeous home with high ceilings, lots of windows, and a huge, sloped lawn. He always went overboard at Christmas with lights, lasers, and his Uncle Jeb in a Santa suit sipping on a flask while handing out candy canes. Miss Mills was JD's only real competition, but whereas JD had Drunk Santa, Miss Mills believed Jesus was the reason for the season. Flying reindeer and magic elves were the work of the devil.

"The eight-footer is what we need," JD said.

We. Gabriel's smile outshone Maggie's. "You know what they say about men who feel the need to buy big trees," he said.

JD lifted the brim of his Stetson, so Gabriel could see his raised eyebrow. "But you know that's not true, don't you, Gabe?"

Gabriel's complexion darkened.

Claire cleared her throat, but neither JD nor Gabriel looked up.

She did it again, less subtly, sounding like an eighty-year-old man choking on a chicken bone.

JD pounded her on the back.

Claire swatted his arm away. "Who's your friend?"

"This is Gabriel, and I imagine you heard all about him as soon as he and I left Travis's last night."

Claire shook Gabriel's hand. "Pleasure to meet you. I've been out of town, so I'm behind on the gossip. Did y'all rob a liquor store last night? Shoot holes in the Rite Aid sign? Pinch the wrong ass at the Purple Pony?"

"We're dating," JD said.

Claire looked behind them. "Dating who?"

"Each other."

It took about three seconds for it to sink in. Then Claire said to Gabriel, "Oh? You must be from Austin then. I knew JD was seeing someone in Austin. How nice. Are you enjoying Big Verde? Will you be staying long? Can I get you a piece of pie?"

"Claire," JD said. "You can stop babbling. It's okay to act surprised."

Claire slumped with relief. "Whew! Oh my God, JD, you're *gay?*"

"Yep."

"I wouldn't mind a piece of pie," Gabriel said with his two-million-dollar smile. "If it's not too much trouble."

Claire looked at him like he was nuts. "I don't have any pie."

"That's just something Southern girls say when they're nervous," JD whispered.

"Who all knows?" Maggie asked. "Did you tell your parents?"

"Yeah. Told the folks last night."

Maggie raised her eyebrows. "And?"

JD removed his hat. "Well, beneath the initial shock, they seemed to think that a lot of my childhood finally made sense."

"Like your fifth-grade obsession with Shania Twain?"

"Shut up. She's a queen and you know it. Anyway, next I told Bubba."

"How'd that go?"

"Once I convinced him he wasn't my type, he didn't much care."

Maggie led them to where the eight-foot tree stood on the lot. Even though it was the only one that size, JD and Gabriel went through the traditional decision-making angst—holding it this way and that, standing back and looking at it from various angles—before deciding they'd take it. Norbert helped them get it loaded onto JD's truck, with Gabriel snapping pictures and posting them to Instagram the entire time.

Maggie refused to let them pay for it.

"Why don't you and Travis come by for some eggnog after work tonight?" JD said.

"Thanks, but we're not really—"

A pickup turned into the lot and parked next to them. It was Bubba. Trista rolled her pregnant self out, looking ready to pop. Bubba got out next, and then they all watched, mesmerized, as the kids clambered out one by one, like clowns from a clown car.

"Merry Christmas, y'all," Bubba said. When he spotted Gabriel, he adopted a formal tone for introductions. "Trista, this is Gabriel, JD's gay boyfriend. I believe I might have mentioned him earlier."

"You mean when you shot through the door like a rocket on steroids this morning? Yes, I think you might have mentioned him." Trista smiled at Gabriel. "So nice to meet a gay boyfriend of JD's. The straight ones were all so boring."

* * *

Travis leaned on the shovel and wiped sweat out of his eyes. It had taken every ounce of willpower he had just to get out of bed and drag himself to work today. He'd been up all night.

Yesterday had started out perfectly. Wonderful Thanksgiving

dinner at Happy Trails. His table surrounded by family and friends—neither of which he'd even *had* a few short weeks ago. And then he and Maggie had made love for the first time.

No, not for the first time, and that was the problem.

As soon as he'd realized what she wanted—*what she needed*—the wolf had come out to play. Maggie had complied so readily, and responded so thoroughly, that he thought he'd pulled it off. That she either hadn't put two and two together, or she had and didn't care.

He'd been wrong. She'd done the math *and* she cared.

The phone calls went straight to voice mail. The texts were ignored. And he felt fucking sick about it. He'd known she wouldn't take it well. How could she? He'd known all along that they'd had sex in the shed—kinky sex, by some standards. And Maggie thought it had been anonymous. He'd let her think that out of cowardice, and then he'd continued the charade out of weakness.

At first, he'd just wanted to avoid awkwardness at work. Later, he was downright fearful she'd blow a gasket, especially since he'd been unable to make himself stop with the sexting. And finally, after they'd grown close and shared their hopes and dreams, he'd been terrified of losing her.

He'd lost her anyway.

Would she stop by today? It was a busy time at Petal Pushers, so probably not. Either way, he had a lot of work to do. He stuck his sweat-drenched bandanna back into his pocket and drove the shovel into a pile of river rocks. Maggie wanted them spread throughout the walking paths of Anna's garden.

His phone rang. With a start, he yanked off his glove and grabbed it out of his pocket. It wasn't Maggie. With his usual lousy timing, Scott was calling. Maybe it was just a *hey, how was your Thanksgiving* call, but Travis doubted it.

"Hello."

"What is this thing I got about garnishing my wages?" Scott demanded.

Gabriel hadn't wasted any time.

"Happy Thanksgiving to you, too."

"I got a job, which is exactly what I was supposed to do—"

"Really? That's great news. Where?"

"Why does it matter? You're going to take all my money!"

"Actually, that money will go to help support your son. It's expensive to raise a kid. I just registered him for soccer. It was sixty-five dollars plus another thirty for the uniform. Want to buy some raffle tickets?"

Maybe Gabriel was right, and rattling Scott's money chain would cause him to drop the threat of taking Henry.

"If I get Henry, I won't have to give anyone any money. Maybe I should just go ahead and pursue that route. Unless, of course, you want to sell the ranch."

"I don't want to sell the ranch. And if you take Henry to punish me, you've got *all* the financial burden. Soccer starts next Thursday. Cleats are on sale at Walmart."

"Why can't you just pay the taxes and sell the ranch? We'll both be rich. And then you can pretend to be Henry's daddy all you want."

"I want to make Happy Trails into something. And I don't want to *pretend* to be Henry's daddy. I want you to give up your rights. If you don't, then the law says you must support your child."

Scott was quiet. Was it working?

"Fuck you. He's probably not my kid anyway."

Travis shook his head in disgust as he stared at the phone. *That's right, motherfucker. He's mine.*

There was no time to sit on this, so Travis texted Gabriel to get the ball rolling. No more procrastinating or avoiding unpleasant situations.

Feeling a little lighter, he put his phone back in his pocket and dug into the rocks with renewed vigor. It only took a few minutes for the endorphins to get pumping. He'd just slayed Goliath for Henry.

Next, he was going to get his woman back.

Chapter
Thirty-Three

❦

Travis watched the gathering storm clouds through the living room window.

It had been four days since Thanksgiving. No word from Maggie. He'd even texted her that he'd found her boot. He suspected she'd blocked him.

He wasn't the kind of guy to creepily stalk a woman, but Henry wouldn't stop asking about her. What was he supposed to do about that?

The Grinch was on TV. This was at least the fifth time Henry had watched the DVD today, all while giving Travis the stinky side-eye for his lack of merrymaking. The naked tree sat in the big front window. He'd bought it at Petal Pushers yesterday, hoping to see Maggie. She hadn't been there, but Claire had. She'd sold him the tree and said, *You're in Big Bad Trouble with a capital T.*

Like he didn't already know that.

"When is Maggie coming to decorate the tree?" Henry asked. Again.

It was Tuesday. Maggie was supposed to come after work, but somehow Travis doubted that was still the plan.

"She's at Petal Pushers," Lupe said, setting out a tray of fresh-baked Christmas cookies. "They close at six, so you've got another hour or so."

Travis gulped. "It's a busy day for Petal Pushers because of the holidays. So, don't be disappointed if she's too tired to come, okay?"

"That's silly, Uncle Travis. Maggie made a promise."

Travis pulled out his phone, looked at it, and tossed it on the couch. But then he had an idea. *Maybe she hadn't thought to block the Big Bad Wolf.*

He went upstairs and pulled the wolf's phone out of his night-stand drawer.

Once upon a time, there was a Big Dumb Wolf.

He sat on the bed and waited. It didn't take long.

And once upon a time there was a fair maiden who made the mistake of following him into the woods.

Travis wanted to remind her that she'd had a banging good time in the woods, but he didn't want to ruin it. He decided to go with what was in his heart.

I miss my moon. The world is dark without her.

Minutes ticked by. He should have known Maggie wouldn't react to romantic bullshit. He was going to have to fight dirty.

Henry wants to know if you're coming tonight.

I'll be there at 7.

When she didn't add anything more, he stood up. It was time to face the music. All of it. He'd been a conflict avoider his entire life. When you lived with a volatile, gambling alcoholic, you lay low, ducked into available open doorways, and waited for storms to pass.

But some storms didn't pass until you weathered them. He was a little old to learn this lesson, but dammit, he'd recently come to realize there were three things that mattered to him—Happy Trails, Henry, and Maggie—and he wasn't going to lose any of them.

"You boys had better get ready for your company," Lupe said when Travis came down the stairs.

He ran his fingers through his mass of hair and rubbed his beard. Lupe was right. He needed to get ready. He went into the bathroom and pulled out a razor and shears. No more hiding.

Twenty minutes later, he emerged to hysterical laughter from Henry. "You look like a plucked chicken!"

Beard: gone. Mass of hair: clipped short.

Lupe walked up and rubbed his cheek. "Very handsome," she said with a wink. "And you, too, Henry."

Henry had put on what he called his fancy clothes: clean jeans with no holes and a long-sleeved blue shirt. He'd even stuffed his feet into the shoes he'd worn to Lisa's funeral. It didn't look like they fit anymore. That gave Travis a lump in his throat the size of Texas and, for some dumb reason, reminded him of the gravity of the situation. There were two possible outcomes: a new beginning, or an ending.

"You know you don't have to get dressed up for Maggie, right? She thinks you're awesome no matter what you wear."

Henry patted his hair and frowned. "I can't get the puffy part to stay down."

"I think Maggie likes the puffy part."

"You don't have to get dressed up either, Uncle Travis. Maggie likes you just the way you are. And that means she loves you."

Travis sighed. Maggie probably thought she didn't know him at all anymore. But she was wrong. She knew him better than anyone ever had.

"I warmed up some chili," Lupe said. "Your bowl is on the bar. You should eat before Maggie gets here."

Travis sat down and pulled the bowl over. He hadn't been able to eat much in the past few days, but now he thought maybe he had an appetite.

Lupe set a manila envelope next to him. "I found this on the gate a couple of days ago. I forgot to bring it in. You might want to open it."

Travis's heart pounded. Had Maggie resorted to leaving him notes on the gate again? And he hadn't even read it? He tried not to be irritated with Lupe—it wasn't her fault he was in this mess. Maggie had never put one of her gate notes in an envelope before. It must be personal. He tried to compose himself as he pulled it out.

AUCTION.

Shit! This wasn't from Maggie. It was from the tax office. He scanned the rest of the letter quickly, searching for a date.

NOVEMBER 29 COURTHOUSE ANNEX LAWN

That was today!

"Travis, what's wrong?" Lupe asked. "You look like you've seen a ghost!"

Travis grabbed his keys and his checkbook. Maybe there was still time. Maybe nobody had bid on Happy Trails, and he could still do something.

"I've got to go."

"But where? Where are you going? Maggie will be here any minute."

It was raining, but he didn't have time to look for an umbrella. He had to get to the courthouse. "Tell Maggie I'll be back as soon as I can. Tell her it's important."

Fifteen minutes later, he pulled up to the courthouse annex. There was absolutely nobody on the lawn, and the place looked closed. He made a run for the courthouse door. It was locked, but he yanked on it anyway. He peered through the glass and saw a woman walking down the hall. He banged on the door.

"The offices are closed," she shouted. "You'll have to come back tomorrow."

"Was there an auction here today? For Happy Trails?"

The woman rolled her eyes and removed a set of keys from her pocket. She opened the door a crack. "Only one person showed up in this weather, but yes, there was an auction."

"Who showed up? Who was it?"

"Gerome Kowalski. He had the winning bid."

Travis took a step back. It was a punch to the gut. To the *heart*. Gerome's kindness had been an act. Travis had been an idiot to think a man like that would want to help a guy like him. Gerome had pretended to be, of all things, *fatherly*. And Travis had soaked it up. No wonder he hadn't wanted money for replacing the fences. He knew they'd be his. He probably had an ingenious plan to incorporate Happy Trails and keep it as a direct line to consumers, hence the farmer's market stall.

"Bye, now," the lady said, closing the door.

The lock clicked. "Wait, how does this work?"

She'd already walked away.

Travis trudged back to his truck, not feeling the rain or the cold or anything at all. Gerome Kowalski had just added two hundred acres to Rancho Cañada Verde . . . *for chump change*.

Chump change that Travis couldn't come up with.

How would he face Henry? He'd fucked it all up.

He started the truck and headed for Tony's. The last barstool on the left already had his name on it.

Chapter

Thirty-Four

The Christmas music was going to be the death of Maggie. "Can we change the station, please?" she begged.

Claire, wearing what Maggie assumed to be a Mrs. Claus outfit if Mrs. Claus was a porn star, stuffed a wreath in a bag. "Yes, we can change it."

"Oh, thank God." Maggie sighed.

"On January first."

"But Claire—"

"Maggie, we're selling trees. We're selling wreaths. We're selling lights and inflatable elves. And we're going to listen to Christmas music, okay?" She smiled at Mrs. Parker as she handed her the bag. "Thank you and Merry Christmas!"

A large hand slapped a box of red and green ornaments on the counter. Maggie looked up to see Bubba peering over four more boxes. "Hey, Bubba. Why all the ornaments?"

"We got a cat," he said. "A cat that climbs Christmas trees. I told Trista that cats are useless animals."

Pop barked from beneath the counter.

"You don't need these then," Maggie said. She looked around for Kristen, the high school senior providing holiday help on weekends. She didn't see the perky blond ponytail anywhere. Which meant Kristen was probably hiding somewhere with her nose glued to her phone. "Come on. We have some that aren't breakable."

"I got the counter," Claire said.

Bubba followed Maggie to the ornaments. "I had to drive Travis home from Tony's last night. He was wasted."

Maggie stopped in her tracks. That asshole had stood her up to go to Tony's and get drunk? It wasn't quite the groveling she'd expected. And to think she'd been ready to forgive him.

I miss my moon. My world is dark without her.

Ha! She'd fallen for that. She really had. But then he hadn't even been at the house last night. She and Lupe had decorated the tree with Henry, looking at the door the whole time because they were freaking idiots. Honey's voice had played in her head on repeat. *That boy done run oft, Maggie.*

Maggie grabbed three boxes of unbreakable ornaments off the shelf and shoved them at Bubba. "You're a married man with kids and a pregnant wife. What were you doing at Tony's?" She really felt like railing on a man, and Bubba was the nearest one.

"Hey, settle down. Trista made eggnog, and I wanted mine with a kick. The liquor store was closed, so Tony slipped a little in a baby bottle for me." He lowered his voice to a whisper. "Don't tell anyone. I think it's illegal."

Maggie rolled her eyes. "I'll try to keep a lid on it."

"What happened with you and Travis? That boy was a mess last night."

Claire came around the corner. "That's just what I was coming back here to ask. Did y'all make up over the Big Bad Wolf thing? Did you pull a pre-surgery Meg Ryan?"

"The Big Bad Wolf? Meg Ryan? What the hell are y'all talking about?" Bubba asked.

"Did I hear something about the Big Bad Wolf?" JD stood at the end of the aisle, smoke coming out of both ears. Nobody had even seen him come in.

"Seriously, JD? Don't you have somewhere else to be? Don't *all of you* have somewhere else to be?"

Claire crossed her arms over her chest. "I work here."

"And I need more tree lights," JD said.

They all looked at Bubba. "I honestly can't remember why I'm here."

Maggie stomped her foot. "Listen, I know you're all curious, and you want to know what happened between me and Travis, but it's my business and for once the entire town of Big Verde doesn't need to know it."

"Know what?" Alice popped up at the opposite end of the aisle, arms full of tinsel.

"That Travis is the Big Bad Wolf who's been sexting Maggie," Claire said.

"Oh, my," Alice said with a grin. "Maggie, aren't you the lucky girl!"

"Wait a minute," JD said. "Are you saying that wolf who had his hands all over you at the gala was Travis? Why, I ought to—"

"Aw, cut out the jealous shit, JD. You're gay now, remember?" Bubba said.

JD yanked on the brim of his hat. "Yes, I remember, and I'm not gay *now*—"

"Well, that didn't last long, did it?" Bubba said.

Maggie wanted to scream. "All of you get out! None of this is any of your business. Travis and I are done. Got it? We are *done*."

"This shit sucks," Bubba said. "After losing Happy Trails, I'm not sure Travis can handle losing you, too. He was even blubbering about Scott and Henry. The poor man thinks he's losing everything."

"One thing at a time," JD said. "He's not going to lose Henry. And no matter how pissed off she is, he's not losing Maggie either."

Maggie started to protest, but JD glared her into silence. "What's this about Happy Trails though?"

Maggie's heart jumped to her throat. No matter how she felt about Travis being the wolf, he and Henry didn't deserve to lose the ranch.

"It was auctioned off yesterday," Bubba said. "Gerome bought it."

Claire gasped. "Daddy bought Happy Trails? That doesn't make any sense."

Bubba shrugged his shoulders. "That's what Travis said."

"That can't be true," Maggie said. Travis hadn't paid the back taxes yet, but would Gerome really take advantage of someone when he was down? Someone who'd been working so hard to dig out? Maggie wrung her hands. It didn't add up. Gerome wasn't that kind of man.

Although she'd recently learned she was a piss-poor judge of character.

"I'm going over there to find out what's really going on," she announced.

"Wait! I'm coming with you," Claire said. "Norbert and Kristen can mind the store."

"I'm coming, too," JD said.

Bubba put the ornaments he was holding back on the shelf. "Oh, hell. Me, too."

* * *

With effort, Travis peeled his lips apart. Next, he forced his eyes open. They felt full of sand, but unless it was a mirage, they were staring at a cup of water. And Tylenol. God bless Lupe.

With a groan, he sat up and popped the pills, downed the water. Yesterday played back like a nightmare. He'd lost the mother-fucking ranch. How much time would they have to move out? And how was he going to tell Henry?

The bedroom door flew open. Travis closed his eyes and covered his ears.

"Uncle Travis, come see the tree!" Henry shouted.

"Talk softly, Henry. I have a headache."

Henry whispered, "Come see the tree."

"Okay," Travis whispered back. "Let me get dressed."

He didn't have the slightest interest in the tree. But he wanted Henry to be happy and carefree for as long as possible, so he'd pretend.

He managed to piss, brush the fur off his teeth, and get a pair of jeans on. Grabbing a T-shirt would involve bending over to open a drawer, so he'd go without.

The smell of strong coffee greeted him at the bottom of the stairs, and Lupe placed a mug in his hand. Holiday shit was everywhere—decorations, photos, an obnoxious musical Christmas village—and it dang near broke his heart. The place finally looked (and felt) like a home. A *real* home. The ones he used to see on TV.

They'd never had a tree at Christmastime. Christmas morning had dawned like every other, with Ben Blake hung over and Travis and Scott fighting over toaster waffles.

"Looks like Santa's elves were busy last night," he said, clearing his throat of whatever was making it difficult to speak.

"It wasn't elves. It was us!" Henry said. "You gots to help us put the angel on top."

"I *have* to help you put the angel on top."

"I know. That's what I said."

Lupe touched Travis's arm. "Come into the kitchen, *mijo*. Let's talk."

The kitchen was warm from the oven. Lupe had made cinnamon rolls, and even though his stomach wasn't in top form, the smell made Travis's mouth water. He reached for one, but Lupe slapped his hand.

"Are you loco? Not good for a hangover."

She grabbed a container out of the refrigerator and stuck it in the microwave. "I went to Rosie's Cocina this morning and picked this up for you. I'd have made it myself, but I didn't know you were going to need it."

Travis inhaled. Dear God. The woman was going to force-feed him *menudo*.

The microwave dinged, and he instinctively checked his phone for a text. Nothing from Maggie. It was over. Everything was over.

Lupe set a bowl and spoon in front of him. "Here you go."

He'd never tasted *menudo*. He didn't reckon himself for a tripe fan. But he knew not to mess with Lupe, especially where food was concerned, so he took a small sip. And it tasted pretty good. The second spoonful was even better. And surprisingly, his stomach was settling down, too.

"Good, right?"

He nodded. Maybe he'd get through this bowl before giving Lupe the bad news.

"I read the notice," Lupe said. "About the auction. Do you know who bought it?"

"It was Gerome."

He expected Lupe's face to reflect the same range of emotions that coursed through him, but she just nodded her head and made a little sound to indicate she wasn't surprised. Was Travis the only one who'd misjudged Gerome's character? The man was a sneaky, slimy bastard.

"Uncle Travis!" Henry shouted.

Travis winced.

"JD's truck is here, and a bunch of people are getting out. Oh! It's Maggie!"

"Shit." Travis jumped up from the table, heart pounding. He needed a shirt. He needed shoes. He needed—

"Hi, Maggie!"

Henry had already let them in. Talk about feeling exposed.

Travis entered the crowded living room like he was on an episode of *Naked and Afraid*. What were they all doing here? His eyes settled on Maggie. She stared at him like she was seeing a ghost. Her cheeks turned pink, followed predictably by her ears. What was she thinking about? Thanksgiving night? The night in the shed? *His betrayal?*

"I told them about the ranch," Bubba admitted.

"How did you know about it?"

"Everybody at Tony's knows about it," Bubba said. "You're quite the showman. And they also know about your deep and meaningful feelings for Maggie and something about a spreader bar."

Maggie gasped, and the ears went to Code Red. Travis was pretty sure he was blushing, too, and he had no beard to cover it up. JD pulled his hat down low, shading the upper half of his face, but his grin was clearly visible.

"What's a spreader bar?" Henry asked.

Jesus. This was great. Travis glared at Bubba.

Bubba shrugged. "They're for lifting engines and other heavy stuff." Bubba gave Travis one of his poker face winks before adding, "The tractor supply place on the highway has some."

Henry had already quit listening, especially since Lupe was holding out a cinnamon roll. "Come into the kitchen, little one. I'll get you some cocoa to go with this." She paused at the door. "My cousin, Herman, works at the tractor place. He'll give you a good deal on the bar."

Wonderful. Travis was soon to be the proud owner of something used to lift tractor engines, right before he presumably moved into an efficiency apartment in Austin.

Maggie grinned at him, but then covered it up with her hand. Hope sparked in his heart. She was here, wasn't she? Her big, brown mood ring eyes couldn't seem to decide between concern, irritation, and something else he couldn't quite put his finger on. He went to rub his beard and realized it was gone. *Oh.* Maybe that was the thing he couldn't put his finger on. Recognition. Maggie was looking at the Big Bad Lying Wolf.

"Maybe you can buy this place back from Gerome," Bubba said, reminding Travis that there were other people in the room.

"With what? Do you know what this place is worth? I can't even afford the taxes on it."

"We'll figure something out," JD said. "Maybe a loan—"

"Someone else is here," Bubba said. "Man, you know how to host a fucking party, Travis."

Claire peeked through the curtains. "It's my dad."

Gerome Kowalski had come to take the ranch.

* * *

Every cell in Maggie's body cried *Wolf!* And judging from the stirring in her heart—*and nether regions*—they didn't feel a bit betrayed. Her mind, however, was another story.

Travis was pale, clearly hungover, and half naked. He shouldn't face Gerome that way. "Go put on a shirt," she whispered.

His eyes searched hers, probably looking for clues as to whether she'd decided he was friend or foe. But she didn't have any to offer up. Not when she was in such turmoil. "Go," she repeated.

Travis bolted up the stairs just as Claire opened the door. "Daddy? Did you have to come so soon?"

Gerome enveloped Claire in a hug. "It's nearly noon. What are you doing here, sweetheart? Your mama's going to be upset that she didn't come along."

Yeah. Because if you're going to rip someone's home out of their hands, why not bring the whole family?

Claire closed the door, and Gerome, wearing a bewildered expression, glanced around the room. "Looks like I walked in on a party," he said. "A sad one."

Lupe came out of the kitchen and offered to take Gerome's coat, which he handed over, along with his hat and a tub of homemade pecan pralines from Claire's mom.

Who did that? Who offered candy in exchange for a family's ranch? This was some seriously weird business, and Maggie didn't dare open her mouth for fear of what might come out of it.

Gerome shook hands with Bubba and JD, both of whom were appropriately curt. Claire, who looked like she'd just discovered her dad had killed Santa, wrung her hands while blinking back tears.

Everyone parted like the Red Sea as Travis came down the stairs. Gerome held out his hand. "Howdy, son."

Travis was fully dressed in Wranglers, a long-sleeved shirt—pressed and starched—and the square-toe boots. Clean-shaven, clipped hair. He looked like a cowboy.

He looked like her wolf.

Travis smiled and shook Gerome's hand as if he were a welcome guest. "Can I get you some coffee?"

"Already had my two cups." Gerome glanced around with apprehension wrinkling his forehead. "Can we go into the kitchen to speak in private?"

Claire stepped forward. "Daddy, whatever you have to say to Travis, you can say in front of us."

JD and Bubba nodded, and JD topped it off with a vicious yank on the brim of his hat, a gesture that could possibly be interpreted as a direct threat.

Gerome shook his head as if trying to clear it of cobwebs and glanced longingly at the couch. "Why don't we all have a seat?"

Bubba took the recliner, leaning back and sighing as if maybe he'd take a nap after Travis was done losing his ranch. JD and Claire took the other two chairs, and Gerome sat on the couch.

Maggie stood next to Travis. She could feel the heat radiating off him. He looked calm and collected, but she knew better.

"I'm not sure how all this is supposed to work, Gerome," Travis said.

Gerome sat up straighter on the couch. "That's what I came to discuss."

Travis cleared his throat. "I'm hoping, on account of Henry, that we can remain in the house through the holidays. Then we'll be on our way."

"What kind of a man do you think I am?" Gerome asked. He stood, joints creaking. "Of course I want you to stay in the house through the holidays. And after."

"I don't understand," Travis said. "Didn't you buy Happy Trails?"

"No. I paid off the taxes and now I own the lien. According to the state of Texas, you've got two years to reclaim the property." He walked over to Travis and placed a hand on his shoulder. "What I did, son, was buy you some time."

Henry ran into the room and threw his arms around Gerome's legs. "Hi, Mr. K! I didn't know you was here."

"*Were* here," Maggie said.

Henry made bug eyes at her. "He's still here, ain't he?"

"Isn't he," Travis said.

"Is there an echo in here?" Henry shouted, sounding just like Lupe.

Travis picked Henry up. His Adam's apple bobbed as he swallowed and searched for words—probably trying to soak in what he'd just heard. Finally, he said, "Why would you do this, Gerome? Why would you spend so much of your own money just to buy me some more time?"

"Well, now, before you go making me a hero, you should know there's a bit of interest involved. But I did it because every boy deserves a chance to be a real cowboy." He pinched Henry's nose, and Henry erupted in giggles.

Travis nodded and ruffled Henry's hair. "Henry deserves a lot of things."

"That he does," Gerome said. "But I was talking about you."

* * *

Travis stood on the porch and watched Gerome drive away. The others, including Maggie, had left earlier, leaving Gerome and Travis alone to discuss the details.

Two years. He had two years to pay off the lien plus interest, and with what he'd already managed to save, it wouldn't take him nearly that long. But Gerome had suggested Travis wait the entire two years—plus one day. Happy Trails would then legally belong to Gerome, and he could sell it back to Travis without Scott's name being on the deed.

Travis wasn't entirely sure how he felt about that. He wanted to be free of Scott, but he didn't want to swindle him. Gerome had scoffed. Said he knew Scott's type and Travis wasn't doing him any favors by giving him money. But he'd agreed to help figure out a fair way to reimburse Scott for his half of the ranch, minus what Scott owed in rent, his share of back taxes, and of course, child support for the past five years.

It would still be a lot of money. But Travis had big dreams for Happy Trails, and he was going after them full throttle.

And those dreams included Henry and Maggie.

He went upstairs and retrieved the phone he kept in his nightstand drawer. Maggie had shown up today. She still had feelings for him. He just knew it. What they had was real, and even if it had started off with role playing and a fictitious *once upon a time*, Travis hoped it would end with a very real *happily ever after*.

The Big Bad Wolf was going to send Little Red Riding Hood one more text.

Chapter
Thirty-Five

❦

Travis leaned against the workbench and admired his handiwork. Bright twinkling lights hung from the shed's rafters. Softly glowing candles surrounded the champagne and glasses he'd set on a small folding table. He clenched a beautiful bouquet of yellow roses—Claire's creation—tightly in his hand. He'd even ordered dinner from the Corner Café. They didn't typically do deliveries, but Bubba's folks owned the place, and he'd offered to bring their steaks to the shed. Travis had no doubt as to Bubba's motives. Five minutes after he left, all of Big Verde would know how the date was going.

Travis shifted nervously from boot to boot and stared at the door. Would Little Red Riding Hood stiff him? It was just past seven o'clock. He dug for his phone and stared at the text he'd sent.

Can we start our 'Once Upon a Time' over? Follow the rose petals to the shed. I'll be there at 7.

She hadn't responded, but the text had been delivered. He stuffed his phone back in his pocket and resumed staring at the door.

Two hours ago, he'd stood up to Scott with Gabriel at his side.

And Scott had consented to relinquish his parental rights. There were still details to work out; the court would have to approve the termination, but Gabriel said it should be no problem since Travis intended to adopt Henry.

Henry would be his son.

Only one element was still needed to turn this fairy tale into a reality, and that was Maggie.

Travis swallowed. Clenched his jaw. *She would come. She had to.*

The First National Bank of Big Verde was holding its annual employee Christmas party at the Chateau, and the music and frivolity floated on the breeze, just as it had the night of the Halloween gala. The night he'd passed up an opportunity to remove his mask and say *Hi. I'm Travis Blake. I know we just met, but I think I might love you.*

Because he'd felt it, even then.

Maggie was something special.

His tie was stifling, so he loosened it. Adjusted the dressy gray Stetson he'd bought special for the occasion. And then he just waited, while his heart threatened to burst through his rib cage.

* * *

Maggie parked next to Travis's truck and stared at the path that led through the cedar trees to the shed. It was covered in yellow petals, which was silly and seemed like a waste of good roses. She slammed her Jeep door and tried to ignore the smile tugging at her lips.

She headed down the path, slowing her pace when she realized she was hurrying. No need to go blasting through the door panting with enthusiasm and drooling forgiveness. Travis was going to have to work for it.

Hopefully he had more than rose petals up his sleeve.

The windows of the shed glowed with an inviting yellow hue.

Candles? Had the man brought candles? Maggie swallowed and walked to the door. Her hand hesitated briefly on the knob, then she inhaled and slowly pushed it open.

Her breath caught at the sight of Travis stepping out of the shadows. The nice suit. The sharp, clean-shaven jaw. *The deep blue eyes.* How had she not known?

"Maggie—" His voice cracked, and he cleared his throat, held out his hand. "Please come inside."

She looked past him to the candles, twinkling lights, roses . . . Was that champagne?

"I promise I won't bite," he said.

He pulled her in gently, shutting the door behind her. His eyes roamed her body, clad in a red sweater dress—*of course she'd worn red*—and added, "Much as I might like to."

Maggie's pulse quickened. He was startlingly handsome. She longed to trace his jaw with her finger, remove the suit jacket, loosen his tie, unbutton his shirt . . .

Travis handed her the roses.

She was twenty-seven years old, owned a mother-luvin' flower shop, and nobody had ever given her roses before. "Oh, Travis. They're beautiful. Thank you." *Dang it, Mackey! Don't be this easy.*

"Claire made the arrangement. She fussed over the color. Said red is for romance, and yellow is for friendship. But yellow reminds me of you and your Jeep, and besides, you're the best friend I've ever had."

Had this conversation really headed so quickly into the friend zone? Maybe she'd made some assumptions—*again*. "Listen, Travis—"

He touched her chin and tilted her face up, gazing intently. "Lupe says that friendship is the basis of true love. That you have to be a true friend to someone before you can ask for their heart. And Maggie, I haven't been a very good friend. I'd like to start over and do better, if you'll let me."

He wanted to ask for her heart? Would it be premature, at this point in the conversation, for her to yank it out of her chest and stick a bow on it?

Yes, it would. He'd *hurt* her. She needed an explanation. And an apology. Until then, there would be no swooning whatsoever. Her shaky knees were getting ahead of themselves. "Why did you carry on this charade for so long? I just don't get it. Were you trying to make a fool out of me?"

Travis closed his eyes as if steeling himself and then opened them with a sigh. "Nobody could ever make a fool out of you, Maggie. You're the strongest, smartest woman I've ever met. I never meant to hurt or—"

"Humiliate?"

"Especially not that," he said. "Never."

"I need to know why."

Travis pulled the brim of his hat down low and stared at his boots. "When I wore the mask, you thought I was a stranger. You were attracted to me—"

"Understatement, and you know it."

He looked up. "You *wanted* me. You didn't know I was Travis Blake, the guy who grew up on the rundown Happy Trails Ranch, accused bracelet thief, son of a man who couldn't afford to keep his fences intact but could afford to drink himself to death. The brother of a criminal. Fresh out of the Army with empty pockets and back taxes to pay and a newly acquired kid..."

But she loved that kid. And she hadn't known Travis had seen himself that way. It wasn't like *she* had seen him that way. She wasn't judgmental.

Previous words and thoughts slowly seeped into her consciousness.

Nice boys, those Blakes.

He's probably a bookie.

I hear he's an ex-con.

He's nothing but a glorified lawn boy.

Her face must have shown the realization, because Travis smiled sadly.

"Travis—"

He put a finger to her lips. "Let me finish. I liked being who-ever you thought I was when I wore the mask. You made me feel like such a man, Maggie. In a way I'd never felt before. And I wanted to *be* that man. When I first saw you at Anna's, I thought you recognized me as the wolf, and that maybe you were a bit embarrassed. But then I realized you didn't, and when you learned who I was…"

Maggie blushed. She'd accused him of abusing Henry. She'd asked Anna to remove him from the project.

"You didn't like me," Travis said, "but you liked the Big Bad Wolf. I had a hard time letting him go for that reason."

"But after I got to know you—"

"You liked me?"

"More than liked you. I even quit messing around with the wolf because of you. You knew it, too. So why didn't you tell me then?"

"I wanted to. Desperately. But I was afraid you wouldn't under-stand. That you'd be humiliated, and angry, and that just when I'd finally earned your respect, I'd lose you entirely."

He was probably right. But it wasn't the *wrong* reaction. It wasn't her fault she'd been lied to, deceived, and made a fool of. It was his. And so far, all she'd heard was excuses.

"Maggie, I am so sorry for hurting you. For lying to you."

Bingo! But was it enough? She'd never been the kind of girl to let go of a grudge very easily.

"If I could do it all over again…" Travis took her hands in his. "I'm Travis Blake. Not some mysterious stranger or intriguing masked lover. I'm just a man. And not always a very good one. But you bring something out in me. Something wild and fierce that wants to have you and protect you and all those things you probably don't like."

But a part of her liked it very much. "You clearly bring something out in me, too," she said, wondering how bright her ears appeared in the dim lighting. "And I'm not a sexy vixen in boots who hooks up with strangers. I'm a woman who'd rather watch basketball than go shopping. I don't need all of this." She looked around the room at the candles, champagne, roses...

"You like it, though."

Yes, she did. "Well, I'm also a control freak who doesn't like to share or be told what to do."

Travis's eyes darkened a shade. "Sometimes you enjoy being told what to do."

Maggie shivered. Travis didn't need the mask to flip her switch.

"I want to be with you, Maggie. I want to be with you when you're bossy and prissy—"

"I am not ever prissy."

Travis grinned. "And argumentative."

The best she could do was produce a disgruntled-sounding harrumph. And try not to smile.

"I want to be with you when you're sweet, kind, and nurturing. And when you're—"

"Ornery and cantankerous?"

"I was going to say sexy. Hot as hell. Naughty in ways I like to think are just for me."

"Oh."

He lowered his eyes. Licked his lips. And then he whispered, "I love you."

There it was. The three little words every girl longed to hear. She felt warm and tingly, as if she'd just guzzled a mixture of sunshine and honey. It made her eyes leak. "Oh, Travis, I—"

They both jumped at a knock on the door.

"Who on earth can that be?" Maggie asked. What if they were about to get in trouble for trespassing?

Travis looked at his phone. "It's seven thirty. I think it's our dinner. I hope you don't mind, I ordered some steaks from the Corner Café."

Maggie hadn't noticed that the table was set for two. Travis opened the door. And there stood Anna.

"Anna," Travis said. "What are you doing here?"

"Freezing my ass off," she answered, pushing him aside and strolling on in. "And delivering dinner."

Travis stood with the door—and his mouth—wide open. After a few awkward seconds, he finally managed to shut both. "Bubba was supposed to do it."

"Well, he can't. Trista popped that baby out right in the middle of St. Luke's *Las Posadas* procession down Main Street. I swear, it's just like her to try and upstage the Virgin Mary."

"Oh my!" Maggie said. "Are she and the baby okay?"

"Of course they are," Anna said. "Another girl. And between you and me, Trista is made for it. Wide hips. But anyway, it happened just as the procession stopped at the Corner Café. They shooed everybody out, and Bubba asked me to pick up your dinner elsewhere. So here I am."

This was a lot to take in.

"You're welcome," Anna added.

"Thank you," Travis said, taking the two large bags.

"I made it easy on myself and picked this up here at the Chateau," Anna said. "Why on earth you're in this shed I'll never know." She glanced around, taking in the lights and candles as if she were in the discount aisle of Walmart.

Maggie saw Travis pale as he pulled out his wallet. Dinner from the Village Chateau would be four times as much as one from the Corner Café.

Anna held up her hand. "No, don't do that. I've got it."

"Now, Anna, I can't let you do that," Travis said, opening his wallet. Maggie hoped there was enough money in it.

Anna crossed her arms over her chest. "Listen. I, um, kind of owe you for…things. I mean, well, there was the bracelet incident. And probably some other stuff."

What other stuff? And did this mean Anna had a heart? Holy cow, did she have a *soul?*

Travis looked at Anna for a minute, and then he put his wallet away. "Thank you," he said. "That's very generous of you, and I accept your apology."

Anna tossed her hair and raised an eyebrow. "It's not like I bought you lobster. It's just a couple of New York strips."

Whatever. A half-assed apology was still an apology, and Travis appeared to be satisfied.

"I'll just be on my way," Anna said. She glanced around the room again, and as Travis opened the door, her eyes met Maggie's. She smiled a little, and for a second, she seemed almost sweet. Then she flipped her hair and headed on out. "Later."

Travis shut the door. "Wow."

"Do you think it's poisoned?" Maggie asked, looking at the bags.

"Probably not," Travis said, taking Maggie in his arms. "Now. Where were we?"

"You just told me you love me, and I was about to say it back."

Travis kissed the tip of her nose. "You might want to get on with it then."

His breath was so warm against her skin. She turned her face up to his and whispered against his lips, "I love you, Travis. So very much."

Kiss me.

He took a small step back and removed his hat, holding it in front of him. "Can you forgive me?"

Maggie's heart melted and pooled at her feet, which was a sure sign she'd already forgiven him. "Of course I can. But no more deception, okay?"

"I swear I'll never hide anything from you again."

She believed him. And she couldn't hold back any longer. She wanted to touch him. Squeeze him. Kiss him. And that was just for starters. Without another thought, she flung herself at her big bad cowboy, wrapping her arms around his neck.

Something large pressed firmly against her tummy.

"My, Travis," she whispered against his lips. "What a big hat you have."

Travis placed it back on his head with a grin. "The better to woo you with, my dear."

Maggie's heart skipped a beat. She rose on her toes as Travis dipped his head, shadowing their faces with the (slightly bent) brim of his Stetson.

And they lived happily ever after.
The End.

Epilogue

Maggie hit the remote and opened the Happy Trails gate with extreme satisfaction. It had been two years and one day, and Happy Trails now officially belonged to Travis and Mary Margaret Blake.

She couldn't help but roll her eyes as she drove past the gigantic wreath on the gate. She'd already spent the day drowning in Christmas at Petal Pushers, or as she liked to refer to it during the holidays, the Little Shop of Ho-Ho-Horrors. But Travis absolutely loved decorating the ranch for the holidays, and even though she cherished her role as Scrooge, she wouldn't deny him that. Or much else, for that matter.

A school bus was parked in front of the hay barn. Goodness, she'd forgotten today was field trip day. And Honey's Cottage was rented out to tourists for the weekend. They'd be arriving any minute, and she hadn't yet left fresh eggs in the fridge or flowers on the table.

She parked between the barn and the country chapel Travis had built for their wedding last April. It had been in constant use ever since. In fact, JD and Gabriel had it booked for Valentine's Day, and Big Verde was going nuts in anticipation of its "first gay wedding," as the newspaper called it.

Maggie and Travis just referred to it as what it was: a wedding.

The tractor rumbled over the hill and Travis waved. Maggie couldn't see his grin, but she felt it. The breeze brought giggles and shrieks from the passengers he towed, snuggled among hay bales and blankets on the trailer. They were coming back from the goat pens, which were currently home to eight baby goats and their mamas. Nothing was more fun and bouncy than baby goats, and Maggie expected their contagious enthusiasm to be reflected in the behavior of the second graders.

Good thing they'd decided against serving hot cocoa.

She went into the barn, where Lupe was ready to hand out educational packets.

"What are you doing out here?" Lupe asked. She insisted on wearing denim overalls for field trip days, which clashed adorably with her teased hair and bright red lips. "You've worked all day. You should be in the house with your feet up."

"I'm hardly lumbering around like one of the pigs. I'm barely pregnant! And this is Henry's class. I'm sure he's being a huge showoff, and I kind of want to see it."

"You should have heard him," Lupe said. "It was awful. Those are *my* cows. Those are *my* turkeys. That is *my* dad."

"How totally obnoxious of him," Maggie said with a huge grin. "Did JD and Gabriel come get their Christmas turkey?"

"They sure did. The rest are being shipped out tomorrow. And Maggie, you wouldn't believe it. One of those birds is going to Maine, and another to Hawaii!"

People came from as far away as Houston to tour the ranch, but Happy Trails did most of its business through a website. Thanks to Gerome and his Rancho Cañada Verde stamp of approval, Happy Trails was cornering a market of its own.

The tractor pulled up noisily to the barn, belching smoke. Travis turned it off and the tailpipe backfired, causing an eruption of shrieks and laughter.

Henry was the first one off. Maggie grabbed him by a belt loop as he ran past. "Hey, aren't you going to say hello?"

"Oh, hi, Mag—" Henry turned pink. "I mean hi, Mama."

They'd decided *Mom* wasn't a good fit. It was what he'd called Lisa.

"Have your classmates had a good time?"

"You bet! They really liked the goats. I had to show them how to hold the babies."

Travis seemed to be having a hard time disentangling himself from a swarm of kids, so Maggie yelled, "Cookies!" to get their attention. She pointed to Lupe, and the swarm moved in unison.

"Did you get the cottage ready for guests yet?" Travis asked.

"Nope. I'm going to head over there now. I just need to grab some eggs. I've got the flowers in the Jeep."

"Forget the eggs," Travis said.

"But why? Guests of Honey's Cottage get fresh eggs. It says so on our website."

"Okay, fine. I'll grab the eggs and meet you there in a few minutes."

Holy cow, she was only a teensy weensy bit pregnant. It was doubtful she'd pop out a baby from picking up a carton of eggs.

As the kids lined up to board the bus, Maggie grabbed the fresh flowers out of the Jeep and walked around to the pasture behind the house, where a familiar cow trail led through the apple orchard. It was the quickest way to the cottage.

A horse neighed behind her. It hadn't taken Travis long to catch up. He sat proudly atop his black gelding, Moonshine II, who he simply called Junior.

Her heart thudded in her chest. *That's my cowboy.*

She offered Junior an apple, which he happily whuffled.

"Did somebody get lost on the way to Grandmother's house?"

Maggie grinned. She was even wearing a red jacket. "Maybe."

"Can I offer you a ride?"

"I'm not sure it's a good idea to go with strangers into the woods," she said.

"It's worked out pretty well for you in the past."

That was true. Maggie put her foot in the stirrup and Travis had her in the saddle in one fell swoop. She settled in snuggly in front of him, grabbing the saddle horn. Travis would do the rest. One large hand pressed against her belly as the other held the reins, and Travis made that adorable little clicking sound with his tongue to get Junior started down the trail.

Maggie's hips rocked back and forth with the horse's stride, causing her rear end to rub against Travis. He shifted in the saddle, and she felt how much he was enjoying the ride.

He kissed her neck, nipped her ear, and ran his hand under her shirt to cup her breast.

"What do you think you're doing?"

"Getting ready to ride," he teased.

"Get that idea out of your head. We've got guests coming. They might be there already."

The cottage came into view. It was lit up with a string of lights, and a tree glowed in the window. Like everything else on Happy Trails, it was awash in Christmas. The guests loved the extra bit of cheer.

Travis pulled the horse to a stop and helped Maggie down. There was no car parked in front, so they entered without knocking. Maggie rushed to put the eggs in the refrigerator, but Travis seemed in no hurry. In fact, he started putting kindling in the wood-burning stove.

"Travis! We can't leave the cottage with the stove going, and I'd prefer to sneak out before the guests arrive."

"They're already here."

"They are?" Maggie went to the window. She didn't see anybody. When she turned around, she noticed a suitcase in the hallway. "Is that my bag? It looks like my bag."

"Welcome to Honey's Cottage," Travis said. "We've got it all to ourselves for the entire weekend."

Maggie almost melted on the spot. That sounded dreamy. Divine, even. She rushed to Travis and jumped on him. He caught her with ease. "I've got all sorts of plans. And there's even a present for you under the tree."

"Really? For me?"

"Yes," he said, setting her on the couch. "Even though you've been naughty."

"I have not."

"Yes, Mrs. Blake, you have. On more than one occasion. And I got you an appropriately naughty gift."

Maggie peeked under the tree. A long, skinny package poked out from beneath its branches. It looked to be about twenty-five inches long. "Is that what I think it is?"

Travis knelt beside her and whispered, "It was Prime. And I promise it's not a telescope."

About the Author

Carly Bloom began her writing career as a family humor columnist and blogger, a pursuit she abandoned when her children grew old enough to literally die from embarrassment. To save their delicate lives, Carly turned to penning steamy, contemporary romance. The kind with bare chests on the covers.

Carly and her husband raise their mortified brood of offspring on a cattle ranch in South Texas.

You can learn more at:
CarlyBloomBooks.com
Twitter @CarlyBloomBooks
Facebook.com/AuthorCarlyBloom
Instagram @CarlyBloomBooks

Looking for more Western romance?
Take the reins with these cowboys from Forever!

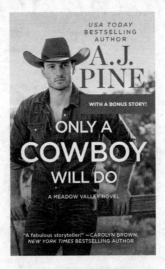

ONLY A COWBOY WILL DO
by A.J. Pine

After a lifetime of helping others, Jenna Owens is finally putting herself first, starting with her vacation at the Meadow Valley Guest Ranch to celebrate her fortieth birthday. Colt Morgan, part-owner of the ranch, is happy to help her have all the fun she deserves, especially her wish for a vacation fling. But will their two weeks of fantasy lead to a shot in the real world, or will their final destination be two broken hearts? Includes a bonus story from Melinda Curtis!

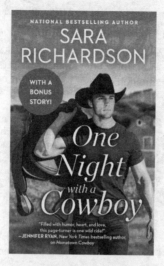

ONE NIGHT WITH A COWBOY
by Sara Richardson

Wes Harding is known as a devil-may-care bull rider—but now, with his sister's pregnancy at risk, Wes promises to put aside his wild ways and take the reins on their ranch's big charity event. Only he didn't count on his co-hostess—and little sister's best friend—being so darn distracting. One kiss with Thea Davis throws his world off-balance. But with her husband gone, Thea's focused only on raising her two rambunctious children. Can Wes convince her that he's the man on whom she can rely? Includes a bonus story by Carly Bloom!

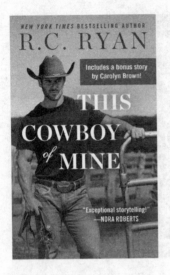

THIS COWBOY OF MINE
by R.C. Ryan

Kirby Regan just quit her career in Washington, D.C., to buy her family's Wyoming ranch. But when a snowstorm hits while she's out hiking in the Tetons, her only option for shelter is a nearby cave. She didn't realize it was already occupied...by a ruggedly handsome cowboy. Casey Merrick doesn't mind sharing his space with a gorgeous stranger, as long as they can both keep their distance—a task that begins to seem impossible as the attraction between them heats up. Includes a bonus story from Carolyn Brown!

BLACKLISTED
by Jay Crownover

In the small Texas town of Loveless, Palmer "Shot" Caldwell lives on the edge of the law. But this ruthlessly hot outlaw follows his own code of honor, and that includes repaying his debts. Which is exactly why icy, brilliant Dr. Presley Baskin is calling in a favor. She once saved Shot's life. Now she needs his help—and his protection.

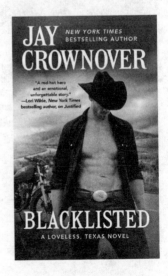